PRAISE FOR A HUGO AWARD-WINNING MASTER OF SCIENCE FICTION ADVENTURE

Angelmass:
"Zahn paints every futuristic detail with gleamy realism . . . scientific dialogue that streams with starship hardware and military trooper talk . . . immensely appealing."
—*Kirkus Reviews*

"Through in-depth characterization, as well as toothsome scientific and political mysteries, Zahn unfolds an intricate tale of adventure sure to please his many fans."
—*Publishers Weekly*

"A serious SF novel sneakily posing as an enormous golden-age thrill ride."
—*Locus*

Dragon and Thief:
"Zahn keeps the story moving at a breakneck pace, maintaining excitement. . . ."
—*Publishers Weekly*

"Characterizations are intriguing, to say the least . . . a romp of a space thriller. . . . Readers will welcome further adventures."
—*Booklist*

"Well paced and smoothly narrated."
—*Kirkus Reviews*

Manta's Gift:
"Zahn's latest effectively combines alien contact, hard science, and action-sf elements. . . . Another thoroughly literate sf yarn from Zahn. . . ."
—*Booklist*

". . . a new twist to a classic tale of human-alien encounter, combining fast-paced action and hard science with personal drama."
—*Library Journal*

Conqueror's Heritage:
". . . is another finely wrought space adventure . . . [the characters] are involved in every sort of social, political and emotional complications, all of which Zahn treats with his usual skill."
—*Booklist*

BAEN BOOKS
by TIMOTHY ZAHN

The Cobra Trilogy
Blackcollar
Blackcollar: The Judas Solution

THE COBRA TRILOGY

TIMOTHY ZAHN

THE COBRA TRILOGY

This is a work of fiction. All the characters and events portrayed in this book are fictional, and any resemblance to real people or incidents is purely coincidental.

Copyright © 2004 by Timothy Zahn. *Cobra* copyright © 1985, *Cobra Strike* copyright © 1986, *Cobra Bargain* copyright © 1988; all by Timothy Zahn.

A Baen Book

Baen Publishing Enterprises
P.O. Box 1403
Riverdale, NY 10471
www.baen.com

ISBN 10: 1-4165-2067-8
ISBN 13: 978-1-4165-2067-2

Cover art by Kurt Miller

First Baen paperback printing, June 2006

Distributed by Simon & Schuster
1230 Avenue of the Americas
New York, NY 10020

Library of Congress Cataloging-in-Publication Data: 200401885

Printed in the United States of America

10 9 8 7 6 5 4 3 2 1

Contents

COBRA

Trainee: *2403*

The music all that morning had been of the militant type that had dominated the airwaves for the past few weeks; but to the discerning ear there was a grim undertone to it that hadn't been there since the very start of the alien invasion. So when the music abruptly stopped and the light-show patterns on the plate were replaced by the face of Horizon's top news reporter, Jonny Moreau clicked off his laser welder and, with a feeling of dread, leaned closer to listen.

The bulletin was brief and as bad as Jonny had feared. "The Dominion Joint Military Command on Asgard has announced that, as of four days ago, Adirondack has been occupied by the invading Troft forces." A holosim map appeared over the reporter's right shoulder, showing the seventy white dots of the Dominion of Man bordered by the red haze of the Troft Empire to the left and the green of the Minthisti to the top and right. Two of the leftmost dots now flashed red. "Dominion Star Forces are reportedly consolidating new positions near Palm and Iberiand, and the ground troops already on Adirondack are expected to continue guerrilla activity against the occupation units. A full report—including official statements by the Central Committee and Military Command—will be presented on our regular newscast at six tonight."

The music and light pattern resumed, and as Jonny slowly straightened up, a hand came to rest on his shoulder. "They got Adirondack, Dader," Jonny said without turning around.

"I heard," Pearce Moreau said quietly.

"And it only took them three weeks." Jonny squeezed the laser he still held. "Three weeks."

3

"You can't extrapolate the progress of a war from its first stages," Pearce said, reaching over to take the laser from his son's hand. "The Trofts will learn that controlling a world is considerably more difficult than taking it in the first place. And we *were* caught by surprise, don't forget. As the Star Forces call up the reserves and shift to full war status, the Trofts will find it increasingly hard to push them back. I'd guess we might lose either Palm or Iberiand as well, but I think it'll stop there."

Jonny shook his head. There was something unreal about discussing the capture of billions of people as if they were only pawns in some cosmic chess game. "And then what?" he asked, with more bitterness than his father deserved. "How do we get the Trofts off our worlds without killing half the populations in the process? What if they decide to stage a 'scorched earth' withdrawal when they go? Suppose—"

"Hey; hey," Pearce interrupted, stepping around in front of Jonny and locking eyes with him. "You're getting yourself worked up for no good reason. The war's barely three months old, and the Dominion's a long way from being in trouble yet. Really. So put the whole thing out of your mind and get back to work, okay? I need this hood plate finished before you head for home and homework." He held out the laser welder.

"Yeah." Jonny accepted the instrument with a sigh and adjusted his de-contrast goggles back over his eyes. Leaning back over the half-finished seam, he tried to put the invasion out of his mind . . . and if his father hadn't made one last comment, he might have succeeded in doing so.

"Besides," Pearce shrugged as he started back to his own work-bench, "whatever's going to happen, there's not a thing in the universe we can do about it from here."

Jonny was quiet at dinner that evening, but in the Moreau household one more or less silent person wasn't enough to change the noise level significantly. Seven-year-old Gwen, as usual, dominated the conversation, alternating news of school and friends with questions on every subject from how weathermen damp out tornadoes to how butchers get the back-blades out of a breaff hump roast. Jame, five years Jonny's junior, contributed the latest on teen-age/high school social intrigue, a labyrinth of status and unspoken rules that Jame was more at home with than Jonny had ever been. Pearce and Irena managed the whole verbal circus with the skill of long practice, answering Gwen's questions with parental patience and generally keeping conversational friction at a minimum. Whether by tacit mutual consent or from lack of interest, no one mentioned the war.

Jonny waited until the table was being cleared before dropping in his studiously casual request. "Dader, can I borrow the car tonight to go into Horizon City?"

"What, there isn't another game there this evening, is there?" the other frowned.

"No," Jonny said. "I wanted to look at some stuff out there, that's all."

" 'Stuff'?"

Jonny felt his face growing warm. He didn't want to lie, but he knew that a fully truthful answer would automatically be followed by a family discussion, and he wasn't prepared for a confrontation just yet. "Yeah. Just . . . things I want to check out."

"Like the Military Command recruitment center?" Pearce asked quietly.

The background clatter of dishes being moved and stacked cut off abruptly, and in the silence Jonny heard his mother's sharp intake of air. "Jonny?" she asked.

He sighed and braced himself for the now inevitable discussion. "I wouldn't have enlisted without talking to all of you first," he said. "I just wanted to go get some information—procedures, requirements; that sort of thing."

"Jonny, the war is a long way away—" Irena began.

"I know, Momer," Jonny interrupted. "But there are people *dying* out there—"

"All the more reason to stay here."

"—not just soldiers, but civilians, too," he continued doggedly. "I just think—well, Dader said today that there wasn't anything I could do to help." He shifted his attention to Pearce. "Maybe not . . . but maybe I shouldn't give up to statistical generalities quite so quickly."

A smile twitched briefly at Pearce's lip without touching the rest of his face. "I remember when the full gist of your arguments could be boiled down to 'because I said so, that's why.' "

"Must be college that's doing it," Jame murmured from the kitchen door. "I think they're also teaching him a little about fixing computers in between the argument seminars."

Jonny sent a quick frown in his brother's direction, annoyed at the apparent attempt to sidetrack the discussion. But Irena wasn't about to be distracted. "What *about* college, now that we're on that topic?" she asked. "You've got a year to go before you get your certificate. You'd at least stay that long, wouldn't you?"

Jonny shook his head. "I don't see how I can. A whole *year*— look at what the Trofts have done in just three months."

"But your education is important, too—"

"All right, Jonny," Pearce cut off his wife quietly. "Go to Horizon City if you'd like and talk to the recruiters."

"Pearce!" Irena turned stunned eyes on him.

Pearce shook his head heavily. "We can't stand in his way," he told her. "Can't you hear how he's talking? He's already ninety percent decided on this. He's an adult now, with the right and responsibility of his own decisions." He shifted his gaze to Jonny. "Go see the recruiters; but promise me you'll talk with us again before you make your final decision. Deal?"

"Deal," Jonny nodded, feeling the tension within him draining away. Volunteering to go fight a war was one thing: scary, but on a remote and almost abstract level. The battle for his family's support had loomed far more terrifyingly before him, with potential costs he hadn't wanted to contemplate. "I'll be back in a few hours," he said, taking the keys from his father and heading for the door.

The Joint Military Command recruiting office had been in the same city hall office for over three decades, and it occurred to Jonny as he approached it that he was likely following the same path his father had taken to his own enlistment some twenty-eight years previously. Then, the enemy had been the Minthisti, and Pearce Moreau had fought from the torpedo deck of a Star Force dreadnaught.

This war was different, though; and while Jonny had always admired the romance of the Star Forces, he had already decided to choose a less glamorous—but perhaps more effective—position.

"Army, eh?" the recruiter repeated, cocking an eyebrow as she studied Jonny from behind her desk. "Excuse my surprise, but we don't get a lot of volunteers for Army service here. Most kids your age would rather fly around in star ships or air fighters. Mind if I ask your reasons?"

Jonny nodded, trying not to let the recruiter's faintly condescending manner get to him. Chances were good it was a standard part of the interview, designed to get a first approximation of the applicant's irritation threshold. "It seems to me that if the Troft advance continues to push the Star Forces back, we're going to lose more planets to them. That's going to leave the civilians there pretty much at their mercy . . . unless the Army already has guerrilla units in place to coordinate resistance. That's the sort of thing I'm hoping to do."

The recruiter nodded thoughtfully. "So you want to be a guerrilla fighter?"

"I want to help the people," Jonny corrected.

"Um." Reaching for her terminal, she tapped in Jonny's name and ID code; and as she skimmed the information that printed out, she again cocked an eyebrow. "Impressive," she said, without any sarcasm Jonny could hear. "Grade point high school, grade point college, personality index . . . you have any interest in officer training?"

Jonny shrugged. "Not that much, but I'll take it if that's where I can do the most good. I don't mind just being an ordinary soldier, though, if that's what you're getting at."

Her eyes studied his face for a moment. "Uh-huh. Well, I'll tell you what, Moreau." Her fingers jabbed buttons and she swiveled the plate around for his scrutiny. "As far as I know, there aren't any specific plans at present to set up guerrilla networks on threatened planets. But if that is done—and I agree it's a reasonable move—then one or more of these special units will probably be spearheading it."

Jonny studied the list. *Alpha Command, Interrorum, Marines, Rangers*—names familiar and highly respected. "How do I sign up for one of these?"

"You don't. You sign up for the Army and take a small mountain of tests—and if you show the qualities they want they'll issue you an invitation."

"And if not, I'm still in the Army?"

"Provided you don't crusk out of normal basic training, yes."

Jonny glanced around the room, the colorful holosim posters seeming to leap out at him with their star ships, atmosphere fighters, and missile tanks; their green, blue, and black uniforms. "Thank you for your time," he told the recruiter, fingering the information magcard he'd been given. "I'll be back when I've made up my mind."

He expected to return home to a dark house, but found his parents and Jame waiting quietly for him in the living room. Their discussion lasted long into the night, and when it was over Jonny had convinced both himself and them of what he had to do.

The next evening, after dinner, they all drove to Horizon City and watched as Jonny signed the necessary magforms.

✧　　　✧　　　✧

"So . . . tomorrow's the big day."

Johnny glanced up from his packing to meet his brother's eyes. Jame, lounging on his bed across the room, was making a reasonably good effort to look calm and relaxed. But his restless fiddling with a corner of the blanket gave away his underlying tension. "Yep," Jonny nodded. "Horizon City Port, *Skylark Lines 407* to Aerie, military transport to Asgard. Nothing like travel to give you a real perspective on the universe."

Jame smiled faintly. "I hope to get down to New Persius some day myself. A hundred twenty whole kilometers. Any word yet on the tests?"

"Only that my headache's supposed to go away in a couple more hours." The past three days had been genuine killers, with back-to-back tests running from seven in the morning to nine at night. General knowledge, military and political knowledge, psychological, attitudinal, physical, deep physical, biochemical—they'd given him the works. "I was told they usually run these tests over a two-week period," he added, a bit of information he hadn't been given until it was all over. Probably fortunately. "I guess the Army's anxious to get new recruits trained and in service."

"Uh-huh. So . . . you've said your good-byes and all? Everything settled there?"

Jonny tossed a pair of socks into his suitcase and sat down beside it on his bed. "Jame, I'm too tired to play tag around the mountain. What exactly is on your mind?"

Jame sighed. "Well, to put it bluntly . . . Alyse Carne is kind of upset that you didn't discuss this whole thing with her before you went ahead and did it."

Jonny frowned, searching his memory. He hadn't seen Alyse since the tests began, of course, but she'd seemed all right the last time they'd been together. "Well, if she is, she didn't say anything to *me* about it. Who'd you find out from?"

"Mona Biehl," Jame said. "And of course Alyse wouldn't have told you directly—it's too late for you to change things now."

"So why are *you* telling me?"

"Because I think you ought to make an effort to go see her tonight. To show that you still care about her before you run off to save the rest of humanity."

Something in his brother's voice made Jonny pause, the planned retort dying in his throat. "You disapprove of what I'm doing, don't you?" he asked quietly.

Jame shook his head. "No, not at all. I'm just worried that you're going into this without really understanding what you're getting into."

"I'm twenty-one years old, Jame—"

"And have lived all your life in a medium-sized town on a frontier-class world. Face it, Jonny—you function well enough here, but you're about to tackle three unknowns at the same time: mainstream Dominion society, the Army, and war itself. That's a pretty potent set of opponents."

Jonny sighed. Coming from anyone else, words like that would have been grounds for a strong denial . . . but Jame had an innate understanding of people that Jonny had long since come to trust. "The only alternative to facing unknowns is to stay in this room the rest of my life," he pointed out.

"I know—and I don't have any great suggestions for you, either." Jame waved helplessly. "I guess I just wanted to make sure you at least were leaving here with your eyes open."

"Yeah. Thanks." Jonny sent his gaze slowly around the room, seeing things that he'd stopped noticing years ago. Now, almost a week after his decision, it was finally starting to sink in that he was leaving all this.

Possibly forever.

"You think Alyse would like to see me, huh?" he asked, bringing his eyes back to Jame.

The other nodded. "I'm sure it would make her feel a little better, yeah. Besides which—" He hesitated. "This may sound silly, but I also think that the more ties you have here in Cedar Lake the easier it'll be to hold on to your ethics out there."

Jonny snorted. "You mean out among the decadence of the big worlds? Come on, Jame, you don't really believe that sophistication implies depravity, do you?"

"Of course not. But someone's bound to try and convince you that depravity implies sophistication."

Jonny waved his hands in a gesture of surrender. "Okay; that's it. I've warned you before: the point where you start with the aphorisms is the point where I bail out of the discussion." Standing up, he scooped an armful of shirts from the dresser drawer and dumped them beside his suitcase. "Here—make yourself useful for a change, huh? Pack these and my cassettes for me, if you don't mind."

"Sure." Jame got up and gave Jonny a lopsided smile. "Take your time; you'll have plenty of chances to catch up on your sleep on the way to Asgard."

Jonny shook his head in mock exasperation. "One thing I'm *not* going to miss about this place is having my own live-in advice service."

It wasn't true, of course . . . but then, both of them knew that.

The farewells at the Horizon City Port the next morning were as painful as Jonny had expected them to be, and it was with an almost bittersweet sense of relief that he watched the city fall away beneath the ground-to-orbit shuttle that would take him to the liner waiting above. Never before had he faced such a long separation from family, friends, and home, and as the blue sky outside the viewport gradually faded to black, he wondered if Jame had been right about too many shocks spaced too closely together. Still, in a way, it seemed almost easier to be changing everything about his life at once, rather than to have to graft smaller pieces onto a structure that wasn't designed for them. An old saying about new wine in old wineskins brushed at his memory; the moral, he remembered, being that a person too set in his ways was unable to accept anything at all that was outside his previous experience.

Overhead, the first stars were beginning to appear, and Jonny smiled at the sight. His way of life on Horizon had certainly been comfortable, but at twenty-one he had no intention of becoming rigidly attached to it. For the first time since enlisting, a wave of exhilaration swept through him. Jame, stuck at home, could choose to see Jonny's upcoming experiences as uncomfortable shocks if he wanted to, but Jonny was going to treat them instead as high adventure.

And with that attitude firmly settled in his mind, he gave his full attention to the viewport, eagerly awaiting his first glimpse of a real star ship.

Skylark 407 was a commercial liner, the majority of its three hundred passengers business professionals and tourists. A handful, though, were new recruits like Jonny; and as the ship made stops over the next few days at Rajput, Zimbwe, and Blue Haven, that number rapidly went up. By the time they reached Aerie, fully a third of the passengers were transferred to the huge military transport orbiting there. Jonny's group was apparently the last batch to arrive, and they were barely aboard before the ship shifted into hyperspace. Someone, clearly, was in a hurry.

For Jonny, the next five days were ones of awkward—and not totally successful—cultural adjustment. Jammed together in communal rooms, with less privacy than even the liner had afforded, the recruits formed a bewildering mosaic of attitudes, habits, and accents, and getting used to all of it proved harder than Jonny had anticipated. Many of the others apparently felt the same way, and within a day of their arrival Jonny noticed that his former shipmates were following the example of those who'd arrived here earlier and were clumping in small, relatively homogenous groups. Jonny made a few halfhearted attempts to bridge the social gaps, but eventually he gave up and spent the remainder of the trip with others of the Horizon contingent. The Dominion of Man, clearly, wasn't nearly as culturally uniform as he'd always believed, and he finally had to console himself with the reasonable expectation that the Army must have figured out how to handle this kind of barrier a long time ago. When they reached the training camps of Asgard, he knew, things would change, and they'd all be simply soldiers together.

In a way he was right . . . but in another way, he was very wrong.

The registration foyer was a room as large as the Horizon City Concert Hall, and it was almost literally packed with people. At the far end, past the dotted line of sergeants at terminals, the slowly-moving mass changed abruptly to a roiling stream as the recruits hurried to their assigned orientation meetings. Drifting along, oblivious to the flood passing him on both sides, Jonny frowned down at his own card with a surprise that was edging rapidly into disappointment.

> JONNY MOREAU
> HORIZON: HN-89927-238-2825p
> ASSIGNED ROOM: AA-315 FREYR COMPLEX
> UNIT: COBRAS
> UNIT ORIENTATION: C-662 FREYR COMPLEX:
> 1530 HOURS

Cobras. The transport had included a generous selection of military reference material, and Jonny had spent several hours reading all he could about the Army's Special Forces. Nowhere had anything called the Cobras been so much as hinted at.

Cobras. What could a unit named after a poisonous Earth snake be assigned to do? Decontamination procedures, perhaps, or else something having to do with antipersonnel mines? Whatever it was, it wasn't likely to live up to the expectations of the past weeks.

Someone slammed into his back, nearly knocking the card out of his hand. "Get the phrij out of the road," a lanky man snarled, pushing past him. Neither the expletive nor the other's accent were familiar. "You want to infiloop, do it out of the phrijing *way*."

"Sorry," Jonny muttered as the man disappeared into the flow. Gritting his teeth, he sped up, glancing up at the glowing direction indicators lining the walls. Whatever this Cobra unit was, he'd better get going and find the meeting room. The local-time clocks were showing 1512 already, and it was unlikely *any* Army officer would appreciate tardiness.

Room C-662 was his first indication that perhaps he'd jumped to the wrong conclusion. Instead of the battalion-sized auditorium he'd expected, the room was barely adequate to handle the forty-odd men already seated there. Two men in red and black diamond-patterned tunics faced the group from a low dais, and as Jonny slipped into a vacant chair the younger of them caught Jonny's eye. "Name?"

"Jonny Moreau, sir," Jonny told him, glancing quickly at the wall clock. But it was still only 1528, and the other merely nodded and made a notation on a comboard on his lap. Looking furtively around the room, Jonny spent the next two minutes listening to his heart beat and letting his imagination have free rein.

Exactly at 1530 the older of the uniformed men stood up. "Good afternoon, gentlemen," he nodded. "I'm Cee-two Rand Mendro, Cobra Unit Commander, and I'd like to welcome you to Asgard. We build men and women into soldiers here—as well as flyers, sailors, Star Forcers, and a few other specialties. Here in Freyr Complex, we're exclusively soldiers . . . and you forty-five have had the honor of being chosen for the newest and—in my opinion—most elite force the Dominion has to offer. *If* you want to join." He looked around, his eyes seeming to touch each of them in turn. "If you do, you'll draw the most dangerous assignment we've got: to go to Troft-occupied worlds and engage the enemy in a guerrilla war."

He paused, and Jonny felt his stomach curling into a knot. An elite unit—as he'd wanted—and the chance to help civilian populations—as he'd also wanted. But to be dropped in where the Trofts already had control sounded a lot more like suicide than service. From the faint stirrings around the room he gathered his reaction wasn't unique.

"Of course," Mendro continued, "we aren't exactly talking about space-chuting you in with a laser rifle in one hand and a radio in the other. If you choose to join up you'll receive some of the most extensive training and *the* absolute top-of-the-line weaponry available." He gestured to the man seated beside him. "Cee-three Shri Bai will be the chief training instructor for this unit. He'll now demonstrate a little of what you, as Cobras, will be able to do."

Bai laid his comboard beside his chair and started to stand up—and halfway through the motion he shot toward the ceiling.

Caught by surprise, Jonny saw only the blur as Bai leaped—but the twin thunderclaps from above and behind him were the gut-wrenching signs of a rocket-assisted flight gone horribly bad. He spun around in his seat, bracing for the sight of Bai's broken body—

Bai was standing calmly by the door, a hint of a smile on his face as he looked around at what must have been some pretty stunned expressions. "I'm sure all of you know," he said, "that using either a lift pack or exoskeleton muscle enhancers would be foolhardy in such a confined room. Um? So watch again."

His knees bent a few degrees, and with the same *thump-thump* he was back on the dais. "All right," he said. "Who saw what I did?"

Silence . . . and then a hand went tentatively up. "You bounced off the ceiling, I think," the recruit said, a bit uncertainly. "Uh . . . your shoulders took the impact?"

"In other words, you didn't really see," Bai nodded. "I actually flipped halfway over on the way up, took the impact with my feet, and continued around to be upright when I landed."

Jonny's mouth felt a little dry. The ceiling was no more than five meters up. To have done that much maneuvering in that small a space . . .

"The point, aside from the power and precision of the jump itself," Mendro said, "is that even you, who knew what was going to happen, couldn't follow Bai's movement. Consider how it would work against a roomful of Trofts who *weren't* expecting it. Next—"

He broke off as the door opened and one more recruit came in. "Viljo?" Bai asked, retrieving the comboard at his feet.

"Yes, sir," the newcomer nodded. "Sorry I'm late, sir—the registration people were running slow."

"Oh?" Bai waved the comboard. "Says here you went through the line at 1450. That's—let's see—seventeen minutes *before* Moreau, who got here seven minutes earlier than you did. Um?"

Viljo turned a bright red. "I . . . guess maybe I got a little lost. Sir."

"With all the signs posted around the complex? Not to mention all the regular Army personnel wandering around? Um?"

Viljo was beginning to look like a hunted animal. "I . . . I stopped to look at the exhibits in the entry corridor, sir. I thought this room was closer than it was."

"I see." Bai gave him a long, chilly look. "Punctuality, Viljo, is a mark of a good soldier—and if you plan to be a Cobra it's going to be an absolute necessity. But even more important are honesty and integrity in front of your teammates. Specifically, it means that when you crusk up, you damn well better not try to push the blame onto someone else. Got that?"

"Yes, sir."

"All right. Now come up here; I need an assistant for this next demonstration."

Swallowing visibly, Viljo unglued himself from the floor and threaded his way through the chairs to the dais. "What I showed you a minute ago," Bai said, once again addressing the entire room, "was essentially a party trick, though with some obvious military applications. This, now, I think you'll find along more practical lines."

From his tunic, he produced two metal disks, each ten centimeters in diameter with a small black inset in the center. "Hold the one in your left hand sideways," Bai instructed Viljo, "and when I give the word, throw the other toward the back of the room."

Mendro had meantime gone to one of the room's back corners. Taking a few steps off to the side, Bai checked positions and bent his knees slightly. "All right: *now.*"

Viljo lofted the disk toward the door. Behind him, Jonny sensed Mendro's leap and catch, and an instant later the disk was shooting back toward Bai. In a smooth motion that was again too fast to follow, Bai fell to the side, out of the disk's path . . . and as he rolled again to one knee, two needles of light flashed in opposite directions from his outstretched hands. Viljo's surprised yelp was almost covered up by the crash of the flying disk against the wall.

"Good," Bai said briskly, getting to his feet and heading over to retrieve the first disk. "Viljo, show them yours."

Even from his distance Jonny could see the small hole just barely off-center through the black inset. "Impressive, um?" Bai said, stepping back up on the dais and presenting the other target. "Of course, you can't always expect the enemy to hold still for you."

This shot hadn't been nearly as clean. Only the very edge of the black showed the laser's mark, and when the light hit it right

Jonny could see that the adjacent metal was rippled with the heat. Still, it was an impressive performance—especially as Jonny had no idea where Bai had been hiding his weapons.

Or where they were now, for that matter.

"That gives you an idea of what a Cobra can do," Mendro said, returning to the front of the room and sending Viljo back to find a seat. "Now I'd like to show you a little of the nuts and bolts involved." Retrieving the comboard, he keyed in an instruction, and a full-sized image of a man appeared beside him. "From the outside a Cobra is virtually indistinguishable from any normal civilian. However, from the *inside*—" The hologram's exterior faded to a blue skeleton with oddly-shaped white spots scattered randomly around. "The blue is a ceramic laminae which makes all the major and most of the minor bones unbreakable, for all practical purposes. That, along with some strategic ligament strengthening, is half the reason Cee-three Bai was able to pull off those ceiling jumps without killing himself. The non-laminated areas you can see are there to allow the bone marrow to continue putting red blood cells into the system."

Another touch on the comboard and the piebald skeleton faded to dull gray, forming a contrast to the small yellow ovoids that appeared at joints all over the hologram. "Servomotors," Mendro identified them. "The other half of the ceiling jump. They act as strength multipliers, just like the ones in standard exoskeletons and fighting suits, except that these are particularly hard to detect. The power supply is a little nuclear goody here—" he pointed to an asymmetric object situated somewhere in the vicinity of the stomach "—and I'm not going to explain it because I don't understand it myself. Suffice it to say the thing works and works well."

Jonny thought back to Bai's incredible jumps and felt his stomach tighten. Servos and bone laminae were all well and good, but a trick like that could hardly be learned overnight. Either this Cobra training was going to take months at the minimum, or else Bai was an exceptionally athletic man . . . and if there was one thing Jonny knew for certain, it was that he himself hadn't been selected for this group because of any innate gymnastic abilities. Apparently the Army was getting set for a long, drawn-out conflict.

On the dais, the hologram had again changed, this time marking several sections in red. "Cobra offensive and defensive equipment," Mendro said. "Small lasers in the tips of both little fingers, one of which also contains the discharge electrodes for an arcthrower—capacitor in the body cavity here. In the left calf is an antiarmor laser; here are the speakers for two different types of sonic weapons; and up by the eyes and ears are a set of optical and auditory enhancers. Yes—question?"

"Recruit MacDonald, sir," the other said with military correctness, a slight accent burring his words. "Are these optical enhancers like the targeting lenses of a fighting suit, where you're given a range/scale image in front of your eyes?"

Mendro shook his head. "That sort of thing is fine for medium- and long-range work, but pretty useless for the infighting you may have to do. Which brings us to the real key of the whole Cobra project." The red faded, and inside the skull a green walnut-sized object appeared, situated apparently directly beneath the brain. From it snaked dozens of slender filaments, most of them paralleling the spinal column before separating off to go their individual ways. Looking at it, Jonny's thoughts flashed back to a picture from his old fourth-grade biology text: a diagram showing the major structures of the human nervous system. . . .

"This," Mendro said, wagging a finger through the green walnut, "is a computer—probably the most powerful computer of its size ever developed. These optical fibers—" he indicated the filament network—"run to all the servos and weapons and to a set of kinesthetic sensors implanted directly in the bone laminae. Your targeting lenses, MacDonald, still require you to do the actual aiming and firing. This nanocomputer gives you the option of having the whole operation done automatically."

Jonny glanced at MacDonald, saw the other nodding slowly. It wasn't a new idea, certainly—computerized weaponry had been standard on star ships and atmosphere fighters for centuries—but to give an individual soldier that kind of control was indeed a technological breakthrough.

And Mendro wasn't even finished with his surprises. "In addition to fire control," he said, "the computer will have a set of combat reflexes programmed into it—reflexes that will not only include evasive movements but such tricks as were demonstrated a few minutes ago. Put it all together—" the hologram became a colorful puzzle as all the overlays reappeared—"and you have the most deadly guerrilla warriors mankind has ever produced."

He let the image stand a few seconds before switching it off and laying the comboard back on one of the chairs. "As Cobras you'll be on the leading edge of the counteroffensive strategy that I expect will ultimately push the Trofts out of Dominion territory . . . but there'll be a definite cost included. I've already mentioned the military dangers you'll be facing; at this point we can't even guess at what kind of casualty percentages there'll be, but I can assure you they'll be high. We'll need to do a lot of surgery on you, and surgery is never very pleasant; on top of that, a lot of what we put inside you will be there to stay. The laminae, for example, won't be removable, which requires you to keep the servos and nanocomputer, as well. There'll undoubtedly also be problems we haven't even thought about yet, and as part of the first wave of Cobras you'll take the full brunt of any design glitches that may have slipped by."

He paused and looked around the room. "Having said all that, though, I'd like to remind you that you're here because we need you. Every one of you has tested out with the intelligence, courage, and emotional stability that mark you as Cobra material— and I'll tell you frankly that there aren't a hell of a lot of you out there. The more of you that join up, the faster we can start shoving this war down the Trofts' throat bladders where it belongs.

"So. The rest of the day is yours to get settled in your rooms, get acquainted with Freyr Complex—" he glanced in Viljo's direction—"and perhaps look through the exhibit halls. Tomorrow morning you're to come back here whenever each of you is ready to give me your decision." Sweeping his gaze one last time around the room, he nodded. "Until then; dismissed."

Jonny spent the day as Mendro had suggested, meeting his roommates—there were five of them—and walking through the buildings and open-air sections of Freyr Complex. The Cobra group seemed to have an entire barracks floor to themselves, and every time Jonny passed the lounge area there seemed to be a different collection of them sitting around arguing the pros and cons of joining up. Occasionally, he paused to listen, but most of the time he simply continued on his way, knowing down deep that none of their uncertainties applied to him. True, the decision ahead wasn't one to be taken lightly . . . but Jonny had gone into this in the first place in order to help the people on threatened planets. He could hardly back down simply because it was going to cost a little more than he'd expected.

Besides which—he was honest enough to admit—the whole Cobra concept smacked of the superhero books and shows that had thrilled him as a kid, and the chance to actually become someone with such powers was a potent enticement even to the more sophisticated college student he was now.

The discussions in his room later that evening went on until lights-out, but Jonny managed to tune them out and get a head start on the night's sleep. When reveille sounded, he was the only one of the six who didn't mutter curses at the ungodly hour involved, but quickly got dressed and went down to the mess hall. By the time he returned, the others—except for Viljo, who was still in bed—had gone for their own breakfasts. Heading upstairs to Room C-662, he discovered that he was the third of the group to officially join the Cobras. Mendro congratulated him, gave him a standard-sounding pep talk, and issued him a genuinely intimidating surgery schedule. He left for the medical wing with a nervous flutter in his stomach but with the confident feeling that he'd made the right decision.

Several times in the next two weeks that confidence was severely strained.

"All right, Cobras, listen up!"

Bai's voice was a rumble of thunder in the half-light of Asgard dawn, and Jonny suppressed a spasm of nausea that the sound and the chilly air sent through what was left of his stomach. Shivering had never made him feel sick before . . . but then his body had never undergone such massive physical trauma before. What pain remained was little more than a dull ache extending from his eyes all the way down to his toes, and in the absence of that outlet his system had come up with these other quirks to show its displeasure. Shifting uncomfortably as he stood in line with the other thirty-five trainees, he felt the odd stresses and strains where his organs squeezed up against the new equipment and supports in his body cavity. The nausea flared again at the thought of all that inside him; quickly, he turned his attention back to Bai.

"—rough for you, but from personal experience I can assure you all the postoperative symptoms will be gone in another couple of days. In the meantime, there's nothing that says you can't start getting used to your new bodies.

"Now, I know you're all wondering why you're wearing your computers around your necks instead of inside your skulls. Um? Well, you're all supposed to be smart, and you haven't had much to do the last two weeks except think about things like that. Anyone want to trot out their pet theory?"

Jonny glanced around, feeling the soft collar-like computer rub gently against his neck as he turned his head. He was pretty sure he'd figured it out, but didn't want to be the first one to say anything.

"Recruit Noffke, sir," Parr Noffke, one of Jonny's roommates, spoke up. "Is it because you don't want our weapons systems operational until we're off Asgard?"

"Close," Bai nodded. "Moreau? You care to amplify on that?"

Startled, Jonny looked back at Bai. "Uh, would it be because you want to phase in access to our equipment—weapons and other capabilities—gradually instead of all at once?"

"You need to learn how to give answers more clearly, Moreau, but that's essentially it," Bai said. "Once the final computer is implanted its programming is fixed, so you'll wear the programmable ones until there's no danger of you slagging yourselves or each other. All right: first lesson is getting the feel of your bodies. Behind me about five kliks is the old ordnance range observation tower. Interworld contenders can run that in twelve minutes or so; we're going to do it in ten. *Move.*"

He turned and set off toward the distant tower at a fast run, the trainees forming a ragged mass in his wake. Jonny wound up somewhere in the middle of the pack, striving to keep his steps rhythmic as he fought the self-contradictory feeling of being both too heavy and too light. Five kilometers was twice as far as he'd ever run in his life—at *any* speed—and by the time he reached the tower his breath was coming in short gasps, his vision flickering with the exertion.

Bai was waiting as he stumbled to a stop. "Hold your breath for a thirty-count," the instructor ordered him briefly, moving immediately to the side to repeat the command to someone else. Strangely enough, Jonny found he could do it, and by the time those behind had caught up, both his lungs and eyes seemed all right again. "Now: that was lesson one point five," Bai growled. "About half of you let your bodies hyperventilate themselves for no better reason than habit. At the speed you were doing your servos should have been doing fifty to seventy percent of the work for you. Eventually, your autonomic systems will adjust, but until then you're going to have to consciously pay attention to all these little details.

"Okay. Lesson two: jumping. We'll start with jumping straight up to various heights; and *you'll* start by watching *me.* You haven't got your combat reflexes programmed in yet, and while you won't be able to break your ankles, if you come down off-balance and hit your heads it *will* hurt. So watch and learn."

For the next hour they learned how to jump, how to right themselves in mid-air when necessary, and how to fall safely when

the righting methods weren't adequate. After that Bai switched their
focus to the observation tower looming over them, and they learned
a dozen different ways of climbing the outside of a building. By
the time Bai called lunch break they had each made the precarious journey up the side and through an unlocked window in the
main observation level; and at Bai's order they returned to the walls
to eat, wolfing down their field rations while clinging as best they
could ten meters above the ground.

The afternoon was spent practicing with their arm servos, with
emphasis on learning how to hold heavy objects so as to put
minimal stress on skin and blood vessels. It wasn't nearly as trivial
a problem as it looked at first blush, and though Jonny got away
with only a few pressure bruises, others wound up with more
serious subcutaneous bleeding or severely abraded skin. The worst
cases Bai sent immediately off to the infirmary; the rest continued training until the sun was brushing the horizon. Another brisk
five-klick run brought them back to the central complex building
where, after a quick dinner, they assembled once more in C-662
for an evening of lectures on guerrilla tactics and strategy.

And finally, sore in both mind and body, they were sent back
to their rooms.

It was the first time Jonny had been in his room since his two-
week stint in surgery had begun, but it looked about as he remembered. Heading straight for his bunk, he collapsed gratefully into
it, wincing at the unexpectedly loud protest from the bed's springs.
Pure imagination, of course—he wasn't *that* much heavier, despite
all the new hardware he was carrying around. Stretching his sore
muscles, he gingerly probed the bruises on his arms, wondering
if he could survive four more weeks of this.

His five roommates arrived a minute or so behind him, coming in as a group and obviously in the middle of comparing notes
on the day. "—tell you *all* Army trainers act like assembly robots,"
Cally Halloran was saying as they filed through the door. "It's part
of the toughening-up process for the recruits. Psychology, troops,
psychology."

"Phrij on psychology," Parr Noffke opined, leaning over the end
of his bunk and doing some halfhearted stretching exercises. "That
whole farrago about eating lunch ten meters up?—you call that
toughening up? I tell you, Bai just likes making us sweat."

"It proved you could hang on without devoting your entire
attention to your fingers, didn't it?" Imel Deutsch countered dryly.

"Like I said," Halloran nodded. "Psychology."

Noffke snorted and abandoned his exercises. "Hey, Druma; Rolon? Get in here and join the party. We've got just enough time for a round hand of King's Bluff."

"In a minute," Druma Singh's soft voice called from the bathroom, where he and Rolon Viljo had vanished. Jonny had noticed the pale blue of heal-quick bandages on Singh's hands when they entered, and guessed Viljo was helping the other change the dressings.

"You, too, Mr. Answer Man," Noffke said, looking in Jonny's direction. "You know how to play King's Bluff?"

Answer Man? "I know a version of the game, but it may be just a local one," he told Noffke.

"Well, let's find out," the other shrugged, stepping to the room's circular table and pulling a deck of cards from a satchel sitting there. "Come on; Reginine rules say you can't turn down a card game when it's not for money."

"Since when do Reginine rules apply on Asgard?" Viljo demanded as he strolled in from the bathroom. "Why not play Earth rules, which state that all games *are* for money?"

"Aerie rules are that you play for real estate," Halloran offered from his bunk.

"Horizon rules—" Jonny began.

"Let's not reach *too* far into the Dominion backwaters, eh?" Viljo cut him off.

"Perhaps we should just go to sleep," Singh said, rejoining the group. "We'll undoubtedly have a busy day tomorrow."

"Come on," Deutsch beckoned, joining Noffke at the table. "A game will help us all settle down. Besides, it's these little things that help mold people into a team. Psychology, Cally. Right?"

Halloran chuckled, rolling out of bed and back onto his feet. "Unfair. All right, I'm in. Come on, Jonny; up. Druma, Rolon—Reginine rules, like the man said. One round only."

The game that Noffke described turned out to be almost identical to the King's Bluff Jonny was familiar with, and he felt reasonably confident as they launched into the first hand. Winning was completely unimportant to him, but he very much wanted to play without making any foolish mistakes. Viljo's gibe about the Dominion backwaters had finally crystallized for him exactly why he felt uncomfortable with this group: with the exception of Deutsch, all the others came from worlds older and more distinguished than Horizon—and Deutsch, as the only Cobra trainee from Adirondack, had obvious status as native authority on one of the two worlds the Trofts had captured. Most of the others weren't as blatant in their condescension as Viljo, but Jonny could sense traces of it in all of them. Proving he could play a competent game of cards might be a first step toward breaking down whatever stereotypes they had of frontier planets in general and Jonny in particular.

Perhaps it was his indifference toward winning aiding his merely average tactical skills, or perhaps it was small differences in body language giving his bluffs an unexpected edge . . . whatever the reason, the round hand wound up being the best he'd ever played. Out of six games he won one outright, bluff-won two others, and lost another only when Noffke stubbornly stayed with a hand that by all rights should have died young. Viljo suggested a second round—virtually demanded one, in fact—but Singh reminded them of the agreed-upon limit, and the game dissolved into a quiet flurry of bedtime preparations.

For several minutes after lights-out, Jonny replayed the game in his mind, searching every remembered nuance of speech and manner for signs that the social barriers were at least beginning to crack. But he was too tired to make much headway and soon gave up the effort. Still, they *could* have left him out of the game entirely; and his last thought before drifting off was that the next four weeks might be survivable, after all.

The first week of training saw a great deal of practice with the servo system, activation of the optical and auditory enhancers, and the first experience with weapons. The small lasers built into their little fingers, the trainees were told, were designed chiefly to be used on metals, but would be equally effective in short-range antipersonnel applications. Bai emphasized that, for the moment, the power outputs were being held far below lethal levels, but Jonny found that of limited comfort as he practiced against the easily melted solder targets. With anywhere up to seventy-two lasers being fired across the range at any given time, it didn't take much imagination to picture what a careless, servo-supplemented twitch of someone's wrist could do. The semiautomatic targeting capabilities, when added, just made things worse: it was all too easy to shift one's gaze with the variable/visual lock activated and wind up firing at the wrong target entirely. But luck—or Bai's training— proved adequate, and by the time the last of those sessions was over, Jonny could stand amid the flickering lights without wincing. At least not much.

At the beginning of the second week, they began putting all of it together.

"Listen up, Cobras, because today'll be your first chance to get yourselves slagged," Bai announced, apparently oblivious to the steady rain coming down on all of them. Standing at attention, Jonny tried to achieve a similar indifference; but the trickles working under his collar were far too cold for him to succeed. "A hundred meters behind me you'll see a wall," Bai continued. "It's part of a quadrangle containing a courtyard and a small inner building. Running along the top of the wall is a photoelectric beam simulating a defense laser; inside the courtyard are some remotes simulating Troft guards. Your objective is a small red box inside the building, which you are to obtain—*quietly*—and escape with."

"Great," Jonny muttered under his breath. Already his stomach was starting to churn.

"Be thankful we're not invading Reginine," Noffke murmured from beside him. "We set *our* wall lasers pointing *up* instead of across."

"Shh!"

"Now, the remotes are programmed with the best estimates of Troft sensory and reflexive capabilities," Bai was saying, "and the operators running them are the best, so don't count on *them* making stupid mistakes. They're carrying dye-pellet guns, and if they get you, you're officially slagged. If you hit the wall photo beam, you're also slagged. If you make too much noise—as defined by the sound pick-ups we've set up—you'll not only lose points, but probably also bring the remotes down on you and get slagged. On top of all that, there are likely to be various automatics and *reasonable* booby-traps in the building you'll need to avoid—and don't bother asking what kind, 'cause I'm not telling. Questions? Um? All right. Aldred, front and center; everyone else to that canvas shelter to your left."

One by one, the trainees moved to Bai's side and headed across the muddy field. Bai had failed to mention that a kill was announced by an alarm horn, and as each man's disappearance over the wall was followed sooner or later by that sardonic bleat the quiet conversation in the shelter took on an increasingly nervous flavor. When the eighth trainee across—Deutsch, as it happened—reappeared over the wall without triggering the alarm, the collective sigh of relief was as eloquent as a standing ovation.

All too soon, it was Jonny's turn. "Okay, Moreau, everything's been reset," Bai told him. "Remember, you're being judged on stealth and observation, *not* speed. Take your time and remember all the stuff I've been lecturing you about the past couple of evenings and you should be okay. Um? Okay; *go*."

Jonny took off across the mud, running hunched-over to give any hypothetical optical sensors a smaller target to work with. Ten meters from the wall he slowed, splitting his attention to search for trip wires, wall-mounted sensors, and possible climbing routes. Nothing hazardous caught his attention; on the debit side, the wall had no obvious handholds, either. At the base Jonny gave the wall one final scan. Then, hoping his height estimate was close enough, he bent his knees and jumped. If anything, he erred on the short side, and at the very peak of his arc his curved fingers slid neatly over the top of the wall.

So far, so good. From his new vantage point, Jonny could see the photoelectric apparatus, from which he could tell that he would need to clear a maximum of twenty centimeters in getting over. A relatively easy task . . . provided he didn't bring the pseudo-Trofts down on him in the process.

Clicking his back teeth together, he activated his auditory enhancers; clicked three times more to run them to max. The sound of impacting rain reached frequency saturation and leveled out at a dull roar; beneath it, fainter noises became audible. None of them, he decided, sounded like remotes slogging through mud. Mentally crossing his fingers, he eased his head above the wall, switching off his super-hearing as he did so.

The inner building was smaller than he'd expected, a single-story structure covering perhaps a tenth of the walled-in area. No guards were visible near it; shifting his attention, he gave the rest of the courtyard a quick sweep.

Empty.

Either he'd been incredibly lucky and all the guards were momentarily on the far side of the building, or else they were all inside, perhaps watching through the darkened windows. Either way, he had little choice but to grab the opportunity. Pulling hard with his right arm, he sent his legs and torso up and over the wall, vaulting horse style, tucking his arms to his chest as he did so to clear the photobeam. Beneath him, he got his first glimpse of the area where he would land—

And of the dull metallic sheen of the remote standing there.

The single thought *unfair!* was all he had time for. Kicking in his targeting lock, he snapped his hands into firing position and gave the remote a double blast. His attention on his shooting, his landing a second later was embarrassingly clumsy; but he had the satisfaction of seeing the guard hit the ground the same time he did.

But there was no reason yet for self-congratulation, and almost before he had his balance back Jonny was running toward the building. Wherever the rest of the remotes were, they would be bound to discover their downed colleague before too long, and he had to move while there was still something left of his initiative. Reaching the nearest wall, he sidled to the corner and took a quick look around it. No one in sight, but he could see the steps leading to an entrance door. Breaking into a run again, he headed for it—

Even without his auditory enhancers on, the buzzer that went off beside him was deafening. Jonny cursed under his breath; obviously, he'd hit one of the automatics Bai had warned them about. In a hurry or not, he still should have taken the time for a careful search. Now, it was too late, and there was nothing to do but prepare for combat. If he could get inside before the remotes reacted to the alarm there might still be a chance . . . he was at the door, aiming his laser at the solder lock, when a remote came around the far corner.

Jonny hurled himself from the building in a flat dive, arm swinging around as he targeted the guard. But even as he squeezed off the shot, the door to his side slammed open; and before he could do more than twist his head to see, he felt the dull punch of a dye-pellet against his ribs.

And, announcing his failure to the world, the alarm horn hooted from the wall. Feeling like an idiot, Jonny got to his feet and looked around for the way out.

"Let that be a lesson to you," someone said from the building, and Jonny turned to see a man with a *Cobra Operations* patch on his coveralls standing behind the remote who'd shot him. "When you've got two or more targets it can actually be faster to slag the first one visually, without the targeting lock."

"Thanks, sir," Jonny sighed. "How do I get out?"

"Right over there—you can head back and get cleaned up. And if it helps, a lot of the others did worse."

Swallowing, Jonny nodded and set off in the indicated direction. It wasn't much comfort to know that others would have died sooner. Dead is still dead.

"So, the great Horizon hope finally crusked one," Viljo said, setting his tray down at the far end of the table and favoring Jonny with an off-cordial smile.

Jonny dropped his eyes to his own lunch and said nothing, concentrating instead on the last few bites of his meal as the blood rushed to his face. Viljo's snide comments had become more and more frequent the past couple of days, and though Jonny was trying hard not to let the other get to him, the tension of the whole thing was becoming increasingly difficult to ignore. Afraid of doing anything that would brand him as overly sensitive or—worse—that would emphasize his frontier origins, he could only sit on his anger and hope Viljo would get tired of his verbal target practice.

Though if he wasn't, possibly others were. Across from Jonny, Halloran hunched over the table to eye Viljo. "I didn't notice you walking away with high honors, either," he said. "Matter of fact, except for Imel, I think we *all* got our egos nicely trimmed for show out there."

"Sure—but Jonny's the one Bai always holds up like he was the ideal trainee. Haven't you noticed? I just wondered if he liked being demoted to mortal."

Beside Viljo, Singh stirred in his seat. "You're exaggerating rather badly, Rolon; and even if you weren't, it would hardly be Jonny's fault."

"Oh, wouldn't it?" Viljo snorted. "Come on—you know as well as I do how this sort of favoritism works. Jonny's family's probably got some fix in with Bai or even Mendro, and Bai's making sure they're getting their money's worth."

And with that, the insults crossed a fine line . . . and Jonny abruptly had had enough.

In a single smooth motion, he stood up and leaped over the table, dimly aware of his chair slamming backwards into the next table as he did so. He landed directly behind Viljo who, apparently caught by surprise, was still seated. Jonny didn't wait for the other to respond; grabbing a fistful of shirt, he hauled Viljo upright and spun him around. "That's it, Viljo—that's the last breaff dropping I'm going to take from you. Now *back off*—understand?"

Viljo eyed him calmly. "My, my; so you have a temper after all. I suppose 'breaff dropping' is just one of those colorful expressions you use out there in the backwaters?"

That final smirk was too much. Letting go of Viljo's shirt, Jonny threw a punch at the other's face.

It was a disaster. Not only did Viljo duck successfully out of the way, but with his servos providing unaccustomed speed to his swing, Jonny was thrown completely off balance and rammed his thigh hard into the table before he could recover. The pain fanned his anger into something white-hot, and with a snarl he twisted around and hurled another blow at Viljo. Again he missed; but even as his arm cocked for a third try, something pinioned it in midair. He shoved against the grip, succeeded only in losing his balance again. "Easy, Jonny; *easy*," a voice murmured in his ear.

And with that the red haze abruptly vanished from his brain and he found himself standing in a roomful of silent Cobra trainees, his arms gripped solidly by Deutsch and Noffke, facing Viljo who—completely unmarked—looked altogether too self-satisfied.

He was still trying to sort it all out when the room's intercom/monitor ordered him to report to Mendro's office.

The interview was short, but excruciatingly painful, and by the time Jonny left he was feeling like one of the solder targets on the laser range. The thought of having to go back out on the practice field—of having to *face* everyone—was a knot of tension in his stomach, and as he walked across Mendro's outer office, he seriously considered turning back and asking for a transfer to a different branch of service. At least then he wouldn't have to endure the other trainees' eyes. . . . But as he debated the decision, his feet kept walking; and outside the office the whole question of hiding suddenly became academic.

Deutsch and Halloran peeled themselves from the wall where they'd been leaning as Jonny closed the door behind him. "You okay?" Deutsch asked, the concern in his face echoed in his voice.

"Oh, sure," Jonny snorted, unreasonably irked by this unexpected invasion of his private shame. "I just got verbally skinned alive, that's all."

"Well, at least it *was* all verbal," Halloran pointed out. "Don't forget, all of *Mendro*'s weapons are functional. Hey, lighten up, Jonny. You're still in the unit, aren't you?"

"Yeah," Jonny said, the hard lump starting to dissolve a bit. "At least as far as I know. Though Bai will probably have something to say about that when he hears what happened."

"Oh, Bai already knows—he's the one who told us to wait here for you," Halloran said. "He said to bring you out to the practice range when you were ready. Are you?"

Grimacing, Jonny nodded. "I suppose so. Might as well get it over with."

"What, facing Bai?" Deutsch asked as they set off down the hall. "Don't worry; he understands what that was all about. So do Parr and Druma, for that matter."

"I wish *I* did," Jonny shook his head. "What has Viljo got against me, anyway?"

Halloran glanced at him, and Jonny caught the other's frown. "You really don't know?"

"I just said that, didn't I? What, he doesn't like anyone who was born more than ten light-years from Earth?"

"He likes them fine . . . as long as they don't show they're better at anything than he is."

Jonny stopped abruptly. "What are you talking about? I never did anything like that."

Halloran sighed. "Maybe not in *your* books, but a person like Rolon does his accounting differently. Look, remember our very first orientation meeting, the one he showed up late at? Who was it Bai used to pop his excuse?"

"Well . . . me. But that was only because I was the last to arrive before him."

"Probably," Halloran conceded. "But Rolon didn't know that. And then the first evening of our actual training you tore the stuffing out of all of us in that game of King's Bluff. People from Earth have a long history of being successful gamers, and I suspect that really put the icing on the cake as far as Rolon was concerned."

Jonny shook his head in bewilderment. "But I didn't mean to beat him—"

"Of course you did—everyone 'means' to win in a game," Deutsch said. "You didn't mean to humiliate him, of course, but in a way that actually makes it worse. For someone with Rolon's competitive streak, being clobbered by a perceived social inferior who wasn't even trying to do so was more than he could take."

"So what am I supposed to do—roll over and play dead for him?"

"No, you're supposed to just continue doing as well as you can and to hell with his ego," Deutsch said grimly. "Maybe maneuvering you into Mendro's kennel will satisfy his lopsided sense of personal honor. If not—" He hesitated. "Well, if he can't learn to work with *you*, I don't think we're going to want him on Adirondack."

Jonny gave him a quick look. For a brief moment Deutsch's air of calm humor had vanished, showing something much darker beneath it. "You know," Jonny said, striving to sound casual, "a lot of times you don't seem very concerned about what's happening on your world."

"You mean because I laugh and joke around?" Deutsch asked.

"Or because I opted to spend a couple of months hanging around Asgard instead of grabbing a laser and rushing back to help?"

"Um . . . when you put it *that* way—"

"I care a lot about Adirondack, Jonny, but I don't see any advantage in tying myself in knots worrying about what the Trofts might be doing to my family and friends. Right now I can help them most by becoming the very best Cobra I can be—and by nudging the rest of you into doing the same."

"I think that's a hint we should get back to practice," Halloran said with a smile.

"Can't fool a psychologically trained mind," Deutsch replied wryly; and with that the momentary glimpse into his deeper self was over. But it was enough, and for the first time Jonny had a real understanding of the kind of men the Army had chosen for this unit.

The kind of men he'd been deemed worthy to join.

And it put the whole thing with Viljo into a final perspective. To risk washing out of the Cobras over what were essentially emotional fly bites would be the absolute depth of stupidity. From now on, he resolved, he would consider Viljo's gibes to be nothing more than practice in developing patience. If Deutsch could bear up under an invasion of his world, Jonny could surely put up with Viljo.

They'd reached an exit now, and Halloran led them outside. "Wait a second—we're on the wrong side of the building," Jonny said, stopping and looking around. "The practice field's that way, isn't it?"

"Yep," Halloran nodded cheerfully. "But for Cobras cross-country's faster than all those hallways."

"Cross-country as in around?" Jonny asked, peering down the eight-story structure heading halfway to infinity in both directions.

"As in over," Halloran corrected. Facing the wall, he flexed his knees. "Last one to the top's a gum-bumbler—and any windows you break come out of your pay."

The second week passed as the first had, with long days of Cobra exercises and equally long—or so it seemed—evenings of military theory. Every day or two they received new neckwrap computer modules, each one allowing a new weapon in their arsenals to be brought into play. Jonny learned how to use his sonic weapons and how to retune them in the event that the Trofts turned out to be particularly susceptible to specific frequencies; learned how to trigger his arcthrower, a blast of high voltage traveling down the ionization path burned by his right fingertip laser, and how to efficiently fry electronic gear with it; and, finally, learned now to handle the antiarmor laser in his left calf, simultaneously the most powerful and most awkward of his weapons. Pointing downward along the tibia, its beam was guided through his ankle by optical fibers to emerge through a flexible focusing lens in the bottom of his heel. Special boots were handed out with the computer modules that day, and as he tried to learn how to shoot while standing on one leg, Jonny joined the rest of the trainees in roundly cursing the idiot who'd been responsible for that particular design. Bai claimed they'd find out how versatile the laser was once they had their programmed reflexes, but no one seriously believed him.

But through all the work, practice, and memorization—through the physical and mental fatigue—two unexpected observations managed to penetrate Jonny's consciousness. First, that Viljo's taunts disappeared almost entirely after the mess hall incident, though the other remained cool toward him; and second, that Bai really *did* tend to single Jonny out for special notice.

The latter bothered him more than he cared to admit. Viljo's suggestion that the Moreau family had somehow bribed the instructor was absurd, of course ... but at least some of the other trainees must have overheard the allegation, and if Jonny could pick up on Bai's pattern so could they. What did they think about it? Did they imagine it implied he was getting special privileges off the training field?

More to the point, why was Bai doing it?

He wasn't the best of the trainees, certainly—Deutsch alone proved that. Nor, he thought, was he the worst. The youngest? Oldest? Closest physically to some old friend/enemy? Or—and it was a chilling thought—did Bai secretly share some of Viljo's biases?

But whatever the reason, there was no response he could think of except the one he was already using: to endure with as much outer stoicism and inner calm as he could manage. It proved more effective than he'd expected it to, and by the time the second week drew to a close he was able to face Bai's comments or work alongside Viljo with only the slightest nervousness. How much the other trainees noticed his new attitude he didn't know, but Halloran made at least one comment on it.

And then the third week began; and all that had gone before paled to the relative significance of a quiet summer's stroll ...

because on the first day of that week they began working with their computerized reflexes.

"It's dead simple," Bai told them, gesturing to the ceiling barely two meters above their heads. "You first key your targeting lock on the spot where you intend to hit, and then jump, giving your body a backward motion as you do so." He bent his knees and straightened them, simultaneously arching his back. "Then just relax and let the computer run your servos. Try not to fight it, by the way; you'll just strain your muscles and make it harder for your subconscious to adjust to having something else in charge of your body. Questions? Um? All right. Aldred, target lock: *go*."

One by one they all performed the ceiling jump that had been their first introduction to Cobra abilities those four long weeks ago. Jonny had thought himself adequately prepared; but when his turn came he found out otherwise. Nothing—not even the now-familiar servo enhancement effect—could quite compare with the essential decoupling of body and mind that the automatic reflexes entailed. Fortunately, the maneuver was over so quickly that he didn't have time to feel more than a very brief panic before his feet were back on the floor and his muscles returned to his control. Only later did he realize that Bai had probably started them with the ceiling jump for precisely that reason.

They went through the exercise five times each, and with each flawless jump Jonny's anxiety and general feeling of weirdness eased, until he was feeling almost comfortable with his new copilot.

As he should have expected, though, he wasn't allowed to feel comfortable for long.

They stood atop a five-story building, looking over the edge at the ground below and the reinforced wall facing them about fifteen meters away. "He's *got* to be kidding," Halloran murmured at Jonny's side.

Jonny nodded wordlessly, his eyes shifting to Bai as the instructor finished his verbal description of the maneuver and stepped to the edge to demonstrate. "As always," Bai said, "you start with a targeting lock to give your computer the range. Then you just . . . jump."

His legs straightened convulsively, and an instant later he was arcing toward the facing wall. He hit it feet first about five meters down, his shoes scraping loudly as they slid a short distance further down along it. The combination of that friction plus the impact-absorbing bending of his knees flipped him partly over;

and when his legs straightened again an instant later, the push sent him back toward the original building in a heels-over-head flip that somehow managed to have him feet forward when he struck the side, another five meters closer to the ground. Again he shoved off, and with one final bounce-and-flip off the far wall, he landed safely on the ground at the base of their building. "Nothing to it," his voice drifted up to the waiting trainees. "I'll be up in a minute, then we'll all try it."

He disappeared inside. "I think I'd rather take my chances with a straight jump," Noffke said to no one in particular.

"That's fine for a five-story building, but you'd never make it with anything really tall," Deutsch shook his head. "We *do* have some real cities on Adirondack, you know."

"I'll bet the Great Horizon Hope could give you a dozen more reasons why this is a good maneuver," Viljo put in, smiling sardonically at Jonny.

"Would you settle for two?" Jonny asked calmly. "One: you're never in free fall for very long this way, and besides making for a softer landing that'll play havoc with any manual *or* autotarget weapon they try shooting at you. And two: with your legs pointing up most of the time, your antiarmor laser's in good position to fire at whatever you were escaping from on the roof."

He had the satisfaction of seeing some of the other trainees nodding in agreement, and of watching Viljo's smirk sour into a grimace.

There was more—much more—and for ten days Bai put them through their paces. Gradually, the daily computer modules began to remove the restraints set onto their most dangerous equipment; just as gradually, the scorch-lasers and dye-pellets used by their metallic opponents were replaced by genuine weapons. Half a dozen of the trainees picked up minor burns and pellet wounds, and a new seriousness began to pervade the general attitude. Only Deutsch retained his bantering manner, and Jonny suspected it was simply because he was already as serious beneath the facade as the man could possibly be. The evening lectures were replaced by extra training sessions, giving them the chance to practice with their enhanced night vision the techniques they had so far used only in daylight and dusk. All of it seemed to be building to a head . . . and then, almost unexpectedly—though they all knew the schedule—it was over.

Almost.

"There comes a time, Cobras," Bai told them that final afternoon, "when training reaches a saturation point; where drills and practice don't hone so much as fine-polish. Fine-polishing is okay if you're a gemstone or an athlete, but you're neither: you're warriors. And for warriors there's no substitute for genuine combat experience.

"So, starting tomorrow morning, combat is what you're going to get. Four days of it: two solitaire and two in units. You'll be up against the same remotes you've been training with; your own weapons and abilities will be identical to what you'll have when your combat nanocomputers are implanted in you five days from now. So. It's sixteen hundred hours now, and you're all officially off-duty until oh-eight-hundred tomorrow, when you'll be taken by transport to the test site. I suggest you eat tonight as if you'll be on field rations for four days—which you will be—and get a good night's sleep. Questions? Unit dismissed."

It was a somber group that gathered in Jonny's room that evening after dinner. "I wonder what it's going to be like," Noffke said, sitting at the table shuffling his cards restlessly.

"Not easy, that's for sure," Singh sighed. "We've already had minor injuries when everyone knew what he and his opponents were doing. We could very well lose someone out there."

"Or several someones," Halloran agreed. He was standing at the window, staring out. Past his shoulder Jonny could see a sprinkling of lights from other parts of Freyr Complex and, further away, the lights from Farnesee, the nearest civilian town. Somehow, it reminded him of his home and family, a thought that added to his gloom.

"They wouldn't make it dangerous enough to actually *kill* us, would they?" Noffke asked, though his tight expression indicated he already knew the answer.

"Why not?" Halloran retorted. "Sure, they've spent a lot on us—but there's no sense letting marginal ones go on to get killed the minute they land on Adirondack. Why do you think they put off implanting our computers until *after* the test?"

"To save some money where possible," Jonny grunted. "Parr, stop shuffling those cards—either deal them or put them away."

"You know what we need?" Viljo spoke up abruptly. "A night out of this place. A few drinks, some music, a little conversation with real people—especially of the female sort—"

"And how exactly do you expect to persuade Mendro to let us out for this little sortie?" Deutsch snorted.

"Actually, I wasn't planning to ask him," Viljo said calmly.

"I think that qualifies as going A.W.O.L.," Halloran pointed out. "There are lots of easier ways to get ourselves crusked."

"Nonsense. Bai said we were off-duty, didn't he? Anyway, has anyone ever *explicitly* told us we were confined to Freyr Complex?"

There was a short silence. "Well, no, now that you mention it," Halloran admitted. "But—"

"But nothing. We can sneak out of here easily enough—this place isn't even guarded as well as a regular military base would be. Come on—none of us is going to sleep well tonight anyway. We might as well have some fun."

Because tomorrow we might die. No one said those words aloud, but from the shifting of feet it was clear everyone was thinking variations of them . . . and after another brief silence Halloran got to his feet. "Sure. Why not?"

"I'm in," Noffke nodded quickly. "I hear there's good card games to be had in the pleasure centers in town."

"Along with lots of other stuff," Deutsch nodded. "Druma; Jonny? How about it?"

Jonny hesitated, his brother's words about decadence and holding onto his ethics flashing through his mind. Still, Viljo was right: nowhere in their verbal or written orders had there been anything about not leaving the complex.

"Come on, Jonny," Viljo said, using his first name for the first time in days. "If you can't justify it as relaxation, think of it as practice infiltrating an enemy-occupied city."

"All right," Jonny said. After all, he wouldn't have to do anything in town he didn't feel right about. "Just let me change into my other fatigues—"

"Phrij on that," Viljo interrupted. "Those look fine. Quit stalling and let's go. Druma?"

"Oh, I guess so," Singh agreed. "But only for a little while."

"You'll be able to leave whenever you want to," Halloran assured him. "Once we're in town everyone's on his own timetable. Well. Out the window?"

"Out and up," Viljo nodded. "Lights out . . . here goes."

It proved far easier to leave the complex grounds than Jonny had expected. From the roof of their wing they dropped to a darkened drill field used by the regular Army recruits in Freyr; crossing it, they arrived at an easily-negotiated perimeter wall. Avoiding the simple photobeam alarms at the top, they went over.

"That's it," Deutsch said cheerfully. "Nothing but ten klicks of field and suburb between us and fun. Race you!"

Even with having to slow down once they hit populated areas, the trip took only half an hour . . . and Jonny got his first taste of what a real city could be.

Afterwards, he wouldn't remember much about that first plunge into mainstream Dominion recreational life. Deutsch took the lead, guiding them on a giddy and tortuous path among the shows, night spots, restaurants, and pleasure centers that he'd become famil-iar with in the weeks between his arrival from an Iberiand univer-sity and his final enlistment in the Cobras. More people than Jonny had ever seen at once in his life seemed to be crowded into the district—civilians in oddly cut, luminescent clothing; other civil-ians whose focus of ornamentation was wild facial makeup, and military personnel of every branch and rank. It was too festive an atmosphere for Jonny to feel uneasy, but by the same token it was too outlandish for him to truly relax and enjoy, either. It made for a lousy compromise, and within a couple of hours he had had enough. Excusing himself from Deutsch and Singh—all that were still together of the original six—he worked his way back through the crowds to the soothing darkness surrounding the town. Getting back into the complex was no harder than sneaking out had been, and soon he was sliding back through the window into their dark and deserted room. Leaving the lights off, he quickly prepared for bed.

He'd been lying in his bunk for perhaps half an hour, trying to will his overactive mind to sleep, when a noise at the window made him open his eyes. "Who's there?" he stage-whispered as the figure eased into the room.

"Viljo," the other murmured tightly. "You alone?"

"Yes," Jonny said, swinging his legs out of bed. Something in Viljo's voice was distinctly off-key. "What's wrong?"

"I thought Mendro and the MPs might be here by now," Viljo said distractedly, flopping onto his back on his own bunk. "I'm not sure, but I think I'm in trouble."

"What?" Jonny bumped his vision enhancers up a notch. In the amplified background light Viljo's expression was tight, but he didn't seem hurt. "What kind of trouble?"

"Oh, I had a little argument with some phrijeater behind one of the bars. Had to bounce him around a bit." Abruptly, Viljo levered himself off the bunk and headed for the bathroom. "Go back to bed," he told Jonny over his shoulder. "If the guy makes trouble we'd both better be innocently asleep when the investigations start."

"Will he recognize you again? I mean—"

"I don't think he was blind or illiterate, no."

"I *meant* was it light enough to read your name off your fatigues?"

"Yeah, it was light enough . . . if he had time to pay attention. Go to bed, will you?"

Heart pounding, Jonny crawled back under his blanket. *Bounced him around a bit.* What did that mean? Had Viljo hurt the other— perhaps even badly? He opened his mouth to ask . . . and then closed it again. Did he really want to know all the details? "What are you going to do?" he asked instead.

"Get undressed and go to bed—what did you think?"

"No, I mean about . . . reporting it."

The sound of running water stopped and Viljo reemerged. "I'm sure as hell not telling anyone else about this. You think I'm crazy?"

"But the guy could be badly hurt—"

"He got away under his own power. Besides, he's hardly the sort of phrijeater worth risking your career over. That goes for *your* career, too."

"I—what?"

"You know what. You go blabbing about this to Mendro and you'll have to admit you were out of Freyr tonight, too." He paused, studying Jonny's face. "Besides which, it'd be a lousy demonstration of team unity for you to turn me in over something this trivial."

"*Trivial?* What was he armed with, a laser cannon? You could've gotten away without fighting. Why'd you stick around?"

"You wouldn't understand." Viljo climbed into his bunk. "Look, I didn't really hurt him; and if I overreacted, it's too late to change things now. So let's just forget it, huh? Chances are he won't even report it."

"But what if he does? If you don't report it first, it'll look like you're trying to cover it up."

"Yeah, well, I'll play the odds—and since it's *my* risk, you're invited to stay out of it."

Jonny didn't answer. Silence again returned to the room, and after a few minutes Viljo's breathing slipped into the slow, steady pattern of sleep. The mark of a clear conscience, Jonny's father would have said, but in this case that hardly seemed likely. For Jonny, though, the immediate problem was not Viljo's conscience but his own.

What *was* the proper thing to do here? If he kept quiet he was technically an accessory after the fact, and if the civilian's injuries turned out to be severe, that could mean real trouble. On the other hand, Viljo's point about team loyalty was well taken. Jonny remembered Bai saying something about such things at the orientation meeting, and if Viljo had in fact simply put a bully in his place, forgetting the incident *would* seem the best course. Point, counterpoint; and with the limited information he had the two arguments could chase each other around his brain all night.

They made a good try at doing just that, keeping him uselessly awake for the next hour and a half. One by one his other four roommates came in the open window, performed their bedtime preparations, and went to sleep. At least none of them had gotten caught; and with that particular worry out of the way Jonny was finally able to force the rest of it far enough back in his mind to fall asleep himself. But his dreams were violent, tension-ridden things, and when reveille put an end to them, he felt worse than if he'd been awake all night.

Somehow, he managed to dress, grab his prepacked combat bag, and head down to the mess hall with the others without his groggy eyes drawing any special comment. No MPs arrived while they were eating, nor was anyone waiting by the transport as they crowded in with the rest of the trainees; and with each kilometer they flew Jonny's load eased a little more. Surely the authorities wouldn't have let them leave if there'd been any complaints of Cobra misbehavior in town. Apparently the other participant in Viljo's fight had indeed decided to let the whole matter slide.

They reached the hundred-thousand-hectare test site an hour later, and after giving them new computer modules, extra equipment, and final instructions, Bai turned them loose on their individual objectives. Putting the entire previous night out of his mind, Jonny set to work surviving the exam.

It was therefore something of a surprise when, returning to field HQ from his first successful exercise, he found an MP transport waiting. It was even more of a shock to find it was waiting for *him.*

The young man fidgeting in his chair next to Mendro's desk certainly looked like he'd been in a fight. Heal-quick bandages covered one cheek and his jaw, and his left arm and shoulder were wrapped in the kind of ribbed plastic cast used to speed broken bone repair. What was visible of his expression looked nervous but determined.

Mendro's expression was merely determined. "Is this the man?" he asked the other as Jonny sat down in the chair his MP guard indicated.

The civilian's eyes flicked once over Jonny's face, then settled onto his fatigue tunic. "It was too dark to see his face well enough, Commander," he said. "But that's the name, all right."

"I see." Mendro's eyes bored into Jonny's. "Moreau, Mr. P'alit here claims you attacked him last night behind the Thasser Eya Bar in Farnesee. True or false?"

"False," Jonny managed through dry lips. Through the haze of unreality filling the room a nasty suspicion was beginning to take shape.

"Were you *in* Farnesee last night?" Mendro persisted.

"Yes, sir, I was. I . . . sneaked out to try and relax before the final exam started today. I was only there for a couple of hours—" he glanced at P'alit—"and I most certainly didn't fight with anyone."

"He's lying," P'alit spoke up. "He was—"

Mendro's gesture silenced him. "Did you go alone?"

Jonny hesitated. "No, sir. All of us in my room went. We split up in town, though, so I don't have any alibi. But . . ."

"But what?"

Jonny took a deep breath. "About a half hour after I got back one of the others came in and told me he'd—well, he said he'd bounced someone around a little behind one of the bars in Farnesee."

Mendro's eyes were hard, unbelieving. "And you didn't report it?"

"He indicated it was a minor argument. Certainly nothing so . . . serious." He looked again at P'alit; only then did the sophistication of the frame-up sink in. No wonder Viljo hadn't wanted Jonny to change clothes before they all left. "I can only conclude that he was wearing my spare tunic at the time."

"Uh-huh. Who was it who told you all this?"

"Rolon Viljo, sir."

"Viljo. The one you attacked in the mess hall awhile back?"

Jonny gritted his teeth. "Yes, sir."

"Obviously just trying to put the blame on someone else," P'alit spoke up scornfully.

"Perhaps. How did the fight start, Mr. P'alit?"

The other shrugged with his free shoulder. "Oh, I made some snide comment about the outer provinces—I don't even know how the topic came up. He took it personally and shoved me out the back door where a bunch of us were standing."

"Isn't that what you targeted Viljo over, Moreau?" Mendro asked.

"Yes, sir." Jonny resisted the almost overwhelming urge to again explain that incident. "I don't suppose any of your companions might have gotten a clear look at your assailant, Mr. P'alit?"

"No, no one saw you clearly—but I don't think that's going to be necessary." P'alit looked back at Mendro. "I think this story's pretty well lost its factory finish, Commander. Are you going to take action on this or not?"

"The Army always disciplines its own," Mendro said, tapping a button on his desk console. "Thank you for bringing this matter to our attention." Behind Jonny, the door opened and another MP appeared. "Sergeant Costas will escort you out."

"Thank you." Standing up, P'alit nodded to Mendro and followed the MP out. Catching the eye of Jonny's guard, Mendro gestured minutely, and the other joined the exodus. The door closed and Jonny and Mendro were alone.

"Anything you'd like to say?" Mendro asked mildly.

"Nothing that would do any good, sir," Jonny told him bitterly. All the work, all the sweat . . . and it was about to come crashing down on top of him. "I didn't do it, but I don't know any way to prove that."

"Um." Mendro gave him a long, searching gaze and then shrugged. "Well . . . you'd better get back to the testing, I suppose, before you get any further behind schedule."

"You're not dropping me from the unit, sir?" Jonny asked, a spark of hope struggling to pierce the rubble of his collapsed future.

"Do you think this sort of misbehavior rates that?" Mendro countered.

"I really don't know." Jonny shook his head. "I know we're needed for the war, but . . . on Horizon, at least, picking on someone weaker than you are is considered cowardly."

"It's considered that way on Asgard, too." Mendro sighed. "It may very well come to expulsion, Moreau; at this point I don't know. But until that decision's made there's no point in depriving your team of your help in the group operations."

In other words, they were going to give him the chance to risk his life—and possibly lose it—and *then* decide whether that risk had any real meaning or not. "Yes, sir," Jonny said, standing up. "I'll do my best."

"I expect nothing less." Mendro touched a button and the MP reappeared. "Dismissed."

✧   ✧   ✧

It wasn't as hard as Jonny had expected to forget his new troubles as the testing continued. The defenses he faced were devilishly tight, and it took every milligram of his concentration to handle his assigned missions. But his luck and skill held out, and he completed the solitaire exercises with nothing more serious than skinned hands and an impressive collection of bruises.

And then he joined his roommates for the group tests . . . and there the disasters began.

Facing Viljo again—working and fighting alongside him— brought out thoughts and feelings that even their danger couldn't suppress . . . and that distraction quickly manifested itself in reduced competence. Twice Jonny got himself into situations that only his computerized reflexes were able to get him out of; more often than that a failure to do his part of the job wound up putting one of the others in unnecessary danger. Singh took a laser burn that had him operating under the sluggishness of heavy pain-killers, while only quick action by Jonny and Deutsch pulled Noffke out of a pincer trap that would almost certainly have left him dead.

A hundred times during those two days Jonny considered having it out with Viljo, either verbally or physically; of letting the others know the kind of vermin they were working with and at least eliminating the lie he was being forced to live. But each time the opportunity arose he choked his anger back down and said nothing. They were all just barely surviving with one of their number under an emotional handicap; to multiply that burden and spread it around would be not only unfair but likely lethal as well.

The other logical alternative occurred to him only once, and for an hour afterward he actually regretted the fact that his ethical training forbade him to simply shoot Viljo in the back.

The missions went on, oblivious to Jonny's internal turmoil. Together the six of them broke into a fortified ten-story building; penetrated and destroyed a twenty-man garrison; disabled the booby-traps around an underground bunker and blew up its entrance; and successfully rescued four remotes simulating civilian prisoners from a Troft jail. They camped overnight in a Troft-patrolled wasteland area, picked up the characteristics of an off-center group of civilians quickly enough and accurately enough to avoid being identified as strangers an hour afterwards, and led a group of Resistance remotes on a simple mission that succeeded despite the often dangerous errors the remotes' operators allowed their machines to make.

They did it all, they did it well, and they lived through it . . .

and as the transport flew them back toward Freyr, Jonny decided it had been worth the risk. Whatever discipline Mendro chose to administer, he knew now that he indeed had what it took to be a Cobra. Whether he was ever allowed to serve as one /or not, that inner knowledge was something they could never take from him.

When they reached Freyr and found the MPs waiting, he was almost glad. Whatever Mendro had decided, apparently it was going to be over quickly.

And it was. What he wasn't expecting was that the commander would invite an audience to watch.

"Cee-three Bai reports you did extremely well," Mendro commented, looking around at the six grimy trainees seated in a semicircle in front of his desk. "Given you're all alive and relatively unscathed, I would tend to agree. Any immediate reactions to the missions that spring to mind?"

"Yes, sir," Deutsch spoke up after a moment of thoughtful silence. "We had some major problems leading that Resistance team—their mistakes were *very* hard to compensate for. Was that simulation realistic?"

Mendro nodded. "Unfortunately, yes. Civilians are always going to make what are—to you—incredibly stupid mistakes. About all you can do is try and minimize that effect while maintaining an attitude of patience. Other comments? No? Then I suppose we'd better move on to the reason I called you here: the charges outstanding against Trainee Moreau."

The abrupt change of subject sent a rustle of surprise through the group. "Charges, sir?" Deutsch asked carefully.

"Yes. He's been accused of attacking a civilian during your unauthorized trip into town four nights ago." Mendro gave them a capsule summary of P'alit's story. "Moreau claims he didn't do it," he concluded. "Comments?"

"I don't believe it, sir," Halloran said flatly. "I'm not calling this character a liar, but I think he must've misread the name."

"Or else saw Jonny that night, got into a fight later, and is trying to stick the Army for his medical costs," Noffke suggested.

"Perhaps," Mendro nodded. "But suppose for the moment it's true. Do you think I would be justified in that event in transferring Moreau out of the Cobras?"

An uncomfortable silence descended on the room. Jonny watched the play of emotion across their faces, but while he clearly had their sympathy, it was also clear which way they were leaning. He hardly blamed them; in their places he knew which answer he would choose.

It was Deutsch who eventually put the common thought into words. "I don't think you'd have any choice, sir. Misuse of our equipment would essentially pit us against the civilian population, certainly in their minds. Speaking as a citizen of Adirondack, we've already got all the opponents we need right now."

Mendro nodded. "I'm glad you agree. Well. For the next couple of days you'll be off-duty again. After that we'll be running through a detailed analysis of your exam performance with each of you, showing you where and how your equipment could have been utilized more effectively." He paused . . . and something in his face abruptly broke through the deadness surrounding Jonny's mind. "That's one of the things we had to keep secret, to avoid excessive self-consciousness," the commander went on. "With the relatively large amount of space available in those neckwrap computers we were able to keep records of all your equipment usage." Almost lazily, he shifted his gaze. "That alley behind the Thasser Eya Bar was dark, Trainee Viljo. You had to use your vision enhancers while you fought that civilian."

The color drained from Viljo's face. His mouth opened . . . but then his eyes flicked around the group, and whatever protest or excuse he was preparing died unsaid.

"If you have an explanation, I'll hear it now," Mendro added.

"No explanation, sir," Viljo said through stiff lips.

Mendro nodded. "Halloran, Noffke, Singh, Deutsch: you'll escort your former teammate to the surgical wing; they already have their instructions. Dismissed."

Slowly, Viljo stood up. He looked once at Jonny with empty eyes, then walked to the door with the remnants of his dignity wrapped almost visibly around him. The others, their own expressions cast in iron, followed.

The brittle silence in the room remained for several seconds after the door closed behind them. "You knew all along I didn't do it," Jonny said at last.

Mendro shrugged minutely. "Not conclusively, but we were ninety percent sure. The computer doesn't record a complete film every time the vision enhancers are used, you know. We had to correlate that usage with servo movements to know whether you'd done it or not—and until you identified Viljo as the probable culprit, we didn't know whose records we also needed to pull."

"You still could've told me then that I wasn't really under suspicion."

"I could've," Mendro acknowledged. "But it seemed like a good opportunity to get a little more data on your emotional makeup."

"You wanted to see if I'd be too preoccupied to function in combat? Or whether I'd just slag Viljo and be done with it?"

"And losing control either way would've had you out of the unit instantly," Mendro said, his voice hardening. "And before you complain about being unfairly singled out, remember that we're preparing you for *war* here, not playing some game with fixed rules. We do what's necessary, and if some people bear a little more of the burden than others, well, that's just the way it goes. Life is like that, and you'd better get used to it." The commander grunted. "Sorry—didn't mean to lecture. I won't apologize for running you an extra turn around the squirrel cage, but having come through the test as well as you did I don't think you've got real grounds for complaint."

"No, sir. But it wasn't just a single turn around the cage. Cee-three Bai's been holding me up for special notice ever since the training began—and if he hadn't done that Viljo might not have gotten irritated enough to try tarnishing my image like he did."

"Which let us learn something important about him, didn't it?" Mendro countered coolly.

"Yes, sir. But—"

"Let me put it this way, then," Mendro interrupted. "In all of human history people from one part of a region, country, planet, or system have tended to look down on people from another. It's simple human nature. In today's Dominion of Man this manifests itself as a faintly condescending attitude toward the frontier planets. Worlds like Horizon, Rajput, even Zimbwe . . . and Adirondack.

"It's a small thing and not at all important culturally, and it's therefore damned hard to test for its influence on a given trainee's personality. So without useful theory, we fall back on experiment: we raise someone from one of those worlds as the shining example of what a good Cobra should be and then watch to see who can't stand that. Viljo obviously couldn't. Neither, I'm sorry to say, could some of the others."

"I see." A week ago, Jonny thought, he'd probably have been angry to learn he'd been used like that. But now . . . *he* had passed his test, and would be remaining a Cobra. They hadn't, and would be becoming . . . what? "What's going to happen to them?

I remember you saying that some of our equipment wouldn't be removable. Will you have to . . . ?"

"Kill them?" Mendro smiled faintly, bitterly, and shook his head. "No. The equipment isn't removable, but at this stage it can be rendered essentially useless." There was something like pain in the other's eyes, Jonny noticed suddenly. How many times, he wondered, and for how many large or small reasons, had the commander had to tell one of his carefully chosen trainees that the suffering and sacrifice was all going to be for nothing? "The nanocomputer they'll be fitted with will be a pale imitation of the one you'll be receiving soon. It'll disconnect the power pack from all remaining weapons and put a moderate upper limit on servo power. To all intents and purposes they'll leave Asgard as nothing more than normal men with unbreakable bones."

"And some bitter memories."

Mendro gave him a long, steady look. "We all have those, Moreau. Memories are what ultimately spell the difference between a trainee and a soldier. When you've got memories of things that haven't worked—of things you could have done better, or differently, or not done at all—when you've got all that behind your eyes but can still do what has to be done . . . *then* you'll be a soldier."

A week later Jonny, Halloran, Deutsch, Noffke, and Singh—now designated Cobra Team 2/03—left with the other newly-commissioned Cobras on a heavily protected skip-transport for the war zone. Penetrating the Troft battle perimeter, the teams were space-chuted into an eight-hundred-kilometer stretch of Adirondack's strategic Essek District.

The landing was a disaster. Reacting far quicker than anyone had expected them to, the Troft ground forces intercepted Jonny's team right on the edge of the city Deutsch had been steering them toward. The Cobras were able to escape the encirclement with nothing more than minor flesh wounds . . . but in the blistering crossfire of that battle three civilians, caught in the wrong place at the wrong time, were killed. For days afterward their faces haunted Jonny's memories, and it was only as the team settled into their cover identities and began planning their first raid that he realized Mendro had been right.

And he was well on his way to collecting a soldier's memories.

Interlude

Halfway around Asgard from Freyr Complex—removed both in distance and philosophical outlook from the centers of military strength—lay the sprawling city known simply as Dome. Periodic attempts had been made in the past two centuries to give it a more elegant name; but those efforts had been as doomed to failure as would have been a movement to rename Earth itself. The city—and the geodesic dome that dominated its skyline—were as fixed in the minds of Dominion citizens as were their own names . . . because it was from here that the Central Committee sent out the orders, laws, and verdicts that ultimately affected the lives of each one of those citizens. From here could be reversed the decisions of mayors, syndics, and even planetary governor-generals; and as all were equal under the law, so in theory could any citizen's complaint or petition be brought to the Committee's attention.

In practice, of course, that was pure myth, and everyone who worked in the dome's shadow knew it. Small, relatively local matters were the province of the lower levels of government, and that was where they generally stayed. Seldom did any matter not directly affecting billions of people come to even a single Committé's attention.

But it *did* happen.

Committé Sarkiis H'orme's office was about average for one of the thirty most powerful men in the Dominion. Plush carpet, rare-wood paneling, a large desk inlaid with artifacts from dozens of worlds—a quiet sort of luxury, as such things went. Beyond the side doors lay his eight-room personal apartment and the miniature haiku garden where he often went to think and plan. Some Committés used their dome apartments but rarely, preferring to

45

leave their work behind in the evening and fly out to their larger country estates. H'orme was not one of those. Conscientious and hard-working by nature, he often worked late into the night . . . and at his age, the strain too often showed.

It was showing now, Vanis D'arl thought, running a critical eye over H'orme as the Committé skimmed through the report he'd prepared. Soon now—probably sooner than either had expected—H'orme would drive himself to an early death or retirement, and D'arl would take his place on the Committee. The ultimate success the Dominion had to offer; but one that carried a twinge of uneasiness along with it. D'arl had been with H'orme for nineteen years—the last eight as chief aide and chosen successor—and if he'd learned one thing in that time, it was that running the Dominion properly took infinite knowledge and infinite wisdom. The fact that no one else possessed those qualities either was irrelevant; the philosophy of excellence under which he'd been raised demanded he strive for the closest approximations possible. H'orme, also born and raised on Asgard, shared that background . . . and D'arl therefore knew how much work those goals entailed.

Pushing the "page" button one last time, H'orme laid down his comboard and raised his eyes to D'arl's. "Thirty percent. After all the preliminary testing thirty percent of the Cobra warrior trainees are still being deemed unfit. I presume you noticed the primary reason listed?"

D'arl nodded. "'Unsuitability for close work with civilian populations.' It's a catch-all category, I'm afraid, but I couldn't get the numbers broken down any further. I'm still trying."

"You see what this implies, though, don't you? For the tests to have missed that badly, *something* must have changed between the prelims and the final cut; and what *that* means is that we're sending fully-activated Cobra warriors to Silvern and Adirondack without truly understanding their psychological state. On general principles alone that's poor policy."

D'arl pursed his lips. "Well . . . it may just be a temporary feeling of power induced by their new abilities," he suggested. "A taste of warfare might make them realize that they're as fallible as any other mortals. Bring any conceit back down to normal."

"Perhaps. But perhaps not." H'orme flipped to the report directory, found an item. "Three hundred of them sent out in the first landing wave; six hundred more in training. Hmmm. I suppose it *could* just be a reflection of the poor statistics available. Any indication the Army's adjusting its prelim testing screen?"

"Too soon to tell," D'arl shook his head.

For a moment the other was silent. D'arl let his attention drift to the triangular windows at H'orme's back and the panoramic view of Dome it provided. Some Committés had the windows permanently blanked in favor of more picturesque holos, and he'd often thought H'orme's choice indicated a firmer commitment to seeking out truth and reality. "If you'd like, sir," he spoke up, "I could place a cancellation order for the whole project on the Considerations List. At the very least it would alert the rest of the Committee that there were potential problems with it."

"Hm." H'orme gazed at his comboard again. "Three hundred already in action. No. No, the reasons the Committee gave its approval in the first place are still valid: we're in a war for Dominion territory and we've got to use every weapon that could possibly help us. Besides, cutting things off now would essentially doom the Cobra warriors already fighting to a losing war of attrition. Still . . ." He tapped his fingers on his desk. "I want you to start gleaning all military intelligence coming from Silvern and Adirondack for data on how they're interacting both with each other and the local civilian populations. If any problems start developing, I want to know about it right away."

"Yes, sir," D'arl nodded. "It might help if I knew exactly what you were looking for."

H'orme waved a hand vaguely. "Oh, call it a . . . a *Titan complex*, I suppose. The belief that one is so powerful that one is above normal laws and standards. The Cobra warriors have been given a great deal of physical power and that *can* be a dangerous thing."

D'arl had to smile at that. Imagine, a Committé of the Dominion worried about too much power in a single individual! Still, he saw the other's point. The Cobra warriors had been handed their power all at once, instead of having to acquire and use it in small increments, which essentially sidestepped the usual adjustment mechanisms. "I understand," he told H'orme. "Do you want me to file that report in the main system?"

"No, I'll do it later. I want to study the numbers more closely first."

"Yes, sir." The unspoken implication being that some of those figures might wind up in H'orme's personal database rather than in the more accessible main Dome system. One of the bases of power, D'arl had long ago learned, was in not letting potential opponents know everything you did. "Shall I have someone bring up dinner for you?"

"Please. And add in an extra pot of cahve; I expect I'll be working late this evening."

"Yes, sir." D'arl got to his feet. "I'll probably also be in my office until later if you need me."

H'orme grunted acknowledgment, already engrossed in the comboard again. Walking silently on the thick carpet, D'arl crossed to the inlaid grafwood door. The Cobra warriors were certainly no danger while occupied in a war; but H'orme wasn't one to jump at sudden noises, and if he was becoming concerned, it was time D'arl did likewise. First step would be a call around the planet to the Cobra training center in Freyr Complex to see about shaking loose some more numbers.

And after that . . . it would probably be best to have the dining service send up two dinners instead of just one. It looked like this could be a long evening for him, too.

Warrior: 2406

The apartment living room was small and cluttered, with the kind of sad dinginess that comes more from lack of time and materials rather than from lack of interest in housekeeping. Seated at the scarred table in the room's center, Jonny let his eyes drift across the far wall, finding an echo of his own weariness in the faded blue paint there. A map of his own soul, he'd frequently thought of it, with its small cracks and chips echoing the effects of nearly three years of warfare on Jonny's psyche. *But it's still standing,* he told himself firmly, as he always did at this point in his contemplation. *The explosions and sonic booms can strain the surface, but beneath it the wall remains solid. And if a stupid wall can do it, so can I.*

"Like this?" a tentative voice asked from beside him.

Jonny looked down at the rumpled piece of paper and the lines and numbers the child had written there. "Well, the first three are right," he nodded. "But the last one should be—"

"I'll get it," Danice interrupted, attacking the geometry problem with renewed vigor. "Don't tell me."

Jonny smiled, gazing fondly at the girl's tangled red hair and determined frown as she redid her work. Danice was ten years old, the same age that Jonny's sister was now, and though Jonny hadn't heard from his family since arriving on Adirondack, he sometimes imagined that Gwen had grown to be a dark-haired version of the girl now sitting beside him. Certainly Gwen's spunk and common-sense stubbornness were here in abundance. Certainly too Danice's ability to treat Jonny as a good friend—despite her parents' quiet reservations over the Cobra's temporary presence in their household—showed the independent streak Jonny had often seen in his sister.

But Danice was growing up in a war zone, and no strength of character could get her through that entirely unscathed. So far she'd been lucky: though crowded into a small apartment with too many people, the simmering guerrilla war outside had otherwise touched her life only indirectly.

Given sufficient time, though, that was bound to change, especially if the Cobras overstayed their welcome in this part of Cranach and brought the Trofts down on the neighborhood. On the negative side, it gave Jonny one more thing to worry about; on the positive side, it was an extra incentive to do his job right and end the war as quickly as possible.

Through the open window came the dull thump of a distant thunderclap. "What was that?" Danice asked, her pencil pausing on the paper.

"Sonic boom," Jonny said promptly. He'd cut in his auditory enhancers halfway through the sound and caught the distinctive whine of Troft thrusters beneath the shock wave. "Probably a couple of kilometers away."

"Oh." The pencil resumed its movement.

Standing up, Jonny stepped to the window and looked out. The apartment was six stories up, but even so there wasn't much of a view. Cranach was a tall city, forced by the soft ground around it to go up instead of out as most of Adirondack's cities had done. Directly across the street was a solid wall of six-story buildings; beyond them only the tops of Cranach's central-city skyrisers were visible. Clicking for image magnification, he scanned what was visible of the sky for the trails of falling space-chutes. The pulse-code message last night from off-planet had sparked a desperate flurry of activity as the underground tried to prepare for their new Cobras—Cobras who, with lousy planning, would be landing virtually in the lap of the Troft buildup going on in and around Cranach. Jonny's jaw tightened at the thought, but there'd been nothing anyone had been able to do about it. Receiving a coded signal that in essence blanketed half a continent was one thing; signaling back again, even if the courier ship could afford to stick around that long, was a whole lot dicier. Jonny knew a round dozen ways of outsmarting radio, laser, and pulse-code direction finders—and each one had worked a maximum of four times before the Trofts came up with a way to locate the transmitter anyway. The underground had one method in reserve for emergencies; the Cobra landing had been deemed not to qualify as such.

"See anything?" Danice asked from the table.

Jonny shook his head. "Blue sky, skyrisers—and a little girl who's not doing her homework," he added, turning back to give her a mock glare.

Danice grinned, the very childlike expression not touching the more adult seriousness in her eyes. Jonny had often wondered how much she knew of her parents' activities out in Adirondack's shifting and impromptu battlefields. Did she know, for example, that they were at this moment on a hastily thrown together diversionary raid?

He didn't know. But if she didn't need a distraction from what was happening out there, *he* certainly did. Seating himself beside her again, he gave his mind over as fully as he could to the arcane mysteries of fifth-grade mathematics.

It was nearly three hours later before the click of a key in a lock came from the outer door. Jonny, his hands automatically curled into fingertip laser firing position, watched with muted anxiety as the six people filed silently into the apartment, his eyes flicking from faces to bodies as he searched for signs of injuries. The survey, as usual, yielded results both better than his fears and worse than his hopes. On the plus side, all those who'd left the apartment at dawn—two Cobras, four civilians—had returned under their own power. On the minus side—

He was across the room before Danice's mother was two steps inside the door, taking her unbandaged left arm from her husband's tired-looking grip. "What got you?" he asked quietly, steering her over to the couch.

"Hornet," Marja Tolan said, her voice heavy with pain-killers. Two of the civilians brushed Jonny aside and got to work with the apartment's bulky medical kit.

"Locked in on the click of her popcorn gun's firing mechanism, we think," Marja's husband Kem added tiredly from the table and Jonny's former chair. Fatigued or not, Jonny noted, he'd made it a point immediately to go over and reassure his daughter.

Jonny nodded grimly. Popcorn guns had hitherto been remarkably safe weapons to use, as such things went. Their tiny inertially guided missiles emitted no radar, sonar, or infrared-reflection that could be picked up by any of the Trofts' myriad detectors and response weapons. The missiles were furthermore blasted inert out of the gun barrels by a solid kick of compressed air, their inboard rockets not firing until they were ten to fifteen meters from the gunner. A lot of the missiles themselves had been destroyed in flight by Troft hornets and laser-locks, but until now the aliens hadn't had a way to backtrack to the gunner himself. Unless Marja had simply suffered a lucky hit . . . ?

Jonny looked at Cally Halloran, raised his eyebrows in a question so common now that he didn't even need to vocalize it. And Halloran understood. "We won't know for sure until popcorn gunners start dropping en masse," the Cobra said wearily. "But it was really too clear a shot to be pure chance. I think we can safely assume popcorn guns are out for the duration."

"For all the good the damn things have done so far," Imel Deutsch growled. Stalking to a window, he stood there facing out, his hands clasped in a rigid parade rest behind his back.

The room was suddenly quiet. Stomach churning, Jonny looked back at Halloran. "What happened?"

"Cobra casualty," Halloran sighed. "One of MacDonald's team, we think, though visibility was pretty poor. The people who were supposed to be guarding one of the approaches to their position apparently lost it and about a dozen Trofts got inside. We got a warning off but were too far away to help."

Jonny nodded, feeling an echo of the bitterness Deutsch was almost visibly radiating . . . of the bitterness he himself had nearly choked on twice since their arrival on Adirondack. Parr Noffke and Druma Singh—both of their team's own casualties had come about through the same kind of civilian incompetence. It had taken Jonny a long time to get over each of the deaths; Halloran, with marginally less tolerance for frontier people, had taken somewhat longer.

Deutsch, born and raised on Adirondack, hadn't gotten over it at all.

"Any idea of casualties generally?" Jonny asked Halloran.

"Low, I think, except for the Cobra," the other said. Jonny winced at the unspoken implication—more common lately than he liked—that Cobra lives were intrinsically more valuable than those of their underground allies. "Of course, we weren't really *trying* to take that stockpile, so no one had to take any unusual chances. Did the fresh troops make it down okay?"

"No idea," Jonny shook his head. "Nothing's come in on the pulse receiver from off-world confirming it."

"It'd be just like those phrijpushers to put a last-minute hold in the drop without telling us."

Jonny shrugged, turned back to the people working on Marja's arm. "How's it look?"

"Typical hornet injury," one of them said. "Lots of superficial damage, but it'll all heal okay. She's out of action for a while, though."

And for that time, at least, Danice would have one parent out of the immediate fray.

If that mattered. Jonny had already seen far too many uninvolved civilians lying dead in the middle of cross fires.

The next few minutes were quiet ones. The two civilians finished with Marja's arm and left, taking the group's small supply of combat equipment with them for concealment. Kem and Danice accompanied Marja to one of the apartment's three bedrooms, ostensibly to put her to bed but mainly—Jonny suspected—to give the three Cobras some privacy to discuss the operation and plan future strategy before the rest of the apartment's occupants returned home from work.

In the first few months, Jonny reflected, they might have done just that. But after three years most of the words had already been said, most of the plans already discussed, and gestures of hand and eyebrow now sufficed where conversations had once been necessary.

For now, the gestures merely indicated fatigue. "Tomorrow," Jonny reminded them of the next high-level tactical meeting as they headed for the door and their own crowded apartments.

Halloran nodded. Deutsch merely twitched a corner of his lip.

And another wonderful day on Adirondack was drawing to a close. *If the wall can stand it,* Jonny repeated to himself, *so can I.*

The three people seated at the table looked very much like everyone else in Cranach these days: tired, vaguely dirty, and more than a little scared. It was hard sometimes to remember that they were among the best underground leaders Adirondack had to offer.

It was even harder, in the face of Cobra and civilian casualties, to admit that they really *were* reasonably good at their jobs.

"The first news is that, despite some crossed signals, the latest Cobra drop was successful," Borg Weissmann told the silent Central Sector underground team leaders seated around the room. Short and stocky, with lingering traces of concrete dust in hair and finger-nails, Weissmann looked indeed like the civilian building contractor he actually was. But he'd retired from the Army twenty years previously as a Chief Tactics Programmer, and he'd been proving for nearly a year now that he'd learned more than computers in that post.

"How many did we get?" someone sitting against the side wall asked.

"Cranach's share is thirty: six new teams," Weissmann said. "Most of those will go to North Sector to replace those that got lost in the airstrip attack a month ago."

Jonny glanced at Deutsch, saw the other grimace at the memory. Their team hadn't been involved in that one at all, but details like that didn't appear to affect Deutsch's reaction. If *anyone* from Adirondack was involved, he seemed to react as if he personally had let his fellow Cobras down. Jonny wondered if he himself would feel similarly if the war was being fought on Horizon; decided he probably would.

"We'll also be getting one of the teams here," Weissmann continued. "Ama's already made arrangements for their living quarters, identity backgrounds, and all. But given the heightened Troft activity these past few weeks, I think it might be a good idea to create a little breathing space while they're settling in."

"In other words, a raid." The tone of Halloran's voice made it clear it wasn't a question.

Weissmann hesitated, then nodded. "I know you don't like to run operations so closely together, but I think it's something we ought to do."

"'We'?" Deutsch spoke up from his usual corner seat. "You mean 'you,' don't you?"

Weissmann licked his lips, a brief flicker of tongue that advertised his discomfort. Deutsch had once been a sort of social buffer zone between the Cobras and Adirondack forces, his dual citizenship—as it were—enabling him to short-circuit misunderstandings and cultural differences. Now, in his current state of disillusionment, he was hell for *anyone* to deal with. "I—uh—assumed you'd want a squad or two along to assist you," Weissmann suggested. "We're certainly willing to carry our part of—"

"*Not* carrying your part is what got another Cobra killed yesterday," Deutsch said quietly. "Maybe we'd better do this one ourselves."

Ama Nunki shifted in her seat. "You, of all people, should know better than to expect too much from us, Imel. This is Adirondack, not Earth or Centauri—we haven't got any history of warfare here to draw on."

"What do you call the past three years—?" Deutsch began hotly.

"On the other hand," Jonny interjected, "Imel may be right on this one. We want a short, tight punch that'll make the Trofts drop door-to-door searches lower on the priority list, not a big operation that may have them calling up support from the Dannimor garrison. A quick Cobra strike would fit the bill perfectly."

Weissmann visibly let out a breath, and Jonny felt an easing of tension throughout the room. More and more lately he seemed to be taking Deutsch's old peacekeeper role in these meetings, a position he neither especially wanted nor felt he was all that good at. But *someone* had to do it, and Halloran had far less empathy for frontier-world people than Jonny did. He could only continue as best he could and hope that Deutsch would hurry up and snap out of his low simmer.

"I guess I have to agree with Jonny," Halloran said. "I presume you have some suggestions as to what might be ripe for picking?"

Weissmann turned to Jakob Dane, the third person at the table. "We've come up with four reasonable targets," Dane said. "Of course, we were thinking there'd be a full assault team going with you—"

"Just tell us what they are," Deutsch interrupted.

"Yes, sir." Dane picked up a piece of paper, the flimsy sheet amplifying the slight trembling of his hands, and began to read. All four, it turned out, were essentially minor objectives; Dane, apparently, had as low an opinion of the underground's troops as Deutsch did.

"Not one of those is worth the fuel it'll take to get there," Halloran snorted when he'd finished.

"Perhaps you'd prefer to take out the Ghost Focus?" Ama suggested acidly.

"Not funny," Jonny murmured as Halloran's expression darkened. It'd been certain for months that the Trofts had a major tactical headquarters somewhere in Cranach, but so far the aptly christened Ghost Focus had proved impossible to locate. It was a particular sore spot for Halloran, who'd led at least half a dozen hunting expeditions in search of the place and come up dry each time.

All of which, belatedly, Ama seemed to remember. "You're right, Jonny," she said, ducking her head in a local gesture of apology that even Jonny found provincial. "I'm sorry; it's not really something to make light of."

Halloran grunted a not-quite-mollified acceptance. "Anyone have any *genuine* suggestions?" he asked.

"What about that shipment of electronics spares that was supposed to come in yesterday?" Deutsch spoke up.

"It's here," Dane nodded. "Locked up in the old Wolker Plant. But that won't be easy to get to."

Deutsch caught Halloran's and Jonny's eyes, cocked a questioning eyebrow. "Sure, why not?" Halloran shrugged. "A commandeered plastics factory's bound to have security loopholes the Trofts haven't plugged yet."

"You'd think they'd have learned that by now," Deutsch said, getting to his feet and glancing around the room at the team leaders. "Looks like we won't be needing the rest of you any more today. Thanks for coming."

Technically, none of the Cobras had the authority to close the meeting, but no one seemed eager to mention that fact. With little conversation and even less loitering, the room emptied, leaving only the Cobras and the three civilian leaders.

"Now," Deutsch said, addressing the latter, "let's see what you've got in the way of blueprints for this plant."

Ama's expression was thunderous, but as it was clear the other two weren't going to make an issue of Deutsch's action, she apparently decided not to do so either. Instead, she stalked to the plate in the corner, bringing both it and a collection of innocuously titled tapes back to the table. Interspersed among the video images were blueprints to major city buildings, sewer and powerline data, and dozens of other handy bits of information the underground had squirrelled away. It turned out that the entry for the Wolker Plastics Plant was remarkably detailed.

The planning session lasted until late afternoon, but Jonny was still able to make it back to the Tolans' apartment before the sundown curfew. Two of the usual occupants—Marja's brother and nephew, refugees from the slagged town of Paris—were away for the night, giving Jonny the unusual luxury of a private sleeping room when the clan went to bed later in the evening. No one had asked about the meeting, but Jonny could sense that they were aware he'd be going on another mission soon. There was a subtle drawing back from him, as if they were building a last-minute emotional shell in case this was the mission from which he didn't return.

Later that night, lying on his thin mattress, Jonny contemplated that possibility himself. Some day, he suspected, he would reach the point where walking into near-certain death wouldn't even bother him. But that day hadn't yet arrived, and he hoped to keep it at bay for a long time. Those who went into battle not caring if they died usually did.

So in the last minutes before drifting off to sleep he mentally listed all the reasons he had to come through this mission alive.

Starting, as always, with his family, and ending with the effect it would have on Danice.

The clock circuit built into their nanocomputers was at the same time the simplest and yet one of the most useful bits of equipment in the entire Cobra arsenal. Like the traditional soldier's chronometer it enabled widespread forces to synchronize their movements; going that instrument one better, though, it could be tied directly into the rest of the servo network to permit joint action on a microsecond scale. It opened up possibilities that had hitherto been the sole province of automatics, remotes, and the most elite mechanized line troops.

And in exactly twelve minutes and eighteen seconds the gadget would once again pay for itself. Wriggling down the long vent pipe he'd entered from the Wolker Plant's unguarded south filter station, Jonny periodically checked the remaining time against his progress. He hadn't been wild about using this back door—enclosed spaces were the single most dangerous environment a Cobra could be trapped in—but so far it looked like the gamble was going to pay off. The alarms the Trofts had installed at the far end had been easy enough to circumvent, and according to the blueprints he should very soon be exiting into a vat almost directly beneath the building's main entrance. He would then have until the timer ran down to find a position from which the inside door guards were visible.

At one point the Trofts had relied heavily on portable black box sensors to defend converted civilian buildings like this, a practice the underground had gone to great lengths to discourage. The aliens quickly learned that, no matter what thresholds the triggers were set at, their opponents soon figured out how to set off false alarms through them. After sufficient effort had been wasted chasing canine "intruders" and hunting for slingshot-and-firecracker-equipped harassers, they'd pulled out the automatics in favor of live guards equipped with warning sensors and dead-man switches. The system was harder to fool and almost as safe.

Almost.

Ahead of him Jonny could see a spot of dark gray amid the black. The grille leading into the main building, probably, the faintness of the background light indicating that particular room was probably unoccupied. He hoped so; he didn't want to have to cut down any aliens this early in the mission.

The crucial question, of course, was whether or not all the

dead-man switches could be deactivated in the microsecond before their owners were wiped out in the synchronized Cobra attack. That task would probably rest on Jonny's shoulders, since any relays for the alarms would be inside. The Trofts had both closed- and open-circuit types of switches, and he would have to determine which kind was being used here before taking action.

He'd reached the grille now. Boosting his optical enhancers, he studied it for alarms and booby-traps. A current detector from his equipment pack located four suspicious wires; jumping them with adjustable-impedance cables, he cut through the mesh with his fingertip lasers and slid through the last two-meter stretch of pipe into an empty vat. There was no provision for releasing its service openings from the inside, but Jonny's lasers took care of that oversight without any trouble. Poking his head out of the opening, he took a careful look around.

He was suspended some five meters above the floor, his vat the largest in a row of similar structures. Four meters away, at eye level, was what looked like the exit from the room, reached from the floor by a set of stairs built into the wall.

Given Troft security thus far, Jonny expected nothing in the way of booby traps to be set up on the floor below. Still, he had just seven minutes to get into position upstairs . . . and to a Cobra a four-meter leap was as easy as a stroll down the walkway. Drawing up his feet, he balanced for a moment on the lip of the vat service opening and pushed off.

The night before he had warned himself of the dangers of apathy. Now, for one awful instant—all the time he had—he recognized that overconfidence extracted an equally bitter price. The sharp *twang* of released springs filled his enhanced hearing, and the servos within his arms snapped his fingertip lasers into position faster than his brain could register the black wall hurtling itself toward him. But it was an essentially meaningless gesture, and even as the pencils of light flashed out he realized the Trofts had suckered him masterfully. A major military target, an enticing backdoor entrance with inadequate alarms, and finally a mid-air trap that used his helpless ballistic trajectory to neutralize the speed and strength advantage of his servos.

The flying wall reached him, and he had just enough time to notice it was actually a net before it hit, wrapping itself around him like a giant cocoon. A split second later he was jerked sharply off his original path as unnoticed suspension lines reached their limit, snapping him back to hang more or less upside down in the middle of the room.

And Jonny was captured . . . which, since he was a Cobra, meant that he was dead.

His body didn't accept that fact so quickly, of course, and continued to strain cautiously against the sticky mesh digging into his clothing. But the limiting factor wasn't his servos' power, and it was all too clear that before the net would break, its threads would slice through both cloth and flesh, stopping only when it reached bone. Above his left foot his antiarmor laser flashed, vaporizing a small piece of the material and blowing concrete chips from the ceiling, but neither his leg or arms could move far enough to cause any serious damage to the net. If he could hit one or more of the lines holding him off the floor . . . but in the gloom, with his eyes covered by two or three layers of mesh, he couldn't even see them.

Somewhere in the recesses of his mind, a direct neural stimulation alarm went off from the sensor monitoring his heartbeat.

He was falling asleep.

It was the enemy's final stroke, as inevitable as it was fatal. Pressed against the skin of his face, the contact drug mixed with the adhesive on the net was soaking into his bloodstream faster than the emergency stimulant system beneath his heart could compensate. He had bare seconds before the universe was forever closed off . . . and he had one vital task yet to perform.

His tongue was a lump of unresponsive clay pressed against the roof of his mouth. With all the will power remaining to him he forced it to the corner of his mouth . . . forced it through wooden lips . . . touched the tip of the emergency radio trigger curving along his cheek. "Abort," he mumbled. The room was growing darker, but it was far too much effort to click up his optical enhancers. "Abort. Walked . . . trap. . . ."

Somewhere far off he thought he heard a crisp acknowledgment, but it was too much effort to try and understand the words. It was too much effort, in fact, to do anything at all.

The darkness rose and swept gently over him.

The nearest building to the Wolker Plant was an abandoned warehouse a hundred meters due north of the plant's main entrance. Crouched on the roof there, Cally Halloran ground his teeth viciously together as he tried to watch all directions at once. A trap, Jonny had said, with sleep or death already near to claiming him . . . but was it a simple booby trap or something more elaborate? If the latter, then Deutsch too would probably never make it off the plant's grounds alive. If the operation was wide enough, even this backstop position could become a deathtrap.

For the moment the fact of Jonny's death hardly touched his thoughts. Later, perhaps, there would be time to mourn, but for now Halloran's duty lay solely with the living. Easing his leg forward, he made sure the antiarmor laser within it could sweep the area freely and waited.

With his light amplification on at full power the night around him seemed no darker than a heavily overcast afternoon, but even so he didn't spot Deutsch until the other was well on his way back from the patch of deep shadow where he'd been waiting for his part of the gate attack. The guards, it seemed, saw him at about the same time, and for an instant that part of the landscape dimmed as laser flashes cut in his enhancers' overload protection. Answering fire came immediately: Deutsch's antiarmor laser firing backwards as he ran. With the unconscious ease of long experience, Halloran raised his own aim to the plant's roof and windows, areas Deutsch's self-covering fire would have trouble hitting.

The precaution proved unnecessary. Even with ankle-breaking zigzags tangling his path, Deutsch took the intervening distance like a ground-hug missile, and in bare seconds he was around the corner of Halloran's warehouse and out of enemy view.

But it was clear the Trofts weren't going to be content with simply driving the Cobras away. Even as Halloran slipped across the roof and down the far side the Wolker Plant was starting to come alive.

Deutsch was waiting for him on the ground, his face tense in the faint light. "You okay?" Halloran whispered.

"Yeah. You'd better get going—they'll be swarming around like ants in a minute."

"Change that 'you' to 'we' and you've got a deal. Come on." He gripped Deutsch's arm and turned to go.

The other shook off his hand. "No, I'm staying here to—to make sure."

Halloran turned back, studying his partner with new and wary eyes. If Deutsch was unraveling . . . "He's dead, Imel," he explained, as if to a small child. "You heard him going under—"

"His self-destruct hasn't gone off," Deutsch interrupted him harshly. "Even out here we should have heard it or felt the vibrations. And if he's alive . . ."

He left the sentence unfinished, but Halloran understood. The Trofts were already known to have live-dissected at least one captured Cobra. Jonny deserved better than that, if it was within their power to grant. "All right," he sighed, suppressing a shiver. "But don't take chances. Giving Jonny a clean death isn't worth losing your own life over."

"I know. Don't worry; I'm not going to do anything stupid." Deutsch paused for an instant, listening. "You'd better get moving."

"Right. I'll do what I can to draw them away."

"Now don't *you* take chances." Deutsch slapped Halloran's arm and jumped, catching the edge of the warehouse roof and disappearing over the top.

Clicking all audio and visual enhancers to full power, Halloran turned and began to run, keeping to the shadows as much as possible. The time to mourn was still in the distant future.

The first sensation that emerged as the black fog faded was a strange burning in his cheeks. Gradually, the feeling strengthened and was joined by the awareness of something solid against his back and legs. Thirst showed up next, followed immediately by pressure on his forearms and shins. The sound of whispering air . . . the awareness that there was soft light beyond his closed eyelids . . . the knowledge that he was lying horizontally . . .

Only then did Jonny's mind come awake enough to notice that he was still alive.

Cautiously, he opened his eyes. A meter above him was a featureless white-steel ceiling; tracing along it, he found it ended in four white-steel walls no more than five meters apart. Hidden lights gave a hospital glow to the room; by it he saw that the only visible exit was a steel door in a heavily reinforced frame. In one corner a spigot—water?—protruded from the wall over a ten-centimeter drainage grille that could probably serve as a toilet if absolutely necessary. His equipment pack and armament belt were gone, but his captors had left him his clothes.

As a death cell, it seemed fairly cheerful. As a surgery prep room, it was woefully deficient.

Raising his head, he studied the plates pinning his arms and legs to the table. Not shackles, he decided; more likely a complex set of biomedical sensors with drug-injection capabilities. Which meant the Trofts ought to know by now that he was awake. From which it followed immediately that they'd *allowed* him to wake up.

He was aware, down deep, that not all the fog had yet cleared away; but even so it seemed an incredibly stupid move on their part.

His first impulse was to free himself from the table in a single servo-powered lunge, turn his antiarmor laser on the door hinges, and get the hell out of there. But the sheer irrationality of the whole situation made him pause.

What did the Trofts think they were doing, anyway?

Whatever it was, it was most likely in violation of orders. The underground had intercepted a set of general orders some months ago, one of which was that any captured Cobras were to be immediately killed or kept sedated for live-dissection. Jonny's stomach crawled at the latter thought, but he again resisted the urge to get out before the Troft on monitor duty belatedly noticed his readings. The enemy simply didn't *make* mistakes that blatantly careless. Whatever was happening, contrary to orders or not, it was being done on purpose.

So what could anyone want with a living, fully conscious Cobra?

Interrogation was out. Physical torture above a certain level would trigger a power supply self-destruct; so would the use of certain drugs. Hold him for ransom or trade? Ridiculous. Trofts didn't seem to think along those lines, and even if they'd learned humans did, it wouldn't work. They would need Jonny's cooperation to prove to his friends he was still alive, and he'd blow his self-destruct himself rather than give them that lever. Let him escape and follow him back to his underground contacts? Equally ridiculous. There were dozens of secure, monofilament line phones set up around the city from which he could check in with Borg Weissmann without ever going near an underground member. The Trofts had tried that unsuccessfully with other captured rebels; trying to follow an evasion-trained Cobra would be an exercise in futility. No, giving him even half a chance to escape would gain them nothing but a path of destruction through their building.

A path of destruction. A path of *Cobra* destruction. . . .

Heart beating faster, Jonny turned his attention back to the walls and ceiling. This time, because he was looking for them, he spotted the places where cameras and other sensors could be located. There appeared to be a *lot* of them.

Carefully, he laid his head back on the table, feeling cold all over. So *that's* what this was all about—an attempt to get lab-quality information on Cobra equipment and weaponry in actual use. Which meant that, whatever lay outside that steel door, odds were he'd have an even chance of getting through it alive.

For a long moment temptation tugged at him. If he *could* escape, surely it would be worth letting the Trofts have their data. Most of what they would get must already be known, and even watching his battle reflexes in action would be of only limited use to them. Only a handful of the most intricate patterns were rigidly programmed; the rest had been kept general enough to cover highly varying situations. The Trofts might afterwards be able to predict another Cobra's escape path from this same cell, but that was about it.

But the whole debate was ultimately nothing more than a mental exercise . . . because Jonny knew full well the proposed trade-off was illusory. Somewhere along the Trofts' gauntlet—somewhere near the end—there would be an attack that *would* kill him.

There's no such thing as a foolproof deathtrap. Cee-three Bai had emphasized that point back on Asgard, hammered at it until Jonny had come to believe it. But it was always assumed that the victim had at least *some* idea of what he was up against. Jonny had no idea how the killing attack would come; had no feeling for the layout of this building; had no idea even where on Adirondack he was.

His duty was therefore unfortunately clear. Closing his eyes, he focused his attention on the neural alarm that would signal an attempt to put him back to sleep. If and when that happened he would be forced to break his bonds, trading minimal information for consciousness. Until then . . . he would simply have to wait.

And hope. Irrational though that might be.

They sat and listened, and when Deutsch finished he could tell they were unconvinced.

Ama Nunki put it into words first. "Too big a risk," she said with a slow shake of her head, "for so small a chance of success."

There was a general shifting in chairs by the other underground and Cobra leaders, but no immediate votes of agreement. That meant there was still a chance. . . . "Look," Deutsch said, striving to keep his voice reasonable. "I know it sounds crazy, but I tell you it *was* Jonny I saw being taken aboard that aircraft, and it *did* head south. You know as well as I do that there's no reason for them to have taken him anywhere but their hospital if they just wanted to dissect him. They *must* have something else in mind, something that requires he be kept alive—and if he's alive he can be rescued."

"But he's got to be found first," Jakob Dane explained patiently. "Your estimate of where the aircraft landed notwithstanding, the assumption that figuratively beating the bushes will turn up some sign of him is at best a hopeful fiction."

"Why?" Deutsch countered. "Any place the Trofts would be likely to stash him would have to be reasonably big, reasonably attack-resistant, and reasonably unoccupied. All right, all right—I *know* that part of the city has a lot of buildings like that. But we've *got* it narrowed down."

"And what if we *do* find the place?" Kennet MacDonald, a Cobra from Cranach's East Sector, spoke up. "Throw all our forces against it in a raid that could easily end in disaster? All they have to do if they lose is kill Moreau and let his self-destruct take out the whole building, rescuers and all."

"In fact, that could very well be what they *want* us to do," Ama said.

"If they wanted to set up a giant deathtrap, they would've left him right there in the Wolker Plant, where we wouldn't have had to work to track him down," Deutsch argued, fighting hard against the feeling that the battle was slipping through his fingers. He glanced fiercely at Halloran, but the other remained silent. Didn't he *care* that Jonny could be saved if they'd just make the effort?

"I have to agree with Kennet," Pazar Oberton, an underground leader from MacDonald's sector, said. "We've never asked you to rescue one of *our* people, and I don't think we should all go rushing south trying to rescue one of yours."

"This isn't a corporation ledger we're running here—it's a *war*," Deutsch snapped. "And in case you've forgotten, we Cobras are the best chance you've got of winning that war and getting these damned invaders off your planet."

"Off *our* planet?" Dane murmured. "Have you officially emigrated, then?"

Dane would never know how close he came to dying in that instant. Deutsch's teeth clamped tightly together as endless months of heartbreak and frustration threatened to burst out in one massive explosion of laser fire that would have cut the insensitive fool in half. None of them understood—none of them even *tried* to understand—how it felt to watch his own countrymen's failures and stupidities cause the deaths of men he'd come to consider his brothers . . . how it felt to be defending people who often didn't seem willing to put forth the same effort to free their world . . . how it felt to share their blame, because ultimately he too was one of them. . . .

Slowly, the haze cleared, and he saw the fists clenched before him on the table. "Borg?" he said, looking at Weissmann. "You lead this rabble. What do you say?"

An uncomfortable rustle went around the table, but Weissmann's gaze held Deutsch's steadily. "I know you feel especially responsible since you were the one who suggested the Wolker Plant in the first place," he said quietly, "but you *are* talking very poor odds."

"Warfare is a history of poor odds," Deutsch countered. He sent his gaze around the room. "I don't *have* to ask your permission, you know. I could order you to help me rescue Jonny."

Halloran stirred. "Imel, we technically have no authority to—"

"I'm not talking technicalities," Deutsch interrupted, his voice quiet but with an edge to it. "I'm talking the realities of power."

For a long moment the room was deathly still. "Are you threatening us?" Weissmann asked at last.

Deutsch opened his mouth, the words *damn right I am* on his lips . . . but before he could speak, a long-forgotten scene floated up from his memory. Rolon Viljo's face as Commander Mendro ordered him removed from the team and the Cobras . . . and Deutsch's own verdict on Viljo's crime. *Misuse of our equipment would pit us against the civilian population of Adirondack.* "No," he told Weissmann, the word taking incredible strength of will to say. "No, of course not. I just—never mind." He sent one last glance around the room and then stood up. "You can all do as you damn well please. I'm going to go and find Jonny."

The room was still silent as he crossed to the door and left. Briefly, as he started down the stairs, he wondered what they would make of his outburst. But it didn't matter very much. And in a short time, most likely, it wouldn't matter at all.

Stepping outside into the night, senses alert for Troft patrols, he headed south.

"I do believe," Jakob Dane said as the sound of Deutsch's footsteps faded away, "that Adirondack's Self-Appointed Conscience is overdue for some leave time."

"Shut up, Jakob," Halloran advised, making sure to put some steel in his voice. He'd long ago recognized that each of the underground members had to deal with the presence of the Cobras in his own way, but Dane's approach—treating them with a faintly supercilious air—was a dangerous bit of overcompensation. He doubted the other had noticed it, but as Deutsch's hands had curled into fists a few minutes ago there had been the briefest pause with thumb resting against ring finger nail . . . the position for firing fingertip lasers at full power. "In case you didn't bother to notice," he added, "just about everything Imel said was right."

"Including the efficacy of a rescue mission?" Dane snorted.

Halloran turned to Weissmann. "*I* notice, Borg, that you haven't given your decision on assigning underground personnel to help locate Jonny. Before you do, let me just point out that there's exactly *one* Troft installation we know exists that we haven't got even a rough locale for."

"You mean the Ghost Focus?" Ama frowned. "That's crazy. Jonny's a ticking bomb—they'd be stupid to put him anywhere that sensitive."

"Depends on what they're planning for him," MacDonald rumbled thoughtfully. "As long as he's alive they're safe enough. Besides, our self-destructs aren't all *that* powerful. Any place hardened against, say, tacnuke grenades wouldn't have any trouble with us."

"On top of that," Halloran added, "it's clear from their slow response to Imel and me that they weren't particularly expecting a raid on Wolker tonight. Jonny's booby trap may have been sitting there for months, and it's as reasonable as anything else to assume they weren't really prepared with another place to put him that we didn't already know about. If the Ghost Focus is like their other tactical bases, they'll have it carved into parallel, independently-hardened warrens. They wouldn't be risking more than the one Jonny was actually in."

"I've never heard that about tactical bases," Ama said, her eyes hard on Halloran.

He shrugged. "There are a lot of things you've never heard," he told her bluntly. "You ever volunteer to penetrate a Troft installation with us and maybe we'll tell you what we know about those hellholes. Until then, you'll have to take our word for it." He had the satisfaction of seeing her mouth tighten; to people like Ama the only real power was knowledge. Turning to Weissmann, he cocked an eyebrow. "Well, Borg?"

Weissmann pressed his fingertips tightly against his lips, staring at and through Halloran. "All right," he said with a sigh. "I'll authorize some of our people for search duty and see if I can borrow a few from other sectors. But it'll be passive work only, and won't begin until after sunup. I don't want anyone getting caught violating curfew—and no one's going into combat."

"Fair enough." It was about as much as Halloran could have expected. "Kennet?"

MacDonald steepled his fingers. "I won't risk my team randomly tearing up the south side of Cranach," he said quietly. "But if you can show me a probable location, we'll help you hit it. Whatever the Trofts want with Jonny, I suspect it's behavior we ought to discourage."

"Agreed. And thank you." Halloran gestured to Ama. "Well, don't just sit there. Pull out the high-resolution maps and let's get to work."

Jonny waited until his thirst was unbearable before finally breaking free of his restraints and going to the spigot in the cell's corner. Without a full analysis kit it was impossible to make sure the water provided was uncontaminated and undrugged, but it didn't especially worry him. The Trofts had had ample opportunity already to pump chemicals into his system, and exotic bacteria were the least of his worries.

He drank his fill, and then—as long as he was up anyway—gave himself a walking tour of his cell. On the whole it was a dull trip, but it *did* give him the chance to examine the walls more closely for remote monitors. The room was, as he'd earlier surmised, loaded with them.

The cell door, up close, proved an intriguing piece of machinery. There were signs at one edge that both an electronic and a tumbler-type combination lock were being used, complementary possibilities to the temptingly exposed hinges he'd already noticed. The Trofts, it appeared, were offering him subtle as well as brute-force escape options. Each of which would give them useful data on his equipment, unfortunately.

Returning to the table, he moved aside the remnants of the monitor/shackles and lay down again. His internal clock circuit, which he hadn't had time to shut off or reset during his capture, provided him with at least the knowledge of how time was passing in the outside world. He'd been unconscious for three hours; since his awakening another five had passed. That meant it was almost ten o'clock in the morning out there. The people of Cranach were out at work in their damaged city, the children—including Danice Tolan—were at school, and the underground . . .

The underground had already accepted and mourned his death and gone on with their business. His death, and possibly Cally's and Imel's as well.

For a long, painful minute Jonny wondered what had happened to his teammates. Had his warning been in time for them to escape? Or had the Trofts been waiting with a giant trap ready to grab all of them? Perhaps they were in similar rooms right now, wondering identical thoughts as they decided whether or not to make their own escapes. They might even be next door to his cell; in which case a burst of antiarmor fire would open a communication hole and let them plan joint action—

He shook his head to clear it of such unlikely thoughts. No help would be coming for him, and he might as well face that fact. If Imel and Cally were alive they would have more sense than to try something as stupid as a rescue, even if they knew where to find him. And if they were dead . . . odds were he'd be joining them soon, anyway.

Unbidden, Danice Tolan's face floated into view. It looked like, barring a miracle, she was finally going to lose a close friend to the war.

He hoped she'd be able to handle it.

The human had been in the cell now for nearly seven *vfohra*, and except for a casual breaking of its loose restraints two *vfohra* ago had made no attempt to use its implanted weaponry against its imprisonment. Resettling his wing-like radiator membranes against the backs of his arms, the City Commander gazed at the bank of vision screens and wondered what he should do.

His ET biologist approached from the left, puffing up his throat bladder in a gesture of subservience. "Speak," the CCom invited.

"The last readings have been thoroughly rechecked," the other said, his voice vaguely flutey in the local atmosphere's unusually high nitrogen content. "The human shows no biochemical evidence of trauma or any of their versions of dream-walking."

The CCom flapped his arm membranes once in acknowledgment. So it was as he'd already guessed: the prisoner had deliberately chosen not to attempt escape. A ridiculous decision, even for an alien . . . unless it had somehow discerned what it was they had planned for it.

From the CCom's point of view, the alien couldn't have picked a worse time to show its race's stubborn streak. The standing order that these *koubrah*-soldiers were to be killed instantly could be gotten around easily enough, but all the time and effort already invested would be lost unless the creature provided an active demonstration of its capabilities for the hidden sensors.

Which meant the CCom was once more going to have to perform that most distasteful of duties. Seating his arm membranes firmly, he reached deep into his paraconscious mind, touching the mass of hard-won psychological data that had been placed there aboard the demesne-lord's master ship . . . and with great effort he tried to think like a human.

The effort left a taste like copper oxide in his mouth, but by the time the CCom emerged sputtering from his dream-walk he had a plan. "SolLi!" he called to the Soldier Liaison seated at the security board. "One patrol, fully equipped, in Tunnel One immediately."

The SolLi puffed his throat bladder in acknowledgment and bent over his communicator. Spreading out his arm membrances—the dream-walk had left him uncomfortably warm—the CCom watched the dormant human and considered the best way to do this.

It was an hour past noon in the outside world, and Jonny was once more reviewing everything he'd ever been taught about prison escapes, when an abrupt creak of metal from the door sent him rolling off the table. Crouching at the edge of the slab, fingertip lasers aimed, he watched tensely as the door opened a meter and someone leaped into his cell.

He had a targeting lock established and lasers tracking before his conscious mind caught up with two important details: the figure was human, and it had not been traveling under its own power. Looking back at the door, he got just a glimpse of two body-armored Trofts as they slammed the heavy steel plate closed again. The *thud* reverberated like overhead thunder in the tiny room, and a possible shot at escaping his cell was gone. Slowly, Jonny got to his feet and stepped around the table to meet his new cellmate.

She was on her feet when he reached her, bent over slightly as she rubbed an obviously painful kneecap. "Damn chicken-faced strifpitchers," she grumbled. "They *could've* just let me walk in."

"You all right?" Jonny asked, giving her a quick once-over. A bit shorter than he was and as slender, maybe seven or eight years older, dressed in the mishmash of styles the war had made common. No obvious injuries or blood stains that he could see.

"Oh, sure." Straightening up, she sent a quick look around the cell. "Though I suppose that could change at any time. What's going on here, anyway?"

"Tell me what happened."

"I wish I knew. I was just walking down Strassheim Street, minding my own business, when this Troft patrol turned a corner. They asked me what I was doing there, I essentially told them to go back to hell, and for no particular reason they grabbed me and hauled me in here."

Jonny's lip twitched in a smile. In the early days of the occupation, he'd heard, it had been possible to fire off multiple obscenities at point-blank range, and as long as you kept your face and voice respectful the Trofts had no way of catching on. With the aliens' advances in Anglic translation, though, only the truly imaginative could come up with something they hadn't heard before.

Strassheim Street. There was a Strassheim in Cranach, he remembered, down in the south end of the city where a lot of the light industry had been. "So what *were* you doing there?" he asked the woman. "I thought that area was mostly deserted now."

She gave him a cool, measuring look. "Shall I repeat the answer I gave the Trofts?"

He shrugged. "Don't bother. I was just asking." Turning his back on her, he hopped back up on the table, seating himself cross-legged facing the door. It really *wasn't* any of his business.

Besides which, he was starting to get an uncomfortable feeling as to the reason for her presence here . . . and if he was right, the less contact he had with her, the better. There was no point in getting to know someone you would probably soon be dying with.

For a moment it seemed like she'd come to a similar conclusion. Then, with hesitant footsteps, she came around the edge of the table and into his peripheral vision. "Hey—I'm sorry," she said, the snap still audible in her voice but subdued to a more civil level. "I'm just—I'm starting to get a little scared, that's all, and I tend to bite heads off when I get scared. I was on Strassheim because I was hoping to get into one of the old factories and scrounge some circuit boards or other electronics parts. Okay?"

He pursed his lips and looked at her, feeling his freshly minted resolve tarnishing already. "Those buildings have been picked pretty clean in the past three years," he pointed out.

"Mostly by people who don't know what they're doing," she shrugged. "There's still some stuff left—if you know where and how to find it."

"Are you part of the underground?" Jonny asked—and instantly wished he could call back the thoughtless words. With monitors all around, her answer could lose her what little chance of freedom she had left.

But she merely snorted. "Are you nuts? I'm a struggling burglar, confrere, not a volunteer lunatic." Her eyes widened suddenly. "Say, you're not, uh—hey, wait a minute; they don't think that I—oh, great. Great. What'd you do, come calling for Old Tyler with a laser in one hand and a grenade in the other?"

"Old Tyler?" Jonny asked, latching onto the most coherent part of that oral skid. "Who or what is that?"

"We're in his mansion," she frowned. "At least I think so. Didn't you know?"

"I was unconscious when I was brought in. What do you mean, you think so?"

"Well, I was actually taken into an old apartment building a block away and then along an underground tunnel to get here. But I got a glimpse through an unblocked window as I was being brought through the main building, and I think I saw the Tyler Mansion's outer wall. Anyway, even without fancy furniture and all you can tell the rooms up there were designed for someone rich."

The Tyler Mansion. The name was familiar from Ama Nunki's local history/geography seminars: a large house with a sort of pseudo-Reginine-millionaire style, he recalled, built south of the city in the days before industry moved into that area. She'd been vague as to the semi-recluse owner's whereabouts since the Troft invasion, but it was generally believed he was holed up inside somewhere, counting on private stores and the mansion's defenses to keep out looters and aliens alike. Jonny remembered thinking at the time that the Trofts were being uncommonly generous to leave the place standing under those conditions, and wondering if perhaps a private deal had been struck. It was starting to look like he'd been right . . . though the deal was possibly more than a little one-sided.

But more interesting than the mansion's recent history were the possibilities inherent in being locked inside such a residence. Unlike a factory, a millionaire's home ought to have an emergency escape route. If he could find it, perhaps he could bypass whatever death-trap the Trofts had planned for him. "You say you came in through a tunnel," he said to his cellmate. "Did it look new or hastily built? Say, as if the Trofts had dug it in the past three years?"

But she was frowning again, a hard look in her eyes. "Who the hell are you, anyway, that you never heard of Old Tyler? He's been written up more than every other celebrity on Adirondack—even volunteer lunatics can't be *that* ignorant. At least, not those who grew up in Cranach."

Jonny sighed; but she *did* have a right to know on whom her life was probably going to depend. And it certainly wouldn't be giving away any secrets to the Trofts eavesdropping on them. "You're right—I grew up quite a ways from here. I'm a Cobra."

Her eyes widened, then narrowed again as they swept his frame. "A Cobra, huh? You sure don't look like anything special."

"We're not supposed to," Jonny told her patiently. "Undercover guerrilla fighters—remember?"

"Oh, I know. But I've seen men masquerade as Cobras before to impress or threaten people."

"You want some proof?" He'd been looking for an excuse to do this, anyway. Hopping off the table, he stepped closer to the rear wall and extended his right arm. A group of suspected sensor positions faced him just below eye level. Targeting it, he turned his head to look at the woman. "Watch," he said, and triggered his arcthrower.

A discerning eye might have noticed that there were actually two components to the flash that lit up the room an instant later: the fingertip laser beam, which burned an ionized path through the air, and the high-amperage spark that traveled that path to the wall. But the accompanying thunderclap was the really impressive part, and in the metal-walled cell it was impressive as hell. The woman jumped a meter backwards from a standing start, mouthing something Jonny couldn't hear through the multiple reverberations. "Satisfied?" he asked her when the sound finally faded away.

Staring at him with wide eyes, she bobbed her head quickly. "Oh, yes. Yes indeed. What in heaven's name *was* that?"

"Arcthrower. Designed to fry electronic gear. Works pretty well, usually." In fact, it worked quite well, and Jonny didn't expect to have to worry about that particular sensor cluster again.

"I don't doubt it." She exhaled once, and with that action seemed to get her mind working as well. "A real Cobra. So how come you haven't broken out of here yet?"

For a long moment he stared at her, wondering what to say. If the Trofts knew he was on to their scheme . . . but surely her presence here proved they'd already figured that out. Tell her the truth, then?—that the aliens were forcing him to choose between betraying his fellow Cobras and saving her life?

He chose the easier, if temporary, solution of changing the subject. "You were going to tell me about the tunnel," he reminded her.

"Oh. Right. No, it looked like it'd been there a lot longer than three years. There also looked to be spots where gates and defensive equipment had been taken out."

In other words, it looked like Tyler's hoped-for escape hatch. And already in alien hands. "How well were the Trofts guarding it?"

"The place was full of them." She was giving him a wary look. "You're not planning to try and leave that way, are you?"

"What if I am?"

"It'd be suicide—and since I plan to be right behind you it'd leave *me* in a bad spot, too."

He frowned at her, only then realizing that she'd apparently figured out more about what was going on than he'd given her credit for. In her own less than subtle way she was saying he need not burden himself physically with her when he chose to escape. That he shouldn't feel responsible for her safety.

If only it were that simple, he thought bitterly. Would she understand as well if he stayed passively in the cell and thereby sentenced her automatically to death?

Or was that option even open to him anymore? Already, despite his earlier resolve, he realized he could no longer see her as simply a faceless statistic in this war. He'd talked to her, watched her eyes change expression, even gotten a little bit inside her mind. Whatever it cost him—life and data too—he knew now that he would eventually have to make the effort to get her out. The Trofts' gambit had worked.

You'll be proud of me, Jame, if you ever find out, he thought toward the distant stars. *My Horizon ethics have survived exposure to even war with all their stupid nobility intact.*

On the other hand . . . he was now locked up with a professional burglar inside what had to be the most enticing potential target Cranach had to offer. In their eagerness to hang an emotional millstone around his neck, it was just barely possible the Trofts had outsmarted themselves. "My name's Jonny Moreau," he told the woman. "What's yours?"

"Ilona Linder."

He nodded, knowing full well that with an exchange of names he was now committed. "Well, Ilona, if you think the tunnel's a poor choice of exits, let's see what else we can come up with. Why don't you start by telling me everything you know about the Tyler Mansion?"

❖   ❖   ❖

"This is hopeless," Cally Halloran sighed, gazing across the urban landscape from the vantage point of an eighth-floor window. "We could sneak in and out of deserted buildings for days without finding any leads."

"You can quit whenever you want to," was Deutsch's predictable answer. Sitting on the floor, the other Cobra was poring over a prewar aerial map of southern Cranach.

"Uh-huh. Well, as long as you're being so grateful for all that we're doing to help, I guess I'll stick around awhile longer."

It was Deutsch's turn to sigh. "All right, all right. If it'll ease your smoldering indignation any, I'll admit I went a little overwrought in selling this to Borg and company. Okay? Can you drop the little digs now?"

"I can drop them any time. But eventually you're going to have to face what you're doing to those people, not to mention what you're doing to yourself."

Deutsch snorted. "You mean undermining morale, while driving myself too hard with unrealistic goals and standards?"

"Well, now that you mention it—"

"I'm not pushing myself any harder than I can handle—you know that. As to the underground—" He shrugged, the movement rustling his map. "You just don't understand the position Adirondack's in, Cally. We're a frontier world, looked down on by everyone else in the Dominion—for all I know, by the Trofts as well. We've got to *prove* ourselves to all the rest of you, and the only way to do that is to throw the Trofts off our world."

"Yes, I know that's the theory you're working under," Halloran nodded. "*My* question is whether or not that's the achievement people will remember most."

Again Deutsch snorted. "What else *is* there in a war?"

"Spirit, for one thing. And Adirondack is showing one hell of a fine spirit." He held up a hand and began ticking off fingers. "One: you haven't got a single genuine collaborationist government anywhere on the planet. That forces the Trofts to tie up ridiculous numbers of troops with administrative and policing duties they'd much rather leave to you. Two: the local governments they *have* coerced into place are working very hard to be more trouble than they're worth. Remember when the Trofts tried conscription from Cranach and Dannimor to repair the Leeding Bridge?"

Almost unwillingly, Deutsch smiled. "Multiple conflicting orders, incompatible equipment, and well-hidden deficiencies in materials. Took them twice as long as the Trofts would have if they'd done it themselves."

"And every one of the people responsible for that fiasco risked their lives to pull it off," Halloran reminded him. "And those are just the things that plain, relatively uninvolved citizens are doing. I haven't even mentioned the sacrifices the underground's shown itself willing to make, the sheer persistence it's demonstrated the past three years. Maybe you're not impressed by your world, but I'll tell you right now that I'd be proud as hell if Aerie did half as well under these conditions."

Deutsch pursed his lips, his eyes on the map now folded over his knees. "All right," he said at last. "I'll concede that maybe we're not doing too badly. But potentials and maybes don't matter in this game. If we lose no one's going to care whether we did the best we could or the worst we could, because no one's going to remember us, period. Only the winners make it into the history books."

"Perhaps," Halloran nodded. "But perhaps not. Have you ever heard of Masada?"

"I don't think so. Was it a battle?"

"A siege. Took place in the first century on Earth. The Roman Empire had invaded some country—Israel, I think it's called now. A group of the local defenders—I'm not sure whether they were even regular military or just guerrillas—they took refuge on top of a plateau called Masada. The Romans encircled the place and tried for over a year to take it."

Deutsch's dark eyes were steady on his. "And eventually did?"

"Yes. But the defenders had sworn not to be taken alive . . . and so when the Romans marched into the camp all they found were dead bodies. They'd chosen suicide rather than capture."

Deutsch licked his lips. "I would have tried to take a few more Romans with me."

Halloran shrugged. "So would I. But that's not the point. They lost, but they weren't conquered, if you see the difference; and even though the Romans wound up winning the war, Masada's never been forgotten."

"Um." Deutsch stared off into space for another moment, then abruptly picked up his map again. "Well, I'd still like to come up with a better ending than that for this game," he said briskly. "Anything out there look particularly promising for our next sortie?"

Halloran directed his attention back out the window, wondering if his pep talk had done any good. "Couple of very obviously gutted buildings to the southwest that might make good cover for a guard house or hidden tunnel entrance. And there's a genuine jungle behind a security wall a little further on."

"The Tyler Mansion," Deutsch nodded, marking locations on his map. "Used to be very nice gardens and orchards surrounding the main house before the war. I suppose all Tyler's gardeners ran off long ago."

"Looks like you could hide an armor division under all that shrubbery. Any chance the Trofts could have taken the place over?"

"Probably, but it's hard to imagine how they'd do that without an obvious battle. That wall's not just decorative, for starters, and Tyler's bound to have heavier stuff in reserve. Besides, no one's ever seen any Trofts going in or out of the grounds."

"That reminds me—we should find a secure phone and check in before we go anywhere else. See if the spotters have anything in the way of Troft movement correlations yet."

"If they haven't found anything in four months they're not likely to have anything now," Deutsch pointed out, folding his map. "All right, though; we'll be good team players and check in. Then we'll hit your gutted buildings."

"Right." *At least,* Halloran thought, *he's got something besides simple win-loss criteria to mull over now. Maybe it'll be enough.*

Only as they were heading down the darkened stairway toward the street below did it occur to him that, in his current state, talking to Deutsch about self-sacrifices might not have been the world's smartest thing to do.

Ilona, it turned out, was a walking magcard of information on the Tyler Mansion.

She knew its outer appearance, the prewar layout of its major gardens, and the sizes and approximate locations of some of its rooms. She could sketch the stonework designs on the five-meter-high outer wall, as well as giving the wall's dimensions, and had at least a general idea as to the total area of both house and grounds. It impressed Jonny tremendously until it occurred to him that all her information would have fit quite comfortably in the sort of celebrity-snoop magazines that seemed to exist in one form or another all over the Dominion. The sort of thing both he and an enterprising gate-crasher would have found more useful—security systems, weapons emplacements, and the like—were conspicuous by their absence. Eventually, and regretfully, he decided she was simply one of those avid followers of the Tyler mystique whose existence she'd already hinted at.

Still, he'd been taught how to make inferences from the physical appearance of structures, and even given that his data was second-hand he was able to form a reasonable picture of what Tyler had set up to defend his home.

And the picture wasn't an especially encouraging one.

"The main gate is shaped like this," Ilona said, sketching barely visible lines with her finger on the tabletop. "It's supposed to be electronically locked and made with twenty-centimeter-thick kyrelium steel, same as the interior section of the wall."

Briefly, Jonny tried to calculate how long it would take to punch a hole through that much kyrelium with his antiarmor laser. The number came out on the order of several hours. "Any of the house's fancy stonework on the outer side?"

"Not on the gate itself, but there are two relief carvings flanking it on the wall. About *here* and *here*." She pointed.

Sensor clusters, most likely, and probably weapons as well. Facing inward as well as outward? No way of knowing, but it wasn't likely to matter with twenty centimeters of kyrelium blocking the way. "Well, that only leaves going over the wall," he sighed. "What's he got up there?"

"As far as I know, nothing."

Jonny frowned. "He's got to have *some* defenses up there, Ilona. Five-meter walls haven't been proof against attackers since ladders were invented. Um . . . what about the corners? Any raised stonework or anything there?"

"Nope." She was emphatic. "Nothing but flat wall all the way around the grounds."

Which meant no photoelectric/laser beam setup along the wall. Could Tyler really have left such an obvious loophole in his defenses? Of course, anything coming over the wall could be targeted by the house's lasers, but that approach depended on temperamental and potentially jammable highspeed electronics; and even if they worked properly, a fair amount of the shot was likely to expend its energy on other than the intended target. Sloppy *and* dangerous. No, Tyler must have had something else in mind. But what?

And then a pair of stray facts intersected in Jonny's mind. Tyler had built his mansion along Reginine lines; and Jonny's late teammate, Parr Noffke, had been from that same world. Had he ever said anything that might provide a clue . . . ?

He had. The day of the trainees' first modest test, the one Jonny had afterward nearly broken Viljo's face over. *Our wall lasers,* Noffke had commented, *point* up, *not across.*

And then, of course, it was obvious. Obvious and sobering. Instead of four lasers arranged to fire horizontally along the walls, Tyler had literally hundreds of the things lined up together like logs in an old palisade, aiming straight up from inside the wall. A horribly expensive barrier, but one that could defend against low projectiles and ground-hug missiles as well as grappler-equipped intruders. Quick, operationally simple, and virtually foolproof.

And almost undoubtedly the Trofts' planned deathtrap.

Jonny swallowed, the irony of it bitter on his tongue. This was exactly what he'd wanted: some insight into how the aliens expected to stop him . . . and now that he knew, the whole thing looked more hopeless than ever. Unless he could somehow get to the control circuitry for those lasers, there was no way he and Ilona would get beyond the wall without being solidly slagged.

He became aware that Ilona was watching him, a look of strained patience on her face. "Well? Any chance of getting through the gate?"

"I doubt it," Jonny shook his head. "But we won't have to. Up and over is a far better bet."

"Up and over? You mean climb a five-meter wall?"

"I mean jump it. I think I can manage it without too much trouble." In actual fact the wall's height was the least of their troubles, but there was no point telling the hidden listeners that.

"What about the defenses you said might be there?"

"Shouldn't pose any real problem," Jonny lied, again for the Trofts' benefit. He didn't dare appear *too* naive; it might arouse their suspicions. "I suspect Tyler's got his wall lasers built into elevating turrets at the corners. With all that stonework available to hide sensors in, there'd be no problem getting them up in time if someone started to climb in. I haven't seen that sort of arrangement on Adirondack before, but it's a logical extension of your usual defense laser setup, especially for someone with the classical aesthetics Tyler seems to have. Actually, I'm a lot more worried about getting *to* the wall in the first place. I want you to tell me everything you can remember about the route the Trofts used to get you to this room."

She nodded, and as she launched into a listing of rooms, hallways, and staircases, he knew she was satisfied with his spun-sugar theory. Now if only he'd similarly convinced the Trofts to let them get all the way to the deathtrap.

And if he could figure out a way through it.

His internal clock said ten p.m., and it was time to go.

Jonny had been of two minds about choosing a nighttime rather than an afternoon breakout. In the afternoon there would have been people beyond the Tyler Mansion's walls; crowds for the two fugitives to disappear into if they got that far, witnesses perhaps to their deaths—and the mansion's significance—if they didn't. But hiding in crowds made little sense if the Trofts were willing to slaughter civilians in order to get the two of them. Besides, forcing the Trofts' outdoor weaponry to rely on radar, infrared, and light amplification for targeting might prove a minor advantage.

Those were the reasons he gave Ilona. One more—that the aliens might not risk letting them even get to the wall in broad daylight— he kept to himself.

He was lying on his back on the table, hands folded across his chest; Ilona sat beside him, her knees pulled close to her chest, apparently contemplating the door. Ilona's inactivity wasn't an act: he'd quoted a ten-thirty jump-off time to her. Whether or not the Trofts could be fooled by so simple a trick he would probably never know, but it had certainly been worth a try.

Taking a deep breath, Jonny activated his omnidirectional sonic weapon.

There was a tingle in his gut, a slight vibration as the buried speakers brushed harmonics of natural body resonances. Straining his ears, he could almost hear the ultrasonic pitch changing as the sound dug into the walls, seeking resonances with the tiny audio and visual sensors open to it. . . .

The full treatment was supposed to require a minute, but Jonny had no intention of giving the Trofts that much warning. He didn't need to knock out the sensors permanently, but just to fog as many of them as possible while he made his move. He gave it five seconds; and just as Ilona began looking around the room with a frown he lifted his left leg slightly and fired.

The upper hinge of the door literally exploded, scattering solid and semisolid bits of itself in a shower to the floor. Beside him, Ilona yelped with surprise; in a single smooth motion, Jonny slid forward so that he could target the lower hinge and fired again. This shot didn't hit the inner sections quite as cleanly, and the explosive vaporization that had taken out the upper hinge didn't

occur. Jonny fired three more times, adding his fingertip lasers to
the assault, and within seconds the hinge was dangling loosely
against the wall. Gripping the edge of the table, he hurled himself feet-first at the hinge side of the door like a self-guided battering ram. The door creaked under the impact, displaced by a
centimeter or two. Regaining his balance, Jonny jumped across the
room, turned and tried it again, his hands providing a last-second
boost from the table as he passed it. The table survived; the door,
fortunately, did not. With a shriek of scraping metal, it popped
out of its frame and sagged at an odd angle, held off the floor
only by its lock mechanism.

"You said *ten-thirty*," Ilona growled. She was already at the door
by the time he got his balance, peering cautiously outside.

"I got impatient," Jonny returned, joining her. "Looks clear
enough; come on."

Stepping past the ruined door, they headed out into a dimly
lit hallway. Enhancers on full, Jonny scanned the walls and floor
quickly as he led Ilona in a quick jog. Nothing seemed to be
there—

They were nearly on top of it when Jonny spotted the slight
discoloration in the wall that indicated a disguised photocell at
knee height. "Detector!" he snapped, slowing to let Ilona catch up.
Pointing it out would have taken unnecessary time; grabbing her
upper arms, he swung her over the invisible beam and then jumped
over himself. *Too easy,* he thought uncomfortably. *Far too easy.* He
knew the Trofts wanted him to get through their gauntlet alive,
but this was ridiculous.

It stopped being ridiculous at the end of the hall.

Jonny paused there, at the threshold of a large room; but neither a complete stop nor a full-speed sprint would have done him
a scrap of good. Flanking the hallway exit were two quarter-circles
of armored Trofts.

Stepping back into the hallway would have been no more than
a temporary solution. Shoving Ilona back into that modest protection, he bent his knees and jumped.

The ceiling here wasn't as sturdy as the one back in Freyr
Complex's Room C-662, the one Bai had first demonstrated on.
But it was sturdy enough, and Jonny hit the floor with balance
intact and only a minor snowstorm of shattered ceiling tiles
accompanying him. Hit the floor, twisted . . . and as the Troft
lasers began to track, he threw himself spinning onto his shoulder-
blades.

Bai had called the maneuver a *break,* for obscure historical reasons; the trainees had privately dubbed it the *backspin.* Curled up in a half-fetal position, knees tucked almost to his chest, Jonny's antiarmor laser swept the line of soldiers, flashing instant death. Only three of the dozen or so soldiers escaped that first salvo, and they died on Jonny's second spin.

The metallic clink of armor-clad bodies hitting floor had barely ceased before Jonny was back in a crouch, eyes darting around. "Ilona!" he stage-whispered. "Come on." Peering into the hall, he saw her leap to her feet and trot toward him.

"Good Lord!" she gasped. "Was all of that *you?*"

"All of it that counted." Which proved all by itself he'd been right about the Trofts' plan. He should at least have picked up some light burns from that exchange. "That door?"

"Right. Remember that it's a stairway."

"Got it."

Like the hallway, the stairs proved to be free of major threats. Probably, Jonny decided, whatever sensors it contained were designed to study his equipment immediately after use, perhaps looking for theoretical limits or emission signatures. Triggering his sonic again, he led Ilona around the two photocells the stairway contained and braced himself for whatever he would find above.

The Trofts' first try had been a straightforward attack. This one was only marginally more subtle. Stretched across the floor, between the fugitives and the room's only exit, was a three-meter-wide black band. Jonny sniffed, caught a whiff of the same smell he remembered from the net at the Wolker Plant. "Glue patch," he warned Ilona, searching the walls with his eyes. A vertical strip of photocells stretched from floor to ceiling at either end of the adhesive; six almost-flat boxes adorned the walls beyond. Unlike the more permanent-looking photocells back in the hall and stairway, this trap had the air of having been hastily set up for the occasion.

Ilona, for a change, was right with him on this one. "So we jump and get hit by something while we're in mid-air?" she murmured tensely.

"Looks like it." Jonny stepped to the side wall near the adhesive and extended his right arm. "I'll try some simple sabotage. Get back into the stairwell, just in case."

His arcthrower flashed even as she obeyed . . . and he discovered just how badly he'd underestimated the Troft ability to learn.

Across the room one of the flat boxes abruptly disintegrated before a spinning mass that shot out directly toward him. The mass flattened as it came, its spin unfolding it into a giant mesh net.

He had no time then to regret having demonstrated his arc-thrower's range a few hours previously; no time to do anything but get out of the way fast.

And his programmed reflexes did their best. Dropping him toward the floor, his servos threw him in a flat dive at right angles to the net's line of motion. But the room was too small, the net too big; and even as he somersaulted into the wall near the stairway door, the edge of the mesh caught his left shoulder, pinning him to the floor.

Ilona was out of her shelter like a shot. "You all right?" she asked, hurrying toward him.

He waved her away and twisted up on one elbow. Cutting the mesh would perhaps be simplest, but if the glue contained a contact soporific again, he didn't want to risk carrying a patch of it along with them. Bracing himself, he jerked abruptly, tearing the trapped sleeve neatly off at the shoulder.

"Now what?" Ilona asked as he scrambled to his feet.

"We give up on the subtle approach. Get ready to move." Sequentially targeting the remaining five wall boxes, he raised his hands and fired.

He was half afraid the attack would trigger the firing mechanisms instead of destroying them. But as each box shattered and the briefly lingering laser beam swept the coiled net behind, it began to look like the Trofts had missed a bet. Until he noticed the pale brown smoke rising from the burning nets. . . .

"Hold your breath!" he snapped at Ilona. Stepping to her side, he grabbed her in a shoulder-and-thigh grip and jumped.

Not simply across the adhesive strip, but all the way to the door at the other end of the room. A potentially disastrous maneuver, but the Trofts fortunately had not hooked any more booby-traps to their photocell strip. The door was closed, but Jonny had no intention of pausing to see whether or not it was locked: he landed on his left foot, his right already snapping out in a servo-powered kick beside the doorknob. The panel shattered with gratifying ease, and—still carrying Ilona—he charged on through.

The room beyond was much smaller and, like the others he'd encountered so far, completely barren of furniture. It would have been nice to pause at the threshold and check for traps, but with expanding clouds of unknown gas in the room just behind, that was a luxury he couldn't afford. Instead, he took the whole five meters at a dead run, avoiding a straight-line path to the door opposite but otherwise relying solely on his combat reflexes to get them through safely.

And whatever the Trofts had set up, they apparently were taken by surprise by his maneuver. Reaching the door unscathed, he wrenched it open and slipped through, dropping Ilona back to the floor and slamming the door behind them. They were, as Jonny had expected, in the middle of a long hallway. Snapping his hands into firing position, he gave the place a quick survey, then focused again on Ilona. "You okay?"

"The bruises from this are going to be interesting," she said, reaching around to rub her rear where he'd been gripping her. "Otherwise okay. I came in that way—second door from the end, I think."

"I hope you're right." It wasn't a trivial point; Trofts routinely sealed off interior doors in buildings they took over, and a wrong turn could put them into a section of maze Ilona knew nothing at all about. At least it *was* a hallway, and therefore—if the Trofts kept to their pattern so far—presumably not booby-trapped. The breather would be nice to have. "Okay; let's go."

And with his attention on the walls, his assumptions firmly in mind, he nearly lost it all right there and then.

It started as a humming in his gut, similar to that caused by his own sonic weaponry, and it was pure luck that they were nearly to a node of the standing wave when he finally woke up to what was happening and skidded to an abrupt halt. "What?" Ilona gasped as she bumped into him.

"Infrasonic attack," he snapped. The humming had become a wave of nausea now, and his head was beginning to throb. "Hallway's a resonance cavity. We're standing at a node."

"Can't stay here," she managed, sagging against him and gripping her own stomach.

"I know. Hang on." There were only seconds, he estimated, before they were both too sick to move, and unfortunately the Trofts had left him only one option for a response. He'd hoped to keep at least one weapon out of their view on this trip, but with no indication where their infrasonic generator was located, his lasers were useless. Clutching the unsteady Ilona to his side, out of the direct line of fire, he activated his sonic disruptor and began sweeping the ends of the hallway.

Either he was very lucky or—more likely—the Trofts had again set him up with an easy victory, because in barely four seconds the sonic beam had hit on the resonance frequency for something in the Trofts' generator. Gritting his teeth—fully aware the sonic hadn't been designed for spaces this big—Jonny held the beam steady as his nanocomputer increased amplitude . . . and abruptly the nausea began fading. Within a dozen heartbeats all that remained of the attack were weak knees and residual aches throughout his body.

"Come on, we've got to keep going," he told Ilona thickly, stumbling toward the door she'd pointed out earlier.

"Yeah," she agreed, and did her best to comply. He wound up mostly carrying her anyway, a task that would have been impossible without his servos. Reaching the door, he pulled it open.

The Trofts had gone back to being unsubtle. This room, unlike all the previous ones, was almost literally loaded with furniture . . . and behind each piece seemed to be an enemy soldier.

It occurred to Jonny in that first frozen millisecond that deviating from Ilona's remembered path might well be disastrous, if for no other reason than panicking the Troft commander. But there was no way he was going to willingly face a roomful of enemies if another possibility existed . . . or could be made.

A single, untuned blast from his sonic was all he had time for before slamming the door to; with luck, it would jar them at least enough to slow any pursuit. Grabbing Ilona's arm, he sprinted to the next door, the last one at this end of the hall.

"This isn't the way I came!" she yelped as he let go and tried the door. It was locked, of course.

"No choice. Hit the ground and yell if you see anyone coming." His fingertip lasers were already spitting destruction at the door's edges, tracing a dashed-line pattern that would yield maximum weakening in minimum time. Halfway through he kicked hard at the door; finishing it, he kicked again. With the second kick he felt it give, and four kicks later the panel abruptly shattered. Ilona right behind him, he ducked through.

And it was instantly clear they were off the path so carefully set up for them. No human-style furniture or equipment here— from floor to ceiling the room was jarringly alien. Long, oddly shaped couches lay grouped around what looked like circular tables with hemispherical domes rising from their centers. On the walls were almost archaic-looking murals alternating with smaller bits of gleaming electronics. Across the room Jonny got just a glimpse of a Troft back-jointed leg as the alien beat a hasty retreat . . . and in the relative silence a sound heretofore conspicuous by its absence could be heard: the thin ululating wail of a Troft alarm.

"Dining room?" Ilona asked, glancing around.

"Lounge." A minor disappointment; he'd rather hoped they would wind up somewhere his arcthrower could be put to use. The control room for the wall defenses, for example.

On the other hand . . .

"Let's get going," Ilona urged, throwing apprehensive glances at the ruined door behind them. "That crowd will be on our backs any minute."

"Just a second," Jonny told her, scanning the walls. Trofts always put lounges and other noncritical facilities on the outer edges of their bases . . . and, half-hidden by the murals, he finally spotted what he was looking for: the outline of a window.

Well boarded up, of course. A dark sheet of kyrelium steel, three meters by one, fitted precisely into the opening, leaving only a hairline crack in the otherwise featureless slate-gray wall. Unbreakable with even Cobra weaponry; but if the designer had followed standard Troft building reinforcement procedures, there might be a chance of getting off this treadmill right here. "Get ready to follow," he called to Ilona over his shoulder. Leaning hard into the floor, he charged the window and jumped, turning feet first in midair and hitting the window shield dead center.

The panel popped neatly from its casing and clattered to the ground outside. Jonny, much of his momentum lost, landed considerably closer to the building. Dropping into a crouch, he activated his light amp equipment and looked quickly around him.

He was in what had probably once been an extensive flower bed, extending most of the way out to where the stunted bushes and trees of an elaborate haiku garden began, the latter shifting in turn to a band of full-sized trees near the outer wall. No cover until the trees—Jonny's rangefinder set the distance at about fifty-two meters. The wall itself . . . thirty meters further.

Behind him came a noise. He twisted around, vaguely aware that the action hurt, to see Ilona jump lightly to the ground. "That was one beaut of a kick," she hissed as she joined him in his crouch.

"Not really. The edges are beveled against impacts from the outside only. Any idea where we are?"

"West side of the house. Gate's around to the north."

"Never mind the gate—we can go over the wall just as easily here." A corner of Jonny's mind considered the possibility that the

Trofts had spy-mikes on them. "First, though," he added for their benefit, "I want to see if the house lasers are set to fire on out-going targets."

Still no sign of enemy soldiers. Moving to the former window cover, he hefted the metal for a quick examination. Kyrelium steel, all right, about five centimeters thick. He had no idea whether it would do for what he had in mind, but there was no time left to find anything better. Bracing himself firmly, he gripped the panel on either side, raised it over his head like a makeshift umbrella . . . and with everything his servos could manage, he hurled it toward the distant wall.

He'd never gone to the limit in quite this way, and for a long, horrifying moment he was afraid he'd thrown the panel too hard. If it cleared the wall—and in the process ruined his pretense of ignorance as to the defensive lasers there—

But he actually had nothing to fear. The panel arced smoothly into the sky and dropped with a crash of breaking branches into the middle of the distant patch of forest, a good twenty meters in from the wall.

And it made the whole trip without drawing any fire.

Jonny licked his lips. So the automatics would most likely leave them alone. Would the live gunners who were undoubtedly up there abstain as well? There was nothing he could do about that but hope that they were still relying on the wall itself to ultimately stop him. If they were . . . and if his plan worked . . .

"Ready for a run?" he whispered to Ilona.

Her eyes were still on the spot where the kyrelium plate had ended its flight. "Phrij and a half," she muttered. "Uh—yeah, I'm ready. Toward the wall?"

"Right. As fast as you can. I'll be behind you where I can theoret-ically handle anyone who tries to stop us." One final look around— "Okay; *go.*"

She took off like the entire Troft war machine was after her, running in a half-crouched posture that offered at best an illu-sion of relative safety. Jonny let her lead him by perhaps five meters, enhanced vision and hearing alert for any sound of pursuit. But the Tyler Mansion might have been deserted for all the response they drew from it. *All lined up on the balcony to watch us slag ourselves, no doubt,* he thought, recognizing as he did so that the strain was beginning to affect him. *A few more seconds,* he told himself over and over, the words settling into the quick rhythm of his footsteps. *A few more seconds and it'll be over.*

At the edge of the forest he put on a burst of speed, catching up to Ilona a few steps later. "Wait a second—I have to find that kyrelium plate."

"What?" she gasped. "Why?"

"Don't ask questions. There it is."

Not surprisingly, the heavy metal was undamaged. Jonny picked it up and balanced it like an oversized door in front of him, searching for the best and safest handholds.

"What . . . you . . . doing?"

"Getting us out of here. Come here—stand in front of me. Come *here*."

She obeyed, stepping between him and the plate. "Arms around my neck—hold on tight . . . now wrap your legs around my waist . . . okay. Hold *tight*, whatever happens. Got it?"

"Yeah." Even muffled by his chest, her voice sounded scared. Perhaps she had a glimmering of what was about to happen.

Twenty meters to the wall. Jonny backed up another ten, getting the feel of the extra weight distribution as he gave himself room for a running start. "Here we go," he told Ilona. "Hang on—"

The whine of the servos was louder in his ears than even the thudding of his pulse as his feet dug deeper into the dirt with each step and his speed increased. Eight steps, nine steps—almost fast enough—*ten* steps—

And an instant later his knees straightened to send them soaring upward.

It was a move Jonny had practiced over and over again back on Asgard: a high-jumper's roll, designed to take him horizontally over whatever barrier stood in his way. Horizontal, face downward, he neared both the top of his arc and the deadly wall . . . and an instant before reaching them, he let go of the plate now directly beneath him and wrapped his arms tightly around Ilona.

The flash was incredibly bright, especially considering that all he was seeing was the fraction of laser light reflected from the underside of the kyrelium plate to the surrounding landscape. There was a rapid-fire cracking sound of heat-stressed metal against the brief hiss of explosive ablation—and then they were past the wall, and Jonny was twisting to bring them upright as they arced toward the ground.

He almost made it, hitting at an angle that probably would have ruined both ankles without his bone and ligament reinforcement. Recovering his balance, he tightened his hold on Ilona and started to run.

He got halfway to the nearest building before the Trofts recovered from their surprise and began firing. Laser blasts licked at his sides and heels as he zigzagged across the open ground. *I guess you're going to get one more datapoint,* he thought in their direction; and, again pushing his leg servos to the limit, he took the last twenty meters in an all-out sprint. One second later they were around the building's corner and out of range.

Jonny kept running, aiming for a second deserted factory a short block away. "Any suggestions as to a hiding place?" he called to Ilona over the wind.

She didn't even bother to raise her face from his shoulder. "Just keep going," she said, and even with the jolting of their run, he could feel her violent shiver.

He ran on, changing direction periodically, searching for a section of the city he could recognize. A kilometer or so later he found a familiar intersection and turned north, heading for one of the underground's secure phones. They were still a block away when the sound of approaching aircraft became audible. Jonny estimated distances and speeds, decided not to risk it, and stepped to the nearest doorway. It was locked, of course: but after what they'd just been through, a locked door was hardly worth noticing. Seconds later, they were inside.

"Are we safe here?" Ilona asked as Jonny set her down. Rubbing her ribs, she peered out the mesh-protected front window.

"Not really, but it'll have to do for the moment." Jonny found a chair and sat down, wincing as he did so. With the danger temporarily at arm's length he finally had time to notice the condition of his own body, and it was clear he wasn't as unscathed as he'd thought. At least five minor burns stung spots on arms and torso, evidence of Troft near-misses. His left ankle felt like it was on fire from the heat leakage buildup of his own antiarmor laser—one of the design flaws, he realized, that Bai had warned them to expect. Sore muscles and bruises seemed to be everywhere, and in several places he couldn't tell whether the clammy wetness of his clothing was due to sweat or oozing blood. "We'll have to wait until the aircraft overhead settle into a pattern I can thread, but then I should be able to get to a phone and alert the underground. They'll figure out where to stash you while I go back to the mansion."

"While you *what?*" She spun around to face him, her expression echoing the odd intensity in her voice.

"While I go back," he repeated. "You didn't know it, but the only reason they let us go was to collect data on my equipment in action. I have to try and get hold of those tapes."

"That's suicidal!" she snapped. "The whole phrijing nest of them will be running around by now."

"Running around out *here*, looking for us," he reminded her. "The mansion itself may not be well defended for a while, and if I'm fast enough I may be able to catch them off guard. Anyway, I've got to at least try."

She seemed about to say something, pursed her lips. "In that case . . . you probably can't take the time to go call the underground, either. If you're going back, you'd better do it right away."

Jonny stared at her. No argument, no real protest . . . and suddenly it occurred to him he really knew nothing at all about her. "Where did you say you lived?" he asked.

"I didn't say. What does *that* have to do with anything?"

"Nothing, really . . . except that I've just noticed I'm at a distinct disadvantage here. *You* know that I'm a Cobra, and therefore which side I'm on. But I don't know the same about you."

She stared at him for a long moment . . . and when she spoke again the usual sardonic undertone was gone from her voice. "Are you suggesting I'm a Troft hireling?" she asked quietly.

"You tell me. All I know about you is what you yourself said— including how exactly you came to be tossed in my cell. Sure, the Trofts *could* have plucked a random citizen off the streets, but they'd have done a lot better to use someone who could be trusted to pressure me if I still refused to perform for them."

"*Did* I pressure you?"

"No, but then that didn't prove necessary. And now you're encouraging me to go back alone, without even calling for underground backup forces."

"If I were a spy, wouldn't I *want* you to get me to the underground?" she countered. "I imagine the Trofts would like to get a solid line on the resistance. And as to encouraging you to go back alone—well, I admit I'm no expert on tactics, but doesn't it seem likely that before your backup forces got organized the Trofts would be back inside and braced for the attack?"

"You've got an answer for everything, don't you?" he growled. "All right. Let's hear *your* suggestion on what I should do with you."

Her eyes narrowed slightly. "Meaning . . . ?"

"If you're a spy I don't want you anywhere near the underground. Nor can I let you loose to tip off the Trofts that I'm coming."

"Well, I'm *not* going back to the mansion with you," she said emphatically.

"I'm not offering. What I guess I'll have to do is tie you up here until I get back."

A muscle twitched in her jaw. "And if you don't?"

"You'll be found by the shop's owner in the morning."

"Or by the Trofts sooner," she said softly. "The patrols looking for us, remember?"

And if she wasn't a spy . . . they'd kill her rather than let word of their mansion HQ get out. "Can you prove you're not a spy?" he asked, feeling new sweat break out on his forehead as he sensed the box closing tightly around his options.

"In the next thirty seconds? Don't be silly." She took a deep breath. "No, Jonny. If you want any chance at all of hitting the mansion tonight, you'll just have to accept my story or reject it on faith alone. If your suspicions are strong enough to justify my death . . . then there's nothing I can really do about it. I suppose it's a question of whether my life's worth risking yours over."

And when put that way, there really wasn't any decision to make. He'd risked his life for her once already . . . and enemy hireling or not, the Trofts had clearly been willing to let her die with him over the wall. "I suggest you find a hiding place before the patrols get here," he growled at her as he moved toward the door. "And watch out for aircraft."

Outside, the sound of thrusters was adequately distant. Without looking back, he slipped out into the night and headed back toward the Tyler Mansion, wondering if he'd just made the last stupid mistake of his life.

It was a much slower trip than before, with aircraft and vehicles forcing him to take cover with increasing frequency the closer he got to his target. Enough so that by the time he finally came within sight of the mansion's outer wall the basic tactical reasoning behind this solo effort was becoming shaky. Nearly three-quarters of an hour had passed since their escape—enough time for the Trofts to begin worrying about a raid and to have drawn their troops back to defensive positions. All around him Jonny's enhanced hearing was starting to pick up a faint background of moving bodies and equipment, all interspersed with the mandible clack of the Trofts' so-called catertalk, as the aliens began barricading the approaches to their base. Forced at last to abandon the ground, Jonny slipped into one of the neighborhood's abandoned buildings, working his way cautiously to an upper floor and a window facing the mansion. With light amps at full power, he studied the scene below.

And knew he'd lost.

The Trofts were everywhere: blocking streets, guarding rooftops and windows, setting up laser emplacements at the base of the wall itself. Beyond them, he could see aircraft drifting over the far wall to join others parked around the mansion. The cordon meant the Trofts were giving up any further hope of disguising their presence in the mansion; the aircraft implied they were preparing to abandon it. A few hours—a day or two at the most—and they would be gone, their tapes of his escape gone with them. Until then—

Until then, the wall's defense lasers would have to be periodically shut down to let the aircraft in and out.

With most of the armed troops *outside* the wall.

An intriguing thought . . . but offhand he couldn't see any way to take advantage of it. With the Troft cordon strengthening almost by the minute, getting to the wall was becoming well-nigh impossible. As a matter of fact, it wasn't even certain anymore that he'd be able to sneak *out* without being spotted and slagged. *I shouldn't have come back,* he thought morosely. *Now I'm stuck here until the ground clutter clears out.*

He was just starting to turn away when a building off to the left emitted a cloud of fire from its base and began collapsing into itself. The thunderclap of the explosion had barely reached him when the streets below abruptly came alive with the stutter-flash of multiple laser weapons.

The unexpectedness of it froze him at the window . . . but for now the *how* of it would keep. He was really too exposed to risk drawing attention with his lasers, but there were other ways he could join the battle.

He watched a few seconds longer, fixing the layout and specific Troft positions in his mind. Then, moving back from the window, he set about collecting the odd chunks of masonry earlier battles in this region had shaken from the walls. Thrown with Cobra accuracy, they could be almost as deadly as grenades.

He was still busily clearing the street of Trofts when a second explosion lit up the sky. Looking up, he was just in time to see the red afterglow fading from an upper window of the Tyler Mansion.

An hour later, the battle was over.

✧　　✧　　✧

Swathed in bandages and IV tubes, Halloran looked more like something out of an archeological dig than a living person. But what was visible of his face looked happier than Jonny had seen it in months. As well it might, considering the lousy odds all three Cobras had somehow managed to survive. "When we get off this rock," Jonny told the other, "remind me to have you and Imel sent up for a complete psych exam. You're both genuinely crazy."

"What—because we pulled the same stupid trick you were going to try?" Halloran asked innocently.

"Stupid trick, nothing," Deutsch retorted from the bed next to Halloran's. Only a few bandages graced his form, mute testimony to superior luck or skill. "We were practically on top of the place when you and Ilona made your break, close enough that we were actually inside their temporary picket ring when they all charged out after you. It was perfectly straightforward, tactically—it was just the implementation that got a bit sticky."

"Sticky, my eyeteeth. *Some* of us lost a lot of skin in there." Halloran jerked his head in Deutsch's direction. "Now *him* you're welcome to have sent up. You should've seen the chances he took in there. Not to mention the way he stared down Borg and got everyone on the streets looking for you."

Which, with a little unconscious help from the Trofts, was what had ultimately saved Jonny's life. He wondered if the aliens had had any idea what Ilona was really doing out there when they'd grabbed her. "I owe you both a lot," he said, knowing how inadequate the words were. "Thank you."

Deutsch waved a hand in dismissal. "Forget it—you'd have done the same for us. Besides, it was pretty much of a group effort, what with half of the Cranach underground taking their share of the risks."

"Including broadcasting the location of that hidden tunnel entrance to us as soon as Ilona phoned in the details," Halloran added. "I don't suppose they mentioned that one to you?—no, I didn't think so. Now *that* was a stupid trick. They're damn lucky the Trofts were too busy to trace the transmission—they certainly had the equipment to do so. I think the whole planet's going to need psychiatric help by the time this is over."

Jonny smiled along with them, hiding the twinge of embarrassment that still accompanied references to Ilona's part in the South Sector underground's counterattack on the Tyler Mansion. "Speaking of Ilona, she's supposed to give me a ride to the new home

Ama's moved me to," he told them. "You guys take it easy, and I'll be back to give you a hand when you're ready to move."

"No rush," Halloran told him airily. "These people treat me with a lot more respect than you two clowns, anyway."

"He's definitely on the mend," Deutsch snorted. "Get going, Jonny; no point in keeping Ilona waiting for *this*."

Ilona was waiting inside the building foyer. "All set?" she asked briskly. "Let's go, then—they're expecting you in a few minutes, and you know how nervous we get when schedules aren't met."

She led the way outside to a car parked by the curb. They got in and she headed north . . . and for the first time since their escape two days earlier they were alone together.

Jonny cleared his throat. "So . . . how's the sifting at the mansion going?"

She glanced at him. "Not too bad. Cally and Imel and that East Sector team left a shambles, but we've found a lot of interesting items the Trofts didn't have time to destroy. I'd say that we've gotten far better than an even trade for those records of Jonny Moreau in action."

"No sign of them, huh?"

"No, but it hardly matters. They'd almost certainly have transmitted the data elsewhere as soon as we escaped."

"Oh, I know. But I'd hoped that if we had the original tapes we could figure out exactly how much they'd learned about our gear and be able to estimate the added danger we'll be working under."

"Ah. Yes, I guess that makes sense. I don't think you're going to have anything to worry about, though."

Johnny snorted. "You underestimate the Trofts' ingenuity. Like you very nearly underestimated my kind heart. You could've *told* me you were with the underground, you know."

He was expecting her to come out with some stiff and wholly inappropriate local security regulation; and so her reply, when it finally came, was something of a surprise. "I could have," she acknowledged. "And if you'd looked like you were making the wrong decision I sure would have. But . . . you'd jumped to a rather paranoid conclusion without any real evidence, and I . . . well, I wanted to find out how far you'd go in acting on that conclusion." She took a deep breath. "You see, Jonny, whether you know it or not, all of us who work and fight with you Cobras are more than a little afraid of you. There've been persistent rumors since you first landed that you'd been given carte blanche by Asgard to do anything you considered necessary to drive the Trofts off—including summary execution for any offense you decided you didn't like."

Jonny stared at her. "That's absurd."

"Is it? The Dominion can't exercise control over you from umpteen light-years away, and *we* sure can't do it. If you've got the power anyway why *not* make it official?"

"Because—" Jonny floundered. "Because that's not the way to liberate Adirondack."

"Depends on whether that's really Asgard's major objective, doesn't it? If they're more interested in breaking the Trofts' war capabilities, our little world is probably pretty expendable."

Jonny shook his head. "No. I realize it's hard to tell from here, but I know for a fact that the Cobras aren't on Adirondack to win anything at the expense of the people. If you knew the screening they put us through—and how many good men were bounced even *after* the training—"

"Sure, I understand all that. But military goals *do* change." She shrugged. "But with any luck the whole question will soon be academic."

"What do you mean?"

She favored him with a tight smile. "We got an off-world signal this morning. All underground and Cobra units are to immediately begin a pre-invasion sabotage campaign."

Jonny felt his mouth drop open. "Pre-invasion?"

"That's what they said. And if it succeeds . . . we owe the Cobras a lot, Jonny, and we won't forget you. But I don't think we'll be sorry to see you go, either."

To that Jonny had no reply, and the rest of the trip was made in silence. Ilona drove several blocks past Jonny's old apartment building, stopping finally before another, even more nondescript place. A tired-eyed woman greeted him at the door and took him to a top-floor apartment, where his meager belongings had already been delivered. On top of the bags was a small envelope.

Frowning, Jonny opened it. Inside was a plain piece of paper with a short, painstakingly written note:

Dear Jonny,
Mom says you're going somewhere else now and aren't going to be staying with us anymore. Please be careful and don't get caught anymore and come back to see me. I love you.
Danice

Jonny smiled as he slipped the note back into its envelope. *You be careful, too, Danice,* he thought. *Maybe you, at least, will remember us kindly.*

Interlude

The negotiations were over, the treaty was signed, ratified, and being implemented, and the euphoric haze that had pervaded the Central Committee's meetings for the past two months was finally starting to fade. Vanis D'arl had expected Committé H'orme to pick this point to bring up the Cobras again; and he was right.

"It's not a question of ingratitude or injustice—it's a question of pure necessity," the Committé told the assembly, his voice quavering only slightly. Seated behind him, D'arl eyed H'orme's back uneasily, seeing in his stance the older man's fatigue. He wondered if the others knew how much the war had taken out of H'orme . . . wondered whether they would consequently recognize the urgency implied by his being here to deliver this message personally.

From their faces, though, it was obvious most of them didn't, an attitude clearly shown by the first person to rise when H'orme had finished. "If you'll forgive the tone, H'orme," the other said with a perfunctory gesture of respect, "I think the Committee has heard quite enough of your preoccupation with the Cobras. If you'll recall, it was at your insistence that we directed the Army to offer them exceptionally liberal reenlistment terms, and in your place *I* would consider it a victory that over seventy percent chose to accept. We've all heard from Commander Mendro and his associates just how much of their equipment the other twenty-odd percent will take back to civilian life with them, and we've concluded the Army's plans are acceptable. To again suggest now that we force those men to remain in the Army strikes me as a bit . . . overconcerned."

Or paranoid, *as the word will be interpreted,* D'arl thought. But

H'orme had one tacnuke yet in reserve, and as the Committé picked up a magcard from his stack, D'arl knew he was about to set it off. "I remember Commander Mendro's visits quite well, thank you," he addressed the other Committé with a nod, "and I've done some checking on the facts and figures he presented." Dropping the magcard into his reader, he keyed to the first of his chosen sections and sent the picture to the other viewers around the table. "You will note here the percentage of Cobra trainees that were actually commissioned and sent into the war, displayed as a function of time. The different colors refer to the continually updated initial screening tests the Army used."

A few frowns began to appear. "You're saying they never got more than eighty-five percent into the field?" a Committé halfway around the table spoke up. "The number *I* remember is ninety-seven percent."

"That's the number that were *physically* able to go after training," H'orme told her. "The rest of them were dropped for psychosociological reasons."

"So?" someone else shrugged. "No testing method's ever perfect. As long as they caught all of the unacceptable ones—"

"I expect H'orme's point is whether or not they *did* catch all of them," another Committé suggested dryly.

"A simple check of eyewitness accounts from Silvern and Adirondack—"

"Will take months to complete," H'orme interrupted. "But there's more. Dismiss, if you'd like, the possibility of antisocial leanings in any of the Cobras. Are you aware they'll be taking their combat nanocomputers back with them?—with *no* reprogramming?"

All eyes turned to him. "What are you talking about? Mendro said . . ." The speaker paused.

"Mendro deflected the question exceptionally well," H'orme said grimly. "The fact of the matter is that the nanocomputers are read-only and can't be reprogrammed, and after being in place even a short time they can't be removed without excessive trauma to the brain tissue that's subsequently settled in around them."

"Why weren't we told?"

"Initially, I presume, because the Army wanted the Cobras and was afraid we'd veto or modify their chosen design. More recently, the point was probably not brought up because there wasn't anything anyone could do about it."

All of which, D'arl knew, was only partly correct. All the data on the nanocomputers *had* been in the original Cobra proposals, had anyone besides H'orme deemed it worth digging out. Perhaps H'orme was saving that fact for future leverage.

The discussion raged back and forth for a while, and long before it was over the remaining air of euphoria had vanished from the chamber. But if the new sense of realism raised D'arl's hopes, the end result dashed them again. By a nineteen to eleven vote, the Committee chose not to interfere with the Cobra demobilization.

"You should know by now that clear-cut victories are as rare as oxygen worlds," H'orme chided D'arl later in his office. "We got them thinking—*really* thinking—and at this stage that's as much as we could have hoped for. The Committee will be watching the Cobras carefully now, and if action turns out to be necessary, it'll take a minimum amount of prodding to get it."

"All of which could've been avoided if they'd just paid attention to the Cobra project in the first place," D'arl muttered.

"No one can pay attention to *everything,*" H'orme shrugged. "Besides, there's an important psychological effect operating here. Most of the Dominion sees the military and the government as essentially two parts of a single monolithic structure, and whether they admit it or not the Committee carries a remnant of that assumption in its collective subconscious. You and I, who grew up on Asgard, have what I think is a more realistic perspective on exactly where and to what extent the military's goals differ from ours. They conceived the Cobras with the sole purpose of winning a war in mind, and every bit of their training and equipment—including the nanocomputer design—made sense within those limited parameters. What the Committee should have done, but didn't, was to remember that all wars eventually end. Instead, we assumed the Army had already done that thinking for us."

D'arl tapped two fingers on the arm of his chair. "Maybe next time they'll know better."

"Possibly. But I doubt it." H'orme leaned back in his chair with a tired sigh. "Anyway, this is the situation we have to live with. What do you suggest as our next move?"

D'arl pursed his lips. H'orme had been doing this a lot lately, and whether it was due to simple mental fatigue or a conscious effort to sharpen the younger man's executive capabilities, it was a bad sign. Very soon now, D'arl knew, H'orme's hot seat was going to pass to him. "We should obtain a listing of all returning Cobras and their destinations," he told H'orme. "Then we should set up local and regional data triggers to funnel all government-accessible news concerning them directly to you, with special flags for criminal or other abnormal behavior."

H'orme nodded. "Agreed. Have someone—Joromo, maybe—get started on it."

"Yes, sir." D'arl stood up. "I think, though, that I'll do this one personally. I want to make sure it's done right."

A ghost of a smile flicked across H'orme's lips. "You humor an old man's obsession, D'arl, and I appreciate it. But I think you'll find—you *and* the rest of the Committee—that the Cobras are going to have far more impact on the Dominion than even I'm afraid of." He turned his chair to gaze out the window at the city below. "I just wish," he added softly, "I knew what form that impact was going to take."

Veteran: *2407*

The late-afternoon sunlight glinted whitely off the distant mountains as the shuttle came to rest with only a slight bounce. Army-issue satchel slung over his shoulder, Jonny stepped out onto the landing pad, eyes darting everywhere. He had never been all that familiar with Horizon City, but even to him it was obvious the place had changed. There were half a dozen new buildings visible from the Port, and one or two older ones had disappeared. The landscaping around the area had been redone with what looked like newly imported off-world varieties, as if the city were making a concerted effort to shake off its frontier-world status. But the wind was blowing in from the north, across the plains and forests that were as yet untouched by man, and with it came the sweet-sour aroma that no cultural aspirations could disguise. Three years ago, Jonny would hardly have noticed the scent; now, it was almost as if Horizon itself had contrived to welcome him home.

Taking a deep breath of the perfume, he stepped off the pad and walked the hundred meters to a long, one-story building labeled "Horizon Customs: Entry Point." Opening the outer door, he stepped inside.

A smiling man awaited him by a waist-high counter. "Hello, Mr. Moreau; welcome back to Horizon. I'm sorry—should I call you 'Cee-three Moreau'?"

"'Mister' is fine," Jonny smiled. "I'm a civilian now."

"Of course, of course," the man said. He was still smiling, but there seemed to be just a trace of tension behind the geniality. "And glad of it, I suppose. I'm Harti Bell, the new head of customs here. Your luggage is being brought from the shuttle. In the meantime, I wonder if I might inspect your satchel? Just a formality, really."

"Sure." Jonny slid the bag off his shoulder and placed it on the counter. The faint hum of his servos touched his inner ear as he did so, sounding strangely out of place against the gentle haze of boyhood memories. Bell took the satchel and pulled, as if trying to bring it a few centimeters closer to him. It moved maybe a centimeter; Bell nearly lost his balance. Throwing an odd look at Jonny, he apparently changed his mind and opened the bag where it lay.

By the time he finished, Jonny's two other cases had been brought in. Bell went through them with quick efficiency, made a few notations on his comboard, and finally looked up again, smile still in place.

"All set, Mr. Moreau," he said. "You're free to go."

"Thanks." Jonny put his satchel over his shoulder once more and transferred the other two bags from the counter to the floor. "Is Transcape Rentals still in business? I'll need a car to get to Cedar Lake."

"Sure is, but they've moved three blocks farther east. Want to call a taxi?"

"Thanks; I'll walk." Jonny held out his right hand.

For just a moment the smile slipped. Then, almost warily, Bell took the outstretched hand. He let go as soon as he politely could.

Picking up his bags, Jonny nodded at Bell and left the building.

Mayor Teague Stillman shook his head tiredly as he turned off his comboard and watched page two hundred of the latest land-use proposal disappear from the screen. He would never cease to be amazed at how much wordwork the Cedar Lake city council was able to generate—about a page a year, he'd once estimated, for every one of the town's sixteen thousand citizens. *Either official magforms have learned how to breed,* he told himself as he rubbed vigorously at his eyes, *or else someone's importing them. Whichever, the Trofts are probably behind it.*

There was a tap on his open door, and Stillman looked up to see Councilor Sutton Fraser standing in the doorway. "Come on in," he invited.

Fraser did so, closing the door behind him. "Too drafty for you?" Stillman asked mildly as Fraser sat down on one of the mayor's guest chairs.

"I got a call a few minutes ago from Harti Bell out at the Horizon Port," Fraser began without preamble. "Jonny Moreau's back."

Stillman stared at the other for a moment, then shrugged slightly. "He had to come eventually. The war's over, after all. Most of the soldiers came back weeks ago."

"Yeah, but Jonny's not exactly an ordinary soldier. Harti said he lifted a satchel that must have weighed thirty kilos with one hand. Effortlessly. The kid could probably tear a building apart if he got mad."

"Relax, Sut. I know the Moreau family. Jonny's a very even-tempered sort of guy."

"*Was,* you mean," Fraser said darkly. "He's been a Cobra for three years now, killing Trofts and watching them kill his friends. Who knows what that's done to him?"

"Probably instilled a deep dislike for war, if he's like most soldiers. Aside from that, it hasn't done too much, I'd guess."

"You know better than that, Teague. The kid's dangerous; that's a simple fact. Ignoring it isn't going to do you any good."

"Calling him 'dangerous' is? What are you trying to do, start a panic?"

"I doubt that any panic's going to need my help to get started. Everybody in town's seen the idiot plate reports on Our Heroic Forces—they all know how badly the Cobras chewed up the Trofts on Adirondack and Silvern."

Stillman sighed. "Look. I'll admit there may be some problems with Jonny's readjustment to civilian life. Frankly, I would have been happier if he'd stayed in the service. But he didn't. Like it or not, Jonny's home, and we can either accept it calmly or run around screaming doom. He risked his life out there; the least we can do is to give him a chance to forget the war and vanish back into the general population."

"Yeah. Maybe." Fraiser shook his head slowly. "It's not going to be an easy road, though. Look, as long as I'm here, maybe you and I could draft some sort of announcement about this to the press. Try to get a jump on the rumors."

"Good idea. Hey, cheer up, Sut—soldiers have been coming home ever since mankind started having wars. We should be getting the hang of this by now."

"Yeah," Fraser growled. "Except that this is the first time since swords went out of fashion that soldiers have gotten to take their weapons home with them."

Stillman shrugged helplessly. "It's out of our hands. Come on: let's get to work."

Jonny pulled up in front of the Moreau home and turned off the car engine with a sigh of relief. The roads between Horizon City and Cedar Lake were rougher than he remembered them, and more than once he'd wished he had spent the extra money to rent a hover, even though the weekly rate was almost double that for wheeled vehicles. But he'd made it, with a minimum of kidney damage, and that was what mattered.

He stepped out of the car and retrieved his bags from the trunk, and as he set them down on the street a hand fell on his shoulder. He turned and looked five centimeters up into his father's smiling face. "Welcome home, Son," Pearce Moreau said.

"Hi, Dader," Jonny said, face breaking into a huge grin as he grasped the other's outstretched hand. "How've you been?"

Pearce's answer was interrupted by a crash and shriek from the front door of the house. Jonny turned to see ten-year-old Gwen tearing across the lawn toward him, yelling like a banshee with a winning lottery ticket. Dropping into a crouch facing her, he opened his arms wide; and as she flung herself at him, he grabbed her around the waist, straightened up, and threw her a half meter into the air above him. Her shrill laughter almost masked Pearce's sharp intake of breath. Catching his sister easily, Jonny lowered her back to the ground. "Boy, you've sure grown," he told her. "Pretty soon you'll be too big to toss around."

"Good," she panted. "Then you can teach me how to arm wrestle. C'mon and see my room, huh, Jonny?"

"I'll be along in a little bit," he told her. "I want to say hello to Momer first. She in the kitchen?"

"Yes," Pearce said. "Why don't you go on ahead, Gwen. I'd like to talk to Jonny for a moment."

"Okay," she chirped. Squeezing Jonny's hand, she scampered back toward the house.

"She's got her room papered with articles and pictures from the past three years," Pearce explained as he and Jonny collected Jonny's luggage. "Everything she could get hard copies of that had anything to do with the Cobras."

"You disapprove?"

"Of what—that she idolizes you? Good heavens, no. Why?"

"You seem a bit nervous."

"Oh. I guess I was a little startled when you tossed Gwen in the air a minute ago."

"I've been using the servos for quite a while now," Jonny pointed out mildly as they headed toward the house. "I really *do* know how to use my strength safely."

"I know, I know. Hell, I used exoskeleton gear myself in the Minthistin War, you know, when I was your age. But it was pretty bulky, and you couldn't ever forget you were wearing it. I guess . . . well, I suppose I was worried that you'd forget yourself."

Jonny shrugged. "Actually, I'm probably in better control than you ever were, since I don't have to have two sets of responses—with power amp and without. The servos and ceramic laminae are going to be with me the rest of my life, and I've long since gotten used to them."

Pearce nodded. "Okay." He paused, then continued, "Look, Jonny, as long as we're on the subject . . . the Army's letter to us said that 'most' of your Cobra gear would be removed before you came home. What did they—I mean, what do you still have?"

Jonny sighed. "I wish they'd just come out and listed the stuff instead of being coy like that. It makes it sound like I'm still a walking tank. The truth is that, aside from the skeletal laminae and servos, all I have is the nanocomputer—which hasn't got much to do now except run the servos—and two small lasers in my little fingers, which they couldn't remove without amputation. And the servo power supply, of course. Everything else—the arcthrower capacitors, the antiarmor laser, and the sonic weapons—are gone." So was the self-destruct, but that subject was best left alone.

"Okay," Pearce said. "Sorry to bring it up, but your mother and I were a little nervous."

"That's all right."

They were at the house now. Entering, they went to the bedroom Jame had had to himself for the last three years. "Where's Jame, by the way?" Jonny asked as he piled his bags by his old bed.

"Out at New Persius picking up a spare laser tube for the bodywork welder down at the shop. We've only got one working at the moment and can't risk it going out on us. Parts have been nearly impossible to get lately—a side effect of war, you know." He snapped his fingers. "Say, those little lasers you have—can you weld with them?"

"I can spot-weld, yes. They were designed to work on metals, as a matter of fact."

"Great. Maybe you could give us a hand until we can get parts for the other lasers. How about it?"

Jonny hesitated. "Uh . . . frankly, Dader, I'd rather not. I don't . . . well, the lasers remind me too much of . . . other things."

"I don't understand," Pearce said, a frown beginning to crease his forehead. "Are you ashamed of what you did?"

"No, of course not. I mean, I knew pretty much what I was getting into when I joined the Cobras, and looking back I think

I did as good a job as I could have. It's just . . . this war was different from yours, Dader. A lot different. I was in danger—and was putting other people in danger—the whole time I was on Adirondack. If you'd ever had to fight the Minthisti face-to-face or had to help bury the bodies of uninvolved civilians caught in the fighting—" he forced his throat muscles to relax—"you'd understand why I'd like to try and forget all of it. At least for a while."

Pearce remained silent for a moment. Then he laid a hand on his son's shoulder. "You're right, Jonny; fighting a war from a star ship *was* a lot different. I'm not sure I can understand what you went through, but I'll do my best. Okay?"

"Yeah, Dader. Thanks."

"Sure. Come on, let's go see your mother. Then you can go take a look at Gwen's room."

Dinner that night was a festive occasion. Irena Moreau had cooked her son's favorite meal—center-fired wild balis—and the conversation was light and frequently punctuated by laughter. The warmth and love seemed to Jonny to fill the room, surrounding the five of them with an invisible defense perimeter. For the first time since leaving Asgard he felt truly safe, and tensions he'd forgotten he even had began to drain slowly from his muscles.

It took most of the meal for the others to bring Jonny up to date on the doings of Cedar Lake's people, so it wasn't until Irena brought out the cahve that conversation turned to Jonny's plans.

"I'm not really sure," Jonny confessed, holding his mug of cahve with both hands, letting the heat soak into his palms. "I suppose I could go back to school and finally pick up that computer tech certificate. But that would take another year, and I'm not crazy about being a student again. Not now, anyway."

Across the table Jame sipped cautiously at his mug. "If you went to work, what sort of job would you like?" he asked.

"Well, I'd thought of coming back to the shop with Dader, but you seem to be pretty well settled in there."

Jame darted a glance at his father. "Heck, Jonny, there's enough work in town for three of us. Right, Dader?"

"Sure," Pearce replied with only the barest hesitation.

"Thanks," Jonny said, "but it sounds like you're really too low on equipment for me to be very useful. My thought is that maybe I could work somewhere on my own for a few months until we can afford to outfit the shop for three workers. Then, if there's enough business around, I could come and work for you."

Pearce nodded. "That sounds really good, Jonny. I think that's the best way to do it."

"So back to the original question," Jame said. "What kind of job are you going to get?"

Jonny held his mug to his lips for a moment, savoring the rich, minty aroma. Army cahve had a fair taste and plenty of stimulant, but was completely devoid of the fragrance that made a good scent-drink so enjoyable. "I've learned a lot about civil engineering in the past three years, especially in the uses of explosives and sonic cutting tools. I figure I'll try one of the road construction or mining companies you were telling me about that are working south of town."

"Can't hurt to try," Pearce shrugged. "Going to take a few days off first?"

"Nope—I'll head out there tomorrow morning. I figured I'd drive around town for a while this evening, though; get reacquainted with the area. Can I help with the dishes before I go?"

"Don't be silly," Irena smiled at him. "Relax and enjoy yourself."

"Tonight, that is," Jame amended. "Tomorrow you'll be put out in the salt mines with the rest of the new slaves."

Jonny leveled a finger at him. "Beware the darkness of the night," he said with mock seriousness. "There just may be a pillow out there with your name on it." He turned back to his parents. "Okay if I take off, then? Anything you need in town?"

"I just shopped today," Irena told him.

"Go ahead, Son," Pearce said.

"I'll be back before it gets too late." Jonny downed the last of his cahve and stood up. "Great dinner, Momer; thanks a lot."

He left the room and headed toward the front door. To his mild surprise, Jame tagged along. "You coming with me?" Jonny asked.

"Just to the car," Jame said. He was silent until they were outside the house. "I wanted to clue you in on a couple of things before you left," he said as they set off across the lawn.

"Okay; shoot."

"Number one: I think you ought to be careful about pointing your finger at people, like you did at me a few minutes ago. Especially when you're looking angry or even just serious."

Jonny blinked. "Hey, I didn't mean anything by that. I was just kidding around."

"*I* know that, and it didn't bother me. Someone who doesn't know you as well might have dived under the table."

"I don't get it. Why?"

Jame shrugged, but met his brother's eyes. "They're a little afraid of you," he said bluntly. "Everybody followed the war news pretty closely out here. They all know what Cobras can do."

Jonny grimaced. It was beginning to sound like a repeat of that last, awkward conversation with Ilona Linder, and he didn't like the implications. "What we *could* do," he told Jame, perhaps a bit more sharply than necessary. "Most of my armament's gone—and even if it wasn't, I sure wouldn't use it on anyone. I'm sick of fighting."

"I know. But they won't know that, not at first. I'm not just guessing here, Jonny; I've talked to a lot of kids since the war ended, and they're pretty nervous about seeing you again. You'd be surprised how many of them are scared that you'll remember some old high school grudge and come by to settle accounts."

"Oh, come on, Jame. That's ridiculous!"

"That's what I tell the ones that ask me about it, but they don't seem convinced. And it looks like some of their parents have picked up on the attitude, too, and—heck, you know how news travels around here. I think you're going to have to bend over backwards for a while, be as harmless as a dove with blunted toenails. Prove to them they don't have to be afraid of you."

Jonny snorted. "The whole thing is silly, but okay. I'll be a good little boy."

"Great," Jame hesitated. "Now for number two, I guess. Were you planning to stop by and see Alyse Carne tonight?"

"That thought *had* crossed my mind," Jonny frowned, trying to read his brother's expression. "Why? Has she moved?"

"No, she's still living out on Blakeley Street. But you might want to call before you go over there. To make sure she . . . isn't busy."

Jonny felt his eyes narrow slightly. "What are you getting at? She living with someone?"

"Oh, no, it hasn't gone that far," Jame said quickly. "But she's been seeing Doane Etherege a lot lately and—well, he's been calling her his girlfriend."

Jonny pursed his lips, staring past Jame at the familiar landscape beyond the Moreau property. He could hardly blame Alyse for finding someone new in his absence—they hadn't exactly been the talk of Cedar Lake when he left, and three years would've been a pretty long wait even if they *had* been more serious about each other. And yet, along with his family, Alyse had been one of his psychological anchors when things on Adirondack had gotten particularly bad; a focal point for thoughts and memories involving something besides blood and death. Just having her around was bound to help in his readjustment to civilian life . . . and besides, to step aside meekly for the likes of Doane Etherege was completely unthinkable. "I suppose I'll have to do something about that," he said slowly. Catching Jame's expression, he forced a smile. "Don't worry; I'll steal her back in a civilized manner."

"Yeah, well, good luck. I'll warn you, though; he's not the drip he used to be."

"I'll keep that in mind." Jonny slid his hand idly along the smooth metal of the car. Familiarity all around him; and yet, somehow it was all different, too. Perhaps, his combat instincts whispered, it would be wiser to stay at home until he knew more about the situation here.

Jame seemed to sense the indecision. "You still going out?"

Jonny pursed his lips. "Yeah, I think I'll take a quick look around." Opening the door, he slid in and started the engine. "Don't wait up," he added as he drove off.

After all, he told himself firmly, he had not fought Trofts for three years to come home and hide from his own people.

Nevertheless, the trip through Cedar Lake felt more like a reconnaissance mission than the victorious homecoming he had once envisioned. He covered most of the town, but stayed in the car and didn't wave or call to the people he recognized. He avoided driving by Alyse Carne's apartment building completely. And he was home within an hour.

For many years the only ground link between Cedar Lake and the tiny farming community to the southwest, Boyar, was a bumpy, one-and-three-quarters-lane permturf road that paralleled the Shard Mountains to the west. It had been considered adequate for so long simply because there was little in or around Boyar that anyone in Cedar Lake would want. Boyar's crops went to Horizon City by way of New Persius; supplies traveled the same route in reverse.

Now, however, all that had changed. A large vein of the cesium-bearing ore pollucite had been discovered north of Boyar; and as the mining companies moved in, so did the road construction crews. The facility for extracting the cesium was, for various technical reasons, being built near Cedar Lake, and a multi-lane highway would be necessary to get the ore to it.

Jonny found the road foreman near a large outcrop of granite that lay across the road's projected path. "You Sampson Grange?" he asked.

"Yeah. You?"

"Jonny Moreau. Mr. Oberland told me to check with you about a job. I've had training in lasers, explosives, and sonic blasting equipment."

"Well actually, kid, I—waitaminit. Jonny Moreau the Cobra?"

"*Ex*-Cobra, yes."

Grange shifted his spitstick in his mouth, eyes narrowing slightly. "Yeah, I can use you, I guess. Straight level-eight pay."

That was two levels up from minimum. "Fine. Thanks very much." Jonny nodded toward the granite outcrop. "You need this out of the way?"

"Yeah, but that'll keep. C'mon back here a minute."

He led Jonny to where a group of eight men were struggling to unload huge rolls of pretop paper from a truck to the side of the new road. It took three or four men to handle each roll and they were puffing and swearing with the effort.

"Boys, this is Jonny Moreau," Grange told them. "Jonny, we've got to get this stuff out right away so the truck can go back for another load. Give them a hand, okay?" Without waiting for an answer, he strode off.

Reluctantly, Jonny clambered onto the truck. This wasn't exactly what he'd had in mind. The other men regarded him coolly, and Jonny heard the word "Cobra" being whispered to the two or three who hadn't recognized him. Determined not to let it throw him, he stepped over to the nearest roll and said, "Can someone give me a hand with this?"

Nobody moved. "Wouldn't we just be in the way?" one of them, a husky laborer, suggested with more than a little truculence.

Jonny kept his voice steady. "Look, I'm willing to do my share."

"That seems fair," someone else said sarcastically. "It was our taxes that paid to make you into a superman in the first place. And I figure Grange is paying you enough money for four men. So fine; we got the first eight rolls down and you can get the last five. That fair enough, men?"

There was a general murmur of agreement. Jonny studied their faces for a moment, looking for some sign of sympathy or support. But all he saw was hostility and wariness. "All right," he said softly.

Bending his knees slightly, he hugged the roll of pretop to his chest. Servos whining in his ears, he straightened up and carefully carried the roll to the end of the truck bed. Setting it down, he jumped to the ground, picked it up again and placed it off the road with the others. Then, hopping back into the truck, he went to the next roll.

None of the other workers had moved, but their expressions had changed. Fear now dominated everything else. It was one thing, Jonny reflected bitterly, to watch films of Cobras shooting up Trofts on the plate. It was something else entirely to watch one lift two hundred kilos right in front of you. Cursing inwardly, he finished moving the rolls as quickly as possible and then, without a word, went off in search of Sampson Grange.

He found the other busy inventorying sacks of hardener mix and was immediately pressed into service to carry them to the proper workers. That job led to a succession of similar tasks over the next few hours. Jonny tried to be discreet, but the news about him traveled faster than he did. Most of the workers were less hostile toward him than the first group had been, but it was still like working on a stage, and Jonny began to fume inwardly at the wary politeness and sidelong glances.

Finally, just before noon, he caught on, and once more he tracked down the foreman. "I don't like being maneuvered by people, Mr. Grange," he told the other angrily. "I signed on here to help with blasting and demolition work. Instead, you've got me carrying stuff around like a pack mule."

Grange slid his spitstick to a corner of his mouth and regarded Jonny coolly. "I signed you up at level-eight to work on the road. I never said what you were gonna do."

"That's rotten. You knew what I wanted."

"So what? What the hell—you want special privileges or something? I got guys who have *certificates* in demolition work—I should replace them with a kid who's never even seen a real tape on the subject?"

Jonny opened his mouth, but none of the words he wanted to say would come out. Grange shrugged. "Look, kid," he said, not unkindly. "I got nothing against you. Hell, I'm a vet myself. But you haven't got any training or experience in road work. We can use more laborers, sure, and that super-revved body of yours makes you worth at least two men—that's why I'm paying you level-eight. Other than that, frankly, you aren't worth much to us. Take it or don't; it's up to you."

"Thanks, but no go," Jonny gritted out.

"Okay." Grange took out a card and scribbled on it. "Take this to the main office in Cedar Lake and they'll give you your pay. And come back if you change your mind."

Jonny took the card and left, trying to ignore the hundred pairs of eyes he could feel boring into his back.

The house was deserted when he arrived home, a condition for which he was grateful. He'd had time to cool down during the drive and now just wanted some time to be alone. As a Cobra he'd been unused to flat-out failure; if the Trofts foiled an attack he had simply to fall back and try a new assault. But the rules here were different, and he wasn't readjusting to them as quickly as he'd expected to.

Nevertheless, he was a long way yet from defeat. Punching up last night's newssheet, he turned to the employment section. Most of the jobs being offered were level-ten laborer types, but there was a fair sprinkling of the more professional sort that he was looking for. Settling himself comfortably in front of the plate, he picked up the pad and stylus always kept by the phone and began to make notes.

His final list of prospects covered nearly two pages, and he spent most of the rest of the afternoon making phone calls. It was a sobering and frustrating experience; and in the end he found himself with only two interviews, both for the following morning.

By then it was nearly dinner time. Stuffing the pages of notes into a pocket, he headed for the kitchen to offer his mother a hand with the cooking.

Irena smiled at him as he entered. "Any luck with the job hunt?" she asked.

"A little," he told her. She had arrived home some hours earlier and had already heard a capsule summary of his morning with the road crew. "I've got two interviews tomorrow—Svetlanov Electronics and Outworld Mining. And I'm lucky to get even that many."

She patted his arm. "You'll find something. Don't worry." A sound outside made her glance out the window. "Your father and Jame are home. Oh, and there's someone with them."

Jonny looked out. A second car had pulled to the curb behind Pearce and Jame. As he watched, a tall, somewhat paunchy man got out and joined the other two in walking toward the house. "He looks familiar, Momer, but I can't place him."

"That's Teague Stillman, the mayor," she identified him, sounding surprised. "I wonder why he's here." Whipping off her apron, she dried her hands and hurried into the living room. Jonny followed more slowly, unconsciously taking up a back-up position across the living room from the front door.

The door opened just as Irena reached it. "Hi, Honey," Pearce greeted his wife as the three men entered. "Teague stopped by the shop just as we were closing up and I invited him to come over for a few minutes."

"How nice," Irena said in her best hostess voice. "It's been a long time since we've seen you, Teague. How is Sharene?"

"She's fine, Irena," Stillman said, "although she says *she* doesn't see me enough these days, either. Actually, I just stopped by to see if Jonny was home from work yet."

"Yes, I am," Jonny said, coming forward. "Congratulations on winning your election last year, Mr. Stillman. I'm afraid I didn't make it to the polls."

Stillman laughed and reached out his hand to grasp Jonny's briefly. He seemed relaxed and friendly . . . and yet, right around the eyes, Jonny could see a touch of the caution that he'd seen in the road workers. "I'd have sent you an absentee ballot if I'd known exactly where you were," the mayor joked. "Welcome home, Jonny."

"Thank you, sir."

"Shall we sit down?" Irena suggested.

They moved into the living room proper, Stillman and the Moreau parents exchanging small talk all the while. Jame had yet to say a word, Jonny noted, and the younger boy took a seat in a corner, away from the others.

"The reason I wanted to talk to you, Jonny," Stillman said when they were all settled, "was that the city council and I would like to have a sort of 'welcome home' ceremony for you in the park next week. Nothing too spectacular, really; just a short parade through town, followed by a couple of speeches—you don't have to make one if you don't want to—and then some fireworks and perhaps a torchlight procession. What do you think?"

Jonny hesitated, but there was no way to say this diplomatically. "Thanks, but I really don't want you to do that."

Pearce's proud smile vanished. "What do you mean, Jonny? Why not?"

"Because I don't want to get up in front of a whole bunch of people and get cheered at. It's embarrassing and—well, it's embarrassing. I don't want any fuss made over me."

"Jonny, the town wants to honor you for what you did," Stillman said soothingly, as if afraid Jonny was becoming angry.

That thought was irritating. "The greatest honor it could give me would be to stop treating me like a freak," he retorted.

"Son—" Pearce began warningly.

"Dader, if Jonny doesn't want any official hoopla, it seems to me the subject is closed," Jame spoke up unexpectedly from his corner. "Unless you all plan to chain him to the speakers' platform."

There was a moment of uncomfortable silence. Then Stillman shifted in his seat. "Well, if Jonny doesn't want this, there's no reason to discuss it further." He stood up, the others quickly following suit. "I really ought to get home now."

"Give Sharene our best," Irena said.

"I will," Stillman nodded. "We'll have to try and get together soon. Good-bye, all; and once more, welcome home, Jonny."

"I'll walk you to your car," Pearce said, clearly angry but trying to hide it.

The two men left. Irena looked questioningly at Jonny, but all she said before disappearing back into the kitchen was, "You boys wash up and call Gwen from her room; dinner will be ready soon."

"You okay?" Jame asked softly when his mother had gone.

"Yeah. Thanks for backing me up." Jonny shook his head. "They don't understand."

"I'm not sure I do, either. Is it because of what I said about people being afraid of you?"

"That has nothing to do with it. The people of Adirondack were afraid of us, too, some of them. But even so—" Jonny sighed. "Look. Horizon is all the way across the Dominion from where the war was fought. You weren't within fifty light-years of a Troft even at their deepest penetration. How can I accept the praise of people who have no idea what they're cheering for? It'd just be going through the motions." He turned his head to stare out the window. "Adirondack held a big victory celebration after the Trofts finally pulled out. There was nothing of duty or obligation about it—when the people cheered, you could tell they knew *why* they were doing so. And they also knew who they were there to honor. Not those of us who were on the stage, but those who weren't. Instead of a torchlight procession, they sang a requiem." He turned back to face Jame. "How could I watch Cedar Lake's fireworks after that?"

Jame touched his brother's arm and nodded silently. "I'll go call Gwen," he said a moment later.

Pearce came back into the house. He said nothing, but flashed

Jonny a disappointed look before disappearing into the kitchen. Sighing, Jonny went to wash his hands.

Dinner was very quiet that evening.

The interviews the next morning were complete washouts, with the two prospective employers clearly seeing him just out of politeness. Gritting his teeth, Jonny returned home and called up the newssheet once again. He lowered his sights somewhat this time, and his new list came out to be three and a half pages long. Doggedly, he began making the calls.

By the time Jame came to bring him to dinner he had exhausted all the numbers on the list. "Not even any interviews this time," he told Jame disgustedly as they walked into the dining room where the others were waiting. "News really does travel in this town, doesn't it?"

"Come on, Jonny, there has to be *someone* around who doesn't care that you're an ex-Cobra," Jame said.

"Perhaps you should lower your standards a bit," Pearce suggested. "Working as a laborer wouldn't hurt you any."

"Or maybe you could be a patroller," Gwen spoke up. "That would be neat."

Jonny shook his head. "I've tried being a laborer, remember? The men on the road crew were either afraid of me or thought I was trying to show them up."

"But once they got to know you, things would be different," Irena said.

"Or maybe if they had a better idea of what you'd done for the Dominion they'd respect you more," Peace added.

"No, Dader." Jonny had tried explaining to his father why he didn't want Cedar Lake to honor him publicly, and the elder Moreau had listened and said he understood. But Jonny doubted that he really did, and Pearce clearly hadn't given up trying to change his son's mind. "I probably would be a good patroller, Gwen," he added to his sister, "but I think it would remind me too much of some of the things I had to do in the Army."

"Well, then, maybe you should go back to school," Irena suggested.

"*No!*" Jonny snapped with a sudden flash of anger.

A stunned silence filled the room. Inhaling deeply, Jonny forced himself to calm down. "Look, I know you're all trying to be helpful, and I appreciate it. But I'm twenty-four years old now and capable of handling my own problems." Abruptly, he put down his fork and stood up. "I'm not hungry. I think I'll go out for a while."

Minutes later he was driving down the street, wondering what he should do. There was a brand-new pleasure center in town, he knew, but he wasn't in the mood for large groups of people. He mentally ran through a list of old friends, but that was just for practice; he knew where he really wanted to go. Jame had suggested he call Alyse Carne before dropping in on her, but Jonny was in a perverse mood. Turning at the next corner, he headed for Blakely Street.

Alyse seemed surprised when he announced himself over her apartment building's security intercom, but she was all smiles as she opened her door. "Jonny, it's good to see you," she said, holding out her hand.

"Hi, Alyse." He smiled back, taking her hand and stepping into her apartment, closing the door behind him. "I was afraid you'd forgotten about me while I was gone."

Her eyes glowed. "Not likely," she murmured . . . and suddenly she was in his arms.

After a long minute she gently pulled away. "Why don't we sit down?" she suggested. "We've got three years to catch up on."

"Anything wrong?" he asked her.

"No. Why?"

"You seem a little nervous. I thought you might have a date."

She flushed. "Not tonight. I guess you know I've been seeing Doane."

"Yes. How serious is it, Alyse? I deserve to know."

"I like him," she said, shrugging uncomfortably. "I suppose in a way I was trying to insulate myself from pain in case you . . . didn't come back."

Jonny nodded understanding. "I got a lot of that on Adirondack, too, mostly from whichever civilian family I was living with at the time."

Alyse seemed to wince a bit. "I'm . . . sorry. Anyway, it's grown more than I expected it to, and now that you're back . . ." Her voice trailed off.

"You don't have to make any decisions tonight," Jonny said after a moment. "Except whether or not you'll spend the evening with me."

Some of the tension left her face. "That one's easy. Have you eaten yet, or shall I just make us some cahve?"

They talked until nearly midnight, and when Jonny finally left he had recaptured the contentment he'd felt on first arriving at Cedar Lake. Doane Etherege would soon fade back into the woodwork, he was sure, and with Alyse and his family back in their old accustomed places he would finally have a universe he knew how to deal with. His mind was busy with plans for the future as he let himself into the Moreau house and tiptoed to his bedroom.

"Jonny?" a whisper came from across the room. "You okay?"

"Fine, Jame—just great," Jonny whispered back.

"How was Alyse?"

Jonny chuckled. "Go to sleep, Jame."

"That's nice. Good night, Jonny."

One by one, the great plans crumbled.

With agonizing regularity, employers kept turning Jonny down, and he was eventually forced into a succession of the level-nine and -ten manual jobs he had hoped so desperately to avoid. None of the jobs lasted very long; the resentment and fear of his fellow workers invariably generated an atmosphere of sullen animosity which Jonny found hard to take for more than a few days at a time.

As his search for permanent employment faltered, so did his relationship with Alyse. She remained friendly and willing to spend time with him, but there was a distance between them that hadn't existed before the war. To make matters worse, Doane refused to withdraw gracefully from the field, and aggressively competed with him for Alyse's time and attention.

But worst of all, from Jonny's point of view, was the unexpected trouble his problems had brought upon the rest of the family. His parents and Jame, he knew, could stand the glances, whispered comments, and mild stigma that seemed to go with being related to an ex-Cobra. But it hurt him terribly to watch Gwen retreat into herself from the half-unintentional cruelty of her peers. More than once Jonny considered leaving Horizon and returning to active service, freeing his family from the cross-fire he had put them into. But to leave now would be to admit defeat, and that was something he couldn't bring himself to do.

And so matters precariously stood for three months, until the night of the accident. Or the murder, as some called it.

Sitting in his parked car, watching the last rays from the setting sun, Jonny let the anger and frustration drain out of him and wondered what to do next. He had just stormed out of Alyse's apartment after their latest fight, the tenth or so since his return. Like the job situation, things with Alyse seemed to be getting worse instead of better. Unlike the former, he could only blame himself for the problems in his love life.

The sun was completely down by the time he felt capable of driving safely. The sensible thing would be to go home, of course. But the rest of the Moreau family was out to dinner, and the thought of being alone in the house bothered him for some reason. What he needed, he decided, was something that would completely take his mind off his problems. Starting the car, he drove into the center of town where the Raptopia, Cedar Lake's new pleasure center, was located.

Jonny had been in pleasure centers on Asgard both before and after the tour on Adirondack, and by their standards the Raptopia was decidedly unsophisticated. There were fifteen rooms and galleries, each offering its own combination of sensual stimuli for customers to choose from. The choices seemed limited, however, to permutations of the traditional recreations: music, food and drink, mood drugs, light shows, games, and thermal booths. The extreme physical and intellectual ends of the pleasure spectrum, personified by prostitutes and professional conversationalists, were conspicuously absent.

Jonny wandered around for a few minutes before settling on a room with a loud music group and wildly flickering light show. Visibility under such conditions was poor, and as long as he kept his distance from the other patrons, he was unlikely to be recognized. Finding a vacant area of the contoured softfloor, he sat down.

The music was good, if dated—he'd heard the same songs three years ago on Asgard—and he began to relax as the light and sound swept like a cleansing wave over his mind. So engrossed did he become that he didn't notice the group of teenaged kids that came up behind him until one of them nudged him with the tip of his shoe.

"Hi there, Cobra," he said as Jonny looked up. "What's new?"

"Uh, not much," Jonny replied cautiously. There were seven of them, he noted: three girls and four boys, all dressed in the current teen-age styles so deplored by Cedar Lake's more conservative adults. "Do I know you?"

The girls giggled. "Naw," another of the boys drawled. "We just figured everybody ought to know there's a celebrity here. Let's tell 'em, huh?"

Slowly, Jonny rose to his feet to face them. From his new vantage point he could see that all seven had the shining eyes and rapid breathing of heavy stim-drug users. "I don't think that's necessary," he said.

"You want to fight about it?" the first boy said, dropping into a caricature of a fighting stance. "C'mon, Cobra. Show us what you can do."

Wordlessly, Jonny turned and walked toward the door, followed by the giggling group. As he reached the exit the two talkative boys pushed past him and stood in the doorway, blocking it.

"Can't leave 'til you show us a trick," one said.

Jonny looked him in the eye, successfully resisting the urge to bounce the smart-mouth off the far wall. Instead, he picked up both boys by their belts, held them high for a moment, and then turned and set them down to the side of the doorway. A gentle push sent them sprawling onto the softfloor. "I suggest you all stay here and enjoy the music," he told the rest of the group as they stared at him with wide eyes.

"Turkey hop," one of the smart-mouths muttered. Jonny ignored the apparent insult and strode from the room, confident that they wouldn't follow him. They didn't.

But the mood of the evening was broken. Jonny tried two or three other rooms for a few minutes each, hoping to regain the relaxed abandonment he'd felt earlier. But it was no use, and within a quarter hour he was back outside the Raptopia, walking through the cool night air toward his car, parked across the street a block away.

He'd covered the block and was just starting to cross the road when he became aware of the low hum of an idling car nearby. He turned to look back along the street—and in that instant a car rolling gently along the curb suddenly switched on its lights and, with a squeal of tires, hurtled directly toward him.

There was no time for thought or human reaction, but Jonny had no need of either. For the first time since leaving Adirondack his nanocomputer took control of his body, launching it into a flat, six-meter dive that took him to the walkway on the far side of the street. He landed on his right shoulder, rolling to absorb the impact, but crashed painfully into a building before he could stop completely. The car roared past; and as it did so needles of light flashed from Jonny's fingertip lasers to the car's two right-hand tires. The double blowout was audible even over the engine noise. Instantly out of control, the car swerved violently, bounced off two parked cars, and finally crashed broadside into the corner of the building.

Aching all over, Jonny got to his feet and ran to the car. Ignoring the gathering crowd, he worked feverishly on the crumpled metal, and had the door open by the time a rescue unit arrived. But his effort was in vain. The car's driver was already dead, and his passenger died of internal injuries on the way to the hospital.

They were the two teen-aged boys who had accosted Jonny in the Raptopia.

The sound of his door opening broke Mayor Stillman's train of thought, and he turned from his contemplation of the morning sky in time to see Sutton Fraser closing the door behind him. "Don't you ever knock?" he asked the city councilor irritably.

"You can stare out the window later," Fraser said, pulling a chair close to the desk and sitting down. "Right now we've got to talk."

Stillman sighed. "Jonny Moreau?"

"You got it. It's been over a week now, Teague, and the tension out there's not going down. People in my district are still asking why Jonny's not in custody."

"We've been through this, remember? The legal department in Horizon City has the patroller report; until they make a decision we're treating it as self-defense."

"Oh, come on. You know the kids would have swerved to miss him. That's how that stupid turkey hop is played—okay, okay, I realize Jonny didn't know that. But did *you* know he fired on the car *after* it had passed him? I've got no less than three witnesses now that say that."

"So have the patrollers. I'll admit I don't understand that part. Maybe it's something from his combat training."

"Great," Fraser muttered.

Stillman's intercom buzzed. "Mayor Stillman, there's a Mr. Vanis D'arl to see you," his secretary announced.

Stillman glanced questioningly at Fraser, who shrugged and shook his head. "Send him in," Stillman said.

The door opened and a slender, dark-haired man entered and walked toward the desk. His appearance, clothing, and walk identified him as an offworlder before he had taken two steps. "Mr. D'arl," Stillman said as he and Fraser rose to their feet, "I'm Mayor Teague Stillman; this is Councilor Sutton Fraser. What can we do for you?"

D'arl produced a gold ID pin. "Vanis D'arl, representing Committé Sarkiis H'orme of the Dominion of Man." His voice was slightly accented.

Out of the corner of his eye Stillman saw Fraser stiffen. His own knees felt a little weak. "Very honored to meet you, sir. Won't you sit down?"

"Thank you." D'arl took the chair Fraser had been sitting in. The councilor moved to a seat farther from the desk, possibly hoping to be less conspicuous there.

"This is mainly an informal courtesy call, Mr. Stillman," D'arl said. "However, all of what I'm going to tell you is to be considered confidential Dominion business." He waited for both men to nod agreement before continuing. "I've just come from Horizon City, where all pending charges against Reserve Cobra-Three Jonny Moreau have been ordered dropped."

"I see," Stillman said. "May I ask why the Central Committee is taking an interest in this case?"

"Cee-three Moreau is still technically under Army jurisdiction, since he can be called into active service at any time. Committé H'orme has furthermore had a keen interest in the entire Cobra project since its inception."

"Are you familiar with the incident that Mr.—uh, Cee-three Moreau was involved in?"

"Yes, and I understand the doubts both you and the planetary authorities have had about the circumstances. However, Moreau cannot be held responsible for his actions at that time. He was under attack and acted accordingly."

"His combat training is that strong?"

"Not precisely." D'arl hesitated. "I dislike having to tell you this, as it has been a military secret up until recently. But you need to understand the situation. Have you ever wondered what the name 'Cobra' stands for?"

"Why . . ." Stillman floundered, caught off guard by the question. "I assumed it referred to the Earth snake."

"Only secondarily. It's an acronym for Computerized Body Reflex Armament. I'm sure you know about the ceramic laminae and servo network and all; you may also know about the nanocomputer implanted just under his brain. This is where the . . . problem . . . originates.

"You must understand that a soldier, especially a guerrilla in enemy-held territory, needs a good set of combat reflexes if he is to survive. Training can give him some of what he needs, but it takes a long time and has its limits. Therefore, since a computer was going to be necessary for equipment monitoring and fire control anyway, a set of combat reflexes was also programmed in.

"The bottom line is that Moreau will react instantly, and with very little conscious control, to any deadly attack launched at him. In this particular case the pattern shows clearly that this is what happened. He evaded the initial attack, but was left in a vulnerable position—off his feet and away from cover—and was thus forced to counterattack. Part of the computer's job is to monitor the weapon systems, so it knew the fingertip lasers were all it had left. So it used them."

A deathly silence filled the room. "Let me get this straight," Stillman said at last. "The Army made Jonny Moreau into an automated fighting machine who will react lethally to anything that even *looks* like an attack? And then let him come back to us without making any attempt to change that?"

"The system was designed to defend a soldier in enemy territory," D'arl said. "It's not nearly as hair-trigger as you seem to imagine. And as for 'letting' him come back like that, there was no other choice. The computer cannot be reprogrammed or removed without risking brain damage."

"What the *hell!*" Fraser had apparently forgotten he was supposed to be courteous to Dominion representatives. "What damn idiot came up with *that* idea?"

D'arl turned to face the councilor. "The Central Committee is tolerant of criticism, Mr. Fraser." His voice was even, but had an edge to it. "But your tone is unacceptable."

Fraser refused to shrivel. "Never mind that. How did you expect us to cope with him when he reacts to attacks like that?" He snorted. "*Attacks.* Two kids playing a game!"

"Use your head," D'arl snapped. "We couldn't risk having a Cobra captured by the Trofts and sent back to us with his computer reprogrammed. The Cobras were soldiers, first and foremost, and every tool and weapon they had made perfect sense from a military standpoint."

"Didn't it occur to anyone that the war would be over someday? And that the Cobras would be going home to civilian life?"

D'arl's lip might have twitched, but his voice was firm enough. "Less powerful equipment might well have cost the Dominion the war, and would certainly have cost many more Cobras their lives. At any rate, it's done now, and you'll just have to learn to live with it like everyone else."

Stillman frowned. " 'Everyone else'? How widespread is this problem?"

D'arl turned back to face the mayor, looking annoyed that he'd let that hint slip out. "It's not good," he admitted at last. "We hoped to keep as many Cobras as possible in the service after the war, but all were legally free to leave and over two hundred did so. Many of those are having trouble of one kind or another. We're trying to help them, but it's difficult to do. People are afraid of them, and that hampers our efforts."

"Can you do anything to help Jonny?"

D'arl shrugged slightly. "I don't know. He's an unusual case, in that he came back to a small home town where everyone knew what he was. I suppose it might help to move him to another planet, maybe give him a new name. But people would eventually find out. Cobra strength is hard to hide for long."

"So are Cobra reflexes," Stillman nodded grimly. "Besides, Jonny's family is here. I don't think he'd like leaving them."

"That's why I'm not recommending his relocation, though that's the usual procedure in cases like this," D'arl said. "Most Cobras don't have the kind of close family support he does. It's a strong point in his favor." He stood up. "I'll be leaving Horizon tomorrow morning, but I'll be within a few days' flight of here for the next month. If anything happens, I can be reached through the Dominion governor-general's office in Horizon City."

Stillman rose from his chair. "I trust the Central Committee will be trying to come up with some kind of solution to this problem."

D'arl met his gaze evenly. "Mr. Stillman, the Committee is far more concerned about this situation than even you are. You see one minor frontier town; we see seventy worlds. If an answer exists, we'll find it."

"And what do we do in the meantime?" Fraser asked heavily.

"Your best, of course. Good day to you."

Jame paused outside the door, took a single deep breath, and knocked lightly. There was no answer. He raised his hand to knock again, then thought better of it. After all, it was *his* bedroom, too. Opening the door, he went in.

Seated at Jame's writing desk, hands curled into fists in front of him, Jonny was staring out the window. Jame cleared his throat.

"Hello, Jame," Jonny said, without turning.

"Hi." The desk, Jame saw, was covered with official-looking

magforms. "I just dropped by to tell you that dinner will be ready in about fifteen minutes." He nodded at the desk. "What're you up to?"

"Filling out some college applications."

"Oh. Decided to go back to school?"

Jonny shrugged. "I might as well."

Stepping to his brother's side, Jame scanned the magforms. University of Rajput, Bomu Technical Institute on Zimbwe, University of Aerie. All off-planet. "You're going to have a long way to travel when you come home for Christmas," he commented. Another fact caught his eye: all three applications were filled out only up to the space marked *Military Service*.

"I don't expect to come home very often," Jonny said quietly.

"You're just going to give up, huh?" Jame put as much scorn into the words as he could.

It had no effect. "I'm retreating from enemy territory," Jonny corrected mildly.

"The kids are dead, Jonny. There's nothing in the universe you can do about it. Look, the town doesn't blame you—no charges were brought, remember? So quit blaming yourself. Accept the fact of what happened and let go of it."

"You're confusing legal and moral guilt. Legally, I'm clear. Morally? No. And the town's not going to let me forget it. I can see the disgust and fear in people's eyes. They're even afraid to be sarcastic to me any more."

"Well . . . it's better than not getting any respect at all."

Jonny snorted. "Thanks a lot," he said wryly. "I'd rather be picked on."

A sign of life at last. Jame pressed ahead, afraid of losing the spark. "You know, Dader and I have been talking about the shop. You remember that we didn't have enough equipment for three workers?"

"Yes—and you still don't."

"Right. But what stops us from having *you* and Dader run the place while *I* go out and work somewhere else for a few months?"

Jonny was silent for a moment, but then shook his head. "Thanks, but no. It wouldn't be fair."

"Why not? That job used to be yours. It's not like you were butting in. Actually, I'd kind of like to try something else for a while."

"I'd probably drive away all the customers if I was there."

Jame's lip twisted. "That won't fly, and you know it. Dader's customers are there because they like him and his work. They don't give two hoots who handles the actual repairs as long as Dader supervises everything. You're just making excuses."

Jonny closed his eyes briefly. "And what if I am?"

"I suppose it doesn't matter to you right now whether or not you let your life go down the drain," Jame gritted. "But you might take a moment to consider what you're doing to Gwen."

"Yeah. The other kids are pretty hard on her, aren't they?"

"I'm not referring to them. Sure, she's lost most of her friends, but there are a couple who're sticking by her. What's killing her is having to watch her big brother tearing himself to shreds."

Jonny looked up for the first time. "What do you mean?"

"Just want I said. She's been putting up a good front for your sake, but the rest of us know how much it hurts her to see the brother she adores sitting in his room and—" He groped for the right words.

"Wallowing in self-pity?"

"Yeah. You owe her better than that, Jonny. She's already lost most of her friends; she deserves to keep her brother."

Jonny looked back out the window for a long moment, then glanced down at the college applications. "You're right." He took a deep breath, let it out slowly. "Okay. You can tell Dader he's got himself a new worker," he said, collecting the magforms together into a neat pile. "I'll start whenever he's ready for me."

Jame grinned and gripped his brother's shoulder. "Thanks," he said quietly. "Can I tell Momer and Gwen, too?"

"Sure. No; just Momer." He stood up and gave Jane a passable attempt at a smile. "I'll go tell Gwen myself."

The tiny spot of bluish light, brilliant even through the de-contrast goggles, crawled to the edge of the metal and vanished. Pushing up the goggles, Jonny set the laser down and inspected the seam. Spotting a minor flaw, he corrected it and then began removing the fender from its clamps. He had not quite finished the job when a gentle buzz signaled that a car had pulled into the drive. Grimacing, Jonny took off his goggles and headed for the front of the shop.

Mayor Stillman was out of his car and walking toward the door when Jonny emerged from the building. "Hello, Jonny," he smiled, holding out his hand with no trace of hesitation. "How are you doing?"

"Fine, Mr. Stillman," Jonny said, feeling awkward as he shook hands. He'd been working here for three weeks now, but still didn't feel comfortable dealing directly with his father's customers. "Dader's out right now; can I help you with something?"

Stillman shook his head. "I really just dropped by to say hello to you and to bring you some news. I heard this morning that Wyatt Brothers Contracting is putting together a group to demolish the old Lamplighter Hotel. Would you be interested in applying for a job with them?"

"No, I don't think so. I'm doing okay here right now. But thanks for—"

He was cut off by a dull thunderclap. "What was that?" Stillman asked, glancing at the cloudless sky.

"Explosion," Jonny said curtly, eyes searching the southwest sky for evidence of fire. For an instant he was back on Adirondack. "A big one, southwest of us. There!" He pointed to a thin plume of smoke that had suddenly appeared.

"The cesium extractor, I'll bet," Stillman muttered. "Damn! Come on, let's go."

The déjà vu vanished. "I can't go with you," Jonny said.

"Never mind the shop. No one will steal anything." Stillman was already getting into his car

"But—" There would be *crowds* there! "I just can't."

"This is no time for shyness," the mayor snapped. "If that blast really *was* all the way over at the extraction plant, there's probably one hell of a fire there now. They might need our help. Come *on!*"

Jonny obeyed. The smoke plume, he noted, was growing darker by the second.

Stillman was right on all counts. The four-story cesium extraction plant was indeed burning furiously as they roared up to the edge of the growing crowd of spectators. The patrollers and fireters were already there, the latter pouring a white liquid through the doors and windows of the building. The flames, Jonny saw as he and the mayor pushed through the crowd, seemed largely confined to the first floor. The *entire* floor was burning, however, with flames extending even a meter or two onto the ground outside the building. Clearly, the fire was being fueled by one or more liquids.

The two men had reached one of the patrollers now. "Keep back, folks—" he began.

"I'm Mayor Stillman," Stillman identified himself. "What can we do to help?"

"Just keep back—no, wait a second, you can help us string a

cordon line. There could be another explosion any time and we've got to keep these people back. The stuff's over there."

The "stuff" consisted of thin, bottom-weighted poles and bright red cord to string between them. Stillman and Jonny joined three patrollers who were in the process of setting up the line.

"How'd it happen?" Stillman asked as they worked, shouting to make himself heard over the roar of the flames.

"Witnesses say a tank of iaphanine got ruptured somehow and ignited," one of the patrollers shouted back. "Before they could put it out, the heat set off another couple of tanks. I guess they had a few hundred kiloliters of the damned stuff in there—it's used in the refining process—and the whole lot went up at once. It's a wonder the building's still standing."

"Anyone still in there?"

"Yeah. Half a dozen or so—third floor."

Jonny turned, squinting against the light. Sure enough, he could see two or three anxious faces at a partially open third-floor window. Directly below them Cedar Lake's single "skyhooker" fire truck had been driven to within a cautious ten meters of the building and was extending its ladder upwards. Jonny turned back to the cordon line—

The blast was deafening, and Jonny's nanocomputer reacted by throwing him flat on the ground. Twisting around to face the building, he saw that a large chunk of wall a dozen meters from the working fireters had been disintegrated by the explosion. In its place was now a solid sheet of blue-tinged yellow flame. Fortunately, none of the fireters seemed to have been hurt.

"Oh, hell," a patroller said as Jonny scrambled to his feet. "Look at that."

A piece of the wall had apparently winged the skyhooker's ladder on its way to oblivion. One of the uprights had been mangled, causing the whole structure to sag to the side. Even as the fireters hurriedly brought it down the upright snapped, toppling the ladder to the ground.

"Damn!" Stillman muttered. "Do they have another ladder long enough?"

"Not when it has to sit that far from the wall," the patroller gritted. "I don't think the Public Works talltrucks can reach that high either."

"Maybe we can get a hover-plane from Horizon City," Stillman said, a hint of desperation creeping into his voice.

"They haven't got time." Jonny pointed at the second-floor

windows. "The fire's already on the second floor. Something has to be done right away."

The fireters had apparently come to the same conclusion and were pulling one of their other ladders from its rack on the skyhooker. "Looks like they're going to try to reach the second floor and work their way to the third from inside," the patroller muttered.

"That's suicide," Stillman shook his head. "Isn't there any place they can set up airbags close enough to let the men jump?"

The answer to that was obvious and no one bothered to voice it: if the fireters could have done that, they would have already done so. Clearly, the flames extended too far from the building for that to work.

"Do we have any strong rope?" Jonny asked suddenly. "I'm sure I could throw one end of it to them."

"But they'd slide down into the fire," Stillman pointed out.

"Not if you anchored the bottom end fifteen or twenty meters away; tied it to one of the fire trucks, say. Come on, let's go talk to one of the fireters."

They found the fire chief in the group trying to set up the new ladder. "It's a nice idea, but I doubt if all of the men up there could make it down a rope," he frowned after Jonny had sketched his plan. "They've been in smoke and terrific heat for nearly a quarter hour now and are probably getting close to collapse."

"Do you have anything like a breeches buoy?" Jonny asked. "It's like a sling with a pulley that slides on a rope."

The chief shook his head. "Look, I haven't got any more time to waste here. We've got to get our men inside right away."

"You can't send men into that," Stillman objected. "The whole second floor must be on fire by now."

"That's why we have to hurry, damn it!"

Jonny fought a brief battle with himself. But, as Stillman had said, this was no time to be shy. "There's another way. I can take a rope to them along the *outside* of the building."

"What? How?"

"You'll see. I'll need at least thirty meters of rope, a pair of insulated gloves, and about ten strips of heavy cloth. *Now!*"

The tone of command, once learned, was not easily forgotten. Nor was was it easy to resist; and within a minute Jonny was standing beneath his third-floor target window, as close to the building as the flames permitted. The rope, tied firmly around his waist, trailed behind him, kept just taut enough to insure that it, too, stayed out of the fire. Taking a deep breath, Jonny bent his knees and jumped.

Three years of practice had indeed made perfect. He caught the window ledge at the top of his arc, curled up feet taking the impact against red-hot brick. In a single smooth motion he pulled himself through the half-open window and into the building.

The fire chief's guess about the heat and smoke had been correct. The seven men lying or sitting on the floor of the small room were so groggy they weren't even startled by Jonny's sudden appearance. Three were already unconscious; alive, but just barely.

The first task was to get the window completely open. It was designed, Jonny saw, to only open halfway, the metal frame of the upper section firmly joined to the wall. A few carefully placed laser shots into the heat-softened metal did the trick, and a single kick popped the pane neatly and sent it tumbling to the ground.

Moving swiftly now, Jonny untied the rope from his waist and fastened it to a nearby stanchion, tugging three times on it to alert the fireters below to take up the slack. Hoisting one of the unconscious men to a more or less vertical position, he tied a strip of cloth to the man's left wrist, tossed the other end over the slanting rope, and tied it to the man's right wrist. With a quick glance outside to make sure the fireters were ready, he lifted the man through the window and let him slide down the taut rope into the waiting arms below. Jonny didn't wait to watch them cut him loose, but went immediately to the second unconscious man.

Parts of the floor were beginning to smolder by the time the last man disappeared out the window. Tossing one more cloth strip over the rope, Jonny gripped both ends with his right hand and jumped. The wind of his passage felt like an arctic blast on his sweaty skin and he found himself shivering as he reached the ground. Letting go of the cloth, he stumbled a few steps away— and heard a strange sound.

The crowd was cheering.

He turned to look at them, wondering, and finally it dawned on him that they were cheering for *him*. Unbidden, an embarrassed smile crept onto his face, and he raised his hand shyly in acknowledgment.

And then Mayor Stillman was at his side, gripping Jonny's arm and smiling broadly. "You did it, Jonny; you did it!" he shouted over all the noise.

Jonny grinned back. With half of Cedar Lake watching he'd saved seven men, and had risked his life doing it. They'd seen that he wasn't a monster, that his abilities could be used constructively and—most importantly—that he *wanted* to be helpful. Down deep, he could sense that this was a potential turning point. Maybe— just maybe—things would be different for him now.

Stillman shook his head sadly. "I really thought things would be different for him after the fire."

Fraser shrugged. "I'd hoped so, too. But I'm afraid I hadn't really counted on it. Even while everybody was cheering for him you could see that nervousness still in their eyes. That fear of him was never gone, just covered up. Now that the emotional high has worn off, that's all that's left."

"Yeah." Lifting his gaze from the desk, Stillman stared for a moment out the window. "So they treat him like an incurable psychopath. Or a wild animal."

"You can't really blame them. They're scared of what his strength and lasers could do if he went berserk."

"He doesn't *go* berserk, damn it!" Stillman flared, slamming his fist down on the desk.

"*I* know that!" the councilor shot back. "Fine—so you want to tell everyone the truth? Even assuming Vanis D'arl didn't jump down our throats for doing it, would you *really* want to tell people Jonny has no control over his combat reflexes? You think that would help?"

Stillman's flash of anger evaporated. "No," he said quietly. "It would just make things worse." He stood up and walked over to the window. "Sorry I blew up, Sut. I know it's not your fault. It's just . . ." He sighed. "We've lost it, Sut. That's all there is to it. We're never going to get Jonny reintegrated into this town now. If becoming a bona fide hero didn't do it, then I have no idea what else to try."

"It's not your fault either, Teague. You can't take it personally." Fraser's voice was quiet. "The Army had no business doing what it did to Jonny, and then dropping him on us without any prepa- ration. But they're not going to be able to ignore the problem. You remember what D'arl said—the Cobras are having trouble all over the Dominion. Sooner or later the government's going to have to do something about it. We've done our best; it's up to them now."

Stillman's intercom buzzed. Walking back to his desk, the mayor tapped the key. "Yes?"

"Sir, Mr. Do-sin just called from the press office. He says there's something on the DOM-Press line that you should see."

"Thank you." Sitting down, Stillman turned on his plate and punched up the proper channel. The last three news items were still visible, the top one marked with a star indicating its importance. Both men hunched forward to read it.

Dominion Joint Military Command HQ, Asgard:
A military spokesman has announced that all reserve Cobras will be recalled into active service by the end of next month. This move is designed to counter a Minthisti build-up along the Dominion's Andromeda border. As yet no regular Army or Star Force reserves are being recalled, but all options are being kept open.

"I don't believe it," Fraser shook his head. "Are those stupid Minthisti going to try it *again*? I thought they learned their lesson the last time we stomped them."

Stillman didn't reply.

Vanis D'arl swept into Mayor Stillman's office with the air of a man preoccupied by more important business. He nodded shortly to the two men who were waiting there for him and sat down without invitation. "I trust this is as vital as your message implied," he said to Stillman. "I postponed an important meeting to detour to Horizon. Let's get on with it."

Stillman nodded, determined not to be intimidated, and gestured to the youth sitting quietly by his desk. "May I present Jame Moreau, brother of Cobra-three Jonny Moreau. He and I have been discussing the Reserve call-up set for later this month in response to the alleged Minthisti threat."

"Alleged?" D'arl's voice was soft, but there was a warning under it.

Stillman hesitated, suddenly aware of the risk they were taking with this confrontation. But Jame stepped into the gap. "Yes, *alleged*. We know this whole thing is a trumped-up excuse to pull all the Cobras back into the Army and ship them off to the border where they'll be out of the way."

D'arl looked keenly at Jame, as if seeing him for the first time. "You're concerned about your brother, of course; that's only natural," he said at last. "But your allegations are unprovable and come perilously close to sedition. The Dominion makes war only in self-defense. Even if your claim was true, what would such an action gain us?"

"That's precisely our point," Jame said calmly, showing a self-control and courage far beyond his nineteen years. "The government is trying to solve the Cobra problem, clearly. But this isn't a solution; it's merely a postponement."

"And yet, the Cobras were generally unhappy in their new civilian roles," D'arl pointed out. "Perhaps this will actually be better for them."

Jame shook his head, his eyes still holding D'arl's. "No. Because you can't keep them there forever, you see. You either have to release them again someday—in which case you're right back where you started—or else you have to hope that the problem will . . . work itself out."

D'arl's face was an expressionless mask. "What do you mean by that?"

"I think you know." For just a second Jame's control cracked, and some of the internal fire leaked out. "But don't you see? It won't *work*. You can't kill off all the Cobras, no matter how many wars you put them through, because the Army will be making new ones as fast as the old ones die. They're just too blasted useful for the brass to simply drop the project."

D'arl looked back at Stillman. "If this is all you wanted, to throw out ridiculous accusations, then you've wasted my time. Good day to you." He stood up and headed toward the door.

"It isn't," Stillman said. "We think we've come up with an alternative."

D'arl stopped and turned back to face them. For a moment he measured them with his eyes, then slowly came and sat down again. "I'm listening."

Stillman leaned forward in his chair, willing calmness into his mind. Jonny's life was riding on this. "The Cobra gear was designed to give extra speed, weaponry, and reflexes to its owners; and according to Jame, Jonny told him the original equipment included vision and auditory enhancers as well." D'arl nodded once, and Stillman continued, "But warfare isn't the only area where these things would be useful. Specifically, how about new planet colonization?"

D'arl frowned, but Stillman hurried on before he could speak. "I've done some reading on this in the last few weeks, and the usual procedure seems to involve four steps. First, an initial exploration team goes in to confirm the planet is habitable. Then a more extensive scientific party is landed for more tests; after that you usually need a pre-colony group to go in with heavy machinery for clearing land and starting settlements. Only then does the first main wave of colonists arrive. The whole process can take several years and is very expensive, mainly because you need a small military base there the whole time to protect the explorers from unknown dangers. That means feeding a few hundred men, transporting weapons and lots of support gear—"

"I know what it involves," D'arl interrupted. "Get to your point."

"Sending in Cobras instead of regular soldiers would be easier and cheaper," Stillman said. "Their equipment is self-contained and virtually maintenance-free, and they can both act as guards and help with the other work. True, a Cobra probably costs more to equip than the soldiers and workers he'll replace—but you've already *got* the Cobras."

D'arl shook his head impatiently. "I listened this long because I hoped you might have come up with something new. Committé H'orme considered this same idea months ago. Certainly, it would save money—but only if you've got some place to use it. There are no more than a half-dozen habitable worlds left within our borders and all have had a preliminary exploration. We're hemmed in on all sides by alien empires; to gain more worlds we would have to go to war for them."

"Not necessarily," Jame said. "We could go *past* the aliens."

"What?"

"Here's what we have in mind," Stillman said. "The Trofts just lost a war to us, and they know that we're still strong enough to really tear into their empire if we decided to invade. So it shouldn't be too hard to talk them into ceding us a corridor of space through their territory, for non-military transport only. All the charts show there's at least *some* unclaimed space on the far side of their territory; that's where we set up the colony."

D'arl was gazing into space, a thoughtful look on his face. "What if there aren't any habitable planets out there?"

"Then we're out of luck," Stillman admitted. "But if there *are*, look at what you've gained. New worlds, new resources, maybe even new alien contacts and trade—it would be a far better return on the Cobra investment than you'd get by killing them off in a useless war."

"Yes. Of course, we'd have to put the colony far enough past the border that the Trofts wouldn't be tempted to sneak out and destroy it. With that kind of long-distance transport, using Cobras instead of an armor battalion makes even more sense." He pursed his lips. "And as the colony gets stronger, it should help keep the

Trofts peaceful—they must surely know better than to start a two-front war. The Army might be interested in that aspect."

Jame leaned forward. "Then you agree with us? You'll suggest this to Committé H'orme?"

Slowly, D'arl nodded. "I will. It makes sense and is potentially profitable for the Dominion—a good combination. I'm sure the . . . trouble . . . with the Minthisti can be handled without the Cobras." Abruptly, he stood up. "I expect both of you to keep silent about this," he cautioned. "Premature publicity would be harmful. I can't make any promises; but whatever decision the Committee makes will be quick."

He was right. Less than two weeks later the announcement was made.

The big military shuttle was surrounded by a surprisingly large crowd, considering that only twenty-odd people would be accompanying Jonny from Horizon to the new colonist training center on Asgard. At least ten times that many people were at the Port, what with family, friends, and general well-wishers seeing the emigrants off. Even so, the five Moreaus and Stillman had little trouble working their way through the mass. For some it seemed to be fear that moved them out of the way of the red and black diamond-patterned Cobra dress uniform; but for others—the important ones—it was genuine respect. Pioneers, Jonny reflected, probably had a different attitude toward powerful men than the general populace. Not surprising; it was on just those men that their lives would soon be depending.

"Well, Jonny, good luck," Stillman said as they stopped near the inner edge of the crowd. "I hope things work well for you."

"Thanks, Mr. Stillman," Jonny replied, gripping the mayor's outstretched hand firmly. "And thanks for—well, for your support."

"You'll tape us before you leave Asgard, won't you?" Irena asked, her eyes moist.

"Sure, Momer." Jonny hugged her. "Maybe in a couple of years you'll all be able to come out and visit me."

"Yeah!" Gwen agreed enthusiastically.

"Perhaps," Pearce said. "Take care, son."

"Watch yourself, Jonny," Jame seconded.

And with another round of hugs it was time to go. Picking up his satchel, Jonny stepped aboard the shuttle, pausing once on the steps to wave before entering. The shuttle was empty, but even as he chose a seat the other colonists began coming in. Almost, Jonny thought, as if his boarding had been the signal they'd been waiting for.

The thought brought a bittersweet smile to his lips. On Adirondack, too, the Cobras had always taken the lead . . . but they'd never really been accepted by the general populace. Would things be different on this new world the survey expeditions had found for them, or would the pattern of Adirondack and Horizon simply be repeated wherever he went?

But in a way, it almost didn't matter anymore. He was tired of being a social pariah, and at least on an untamed planet that kind of failure was unlikely. Out there, the alternative to success was death . . . and death was something Jonny had long ago learned how to face.

Still smiling, he leaned back in his seat and waited calmly for takeoff.

Interlude

The haiku garden in H'orme's dome apartment was a minor miracle of horticultural design, a true example of the melding of nature with technology. Somehow, D'arl had never before noticed the harmony of the place—the ease, for example, with which the holographic walls and ceiling complemented the pattern of the walkways to give the illusion of a much larger garden than was actually here. The gently shifting winds, the whispered hints of distant waterfalls and birds, the genuine sunshine brought in via mirrors from outside—D'arl was impressed by the richness of it all. Had H'orme, he wondered, always kept these sensory distractions at a minimum whenever the two men had walked here together in the past? Probably. But today there were no reports for H'orme to concentrate on. Only small talk . . . and good-byes.

"You'll need particularly to watch out for Committé Pendrikan," H'orme commented as he stooped briefly to examine a particularly well-textured saqqara shrub. "He's never liked me and will probably transfer that animosity to you. Illogical, really, but you know the multi-generational grudges they like to hold on Zimbwe."

D'arl nodded; he was well aware of Pendrikan's attitude. "I've watched you handle him often enough, sir. I think I know the levers to use on him."

"Good. But don't go out of your way to pick any fights for a while. The Committee's a surprisingly conservative body, and it'll be a bit before they feel at ease with you sitting *at* the table instead of behind it."

"And vice versa," D'arl murmured.

H'orme smiled, the expression becoming wistful as he looked around the garden. "I have no fears for you, D'arl. You have a natural talent for the job of Committé, the ability to see what needs to be done and how to do it. This whole resolution of the immediate Cobra problem showed that: your campaign was masterfully executed, from original concept to final Committee approval."

"Thank you, sir. Though as I've said before the basic idea came from elsewhere."

H'orme waved aside the distinction. "You're not supposed to reinvent the fusion plant every time you need something. It's your staff's job to come up with ideas; it's *your* job to evaluate them. Don't ever fall into the trap of trying to do it all yourself."

D'arl suppressed a smile. "Yes, sir."

H'orme gave him a sideways glance. "And before you savor the irony of that too much, remember how much work *I've* dumped on you alone. Pick your aides well, D'arl—in all too many cases, they're what make or break a Committé."

D'arl nodded silently and the two men continued their walk. Looking around, D'arl found his mind drifting back and forth across his thirteen years as H'orme's aide. It didn't seem nearly long enough to prepare him for the task ahead.

"So . . . what's the latest word from Aventine?"

Startled, D'arl tried to put his brain back online. Aventine . . . ? Oh, right—the new colony world. "The first wave of colonists seems to be settling in well enough. No major problems or overly dangerous fauna."

"At least as of three months ago," H'orme nodded.

"True," The communications time lag, D'arl had already realized, was going to be a problem in governing the new colony. Choosing a competent and reliable governor-general was going to be a major Committee task soon.

"And how do the Trofts seem to be taking it?" H'orme asked.

"No trouble at all, so far. Not even any boarding of ships going down the Corridor to check for military hardware."

"Um. Not what I expected. Still, all the ships up to now have been carrying Cobras as well as colonists. They may not have wanted to tangle with them again. But that can't last." H'orme walked for a moment in silence. "Somewhere along the line the Trofts are bound to realize Aventine is a potential threat to them. When that happens . . . the colony has to be strong enough to defend itself."

"Or spread out enough that it can't be taken in a single blow," D'arl suggested.

H'orme sighed. "A less acceptable position, but probably a more realistic one. Certainly in the short run."

They'd come full circle around the garden now, and H'orme paused at the office door for one last look. "If you'll sit still for one final word of advice, D'arl," he said slowly, "I'd recommend you find someone for your staff who really understands the Cobras. Not their weaponry, specifically, but the Cobras themselves."

D'arl smiled. "I believe I can do even better than that, sir. I've already been in touch with the young man who suggested the Aventine colony in the first place. His brother, as it happens, is one of the Cobras out there."

H'orme returned the smile. "I see I've trained you better even than I thought. I'm proud to have you as my successor . . . Committé D'arl."

"Thank you, sir," the younger man managed to say. "May you always be so proud of me."

Together they left the garden, to which H'orme would never return.

Loyalist: 2414

The boundary between field and forest was as sharp as a laser beam, the giant blue-green cyprenes running right up to the half-meter of orange vegebarrier insulating the tender wheat shoots from native plant encroachment. In his more philosophical moments, Jonny saw a multi-leveled yin/yang in the arrangement: tall versus short, old versus young, native versus man-made. At the moment, though, his mood was anything but philosophical.

Looking up from the note, he found the youth who had delivered it standing in a rigid imitation of military attention. "And what exactly is this supposed to mean?" he asked, waving the note paper gently.

"The message is self-explanatory, sir—" the boy began.

"Yes, I can read," Jonny interrupted him. "And one more 'sir' out of you, Almo, and I'm going to tell your father on you. What I meant was, why did Challinor send you all the way out here just to invite me to a meeting? That's what these things are supposed to be for." He tapped the compact phone resting on his hip.

"Cee-two Challinor didn't want to take any chances on word leaking out about this, sir—Jonny," Almo corrected himself hastily. "It's a private meeting, for Cobras only."

Jonny studied the other's face a moment, then folded the paper and stuck it in his pocket. Whatever Challinor was trying to prove, browbeating his messenger boy wouldn't do any good. "You can give Challinor a definite 'maybe,'" he told Almo. "There's a spine leopard that's been poking around the edge of the forest lately. If I don't get it today, I'll have to ride guard with Chin's planter tonight."

"Cee-two Challinor said I should emphasize the meeting was very important."

"So's my word—and I promised Chin he could start his second seedling run by tonight." Jonny reached for his phone. "If you'd like, I can call Challinor and tell him that myself," he suggested.

"No—that's all right," Almo said hastily. "I'll tell him. Thank you for your time." With that he took off across the field toward where his car was waiting.

Jonny felt a smile touch his lips, but his amusement quickly faded. There weren't a lot of teenagers in this part of Aventine—the first two waves of colonists had all been childless, and two succeeding waves of families hadn't made up the deficit—and Jonny had always felt a twinge of pain for the enhanced loneliness he knew Almo and his peers must feel. The four Cobras assigned to Almo's town of Thanksgiving were obvious role models for the teen-aged boys, at least, and Jonny was glad Almo had found a friend in Tors Challinor. At least he used to be glad. Now, he wasn't entirely sure.

Almo's car took off with minimal dust, and Jonny turned both his face and attention to the towering trees. He'd worry about Challinor's cloak and laser later; right now he had a spine leopard to kill. Making sure all the equipment on his belt was secured, he crossed the vegebarrier and entered the forest.

Even after seven years on Aventine Jonny felt a sense of awe whenever he stepped under the ancient canopy of oddly shaped leaves that turned the day into a diffuse twilight. Partly it was the forest's age, he had long ago decided; but partly also it was the humbling reminder of how little mankind knew about the world it had so recently claimed as its own. The forest was teeming with plant and animal life, virtually none of which was really under-stood. Clicking on his vision and auditory enhancers, Jonny moved deeper into the woods, trying to watch all directions at once.

The extra-loud snap of a branch above and behind him was his only warning, but it was enough. His nanocomputer correctly interpreted the sound as being caused by a large airborne body, and almost before Jonny's brain had registered the sound, his servos had taken over, throwing him to the side just as four sets of claws slashed through the space he'd vacated. Jonny rolled through a somersault—barely missing a gluevine-covered tree—and came up into a crouch. He got a glimpse of the spine leopard as it leaped toward him, razor-edged quills tucked tightly against its forelegs—and again his computer took over.

Standing flatfooted in the open, the only weapons Jonny could bring to bear were his fingertip lasers; but even as it again threw him to the side his computer used them with deadly efficiency. The twin needles of light lanced out, sweeping across the alien creature's head.

The spine leopard screamed, a full-bodied ululation that seemed to bounce off the inside of Jonny's stomach, and its spines snapped reflexively upright on its legs. The instinctive defensive move proved useless; Jonny was already beyond reach of the spine tips. Again he hit the ground, but this time he didn't roll back to his feet. Looking back over his shoulder, he saw the spine leopard struggling to get up, apparently oblivious to the black lines crisscrossing its face and to the brain damage behind them. A wound like that would have killed a human outright, but the less centralized alien metabolism wasn't as susceptible to localized destruction. The creature rose to its feet, spines still fully spread.

And the brilliant flash of his antiarmor laser caught the spine leopard in the head . . . and this time the destruction was more than adequate.

Carefully Jonny got to his feet, wincing at the fresh bruises the battle had given him. His ankle felt warmer than it should have after only a single shot from the antiarmor laser—a heat-sensitization, he'd long suspected, due largely to his overuse of the weapon during the Tyler Mansion escape.

Even on Aventine, it seemed, he couldn't entirely escape the aftereffects of the war.

Taking one last look around him, he pulled out his phone and punched for the operator. "Ariel," the computer's voice said.

"Chin Reston," Jonny told it. A moment later the farmer's voice came on. "Reston here."

"Jonny Moreau, Chin. I got your spine leopard. I hope you didn't want it stuffed—I had to burn its head off."

"Hell with the head. Are *you* okay?"

Jonny smiled. "You worry too much—you know that? I'm fine; it never laid a spine on me. If you want, I'll put a beacon on it and you can come get the pelt whenever you want."

"Sounds good. Thanks a lot, Jonny—I really appreciate it."

"No charge. Talk to you later." Pressing the off switch, Jonny again punched for the operator. "Kennet MacDonald," he told the computer.

There was a moment of silence. "No answer," the operator informed him.

Jonny frowned. Like all Cobras on Aventine, MacDonald was supposed to carry his phone with him at all times. He was probably out in the forest or somewhere equally dangerous and didn't want to be distracted. "Record a message."

"Recording."

"Ken, this is Jonny Moreau. Call me as soon as you get a chance—preferably before this evening."

Switching off, Jonny returned the phone to his belt and unfastened one of the two tiny transponders from the underside of his emergency pouch. A flick of a switch set it in "operate" mode; stepping over the dead spine leopard, he dropped the device on its flank. For a moment he looked down at the creature, his eyes drawn to the foreleg spines. Aventine's biologists were unanimous in the opinion that the spines' placement and range of angles made them defensive rather than offensive weapons. The only problem was that no one had ever found any creature on the planet that a spine leopard might need such weapons to outfight. Personally, Jonny had no desire to be around when the first of that unknown species was discovered.

Reactivating his sensory enhancers, he began working his way back out of the forest.

MacDonald's call came in late in the afternoon, just as Jonny was looking over his pantry and trying to decide what to have for dinner.

"Sorry about the delay," MacDonald apologized after identifying himself. "I was out in the forest near the river most of the day with my phone turned off."

"No problem," Jonny assured him. "Spine leopard hunting?"

"Yeah. Got one, too."

"Likewise. Must be another migration; they don't usually find the territories we've cleared out quite this fast. We're probably going to be busy for a while."

"Well, things were getting dull, anyway. What's on your mind?"

Jonny hesitated. There *could* be a good reason why Challinor didn't want any word of his meeting going out on the airwaves. "Did you get any unusual messages today?" he asked obliquely.

"Matter of fact, I did. You want to get together and talk about it? Wait a second—Chrys's trying to get my attention." A voice spoke unintelligibly in the background. "Chrys says you should join us for dinner in about half an hour, at her place."

"Sorry, but I've already got my own started," Jonny lied. "Why don't I come over when I've finished eating?"

"Okay," MacDonald said. "About seven, say? Afterward, maybe we can all go for a drive together."

Challinor's meeting was scheduled for seven-thirty. "Sounds good," Jonny agreed. "See you at seven."

Replacing his phone, Jonny grabbed a package at random from the pantry and took it over to the microwave. He would have liked to have joined the others for dinner—MacDonald and Chrys Eldjarn were two of his favorite people—and if Chrys's father hadn't been out of town doing emergency surgery, he would have jumped at the invitation. But Chrys and MacDonald were a pretty steady couple, and they got little enough time to be alone together as it was. With only two Cobras to guard Ariel's four hundred sixty colonists from both Aventine's fauna and, occasionally, each other, spare time was at a premium.

Besides which, he thought wryly, spending more time in range of Chrys's smile would only tempt him to try and steal her away from MacDonald again, and there was no point in making trouble for himself like that. Their friendship was too valuable to him to risk messing it up.

He had a—for him—leisurely dinner and arrived at the Eldjarn's home at seven o'clock sharp. Chrys let him in, treating him to one of her dazzling smiles, and led the way to the living room, where MacDonald waited on the couch.

"You missed a great dinner," MacDonald greeted him, waving him to a chair.

"I'm sure you made up for my absence," Jonny said blandly. Half a head taller than Jonny and a good deal burlier, MacDonald had an ability to put food away that was known all through the district.

"I tried. Let's see your note."

Digging it out, Jonny handed it over. MacDonald scanned it briefly, then passed it to Chrys, who had curled up on the couch beside him. "Identical to mine," he told Jonny. "Any idea what it's all about?"

Jonny shook his head. "The *Dewdrop*'s been out surveying the nearest system for the past couple of months. Do you suppose they found something interesting?"

" 'Interesting' as in 'dangerous'?" Chrys asked quietly.

"Possibly," MacDonald told her, "especially if this news is really only for Cobras. But I doubt it," he said, addressing Jonny.

"If this were a war council or something we should all be meeting at Capitalia, not Thanksgiving."

"Unless they're passing the news out piecemeal, to the individual villages," Jonny suggested. "But that again drops it out of the 'emergency' category. Incidentally, who brought you the message? Almo Pyre?"

MacDonald nodded. "Seemed awfully formal, too. Called me 'Cee-two MacDonald' about four times."

"Yeah, me too. Has Challinor instituted the old rank system over there, or something?"

"Don't know—I haven't been to Thanksgiving for weeks." MacDonald glanced at his watch. "I suppose it's time to remedy that deficiency, eh? Let's go see what Challinor wants."

"Come back after it's over and tell me what happened," Chrys said as they all stood up.

"It could be late before we get back," MacDonald warned as he kissed her good-bye.

"That's okay—Dad's coming home late, too, so I'll be up."

"All right. Car's out back, Jonny."

Thanksgiving was a good twenty kilometers east-northeast of Ariel along a dirt-and-vegebarrier road that was, so far, the norm in the newer areas of the human beachhead on Aventine. MacDonald drove, guiding the car skillfully around the worst of the potholes while avoiding the occasional tree branch reaching out from the thick forest on either side.

"One of these days a spine leopard's going to jump a car from one of those overhangs and get the surprise of his life," MacDonald commented.

Jonny chuckled. "I think they're too smart for that. Speaking of smart moves, you and Chrys to the point of setting a date yet?"

"Umm . . . not really. I think we both want to make sure we're right for each other."

"Well, in my opinion, if you don't grab her while you've got the chance you're crazy. Though I'm not sure I'd give her the same advice."

MacDonald snorted. "Thanks a kilo. Just for that I may make you walk home."

Challinor's house was near the outskirts of Thanksgiving, within sight of the cultivated fields surrounding the village. Two other cars were already parked there; and as they got out and headed for the house, the front door opened, revealing a slender man in full Cobra dress uniform. "Good evening, Moreau; MacDonald," he said coolly. "You're twenty minutes late."

Jonny felt MacDonald stiffen beside him and hurried to get in the first word. "Hello, L'est," he said, gesturing to the other's outfit. "I didn't realize this was a costume party."

Simmon L'est merely smiled thinly, a mannerism whose carefully measured condescension had always irritated Jonny. But the other's eyes showed the barb had hit its target. MacDonald must have seen that, too, and brushed silently by L'est without delivering the more potent blast he'd obviously been readying when Jonny stepped in. Breathing a bit easier, Jonny followed his friend in, L'est closing the door behind them.

The modest-sized living room was comfortably crowded. At the far end, on a straight-back chair, sat Tors Challinor, resplendent in his own Cobra dress uniform; at his right, looking almost drab in their normal work clothes, were Sandy Taber and Barl DesLone, the two Cobras stationed in Greensward. Next to them, also in dress uniforms, were Hael Szintra of Oasis and Franck Patrusky of Thanksgiving.

"Ah—MacDonald and Moreau," Challinor called in greeting. "Come in; your seats are right up here." He indicated the two empty chairs to his left.

"I hope this is really important, Challinor," MacDonald growled as the two men crossed the room and sat down. "I don't know what things are like in Thanksgiving, but we don't have a lot of time in Ariel for playing soldier." He glanced significantly at the uniforms.

"As it happens, your lack of spare time is one of the topics we want to discuss," Challinor said smoothly. "Tell me, does Ariel have all the Cobras it deserves? Or does Greensward, for that matter?" he added, looking at Taber and DesLone.

"What do you mean, 'deserves'?" Taber asked.

"At last count there were about ten thousand people in Caravel District and exactly seventy-two Cobras," Challinor said. "That works out to one Cobra per hundred-forty people. Any way you slice it, a town the size of Greensward ought to have *three* Cobras assigned to it, not two. And that goes double for Ariel."

"Things seem reasonably calm at the moment in Ariel," MacDonald said. "We don't really need any more firepower than we've got." He looked at Taber. "How are conditions around Greensward?"

"Firepower isn't the issue," Szintra put in before Taber could answer. "The point is that we're required to do a lot more than just guard our villages against spine leopards and falx. We have to hunt down wheat snakes, act as patrollers in domestic squabbles—and if we have any spare time left, we're supposed to help cut down trees and unload supply trucks. And we get *nothing* in return!"

Jonny looked at Szintra's flushed face, then at the other three uniformed men. A cold knot was beginning to form over his dinner. "Ken, perhaps we should get back to Ariel," he said quietly to MacDonald.

"No—please stay a while longer," Challinor spoke up hastily. "Cee-three Szintra was a bit more forceful than necessary, but stuck all alone out in Oasis he perhaps sees matters more clearly than some of the rest of us."

"Let's assume for the present that he's right, that we don't get the respect we deserve," MacDonald said. "What solution are we discussing here?"

"It's not simply lack of respect, or even the way we always seem to be taken for granted," Challinor said earnestly. "It's also the way the syndic's office takes forever to process the simplest requests for equipment or supplies—though they're prompt enough when it comes to picking up surplus wheat and gluevine extract when we have it. They seem to have forgotten that the whole planet isn't as comfortable as Rankin and Capitalia, that when a frontier town needs something we need it *now*. Add to that the mania for making lots of little frontier settlements instead of consolidating the territory we've got—which is why we're spread so damn thin—and you get a picture of a government that's not doing its job. To put it bluntly, we feel something has to be done about it."

There was a long moment of silence. "What do you suggest?" DesLone asked at last. "That we send a petition to the Dominion with the next courier ship?"

"Don't be denser than you have to, Barl," Taber growled. "They're talking about replacing Governor-General Zhu themselves."

"Actually, our thinking is that more than the governor-general needs changing," Challinor said calmly. "It's painfully clear that the centralized system that works so well once a world is established is failing miserably on Aventine. We need something more decentralized, something more responsive to the planet's needs—"

"Governed by those who'd do the best job?" Jonny cut in. "Us, for instance?"

"In many ways, our struggle to tame Aventine is analogous to the guerrilla war we waged against the Trofts," Challinor said. "If I do say so myself, we did a hell of a job back then—don't you agree? Who on this planet could do better?"

"So what are you suggesting?" MacDonald asked, his tone far more interested than it had any business being. "We carve Aventine into little kingdoms, each one run by a Cobra?"

"Basically," Challinor nodded. "It's a bit more complicated than that—there'd have to be a loose hierarchy to settle disputes and such—but that's the general idea. What do you say? Are you interested?"

"How many of you are there?" MacDonald asked, ignoring the question.

"Enough," Challinor said. "The four of us here, plus the three from Fallow, two from Weald, and three more from Headwater and the lumber camps upslope of the Kerseage Mines."

"You propose to take over an entire world with twelve Cobras?"

Challinor's brow furrowed slightly. "No, of course not. But I've talked to a lot of other Cobras, both in and out of Caravel District. Most of them are willing to wait and see what happens with our experiment."

"In other words, to see how hard Zhu comes down on you when you declare independence?" MacDonald shook his head. "Your thinking's got loose connections, Challinor. No Cobra's going to be allowed to stay neutral in something like that—they'll be ordered to come here and restore the syndic's rule, and their answer to that order will put them on one side or the other. With the odds at—let's see; twelve Cobras out of six hundred twenty makes it about fifty to one—which way do you think they'll jump?"

"Which way are *you* jumping, MacDonald?" L'est cut in suddenly from his seat by the door. "You ask a lot of questions for someone who hasn't committed himself yet."

MacDonald kept his eyes on Challinor. "How about it, Challinor? This is going to take more than an ace or two up your sleeve."

"I asked you a question, damn it!" L'est snapped.

Deliberately, MacDonald turned to face the other; just as leisurely he got to his feet. "I stand where I and my family have always stood: with the Dominion of Man. What you're talking is treason, gentlemen; I won't have any part of it."

L'est was on his feet now, too, standing sideways to MacDonald in a Cobra ready stance. "The loyalty of an EarthScot or a fine dog," he sneered. "In case you haven't noticed, EarthScot, this Dominion you're so eager to please is treating you like dangerous garbage. It's thrown you just as far away as it possibly could, with a hundred fifty light-years and two hundred billion Trofts between you and civilization."

"We're needed here for the colonization effort," Jonny interjected, wanting to stand in MacDonald's support but afraid the action might be misinterpreted. In such close quarters an all-out fire fight between the two Cobras would probably be lethal to everyone in the room.

"That's donk dung, Moreau—we're here because it was cheaper than starting a new war just to kill us off," L'est ground out. "The Dominion doesn't care if we live or die out here. It's up to us to insure our own survival—no matter what sort of short-sighted fools get in our way."

"You coming, Jonny?" MacDonald asked, taking a step toward the door.

L'est took a step of his own, putting himself directly in front of the door. "You're not leaving, MacDonald. You know too much."

"Take it easy, Simmon," Challinor said, his tone calm but with steel underlying it. "We're not giving these gentlemen a choice between joining us or death."

L'est didn't move. "You don't know this clown, Tors. He's a troublemaker."

"Yes, you told me that earlier. Cee-two MacDonald, please understand that we're not doing this simply for our own personal gain." Challinor's voice was pure sincerity. "The people of Aventine need strong, competent leadership, and they're not getting it. It's our *duty* to these people—these citizens of the Dominion—to save them from disaster."

"If your friend over there doesn't get out of the way, I'm going to have to move him myself," MacDonald said.

Challinor sighed. "Simmon, step aside. MacDonald, will you at least think about what I've said?"

"Oh, I'll think about it all right." With his eyes still on L'est, MacDonald moved toward the door.

Carefully, his attention on the still-seated Patrusky and Szintra, Jonny got to his feet and followed. "If you'd like to stay, Moreau," Challinor called after him, "we can get you back to Ariel later."

"No, thanks," Jonny said, glancing back over his shoulder. "I have some work I need to finish up tonight."

"All right. But think about what I've said, all right?"

The words were friendly, but something in the tone made the hairs on Jonny's neck tingle. Suppressing a shiver, he got out fast.

✧   ✧   ✧

The drive back to Ariel was quiet. Jonny, expecting MacDonald to be somewhere on the far side of furious, braced himself for a hair-raising ride on the bumpy road. To his surprise, though, MacDonald drove with a calmness that bordered on the sedate. But the backwash of the car's headlights showed clearly the tension in his jaw and around his eyes. Jonny took the cue and kept his mouth shut.

Lights were still showing in the Eldjarn house when MacDonald brought them to a stop across the street. Parked in front of them was the car Chrys's father had taken to Rankin; obviously, he'd arrived home too late to take it back to the village garage.

As before, Chrys answered the door. "Come on in," she invited, stepping to one side. "You're earlier than I expected—short meeting?"

"Too long," MacDonald growled.

Chrys's eyes took on a knowing look. "Uh-oh. What happened— Challinor want you to petition for more Cobras again?"

MacDonald shook his head. "Nothing so amusing. They want to take over the planet."

Chrys stopped in mid-stride. "They *what?*"

"You heard me. They want to overthrow the governor-general and set up a warlord system with little fiefdoms for all of the Cobras who join him."

Chrys looked at Jonny. "Is he kidding me, Jonny?" she asked.

Jonny shook his head. "No. Challinor's dead serious about it. I don't know how they hope to do anything but get themselves slagged, though—"

"Just a second," she interrupted, moving toward the door to the bedroom wing. "I think Dad had better hear this."

"Good idea," MacDonald grunted, stepping to the corner liquor cabinet and pouring himself a drink. Holding up the bottle, he looked questioningly at Jonny, who shook his head.

A couple of minutes later Chrys was back, a dressing-gowned man in tow. "Ken; Jonny," Dr. Orrin Eldjarn nodded to them, looking wide awake despite his sleep-tousled hair. "What's this about some kind of cabal being formed?"

They all sat down, the Eldjarns listening intently as MacDonald gave them a capsule summary of Challinor's proposal. "But as Jonny said," he concluded, "there's just no way they can succeed. One Cobra's fighting strength is essentially the same as another's, after all."

"But orders of magnitude higher than anyone else's," Eldjarn commented. "If Challinor announced he was taking over Thanksgiving, there's really nothing the people there could do to stop him."

"Surely there are a few other weapons there," Chrys argued. "We've got at least a half dozen pellet guns here in Ariel, and Thanksgiving's bigger than we are."

"Pellet guns would be essentially useless against a Cobra except in cramped quarters where he couldn't maneuver," Jonny told her. "The firing mechanism has a distinctive click that's loud enough for us to hear, and we'd normally have no trouble getting out of the line of fire. The Trofts on Silvern took forever to learn that lesson."

"But that's not the point," MacDonald said. "To kill twelve rebel Cobras, all it should take is twelve loyal Cobras."

"Unless the rebels manage to target all the others before the battle starts," Chrys suggested suddenly. "Couldn't they kill everyone in one quick volley if they did that?"

MacDonald shook his head. "The optical enhancers we've got now don't have the multiple targeting capability of our old ones. But okay—let's say it'll even take *fifty* Cobras if the rebels are dug in and you want an absolutely sure victory. That's still only a twelfth of Zhu's forces. Challinor has to know that."

"So the question is, what else does he know—that we don't." Eldjarn stroked his chin thoughtfully. "Anything happening elsewhere on Aventine that might be pinning down large numbers of Cobras? Civil unrest in one of the other districts or something?"

Jonny and MacDonald exchanged glances, and the latter shrugged. "Nothing we've heard of," he said. "I suppose it's conceivable that Challinor's organized groups in other towns for a simultaneous declaration, but I don't really believe it."

"The spine leopards are on the move again," Jonny suggested doubtfully. "That'll keep a lot of Cobras on patrolling and hunting duty unless the farmers went to stay out of their fields for a few days. I can't see that worrying the governor-general, though. Maybe Challinor's just lost his mind."

"Not Challinor." MacDonald was definite. "He's as sharp and level-headed as they come. And L'est wouldn't have come in on this on the strength of Challinor's sales talk alone, either—that one was a weasel even before we hit Aventine."

"I'm inclined to agree," Eldjarn said slowly. "The timing here is too good for megalomaniacs to have come up with. As you pointed out, Jonny, the spine leopard migration will hinder any official counter-measures, at least a little. Less coincidental, I'm sure, is the fact that the Dominion courier ship left Capitalia just a few days ago, which means it'll be six months before anyone from the Dominion touches down here again."

"Plenty of time to consolidate a new regime," MacDonald growled. "They can present the courier with a *fait accompli* and dare Dome to do something."

"And the *Dewdrop*'s out somewhere in deep space," Jonny said with a grimace.

"Right," Eldjarn nodded. "Until it gets back, there's no way for Zhu to get in touch with anyone—and even then, if the *Dewdrop* can't land somewhere secure for fuel and provisions, it won't be able to go for help. No, Challinor's thought this out carefully. It's a shame you couldn't have played along a little longer and found out the rest of his plan."

"I did what I could," MacDonald said, a bit stiffly. "I won't lie about my loyalty to anyone."

"Sure—I understand," Eldjarn said.

For a moment the room was silent. "I suppose *I* could go back to them," Jonny said hesitantly. "I never really stated where I stood."

"They'd be suspicious," MacDonald said, shaking his head. "And if they caught you passing information to us they'd treat you as a spy."

"Unless, of course," Chrys said quietly, "you *want* to go back."

Her father and MacDonald looked at her in surprise, but her gaze remained on Jonny. "After all, we've been assuming Jonny was solidly on our side," she pointed out calmly. "Maybe he hasn't really made up his mind. This isn't a decision that we should be making for him."

Eldjarn nodded agreement. "You're right, of course. Well, Jonny? What do you say?"

Jonny pursed his lips. "To be completely honest, I don't know. I swore an oath of allegiance to the Dominion, too—but the government here really *is* doing some potentially disastrous things, especially the overextending of people and resources. What Challinor said about our duty being to the *people* of Aventine isn't something I can dismiss out of hand."

"But if the legal avenues for political change are ignored—by anyone—you open the way for total anarchy," MacDonald argued. "And if you really think Challinor and L'est would do a better job—"

"Ken." Chrys put a restraining hand on his arm. To Jonny, she said, "I understand your uncertainties, but I'm sure you realize this isn't an issue you'll be able to stay neutral on."

"And you'll need to make your decision soon," Eldjarn pointed out. "Challinor wouldn't have risked telling such a long-shot as Ken about the plot unless they were almost ready to move."

"I understand." Jonny got to his feet. "I think perhaps I'd better go home. If I decide to actively oppose Challinor you can always fill me in later on anything you come up with tonight. At any rate—" he met MacDonald's gaze firmly "—what's been said here already is between the four of us alone. Challinor won't hear any of it from me."

Slowly, MacDonald nodded. "All right. I guess that's all we can expect. You want a ride home?"

"No, thanks; I'll walk. Good night, all."

Like the farming communities Jonny had known on Horizon, Ariel generally closed down fairly early in the evening. The streets were dark and deserted, with the only illumination coming from occasional streetlights and the brilliant stars overhead. Usually, Jonny liked looking at the stars whenever he was out this late; tonight, he hardly noticed they were there.

There had been a time, he thought wryly, when simply gazing into Chrys's eyes would have immediately brought him back onto her side, no matter what the cause or topic at issue. But that time lay far in his past. The war, his failed attempts to reenter mainstream society afterwards, and seven long years of working to build a new world had all taken their toll on the rashness of youth. He had long ago learned not to base his decisions on emotional reasoning.

The trouble was that, at the moment, he didn't have a terrific number of facts on which to base an intelligent decision. So far everything pointed to a quick defeat for Challinor's group . . . but there *had* to be more to it than the obvious. Whatever his other irritating characteristics, Simmon L'est was an excellent tactician, his father having been an Army training instructor on Asgard. He wouldn't join any venture that was obviously doomed—and a long, bloody war would be disastrous for the colony.

On the other hand, Jonny's allegiance *was* technically to the government of the Dominion and, by extension, to Aventine's governor-general. And despite L'est's sneers, MacDonald's sense of loyalty had always been something Jonny admired.

His brain was still doing flip-flops when he reached home. The

usual bedtime preparations took only a few minutes; then, turning off the light, he got into bed and closed his eyes. Perhaps by
morning things would be clearer.

But he was far too keyed up to sleep. Finally, after an hour of
restlessly changing positions, he went to his desk and dug out the
tape from his family that had come with the last courier. Putting
it on the player, he adjusted the machine for sound only and crawled
back into bed, hoping the familiar voices would help him relax.

He was drifting comfortably toward sleep when a part of his
sister's monologue seemed to pry itself under a corner of his
consciousness. " . . . I've been accepted at the University of Aerie,"
Gwen's playful voice was saying. "It means finishing my schooling away from Horizon, but they've got the best geology program
in this part of the Dominion and offer a sub-major in tectonic
utilization. I figure having credentials like that's my best chance
of getting accepted as a colonist to Aventine. I hope you'll have
enough pull out there by the time I graduate to get me assigned
to Ariel—I'm not just coming out there to see what the backside
of the Troft Empire looks like, you know. Though Jame ought to
be able to pull any strings from Asgard by then, too, come to think
of it. Speaking of the Trofts, there was a sort of informal free-for-
all debate in the hall at school the other day on whether the
Aventine project was really just an Army plot to outflank the Trofts
so that they wouldn't try to attack us again. I think I held up our
end pretty well—the stats you sent on the output of the Kerseage
Mines were of enormous help—but I'm afraid I've ruined any
chance I might ever have had of passing myself off as demure or
ladylike. I hope there's no ban on letting in rowdies out there. . . ."

Getting up, Jonny switched the player off . . . and by the time
he got back into bed he knew what his decision had to be. Gwen's
cheerful tapes to him, full of confidence and borderline hero
worship, had helped him over the roughest times out here in a
way that the quieter support of his parents and Jame hadn't been
able to duplicate. To willingly take on the label of traitor—especially
when the situation was by no means desperate yet—would be a
betrayal of both Gwen's pride and his family's trust. And that was
something he would never willingly do.

For a moment he considered calling MacDonald to tell the other
of his decision . . . but the bed felt more and more comfortable
as the tension began to leave him. Besides, it was getting late.
Morning would be soon enough to join the loyalist cause.

Five minutes later, he was sound asleep.

✧　　✧　　✧

He woke to the impatient buzz of his alarm, and as he rubbed the sleep from his eyes, the answer popped into his mind. For a moment he lay still, his mind busy sorting out details and possibilities. Then, rolling out of bed, he snared his phone and got the operator. "Kennet MacDonald," he told it.

The wait was unusually long; MacDonald must have still been asleep. "Yes; hello," his voice finally came.

"It's Jonny, Ken. I know what Challinor's up to."

"You do?" MacDonald was suddenly alert. "What?"

"He's going to take over the Kerseage Mines."

Another long pause. "Damn," MacDonald said at last. "That has to be it. Over half of Aventine's rare-earth elements alone come from there. All he'd have to do is use the mine's explosives cache to doomsday the shafts and entrances—Zhu would have to think long and hard about sending a massive force to evict him."

"And the longer Zhu hesitates the weaker he looks," Jonny said, "and the more likely some of Challinor's 'neutral' Cobras will see him as the probable winner and shift sides. If enough do that, Zhu'll either have to capitulate or risk civil war."

"Yeah. *Damn.* We've got to alert Capitalia, get them to send a force up there before Challinor makes his move."

"Right. You want to call them or shall I?"

"It'd be better if we were both on the line. Hang on; let's see if I remember how to do this—"

There was a double click. "Ariel," the operator said.

"The governor-general's office in Capitalia," MacDonald told it.

"I'm sorry, but I am unable to complete the call."

Jonny blinked. "Why not?"

"I'm sorry, but I am unable to complete the call."

"Do you suppose the satellite's out of whack?" Jonny suggested hopefully.

"Not likely," MacDonald growled. "Operator: Syndic Powell Stuart's office in Rankin."

"I'm sorry, but I am unable to complete the call."

And Rankin wasn't far enough away to require the communication satellite. "So much for coincidence," Jonny said, feeling a knot forming in his stomach. "How did Challinor get to the phone computer so fast?"

"He could have done this any time in the past few days," MacDonald grunted. "I doubt if anyone's needed to talk to Capitalia or Rankin lately; certainly not since the courier ship left."

"Maybe that's why he sent Almo Pyre with notes instead of calling us from Thanksgiving," Jonny suggested, suddenly remembering. "Maybe all out-of-town contact's been halted."

"Maybe. Listen, I don't like using this phone, all of a sudden. Let's meet at Chrys's shop in, say, half an hour."

"Right. Half an hour."

Jonny clicked off the phone, and for a moment he stared at the little box, wondering if anyone had been eavesdropping on the conversation. Unlikely . . . but if Challinor could fix the computer to block out-of-town calls, why not also set up something to monitor all in-town ones?

Jumping out of bed, he began pulling on his clothes.

One of Ariel's two fully qualified electronics technicians, Chrys shared a two-floor combination office/shop/storeroom near the roughly circular area in the center of town which was known, presumably for historical reasons, as the Square. Jonny got there early and waited nervously outside until Chrys and MacDonald arrived with the keys.

"Let's get inside," MacDonald urged, glancing around at the handful of other people that had appeared on the streets as the village began its preparations for the new day. "Challinor may have hired a spy or two in town."

Inside, Chrys turned on some lights and sank into her workbench chair, yawning prodigiously. "Okay, we're here," she said. "Now would you care to explain what we needed me to do here on five hours' sleep and ten minutes' notice?"

"We're cut off from both Rankin and Capitalia," MacDonald told her. "Challinor's apparently jinxed the phone computer." He went on to describe Jonny's idea about the Kerseage Mines and their attempt to alert the authorities. "Besides the water route up the Chalk River, the only land routes to the Mines are the roads from Thanksgiving and Weald," he explained. "Challinor's in position to block both of them, and if he can control the river here at Ariel, the governor-general won't have any way to move in forces or equipment except by aircar."

"*Damn* him," Chrys muttered, her eyes wide awake now and flashing sparks. "If he's fouled up all the long-distance circuits, it'll probably take a week to repair the damage."

"Well, that answers my first question," MacDonald said grimly. "Next question: can you build a transmitter of any kind here that can bypass the operator entirely and run a signal to Capitalia via the satellite?"

"In theory, sure. In practice—" She shrugged. "I haven't built a high-frequency focused-beam transmitter since my first year at school. It would take at least two or three days' work, even assuming I've got all the necessary equipment."

"Can you use some of your spare telephone modules?" Jonny suggested. "That should at least save you some assembly time."

"Provided I don't overlap one of the regular frequencies and trigger a squelch reaction from the phone computer, yes," she nodded. "Readjusting built-in freq settings may take just as long as building from scratch, but it's worth a try."

"Good. Get to work." MacDonald turned to Jonny. "Even if Challinor didn't set up a flag to let him know when anyone tries to call Capitalia, we should assume he'll be moving against us soon. We'll need to alert Mayor Tyler and organize whatever we can in the way of resistance."

"Which is basically you and me," Jonny said.

"Plus those half-dozen pellet guns Chrys mentioned last night." He saw Jonny's expression and shrugged uncomfortably. "I know— living clay pigeons. But you know as well as I do that our nanocomputers react more slowly when faced with two or more simultaneous threats. It might just give us the edge we'll need."

"Maybe." All the ghosts of Adirondack were rising behind Jonny's eyes. Civilians getting killed in cross-fires . . . "What would we be doing, trying to guard the road from Thanksgiving?"

MacDonald shook his head. "There's no way we can keep them out—they can abandon the road whenever they please if they don't mind having to kill a spine leopard or two on the way into town and don't need to bring in any heavy equipment. No, the best we can hope for is to hold this building until Chrys can finish a transmitter that'll bring help from Capitalia."

"Maybe we should try the innocent approach, too," Chrys suggested, looking up from the book of circuit diagrams she'd been paging through. "As long as they haven't actually invaded yet, why don't we have someone—Dad, for instance—try to drive through Thanksgiving to Sangraal and call Capitalia from there?"

"I doubt if Challinor's letting any traffic travel east from here," MacDonald said, "but it's worth a try. You think your dad would be willing?"

"Sure," she reached for her phone . . . hesitated. "Maybe I'd better just ask him to come over and then explain things once he gets here. Challinor may have put a monitor in the system."

The call took half a minute; Eldjarn asked no questions and said he'd be there right away. As Chrys broke the connection MacDonald started for the door. "I'm going to find the mayor," he said over his shoulder. "Jonny, you stay here—just in case. I'll be back as soon as I can."

Eldjarn had come and gone and Chrys had been working for an hour and a half when they heard the shot.

"What was *that?*" Chrys asked, looking up from her breadboard.

"Pellet gun," Jonny snapped, already moving toward the door. "You'd better stay here while I—"

"Forget it," she said, setting her solderer down carefully and racing after him. "Ken's out there!"

There was no second shot, but even so they had no problem locating the scene of the trouble. Already thirty or more people had gathered around the edge of the Square; more, like Jonny and Chrys, were hurrying in that direction. Off to the side, at one corner of the building housing the mayor's office, lay a crumpled figure. Kneeling over him was MacDonald.

"Halt!" an authoritative voice barked, as Jonny and Chrys pushed through the clump of spectators and headed for MacDonald. "Stay away from him."

Jonny glanced at the speaker without slowing. "The hell with you, L'est," he said. "The man's hurt!"

The laser blast Jonny had half expected to take in the back didn't come, and they reached MacDonald without further incident. "What can we do?" he asked as they dropped to their knees beside him. The other Cobra, Jonny saw now, was pumping rhythmically on the injured man's sternum with the heel of his hand.

"Ventilate him," MacDonald snapped; but Chrys had anticipated the order and was already beginning mouth-to-mouth. Jonny opened the charred shirt gingerly, wincing as he saw the location of the burn. "What happened?"

"Challinor got here about fifteen minutes ago and told Mayor Tyler they were taking over," MacDonald said tightly. "We weren't in any kind of defense posture yet, but Insley tried to take a shot at him anyway." He swore viciously. "Challinor got out of the way and behind cover. There wasn't any reason to shoot to kill—but L'est apparently felt we needed an object lesson."

Jonny looked over MacDonald's shoulder. L'est was still standing near the center of the Square, watching them. Glancing around, he noticed for the first time that four more Cobras were also present, spaced more or less evenly around that end of the Square:

the two men who besides L'est had been at Challinor's the night before, Challinor himself, and—"Sandy Taber's joined them," he said.

MacDonald grunted. "Chrys?" he asked

She moved her face away from Insley's and shook her head. "There's no pulse in the carotid artery," she said gently. "Hasn't been since we got here. I'm sorry, Ken."

For a long moment MacDonald looked at her, his hands still in position on the dead man's chest. Then, slowly, he stood up and turned back toward the Square, his face like a thundercloud sculpted from stone. "Keep her clear, Jonny," he murmured, and started walking toward L'est.

The action was so casual that he was four steps away before Jonny understood exactly what the Cobra was planning. Simultaneously, a hissing intake of air behind him told him Chrys also had suddenly realized what was going to happen. "Ken!" she blurted, leaping to her feet.

Jonny was faster, standing up and grabbing her in an unbreakable grip before she could get past him. "Stay here," he whispered urgently into her ear. "You can't do anything for him out there."

"Jonny, you have to stop him!" she moaned as she struggled against him. "They'll kill him!"

For Jonny, it was the hardest decision he'd ever made in his life. Every instinct screamed at him to step into the Square and begin shooting, to try and knock out one or more of the Cobras waiting silently in their circle. To him it was obvious that Insley's death had been a deliberate effort on L'est's part to provoke precisely this reaction; to goad MacDonald into a confrontation where all the numerical and tactical advantages were theirs. But equally obvious was the fact that there was nothing he could do to change the coming battle's outcome. At five-to-two odds he and MacDonald together would die just as surely as MacDonald alone . . . and with both of their Cobra defenders gone, the people of Ariel would have no way at all to fight back against Challinor's fledgling warlords. Even more than it had been the previous night, it was clear where his duty lay.

And so he clung tightly to Chrys and watched as they killed his friend.

It was a short battle. Even burning with rage, MacDonald had enough sense not to simply come to a halt and try to gun L'est down. Halfway through one of his strides he abruptly let his right leg collapse beneath him, dropping straight down onto the ground.

Simultaneously, his arms snapped up, fingertip lasers sending fire
to both sides. Patrusky and Szintra, at the receiving ends of the
two blasts, reacted instantly, twisting aside as their own nanocomputers responded with return fire. An instant later there were
twin howls of pain as the renegade Cobras' shots crossed the Square
and hit each other . . . and from his prone position on the ground,
MacDonald brought his left leg to bear on L'est.

He never got a chance to fire. With his own lightning reflexes
and servo-augmented muscles, L'est leaped up in a six-meter-high
arc that took him almost directly over his opponent. MacDonald
moved with desperate speed to get his hands up . . . but L'est's leg
got to firing position first.

The square lit up for an instant, and it was all over.

Beside him, Jonny felt the tension drain out of Chrys's body.
For a moment he thought she would either faint or become
hysterical . . . but when she spoke her voice was quiet and firm.
"Let me go to him, Jonny. Please."

He hesitated, knowing what it would look like. "It'll be pretty
bad—"

"Please."

They went together, Jonny with his arm still around her.

It was, indeed, pretty bad. L'est's antiarmor blast had caught
MacDonald high in the chest, destroying his heart and probably
a good percentage of his lung tissue. His arms lay limply on the
ground, indicating that the connections between nanocomputer
and arm servos had also been destroyed, denying the Cobra even
the satisfaction of one last dying shot.

"Such a terrible waste."

Jonny turned slowly, disengaging his arm from Chrys's shoulders and taking a half step away from her. "Yes, it is, isn't it,
Challinor?" he said to the man standing before him, a white-
hot anger beginning to burn through his mind. "A shame he
didn't try for you and your chief butcher instead of your two
dupes."

"He attacked first. You saw that—you all saw that," Challinor
added, raising his voice for the benefit of the stunned crowd. "Cee-
three L'est was protecting you, as is his duty."

All the possible responses collided deep in Jonny's throat; what
came out was an animalistic growl. Challinor regarded him
thoughtfully. "I'm sorry about your friend—truly I am," he said
quietly. "But we can't allow opposition to our plan. We're going
to remake Aventine, Moreau; and the faster and stronger our first

stroke, the more likely the governor-general will capitulate without unnecessary bloodshed."

Taber came up to Challinor's side. "Szintra is dead," he reported, avoiding Jonny's eyes. "Patrusky's going to be out of action for a few days, but none of his burns are really dangerous."

Challinor nodded. "I underestimated him rather badly," he mused. "I thought he was too angry to be thinking tactically. A dangerous man—I wish he'd been on our side."

"I'm going to kill you, Challinor," Jonny ground out. "You set Ken up to be killed, and you're going to die for that."

Challinor didn't move, but his gaze tightened slightly. "You're welcome to try," he said softly. "But you can't stop us. L'est will carry on in my place if I die; would you rather he be in charge? And don't expect you'll get all of us. MacDonald was lucky to do as much damage as he did."

Jonny didn't reply. Like a surfer on a wave, his tactical sense was riding the crest of his rage, calculating odds and possibilities with abnormal speed and clarity. Challinor stood before him, Taber slightly to his left, L'est somewhere behind him. An imperceptible bending of the knees could let him jump high enough to deliver lethal head kicks to the two in front of him, especially if the attack were preceded by a numbing blast from his sonic. L'est was far out of the sonic's outdoor range, but if he was watching the crowd for signs of hostility Jonny might be able to get in the first shot there, too—

"No!" Chrys's unexpected grip on his arm froze his thoughts in mid-stride. "Don't do it, Jonny. I've lost Ken already—I don't want to lose you, too."

Jonny closed his eyes and took a deep, ragged breath. *My duty to Ariel does not include throwing my life away in anger,* he thought at the white heat within him . . . and slowly the bonfire cooled to more controllable embers.

He opened his eyes. Challinor and Taber were watching him tensely. "Dr. Eldjarn had to go to Sangraal this morning," he told Challinor evenly. "You'll need to release our phone system so that we can call him back."

The two renegade Cobras relaxed fractionally. "No need," Challinor said. "He'll be back at home in a few minutes, if he's not there already. Our roadblock stopped him on the way out of Thanksgiving, of course. You really shouldn't have tried to get a message out like that—you left us no choice but to move in."

There was nothing to say to that. Taking Chrys's arm, Jonny led her away.

"His great-grandfather was the last of six MacDonald generations to hold commissions in the Fifty-First Highland Division on Earth—did you know that?"

Jonny nodded silently. Chrys had been curled up on the couch, talking almost nonstop about MacDonald, since their arrival back at her home several hours previously. At first Jonny had been worried, wondering whether she was retreating into some sort of personal fantasy world. But it soon became apparent that it was simply her way of saying good-bye.

So he sat quietly in his chair, making verbal responses where necessary, and watched as she purged herself of her grief.

The afternoon was nearly gone before she finally fell silent, and for a long time afterwards they sat together in the stillness, looking out the window at the lengthening shadows. What Chrys's thoughts were during that time Jonny never found out; but his own were a slowly flowing river of bitterness and unreasoning guilt. Over and over the whole scene replayed itself in his mind, nagging at him with unanswered questions. Had MacDonald really been crazy with rage, or thinking perfectly clearly? Had he seen the opportunity to take Szintra and Patrusky out simultaneously and acted accordingly? Had he expected Jonny to back him up in his play? *Could* the two of them actually have defeated Challinor's group?

The sound of the front door broke the cycle of recrimination and guilt. "Dad?" Chrys called.

"Yes." Eldjarn came in and sat down next to his daughter. He looked tired. "How are you doing?"

"I'm all right. What's happening in town?"

"Not much." Eldjarn rubbed his eyes. "Mayor Tyler has basically promised Challinor none of us will make trouble. I don't know, though—I've heard a lot of rumblings to the effect that someone ought to do something."

"That someone being me," Jonny said. "I gather they think I'm afraid to act?"

Eldjarn looked up at him, shrugged uncomfortably. "No one blames you," he said.

"In other words, they do," Jonny said, a bit too harshly.

"Jonny—"

"It's all right, Chrys," Jonny told her. He could hardly blame the others; they didn't know why he'd held back. He wasn't even sure why himself, now. . . . "Orrin, how many men does Challinor have in Ariel? Any idea?"

"At least ten Cobras that we know of, and probably a dozen of those teen-aged arrogants manning roadblocks," Eldjar said.

Jonny nodded. Challinor had said he had twelve Cobras on his side. Add Taber and maybe a couple more, subtract Szintra, and it still looked like nearly all the rebels were now in Ariel. The conclusion was obvious. "They're not ready to move against the Mines yet. So unready that they'd rather try and box up a whole town than move up their timetable. Any guesses as to why?"

For a moment the room was silent. "The miners usually work a two-week shift and then have a week off in Weald, don't they?" Chrys asked. "Maybe Challinor wants to move in during the shift change."

"That sounds reasonable," Jonny agreed. "Depending on how the routine goes, Challinor would hit the mines with either a single shift there or else all three of them. If the former, he has an easier takeover; if the latter, he gets extra hostages, so it makes sense either way." He glanced at his watch. "Three days to go, if they're on a rational system up there. Should be enough time."

"For what?" Chrys asked suspiciously.

"For me to go upriver to the mines and blow the whistle, of course—and I'd better get started right away." He stood up.

"Hold it, Jonny; this is crazy," Eldjarn said. "In the first place, there are forty kilometers of extremely hostile forest between us and them. In the second place, you'd be missed long before you could get there."

Slowly, Jonny sat back down. "I hadn't thought of that last," he admitted. "You really think Challinor will keep such close track of me?"

Eldjarn shrugged. "Despite your . . . Um . . . inactivity this morning, you're still the only person in town who can be a threat to him. Your disappearance would certainly be discovered by morning, and I hate to think what desperate steps he might consider it necessary to take. It's a good idea, but someone else is going to have to do it. Me, for instance."

"You?" Chrys looked startled. "That's ridiculous—suicidal, too. Without weapons and with the spine leopards on the move you wouldn't have a chance."

"I have to try," her father told her. "A boat would protect me from all but the most determined spine leopards. And there is a weapon still in town that I can take."

"What—Seth Ramorra's machete?" she scoffed.

"No." Eldjarn paused, and Jonny saw a muscle twitch in his cheek. "Ken's antiarmor laser."

Chrys's jaw dropped. "You mean the one in—Dad! You're not serious!"

"I am." He looked at Jonny. "Is it possible to remove the laser without amputating the leg? That would be too obvious for Challinor to miss."

"It was done once before, during our brief foray into civilian life," Jonny said mechanically. All of MacDonald's Cobra gear available—and he'd never once thought about using it. "Have you talked to Father Vitkauskas about the funeral arrangements yet?"

Eldjarn nodded. "It'll be a combined service, for both Ken and Ra Insley, tomorrow at nine in the Square. Most of the town is going to come, I think—and in a crowd that size, Challinor would never realize I was missing."

Jonny stood up. "Then we've got to get that laser out now. Ken's body's back there, isn't it? Good; let's go."

As in most frontier towns on Aventine, Eldjarn's job as Ariel's doctor also required him to act as undertaker when necessary, and the modest office/surgery attached to the house included a small room in the rear for preparation of the dead for burial. Leaving Chrys to stand guard in the office, Jonny and Eldjarn went back there.

Laid out on a table, MacDonald's body didn't look any better than it had sprawled in the street, but at least the odor of burned flesh was gone, either dissipated or artificially neutralized. Jonny looked at the chest wound only once, then turned away, concentrating deliberately on the leg. "The laser lies right here, beneath most of the calf muscle," he told Eldjarn, tracing the position lightly on MacDonald's leg. "There's probably no scar—I haven't got one— but the last time they took it out, the incision line was about here." He indicated it.

Eldjarn nodded. "I see how they inserted it now. All right; I'll get an instrument tray and we'll get started."

The faint sound of footsteps was their only warning. Jonny looked over his shoulder just in time to see the door swing open as L'est and Taber strode into the room, a white-faced Chrys trailing behind them.

"Good evening, Doctor Eldjarn; Moreau," L'est said, giving the room a quick once-over. "I trust we're not interrupting anything?"

"We're preparing Mr. MacDonald's body," Eldjarn said shortly. "What do you want?"

"Oh, just a little insurance against heroics." L'est glanced over Eldjarn's shoulder. "It occurred to me that perhaps we ought to remove our late compatriot's weapons before someone else took it into his head to do so. If you'll just step aside, this will only take a minute."

Eldjarn didn't move. "No," he said, his tone allowing no argument. "I'm not going to permit you to mutilate the dead."

"You don't have any choice. Move aside."

Eldjarn snorted. "I realize you're new to this warlord business, but if you think you can kill or imprison a town's only doctor and then expect to get even grudging cooperation from the rest of the populace you're in for a very rude shock."

For the first time L'est's confidence seemed to waver. "Look, Doctor—"

"Doctor, would *you* remove the lasers for us?" Taber put in suddenly. "You're a surgeon—you could do it without leaving any marks."

Eldjarn hesitated. "Jonny?" he asked.

Jonny shrugged, trying to hide his disappointment at L'est's rotten sense of timing. "Either you do it or L'est will. I'd rather you did, personally." He impaled L'est with his eyes. "But Orrin's right: we'll have no mutilation. Specifically, we're not going to let you cut off his fingers."

"But the lasers—" L'est began.

"No buts. His hands are going to be in plain sight in the casket."

Taber nudged L'est. "As long as we can confirm the fingertip lasers are still there in the morning, that should do," he murmured. "You can always take them and the power supply out before the actual burial, if you really think it's necessary."

Slowly, L'est nodded. "All right. But if those fingers are missing in the morning, we'll hold you responsible, Doctor."

"I understand. Jonny, perhaps you and Chrys would go over to Ken's house and bring me his Cobra dress uniform?"

Jonny nodded. Bad enough that Chrys had had to stand there and listen while MacDonald's body was discussed like a military bargaining chip; there was no need for her to watch as it was cut up as well. "Sure. I think both of us could use a walk. Come on, Chrys."

"Just be sure and stay where you're supposed to," L'est warned.

"The roads out of town are closed—and there are Cobras on each barricade."

Jonny didn't bother to reply. Brushing past them, he took Chrys's arm and left.

MacDonald's house wasn't too far away, but Jonny was in no particular hurry, and the house held a lot of memories for both of them to linger over. By the time they emerged with the carefully folded uniform, it was dark enough for the brightest stars to be visible. "Let's walk for a while," he suggested as Chrys turned in the direction of home.

"That's not necessary," she said tiredly. "Dad will be finished by now."

"But it's such a nice night," he said, steering her gently but firmly toward the center of town.

She resisted only a moment before falling into step beside him. "You have an idea?" she whispered.

Jonny nodded. "I think so. You have the key to your office with you?"

"Yes . . . but I hadn't gotten very far on my tight-beam transmitter."

"That's okay. Do you have any of those tiny electrical gadgets you can install in a vehicle's control circuits that let you run it by remote control?"

"Radio microrelays? Sure. The miners at Kerseage use them all the time for boring machines and slave-controlled ore barges going downriver—" She broke off. "A boat going upriver? With a message in it?"

"Keep your voice down—the guy following us might hear you."

He doubted it, actually; he'd already confirmed that the tail was one of Challinor's teen-agers, who was much too far back to hear anything except a loud scream. But he wasn't at all sure how Chrys was going to react to the plan that was slowly gelling in the back of his mind and wanted to put that explanation off as long as possible.

They were almost to the edge of the Square and within sight of Chrys's shop when she suddenly tugged on his arm. "There's someone standing at the door!" she hissed.

Jonny nudged his vision enhancers up. "It's Almo Pyre," he identified the guard. "With a pellet gun. Challinor's probably worried about you or Nedt putting together something to ungimmick the phone system." Though the fact that Challinor had apparently deployed the bulk of his forces with an eye to keeping anyone from slipping out of town showed how small a threat he considered Chrys's equipment to be. "This shouldn't be too hard."

"What about the tail?" Chrys asked anxiously. "And you're not going to hurt Almo, are you? He's just a boy."

"Who's old enough to face the consequences of his choices," Jonny pointed out. "Oh, don't worry—I like the kid, too. As for the tail, I think a hard right turn around the drugstore here and a little brisk walking will lose him without tipping him off that we were on to him. Then we'll circle around and come up on your shop from behind. Once we move there'll be no talking, so I need some information right now. . . ."

As far as Jonny could tell, the trick worked, and they reached Chrys's building with Challinor's spy nowhere in sight. The rear of the shop, with no door that required guarding, was deserted. Stepping directly underneath the second-floor window Chrys pointed out, Jonny took one final look around him and jumped. His leg servos were more than equal to the task, landing him on the narrow window ledge in a crouched position, knees spread to the sides to avoid breaking the glass and hands finding good purchase on the wooden frame. The window, open a few centimeters for ventilation, slid all the way up with only token resistance. Seconds later, Jonny was inside.

The search was short—all the items he sought were right where Chrys had said they were—and within two minutes he was back on the ledge, closing the window behind him. Seconds after that he was walking away from the building as nonchalantly as possible. Chrys, at his side, was breathing harder than he was.

"No problem," he assured her, answering her unasked question. "No one'll ever know I was there. Let's get back home—you and your father have a lot of work yet to do tonight."

L'est and Taber had long since left by the time they reached the Eldjarn home, but Jonny knew better than to stay inside too long. Fortunately, explaining what he wanted them to do took less than five minutes. Neither Chrys nor her father was especially happy with the plan, but with obvious reluctance they agreed.

He left immediately afterwards, and as he walked down the street toward his own house, his peripheral vision caught a glimpse of a shadow detaching itself from a bush near the Eldjarn home and falling into step behind him, somewhat closer than before.

He sighed, and for the first time since MacDonald's death a tight smile flickered across his face. So the gamble had worked: the tail was back on the job, and the absence of nervous Cobras scouring the area indicated the boy had decided that losing his quarry for a few minutes wasn't worth reporting. An understandable reaction, Jonny thought, given the earlier demonstration of Cobra killing power. And as far as he was concerned, the kid was welcome to watch him the rest of the night.

He just hoped Challinor hadn't thought to have someone watch the Eldjarns, too.

The morning dawned crisp and clear, with only a few scaly cirrus clouds to mar the deep blue sky. To Jonny it seemed wrong, somehow, that Aventine's sky should appear so cheerful on the day of MacDonald's funeral and after Jonny's own restless, nightmare-filled sleep. Still, good weather should mean a large turnout at the funeral, and that should draw a lot of Challinor's Cobras. Perhaps Aventine was on his side after all.

Feeling a bit more encouraged, he ate a good breakfast, showered and shaved, and at eight-thirty emerged from his house in full Cobra dress uniform.

L'est and Taber, looking as tired as he felt, were waiting for him. "Morning, Moreau," L'est said, looking him up and down. "Neatest I've seen you since the day of the landing."

"You're too kind," Jonny said shortly. "Now if you don't mind, I have a funeral to attend. I'm sure you have somewhere you have to be, too." He stepped between them and stalked down the street.

They fell into step on either side and a pace behind him. "There are about a hundred places I'd rather be going," L'est said, "and about a thousand people whose company I'd prefer. But Tors seems to think you need someone to hold your leash."

Jonny snorted. "Challinor always did have a way with words. What the hell are you afraid of—that I'll start a riot or something at Ken's funeral?"

"There's no point in taking chances," Taber said dully. "So far Ariel's been peaceful, but mass meetings are always potentially explosive. A show of force is the best way to make sure no one gets crazy ideas."

Jonny glanced back at him. "You don't sound thoroughly convinced anymore," he suggested. "Challinor's high-handed methods getting to you?"

Taber was silent for several steps. "I liked MacDonald, too," he said finally. "But Challinor's right: the government here *isn't* working."

"There are ways to improve it that don't involve rebellion—"

"That's enough," L'est interrupted. "The time for talking politics is over."

Jonny clamped his jaw tightly, but he really hadn't expected any other reaction. L'est wasn't just going to stand quietly and let him sprinkle extra water on the seeds of uncertainty that Taber was beginning to show. But maybe—just maybe—there was enough there already for them to sprout on their own. Whether they would do so in time was another question entirely.

Not since the last Landing Day festival had Jonny seen the Square so crowded. In the center, resting on two waist-high stands, were the open coffins; from the edge of the Square, MacDonald's face and folded hands were just visible. Between the coffins, sitting on the only chair in sight, was Father Vitkauskas. Without pausing, Jonny turned to his left, circling the crowd until he was standing in line with the foot of MacDonald's coffin. Looking around, he spotted at least six more of Challinor's Cobras grouped loosely together on the fringes of the crowd near him, their positions obviously having been chosen to take advantage of the slight rise there that would permit a better view of the area. Apparently Challinor really *was* worried about trouble with the crowd.

"Good morning, Moreau," a voice murmured behind him. Turning, Jonny saw Challinor step up next to L'est. "A good turnout, wouldn't you say?"

"Very good," Jonny said coldly. "Ken was a very popular person. Killing him was probably one of your biggest mistakes."

Challinor's gaze flicked over the crowd before returning to Jonny. "I trust you won't be foolish enough to try and take advantage of that," he said, with the faintest edge to his voice. "L'est, Taber, and I will be standing behind you the whole time, and if you even look like you're about to make trouble, it'll be the last thing you ever do. *And* probably the last some of these other people do, too." He glanced significantly at the Cobras standing to either side.

"Don't worry," Jonny growled. "I have no intention of starting anything."

Abruptly, the low murmur of conversation in the Square faded into silence. Turning back, Jonny saw Father Vitkauskas had risen to his feet.

And the funeral began.

Jonny remembered afterwards very little of what was said that morning. He sang mechanically with the other people when necessary, and bowed his head at the proper times . . . but mostly his attention was on the crowd, picking out those people he knew best and trying to gauge their mood. Chrys and her father he found easily, standing in the front row a quarter of the way around the circle from him. Mayor Tyler was near them, looking grimly dignified, a man determined not to show his shock at the sudden inverting of his world. A lot of the people were wearing that same expression, Jonny noted, and he could hardly blame them. The Cobras, their helpers and protectors, had seemingly turned against them, and no one was quite sure how to react. Some showed more uncertainty than others; Jonny noticed Almo Pyre shifting uneasily from foot to foot. Like Taber, the teen-ager seemed to be having second thoughts about the side he'd chosen.

A sudden rustle of cloth brought Jonny's attention back to the priest. The service was drawing to a close, he saw, and the crowd was kneeling for the final prayer. Hastily, Jonny dropped to his knees, glancing around as he did so. Challinor's Cobras were still on their feet, whatever feelings of respect they might have had overridden by the tactical necessity of keeping close watch on the crowd. Out of the corner of his eye he saw Almo hesitate and then, with a glance in Jonny's direction, kneel with the rest of the people around him. Between the coffin stands Father Vitkauskas had himself knelt . . . and as he began the requiescat, Jonny's eyes sought Chrys, saw her hand slip under the hem of her long skirt to the device strapped to her leg. . . .

And MacDonald sat up in his coffin.

Behind Jonny someone gasped—but that was all the reaction anyone had time for. MacDonald's hands unfolded themselves, settling smoothly down into what looked like the ready position for a double handshake . . . and the lasers in his little fingers abruptly spat flame.

Taber, standing directly in the line of fire, crumpled without a sound. Challinor and L'est, their programmed reflexes finally breaking them free of their astonished paralysis, dodged to either side, raising their own lasers to counterattack. But MacDonald's forearms were already swinging rapidly to his sides, sweeping twin fans of death over the heads of the kneeling crowd. L'est made a choking sound as the beam caught him across the chest and he fell, lasers still firing uselessly at the man he'd already killed once. Challinor broke off his own attack barely in time to duck down— and fell all the way to the ground as Jonny's antiarmor laser flashed. The rest of the Cobras around the Square, their reflexes and targeting locks already keyed to the futile task of avoiding

MacDonald's attack, reacted far too slowly to Jonny's entry into the battle; many, in fact, probably never realized anyone else was shooting at them until it was too late. Between MacDonald's wild spray and Jonny's more accurate sniping, they made a clean sweep.

It was over before anyone in the crowd thought to scream.

"We're not going to be able to keep this secret, you know," Mayor Tyler said, shaking his head. His hands were shaking, too. "If nothing else, we—and about a quarter of the towns in Caravel District, for that matter—are going to have to ask the governor-general for new Cobras."

"That's okay," Jonny said, wincing slightly as Eldjarn applied salve to his shoulder, where a near miss had burned him. "No one's going to try and avenge Challinor or pick up where he left off, if that's what you're worried about. All the fence-straddlers he said he had standing by will be moving like crazy to make sure they come down on the right side. The warlord movement is dead." He cocked an eye at the mayor. "You just make sure your report shows that only a very small minority was involved in the plot. We can't have people getting paranoid about us—there's still too much work on Aventine that only Cobras can do."

Tyler nodded and moved toward the door to his private office. "Yeah. I just hope Zhu doesn't take the whole thing wrong. I'd hate for Ariel to get stuck with the blame for Challinor's ambition."

The door closed behind him, and Chrys stood up. "I suppose I'd better go, too—I've got to get busy fixing the phone system."

"Chrys—" Jonny hesitated. "I'm sorry that had to be done at Ken's funeral, and that you had to . . . to see all of that . . ."

She smiled wanly. "That extra damage?" She shook her head. "Ken was long gone from that body, Jonny. He couldn't feel those lasers. *You* were the one I was worried about—I was scared to death you'd be killed, too."

Jonny shook his head. "There wasn't really much danger of that," he assured her. "You, Orrin, and Father Vitkauskas set things up perfectly for me. I just hope Ken's reputation doesn't . . . I don't know."

"It already has," she sighed. "The rumors are already starting to travel out there, to the effect that Ken was faking death so that he could get in one last shot."

Jonny grimaced. Yes, that *would* be what they thought—and within a few days and a hundred kilometers that story would probably be bent completely past recognition. The Avenging Cobra, perhaps, who'd returned from the dead to defend his people from oppression? "A legend like that might not be all bad, though—it ought to at least slow down future Challinors," he murmured, thinking out loud. "I don't think that's something Ken would dislike having attached to his name."

Chrys shook her head. "Maybe. I can't think that far in the future right now."

"You sure you really feel like working?" he asked, studying her strained face. "Nedt could start the phone repairs alone."

"I'm all right." She reached for Jonny's hand, squeezed it briefly. "I'll see you later, Jonny—and thank you."

She left, and Jonny sighed. "The real thanks goes to you two," he told Eldjarn. The reaction was beginning to hit him, and he suddenly felt very tired. "I don't think I could have faced having to wire all those sequential relays to Ken's servos, even if I'd known how to do it. It must have been pretty hard on Chrys, especially."

"We all did what we had to," Eldjarn said obliquely. "You know, though, that it's not over yet—not by a long shot. Zhu's going to react to this, all right. If he's smart, part of his reaction will be to start listening to what Cobras have to say on governmental policies and procedures. You'll need to take advantage of the opportunity to offer some good, concrete suggestions."

Jonny shrugged wearily. "I'm like Chrys: I really can't think that far ahead right now."

Eldjarn shook his head. "Chrys can get away with that excuse; you can't. As long as there are Cobras on Aventine, the threat of something like this happening again will always be with us. We have to act *now* to make sure that possibility stays small."

"Oh, come on, Orrin—you're talking politics now, and that's light-years out of my experience. I wouldn't even know where to start."

"You start by making the Cobras feel that an attack on the government is an attack on them personally," Eldjarn said. "Ken fought Challinor because the rebellion was an attack on his family pride; you probably had similar reasons." He hesitated. "For most of you, I suspect, we'll have to appeal to enlightened self-interest . . . once your self-interest has been properly linked with the government's."

Jonny frowned as understanding began to come. "You're suggesting we be brought directly into the government somehow?"

"I think it's inevitable," Eldjarn said; and though his voice was firm, his restless hands indicated his uneasiness. "You Cobras have a lot more of the power on this world than the system has taken into account, and one way or another the system has to adjust to reflect that reality. We either give it to you in a controlled, orderly way or risk the chaos of Challinor's method. Like it or not, Jonny, you're an important political force now—and your first political responsibility will be to make sure Zhu understands that."

For just a second Jonny grimaced at the irony. Perhaps, in a small and unexpected way, Challinor had won after all. "Yes," he sighed. "I guess I'll have to."

Interlude

To the trained and observant eye, the signs were all there.

They weren't obvious, of course. An unnecessary phrase in an official Troft message to the Committee, certain small shiftings of both merchant and perimeter guard star ships, comments coming from the Minthisti at obvious Troft prodding—small things, each in itself completely meaningless. But taken as a group, all the tiny pieces pointed unidirectionally to the same conclusion.

After fourteen years of allowing Dominion ships to pass freely through their territory, the Trofts were getting tired of it.

Vanis D'arl scowled blackly as he stared at the nighttime view of Dome visible through his office window. It wasn't exactly a startling development—half the Committee was frankly surprised the Corridor had remained open as long as it had. The Star Force, in fact, had been updating its contingency plans for eleven years now . . . and unless something was done, it looked like they'd get the chance to test its strategies within the year.

It went without saying that, win or lose, one of the first casualties of a new war would be Aventine and its own two fledgling colonies . . . precisely the worlds the war would theoretically be fought to defend. Which, in D'arl's opinion, made the looming conflict an exercise in near-perfect futility.

But what were the alternatives? The Committee, which had had to be virtually dragged by the nose to accept the colony plan in the first place, had in recent years done a complete turnaround as rare minerals and new pharmaceuticals began flowing the other way down the Corridor. With military ships barred by treaty from entering Troft territory, the Dominion had no way to defend Aventine except by the threat of warfare if the colony was attacked—a threat which had been delivered both publicly and privately over the years.

And if there was one universal rule of politics, it was that a threat that wasn't followed through on would always cost more in the long run.

Reaching over, D'arl touched his intercom. "Yes, Committé?" the young man looked up at him from the screen.

"Have you cross-correlated the Aventine botanical data yet?"

"Yes, sir," Jame Moreau nodded. "It's on your desk, marked 'Aventine Bot/Phys III.' I put it in there while you were at your General Policy meeting."

"Thank you." D'arl glanced at his watch. "You might as well go on home, Moreau; the night staff can help me if I need anything more."

"Yes, sir. Let me mention first that there's one item on that magcard I think might be worth following up, if I understand what you're looking for. It's marked with a double star."

"Thank you," D'arl repeated, and broke the connection. *If you understood what I was looking for?* he thought wryly at the blank screen. *If I understood what I was looking for I'd probably have found it years ago.* The self-sufficiency studies, the deterrent proposal—it all worked, it all made sense, and D'arl was ready at any time to try implementing it. But *something* was missing; a political keystone to insure he could sell the package both here and on Aventine. It *had* to exist . . . but at this point D'arl had no idea what it might be.

Sifting through the ordered mess on his desk, he located Moreau's magcard and slid it into his comboard, keying for the double star. It turned out to be an analysis of some reedy plant called blussa that apparently thrived in damp lowland regions on Aventine, busily concentrating one of the strategic metals on D'arl's self-sufficiency list. Growth cycle, ecological niche, biochemistry—he skimmed the overview Moreau had copied directly from the master files.

—biochemical response to climatological changes.

He slowed down and read carefully. Backed up and read it again. Called up the last climatological data Aventine had sent, read those, and contacted the dome's night computer staff for a search/simulation with the colony's fauna records. The chief programmer listened carefully, informed D'arl the task would take several hours to complete, and signed off.

And at that point there was nothing for the Committé to do

but wait. If he had indeed found his elusive keystone . . . but even then there would be a long way to go, on both of the affected worlds. And on top of that, the scheme might not work even if he succeeded completely in implementing it.

In his early days on the Committee, he would probably have felt the uncertainties as a crushing weight around his shoulders. Now, after more than a decade, the emotional reaction was more reasonable. He would do what he could, to the best of his ability, and leave the rest to the universe.

And in this instance, the universe was kind. Six hours later, when he awoke from a short night's sleep, the results of the simulation were waiting.

Positive.

He read the entire report through carefully. Yes, the keystone was there. Unexpected; unlooked for, really—but there . . . and now it was time to see if the other pieces he'd assembled would indeed fit together. And if so—

If so, the Dominion was about to see just how the Trofts reacted to a change in the game's rules.

Politician: *2421*

Jonny shook his head. "I'm sorry, Tam, but you'll just have to make do without me. I'm starting my vacation in exactly—" he consulted his watch "—four minutes."

Peering out through the phone's screen, Tamis Dyon's face had already finished the plunge from excitement to shock and was beginning to edge back toward disbelief. "You're *what?* Jonny, that's a *Dominion Committé* out there!"

"I heard you. So what does Zhu want to do, hold a full military inspection of the planet? If the guy wanted pomp, he should've given us more than six hours' notice he was coming."

"Jonny, I realize you and I are new to this politics business, but don't you think it'll be expected that we'll at least be on hand in Capitalia to greet the Committé's ship?"

Jonny shrugged, suppressing a smile. Watching Dyon try to operate in "patient" mode was always an amusing sight. "I doubt seriously that *all* the syndics are going to make it in," he pointed out. "And if it's not going to be unanimous, what difference does one more make?"

"What makes the difference," Dyon ground out, "is that *we* have the honor of the Cobras to uphold."

"So *you* uphold our honor. Seriously, Tam, what's the big deal whether one, both, or neither of us shows up? Unless Zhu's planning a laser light show or something."

Dyon snorted, but even he had to crack a smile at the image of the dignified governor-general pulling a stunt like that. "He's going to be furious, you know, if you're not there. What's so important about this vacation, anyway? Chrys threatening to leave you if you don't take some time off?"

"Don't be absurd," Jonny snorted in turn. Though there *had* been small problems in that area in the past. . . . "In point of fact, the ship that's making orbit just about now has someone more important than a mere Committé aboard: my sister Gwen. I want to give her a tour of the bright lights and then help her settle in with the Molada Mountain geological group in Paleen."

Dyon made a face. "Dawa District, right? Grumf. You're right; she *does* deserve *something* approaching civilization before disappearing into the cultural depths." He exhaled loudly, shaking his head. "You win. Get out of there and forget your phone. You've got half an hour's head start before I notify Zhu's office that you're gone."

"Thanks—I owe you one. And tell Zhu to relax—I'll be back in a week, and the Committé's hardly likely to be gone by then. He'll have plenty of formal dinners left to inflict on me."

"I'll quote you exactly. So long." Dyon disappeared from the screen.

Grinning, Jonny got to his feet, fingering the portable field phone in his belt. He *could* leave it behind, as Dyon had suggested . . . but even though he was no longer on round-the-clock call, he *was* still a Cobra. He compromised, switching the phone off but leaving it in his belt, and left his office.

Chrys was already in the anteroom, chatting with Jonny's assistant. "All set?" she asked as he entered.

"All set," he nodded. "I'm officially off-duty, leaving the fate of Caravel District in Theron's capable hands."

Theron Yutu grinned. "With any luck the district'll still be here when you come back, Syndic," he said. "How off-duty are you?"

"I'm taking my phone, but it's going to be off," Jonny told him. "You reveal the override code to anyone short of a genuine emergency and I'll take you to Dawa District and let the gantuas walk on you."

"A fate worse than debt," Yutu agreed solemnly. "Have a good time, sir; Mrs. Moreau."

Chrys had left the car poised for a quick getaway, and a minute later they were driving through the moderate Rankin traffic, heading for the local aircar field. "Any problem with Corwin I should know about?" he asked Chrys.

She shook her head. "Tym and Sue said they can keep him overnight if we don't make it back by then. How about you? Any problems because of the other ship out there?"

He glanced at her. "You never cease to amaze me, Hon—I just heard about that a few minutes ago myself."

She smiled. "That *is* all I know, though—the bare fact of a second incoming ship was coming through on Theron's net as I got to the office. Is it bad news?"

"Not as far as I know. There's a member of the Central Committee aboard who I gather wants to tour the Dominion's colonies out here. I've included myself out of any ceremonies for this next week."

"I wonder if the Dominion's planning to cut our supply shipments," Chrys mused. "Or whether the Trofts are making trouble."

"If there's anything I need to know, Theron can find me," Jonny shrugged. "Until then, let's assume the visit is just political and act accordingly."

They reached the airfield a few minutes later, and a few minutes after that they were heading for Capitalia at a shade under Mach Two. There had been times—a lot of them, in fact—when Jonny had regretted accepting the position of syndic, of having exchanged the day-to-day problems of a single village for the executive headaches of an entire district. But having an aircar on permanent call was one of the spangles of the job that occasionally made it worthwhile.

Not having to risk his life fighting spine leopards and falx, of course, was another big plus.

The last of the star ship's passengers had been down for some time when Jonny and Chrys arrived at the starfield, but with processing and all the first of them were only then beginning to emerge from the entrypoint building. Taking up a position off to the side, they waited.

But not for long. Suddenly, Gwen Moreau was there . . . and Jonny, a corner of his mind still expecting the ten-year-old girl he'd left back on Horizon, nearly tripped over his tongue calling to her. "Gwen! Over here!"

"Jonny!" she smiled, bounding over with an echo of the high spirits he'd always associated with her. For an instant he was tempted to respond by tossing her into the air, as he'd always done back home. Fortunately, probably, he resisted the urge.

The introductions and greetings were a flurry of smiles, hugs, and general giddiness. Chrys and Gwen had known each other well enough through tapes back and forth that the awkwardness Jonny had half feared never materialized. Gwen asked about her nephew, was assured he was like any other two-year-old—except smarter, of course—and Jonny was just turning to lead the way out when she stopped him with a hand on his arm and a mischievous grin.

"Before we go, Jonny, I've got a little surprise for you," she said. "Someone I met on the ship who's going to be working in the same town I am." Her eyes flicked over his shoulder.

A ship-met fiancé? Jonny thought. He turned, expecting a stranger . . . and felt his mouth drop open. "Cally!"

Cally Halloran's grin was a thing of truly massive proportions. "Hi, Jonny. *Damn*, but it's good to see you."

"Same to you with spangles," Jonny grinned. "Chrys, this is Cally Halloran, one of my teammates in the Adirondack war. I thought you and Imel were planning to stay in the Army for the rest of your natural lives."

"Imel's still there," Halloran nodded, "but you clowns out here gave the brass too many ideas of what Cobras could be used for. I finally had one Iberiand forest-patrol mission too many and put in for a transfer here."

"If you're expecting palace guard duty work in Dawa District, you can forget it," Jonny warned. "Chances are you'll be doing jungle duty *and* heavy manual labor besides."

"Yeah, but here I'll at least be working more on my own, without some middle-level Army officer looking over my shoulder." He waved a hand skyward. "Or maybe even get to help open up a new world like you did."

"Palatine and Caelian?" Jonny shook his head in mild disgust. "You want Army thinking, there it is in spades. We've barely got a third of Aventine even surveyed, let alone settled, and they open up beachheads on two other worlds. Talk about straining resources and manpower—especially Cobra manpower—"

"Jonny," Chrys interrupted smoothly, "you promised you wouldn't plunge us into Aventine's politics for at least the first hour. Remember?"

They all laughed. Jonny had not, in fact, made any such promise, but the hint was well taken. "Chrys is right—I *do* tend to go overboard sometimes," he admitted, pointing them all toward the door. "If you're all adequately tired of standing around here, let's go get some dinner. Chrys and I don't get to Capitalia too often, but we know where the best restaurant is."

The meal was a resounding success, the food and atmosphere of the restaurant as good as Jonny had remembered. They spent some time catching up on Halloran's and the Moreau family's recent histories, the conversation then shifting to Aventine in general and Dawa District in particular. Jonny knew relatively little about the latter, Dawa being one of the most recently incorporated parts of the planet, and he was rather surprised to find that he and Chrys still knew far more than the supposedly up-to-date information the colonists had been given.

They were working on dessert and the Aventine version of cahve when Chrys casually mentioned the mysterious Dominion craft coming in fast on the colony ship's wake. "No mystery there," Halloran shook his head. "*I* heard about it back on Asgard; I assumed you'd been told, too. That's Committé Vanis D'arl and some sort of special Cobra project that the Army and Central Committee have cooked up."

"*D'arl?*" Gwen's eyes were wide. "Jonny—that's the Committé Jame's working for."

"You're right." The name hadn't immediately registered, but now he remembered. Jame had been with D'arl's staff for, what, twelve years now? "Any idea who D'arl brought with him, Cally?"

"Boy, you Moreaus really get around," Halloran said, shaking his head in amazement. "No, I don't know who else is aboard— I only know it involves Cobras because Mendro and Bai had Freyr Complex tied up in knots for a month while Committee people crawled all over the place."

"Doing what?"

"All I heard were rumors. But they had a lot of trucks moving in and out . . . and parking by the surgery wing."

"Sounds like they're updating the Cobra equipment," Jonny frowned. "Have the Trofts and Minthisti been behaving themselves?"

"Far as I know. Maybe the Dominion's thinking about really pushing the colonization effort out here and wants to have more Cobras available."

"With D'arl coming here for a final assessment?" Jonny suggested. "Could be."

"Ah-ah," Gwen put in warningly. "That's politics, you guys. Technical foul; Chrys gets a free change of topic."

They all smiled, and the conversation shifted to the sorts of geological and tectonic utilization work Gwen hoped to be doing on her new world. But for Jonny, the relaxed mood of a few minutes earlier proved impossible to totally recapture. Tors Challinor's attempted rebellion seven years ago hadn't been repeated, but Jonny had lived those years waiting for that other shoe to drop, knowing that if Aventine could survive another few decades, the Cobras would all be dead and the society could at last get back to normal. But if the Dominion was planning to send them a new batch . . .

But the evening, if no longer scintillating, nevertheless remained pleasant as Jonny and Chrys gave the others a brief tour of Capitalia's night life. It was odd, though perhaps inevitable, that Jonny found himself mentally comparing everything to their hazily remembered counterparts on Asgard and Horizon; but if Gwen and Halloran found it all quaint and primitive, they were far too polite to say so.

It was after midnight when they finally called it quits, and as there was no point in returning to Rankin at such an hour, they checked into one of Capitalia's small selection of hotels. Gwen and Halloran had disappeared to their rooms, and Jonny was just starting to undress when he noticed the red "message waiting" light on his phone was glowing. "Uh-oh," he muttered.

Chrys followed his gaze. "Ignore it," she advised. "At least until morning. Theron would've risked waking you up if it was urgent."

"Ye-e-e-s," Jonny agreed, almost unwillingly picking up the instrument. "But he wouldn't have bothered us at all if it wasn't at least important. Might as well get it over with."

The message, as he'd expected, was simply to phone his assistant whenever convenient. Jonny looked at his watch, shrugged, and made the call.

Yutu answered promptly, without any of the grogginess that would have indicated a sound sleep. "Sorry to bother you, Syndic," he apologized, "but something came in on the net a half hour ago that I thought you should know about. Late this afternoon a dead spine leopard was found in the plains a couple of kilometers west of Paleen in Dawa District. It had been mauled pretty badly . . . and apparently *not* by scavengers."

Jonny looked up to see Chrys's suddenly tense eyes, felt his own jaw tighten. The elusive predator that even spine leopards needed defenses against had finally made its long-overdue appearance. So to speak. . . . "Any sign of what had killed it?" he asked Yutu.

"There's nothing more yet than what I've told you, sir. The carcass has been taken to Niparin, where I gather they're going to bring some experts in to study it. I just thought you might want to issue some orders immediately."

"Yeah." Caravel District was getting more built up every day, but there were still vast tracts of forest area surrounding the towns . . . and if the new predator migrated like the spine leopards did, the region could have unwelcome company at any time. "Put all the Cobras on alert, and have them keep an eye out for any unusual tracks or signs if business takes them into the forest," he instructed Yutu. "Everyone else is to stay *out* of the forest, period, and farmers working near the edges are to keep their cabs sealed."

"Yes, sir; I'll have these on the public net in half an hour. Uh— Governor-General Zhu also called this evening. He wants all the syndics at a special meeting at the Dominion Building tomorrow morning at eleven."

Jonny snorted. "A ceremonial brunch for the visiting Committé, no doubt."

"I don't think so, actually," Yutu said. "Committé D'arl will be there, but it sounded a lot more important than that. The governor-general seemed preoccupied, for one thing. Anyway, I told him I'd try to get in touch with you, but I didn't promise anything."

"Thanks." Jonny glanced at Chrys, mindful of his promise of a vacation. But her eyes were worried, and she nodded fractionally. "All right, I'll try to show up. Start collecting everything that comes through on that dead spine leopard for me—we're going to want to ID its killer as fast as possible."

"Understood, sir."

"Thanks for calling. Good-night." Jonny broke the connection and again shut off the phone. Looking up at Chrys, he opened his mouth to apologize . . . but she got in the first word.

"Gwen and Cally are both going to Paleen," she said quietly. "If something that dangerous is in the vicinity . . ." She shuddered. "Should I go ahead and take them back to Rankin in the morning?"

Jonny sighed. "Yeah, probably. No telling how long that meeting will take. Though on second thought . . . if I was running Dawa District, I'd probably cancel Cally's orientation week and hustle him right down to Paleen for guard duty. Maybe you'd better just take Gwen and leave Cally here. If he gets his orders, I can run him down there and get a firsthand look at the spine leopard while I'm at it."

"And maybe join in the hunt?" She held up a hand against his protests. "No, I understand. I don't have to like your risking your life to know that you have to do it. Even middle-aged Cobras are safer out there than younger men."

"Thanks a raft," he snorted. "Thirty-nine is *hardly* middle-aged."

She smiled. "Why don't you quit protesting, then, and come to bed . . . and *show* me just how young you are."

Afterward, they lay side by side in the dark, and Jonny's thoughts drifted back to Adirondack. There, the people he cared for had always drawn back when they feared they might never see him again. Chrys's response to the same situation was far more pleasant . . . though the underlying reality wasn't any easier to face. Still, he'd faced danger a thousand times before. Even Chrys should know by now that he was too lucky to get himself killed.

But his dreams that night were frightening things, centering around a giant creature that walked in haze, killing spine leopards and Cobras and disappearing without a trace.

Seated beside Governor-General Zhu at the conference room table, Committé Vanis D'arl could at first glance have passed for any other Aventine citizen. Middle-aged and reasonably fit, his dark hair cut in a conservative pattern, he gave no immediate sense of his awesome power. But his name labeled his home planet as Asgard, and to Jonny's eyes there were disturbing similarities between him and the failed rebel Cobra Simmon L'est. There was a quiet hardness about his face, the feeling that he would stop at nothing to get his own way. And underlying it all was an odd sense of urgency.

Zhu's introduction was a subtle underscoring to the latter, lasting only a fraction of the time the occasion should have dictated. "Thank you, Governor-General Zhu," D'arl said, rising to his feet as Zhu reseated himself. His voice was heavy with the subtle accents of Asgard. "I would first of all like to congratulate you on behalf of the Central Committee on your truly outstanding accomplishment in the development of this new Dominion world. In barely fifteen years, you've achieved a solid foothold on Aventine and are even looking ahead to the future colonization of Caelian and Palatine. The natural resources for these endeavors are, of course, readily available, and it is obvious as well that you are not lacking in spirit. As the Committee has studied your progress, in fact, it has become apparent that the limiting factor in your expansion has been—and continues to be—the lack of Cobras to spearhead your efforts."

Jonny felt his breath catch. D'arl's eyes, sweeping the table, shifted to him, and for an instant the two men locked gazes. "Your reports," D'arl continued coolly, "have from almost the beginning contained requests for more Cobras, and the Committee has done its best to accommodate you. We've encouraged Cobra transfers to this colony, to the point where the Army has barely two companies left for general Dominion defense. Obviously, this drain cannot continue indefinitely; and the Committee has therefore come up with the following solution."

Here it comes, Jonny thought, his stomach tensing. *A steady stream of Cobras through the Corridor, maybe forever.*

But even he was unprepared for D'arl's next words. "Since it seems inefficient for the Dominion to equip and train Cobras only to send them here, we've decided to shift the entire operation to Aventine instead."

Jonny's jaw dropped. *No!* he shouted . . . though the word never made it past his frozen tongue. But D'arl nevertheless noticed, and his eyes were steady on Jonny's face as he continued. "Aboard my ship is all the necessary surgical and implant equipment, as well as specialists trained in its use. The procedure takes from two to six weeks, depending on how much discomfort you deem acceptable, and training by your own Cobras will probably take no more than four weeks more. This is far better than the seven to nine month response time for getting new Cobras from Asgard, and will in addition put the operation entirely under your control. I could continue . . . but I sense there is a comment waiting impatiently to be made, so I'd like to pause now for at least a brief discussion."

Jonny was on his feet almost before the last word was out of D'arl's mouth. "With all due respect and gratitude, Committé D'arl," he said carefully, "I feel that perpetuating the line of Cobras would be detrimental to the social and political development of Aventine."

D'arl's eyebrows rose politely. "How so, Syndic Moreau? It seems to me your government has adapted remarkably well to the presence of a disproportionate number of Cobras among its citizens. Your own position here would seem evidence of that."

"If you're referring to the Challinor rebellion, yes, we've managed to avoid a repeat of that," Jonny said. "But the cost has been an unnatural distortion of basic Dominion political theory."

"You speak, I presume, of the fact that at all levels of government Cobras have more than the single vote given to ordinary citizens." D'arl's face was expressionless, his voice giving no hint as to his opinion of that practice. "I believe a study of history will show, Syndic, that numerous adjustments of ideal theory have been made when circumstances required it."

Across the table, Brom Stiggur of Maro District rose slowly to his feet. "Perhaps then, Committé, a more concrete objection should be raised," he said. "You speak of perpetuating the Cobra presence on Aventine, and of putting the selection of Cobra candidates under our control. Under *whose* control, though, would it be? The governor-general's? A syndic majority's? Direct vote of the citizens? How do we guarantee, for obvious example, that this Cobra factory doesn't come under the influence of another Challinor?"

"You seem to have a pretty low opinion of the sort of man who'd volunteer to be a Cobra in the first place," Tamis Dyon said stiffly from a few seats down. "You'll notice that the psychological screening methods were perfectly successful with most of us—and as to Challinor, you might remember it was Syndic Moreau and his companions who defeated him, not official paranoia." He shifted his eyes to D'arl. "I, for one, would be delighted to have another dozen Cobras available to station in my outlying villages."

"You're oversolving the problem," Jonny spoke up as murmurs of both agreement and disagreement rippled across the table. "We simply don't *need* full-fledged Cobras for most of the work that's being done. Fitting the lasers Committé D'arl has brought into hand weapons would do perfectly well against falx or wheat snakes. Spine leopards are trickier, I'll admit, but they're a problem only on the very edges of human territory, and the Cobras we have now can control them well enough."

"And how about the spine leopard killers?" Jor Hemner spoke up quietly. "Can you handle *them*, as well?"

All eyes turned to him. "What are you talking about?" Zhu demanded.

"My office put the bulletin on the net late last night," Hemner said. "We found a spine leopard dead yesterday near Paleen, mauled by something as big as a gantua but obviously far more aggressive. The leopard's foreleg spines, incidentally, were rigored into their extended, defensive, position."

From the shocked looks around the table Jonny gathered the report was news to nearly all the other syndics. "We certainly don't want to make any decisions on the basis of a single unexplained event," he said quickly, hoping to diminish the shock effect of the incident. "For all we know, the spine leopard might have been poisoned by some kind of snake and killed by extra-bold scavengers."

"The evidence—" Hemner broke off suddenly, and Jonny turned to see D'arl standing with hand raised for silence.

"I must point out that Syndic Moreau is perfectly correct in warning against a hasty decision," the Committé said. "I've given you some of the reasons the Committee is offering you this equipment; there are others which are listed in the complete report I've brought. But the decision is yours, and I expect you to give this issue the careful consideration the Dominion expects from its leaders. I will be here for another few weeks, and you will have that long, if necessary, to determine what course to take." Looking down, he murmured something to Zhu, who nodded and got to his feet.

"I'm declaring a short recess so that we can all have time to examine the information Committé D'arl mentioned," the governor-general announced. "The relevant magcards are down the hall in your offices. Please take some time to study them, and we'll continue this discussion in two hours."

Jonny joined the general exodus to the building's office wing, but unlike the other syndics, he didn't stay there long. Picking up his copy of D'arl's magcard, he made two quick calls and then left.

Twenty minutes later he and Cally Halloran were on an aircar, heading southeast for Dawa District.

The last page flicked from the screen of Jonny's comboard, and with a snort he flicked off the instrument and tossed it onto the next seat. Across from him, Halloran looked up from his own comboard. "Well?"

"Not a single argument that could hold vacuum in space," Jonny growled. "We can answer all the problems D'arl raises without resorting to a Cobra assembly line."

"But your solutions come from an Aventine syndic, while his come from a Dominion Committé?"

"You got it." Sighing, Jonny gazed out the aircar window at the lush Aventine landscape below. "I don't think I've got a hope in hell of pushing a no-vote through unless we can identify this spine leopard killer fast."

"I'm not sure what that'll accomplish, actually," Halloran said, tapping his comboard. "If the stuff in here on spine leopards isn't exaggerated, you may well *need a* Cobra assembly line to fight its killer."

Jonny remained silent a long moment, wondering whether he should give Halloran the rest of it. At best his suspicions were slanderous; at worst they could possibly be construed as treason. "Has it occurred to you," he said at last, "how remarkably handy the timing has worked out for D'arl? Here he is, pushing us to accept a permanent Cobra presence here, and he's barely landed when this mysterious super-predator suddenly decides to pop up.

He couldn't have found a better argument for his side if he'd manufactured it himself."

Halloran's eyebrows rose. "Are you implying he *did* manufacture it?"

Jonny shook his head slowly. "No, of course not. Probably not. But I still can't get over the timing."

Halloran shrugged. "That part of Dawa District's undergoing a pretty severe drought right now, with the Kaskia branch of the Ojaante River dried up and all. Could that have hurt the gantuas' food supply to the point where they'd risk taking on a spine leopard?"

"Not a chance. Gantuas are pure herbivores, with no meat-eating capability at all. There are a couple of that type of pseudo-omnivore here, but they're far too small to bother even a sick spine leopard."

"Then maybe the drought drove some other creature down from the mountains," Halloran persisted. "I'm keying on the drought, you see, because that's also an unusual occurrence, at least in the occupied areas of Aventine."

"And you think D'arl's visit just happened to coincide with our first drought?" Jonny said almost reluctantly. "Well . . . maybe. But I still don't like it."

Again Halloran shrugged. "I'll be happy to keep the possibility of foul play in mind," he said. "But until and unless we come up with something approaching hard evidence, we ought to keep such thoughts to ourselves."

In other words, he thought Jonny was making a dangerously big deal out of nothing. And he was probably right. Still . . .

Fifteen minutes later, they landed at the village of Paleen.

A visiting syndic generally called for a minor official fuss, or at the very least the welcoming presence of the local mayor. But Jonny had called ahead with explicit instructions to the contrary, and as he and Halloran left the aircar they found a lone man waiting. "Syndic Moreau?" he said. "I'm Niles Kier, resident Cobra."

Jonny nodded acknowledgment and indicated Halloran. "This is Cally Halloran, your soon-to-be teammate here. What have you got on the dead spine leopard?"

"Not much more than we had yesterday," Kier admitted, leading them toward an open car parked at the edge of the field. "The experts are still studying it up at Niparin, but haven't come to any conclusions yet."

"You're the one who found it, right?"

Kier nodded. "I was out doing a water survey when I spotted the carcass lying in a small hollow."

"Water survey?" Halloran put in. "You were hauling a sounder around by yourself?"

"Here you just measure the diameters of the gluevines that climb around some of the trees," Jonny explained absently. "It gives you a direct reading of the soil moisture and an indirect indication of where the water table is. Any tracks around it?"

"The ground was pretty badly torn up," Kier said as they got into the car. "I spotted some marks nearby that looked like gantua tracks, but if they were the thing was either huge or running faster than any I've ever heard of."

"From the tapes I've seen I can't see any reason a gantua should ever bother to run," Halloran commented.

Jonny nodded. As big as elephants, their bodies armored with snake-patterned horny plates, gantuas were the closest thing to living tanks he'd ever seen. "A dignified trot is about as close as they get," he told Halloran uneasily. "If this thing scared a *gantua* enough to make it run, we *are* in trouble. Let's go to the spot, Niles, and poke around a little. I gather you didn't do much exploring at the time."

"No," Kier said as he turned the car and headed west. His tone sounded more than a little defensive. "I thought my immediate duty lay in sounding the alarm . . . and in *not* leaving Paleen defenseless."

Jonny nodded grimly. It was a rationale he well remembered—and logical though it was, he knew how cowardly it could make a Cobra feel. Perhaps Kier would get the chance later to redeem himself.

They left the car at a section of reasonably dense forest at village's edge and headed into the trees on foot. The forest gave way barely a hundred meters later into a tree-dotted grassland which was the norm for the Kaskia Valley as a whole. Jonny looked around, feeling strangely more exposed and vulnerable than he ever had in the thicker woods back at Ariel. "Which way?" he asked Kier, fighting the urge to whisper.

"Uh . . . over there, I think. It's near a—"

"Shh!" Halloran hissed suddenly. All three men went instantly rigid . . . and in the silence, Jonny's auditory enhancers picked up a strange rustling of grass and a quiet snuffling snort. Turning his head slowly, he located the sound: beyond a wide stand of blussa reeds. Kier had placed it, too. Catching Jonny's eye, he pointed and gave a thumbs-up sign. Jonny nodded; gesturing to Halloran, he moved a few meters to the side and raised his hands in laser-ready position. Halloran did likewise . . . and Kier jumped.

The twenty-meter reconnaissance jump had usually been considered too dangerous to use during the war, leaving the Cobra as it did in a helpless ballistic trajectory for a shade over four seconds. On Aventine, with no Troft gunners around, the trick was often more useful.

"Gantua," Kier said as he hit the ground, knee servos taking the impact. "Looked sort of sick—"

And with a crash of breaking blussa, the brown-gray monster appeared across the plain . . . and charged.

"Scatter!" Jonny snapped, his own feet digging into the ground as he sprinted in the general direction of a tall cyprene. He would never have believed a gantua could move so *fast*—

Veering like a hill on legs, the creature shifted to an intercept course.

Jonny picked up his own speed, raising his hands as he did so to send twin bursts of laser fire at the gantua's head. Other flickers of light, he noted, were playing about its side, but if the creature was bothered it gave no sign. Jonny's target tree was seeming less and less likely to be a place of real safety; but on the other hand, if he could get the gantua to blast full tilt into it, the impact should at least stun the beast. Shifting his attention back and forth, he adjusted his speed . . . and a bare instant ahead of his pursuer he leaped high into the cyprene's branches—

And lost his grip completely as the tree swayed violently in time with the thunderous crash from below.

The programmed Cobra reflexes included a catlike maneuver for righting oneself in midair, but Jonny was far too close to the ground for it to be effective. He landed off-balance, crashing down onto his left shoulderblade, the impact driving most of the air out of his lungs.

For several seconds he just lay there, fighting to clear away the spots twinkling in front of his eyes. By the time he was able to force himself to his knees, the gantua had managed to halt its charge and was wheeling around for a second try. From behind Jonny two spears of light lanced out to catch the beast's head— the other Cobras' antiarmor lasers—and this time the gantua noticed the attack enough to emit a bellow in response. But it kept coming. Jonny climbed shakily to his feet, still struggling to get his wind back. He was still too weak to move . . . but somewhere along here his nanocomputer should recognize the danger and get him out of the way—

And abruptly he was hurled in a flat dive to the side. Rolling back to his feet, he turned just in time to see Halloran and Kier launch their attack.

For something that spur-of-the-moment, it was as tight a maneuver as Jonny had ever seen. Halloran, waving his arms and shouting to attract the gantua, waited until the last second before leaping to the right, his raised left leg raking the gantua's side with antiarmor laser fire as it swept past. At the same moment, Kier leaped over the beast, directing his own antiarmor blast at the juncture of head and body. Again the creature bellowed, and this time Jonny could see a line of blackened plates when it turned. But even as it paused, he could see its sides pumping rhythmically as it regained its wind, and the barely visible eyes sweeping the three Cobras showed no sign of either fear or imminent death.

Pulling his phone from his belt, Jonny keyed for local broadcast. "Hold your fire," he murmured into it as, across the plain, Halloran and Kier fumbled out their own phones. "We're not going to kill it by brute force alone."

"What the hell is that thing *made* of?" Halloran asked tightly. "That blast would've taken out a Troft APC."

"Gantua plates are highly ablative," Kier told him. "The cloud of vaporized material scatters all but the first couple of milliseconds of beam—and the damn things are *thick*, too. Jonny—Syndic—we're going to have to call Capitalia and see if anyone up there's got a rocket launcher."

"Even if they did, it'd take too long to get it here," Jonny shook his head. "If the gantua bolts, we could lose it for good."

"We go for head shots, then?" Halloran asked.

"Take a long time to kill it that way," Kier said doubtfully. "Gantua central nervous systems are a lot more decentralized than anything you're probably used to. Underbelly and heart-lung would be a better target."

"Only if we can get it to roll over," Jonny pointed out. The gantua's panting, he noticed uneasily, was already slowing down. Another minute or two and it would be ready to either attack or flee. His eyes flicked around the plain, looking for inspiration . . . fell on a gluevine-wrapped cyprene. "Miles, that tree to your left has a long gluevine on it. See if you can ease over and cut us a good length of it."

Moving carefully, attention on the gantua, Kier glided toward the tree. "Cally," Jonny continued, "when Niles gets the gluevine free, he's going to toss you one end. *Don't* touch the cut part; it'll stick like crazy to you. You two will hold it stretched between you at about knee height and I'll try and attract the gantua into it. Clear?"

"Clear," Halloran acknowledged. "Do we slice the vine open in the middle with fingertip lasers?"

"If we have time," Kier told him. "Otherwise we'll just have to hope the impact will open enough of the skin to release the glue."

Kier was at the tree now, judging with his hands the best places to cut the vine. "What happens if it charges one of us instead of you?" Halloran asked.

Jonny was almost in position now, between the other Cobras and perhaps fifty meters behind them. "Wait as long as you can, then throw your end of the vine at its legs and jump," he said. "Niles?"

"Ready." Kier took an audible breath. "Okay, Cally—look sharp."

And with twin flashes of laser fire the vine came loose.

The light, or Kier's sudden movements, triggered the gantua. With a hoarse roar it lumbered forward. Jonny yelled at it, waving his arms, and the creature changed direction toward him. At the bottom of his peripheral vision, Jonny saw the vine snake over to Halloran . . . erupt with laser sparkle along much of its length . . . go rigid just above the grass—

The gantua hit it full tilt, and with a crash that shook the area like a minor earthquake, it slammed headlong to the ground.

Down, but not out. Even as Jonny raced toward it, the creature rolled to its side, treetrunk legs straining against the vine wrapped around them. Lousy leverage or not, the vine was already showing signs of strain. This would have to be done fast. . . .

And as he raised his antiarmor laser, Jonny abruptly realized the gantua's legs were blocking his intended target.

"Uh-oh," Kier muttered as he and Halloran joined Jonny. "We may have outsmarted ourselves on that one."

"Let's try wrapping more gluevine around it," Halloran suggested. "Maybe we can take it alive."

"Taking a berserk gantua alive is *not* my idea of a solution," Jonny told him. "There isn't a facility within a hundred kilometers for a quiet one, let alone this beast." He gritted his teeth. "Okay; there's one more thing we can try. Cally, when I give the word, cut the vine between its front legs. Niles, you and I'll see what we can do in the half second or so we'll have. If it doesn't work, scatter and we'll try to come up with something else. Ready? Okay, Cally; *now.*"

The vine disintegrated in a flicker of light—and the gantua's legs, straining against it, flew wide apart to expose its abdomen.

Afterward, Jonny would shudder at the risk none of them had quite known they were taking. The gantua's underbelly was relatively unprotected, the two antiarmor lasers firing their deadly blasts at point-blank range—and still the creature was able to struggle nearly to its feet before they finally penetrated to a vital spot. Even then, its death convulsions nearly caught Kier, saved only by a combination of luck and programmed reflexes.

Halloran summed it up for all of them when the gantua finally lay still. "Good *God,* those things are built tough."

"I don't remember ever hearing of anyone killing one before," Jonny said. "Now I know why."

"I sure hope he was a rogue," Kier agreed, rubbing his shin where the creature's death throes had touched it. "If they've all gone crazy, we'll have to evacuate half of Dawa District alone."

"Or get a whole lot of new Cobras," Jonny muttered. Ignoring Halloran's suddenly thoughtful look, he pulled out his phone.

Governor-General Zhu had the pained look of a man caught between two opposing but equally valid requirements. "But the vote has already been taken," he said. "Committé D'arl's people are already unloading their equipment."

"So negate the vote on the grounds of new evidence," Jonny argued, staring hard at the other through the phone screen. He'd borrowed the Niparin mayor's office specifically for the use of the vision attachment, but so far the face-to-face advantage hadn't gained him a thing. "Or on the grounds that neither I nor the syndics of Palatine and Caelian were present. Come on, Zhu—this vote wasn't even supposed to be taken for a week or so."

"The others were ready to vote—what was I supposed to do? Anyway, you and the other two missing syndics wouldn't have made a difference. The vote was eleven to five, and even with your Cobra's double vote, the end result would have wound up the same. And as for new evidence, all you've said so far merely reinforces the decision. If one or more gantuas have gone crazy, we certainly *are* going to need more Cobras to defend ourselves."

"Doesn't that depend on *why* they went crazy?"

Zhu's eyes narrowed. "What does *that* mean?"

"I don't know—yet. The scientific people are just starting a biochemical study of the gantua we killed to see if there are any foreign substances in its system."

" 'Foreign substances'? Moreau, it strikes me you're being unnecessarily mysterious. What, in plain language, are you driving at?"

Jonny took a deep breath. "I'm not being mysterious; I simply don't *know* anything for certain. I have . . . suspicions . . . but I'd rather not air them without proof."

Zhu studied his face for a long minute. "All right," he said at last. "I'll tell you what I'll do. I'll call another council meeting for tomorrow morning at ten. Ostensibly it'll be so you can describe your battle with the gantua and present the scientific team's preliminary data. *If* you have whatever proof you seem to expect, we'll listen to your accusations or whatever then; and *if* it seems warranted, I'll call for a new vote. *If*. Is that satisfactory?"

"Yes, sir," Jonny nodded.

"Good. Ten tomorrow, then. Good-bye."

For a moment Jonny stared at the blank screen, trying to form his strategy for the meeting. But there were still too many unknowns. Giving up, he flicked on the phone again and called home.

Chrys answered on the second ring. "Hi," she said, the slight tension lines leaving her face as she saw him. "How are things going?"

"Slow, at the moment," he told her. "I'm just sitting around Niparin waiting for the scientific types to give us something solid to use. Cally went back to Paleen with Niles for the night in case something else happens there. Though there aren't a lot of approaches to the village even a crazed gantua could get through."

"That helps," Chrys nodded. "Is Niles's leg okay?"

"Oh, sure. Bruised, but I'm sure he's had worse."

She smiled faintly. "Listen, Jonny, about a half hour ago we got a call from Capitalia. It was your brother Jame."

So D'arl *had* brought him along. "Well! How was he?"

"Fine, he said. He wanted to know if you and Gwen could meet him at about eleven tonight for a late supper."

Jonny grinned. Imagine Jame Moreau, late of Cedar Lake, Horizon, casually inviting relatives to fly two thousand kilometers for a meal! Life on Asgard had affected him, all right. "What did Gwen say?"

"She said sure, made me promise to call you in plenty of time, and hopped an aircar for Capitalia."

"On my syndic's authority, I presume." He looked at his watch: two hours before he'd have to leave. Well, he could always have the gantua data phoned to him at Capitalia if it wasn't ready before then. "Okay," he told Chrys. "You want to try and scare up a short-notice sitter for Corwin and join us?"

She shook her head. "Jame already asked me that, but I think this one should be for Moreaus only. I'll get to meet him before he leaves Aventine. Oh, Gwen suggested you meet at the restaurant we took Cally and her to yesterday."

"Sounds good." He grimaced. "This is some vacation for you, isn't it? I'm sorry."

"Don't worry about *me*," she said softly. "You just be careful yourself."

"I will. Love you, Chrys."

"Love you, Jonny. Say hi to Jame for me."

He broke the connection and again glanced at his watch. Two hours . . . and nothing he could do to help with the gantua autopsy. And whatever they found . . .

Would not in and of itself be proof that D'arl was behind it all.

But at least a part of that proof might still be available. Heading outside, he picked up his aircar and flew back down to Paleen. It was getting dark by the time he and Halloran returned to the place where they'd killed the gantua, but with their vision and auditory enhancers it was unlikely even a spine leopard could sneak up on them. Still, the events of the afternoon had left Jonny a bit jumpy, and he was glad their task took only a few minutes.

An hour and a half later, he was flying over the starlit landscape toward Capitalia . . . with information that would turn the ill-considered council vote on its ear.

Gwen and Jame were already seated at a table when Jonny arrived at the restaurant. "Jonny!" Jame exclaimed, rising for a firm handshake as he joined them. "It's been more than just a couple of years, but you see we *did* finally get here to see you."

It took Jonny a few seconds to track down the reference. "Oh—right. The day I left Horizon. You're looking good, Jame."

His brother grinned. "Hard but useful work. Same prescription you've been following. Let's sit down, shall we? Gwen's been trying to translate this menu for me, but I think we're going to need an expert."

They sat down together and the conversation continued . . . and as they talked, Jonny studied the man his brother had become.

Physically, of course, Jame's transition from nineteen to thirty-five was less of a jolt than Gwen's maturing had been; but like Gwen, there was something about him that all his tapes had left Jonny unprepared for. Jame's teen-aged self-confidence had blossomed into an almost tangible air of authority and competence—an air which, almost paradoxically, had no hint of condescension to it. Accustomed to dealing with the Dominion elite, he had nevertheless not forgotten how to talk with ordinary citizens.

Or else he's gone beyond even arrogance and learned how to fake *sociability,* he thought, and felt immediately ashamed. This was *Jame,* after all; the one who'd warned *him* not to abandon his ethics. No matter who or what D'arl was, he could surely not have corrupted the younger man so thoroughly as to have left not even a trace of the tampering.

From which it followed that Jame didn't really know what kind of man he was working for. And if that was the case . . .

Jonny waited for an appropriate opening, as a good soldier should, and as the meal drew to a close it presented itself.

" . . . so when I found out Committé D'arl was going to personally supervise the whole thing here, I naturally made sure to get my bid in early to come with him." Jame took a sip of cahve. "He worked very hard to get the Central Committee to go along with the plan; I'm glad to see you're going to accept it, too."

"So D'arl's got his political reputation on the line here, does he?" Jonny asked casually.

A flicker of uncertainty passed across Jame's face. "He's got some prestige at stake, but nothing quite that crucial."

"As far as you know, you mean."

Jame set his mug down carefully and lowered his voice. "All right, Jonny; you don't have to prod around the edges like that with *me.* What's on your mind?"

Jonny pursed his lips. "I expect you've heard by now that we killed a berserk gantua southeast of here today." The other nodded. "You may also know that in the fifteen years we've been here no gantua has ever shown even the slightest aggressiveness. All right. What would you say, then, if I told you I have proof the gantua we killed had been drugged?"

Gwen inhaled sharply. Jame's eyes narrowed. "Drugged how?"

"A potent hallucinogen-stimulant chemical had been sprayed over the blussa reeds near where it attacked us. That's all the gantuas ever eat, so it was a perfect way to get the stuff into their systems."

"A perfect way for whom?"

Jonny hesitated. "I don't know, specifically. But I'll point out that it gave D'arl a lot of extra push in the vote today. *And* that it happened right after your ship got in."

Jame leaned back in his seat and regarded Jonny thoughtfully. "I could remind you that I've worked with the Committé and his staff for several years now and that I'm a reasonably good judge of character. I could also point out that unsupported accusations could get you in a lot of trouble. But I'd rather tackle the whole issue logically. Assuming someone aboard our ship sprayed this drug from orbit, why hasn't every other animal in that area gone crazy as well? Even if we dropped a mist bomb or something— and I don't even know if our approach path was anywhere near there—there should've been *some* dispersion."

Jonny exhaled through clenched teeth. "All right, then. Someone on your ship must have had an agent down here with the stuff all ready to spray."

"You only had a few hours' warning, though, didn't you?" Gwen spoke up. "Could something the size of a gantua ingest enough of the drug that fast?"

"It would probably have needed a massive initial dose," Jame agreed. "And in that case, why coat the blussa plants at all?" He frowned. "Though I'll admit the Committé has been very interested in Aventine flora and fauna recently, and I remember blussa reeds showing up in some of the studies I worked on."

"How were they mentioned, specifically?" Jonny asked, leaning forward.

"Let's see...." Jame stared into his cahve. "If I remember correctly, it was part of a strategic minerals study he was having us do. Something about Aventine becoming self-sufficient in case the Troft Corridor was closed. I dug out the fact that your blussa plant is unusually good at concentrating some metal—I forget which one—especially in late autumn."

"And from this study he almost undoubtedly learned that gantuas are the only things larger than insects that feed on blussa plants," Jonny said grimly. "So his agents inject massive doses of hallucinogen into a few gantuas and spray the blussa nearby to ensure they don't come down from their high until they've attracted our attention."

"Jonny, you're edging *very* close to sedition here." Jame's voice was barely audible, his hand rigid as it clutched his mug. "Even if what you're saying is true, you haven't got a shred of evidence to point to the Committé himself."

"Not yet. But maybe you can get that evidence for me."

Jame's face seemed to become a mask. "What do you mean?"

"If anyone aboard your ship is involved in this, they'll almost certainly have had communication with their agents here. You can pull the radio log and look for coded transmissions."

For a long moment Jame locked eyes with his brother. "You're asking *me* to be disloyal now," he said at last.

"Am I? If D'arl's implicated, shouldn't that fact be brought to the attention of the entire Central Committee? And if someone's working behind his back—for whatever reason—shouldn't you find out and let him know?"

"And if the whole thing's some home-grown Aventine plot, wouldn't I be betraying the trust Committé D'arl's placed in me?" Jame retorted.

"Jame, you've got to help me," Jonny said carefully, fighting to keep any hint of his desperation from creeping into his voice. Jame was right: he *hadn't* any proof that D'arl was manipulating Aventine politics, and unless he could get it, the Committé's plan would go ahead unchecked. "Don't you see how the continual presence of Cobras is going to warp our society? I don't want D'arl's Cobra factory set up on Aventine—and I sure as *hell* don't want it here for a fraudulent reason."

He stopped abruptly, embarrassed by his outburst. Jame ran his finger absently around the rim of his mug, then looked up at Gwen. "What are *your* thoughts on this?" he asked her.

She shrugged fractionally. "I've barely been here a day, Jame— I really can't say anything about the benefits versus drawbacks of this so-called Cobra factory. But if Jonny says it'd be bad—" She grinned. "You *know* how everything Jonny says and does is right."

Jame relaxed, smiling back. "That's only because he wasn't around during those critical formative years when you were busy fighting with *me*," he said.

"Jonny was doing a lot for the Dominion during those years," she replied softly.

Jame looked down at his cahve again. "He was, wasn't he?" He took a deep breath, pursed his lips. "All right," he said at last, looking Jonny in the eye. "I guess I can risk the Committé's anger for something that's this important to you. But I won't be able to simply give you any logs I find. I'll analyze them myself and let you know if there's anything out of the ordinary. They're all technically confidential, after all."

Jonny nodded. "I understand. And I wouldn't be asking you to do this if there was any other way."

"Sure." Raising his mug, Jame drained the rest of his cahve and stood up. "I'll call you as soon as I have anything." He nodded to them both and left.

Jonny leaned back with a sigh of relief. If this worked . . .

"I hope you know what you're doing."

He looked over to find Gwen's eyes on him. "If it works, I should have at least enough indirect evidence to get Zhu and the council thinking about what they're doing to Aventine."

"And if it doesn't," she rejoined quietly, "you'll have risked—maybe ruined—Jame's career for nothing."

Jonny closed his eyes. "Don't remind me." He sat like that for a moment, feeling the tension of the day turning to fatigue and soaking into his bones. "Well," he said, opening his eyes and getting to his feet, "what's done is done. Let me get a car to take you to a hotel for the night."

"What about you?" she asked as they headed for the exit.

"I'm staying at the Dominion Building office tonight," he told her grimly. "It occurs to me that I've got information there that someone may think worth stealing. I almost hope they try it."

But the packet from the scientific team in Niparin was untouched when he arrived, and nothing but uncomfortable dreams disturbed his sleep.

It was quickly clear that, whether he'd intended such a result or not, Zhu had given Jonny the best opening he could possibly have come up with. The other syndics listened closely—even raptly—as Jonny described in detail the Cobras' battle with the gantua the previous afternoon. He hadn't had that kind of attention in weeks; and if it emphasized how much Aventine needed Cobra power, it surely also reminded them that Cobra good will and cooperation were equally vital. It was, he decided, a fair psychological trade-off.

"The important question, of course," he said when he'd finished, "is what could cause a gantua to behave like that. As of late yesterday evening we have the answer." He paused, flicking a glance at D'arl. The Committé was as attentive as the others, but if he saw his scheme unraveling, his expression gave no hint of it. "It appears," Jonny continued, "that the gantua was deliberately drugged with a hallucinogenic chemical sprayed directly on its food supply."

He paused again, but the dramatic outburst he'd half expected never materialized. "That's ridiculous," Jor Hemner spoke up into the silence. "Why would anyone do something like that?"

Jonny took a deep breath. This was it. "Perhaps," he said, locking eyes with D'arl, "to persuade us to accept a Cobra presence we don't really need."

D'arl returned his gaze steadily. "Are you accusing *me* of drugging your gantuas, Syndic?"

"And have you got any proof?" Zhu added tartly before Jonny could answer. "Because you'd damn well better not be even *suggesting* Committé D'arl has any connection with this unless you do."

The proof is on his ship, Jonny wanted to say . . . but until and unless Jame contacted him, he didn't dare invite any scrutiny in that direction. "I'm not accusing anyone specifically, gentlemen," he said, shifting his gaze between Zhu and D'arl. "But since it seems obvious a crime has been committed—and since it's unarguable that the drugged gantua's existence had at least an indirect effect on yesterday's vote—I would like to suggest the vote be rescinded and a new vote not be taken until all the facts are in on this case."

"What other facts do you expect to find?" an older syndic put in. "Or should I say *hope* to find? It seems to me you've got nothing but a soap-bubble of—"

"Gentlemen." D'arl's voice was quiet, but there was an edge to it that cut off the syndic in mid-sentence. "If I may make a suggestion, it seems to me you're putting too much emphasis on guarding my honor and too little on solving the genuine mystery Syndic Moreau's uncovered. If there is indeed clandestine activity underway, it must be stopped, no matter who is involved. If, on the other hand, what we have here is a purely natural phenomenon, you should similarly learn all that you can about it, and as quickly as possible."

"Natural phenomenon?" Jonny snorted. "If the Committé will excuse my skepticism—"

"Skepticism is a natural part of science," D'arl interrupted him calmly. "But before you announce your disbelief too loudly, I suggest you check on the following: one, are all the blussa plants in the Kaskia Valley coated by this drug; two, is there any trace of it on the surrounding foliage; three, are there any conditions under which the plants could themselves naturally produce such a drug; and four, are such conditions currently present. The answers to these questions might prove interesting." He stood up and nodded to Zhu. "With your permission, I will continue the equipment setup begun yesterday. If a later vote requires its removal, it can be done easily enough."

"Of course, Committé," Zhu agreed quickly. "Thank you for coming today. Syndics: the meeting is adjourned."

And that was it. In half a minute, D'arl had completely blunted his attack. An attack the Committé had been remarkably well prepared for. . . .

Tight-lipped, Jonny collected his magcards and left the room.

Halloran, still in Niparin, listened quietly as Jonny described the fiasco over the phone. "He sounded awfully sure of himself," he commented thoughtfully. "What chance that he's right about this being a natural phenomenon?"

Jonny exhaled loudly. "It's hard to imagine him going that far out on a purely speculative limb," he admitted. "But if that's what's happening, how come *he* knew about it and we didn't?"

Halloran shrugged. "You've been sending samples and data back to Asgard for a long time, and they've got far better test and computer simulation equipment than you'll ever see here. Or maybe it was something even simpler; maybe some of the live plants got dehydrated during the trip."

"Dehydrated. So you think it's the drought?"

"I don't know what other condition he could have been referring to. It's the only environmental factor that's new to you."

Jonny gnawed the inside of his cheek. "The drought. All right, then. If that's the problem, we'll just have to eliminate it."

Halloran cocked an eyebrow. "You know a rainmaker who specializes in getting clouds over mountains?"

"Actually, I can do better than that. Hang on." He pressed the lock key on the phone and got a connection to Rankin. Chrys answered, the screen splitting to include her image. "Hi, Hon," he greeted her. "Is Gwen there?"

"Hi, Jonny; Cally. Yes, she's in the kitchen. Gwen?"

A moment later Gwen's face replaced Chrys's. "Hi, guys. What's up?"

"Your vacation," Jonny told her. "I've got a little job for you and Cally."

Describing what he had in mind took only a few minutes . . . and it turned out to be the easy part.

"Jonny, that's *crazy*," Gwen told him flatly. "Do you have any *idea* of what you're asking?"

"Syndic Hemner will be furious if he catches them," Chrys put in from off-camera.

"Why?" Jonny countered. "They're both *supposed* to be in his district, remember?"

"But under *his* authority, not yours," Halloran said.

"So you leave your field phones off and plead ignorance," Jonny shrugged. "What's he going to do, bust me back to cee-five?"

"Probably have you arrested and sent to the Palatine beachhead," Halloran said bluntly. "Especially if it doesn't work."

"But if it *does* work he won't be able to do a thing without looking like a petty legalist," Jonny said. "And I have confidence in you two."

"Well, *I* don't," Gwen admitted. "Jonny, you can't do something like this on ten minutes' notice. It takes *time*—time for studies, time for mapping and emplacement—"

"Maps we've got—the Molada mountain range has been extensively studied. As to the rest, we can surely risk a little environmental damage."

"Jonny, there's still one major point you're missing." Chrys moved back into camera range, and Jonny was struck by the odd intensity in her face. "What you're doing," she continued softly, "is planning to bypass legal channels, to take a major policy decision away from Zhu and the other syndics and handle it yourself. Don't you see?—that's exactly what you and Ken fought to keep Challinor from doing seven years ago."

Jonny's mouth felt suddenly dry. "No. No, it's different, Chrys. He was trying to take over the whole planet, to totally eliminate the Dominion authority."

"It's different only in degree," she shook her head minutely. "You'll still be setting a precedent that a syndic—or a Cobra— who doesn't like a legal governmental decision can simply ignore it and go his own way."

But it's not the same, the words echoed through Jonny's mind. *The government's doing something stupid just because an important outsider wants them to. My responsibility is to the people of Aventine—*

To the *people* of Aventine.

Challinor's old argument.

The three faces crowded together in the phone screen were watching him closely. "All right," he said with a sigh. "Gwen, you and Cally will head out for the Kaskia Valley, but to do feasibility studies only. I'll bring it up with the whole council before we take any real action, but I want to be able to at least show them a solid alternative."

Chrys seemed to sag as the tension left her. "Thank you," she murmured.

He smiled tightly. "Don't thank *me*. *You're* the one who was right." He focused on Gwen. "Chrys'll get you in touch with Theron Yutu, my assistant, who'll find you an aircar and pilot and whatever else you'll need. Check with Chrys for anything electronic—if she can't find it, she can probably build it. You can rendezvous with Cally in Niparin and go from there. As for you, Cally—" He held up a finger for emphasis. "No matter what Theron or Gwen tell you, any equipment you take *is* replaceable. If you run into a crazed gantua up there, don't hesitate to grab Gwen and run for it. Got it?"

"Got it." Halloran hesitated. "If it helps any, I think you're making the right decision."

"Not really, but thanks anyway. Chrys?"

"I'll call Theron right away," she nodded, all business now. "We can probably have Gwen down to Niparin in three hours or less."

"Good. Well . . . keep me posted, everyone, and I'll let you know when you're needed here. And be careful."

They all signed off, and for several minutes Jonny just sat there, feeling oddly alone in the quiet office. As if his own career and Jame's weren't enough, he'd now put Gwen's and Cally's on the target range, too. Could he really be *that* sure he was right about all this?

There wasn't any answer for that . . . but at the moment there was something he needed more than answers, anyway. Flipping on the phone, he called D'arl's ship. "Jame Moreau," he told the young ensign who answered. "Tell him it's his brother."

The other nodded and faded; a minute later the screen lit up with Jame's image. "Yes, Jonny?" he said. His voice was casually friendly, but there was an edge of wariness to his expression.

"I'd like to get together with you later," Jonny said. "Dinner tonight, maybe, whenever you get off duty?"

The wariness deepened. "Well . . ."

"No inquisitions, no favors, no politics," Jonny promised. "I'd just like to be with family for a while. If you've got the time."

Jame smiled faintly, the tension easing from his face. "There's always time for the important stuff," he said quietly. "Let's make it lunch—that same restaurant in half an hour?"

Jonny smiled back. Already the weight around his shoulders was lifting a little. "I'll be there."

✧   ✧   ✧

It took a week, but at last the results of the various blussa reed tests began to coalesce . . . and they were indeed just as D'arl had suggested.

"It seems to be a response to severe lack of available ground water," the senior botanist told the council, his hand trembling noticeably as he shifted graphs, complex formulas, and photos on the syndics' comboards. He'd probably never before addressed even a single syndic before, Jonny thought, let alone a group of them plus a Dominion Committé. "One of the components in the cutin—that's the layer that protects against water loss—alters chemically from *this* form to *this* one." The two molecular diagrams appeared on the comboards. "It turns out that this makes good biological sense in two complementary ways," the botanist continued. "Not only is the new cutin fifteen to twenty percent better at controlling transpiration, but the chemical reaction involved actually releases two molecules of water, which are then available for the plant to use."

"In other words, the drier it gets, the crazier the gantuas become?" Syndic Hemner asked.

"Basically, yes," the scientist nodded. "There may be a cutoff somewhere where the gantuas switch to a different plant species for food, but if there is, we don't seem to have reached it yet."

Seated beside Gwen against the side wall, Halloran caught Jonny's eye and wrinkled his nose. Jonny nodded fractionally in agreement: if the gantua they'd fought wasn't fully berserk, he had no wish to meet one that was.

"Well, then, our alternatives seem pretty clear," Hemner said grimly. "We either get Committé D'arl's new Cobras into service as quickly as possible or pull completely out of the Kaskia Valley until the drought ends. If it ever does."

"There's one more possibility," Jonny said into the growing murmur of agreement.

"And that is . . . ?" Zhu prompted.

"End the drought now." Jonny gestured to Gwen. "May I present Dr. Gwen Moreau, recently returned from the mountains surrounding the Kaskia Valley."

Gwen stood. "With your permission, Governor-General Zhu, I would like to present the results of a study Syndic Moreau asked me to make a week ago."

"Concerning what?" Zhu asked suspiciously.

"Concerning a proposal to break a pass in the Molada

Mountains that would divert water from Lake Ojaante directly into the currently dry Kaskia riverbed."

Jaw sagging slightly, Zhu waved her wordlessly to the table.

"Thank you. Gentlemen," she addressed the syndics, sliding her magcard into its slot, "let me show you how easily this proposal could be carried out. . . ."

And for the better part of an hour she did just that, punctuating her talk with more charts and diagrams than even the botanist who'd preceded her. She spoke authoritatively and coherently, slipping in enough about the basic methods of tectonic utilization to painlessly educate even the most ignorant of the syndics . . . and slowly Jonny sensed the silence around the table change from astonishment to interest to guarded enthusiasm.

For him the changes went even deeper, as his mentally superimposed image of Gwen The Ten-Year-Old vanished forever from her face. His little sister was an adult now . . . and he was damn proud of what she'd become.

The final picture faded at last from the comboard screens and Gwen nodded to the syndics. "If there are any questions now, I'll do my best to answer them."

There was a moment of silence. Jonny glanced at D'arl, bracing for the attack the Committé would surely launch against this rival scheme. But the other remained silent, his look of admiration matching others Jonny could see around the table.

"We will need more study, if merely to confirm your evaluations," Zhu spoke up at last. "But unless you've totally missed some major problem, I think it safe to say that you can start drawing up detailed plans immediately for the precise fault-line charge placements you'll need." He nodded to her and glanced around the table. "If there's no further business—" He paused, almost unwillingly, at the sight of Jonny's raised forefinger. "Yes, Syndic Moreau?"

"I would like to request, sir, that a new vote be taken on Committé D'arl's proposal," Jonny said with polite firmness. "I believe the study just presented has borne out my earlier contention that our problems can be solved without the creation of a new generation of Cobras. I'd like to give the council a new opportunity to agree or disagree with that contention."

Zhu shook his head. "I'm sorry, but in my opinion you've shown us nothing that materially changes the situation."

"What? But—"

"Governor-General." D'arl's voice was calm as always. "If it would ease your official conscience, let me state that I have no objection to a new vote." His eyes met Jonny's and he smiled. "In my opinion, Syndic Moreau's earned a second try."

The vote was taken . . . and when it was over, the tally was eleven to seven in favor of D'arl's proposal.

Parked at one end of Capitalia's starfield, D'arl's ship was an impressive sight—smaller than the big space-only transports, of course, but still more than twice the size of Aventine's own *Dewdrop*. A sensor-guard perimeter extended another fifty meters in all directions, and as Jonny passed its boundary, he noticed an automated turret atop the ship rotate slightly to cover him. The two Marines at the closed entry way made no such obvious moves, but Jonny saw that the muzzles of their shoulder-mounted parrot guns stayed on him the entire way. "Syndic Jonny Moreau to see Committé D'arl," he told them, coming to a halt a few meters away.

"Are you expected, sir?" one of the guards asked. He could afford to be courteous; in full exoskeleton armor he was more powerful than even a Cobra.

"He'll see me," Jonny said. "Tell him I'm here."

The other guard glanced at his partner. "The Committé's quite busy, sir, with the departure tomorrow and all—"

"Tell him I'm here," Jonny repeated.

The first guard pursed his lips and touched a control at his throat. His conversation was brief and inaudible, but a moment later he nodded. "The Committé will see you, Syndic," he told Jonny. "Your escort will be here shortly."

Jonny nodded and settled down to wait; and when the escort arrived, he wasn't surprised to see who it was.

"Jonny," Jame nodded in greeting. His smile was cordial but tight. "Committé D'arl's waiting in his office. If you'll follow me. . . ."

They passed through the heavy kyrelium steel entryway and between another pair of armored Marines. "I was hoping to see you again before we left," Jame said as they started into a maze of short corridors. "Your office said you were on vacation and couldn't be reached."

"Chrys thought it would help me to get away for a couple of weeks," Jonny told him evenly. "Try to come to grips with what your Committé's done to us."

Jame looked sideways at him. "And . . . did you?"

"You mean do I intend to attack him?" Jonny shook his head.

"No. All I want is to understand him, to find out *why*. He owes me that much."

Ahead, two more Marines—this pair in dress uniforms—flanked an obviously reinforced door. Jame led the way between them and palmed the lock, and the panel slid soundlessly open.

"Syndic Moreau," D'arl said, rising from the desk that dominated the modest-sized room. "Welcome. Please sit down." He indicated a chair across the desk from him.

Jonny did so. Jame took a chair by the desk's corner, equidistant from the other two men. Jonny wondered briefly if the choice was deliberate, decided it probably was.

"I'd hoped you'd come by this evening," D'arl said, sitting back down himself. "This will be our last chance to talk—shall we say 'honestly'?—before the tedious departure ceremonies Zhu has scheduled for tomorrow."

"'Tedious'? I take it it's not the public acclaim or adoration that makes all this worthwhile to you, then." Jonny took a moment to glance around the room. Comfortable, certainly, but hardly up to the standards of luxury he would have expected in a Dominion Committé's personal quarters. "Obviously, it's not the wealth, either. So what is it? The power to make people do what you want?"

D'arl shook his head. "You miss the whole point of what happened here."

"Do I? You *knew* the gantuas would be going on a rampage just at the time you came dangling your Cobra bait in front of our faces. You knew all along it was the dehydrated blussa reeds, yet you said nothing about it until I forced your hand."

"And what if I had?" D'arl countered. "It's not as if I could be blamed for causing the situation."

Jonny snorted. "Of course not."

"But as you said outside," D'arl continued, as if he hadn't noticed the interruption, "the important question is *why*. Why did I offer and why did Aventine accept?"

"Why the council accepted is easy," Jonny said. "You're a Dominion Committé and what you say goes."

D'arl shook his head. "I told you you were missing the point. The gantua problem helped, certainly, but it was really only part of a much more basic motivation. They accepted because it was the solution that required the least amount of work."

Jonny frowned. "I don't understand."

"It's clear enough. By placing the main burden and danger of Aventine's growth on you Cobras, they've postponed any need to shift the responsibility to the general population. Given a chance to continue such a system, people will nearly always jump at it. Especially with an excuse as immediate and convenient as the gantuas to point to."

"But it's only a short-term solution," Jonny insisted. "In the long run—"

"*I* know that," D'arl snapped. "But the fraction of humanity who can sacrifice their next meal for a feast two weeks away wouldn't fill this city. If you're going to stay in politics, you'd damn well better learn that."

He stopped and grimaced into the silence. "It's been years since I lost my temper in anything approaching public," he admitted. "Forgive me, and take it as a sign that I'm not any happier than you are that this had to be done."

"Why *did* it?" Jonny asked quietly. Two weeks ago he would have shouted the question, putting into it all the frustration and fury he'd felt then. But now the anger was gone and he'd accepted his failure, and the question was a simple request for information.

D'arl sighed. "The other *why*. Because, Syndic Moreau, it was the only way I could think of to save this world from disaster." He waved his hand skyward. "The Troft threats to close the Corridor have been getting louder and more insistent over the past year or so. Only one thing keeps them from doing it tonight: the fact that it would mean a two-front war. And for Aventine to be a credible part of that two-front threat, you *must* have a continued Cobra presence."

Jonny shook his head. "But it doesn't work that way. We have no transport capability to speak of—we can't possibly threaten them. And even if we could, they could always launch a pre-emptive strike and wipe us out from the sky in a matter of hours."

"But they wouldn't. I once thought that myself, but the more I study the indirect psychological data gleaned over the years, the more I suspect mass destruction simply isn't the Troft way of making war. No, they'd be much more likely to invade, as they did on Silvern and Adirondack."

"But you still don't need *Cobras* to defend against that," Jonny persisted, feeling frustration stirring to life in him again. "You brought in antiarmor lasers—you could just as easily have brought in standard laser rifles and organized a militia or even a standing army. Why can't I make you understand that?"

D'arl smiled sadly. "Because the Trofts aren't afraid of human militias or armies. They're afraid of Cobras."

Jonny blinked. He opened his mouth to disagree . . . but all that came out was a single whispered syllable: "Damn."

D'arl nodded. "And you see now why I had to do all this. Aventine may never have the ability to truly defend itself against an invasion, but as long as a deterrent exists, even a purely psychological one . . . well, you at least have a chance."

"And the Dominion is spared the trouble and expense of a punitive war?" Jonny suggested acidly.

Again, D'arl smiled. "You're beginning to understand the mechanisms of politics. The greatest good for the greatest number, and immediate benefits for as many as possible."

"Or at least for those whose support you need?" Jonny asked quietly. "Those whose objections don't count can be ignored?"

"Jonny, it's your safety we're talking about here," Jame put in earnestly. "Yes, it's going to cost you something, but everything in life *does*."

"I know that." Jonny stood up. "And I'll even accept that the Committé had our interests at least somewhat at heart. But I don't have to like his solution, and I don't have to like his method of pushing it on us. You withheld information about the gantuas from us, Committé, maybe for months—and someone could have been killed because of it. If I could see it making a scrap of difference, I'd have that fact on the public net tonight. As it is, I suppose I'll just have to leave you to your own conscience. If you still have one."

"Jonny—" Jame began angrily.

"No, it's all right," D'arl interrupted him. "An honest enemy is worth a dozen allies of expediency. Good-bye, Syndic Moreau."

Jonny nodded and turned his back on the Committé. The door slid open as he approached it and he stepped through, relying on his memory to get him back through the corridors to the ship's exit. Thoughts churning, he didn't notice Jame had followed him until the other spoke. "I'm sorry it had to end that way. I would have liked you to understand him."

"Oh, I understand him," Jonny replied shortly. "I understand that he's a politician and can't bother to think through the human consequences of his chess moves."

"You're a politician now yourself," Jame reminded him, guiding him through a turn he'd forgotten. "Chances are you'll be stuck with a similar no-win situation yourself someday. In the meantime, I hope you have enough wins and losses to be able to handle both a bit better."

They said their good-byes at the entryway—cool, formal words of farewell Jonny would never have envisioned saying to his own brother—and a few minutes later the Cobra was back in his car.

But he didn't drive off immediately. Instead, he sat behind the wheel and stared at the muted sheen of the Dominion ship, his mind replaying over and over again Jame's last words to him. Could he really be reacting so strongly simply because he'd lost a minor power struggle? He *was* unused to defeat, after all. Could his noble-sounding concern for Aventine's future be truly that petty underneath?

No. He'd suffered defeats many times: on Adirondack, on Horizon after the war, even in the opening round of the brief struggle against Challinor. He knew how losing felt, knew how he reacted to it . . . and knew it was often only temporary.

Temporary.

With one final glance at D'arl's ship, Jonny started the car. No, it wasn't over yet. Aventine would survive and grow; and he, not D'arl, would be best in position to guide that growth. And if learning the art of politics was what he needed to do, he would become the best damn politician this side of Asgard.

In the meantime . . . there were a woman, a child, and a district who deserved his full attention. Turning the car around, he headed for home. Chrys, he knew, would be waiting up.

Interlude

The haiku garden had changed over the years, slowly and subtly enough that D'arl no longer remembered exactly how it had been when he had succeeded Committé H'orme. One stretch, however, showed D'arl's hand clearly: a series of blussa reeds, stunted cyprene trees, and other flora from Aventine. As far as he knew, he was the only Committé to incorporate plant life of the Outer Colonies in his haiku garden . . . and it looked very much like no one else would ever have the chance to do so.

Jame Moreau, at his side, correctly interpreted his gaze. "This time they mean it, don't they," he said. It was more statement than question.

D'arl hesitated, then nodded. "I can't see any other interpretation for such a clear-cut demand. We're going to be lucky if the ship we're sending doesn't get stranded on Aventine."

"Or halfway back." Jame squatted down to straighten a blussa reed that was trying to fall over.

"Halfway back *would* be a problem," D'arl agreed. "But we can't let the Trofts close the Corridor without at least giving Aventine a little warning."

"For all the good it'll do." Jame's voice was controlled, but D'arl knew what he was thinking. The younger man's brother and sister were out there; and if the relationships were a bit cooler than they'd once been, Jame still cared deeply for them both.

"They'll survive," the Committé told him, wishing the words could be more than ineffectual puffs of air. "The Troft concept of hostage seems to involve land and property instead of people. If they behave themselves, the Trofts aren't likely to hurt them."

Jame straightened up, brushing bits of dirt from his fingers.

209

"Except that they *won't* behave themselves," he said quietly. "They'll fight, especially Jonny and the other Cobras—and that *is*, after all, just what the Committee and Joint Command want them to do."

D'arl sighed. "That's always been the fate hanging over their heads, Moreau. We knew it when we sent them out—you probably knew it, down deep, when you first came up with the plan. Whatever happens now, it was still worth the risk."

Jame nodded. "I know, sir. But I can't help wishing there was something we could do for them here."

"I'm open to suggestions."

"How about letting the Trofts close the Corridor in exchange for leaving the colonies alone?"

D'arl shook his head. "I've thought of that, but the Committee would never go for it. Impossible to verify, for starters. Besides which, we've put a lot of money, people, and effort into those worlds, and we couldn't simply cut them adrift without a fight."

Jame sighed and nodded in reluctant agreement. "I'd like to request a place on the courier ship, sir, if you can get me aboard. I know it's short notice, but I can be ready before the scheduled lift from Adirondack."

D'arl had suspected the request was coming, but that didn't make his answer any easier to give. "I'm sorry, Moreau, but I'm afraid I can't allow you to go. You've pointed out yourself the danger of Troft capture or destruction on the return trip—and before you tell me you're willing to take the risks, let me say *I'm* not willing for you to do so. You know too much about the internal workings and frictions of the Committee, and I'd hate to have the Trofts using our own most petty politics against us."

"Then let me take a fast recall-blockage treatment," Jame persisted. "It wouldn't delay the lift by more than a day if I can schedule my recuperation period to be aboard ship."

D'arl shook his head. "No—because you could lose it all permanently with a hasty treatment like that, and I'm not risking *that*, either."

Jame exhaled in defeat. "Yes, sir."

D'arl gazed off across the haiku garden. "I'm not insensitive to your feelings," he said quietly, "but such a hurried meeting with your family under these conditions would be bittersweet at best and certainly unproductive. The best thing you can do for them is to stay here and help me hold off the diplomatic breakdown as long as I can. The longer we have before actual hostilities begin, the more time they'll have to prepare."

And the more time—he didn't add—the Dominion would have to prepare its own defenses. Because important as they were, the Outer Colonies represented less than four hundred thousand people . . . and from the perspective of the dome, the Dominion's seventy other worlds and hundred billion other people were vastly more important. In the defense of those people, Aventine and its sister worlds were ultimately expendable. *The greatest good for the greatest number* was still the most stable guidepoint D'arl knew.

He was careful not to spell it all out for Jame . . . but then, the other had probably already figured it out. Why else would he have wanted to go to Aventine and say good-bye?

With a sigh, D'arl continued down the path. One more curve and he would be back to his office door. Back to the real world, and to the looming specter of war.

And to waiting for a miracle he knew wouldn't happen.

Statesman: 2432

The bedside phone's signal was a loud, directional buzz scientifically designed to wake even deep sleepers. But it had been months since Jonny slept merely deeply, and his mind barely noticed the sound enough to incorporate it into his current dream. It wasn't until Chrys's gentle prodding escalated to a vigorous shake that he finally drifted up to partial wakefulness. "Um?" he asked, eyes still closed.

"Jonny, Theron Yutu's on the phone," she said. "He says it's urgent."

"Uff," Jonny sighed, rolling heavily onto his side and punching at the hold-release button. "Yeah?"

"Governor, I'm at the starfield," Yutu's voice came. "A Dominion courier ship's on its way in—ETA about an hour. They want you, Governor-General Stiggur, and as many syndics as possible assembled here when they arrive."

"At—what is it, three in the morning? What's the rush?"

"I don't know, sir—they wouldn't say anything more than that. But the starfield night manager said they wanted no more than a twelve-hour turnaround."

"They want to leave in twelve *hours*? What the hell is—? Oh, never mind; I'm sure they wouldn't tell you." Jonny inhaled deeply, trying to clear the ground clutter from his brain. "Have you gotten in touch with Stiggur yet?"

"No, sir. The Hap-3 satellite's still out, and it'll be another half hour before Hap-2 is in position to make the call."

And once he *was* notified it would be another three hours before he could get back from the outland district he was touring. Which meant the whole burden of greeting this mysterious and apparently impatient Dominion representative was going to fall on Jonny. "Well, you'd better get some people calling all the syndics—even the ones who can't get here in an hour should come as soon as they can. Uh . . . any idea of what rank this guy is?"

"No, sir, but from his attitude I doubt he's looking for much in the way of ceremony."

"Well, that's one bright spot, anyway. If it's efficiency he wants, we'll give it to him with spangles. We'll skip the Dominion Building altogether and meet at the starfield's entrypoint building. Can you get us a decently sized office or conference room and set up some security around it?"

"Almo Pyre's already down there—I'll have him find you a room."

"Good." Jonny tried to think of anything else he should suggest, but gave up the effort. Yutu generally knew what he was doing, anyway. "All right, I'll be at the starfield in half an hour. Better get out there yourself—I might need you."

"Yes, sir. Sorry about all this."

"S'okay. See you."

Jonny flicked off the phone with a sigh and lay quietly for a moment, gathering his strength. Then, trying not to groan audibly, he sat up. It wasn't as bad as he'd expected: he felt the usual stiffness in his joints, but only one or two actual twinges of pain. The lightheadedness left quickly, and he got to his feet. The hemafacient pills were on his nightstand, but he technically wasn't supposed to take one for another four hours. He did so anyway, and by the time he finished his shower the last remnants of his anemic fatigue were gone. At least for a while.

Chrys had been busy in his brief absence, finding and laying out his best formalwear. "What do you think it's all about?" she asked, keeping her voice low. The eight-year-olds, Joshua and Justin, were in the next room, and both had a history of light sleeping.

Jonny shook his head. "The last time they sent someone without at least a couple months' warning, it was to stick us with the Cobra factory. I suppose it could be something like that . . . but a twelve-hour turnaround sounds awfully ominous. He either wants to get back home as fast as possible or doesn't want to spend any more time here than absolutely necessary."

"Could some disease have shown up in our last shipment?" Chrys asked, holding his shirt for him. "A lot of those commercial carriers only take minimal precautions."

"If it had, they'd probably have specified that they'd stay aboard their ship while it was being serviced." Jonny grimaced as he backed into the sleeves, trying to keep the sudden pain from showing.

Chrys noticed anyway. "Dad called this afternoon to remind you again about getting that checkup," she said.

"What for?" Jonny growled. "To hear him tell me my anemia and arthritis are still getting worse? I already know that." He sighed. "I'm sorry, Chrys. I know I should go see Orrin, but I truly don't know what good it would do. I'm paying the price for being a superman all these years, and that's all there is to it."

She was silent for a long moment, and in a way her surface calm was more disturbing than the periodic outbursts of bitterness and rage that had occurred over the first months of his condition. It meant she'd accepted the fact that he couldn't be cured and was sublimating her own pain to help him and their three sons handle theirs. "You'll call when you know what's going on?" she asked at last.

"Sure," he promised, relieved at the change of subject. But only for a moment . . . because there was only one reason he could think of for the behavior of that ship out there. And if he was right, progressive anemia was likely to be the least of his worries.

Five minutes later he was driving toward the starfield. Beyond the glow of the streetlights, in the darkened city, the ghosts of Adirondack seemed to be gathering.

Tammerlaine Wrey was the image of the middle-level Dome bureaucrats that had been the favorite target of political caricaturists when Jonny was growing up. Paunchy and soft, with expensive clothes in better shape than he was, he had that faintly condescending air that frontier people often claimed to sense in all mainstream Dominion citizens.

And his news was as bad as it could possibly be.

"Understand, we'll be doing what we can to draw off the bulk of the Troft forces," he said, waving a finger at the curved battle front on the Star Force tactical map he'd brought with him. "But while we'll be keeping them pretty busy, it's unlikely they'll forget about you completely. The Joint Command's best estimate is that you can expect anywhere from twenty to a hundred thousand troops on your three planets within a year."

"My God!" Syndic Liang Kijika gasped. "A hundred *thousand?* That's a *quarter* of our combined populations."

"But you have nearly twenty-four hundred Cobras," Wrey pointed out. "A hundred thousand Trofts shouldn't be too much for them to handle, if past experience proves anything."

"Except that almost seventy percent of those Cobras have never seen any sort of warfare," Jonny put in, striving to keep his voice calm as the memories of Adirondack swirled like swamp vapor through his mind. "And those who have are likely to be unfit for duty by the time the attack comes."

"'Those who can't do, teach,'" Wrey quoted. "Your veterans ought to be able to whip them into shape in a few months. Gentlemen, I didn't come here to run your defense for you—it's *your* people and *your* world and you'll undoubtedly do a better job of it than I or anyone else on Asgard could. I came here solely to give you a warning of what was coming down and to bring back the dozen or so Dominion citizens that the ban on commercial travel has stranded here."

"We're *all* Dominion citizens," Tamis Dyon snarled.

"Of course, of course," Wrey said. "You know what I mean. Anyway, I'll want those people packed and on my ship within six hours. I have their names, but you'll have to find them for me."

"What's being done to try and prevent the war?" Jonny asked.

Wrey frowned slightly. "It's beyond prevention, Governor—I thought I'd made that clear."

"But the Central Committee is still talking—"

"In order to delay the outbreak long enough for you to prepare."

"What do you mean, *prepare*?" Dyon snapped, rising half out of his seat. "What the hell are we going to do—build antiaircraft guns out of cyprene trees? You're condemning us to little more than a choice of deaths: murder by the Trofts or the slow strangulation of a closed supply pipeline."

"*I* am not responsible for what's happened," Wrey shot back. "The Trofts started this, and you ought to be damned glad the Committee was willing to back you up. If it hadn't, you'd have been overrun years ago." He paused, visibly regaining his control. "Here's the list of people I'm authorized to bring back," he said, sliding a magcard across the table toward Jonny. "Six hours, remember, because the *Menssana*'s leaving in—now—eleven."

Slowly, Jonny reached across the table and picked up the magcard. The die was apparently cast . . . but there was too much at stake to just sit and do nothing. "I'd like to talk to Governor-General Stiggur about sending an emissary back with you," he said. "To find out what's really going on."

"Out of the question," Wrey shook his head. "In the first place we stand an even chance of getting hit by the Trofts before we ever reach Dominion space; and even if we get through, your emissary would just be trapped there. The Corridor hasn't a prayer of staying open long enough for him to return, and he'd just be dead weight on Asgard."

"He could function as a consultant on conditions here," Jonny persisted. "You admitted yourself you don't really know us."

"A consultant to what end? Are you expecting the Star Force to launch a backup assault through a hundred light-years of Troft territory?" Wrey glanced around the table at the others and stood up. "Unless there are any more questions, I'm going back to the *Menssana* for a while. Please inform me when Governor-General Stiggur arrives." Nodding, he strode briskly from the room.

"Doesn't care falx droppings for us, does he?" Kijika growled. His fingertips were pressed hard enough against the tabletop to show white under the nails.

"It's not going to matter much longer what he or anyone else in the Dominion thinks about us," Dyon said grimly.

"Maybe we can postpone that a bit," Jonny told him, handing Dyon the magcard. "Would you give this to Theron Yutu and have him start locating these people? I have an important call to make."

Governor-General Brom Stiggur was still en route to Capitalia, but he was within constant range of the Hap-2 communications satellite now and the picture was crystal clear. Not that it mattered, really—Stiggur's expression was exactly as Jonny had expected it to be. "So that's it, then," the other said when Jonny had summarized Wrey's doomsday message. "The Trofts have finally gotten their courage up for round two. Damn them all to hell." He snorted. "Well, what's it going to take to get us ready for a siege?"

"More time than we've got," Jonny said bluntly. "To be brutally honest, Brom, I don't think we've got an icecube's chance on Vega if the Trofts decide they really want us. The new Cobras are our only defense and they know less than nothing about warfare."

Stiggur grimaced. "Should we be discussing this on a broadcast signal—?"

"We're going to keep all this a secret?"

"Not hardly," Stiggur conceded. "All right, Jonny—you didn't call just to give me advance notice of Armageddon. What do you want?"

Jonny swallowed hard. "Permission to return with Wrey to Asgard and see what can be done to hold off the war."

Stiggur's eyebrows lifted toward his hairline. "Don't you think they've done everything possible in that direction already?"

"I don't know. How can we unless we talk directly to the Central Committee or Joint Command?"

Stiggur exhaled loudly. "We need you here."

"You know better than that. I can't fight worth a damn anymore, and there are a lot of First Cobras with better military and tactical knowledge."

"What about your family, then?" Stiggur asked quietly. "*They* need you."

Jonny took a deep breath. "Twenty-nine years ago I left all the family I had then to fight for people I didn't even know. How can I pass up even the slimmest chance now to save the lives of not only my wife and children, but virtually all the friends I've ever had?"

Stiggur gazed at him for a long minute, his expression giving away nothing of what was going on behind it. "Much as I hate to admit it, I suppose you're right," he finally said. "I'll recommend to this Wrey character that he take you along. Uh . . . another half-hour to Capitalia, looks like. I should have his answer in an hour or so. In the meantime—" He hesitated. "You'd better let Yutu handle things and go discuss this with Chrys."

"Thanks, Brom. I'd already planned to do that."

"I'll talk to you whenever I know something." He nodded and the screen went blank.

Sighing, Jonny carefully flexed his rebellious elbows and punched for Yutu.

They all sat quietly in the softly lit living room as Jonny explained both the bad news and his proposed response to the crisis; and as he gazed at each member of his family in turn, he was struck as never before by the contrasting personalities their expressions revealed. Justin and Joshua, huddled together on the couch, showed roughly equal parts of fear and unquestioning trust, a mixture that was painfully reminiscent of his sister Gwen's childhood hero-worship. By contrast, Corwin's face belied his thirteen years as he clearly struggled to find an adult perspective into which he could submerge his own feelings of dread. Very like Jame, who'd always seemed older than his own biological age. And Chrys . . .

Chrys was as she always was, radiating a quiet strength and support toward him even while her eyes ached with the fear and pain a permanent separation would bring her. An acceptance of his plan based not on submission of any kind, but on the simple fact that her mind worked the same as his did and she could see just as clearly that it was something that had to be tried.

He finished his explanation, and for a few moments the silence was broken only by the soft hum of the air conditioning. "When'll you be leaving, Dad?" Corwin asked at last.

"If I go, it'll be today," Jonny answered. "They'll want to leave as soon as the ship's refueled and all."

"Are you going to take Almo or someone with you?"

Jonny smiled briefly. Almo Pyre had been one of the first volunteers through D'arl's Cobra factory, and with his fierce loyalty toward Jonny and the entire Moreau family, he'd been a natural role model for Corwin to latch onto. "I don't think we'll have any problems on the way back," he told his son. "Besides which, your father's not *that* helpless yet." Steeling himself, he turned to Chrys. Her loyalty toward him deserved at least as much back. "I've explained all of what I know and think, and why I feel I should go," he told her. "But if, after hearing it, you think I should stay, I'll do so."

She smiled sadly. "If you don't understand me better than that by now—"

The abrupt ring from the phone made them all jump. Getting carefully to his feet, Jonny went to his desk and flipped the instrument on. "Yes?"

It was Stiggur. "Sorry, Jonny, but no go. Wrey steadfastly refuses to clutter his ship with useless colonial officials. His words."

Jonny exhaled slowly. "Did you explain how important it could be?"

"Loudly enough to scare a gantua. He simply refuses to consider anything even marginally outside his orders."

"Then maybe I'd better talk to him again myself. Do I still have *your* authorization to go?"

"I guess so. But it's all academic now."

"Perhaps. I'll get back to you."

He disconnected and started to punch for the starfield . . . but halfway through the motion he paused and turned to look at Chrys.

Her eyes gazed at his, and through them to whatever pain she saw in the future. But though her lips seemed made of wood, her voice was firm enough. "Yes. Try."

He held her eyes another second, then turned back to the phone.

A few moments later Wrey's face appeared. "Yes? Oh, it's you. Look, Governor—"

"Mr. Wrey, I'm not going to repeat Governor-General Stiggur's arguments," Jonny interrupted him. "I don't care whether you can't see past your own nose and understand why this is important. The fact of the matter is that I'm coming with you to Asgard, and you can like it or not."

Wrey snorted. "Oh, really? They call that a Titan complex back in Dome, Moreau—the belief that you can go ahead and defy authority any time you want to. I suggest you check on my status here and consider what would happen if you tried to barge past my Marines against my orders."

Jonny shook his head. "I'm afraid it is *you*, sir, who's misunderstanding the legal situation here. Our charter clearly states that the governor-general may requisition a berth on any outgoing ship for purposes of consultation with Dominion officials. The charter makes *no* provision for exceptions."

"I claim an exception anyway. If you don't like it, you can file a grievance with the Central Committee when the war's over."

"I'm sorry, but it doesn't work that way. If you want to claim a legitimate exception, you'll have to present your case here, to Aventine's Council of Syndics."

Wrey's eyes narrowed. "What does that entail?"

Which meant the other had been on Asgard so long he'd forgotten how planet-level politics worked. For an instant Jonny was tempted to spin a genuine horror story, but quickly decided against it. Playing it straight was safer, and the truth was bad enough. "We'll first need to assemble all the Syndics—that's the easy part; they're all on the way here already. Then you'll present your credentials and your case and Governor-General Stiggur will present his. The council will discuss the situation and probably recess to make individual studies of the charter and try to find precedents in whatever Dominion records we have on file. Then they'll reassemble for a full debate, and when that's finished they'll vote. If the law seems to allow both sides of the case, a simple majority will suffice; but if the charter regulation I mentioned seems unopposed, then you'll need a three-quarters vote to grant you a one-time exception. The whole process will take—oh, maybe three to five days, minimum."

From the look on Wrey's face, the other had already added up the times. "Suppose I refuse to cooperate with this little delaying tactic?"

"You're free not to cooperate . . . but your ship doesn't lift until all this is resolved."

"How are you going to stop me?"

Reaching to the phone, Jonny tapped some keys, and a second later a new voice joined the circuit. "Pyre here."

"Almo, this is Jonny Moreau. How's security setup going?"

"All locked down, Governor," the younger Cobra told him.

"Good. Please inform the night manager that there's no longer any rush to service the Dominion ship. It won't be leaving for a few more days."

"Yes, sir."

"Hold it, soldier," Wrey snapped. "I am a direct representative of the Central Committee, and on that authority I'm countermanding that order. Understand?"

There was a short pause. "Governor, is his claim legitimate?"

"Yes, but this specific action seems to violate a clear charter provision. It looks like it'll be going to the council."

"Understood, sir. Servicing operations will be suspended immediately."

"What?" Wrey barked. "Just a damned—"

"Out, sir."

A click signaled Pyre's departure, leaving the rest of Wrey's outburst to expend itself in thin air. He broke off, fixing Jonny with a furious glare. "You're not going to get away with this, Moreau. You can throw your Cobras against my armored Marines all day without—"

"Are you suggesting a firefight in the vicinity of your ship, sir?" Jonny asked mildly.

Wrey fell suddenly silent. "You won't get away with it," he repeated mechanically.

"The *law* is on my side," Jonny said. "Frankly, Mr. Wrey, I don't see why this is really a problem. You obviously have the room to spare for me, and I've already showed you that you'll be both morally *and* legally in the clear if your superiors become annoyed. And who knows? Maybe they'll actually be glad I came along . . . in which case you'll get all the credit for such foresight."

Wrey snorted at that, but Jonny could see in his face that he'd already opted for the simpler, safer course. "All right, what the hell. You want to cut out and spend the war on Asgard, that's none of *my* business. Just be here when the rest of the passengers show or I'll leave without you."

"Understood. And thank you."

Wrey snorted again and the screen went blank.

Jonny exhaled slowly. Another minor victory . . . and as emotionally unsatisfying as all such political wins seemed to be. Perhaps, he thought, it was because no opponent was ever fully vanquished in this form of combat. They always got back up out of the dust, a little smarter and—often—a little madder each time. And Jonny would now be spending the next three months heading straight for Wrey's political domain, while Wrey himself had those same months to plan whatever revenge he chose.

So much for victory.

Grimacing, Jonny punched again for Almo Pyre. His order halting the ship's servicing would have to be rescinded.

There was a great deal of work involved in turning over his duties on such short notice, and in the end Jonny wound up with far less time than he'd wanted to tell his family good-bye. It added one more shade of pain to the already Pyrrhic victory, especially as he had no intention of letting Wrey know how he felt.

The worst part, of course, was that there was very little aboard ship to occupy his thoughts. On the original trip to Aventine a quarter century earlier, there'd been fellow colonists to meet as well as magcards of information compiled by the survey teams to be studied. Here, even with the fourteen business passengers Wrey was bringing home, the ship carried only thirty-six people, none of whom Jonny was especially interested in getting to know. And if the ship carried any useful information on the impending war, no one was saying anything about it.

So for the first couple of weeks Jonny did little except sit alone in his cabin, reread the colonies' data he'd brought to show the Central Committee, and brood . . . until one morning he awoke with an unexpected, almost preternatural alertness. It took him several minutes to figure out on a conscious level what his subconscious had already realized: during ship's night they had passed from no-man's space into the Troft Corridor. The old pattern of being in hostile territory evoked long-buried Cobra training; and as the politician yielded to the warrior, Jonny unexpectedly found his helpless feelings giving way to new determination. For the time being, at least, the political situation had become a potentially military one . . . and military situations were almost never completely hopeless.

He began in the accepted military way: learning the territory. For hours at a time he toured the *Menssana,* getting to know everything about it and compiling long mental lists of strengths, weaknesses, quirks, and possibilities. He learned the names and faces of each of the fourteen crewers and six Marines, evaluating as best he could how they would react in a crisis. Doing the same with the passengers actually proved a bit easier: with the same excess of free time he himself had, they were eager to spend time with him, playing games or just talking. More than once Jonny wished he'd brought Cally Halloran along, but even without the other's knack at informal psych analysis, he was soon able to divide the passengers into the old "float/freeze" categories: those who could probably deal with and adapt to a crisis, and those who couldn't. Heading the former were two executive field reps Jonny soon learned to consider friends as well as potential allies: Dru Quoraheim, a pharmaceutical company executive whose face and dry humor reminded him vaguely of Ilona Linder; and Rando Harmon, whose interests lay in rare metals and, occasionally, Dru Quoraheim. For a while Jonny wondered if Dru had latched onto him to use as a partial shield against Harmon's advances, but as it became clear that those advances were entirely non-serious he realized the whole thing was an elaborate game designed to give the participants something to concentrate on besides the mental picture of silent Troft warships.

And when his survey was complete . . . it was back to waiting. He played chess with Dru and Harmon, kept abreast of the ship's progress, and—alone, late at night—tried to come up with some way to keep the war from happening, or at least to keep it from happening to Aventine. And wondered if and when the Trofts would move against the *Menssana*.

Twenty-five light-years from Dominion space, they finally did.

It was evening, ship's time, and most of the passengers were in the lounge, grouped in twos and threes for conversation, social drinking, or the occasional game. At a table near the back Jonny, Dru, and Harmon had managed a synthesis of all three in the form of a light Aventine sherry and a particularly nasty round of trisec chess.

A game Jonny's red pieces were steadily losing. "You realize, of course," he commented to his opponents, "that such friendly cooperation between you two is prima facie evidence of collusion between your two companies. If I lose this game, I'm swearing out a complaint when we get to Asgard."

"Never stand up in court," Harmon rumbled distractedly. His

attention had good reason to be elsewhere; Dru was slowly but inexorably building up pressure on his king side and too many of his own pieces were out of position to help. "Dru's the one who's apparently moonlighting from the Joint Command's tactical staff."

"I wish I was," Dru shook her head. "At least I'd have something to *do* during the war. Market developers don't get much work when the market shrinks."

For a few minutes the only sound was the click of chess pieces as Dru launched her attack, Harmon defended, and Jonny took advantage of the breather to reposition his own men. Harmon was a move behind in the exchange and wound up losing most of his cozy castle arrangement. "Tell me again about this collusion," he said when the flurry of moves was over.

"Well, I *could* be mistaken," Jonny admitted.

Harmon grunted and took a sip of his drink. "Going to be the last Aventine sherry anyone back home gets for a long time," he commented. "A real pity."

"War usually is." Jonny hesitated. "Tell me, what does the Dominion's business community think of the upcoming hostilities?"

Dru snorted. "I presume you're not talking about the shipyards and armaments manufacturers?"

"No, I mean companies like yours that've been working with Aventine. Maybe even the Trofts, too, for all I know. Like you said, Dru, you're losing a growing market out here."

She glanced at Harmon. "With Aventine, yes, though I'll point out for the record that neither of our companies deals with the Trofts—Dome is very stingy with licenses for that kind of trade. You're right, though, that the Outer Colonies are going to be missed."

"Anyone who deals with you feels pretty much the same way," Harmon added. "But there's nothing obvious we can do about it."

"About all we can do is hope our first attack is so brilliant and decisive that it ends the war before too much damage is done." Dru moved a pawn, simultaneously opening Harmon's king to a new threat and blocking an advance from Jonny's remaining rook.

Harmon waved at the board. "And if the Star Force has any brains, they'll put Dru in charge—what was that?"

Jonny had felt it too: a dull, almost audible thump, as if someone had dropped an exceptionally heavy wrench in the *Menssana's* engine room. "We've just dropped out of hyperspace," he said quietly, sliding his chair back and looking around. None of the others in the lounge seemed to have noticed the jolt.

"Out *here?*" Dru frowned. "Aren't we still two weeks inside Troft territory?"

"It may not have been voluntary." Jonny stood up. "Stay here; I'm going to the bridge. Don't say anything to the others yet— no sense panicking anyone until we know what's going on."

He reached the bridge to find Captain Davi Tarvn presiding over a scene of controlled chaos. "What's the situation?" he asked, stepping to the other's command station.

"Too soon to really tell," Tarvn replied tightly. "Looks like we hit a Troft flicker-mine web, but so far the usual spider ships haven't shown up. Maybe they won't."

"Wishful thinking."

"Sure, but that's about all we've got," Tarvn nodded. "If a Troft shows up before the drive's recalibrated, we've had it. You know as well as I do how long our weaponry and plating would hold against attack—you've been studying the ship enough lately."

Jonny grimaced. "About half a minute if they were determined. What can I do?"

"You can get the hell off the bridge," a new voice snapped, and Jonny turned to see Wrey crossing the floor toward them. "Status, Captain?"

"Minimum of an hour before the drive can be fixed," Tarvn told him. "Until then we try to be as inconspicuous as possible—"

"Hostile at ninety-seven slash sixty," the navigator interjected suddenly. "Closing, Captain."

"Battle stations," Tarvn gritted. "Well, gentlemen, so much for staying inconspicuous. Mr. Wrey, what do you want me to do?"

Wrey hesitated. "Any chance of outrunning him?"

"Second hostile," the navigator said before Tarvn could reply. "Two-ninety slash ten. Also closing."

"Right on top of us," Tarvn muttered. "I'd say our chances are slim, sir, at least as long as we're stuck in normal."

"Then we have to surrender," Jonny said.

Wrey turned a murderous glare onto him. "I told you to get lost," he snarled. "You have no business here—this is a *military* situation."

"Which is exactly why you need me. *I've* fought the Trofts; you almost certainly never have."

"So you're an overage reservist," Wrey grunted. "That still doesn't—"

"No," Jonny said, lowering his voice so that only Wrey and Tarvn could hear. "I'm a Cobra."

Wrey's voice died in mid-word, his eyes flicking over Jonny's form. Tarvn muttered something under his breath that Jonny didn't bother notching up his enhancers to catch. But the captain recovered fast. "Any of the passengers know?" he murmured.

Jonny shook his head. "Just you two—and I want it kept that way."

"You should have told me earlier—" Wrey began.

"Be quiet, sir," Tarvn said unexpectedly, his eyes still on Jonny. "Will the Trofts be able to detect your equipment, Governor?"

"Depends on how tight a filter they put all of us through," Jonny shrugged. "A full bioscan will show it, but a cursory weapon detector check shouldn't."

Behind Jonny the helmsman cleared his throat. "Captain?" he said, his voice rigidly controlled. "The Trofts are calling on us to surrender."

Tarvn glanced at his screens, turned back to Wrey. "We really don't have any choice, sir."

"Tell them we're an official Dominion courier and that this is a violation of treaty," Wrey said tightly, his own eyes on the displays. "Threaten, argue—do your damnedest to talk our way out. Then—" He exhaled between clenched teeth. "If it doesn't work, go ahead and surrender."

"And try to get terms that'll leave all of us aboard the *Menssana*," Jonny added. "We may need to get out in a hurry if we get an opening."

"We damn well better *get* that opening," Wrey murmured softly. "All of this is *your* idea, remember."

Jonny almost laughed. Middle-level bureaucrat, indeed—the operation had barely begun and already Wrey was scrambling to place any possible blame elsewhere. Predictable and annoying; but occasionally it could be used. "In that case, I presume I'm authorized to handle the whole operation? Including giving Captain Tarvn orders?"

Wrey hesitated, but only briefly. "Whatever you want. It's your game now."

"Thank you." Jonny turned back to Tarvn. "Let's see what we can do now about stacking the deck and maybe providing a little diversion at the same time."

He outlined his plan, got Tarvn's approval, and hurried to the Marine guardroom to set things up. Then it was back to the lounge and a quiet consultation with Dru and Harmon. They took the news calmly, and as they all collected and put away the chess pieces, he outlined the minor and—theoretically—safe roles he wanted them to play. Both agreed with a grim eagerness that showed he'd chosen his potential allies well.

He was back in his cabin fifteen minutes later, hiding the most sensitive of his Aventine data on random sections of unrelated magcards, when Tarvn officially announced the *Menssana*'s surrender. Obeying the captain's instructions, he went to the lounge with the others and tried to relax. He succeeded about as well as everyone else.

A half hour later, the Trofts came aboard.

The lounge was the largest public room on the ship, but fifteen passengers, thirteen crewers, and four Marines made for cozy quarters even without the seven armed Trofts lined up along the wall. Wrey and Tarvn were absent, presumably having been taken elsewhere; Jonny kept his fingers crossed that anyone who noticed would assume the two missing Marines were with them.

There had been few communications with the Trofts during the war to which Jonny had been privy, but back then he'd gotten the impression the aliens weren't much for social or even political small talk, and the boarding party's spokesman did nothing to shake that image. "This ship and its resources are now possessions of the Drea'shaa'chki Demesne of the Trof'te Assemblage," the alien's translator repeater stated in flat tones. "The crew and passengers will remain aboard as tokens of human consensus-order violations. The so-named Trof'te Corridor has been reclaimed."

So they *were* to be held aboard. That was a stroke of luck Jonny had hoped for but not dared to expect. If Wrey had wangled this concession, perhaps he was good for something, after all—

His thoughts were cut off abruptly as an armored but weaponless Marine was hauled through the door by two Trofts and put into line with the other prisoners. Mentally, Jonny shrugged; he'd expected the better equipped of his two sleepers to be found fairly quickly. The other Marine, in shirtsleeves and armed only with a knife and garotte, should withstand the search somewhat better. Not that his freedom or capture ultimately made much difference. As long as he drew the Trofts' attention away from the civilians, he was serving his purpose. Though Jonny doubted that he realized that.

The prisoners were kept in the lounge another hour, leading Jonny to wonder whether they would be staying there until the Trofts were satisfied everyone had been found. But as they were led back to the passenger cabin section without the second

Marine making his appearance, he decided the reason for the delay was probably more prosaic: that the aliens had been conducting careful sensor searches of their rooms with an eye toward turning them into cells. The guess turned out to be correct, and a few minutes later Jonny found himself back in his cabin.

Though not *quite* alone.

The three sensor disks the Trofts had attached to selected sections of wall and ceiling were rather conspicuous as such things went, nearly two centimeters across each with faintly translucent surfaces. A quick check showed that the bathroom and even the closet were equipped with disks of their own. What they might pick up besides an optical picture Jonny didn't know, but it hardly mattered. As long as they were in place, he was unable to act; ergo, his first task was to get rid of them.

It was probably the first time in twenty-seven years that his arcthrower might have done him some good; but then, he hardly could have used it without announcing in large red letters that he was a Cobra. Fortunately, there were other ways to accomplish what he had in mind. Returning to the bathroom, he selected a tube of burn salve from the cabinet first-aid kit. He was in the process of coating the second of the main room's disks with a thick layer of cream when the inevitable Troft charged in.

"You will cease this activity," the alien said, the monotone translator voice editing out whatever emotion lay behind the words.

"I'll be damned if I will," Jonny snarled back, putting all the righteous indignation he could into both voice and body language on the off-chance this was one of those Trofts who could read such nuances. "You attack us, pirate our ship, paw through our cabins—just *look* at the mess you left my magcards in—and now you have the damned nerve to *spy* on us. Well, I'm not going to stand for it—you hear me?"

The alien's upper-arm membranes rippled uncertainly. "Not all of you seem bothered by our security needs."

Not all of you... which implied Dru and Harmon had followed his instructions to kick up similar fusses. Three wasn't a very big crowd to hide in, but it was better than being blatantly unique. "Not all of us grew up with private bathrooms, either," he retorted, "but those who did can't do without them. I want my privacy and I'm going to get it."

"The sensors will remain," the Troft insisted.

"Then you're going to have to chain me up," Jonny snarled, crossing his arms defiantly.

The alien paused, and Jonny's enhanced hearing caught a stream of high-speed Troft catertalk. It was another minute before the translator came back on-line. "You spoke of privacy in the bathroom. If the sensor is removed from in there, will that satisfy your needs?"

Jonny pursed his lips. It *would*, actually, but he didn't want to accept the compromise too eagerly. "Well . . . I could try that, I suppose."

The Troft stepped past him and disappeared into the bathroom, returning a moment later with the sensor disk in one hand and some tissues from the dispenser in the other. He offered the latter to Jonny. It took the Cobra a second to understand; then, taking them, he proceeded to wipe clean the two disks he'd disabled. When he was finished, the Troft strode to the door and left.

He gave in awfully easily, was Jonny's first thought. A careful check of the bathroom, though, showed it was indeed clear of all sensors. Returning to the main room, he sat back down with his comboard—remembering to maintain an air of discomfort—and pretended to read.

He waited an hour, ten minutes of which time was spent in the bathroom to see if the Trofts would get nervous and send in a guard. But they'd evidently decided there was nothing dangerous he could do in there and no one disturbed him. Taking slightly higher than normal doses of his anemia and arthritis medicines, he returned to his comboard . . . and when the drugs took effect it was time to go.

He began with the normal human pattern for a pre-bedtime shower: pajamas carried into the bathroom accompanied by the hiss of water against tile. But under cover of the sound, Jonny's fingertip lasers traced a rectangular pattern on the thin metal panel between sink and shower stall, and within a minute he had a passable opening to the cramped service corridor behind the row of cabins. Leaving the water running, he squeezed into the corridor and began sidling his way forward.

The *Menssana*'s designer had apparently felt that separate ventilation systems for the various service lane levels would be a waste of good equipment and had opted instead for periodically spaced grilles to connect all of them together. It was a quirk that would ordinarily be of no use to anyone in Jonny's position, as the cramped quarters and high ceilings discouraged vertical movement almost as much as solid floors would have. But then, the designer hadn't been thinking about Cobras.

Jonny passed three more cabins before finding a grille leading
to the deck above. Bending his knees the few degrees the walls
allowed, he jumped upward, stifling a grunt as a twinge of pain
touched the joints. Catching the grille, he hung suspended for a
moment as he searched out the best spots to cut. Then, with leg
servos pressing his feet against the walls in a solid friction grip,
he turned his lasers against the metal mesh. A minute later he was
through the hole and sidling down that level's service corridor;
two minutes after that he was peering out the corridor's access
door at the darkened equipment room into which it opened. Next
door would be the EVA-ready room. Beyond that was the main
hatch and the probable connection to the Troft ship.

Jonny eased out the equipment room door into the deserted
corridor, alert for sounds of activity that weren't there. The main
hatch was indeed open, the boarding tunnel beyond snaking
enough to block any sight of the alien ship's own entryway.
Whatever security the Trofts had set up was apparently at the far
end of the tunnel, an arrangement that would be difficult but not
impossible to exploit. But any such operation required first that
the *Menssana* be under human control again . . . and to accomplish *that,* he would have to retake the bridge. Passing the hatch,
he continued on forward.

The spiral stairway leading to the bridge had not been designed
with military security in mind, but the Trofts had added one of
their sensor disks to the spiral in a position impossible to bypass.
From a semi-shadowed position down the hall, Jonny gritted his
teeth and searched his memory for a way to approach the stairway from behind. But any such route would take a great deal of
time, and time was in short supply at the moment. On the other
hand . . . if the Trofts saw an apparently unarmed man approaching
their position, they were unlikely to greet him with an automatic
blaze of laser fire. They would probably merely point their weapons
and order him to surrender, after which they would return him
to his cell and find out how he'd escaped. If they followed safe
military procedure and called in before confronting him . . . but
he'd just have to risk that. *Now,* while the *Menssana* was still in
or near the Corridor, was their best opportunity for escape. Gritting
his teeth, he started for the staircase.

He moved quickly, though no faster than a normal human could
have, and no challenges or shots came his way before he reached
the stairs and started up. His catlike steps were small bomb blasts
in his enhanced hearing, but between them he could hear the

unmistakable sounds of sudden activity overhead. He kept going . . . and when he raised his head cautiously above the level of the bridge floor he found himself facing a semicircle of four Troft handguns. "You will make no sudden movements," a translator voice ordered as he froze in place. "Now: continue forward for questioning."

Slowly, Jonny continued up the stairs and into the bridge, keeping his hands visible. The four guards were backed up by three more at the *Menssana*'s consoles, armed but with weapons holstered. Sitting atop the communications board was a small box of alien design. The Trofts' link with their own ship and translator, most likely . . . and in a highly vulnerable position.

"How did you escape from your quarters?" one of the guards asked.

Jonny focused on the semicircle. "Call your captain," he said. "I wish to speak to him about a trade."

The Trofts' arm membranes fluttered. "You are in no position to trade anything."

"How do you know?" Jonny countered. "Only your captain can make that assessment."

The Troft hesitated. Then, slowly, he raised a hand to a collar pin and let loose with a stream of catertalk. Another pause . . . and the communications box abruptly spoke. "This the Ship Commander. What do you propose to trade?"

Jonny pursed his lips. It was a question he'd been working on since the Trofts first came aboard . . . and he had yet to come up with a really satisfactory answer. Trade back the Trofts aboard the *Menssana*? But the aliens didn't think of *hostage* as a word applicable to living beings. The *Menssana* itself? But he hardly had real control of the ship. Still, if politics had taught him anything, it was the value of a plausible bluff. "I offer you your own ship in return for the humans you hold plus the release of this vessel," he said.

There was a long pause. "Repeat, please. You offer me my own demesne-ship?"

"That's right," Jonny nodded. "From this ship I have the power to destroy yours. For obvious example, a hard starboard yaw would tear out the boarding tunnel, depressurizing that part of your demesne-ship, and a simultaneous blast with the drive at this range would cause extensive damage to your own engines. Is this possibility not worth trading to avoid?"

His captors' arm membranes were fluttering at half-mast now.

Either the room temperature had risen dramatically or he had indeed hit a sensitive nerve. "Commander?" he prompted.

"The ability you claim is nonexistent," the box said. "You are not in control of that ship."

"You're wrong, Commander. My companion and I are in full control here."

"You have no companion. The soldier hiding in the dining-area ventilation system has been returned to his quarters."

So the other Marine *had* been found. "I'm not speaking of him."

"Where is your companion?"

"Nearby, and in control. If you want to know any more you'll have to come here and negotiate the trade I've suggested."

There was another long pause. "Very well. I will come."

"Good." Jonny blew a drop of sweat from the tip of his nose. Perhaps it *was* just getting hot.

"You will reveal your companion to us before the Ship Commander arrives," one of the guards said. It didn't sound like a request.

Jonny took a careful breath . . . prepared himself. "Certainly. She's right here." He gestured to his left, the arm movement masking the slight bending of his knees—

And he ricocheted off the ceiling to slam to the deck behind the four guards, fingertip lasers blazing.

The communications box went first, fried instantly by a blast from his arcthrower. Two of the guards' guns hit the deck midway through that first salvo; the other two guards made it nearly all the way around before their lasers also erupted with clouds of vaporized metal and plastic and went spinning from burned hands. A sideways jump and half turn and Jonny had the last three Trofts in sight. "Don't move," he snapped.

With the translator link down his words were unintelligible, but none of the aliens seemed to mistake his meaning. All remained frozen where they stood or sat, arm membranes stretched wide, as Jonny disarmed the last three and then tore the communicator pins from the uniforms of all seven. Herding them down the staircase, he got them into a nearby water pumping room—spot-welding the latch to make sure they stayed put—and hurried aft toward the main hatch. The Troft commander wasn't likely to come alone, and Jonny needed at least a little advance notice as to what size force he'd have to handle. The possibility that the other would simply veer off, trading his occupation force for two humans, wasn't one Jonny wanted to consider.

He heard them coming down the boarding tunnel long before they actually appeared: ten to fifteen of them, he estimated, from the sound. Hidden in an emergency battery closet a dozen meters down the hall, he watched through a cracked door as they approached. The commander was easy to spot, keeping to the geometric center of his guard array: an older Troft, by the purple blotches on his throat bladder, his uniform fairly dripping with the colored piping of rank. Six guards ahead of him, six behind him, their lasers fanned to cover both directions, the procession moved down the corridor toward Jonny's hiding place and the bridge. The vanguard passed him . . . and Jonny slammed open the door and leaped.

The door caught the nearest Troft full in the back, jolting him forward and clearing just enough room for Jonny's rush to get him through the phalanx unhindered. With one outstretched arm he caught the commander around his torso, the action spinning them both around as Jonny's initial momentum drove them toward the far wall. Slipping between the two guards on that side, they slammed against the plating, Jonny's back screaming with agony as it took the brunt of the impact.

And then, for a long moment, the corridor was a silent, frozen tableau.

"All right," Jonny said as his breath returned, "I know you don't apply the idea of hostage to yourselves, Commander, so we'll just think of this as a matter of your personal safety. All of you—lay your weapons down on the deck. I don't especially want to hurt your commander, but I will if I have to."

Still no one moved, the twelve laser muzzles forming shining counterpoint to the arched arm membranes spread out behind each of them. "I told you to drop your guns," Jonny repeated more harshly. "Don't forget that you can't hit me without killing your commander."

The Troft leaning against him stirred slightly in his grip. "They have no concern for my life," the translator voice said. "I am not the Ship Commander, merely a Services Engineer in his uniform. A crude trick, but one which we learned from humans."

Jonny's mouth went dry. His eyes swept the circle of Trofts, the steadiness of their weapons an unspoken confirmation of the other's words. "You're lying," he said, not believing it but driven to say *something.* "If you're not the commander, then why haven't they opened fire?" He knew the answer to that: they wanted him alive. History—personal history, at least—had repeated itself . . . and even more than on Adirondack, he knew the knowledge he held this time was too valuable to allow the enemy to have. *Chrys, a* detached fragment of his mind breathed in anguish toward the distant stars, and he prepared for his last battle—

"They will not shoot," the Troft in his grip said. "You are a *koubrah*-soldier from the Aventine world, and if killed you would merely fight on until all aboard were dead."

Jonny frowned. "How's that?"

"You need not deny the truth. We have all heard the report."

What report? Jonny opened his mouth to ask the question aloud . . . and suddenly he understood.

MacDonald. Somehow they'd heard about MacDonald.

He looked at the circle of Trofts again, seeing their rigidly stretched arm membranes with new eyes. Determination, he'd thought earlier, or perhaps rage. But now he recognized the emotion for what it was: simple, naked fear. *D'arl was right,* that same detached fragment of his mind realized. *They* are *afraid of us.* "I don't wish to kill anyone," he said quietly. "I want only to free my companions and to continue on my way."

"To what end?" the same flat voice came from the direction of the boarding tunnel. Jonny turned his head to see another middle-aged Troft walking slowly toward them. His uniform was identical to the one wrapped in Jonny's arms.

"That of protecting my world, Commander," Jonny told him. "By diplomatic means if possible, military ones if necessary."

The other said something in catertalk, and slowly the circle of laser muzzles dipped to point at the floor. His eyes on the Troft commander, Jonny released his captive and stepped out from behind him. A trick to put the Cobra off-guard, perhaps; but the politician within Jonny recognized the need to respond to the gesture with a good-faith one of his own. "Have we any grounds for negotiation?" he asked.

"Perhaps," the commander said. "You spared the lives of the Trof'tes in your control center when you could as easily have killed them. Why?"

Jonny frowned, realizing for the first time that he had no idea why he'd handled things that way. Too long in politics, where one never killed one's opponent? No. The real reason was considerably less colorful. "There wasn't any need to kill them," he said with a shrug. "I suppose it never really occurred to me."

"*Koubrah*-soldiers were created to kill."

"We were created to *defend*. There's a difference."

The other seemed to ponder that. "Perhaps there *are* grounds for compromise," he said at last. "Or at least for discussion. Will you and your companion come to my bridge?"

Jonny nodded. "Yes . . . but the companion I mentioned won't actually be there. She's an insubstantial entity we humans call Lady Luck."

The commander was silent a moment. "I believe I understand. If so, I would still invite her to accompany us."

Turning, he disappeared into the boarding tunnel. Hesitating only a moment, Jonny followed. The escort, weapons still lowered, fell into step around him.

He was back on the *Menssana* side of the tunnel four hours later when Wrey and Tarvn were brought aboard. "Good evening, gentlemen," Jonny nodded as their Troft escort silently disappeared back down the tunnel. "Captain, if you'll seal that hatch we're almost ready to be on our way."

"What the hell happened?" Wrey asked, his bewildered tone making the words more plaintive than demanding. "No questioning, no demands—no talk, period—and suddenly they're letting us go?"

"Oh, there was talking, all right," Jonny said. "Lots of it. That hatch secure? Good. Captain, I believe the drive repairs are finished, but you'll need to confirm that from the bridge. And make sure we're all ready before you pull away—the other Troft ship isn't in on this and they might try and stop us."

Tarvn's eyebrows arched, but all he said was, "Got it," before heading forward at a fast trot.

"What's going on?" Wrey demanded as Jonny started to follow. "What do you mean, there was lots of talking?"

"The Ship Commander and I had a discussion, and I convinced him it was in his best interests to let us go."

"In other words, you made a deal," Wrey growled. "What was it?"

"Something I'll discuss only with the Central Committee and only when we reach Asgard," Jonny told him flatly.

Wrey frowned at him, irritation and growing suspicion etching his face. "You're not authorized to negotiate for the entire Dominion of Man."

"That's okay—the Ship Commander wasn't authorized to negotiate for the Troft Assemblage, either." A gentle thump rippled through the deck and Jonny relaxed muscles he hadn't realized he'd had tensed. "But what authority he did have seems to have been adequate to get us away."

"Moreau—"

"Now if you'll excuse me, it's been a long night and I'm very tired. Good-night, Mr. Wrey; you can figure out on your own how you'll write this incident up. I'm sure you'll come out the hero in the final version."

Which was a rather cheap shot, Jonny admitted to himself as he headed aft toward his cabin. But at the moment his body was aching more than Wrey would ever know and he had no patience left for mid-bureaucratic mentality.

Or, for that matter, for illegal business practices and deliberate evasions. Which was why he planned to take a few days to recuperate before confronting Dru and Harmon with the half-truth the Troft Ship Commander had popped. Allies they had been; allies they might yet be . . . and he would like if possible to also keep them as friends.

It was another two weeks' travel to the Troft-Dominion border, fourteen of the longest days Jonny had ever suffered through this side of the last war. The cooling attitude toward him aboard the *Menssana* was part of it, of course, bringing back painful memories of those last months on Horizon. Jonny had all but forgotten the fear mainstream Dominion society felt toward Cobras, and on top of that he suspected Wrey of spitefully dropping hints that he'd made some terrible deal to buy their freedom. Only Harmon and Dru seemed relatively untouched by the general aloofness, and even with them Jonny could tell their friendliness had a large wedge of self-interest mixed in. After the long and painful confession session Jonny had forced them through shortly after their escape, he had the power to bring a fair amount of official flak down on them, and they both knew it.

But the social isolation was only a minor part of the frustration Jonny felt with the slowness of their progress. He had a real chance of sidetracking the war completely, but only if he could get to Asgard before the actual shooting began. To Asgard, and in front of the Central Committee. He hoped Jame would be able to arrange that; Wrey wasn't likely to be of any help.

And at last the *Menssana* touched down on Adirondack, the terminus point for Corridor traffic . . . and Wrey played his trump card.

"I'm sorry for whatever inconvenience it'll cost you to have to find your own ways back to your ultimate destinations," Wrey told the group of passengers as they gathered in the Dannimor starfield's customs building. "Unfortunately, the fast courier I'll be taking to Asgard hasn't room for anyone besides myself and Captain Tarvn."

"And me, I presume," Jonny spoke up.

"Afraid not," Wrey said blandly. "But then, you'll remember I warned you against inviting yourself along."

For a heartbeat Jonny simply stood there, unable to believe his ears. "You can't do that, Wrey—"

"Can't I?" the other retorted. "I suggest you check the statutes, Moreau—if you know how to look up *real* law, that is."

Jonny gazed at the other's self-satisfied expression, the small gloating smile playing at the corners of the paunchy man's mouth—the small mind having its big moment. And Jonny, his own mind occupied by too many other things, had failed completely to anticipate this move. "Look," he said quietly, "this is foolish, and you know it. The Committee needs to hear what the Troft Ship Commander told me—"

"Oh, yes—the 'secret plan' to stop the war that you won't tell anyone about," Wrey almost-sneered. "Maybe you'd better finally loosen up and give me at least the basic outline. I'd be sure and mention it to the Committee."

"I'm sure you would," Jonny grated. "You'll forgive me if I don't trust you to do the job right. Of course, you realize leaving me stranded here with vital information is likely to land you in very deep water very fast."

"Oh, I wouldn't worry about that." Wrey raised a finger and four men in Army uniforms detached themselves from various walls and stepped forward, halting in a loose box formation about Jonny. "I wouldn't worry about yourself, either," Wrey added. "You're going to be well taken care of."

Jonny glanced at the guards, his eyes slipping from the quietly alert faces to the collar insignia beneath. Interrorum, the Army's crack anti-espionage/anti-terrorist squad. "What the hell is this?" he demanded.

"You'll be getting a first-class military ride to Asgard," Wrey told him. "*After you've* been checked for hypnotic and subliminal manipulation, of course."

"What? Look, Wrey, unless basic citizen rights have been suspended recently—"

"You were alone with the Trofts for several hours, by your own admission," Wrey interrupted harshly. "Maybe they let us go because you'd been programmed for sabotage or assassination."

Jonny felt his jaw drop. "Of all the *ridiculous*—you can't make a charge like that stick for ten minutes."

"Take it easy, Governor. I'm not trying to make anything 'stick'— I'm merely following established procedures. You'll be released in— what were those numbers? Three to five days minimum? It takes a three-quarters majority of the examiners to clear you, of course."

Jonny ground his teeth. Wrey was really taking his pound of flesh. "And suppose while I'm sitting around hooked to a biomedical sensor your news of the Troft hijacking starts a war that could have been prevented? Or didn't that occur to you?"

For just an instant Wrey's eyes lost some of their insolence. "I don't think there's any danger of that. You'll get to Asgard in plenty of time." He smiled slyly. "Probably. All right, take him."

For a long second Jonny was tempted. But the soldiers were undoubtedly backed up by plainclothesmen elsewhere, and there were lots of innocent civilians in the building who'd be caught in any crossfire. Exhaling through his teeth, he let them take him away.

The first part of this kind of testing, Jonny remembered from his Cobra lectures, was to establish a physiological baseline by giving the subject several hours of solitary while hidden sensors piled up data. A side effect, especially for those who didn't know the procedure, was to raise the subject's tension level as he contemplated the unknown future awaiting him.

For Jonny, the wasted hours ticking by were maddening.

A dozen times in the first hour he seriously considered breaking out and trying to commandeer a star ship, and each time it was the sheer number of uncertainties that finally stopped him. By the end of the second hour the first twinges of pain began to intrude on his planning. He called the guard, was politely but firmly told his medicine would be returned once it had been analyzed. Protests were of no avail, and as he settled back on his cot to wait, the simmering anger within him began to slowly change into fear. In a very short time he would lose the ability to function . . . and when that happened he truly *would* be at Wrey's mercy.

He'd been in the cell nearly three hours when a shadow passed across the observation window and his enhanced hearing picked up a quiet click from the direction of the door.

He turned his head to see, muscles tensing . . . but the door wasn't being opened. Instead, a small hemispherical dome near the floor beside it rotated open to reveal a tray of food.

At the observation window a guard's face appeared. "Thanks," Jonny said, easing from the cot and retrieving the meal. The old familiar Adirondack cooking, his nostrils told him as he carried the tray back and sat down.

"No problem." The guard hesitated. "Are you really one of the Cobras that saved Adirondack from the Trofts?"

Jonny paused, spoon halfway to his mouth. "Yes," he acknowledged. "Are you a native?"

The guard nodded. "Born and raised right here in Dannimor. Where were you stationed?"

"Over in Cranach." The mesh in the window made the guard's face hard to see, but Jonny estimated his age in the low thirties. "You were probably too young to remember the war much."

"I remember enough. We had relatives in Paris when it was destroyed." He pursed his lips at the memory. "I had an uncle in Cranach then, too. Did you know a Rob Delano?"

"No." Memories flooded back of the people he had known . . . and with the mental pictures came an idea. "Tell me, just how isolated am I supposed to be?"

"What do you mean—visitors or something?"

"Or even phone calls. There are people probably still living nearby who I once thought I'd never see again. As long as I'm stuck here for a while maybe I can at least say hello to some of them."

"Well . . . maybe later that'll be possible."

"Can you at least get me a directory or something so I can find out who still lives in the area?" Jonny persisted. "This dose of solitary isn't a punishment, after all—it's just part of the deep-psych test preparation. I ought to be allowed to have reading material in here."

The guard frowned at that, but then shrugged. "I'm not sure that really qualifies as reading material, but I'll check with the guard captain."

"Be sure to remind him that I *am* a high Dominion official," Jonny said softly.

"Yes, sir." The guard disappeared.

Jonny returned his attention to his dinner, striving to keep his new spark of hope in check. What he could accomplish with a directory—or even with the hoped-for contact with his old allies—wasn't immediately clear, but at least it was somewhere to start. If nothing else, it might give him a feel for exactly how big an official cloud Wrey had put him under.

He had finished his meal and returned the tray to its place by the door, and was considering lying down again, when the guard returned. "The captain wasn't available," his disembodied voice came as the tray disappeared and a small comboard showed up in its place. "But since you're a Dominion official and all, I guess it'll be all right." His face reappeared at the window, and he watched as Jonny brought the instrument back to his cot.

"I really appreciate it," Jonny told him. "The directory's on the magcard here?"

"Yes—it covers Cranach, Dannimor, and the ten or so smaller towns around." He paused. "You Cobras were pretty effective, from all I've read about you."

Something in his tone caught Jonny's attention. "We did all right. Of course, we couldn't have done it without the civilian underground."

"Or vice versa. We're not going to have Cobras for the next war—did you know that?"

Jonny grimaced. "I didn't, but I guess I'm not surprised. The Army just going to set up normal guerrilla teams if war breaks out?"

"*When*, not *if*," the other corrected. "Yeah, we've got a whole bunch of Ranger and Alpha Force groups here now, some of them setting up civilian resistance networks."

Jonny nodded as he finally placed the guard's tone. "Scary, isn't it? War always is . . . but this one doesn't have to happen."

"Yes, I heard the Interrorum guys talking about that. They said a Cobra would blow up if he'd been hypno-conditioned."

"No, they took those self-destruct triggers out right after the war. But I *wasn't* hypno-conditioned; by the Trofts or anyone else."

"That Committee man, Wrey, seems to think so."

Jonny smiled bitterly. "Wrey's a short-sighted idiot who's nursing a bruised pride. I had to practically force him to bring me from Aventine in the first place, and then I saved his spangles for him when the Trofts captured the *Menssana*. This is his way of putting me in my place."

"But would you necessarily *know* if your mind had been tampered with?"

"*I* would, yes. That kind of thing requires that the subject be put into an unconscious or semiconscious state, and I've got internal sensors that would warn me of any chemical, optical, or sonic attempts to do that."

The guard nodded slowly. "Does Wrey know that?"

"I wasn't given the chance to tell him."

"I see. Well . . . I'd better get back to my duties. I'll be back later for the comboard."

"Thanks again," Jonny said; but the other had gone. *Now what,* he wondered uneasily, *was that all about? Information? Reassurance? Or was someone pulling his strings, trying to see how much I'd say?* Maybe Wrey had decided to hang around a few more hours hoping to be spared the trouble of shipping Jonny to Asgard. If so, Jonny knew, it would be a long wait. Balancing the comboard on his knees, he started his search.

Weissmann, Dane, Nunki; the names of a dozen temporary families and twice that many temporary teammates; the names *and* faces of Cobras living and dead—all of them tumbled out together with an ease that belied the twenty-six-year gap. For nearly half an hour he bounced back and forth through the directory as fast as his stiffening fingers would allow; for an hour after that he went more slowly as the flood of names became a trickle and finally ceased entirely.

And none of them were listed.

He stared at the comboard, mind unwilling to accept the evidence of his eyes. Adirondack was still classified as a frontier world, yes, with new areas constantly being developed—but even in twenty-six years how could *everyone* he'd known here have moved somewhere else?

He was still trying to make sense of it all when a movement outside his cell made him look up. The click of multiple bolts being withdrawn gave him just enough time to slide the comboard under his pillow before the cell door opened to reveal a young woman. "Governor Moreau?" she asked.

"Yes," Jonny nodded. "I hope you're someone in authority here."

Something crossed her face, too quickly to identify. "Not hardly. Thank you," she said, turning to the guard hovering at her shoulder—a different one, Jonny noted, than the one he'd talked with earlier. "I'll call when I'm done."

"All right, Doctor." The door swung shut behind her.

"Well, Governor, your medicine's been cleared," she said briskly, reaching into a pouch on her belt and producing the two vials that had been taken from him earlier. "I imagine you'd like to get some into your system before the examination."

Jonny frowned. "Examination?"

"Just routine. Take your pills, please."

He complied, and she sat down beside him on the cot. "I'll be taking some local/gradient readings," she said, producing a small cylinder from her pouch. "Just hold still and don't talk."

She flipped the instrument on and an oddly pervasive humming filled the room. "You've changed a lot," she said, just barely over the noise. "I wasn't sure it was you until I heard you speak."

"What?"

"Talk without moving your lips, please." She moved the instrument slowly across his chest, eyes on the readout.

Jonny felt a cold sweat break out on his forehead. Again, the possibility that this was a test sprang to mind . . . but if so the stakes had been jumped immensely. Even passive cooperation with this woman might be worth a conspiracy charge. "Who are you?" he mumbled, lips as motionless as he could keep them.

Her eyes met his for the first time and a strangely mischievous smile tugged at the corners of her lips. "Don't you remember your star geometry pupil?"

Geometry? "*Danice?* Danice Tolan?"

Her smile widened a bit. "I *knew* I hadn't changed that much." Abruptly, she became serious again. "Now: what are you doing in a Dominion military prison?"

"Officially, I'm here because I've been talking about peace with the Trofts and am therefore considered a security risk. In actuality, I'm here for stepping on a little man's pride."

"Peace." Danice said the word as if tasting it. "Anything come of those talks that could be considered progress?"

"It wasn't exactly a formal negotiation: but yes, I think I can keep the war from happening. If I can get the Central Committee to go along, that is."

"Which you obviously can't do from here." Her eyes were hard, measuring. "How long are you in for?"

"Wrey said three to five days or more. But he's already gone on to Asgard and there's no telling what the Committee'll do when he tells them we were stopped and boarded by the Trofts."

"You think they might declare war right then and there?"

"You tell me—you must know more about Dominion politics these days than I do."

Danice chewed gently at her lip, and for a long minute the only sound in the cell was the hum of her probe. Twice she paused to reset the instrument, and Jonny noticed a worried frown gradually spreading across her face. "All right," she mumbled abruptly. "We'll do it now. I'm registering a possible aneurysm in the hepatic artery—that should buy us a trip to the hospital for a closer look. Just try and play off of any cues." Without waiting for a reply she flicked off the instrument and called for the guard captain.

The captain wasn't wildly enthusiastic about her proposed hospital trip, but it was clear from his tone and worried glances that he considered the Cobra an important prisoner. Barely fifteen minutes later Jonny and Danice were heading under heavy guard through the gathering dusk toward the city's newest and best-equipped hospital.

Jonny's last experience with full mainstream medical care had been just before leaving for Aventine, and he was thoroughly impressed by the added sophistication and power the equipment had achieved in the intervening time. Multiple-layer, real-time holographic displays of his body were available at anything from a quarter- to twenty-thousand-power magnification, with structural and chemical highlighting available. Danice handled the controls with the skill of obvious practice, locating and displaying the alleged aneurysm so clearly that even Jonny could spot it in the holo.

"We'll have to operate," Danice said, turning to the senior guard who'd accompanied them. "I suggest you check with your superiors for instructions—see if there's a particular surgeon they'd prefer to use or whatever. In the meantime I'm going to sedate him and give him a shot of vasodepressor to relieve pressure on that aneurysm."

The guard nodded and fumbled out his phone. A floating table, looking uncomfortably like a coffin with a long ground-effect skirt, was brought up. Jonny was hoisted onto it and strapped down, and from a cabinet in its side Danice withdrew a hypospray and two vials. Injecting their contents into Jonny's arm, she replaced the hypospray and brought out a full-face oxygen mask. "What's that for?" one of the guards asked as she slipped the milky plastic over Jonny's head.

"He needs a slightly enhanced air supply to compensate for his suppressed circulation," she said. "What room, orderly?"

"Three-oh-seven," the man who'd brought in the floating table told her. "If you'll all get out of the way . . . thank you."

Danice at his side, Jonny was pushed out into the hospital's corridor maze, arriving eventually at room 307, the numbers barely legible through the mask. "Wait here until he's settled," Danice told the guards curtly. "There's not enough room to accommodate spectators in there."

Jonny was maneuvered alongside a bed in a crackerbox-sized

alcove. Stepping to the far side of his table—the side between him and the guards at the door—Danice and the orderly reached down—

And he was flipped over into total darkness.

The action was so unexpected that it took Jonny several heartbeats to realize exactly what had happened. The flat top of the floating table had apparently rotated a half turn on its long axis, concealing him in a hollowed-out part of the table's upper section. Above him he could hear the faint sounds of something heavy being lifted from the table . . . felt the table moving away from the bed . . . indistinct voices holding a short conversation . . . then moving again, through several turns and a long elevator ride. . . .

When he was finally rotated into the open again, he and Danice were alone in an underground parking garage. "Hurry," she whispered, her hands shaking as she unfastened his restraints. "We've got to get you off-planet before they realize that's not you in that bed."

"Who is there?" Jonny asked as they jogged to a nondescript gray car.

"Fritz—one of the hospital's medical practice robots." She got behind the wheel, took a deep breath. "We had a few minutes to touch up his features a bit, but the minute someone pulls off that mask, it's all over."

"You want me to drive?" Jonny asked, eyeing the tension lines in her face.

A quick shake of the head. "I need to get used to this sometime. It might as well be now."

She drove them through the garage, up a ramp, and out into the bustle of early-evening traffic. Jonny let her drive in silence for a few minutes before asking the obvious question. "Where are we going?"

"There's a freighter leaving for Palm in about two hours," she said, not looking at him. "We've bumped some ungodly number of high-stress plastic whosies to put aboard a yacht and pilot for you—you can tell him exactly where and when to part company with the freighter."

Jonny nodded, feeling slightly dazed by the speed at which this was all happening. "Do I get to ask who I have to thank for all this?"

"Do you really want to know?" she countered.

Jonny thought that one over. It *wasn't* a trivial question. "Yes," he said at last.

She sighed. "Well. First of all, you can lay your worst fears to rest—we're not in any way a criminal group. In fact, in one sense we're actually an official arm of the Dominion Joint Command." She snorted. "Though that may change after this. We're what's known as the Underground Defense Network, an organization that's supposed to do in this war what you and my parents' underground did in the last one. Except that we won't have any Cobras."

"You sound like one of my guards," Jonny murmured. "He the one who told you about me?"

Danice glanced at him in obvious surprise. "You're as quick as I always remembered you being. Yes, he's one of the handful of quiet liaisons between the military and the UDN, though I don't think his immediate superiors know. He's the one who put word of your arrest on our communications net."

"And convinced all of you I was worth defying the authorities over?"

She smiled bitterly. "Nothing of the kind. Everyone helping us thinks this is just another training exercise. Rescuing Prisoner From Under Enemy's Nose 101; final exam."

"Except you." The question was obvious; he didn't bother to voice it.

"I was just a kid in the last war, Jonny," she said quietly, "but I remember enough about it to haunt two or three lifetimes. I don't want to go through it again . . . but if the Dominion goes to war I'll have to."

"Maybe not—" Jonny began cautiously.

"What do you mean, 'maybe not'?" she flared. "You think they're going to all this trouble for the fun of it? They *know* Adirondack's going to be a major Troft target, and they've as good as admitted they won't be able to defend us. The plain, simple truth is that they're writing our world off and preparing us to sink or swim on our own. And for *nothing*."

She broke off and took a deep breath. "I'm sorry, Jonny. I'm sure Aventine means a lot to you. But I just can't see sacrificing Adirondack and maybe Silvern and Iberiand too in what amounts to a war of retribution."

"No need to apologize," he assured her, "No world should have to fight for its life twice in one generation."

Danice shook her head wearily. "You don't know the half of it. The social upheaval alone . . . There were a lot of books written about us after the war, you know, books that listed a lot of the underground people by name. Well, the Joint Command decided those people's lives might be in danger when the Trofts came in again, so five years ago they took everybody mentioned in any of the books and gave them new identities somewhere else on the planet. I was just barely able to find my own parents, and they *still* don't know where half of their oldest friends are."

Ahead, Jonny could see the starfield's control tower silhouetted against the last traces of red in the southwestern sky. "This pilot you've picked out also thinks this is a training exercise?"

"Theoretically. But Don is pretty smart—he may have figured out something else is up. Anyway, you'll have several days to discuss it." She favored him with a thoughtful look. "You really don't like this business of trusting other people with your life, do you? I suppose the habits of being a Cobra die hard."

"Not as hard as you'd think," Jonny shook his head. "You're remembering me with the eyes of a ten-year-old. Even then, I wasn't really any less dependent on other people than you are now."

Which was not, of course, an answer to her question. He *didn't* like depending on others, especially with so much at stake.

But it was something he could get used to.

"Committé Vanis D'arl's office," the bored face in the phone screen announced.

"Jame Moreau," Jonny told her, watching her closely. If she gave even the slightest indication she recognized him . . .

"Who's calling, please?" she asked.

"Teague Stillman—I used to be mayor of his home town. Tell him it's important."

Jonny held his breath; but, "Just a minute, please," was all she said before her face was replaced by a stylized dome. The local "hold" symbol, Jonny supposed, automatically starting his nanocomputer clock circuit. He'd give Jame two minutes to answer before assuming the woman had called the cops instead and getting the hell out of the area—

"Hello, Jonny."

Jonny wrenched his gaze back from its survey of possible escape routes. If Jame was surprised to see him, it didn't show. "Hi, Jame," he said cautiously. "Uh . . ."

"The line's secure," his brother said. "You all right?"

"I'm fine, but I need your help. I have to—"

"Yeah, I know all about it. Damn it all, Jonny—look, where are you?"

Jonny felt icy fingers closing around his gut. "Why?"

"Why do you think?" Jame waved a hand in irritation. "Never mind—do it your own way. My neck's stuck far enough out as it is."

Jonny gritted his teeth. "I'm at a public phone on V'awter Street, just north of Carle Park."

Jame sighed. "All right. I'll be there in half an hour or less to get you. And *stay put* this time—understand?"

"Okay. And—thanks."

Some of the steel seemed to go out of Jame's backbone, and a small, guarded smile even touched his face. "Yeah. See you soon."

He was there in twenty minutes flat, and even with Jonny's lack of familiarity with current styles, it was obvious the younger Moreau's car was a top-of-the-line model. "Nice," Jonny nodded as he got in beside Jame and sank into the rich cushioning. "A step or two up from Dader's old limper."

"It won't stay that way long if anyone spots us," Jame replied tartly as he pulled into the traffic flow. "We're just lucky the alert on you was limited to the military and not made public. What did you think you were up to, anyway, breaking confinement like that?"

"What did you expect—that I'd just sit there in Wrey's private limbo while the pompous idiot got a war going?"

"Granted Wrey's a self-centered grudge-holder, credit him with at least the intelligence to guard his own skin," Jame growled. "He wouldn't have left you there more than two days at the most— *and* he'd arranged for a Star Force scoutship to bring you here after you'd been cleared. With the extra speed scouts can make, you'd have been here four days ago—barely a day, if that, behind Wrey."

Jonny's hands curled into fists. Could he really have misread Wrey *that* badly? "Damn," he murmured.

Jame sighed. "So instead of being brought before the Committee to have your say, you're right up there on the military's must-find list. I don't think even Wrey really believed his innuendo about you making a private deal with the Trofts, but the ease with which your friends got you loose has a lot of people very nervous. How'd you organize all that, anyway?"

"I didn't." Jonny sighed. "Okay. I admit I crusked up good. But it doesn't change the fact that the Committee needs to hear what I've brought."

Jame shook his head. "Not a chance. You wouldn't get past the first door of the dome."

Abruptly, Jonny realized that they were heading further *out* of the city instead of inward. "Where are we going?"

"To Committé D'arl's country estate."

Jonny's mouth went dry. "Why?"

Jame frowned at him. "You're the one who just said you wanted to talk to someone. Committé D'arl's agreed to hear you out."

"At his private estate." Where Jonny could quietly and conveniently disappear, if necessary, with no one the wiser.

Jame sighed. "Look, Jonny, I know you don't like the Committé, but this is the only way you're going to get a hearing. And I'll tell you flat out that you couldn't find a more receptive audience anywhere in Dome." He glanced at his older brother. "Come on— settle back and relax. I know it probably looks like the whole universe is against you right now, but if you can't trust your old pillow-fight partner, who *can* you trust?"

Almost unwillingly, Jonny felt a smile touch his lips. "You may be right," he admitted.

"Of course I'm right. Now: we've got just under an hour for you to bring me up-to-date on the Aventine branch of the Moreau family. So start talking."

D'arl's country estate was at least as large as the entire city of Capitalia; a rich man's version, Jonny thought once, of the Tyler Mansion and grounds of Adirondack. With a rich man's version of security, too. The car was stopped six times by pairs of variously armed guards, and at each roadblock Jonny's enhanced vision picked out hidden remotes and backups lurking near trees or oddly-shaped statues. But the Moreaus were clearly expected, and the guards passed them through without question.

The main house was as impressive as the grounds, its exterior magnificent and imposing, its interior carrying the same underplayed sense of luxury Jonny had noticed on the Committé's star ship so long ago. Personal taste, he'd thought then; but with eleven more years of politics behind him he could now recognize the additional subtle warning the decor conveyed: its owner was not a man who could be bought.

D'arl was waiting for them in a small study clearly designed for personal work rather than for public or private audiences. He looked up as they entered, waved them silently to the chairs already pulled up to face his. They sat down, and for a moment the Committé gazed at Jonny. "Well, Governor—it *is* Governor, isn't it?" he said at last. "You seem to have made a genuine mess of your little diplomatic trip. I presume your brother has already dragged you through the roasting pit over that asinine escape from Adirondack, so I'll dispense with any further remarks about that. So now tell me why you're worth sticking my neck out."

"Because I have information about the Troft Assemblage I think you don't," Jonny said calmly. "And what may be a good chance to prevent a war. The greatest good for the greatest number—wasn't that the criterion you've always followed?"

D'arl's lip twitched in a brief smile. "Your political skills have definitely improved, Governor. All right. Let's start with why you called the Troft Empire an Assemblage a minute ago."

"Because that's what the Trofts call it, and because that's exactly what it is. There's no centralized government, at least nothing corresponding in authority to Dome or the Committee. The Assemblage is actually nothing more than a loose-knit fraternity of two- to four-planet demesnes."

D'arl frowned. "You'll forgive me if I'm skeptical. A collection of systems working at cross-purposes could hardly have held off the Dominion's military might for three years."

"True—but I never said they always worked at cross-purposes."

D'arl shook his head. "Individual self-interest alone would guarantee disunity among that many demesnes."

"Unless there were some issue of overriding importance to all of them," Jonny said quietly. "Such as an invasion by an alien race. Us."

"Jonny, the Trofts started the war, not us," Jame spoke up. "That's not just an official line, you know—I've personally seen the records."

"Then perhaps you've also seen the records of the 471 Scorpii exploration," Jonny said. "That, according to the Trofts, is what started the war."

D'arl started to speak, reached instead for a comboard resting on a low table beside his seat. "I don't think I know the reference," Jame said.

"It was a minor double star system the Dominion thought might be worth a mining development," D'arl told him. "But according to this, the initial probe took place almost ten years before Silvern was hit."

"Yes, sir," Jonny nodded. "It took the affected demesnes that long to convince the others a war was necessary."

For a moment D'arl gazed at the comboard, fingers drumming on the chair arm. "You're implying the Committee's been blind for the past thirty years." His tone was less accusing than it was thoughtful.

Jonny shrugged. "The Trofts would hardly have advertised what they probably saw as a major military disadvantage. And any dealings since then on a planetary scale or less really *would* look very similar to how the Dominion does things, too. But the indications were there, if the figures the Troft Ship Commander gave me are correct. Do you have the number of representatives the Trofts sent to the peace talks after the war?"

D'arl busied himself with his comboard. "They had—let's see: twenty-six Senior Representatives. Another eighty-four aides and support personnel came to Iberiand with them."

"Twenty-six. What size team did the Dominion send, about ten?"

"Twelve—and I remember Committé H'orme complaining at the time that that seemed top-heavy." D'arl's eyes met Jonny's. "Twenty-six Troft demesnes?"

Jonny nodded. "One each from the border demesnes, the only ones whose territory would be directly affected by any settlement. But then a year later you began negotiations for the rights to the Troft Corridor, which I estimate affected eighty or so additional demesnes."

D'arl was already punching keys. "One hundred six Senior Representatives," he said, shaking his head slowly. "Eighty more, exactly."

"There were other indications, too," Jonny said into the silence that followed. "The Ship Commander who let us go obviously felt entitled to disobey his orders when he had sufficient reason to do so. And even during the war I was captured by a local officer who kept me alive almost certainly against orders. You may remember me telling you about that one, Jame."

The younger Moreau was frowning. "I remember . . . but I don't buy your explanation. This wide-open autonomy between demesnes is bad enough, but if you run it to upper military command level, too, you're going to wind up with complete anarchy."

Jonny shrugged. "I frankly don't understand it myself," he admitted. "The Ship Commander tried to explain how a graduated system of respect or obedience based on an individual's past record kept their society running smoothly, but it still sounds like magic to me."

"All right," D'arl said abruptly. "Assume for the moment all this is true. Then what?"

Jonny turned back to face him. "Then avoiding a war becomes

simply a matter of removing the issue the demesnes are uniting over. Specifically, allowing them to close the Corridor."

"Out of the question." D'arl's voice was flat. "Official Dominion policy says the Corridor stays open or the Trofts pay heavily for closing it."

"Dominion policy isn't carved into bedrock," Jonny countered. "The *purpose* of that threat was to protect Aventine from attack. Fine—but right now we have a better chance of surviving *without* your protection; and if loss of contact with you is the price, we're willing to pay it."

"Are you, now," D'arl said. "And what happens when your machines and electronics start breaking down? Aventine hasn't got an extensive enough technological base to maintain things for long."

"No, but the Trofts do. We can undoubtedly trade with them as well as you do."

"*Our* trade has been extremely minimal, for intelligence purposes only—"

"Oh, come on," Jonny snorted. "We both know what I'm talking about. Practically every one of your licensed carriers routinely stops off for trade en route to Aventine. Why else do you think the Corridor demesnes have put up with the arrangement all these years? They get goods *and* information that they would normally have to buy—with heavy tariffs, no doubt—from their brother demesnes."

D'arl had a sour look on his face. "As it happens, we've been trying to come up with a good way to end that clandestine trade for years."

Jonny spread his hands. "Well, here's your chance."

D'arl sighed. "Governor, you still don't understand the political realities here. The Committee has taken a stand; we cannot back down without a damn good reason."

"So make one up," Jonny snapped, his patience beginning to fray. "You're a consummate politician—surely you won't let a little matter of truth stand in the way of what you want." D'arl's brow darkened, but Jonny rushed on before the other could speak. "Aventine doesn't want war, the Trofts don't especially want war, your own *people* don't want war. Is the Committee so hell-bent on fighting someone that not even that will stop them?"

"Jonny!" Jame snapped.

"It's all right, Moreau, I'll handle it," D'arl said. "Governor, I'll take your recommendation to the Committee tomorrow. That's the best that I can do."

"A Committé with your experience?" Jonny scoffed. "You can do better than just playing court reporter."

"I can push any solidly-based, politically plausible reason for closing the Corridor," D'arl bit back. "You've yet to give me anything that qualifies."

"You want a good political reason? Fine; I'll give you one right now." Jonny stood up, dimly aware that his anger was near to overwhelming all control over it. "What do you think the Committee would do if a visiting dignitary from Aventine shot down one of its members?"

"Jonny!" Jame jumped to his feet.

"Stay back, Jame." Jonny kept his eyes on D'arl. "Well, Committé? It would mean economic sanctions against the colonies, wouldn't it, which for all practical purposes means closing the Corridor."

"It would." D'arl was glacially calm. "But you wouldn't shoot me down in cold blood just for that."

"Wouldn't I? The greatest good for the greatest number, remember? What does it matter that you and I would be sacrificed? And I've got more than just that, anyway. For what you've done to thousands of Aventine boys alone I could hate you enough to kill. Jame, get *back*."

The younger Moreau ignored the order. Quietly, he walked over to stand squarely between the other two men. For a long moment the brothers locked gazes. Then Jonny reached forward and effortlessly lifted Jame into the air by his upper arms, setting him to the side. The brief burst of anger was gone, leaving only determination and the cold knowledge that he'd come too far to back out now. "Committé, I want you to get on the phone and start calling in all the favors you've undoubtedly been accumulating through the years," he told D'arl grimly. "Now. You *are* going to get the Corridor closing accepted."

D'arl didn't move. "Under threat to my life? No. And certainly not because of your unreasonable feelings about the Aventine Cobra project."

He said the last so casually that Jonny was taken aback. Fury threatened to drown him . . . but abruptly he understood. "You don't know, do you?" he said, more in bitterness than in anger. "I suppose it hasn't happened yet to your own Cobras."

"Know what?"

Jonny dug into his pocket for his medicine, tossed the two vials into D'arl's lap. The Committé frowned at the labels and keyed the names into his comboard. A moment later he looked up to meet Jonny's eyes. "Anemia and arthritis," he almost whispered.

"Yes," Jonny nodded, wondering at the oddly intense reaction. "Every one of the First Cobras in the colonies is coming down with those diseases, as a direct result of our implanted servos and laminae, and there are indications our immune systems are starting to be affected, as well. Best estimates give me barely twenty years left to live, if that long. *That's* the ultimate legacy your Cobra project has left on Aventine."

D'arl stared down at the vials in his hand. "It's starting here, too, Governor. Reports of chronic Cobra illnesses have dribbled in for the past year or so. Statistically inconclusive as yet . . . I'd hoped my suspicions were wrong." He looked up at Jame's stunned expression. "I ran the reports through Alveres, Moreau—I didn't see any point in worrying you about your brother's health."

Jame took a deep breath. "Committé . . . if what Jonny said about secret trade helping to keep the Corridor open is true, then it follows that the whole Aventine Cobra project was indeed unnecessary, or at least premature."

"The Cobras will be needed now."

"No," Jonny shook his head. "We'll be maintaining the trade relationship with the Trofts, and with the Corridor closed we're no longer a military threat. They won't attack us—and *we* won't provoke *them*, either. There's another point for you, Committé: if war starts, you won't be able to count on those hundred thousand Troft troops being tied up on Aventine."

"*My* point, sir—" Jame cut off as D'arl raised a hand.

"Peace, Moreau," the Committé said quietly. "I never said I didn't want to help, just that I needed a stronger case. And now I've got it. Excuse me."

Standing, he brushed by Jonny and stepped to a small desk off to one side. "Starport," he said to the phone screen. " . . . This is Committé D'arl. Number one star ship is to be prepared for travel, under the direction of Jame Moreau. Passenger and cargo lists to be supplied by him; ultimate destination Adirondack. . . . Thank you."

He keyed the phone off and turned to face the two Moreaus. "I'm heading back to Dome to get things started. Governor, you and your brother need to make a list of whatever you'd like as your last shipment of goods to the Outer Colonies. You can go whenever you're ready; I'll contact you on Adirondack before you leave there with any final messages." He turned to go.

"Committé," Jonny called after him. "Thank you."

The other turned back, and Jonny was surprised to see an ironic smile tugging at his lips. "I'll stop the war, Governor. But save your thanks until you see how I do it." He left the room, closing the door gently behind him.

Jonny never saw him again.

It was the end of the road for them, and both men knew it. So for a long moment they stood beside the *Menssana*'s entry ramp and just looked at each other. Jonny broke the silence first. "I saw on the newscast this morning that Aventine's apparently starting to complain about the way Dome's been running the Outer Colonies. The announcer seemed a bit on the indignant side."

Jame nodded. "It's going to get worse, too, I'm afraid. By the time we're finished with you, banning all trade or other contact with the colonies is going to seem like a remarkably restrained response by the Committee."

"In other words, history's going to put the blame squarely on Aventine."

Jame sighed. "It was the only way—the only *political* way—to let the Committee back away from such a long-established stance. I'm sorry."

Jonny looked back across the city, his memory superimposing Adirondack's battered wartime appearance against what was there now. "It's not important,' he told his brother. "If vilifying us is what it takes to save face, we can live with it."

"I hope so. You haven't heard yet one of the more secret reasons the Committee accepted Committé D'arl's proposal."

Jonny cocked an eyebrow. "Which is . . . ?"

"A slightly edited version of your confrontation at the estate. He convinced them the Aventine Cobras might get angry enough to seek revenge against them in the near future if contact with the Outer Colonies was maintained." Jame snorted gently. "It's strange, you know. Almost from the end of the last war the Committee's been trying to figure out a safe way to get rid of the Cobras; and now that they've got one, it had to practically be drop-kicked down their throats."

"No one said politics was self-consistent," Jonny shrugged. "But it worked, and that's all that matters."

"So you heard the courier report already," Jame nodded. "The Troft response was very interesting to read—the experts say the phrasing indicated our capitulation on the Corridor issue really caught them off-guard."

"I'm not surprised," Jonny said. "But I wouldn't worry about this setting any precedents. Remember how hard it is for the demesnes to get together on any future demands." He glanced around the visible sections of the starfield, hoping against hope that Danice Tolan would make a last-minute appearance.

Jame followed his gaze and his thoughts. "I wouldn't count on seeing your friend before you have to go. She's probably up to her cloak and laser in the Joint Command's decommissioning procedure—I think they've suddenly decided they don't like having independent paramilitary units running around the Dominion." He smiled briefly, but then sobered. "Jonny . . . you're not condemning your own world to slow death just to prevent a war, are you? I mean, trading with the Trofts is all very well on a theoretical level, but none of you has ever actually done it before."

"True, but we'll pick up the techniques fast enough, and with the *Menssana* to double our long-range fleet, we'll have reasonable capacity. Besides, we're not exactly starting cold." He patted his jacket pocket and the list of Troft contacts and rendezvous points Rando Harmon and Dru Quoraheim had supplied. "We'll do just fine."

"I hope you're right. You haven't got much going for you out there."

Jonny shook his head. "You've been on Asgard too long to remember how it feels to be a frontier world. Horizon, Adirondack, and now Aventine—I've never lived on anything but. We'll make it, Jame . . . if for no other reason than to prove to the universe that we can."

"Governor Moreau?" a voice drifted down from the ship beside them. "Captain's compliments, sir. Control's given us permission to lift any time."

And it was time to say good-bye. "Take care of yourself, Jonny," Jame said as Jonny was still searching for words. "Say hello to everyone for me, okay?"

"Sure." Jonny stepped forward and wrapped his brother in a bear hug. Tears blurred his vision. "You take care of yourself, too. And . . . thanks for everything."

Two minutes later he was on the *Menssana*'s bridge. "Ah— Governor," the captain said, attempting with only partial success to hide his bubbling enthusiasm beneath a professional demeanor. The entire crew was like that: young, idealistic, the whole lot barely qualified for the trip. But they were the most experienced of those who'd volunteered for this one-way mission. The last colonists the Dominion would be sending for a long, long time—they, like the *Menssana* and its cargo, a farewell gift from D'arl and the Committee. "We're all set here," the young officer continued. "Course is laid out, and we've got the special pass the Trofts sent already programmed into the transmitter. Whenever you're set, we can go."

Jonny's eyes searched out a ground-view display, watched the tiny image of Jame just disappearing into the entrypoint building. "I'm ready any time," he told the captain quietly. "Let's go home."

COBRA STRIKE

Chapter 1

The whine of Troft thrusters drifted in through the window on the late-summer breezes, jarring Jonny Moreau awake. For one heart-wrenching moment he was back in the midst of the Adirondack war; but as he tipped his recliner back to vertical the abrupt stab of pain in elbows and knees snapped him back to the present. For a minute he just sat there, gazing out the window at the Capitalia skyline and trying to bring his brain and body back on-line. Then, reaching carefully to his desk, he jabbed at the intercom button on his phone. "Yes, Governor?" Theron Yutu said.

Jonny leaned back in his chair again, snagging a bottle of pain pills from the desktop as he did so. "Is Corwin back from the Council meeting yet?"

The image jumped to another desk and Jonny's 27-year-old son. "Haven't gone yet, Dad," he said. "The meeting's still an hour away."

"Oh?" Jonny squinted at his watch. He'd have sworn the meeting was scheduled for two . . . sure enough, it was just a few minutes past one. "Felt like I'd slept longer," he muttered. "Well. You all set to go?"

"Pretty much, unless there's something new you want me to bring up. Hang on—I'll come in there and we can talk."

The screen went blank. Flexing his elbows experimentally, Jonny eyed the pain pills. *Later,* he decided firmly. His arthritis would ease some as he started moving around again, and the drugs invariably left his brain fuzzier than he liked.

The door opened and Corwin Jame Moreau strode into the room, the inevitable comboard tucked under his arm. The boy—the *man,* Jonny reminded himself—had taken to the world of politics with a zest the older Moreau had never been able to generate. More and more Corwin reminded Jonny of his own brother Jame, working up through the ranks of the Dominion of Man's highest political power. Fourteen years ago Jame had been a trusted aide to a member of the Central Committee itself. What was he now, Jonny often wondered—aide, designated successor, a Committé himself?

Jonny would never know. It was one of the few results of the Troft Corridor closing that he was still able to wholeheartedly regret.

Setting his comboard on a corner of Jonny's desk, Corwin pulled up a chair. "Okay, let's see. The main points you wanted me to present were the exclusivity clause of the new trade agreement with the Hoibe'ryi'sarai—" the Troft demesne-name flowed smoothly from Corwin's tongue—"the need for more Cobras to be shifted to spine leopard duty in the outer districts, and the whole question of whether Caelian is really worth hanging onto."

Jonny nodded, feeling a twinge of guilt for once again skipping the Council duties a governor emeritus was supposed to perform or at least put up with. "Lean on the latter two especially—I don't know how the spine leopards figure out their numbers are down, but their breeding rate sure shows that they know *somehow*. Make sure even the densest syndics understand that we can't take on a full-scale spine leopard resurgence *and* also make any headway on Caelian without lowering the standards at the Cobra factory."

A frown flickered across Corwin's face. "Speaking of the academy. . . ." He stopped, looking uncomfortable.

Jonny closed his eyes briefly. "Justin. Right?"

"Well . . . yes. Mom wanted me to try and get you to change your mind about using your Council veto on his application."

"To what end?" Jonny sighed. "Justin is smart, exceptionally stable emotionally, adaptable, and with a strong desire to serve his world this way. You'll forgive a father's pride, I trust."

"I know all that—"

"More to the point," Jonny interrupted, "he's 22 years old and has been wanting to be a Cobra since he was 16. A period, you'll notice, in which he's had ample opportunity to mull over exactly what a few decades of Cobra gear does to a man." He raised his hands slightly as if offering his body for inspection. "If that hasn't dampened his resolve—and the tests show it hasn't—then I'm not about to veto his admission. He's exactly the kind of man we need in the Cobras."

Corwin waved a hand in a gesture of defeat. "I almost wish I could argue with you, for Mom's sake. But I'm afraid I have to agree."

Jonny looked out the window. "Your mother's had a lot of this kind of pain in her life. I wish I knew how to make it up to her."

For a long moment the room was silent. Then Corwin stirred, reaching for his comboard. "Spine leopards and Caelian it is, then," he said, standing up. "You going to be here or the therapy room when the meeting's over?"

Jonny looked back at his eldest son, grimacing. "You *had* to bring that up, didn't you? Oh, all right; I'll go make the torturers happy. What's left of me will be back here by the time you're through."

Corwin nodded. "Okay. But be nice to them—they're just trying to do their jobs."

"Sure. See you later." Jonny waited until the other had closed the door behind him and then snorted. "Their jobs, indeed," he muttered under his breath. "Bunch of experimentalists poking around with human white-rats." All in hope that they could come up with a therapy that would someday be able to help the rising generations of Cobras.

One of whom was going to be his own son.

Sighing, Jonny gripped the arms of his chair and got carefully to his feet. He would get outside to his car on his own, and without his pills, even if it killed him. The old man, as he was fond of saying, wasn't helpless *yet*.

Even with traffic in the Cobra Worlds' capital as dense as it was these days, it would be only a ten-minute drive to the Dominion Building for the Council meeting. Corwin nevertheless gathered together his magcards and other paraphernalia as quickly as possible, hoping to get there early enough for some cloakroom soundboarding with the other Council members. His father had left for his therapy session, and Corwin was about ready to leave himself, when his mother came in.

"Hello, Theron," she smiled at Yutu. "Corwin, is your father still here?"

"He just left." Corwin felt his muscles tense in anticipation of the confrontation he knew was ahead. "He'll be coming back after his physical therapy."

"What did he say?"

Corwin consciously unclenched his jaw. "Sorry, Mom. He's not going to block it."

The age lines framing her features seemed to deepen. "You'll be casting the vote," she said, her meaning clear.

"Let me restate it, then: *We* are not going to block it."

"So that's it, is it?" she said coldly. "You're just going to let them condemn your brother to—"

"Mother." Corwin stood up, gesturing to his chair. "Sit down, will you."

She hesitated, then complied. Corwin pulled up a guest chair to face her, noting peripherally that Yutu had apparently just discovered something that needed to be done in Jonny's office. Sitting down, Corwin took a moment to look—*really* look—at his mother.

Chrys Moreau had been beautiful when she was younger, he knew from old pictures and tapes, and even with the assorted physical changes of middle age she was still strikingly attractive. But there were other changes, not all of them explained by simple maturation of viewpoint or even a response to her husband's long illness. She seemed to smile less these days, and to move with the restricted motions of one deathly afraid of knocking something over. This business with Justin was part of it, that much Corwin knew . . . but there was more, and so far he hadn't found the right words to open up that section of his mother's thoughts.

Nor was this time going to be any different. "If you're going to give me the old arguments why Justin should be a Cobra, please don't bother," Chrys began. "I know them all, I still don't have any logical counters for them, and I'll even admit that if he weren't my son I'd probably agree with them. But he *is* my son, and irrational as it may seem, I don't think it fair that I should lose *him* to the Cobras, too."

Corwin let her finish, though her words represented no new ground either. "Have you asked Joshua to talk with him?" he asked.

Chrys shook her head minutely. "He won't. *You* should know that better than anyone else."

Despite the seriousness of the moment Corwin felt a brief smile touch his lips at the memories evoked. Five years older than the twins, he had nevertheless been successfully ganged up on more times than he cared to remember. Their unshakable loyalty to each other even in the face of parental punishments had made for equally unshakable alibis. "Than I'm afraid it's out of our hands," he told his mother gently. "Legally—not to mention ethically— Justin has a perfect right to choose his life's work. Besides, the political fallout of such a nepotistic veto would be awfully messy to clean up."

"Politics." Chrys turned her head to stare out the window. "I'd hoped your father would be finished with it when he retired from the governorship. I should have realized they wouldn't let him escape that easily."

"We need his wisdom and experience, Mom." Corwin glanced at his watch. "And speaking of that, I'm afraid I'm going to have to go give the Council its monthly dose now."

A shadow briefly crossed Chrys's face, but she nodded and stood up. "I understand. Will you be coming by for dinner tonight? The twins have said they'll be able to make it."

And it would be the last time until Justin's Cobra training was over that they'd all have a chance to be together. "Sure," Corwin said, walking her toward the door. "I'll be talking to Dad after the meeting, so I'll just come with him when we're finished."

"All right. Around six?"

"Fine. See you then."

He walked her to her car and watched as she drove off. Then, with a sigh, he went to his own car and headed for the Dominion Building. Why, he wondered, did the internal problems of his own family always seem more insurmountable than those facing three entire worlds? *Probably*, he thought flippantly, *because there isn't anything the Council can do anymore to surprise me.*

He would afterward recall that thought and its unfortunate timing . . . and wince.

Chapter 2

The Council of Syndics—its official title—had in the early days of the colony been just that: a somewhat low-key grouping of the planet's syndics and governor-general which met at irregular intervals to discuss any problems and map out the general direction they hoped the colony would grow in. As the population increased and beachheads were established on two other worlds, the Council grew in both size and political weight, following the basic pattern of the distant Dominion of Man. But unlike the Dominion, this outpost of humanity numbered nearly three thousand Cobras among its half-million people. The resulting inevitable diffusion of political power had had a definite impact on the Council's makeup. The rank of governor had been added between the syndic and governor-general levels, blunting the pinnacle of power just a bit; and at *all* levels of government the Cobras with their double vote were well represented.

Corwin didn't really question the political philosophy which had produced this modification of Dominion structure; but from a purely utilitarian point of view he often found the sheer size of the 75-member Council unwieldy.

Today, though, at least for the first hour, things went smoothly. Most of the discussion—including the points Corwin raised—focused on older issues which had already had the initial polemics thoroughly wrung out of them. A handful were officially given resolution, the rest returned to the members for more analysis, consideration, or simple foot-dragging; and as the agenda wound down it began to look as if the meeting might actually let out early.

And then Governor-General Brom Stiggur dropped a pocket planet-wrecker into the room.

It began with an old issue. "You'll remember the report of two years ago," he said, looking around the room, "in which the Farsearch team concluded that, aside from our three present worlds, no planets exist within at least a 20-light-year radius of Aventine that we could expand to in the future. It was agreed at the time that our current state of population and development hardly required an immediate resolution of this long-term problem."

Corwin sat a bit straighter in his seat, sensing similar reactions around him. Stiggur's words were neutral enough, but something explosive seemed to be hiding beneath the carefully controlled inflections of his voice.

"However," the other continued, "in the past few days something new has come to light, something which I felt should be presented immediately to this body, before even any follow-up studies were initiated." Glancing at the Cobra guard standing by the door, Stiggur nodded. The man nodded in turn and opened the panel . . . and a single Troft walked in.

A faint murmur of surprise rippled its way around the room, and Corwin felt himself tense involuntarily as the alien made its way to Stiggur's side. The Trofts had been the Worlds' trading partner for nearly 14 years now, but Corwin still remembered vividly the undercurrent of fear that he'd grown up with. Most of the Council had even stronger memories than that: the Troft occupation of the Dominion worlds Silvern and Adirondack had occurred only 43 years ago, ultimately becoming the impetus for the original Cobra project. It was no accident that most of the people who now dealt physically with the Troft traders were in their early twenties. Only the younger Aventinians could face the aliens without wincing.

The Troft paused at the edge of the table, waiting as the Council members dug out translator-link earphones and inserted them. One or two of the younger syndics didn't bother, and Corwin felt a flicker of jealousy as he adjusted his own earphone to low volume. He'd taken the same number of courses in catertalk as they had, but it was obvious that foreign language comprehension wasn't even close to being his forte.

"Men and women of the Cobra Worlds Council," the earphone murmured to him. "I am Speaker One of the Tlos'khin'fahi demesne of the Trof'te Assemblage." The alien's high-pitched catertalk continued for a second beyond the translation; both races had early on decided that the first three parasyllables of Troft demesne titles were more than adequate for human use, and that a literal transcription of the aliens' proper names was a waste of effort. "The Tlos'khin'fahi demesne-lord has sent your own demesne-lord's request for data to the other parts of the Assemblage, and the result has been a triad offer from the Pua'lanek'zia and Baliu'ckha'spmi demesnes."

Corwin grimaced. He'd never liked deals involving two or more Troft demesnes, both because of the delicate political balance the Worlds often had to strike and because the humans never heard much about the Troft-Troft arm of such bargains. That arm *had* to exist—the individual demesnes seldom if ever gave anything away to each other.

The same line of thought appeared to have tracked its way elsewhere through the room. "You speak of a triad, instead of a quad offer," Governor Dylan Fairleigh spoke up. "What part does the Tlos'khin'fahi demesne expect to play?"

"My demesne-lord chooses the role of catalyst," was the prompt reply. "No fee will be forthcoming for our role." The Troft fingered something on his abdomen sash and Corwin's display lit up with a map showing the near half of the Troft Assemblage. Off on one edge three stars began blinking red. "The Cobra Worlds," the alien unnecessarily identified them. A quarter of the way around the bulge a single star, also outside Troft territory, flashed green. "The world named Qasama by its natives. They are described by the Baliu'ckha'spmi demesne-lord as an alien race of great potential danger to the Assemblage. Here—" a vague-edged sphere appeared at the near side of the flashing green star—"somewhere, is a tight cluster of five worlds capable of supporting human life. The Pua'lanek'zia demesne-lord will give you their location and an Assemblage pledge of human possession if your Cobras will undertake to eliminate the threat of Qasama. I will await your decision."

The Troft turned and left ... and only slowly did Corwin realize he was holding his breath. Five brand-new worlds ... for the price of becoming mercenaries.

He wondered if the Troft had any idea of the size snakepit he'd just opened.

If the alien didn't, the Council certainly did. For the better part of a minute the room was silent as an isolation tank as each member apparently tried to track through the tangle of implications. Finally, Stiggur cleared his throat. "While we of course have no intention of replying to this offer today, or even to fully discuss its relative merits, I would nevertheless appreciate hearing whatever initial reactions you might have."

"I, for one, would like a little more information before we listen to any hard-wired-reflex comments," Governor Lizabet Telek said. Her perennially gravelly voice gave no clue to her own reaction. "Something about these new aliens would be nice for starters— bio specs, tech level, specifics of their alleged threat; that sort of thing."

Stiggur shook his head. "Speaker One either doesn't have any more data or won't give it away free—I've already pressed him on that. I suspect the former, personally; there's no particular need for the Tlos demesne to buy what would be little more than abstract knowledge to them. Same goes for information on these five alleged worlds the Pua demesne's offering, before anyone asks."

"In other words, we're being asked to sign an essentially blank agreement?" one of the newer syndics asked.

"Not really." Governor Jor Hemner shook his head, the movement looking risky on one so frail. "There are lots of intermediate possibilities, including buying the Baliu's data or sending our own survey team out to take a look. Standard Troft trade procedure assumes we'll come up with these suggestions ourselves. What *I'm* worried about is whether setting a precedent of this kind is a good idea."

"Why not?" someone else spoke up from Corwin's side of the room. "It's the fear of the Cobras that keeps the Trofts friendly, isn't it? How better to show them that kind of caution is good policy?"

"And if we lose?" Hemner asked stiffly.

"The Cobras haven't lost anything yet."

Corwin glanced at Governor Howie Vartanson of Caelian, wondering if he'd comment. But the other merely curled his lip slightly and kept silent. Politicians from Caelian tended to adopt that low-profile position when they came to Aventine, Corwin had noticed; but the point, he felt, ought to be made. Subtly, if possible. . . . "I'd like to point out," he spoke up, "that one or more new planets would enable us to solve the problem of Caelian without depriving the 19,000 people there of the right to their own world."

"Only if they'd be willing to leave," Stiggur said; but the mention of Caelian, as Corwin had planned, seemed to bring the members' thoughts to the current stalemate between the Cobras and that strange world's hostile ecology. "Fluid genetic adaptation," the official reports elegantly called, it. The Caelians' own term was considerably cruder: *Hell's Blender.* Every species on the planet, from the simplest lichen to the largest predator, seemed mindlessly determined to hold onto its ecological and territorial niche against all efforts to dislodge it. Clear some land and soak it with vegebarrier, and within days there would be a dozen new plant variants attempting to reclaim it. Build a house where a thicket had been, and before long the local fungi would be growing on the walls. Create a city, or even a small town, and the displaced animals would find their way in somehow . . . and not only the small ones. A world under perpetual siege, Corwin had once heard Jonny call it. Only the Caelians themselves knew how—or why— they put up with it.

For another long moment the room was again silent. Stiggur looked around, nodded at what he saw. "Well. I think we can safely agree with Governor Telek that considerably more information is needed before we can even consider acting. For the moment, then, you're to keep this proposal a secret from the general populace while you work out the various pros and cons for yourselves. Now, then—one final item and we'll be adjourned. I have a list of Cobra applicants awaiting final Council approval." The twelve names— an unusually high number—appeared on Corwin's screen, along with their home towns and districts. All the names were familiar ones; the Cobra Academy screeners had sent in their test results nearly a month ago. Justin Moreau was the seventh one listed.

"Do I hear any votes against these citizens becoming Cobras, either individually or as a group?" Stiggur asked the standard question. A couple of nearby heads turned in Corwin's direction; clamping his jaw tightly, he kept his eyes on the governor-general and his hands in his lap. "No? Then this Council affirms the decision of the Cobra Academy officials, and hereby directs them to begin the irreversible stages of the Cobra process." Stiggur pushed a button and the room's screens blanked. "This Council session is adjourned."

Irreversible stages. Corwin had heard those words at least twenty times before at these meetings, but somehow they'd never sounded so final. But then, he'd never heard them applied to his own younger brother before, either.

Justin Moreau let the car roll to a stop in front of the house, feeling the tension in his shoulders translate along his arms to a brief white-knuckled squeeze on the wheel. The word had come by phone only an hour ago that the Council had given final approval to his application. Tomorrow the surgery would begin that would finally and firmly set him down in his father's footsteps . . . but tonight he would have to face his mother's pain.

"You ready?" Joshua asked from the seat next to him.

"As ready as I'll ever be." Opening the door, Justin got out and headed toward the house, his brother falling into step beside him.

Corwin answered Joshua's knock, and despite his tension Justin found himself enjoying the inevitable half-second it took their older brother to figure out which was which. Even among identical twins Joshua and Justin were unusually hard to tell apart, a fact that had caused untold confusion throughout their lives. Family and close friends were generally able to manage the trick, but even with them a secret swap of tunics could sometimes go undetected for hours. They'd pulled such stunts innumerable times when they were younger, a game they'd given up only after their father threatened to color-code them with liberal applications of paint.

"Joshua; Justin," Corwin nodded, looking at each in turn as if to prove he'd gotten them straight. "Abandon all hope of light conversation, you who enter here. The Moreau War Council is in session tonight."

Oh, great, Justin groaned inwardly. But Corwin had stepped aside, and Joshua was already heading in, and it was too late to back out now. Squaring his shoulders, Justin followed.

His parents were already seated together on the living room couch, and from long habit Justin gave his father a quick once-over. A little weaker-looking, perhaps, than the last time he'd seen him, but not much. Of more significance was the slight flicker of pain that crossed Jonny's eyes as he gave the twins an abbreviated wave in greeting. The pain pills for his arthritis really didn't affect his mental facilities all *that* much; if he'd opted to do without them there was some high-powered thought going on in here indeed. A glance at his mother's grim face confirmed it, and for a long minute Justin wondered if he'd drastically underestimated the level of family opposition to his Cobra ambitions.

But that assumption didn't last long. "Dinner'll be ready in about half an hour," Jonny told the twins as they chose chairs and sat down. "Until then, I want to feel you out on a proposal Stiggur dropped on the Council session today. Corwin?"

Corwin took a seat where he could see all the others' faces. "This is all to be kept secret, of course," he said . . . and then launched into the damnedest story Justin had ever heard.

Jonny let a few seconds pass after his eldest had finished and then cocked an eyebrow at the twins. "Well? Reactions?"

"I don't trust them," Joshua said promptly. "Especially the Tlos demesne. Why should they offer their set-up services for nothing?"

"That much is obvious," Jonny told him. "This is what's known as a free sample—and running both ways. If we take the job and the Baliu demesne likes our work, the Tlossies will undoubtedly offer themselves as our agents to any other interested demesnes."

"And if *we* like the deal, they'll offer us their services in find-ing new jobs," Corwin nodded. "They pulled the same type of inducement scheme when we were first opening up trade with the Trofts generally, which is one reason they now handle so much of it."

"All right," Joshua shrugged. "Assume the offer's legitimate. Are five planets of dubious value worth fighting a war for? An unprovoked war, yet?"

"Flip that over, though," Corwin said. "Suppose this new alien is a genuine and imminent threat. Do we dare simply ignore it and hope it won't find us? Maybe it *would* be better to take it out now while it can be done relatively easily."

"And what does 'relatively easily' mean?" Joshua countered.

Justin glanced at his mother's tight-lipped expression. The pattern was now a familiar one: Corwin usually took the devil's advocate position in these round tables, which implied Jonny was leaning toward the nay side on the issue. His reasons would be interesting to hear, but he was unlikely to voice them until the twins had had their say. But Chrys might not be so reticent. "Mom, *you* haven't said anything yet. How do *you* feel?"

She looked at him, a tired smile touching the corners of her mouth. "With you about to become a Cobra? Of course I don't want to risk your life for worlds we won't even need for another millennium. But aside from that emotional reaction, my logic center can't help but wonder *why* the Trofts want *us* to do this. They have a war machine the equal of the Dominion's—if they can't handle this alien threat, what do they expect *us* to do?"

Justin looked at Joshua, saw his own sudden thoughtfulness only hinted at in his brother's face. Understandable; Justin knew much more about both Cobra capabilities *and* limitations than Joshua did. He turned to his father, who seemed in turn to be watching him. "Odd," he said.

"Indeed," Jonny agreed. "The only advantage Cobras have over combat-suited troops is the fact that our weapons are concealed. It's hard to imagine a normal, non-guerrilla war where that's a deciding factor."

"Of course, the nearest known combat suits are way over in the Dominion—" Corwin began.

"But if they can hire *us* they can just as easily hire *them*," Justin finished for him. "Right?"

Corwin nodded. "Which leads me, at least, to only one answer for Mom's question."

There was a brief pause. "A test," Joshua said at last. "They want another crack at seeing just how powerful Cobras really are."

Jonny nodded. "I can't see any other explanation. Especially since the demesnes at this end of the Assemblage probably didn't have any direct contact with human forces during the war. All they've got are the farside demesnes' reports, and they may think those are exaggerated."

"So . . . what do we do?" Joshua asked. "Play it safe and say we're above mercenary work?"

"That would be my recommendation," his father sighed. "Unfortunately—well, you tell them, Corwin."

"I took a quick sample of Council opinion right after the meeting," Corwin said. "The eight syndics and two governors I talked to who'd followed this same line of reasoning were split straight down the middle on whether backing down would be a dangerous signal of weakness."

"If we try it and fail, what kind of a signal is *that?*" Joshua snorted.

Justin looked at Corwin. "What about the other Cobras on the Council?" he asked. "Did you talk to them?"

"One of them, yes. He was more interested in discussing the various modifications that would be needed to bring the Cobras back to full war footing."

"Actually, it wouldn't take much more than a replacement of the optical enhancement system," Jonny said. "The ones we've got now don't have the multiple targeting lock we'd need in combat. We'd have to change the academic and some of the practical content of the training, too, but aside from that a changeover would be easy. The nanocomputers still carry all the combat reflex programming, certainly."

Justin's tongue swiped briefly at his lips. *Combat reflexes.* The Cobra information packets were never quite that blunt; but that was, after all, what the Instant Defense Capabilities really were. *Combat reflexes.* What had sounded perfectly reasonable for a one-on-one confrontation with a spine leopard didn't seem nearly as reliable for the confusion of full warfare.

Still . . . one of those same little computers had helped keep his father alive through three years of guerrilla war against the Trofts; his father and Cally Halloran and hundreds of others. The computer, and the bone-strengthening laminae, and the servo motor network, and the lasers, and the sonics. . . . He found his eyes ranging over his father's form as he catalogued the weaponry and equipment implanted there . . . the equipment that the surgeons at the Cobra Academy would start putting into his own body tomorrow . . .

Someone was calling his name. Snapping out of his reverie, Justin focused on his older brother. "Sorry," he said. "Thoughts were elsewhere. What did you say?"

"I was asking what you thought of the idea of being a mercenary, if that's what it ultimately boils down to," Corwin said. "Ethically, I mean."

Justin shrugged uncomfortably, avoiding his mother's eyes. "Actually, it doesn't look to me like we *can* be pure mercenaries on this one. We *may* be defending the Worlds against an alien threat; we *will* be making a statement to the whole Troft Assemblage as to what kind of defensive capabilities we have here. Either way, we're ultimately serving our own people . . . which is what Cobras are supposed to do."

"In other words, you wouldn't mind going off to fight?" Chrys asked quietly.

Justin winced at her tone, but kept his voice steady. "I don't mind fighting if it's necessary. But I don't think we should hand that decision to the Trofts, either. The Council should get all the data on these aliens that we can and then make their decision without regard to these five planets being dangled in front of us."

In the kitchen a soft tone sounded. "Dinner time," Jonny announced, levering himself carefully out of the couch. "And with the food comes an end to political talk. Thank you for your feedback—it's nice to know we have a family consensus on this. Now hop to the kitchen and give your mother a hand. Table needs setting, vegetables a final rinse, and I believe it's your turn, Corwin, to carve the roast."

Corwin nodded and headed for the kitchen, Joshua hard on his heels. Chrys stayed at Jonny's side; and Justin lingered long enough to see his father fumble out his vials of pain pills. *The political talk is indeed over,* he told himself.

Leaving his parents to themselves, he hurried toward the kitchen to assist his brothers.

Chapter 3

Sometime in the past year or two one of Aventine's violent springtime thunderstorms had swept this part of the Trappers Forest, and the region's highest hill had taken a real beating. At least one tree had been blown to kindling by the lightning; six others had been knocked flat by either lightning or wind. The result was a hilltop which, despite its lousy footing, provided a clear line of sight for thirty meters in every direction. An unnecessary luxury for the average Cobra command post . . . but then, the average Cobra mission didn't have civilian observers to watch out for, either.

Audio enhancers at full power, Almo Pyre sent his gaze slowly around the edges of the informal clearing, acutely conscious of the middle-aged woman standing at his side. A civilian was bad enough; but to have one of Aventine's three *governors* out here was the sort of unnecessary—not to say damnfool—risk no Cobra leader in his right mind would take. *I should have left her behind,* Pyre though irritably. *The official mayhem would've been nothing to what'll happen if she gets killed.*

A soft hum—three brief notes—sounded from the receiver in his right ear: Winward had spotted one of their target spine leopards. Pyre hummed an acknowledgement into the wire-mike curving along his cheek, adding an alert to the others. Limited and sometimes awkward to use, the humming code had the advantage that it wasn't loud enough to kick in the cutoffs in the listener's audio enhancers.

"Hmm?" Governor Lizabet Telek hummed. The sound was louder than another Cobra would've used, but at least she knew enough not to ask her questions out loud.

Pyre notched back the audio, automatically shifting more

274

attention to his visual scan as he did so. "Michael's found one," he explained quietly. "The others will be sweeping in with a net pattern, watching for cubs and other adults."

"Cubs." Telek's voice was even, but there was more than a touch of dissatisfaction beneath it.

Pyre shrugged fractionally. Had he seen a flicker of movement in the shadow between two trees? "This year's cubs will be next year's breeders," he reminded her. "If you biology people can come up with a way—"

A *swoosh* of branches came from his right, and he spun to see a large feline body shooting down at them from the trees.

The leap would be short—that much was instantly obvious—but Pyre knew the predator would hit the ground running. His hands were already in firing position—little fingers pointed toward the spine leopard, thumbs resting against ring fingers' nails—and as the animal stretched its hind legs downward for a landing he squeezed.

The lasers in his little fingers spat needles of light into the spine leopard's face, burning fur and bone and brain tissue. But Pyre's intended target, its eyes, escaped destruction, and the creature's more decentralized nervous system shrugged off the brain damage as if not noticing it. The spine leopard landed, feet stumbling slightly on the branch-littered surface—

Pyre had twisted and was swinging his left leg to bear when Telek gasped. "Behind you!" she snapped.

A glimpse over his shoulder was all Pyre could get from his angle, but it was enough. The flicker he'd seen in the forest had become a second spine leopard, charging them like a furry missile.

And spinning the direction he was, Pyre was out of position to do anything about it. "Down!" he barked at Telek, hoping desperately he could attract the spine leopard's attack to himself. His programmed reflexes gave him a fighting chance, but they had no provision for defending bystanders, as well. An instant later his left leg reached firing position, and from the heel of his boot the brilliant spear of his antiarmor laser lanced out.

There was no time to assess the damage—he would just have to assume the first spine leopard was at least temporarily stopped. Continuing his spin, he dropped his left leg back to the ground and brought up his right—

In time to catch the second spine leopard full in the face with his foot.

There was no way Pyre's precarious balance could absorb the

full impact of the predator's charge—and even as the animal's teeth scrambled for a grip on his boot he felt himself falling sideways. Letting his left leg buckle beneath him, he drew his right back from the fangs . . . and as spine leopard sailed over him he straightened the leg sharply to send a servo-augmented kick hard into the creature's belly.

It shrieked, and even through the blur of motion Pyre saw its foreleg spines snap outward into defense position. It knew it was hurt . . . though perhaps not that it was doomed. For whatever incidental damage Pyre's kick had caused, it had also pushed the creature higher into the air—and the extra half second it took the spine leopard to reach the ground was all the time Pyre needed to again bring his left leg to bear. The antiarmor laser flashed twice, and the predator landed in a smoking heap.

Pyre scrambled to his feet, eyes automatically searching out the unmoving figure of the first spine leopard. Only then did he turn back to see what had happened to Telek.

The governor was on hands and knees in the small hollow between two fallen tree limbs, the small pellet pistol she'd been carrying clutched in one hand. "Is it safe to come out yet?" she asked, only a slight quaver in her voice.

Pyre gave the edge of the forest a careful scan. "I think so," he said, stepping forward to help her up. "Thanks for the warning."

"No problem." She waved off his assistance, brushing off dead leaves as she got to her feet. "I'd heard reports from other areas that the spine leopards were occasionally hunting in pairs these days, but I didn't think it'd started here yet. Survival pressure's supposed to be lighter in the major forests."

"It's strong enough," Pyre told her grimly. "And as I was saying, unless you biologists can come up with a way to counteract it, these hunts are going to have to continue."

"I'm hardly on the forefront of biological research these days—"

She broke off as Pyre held up his hand. "Report," he said quietly into his wire-mike. " . . . yes. Need any help? . . . all right. Return here when you're done."

Telek was watching him. "They found the den site," he told her. "Ten cubs in it."

Her mouth compressed into a tight line. "Ten. Twenty years ago a spine leopard litter never exceeded two or three. Never."

Pyre shrugged uncomfortably, running a hand through his thinning hair. *Forty-seven years old, and chasing through the forests like a newly-commissioned kid.* He might have been bitter if the duty wasn't so vital. "We've cleared out too many of their territories," he said with a shake of his head. "However it is they sense these things, they *know* there's room on Aventine for a whole lot more spine leopards. Theoretically."

Telek snorted gently. "Theoretically, indeed. Spine leopards in the streets of Capitalia." She shook her head in turn. "If you only knew, Pyre, how often biologists have yearned for a truly self-healing planetary ecology. And now we've got two . . . and they're a damn bloody nuisance."

" 'Nuisance' is hardly a word I'd apply to Caelian, Governor," Pyre murmured.

"True." Something in her tone made him glance over, and he found her gazing tight-lipped into the forest. "Well . . . maybe there's something we can do about it."

"About all we could do about Caelian is abandon it," he retorted.

"That's exactly what I had in mind," she nodded. "Tell me, would you be available for some consultation before the Council meeting the day after tomorrow? I need some expert advice from an experienced Cobra team leader."

"I suppose so," he said reluctantly. "But only if we're finished completely out here."

"Fine," she agreed. "I think you'll find my proposal very interesting."

I doubt it, he told himself morosely, turning his attention back to the forest. *Another political mind with another political solution. Once—just once—I'd like to hear something else. Anything else.* Unbidden, the face of Tors Challinor rose before him: Challinor, who had tried years ago to take military control of Aventine. *Well, all right,* he told the memory with a shudder. *I'd like* almost *anything else.*

Chapter 4

"This meeting is officially come to order," Governor-General Stiggur announced, bringing his hand down in a dramatic gesture to start the sealed recorder.

Somehow, Corwin thought, the whole thing lost a lot of effect when translated to a room the size of a large office and an audience of six. "I've called you here," Stiggur continued, "to discuss the issue raised at the Council meeting two weeks ago: namely, whether to undertake the job the Tlos demesne has offered us."

Corwin glanced surreptitiously around the table at the five governors, feeling as he never had at Council meetings the sheer *weight* of political authority assembled around him. An oppressive, almost suffocating presence—

Until Governor Lizabet Telek spoke up and broke the bubble. "I realize, Brom, that you're speaking for posterity here," she said to Stiggur, "but can we try to do without the heavy historical phrasings?"

Stiggur tried to glare at her, but his heart clearly wasn't in it. None of them had come to Aventine all those years ago with any political aspirations, and while they'd stepped into these positions with reasonable success, they were all still non-politicians beneath the trappings. "All right—point taken," Stiggur sighed. "Fine. So who's got anything to report?"

"I'd like to know first of all where Governor Emeritus Moreau is," Caelian's Governor Howie Vartanson spoke up. "It seems to me this issue should take priority over therapy sessions or whatever."

"My father's in the hospital at the moment," Corwin said,

resisting the urge to say something nasty about the other's unthinking callousness. He *knew* Jonny was a first-generation Cobra, after all. "Immune system trouble, the doctors think."

"How serious is it?" Stiggur asked, frowning.

"Apparently not very. It came on rather suddenly last night, though."

"You should have let someone know," Jor Hemner said, one frail hand playing restlessly with his wispy beard. "We could have postponed this meeting."

"Not if we want to have a recommendation for the full Council meeting this afternoon," Corwin said, glancing at Hemner before returning his gaze to Stiggur. "I know my father's thoughts on this matter, sir, and have his authority to act for him. I presume you'll accept my council proxy in this session?"

"Well, the strict legality—"

"Oh, for heaven's sake, Brom, let him sit in and be done with it," Telek put in. "We've got a lot of ground to cover this morning, and I want to get to it."

"Fine." Stiggur raised his eyebrows at the others. "Any objections? All right. Anyone managed to find out anything from the Trofts about this Qasama?"

Olor Roi of Palatine cleared his throat. "I tried playing the old independent-planets routine on Speaker One, but I think it's starting to wear thin. They're finally tumbling to the fact that we're a political unit even though we can all make our own trade agreements. Still, I think he was being honest when he said he'd already given us all he had."

"Maybe he was just holding out in hopes we'd outbid you," suggested Dylan Fairleigh, the third Aventine governor. It was a rather naive comment, Corwin thought, betraying the lack of experience with Troft trade that almost automatically came with the other's Far West Region jurisdiction.

Vartanson, predictably, didn't bother to take that into account. "Don't be ridiculous," he snorted. "Trofts don't *hold out* without making it known that they *have* something for sale. Where've you been the past 14 years, anyway?"

Fairleigh's forehead darkened, but before he could speak Telek cut in. "Okay—so it's established the Tlossies haven't got anything. Next step is obviously to get to someone who *does*. I see two choices: the Baliu demesne or Qasama itself."

"Just a second," Corwin spoke up. "Isn't the next step to see whether we're going to *need* this information?"

Telek frowned at him. "Of *course* we need it. How else can we make a rational decision?"

"The most rational decision would be to give the Tlossies a simple no sale right now," Corwin answered. "If we do—"

"Since when is hiding from reality a rational decision?" Telek interrupted tartly.

"Saying no now is a statement of principle," Corwin told her, feeling sweat break out on his forehead. Jonny had warned him this view was unlikely to be well received, but Corwin hadn't been prepared for so strong a negative reaction. "It says we're not interested in becoming mercenaries for—"

"What about our own interests?" Vartanson put in. "If Qasama is a threat to the Trofts it's probably a threat to us, too."

"Yes, but . . ." Corwin stopped as words and logic suddenly tangled into a knotted mess. *Relax,* he ordered himself. *No one here's anyone to be afraid of.*

But even as he fought his sudden shyness Stiggur came to his rescue. "I think the point Corwin's trying to make is that we can still send expeditions to Qasama or wherever once we've turned down the Baliu demesne's deal," he said. "At that point we're not constrained by what the Trofts want done, but are free to take action as *we* see fit."

"Sounds very noble," Telek nodded. "Unfortunately, it runs very quickly into one important practical detail. Namely, who pays for this if the Trofts don't?"

Fairleigh shifted in his seat. "I was under the impression the Trofts were offering only those five planets, not payment of costs too."

"No deal's been officially struck—we could demand costs as part of the package," Roi pointed out thoughtfully. "But it would still take a lot of Cobras out of circulation for up to several years. How fast can the academy replace them?"

"Surgery and training together take three months," Corwin spoke up, feeling better on balance. "Candidate screening adds another two weeks."

"But the whole process can be shrunk to less than seven weeks," Telek said, brandishing a magcard for a moment before dropping it into her reader. "In the past few days I've spoken with two authorities on Cobra matters: Cally Halloran, who was Jonny's old teammate in the Troft War; and Almo Pyre, currently head of Cobra operations in Syzra District. Together they've provided the data necessary for a cost analysis of both the initial scouting expedition and the three most likely types of military operation."

Corwin stared at the figures that appeared on his display, the two names she'd dropped so casually into the discussion bouncing like unexploded grenades around his numbed brain. *Cally Halloran*—one of his father's oldest and most trusted friends; and *Almo Pyre*—a Moreau family friend for as long as Corwin could remember. Sneaking a glance over his screen, he found Telek's calm eyes on him . . . and suddenly he realized what she was trying to do.

By choosing Jonny's friends as her experts, she hoped to stifle any disagreement the only Cobra in this inner circle might have had with her numbers . . . and as he began studying those numbers he saw the conclusion they inevitably led to.

For even the smallest of the projected military actions the costs were simply staggering. Halloran and Pyre had estimated a minimum of nine hundred Cobras—a full third of the three Worlds' current contingent—on or near Qasama for six to twelve months. Equipment, transport, supply, replacement of casualties—it was far more than the Worlds could hope to scrape together from their modest economies. The abrupt loss of that many Cobras alone would bring to a dead halt all territorial expansion on Aventine and Palatine; on Caelian it could easily precipitate the final destruction or abandonment of that beleaguered colony.

Fairleigh broke the silence first. "We'd better hope the Qasamans aren't *too* immediate a threat," he muttered. "Nine hundred to three *thousand* Cobras. How long would it take to replace—? Oh, there it is."

Corwin found the line on his own display. "That assumes an unlimited supply of qualified candidates," he said.

"Well, if that pool doesn't exist—or can't be generated—we're in serious trouble already," Roi growled. "Our safety from the Trofts themselves depends on a healthy respect for Cobra fighting skills. If they thought our paltry twenty-eight hundred were all they'd ever have to deal with . . ." He shook his head.

"All the more reason to show them how easily expandable the Cobra program is," Telek argued. "We *can* do it—especially with the Trofts paying for the demonstration."

The discussion raged on for a half hour more, but Corwin could see the battle was lost. Of the six others in the room, only Hemner and Roi seemed at all willing to consider Jonny's position. If neither of them switched sides, Corwin's double vote would deadlock the issue at four to four, which would mean throwing it to the full Council without any official recommendation. The Council's handling of matters even with a recommendation was chancy enough; without one, the results were impossible for anyone to predict.

And as the probability of victory slipped ever closer to zero, Corwin realized that, for the first time since obtaining his father's proxy, he was going to have to make a deal on his own initiative. A deal he wasn't at all certain Jonny would approve of. . . .

He waited until the last minute, hoping against the odds; but as the governor-general called for a vote he raised his hand. "I'd like to ask for a short break before we go any further," he said. "It seems to me some private thought or discussion might be useful before we commit our votes to the record."

Stiggur's eyebrows lifted slightly, but he nodded without hesitation. "All right. We'll meet back here in 20 minutes."

The general exodus was quiet—apparently the others felt in need of a break, as well—and a minute or two later Corwin was sitting in his father's Dominion Building office. For a long moment he stared at the phone on the desk, wondering if he should discuss this with anyone before he went ahead and did it. But his father would still be in the depths of biochemical surgery, and he could guess what his mother would say. Theron Yutu, across town in Jonny's main office? No. The twins—he ought to discuss it with them. But Justin was incommunicado in the surgery wing of the Cobra Academy, and to tell only Joshua would be unfair . . . and Corwin realized he was stalling. Taking a deep breath, he got up from his father's chair and headed down the hall to Governor Telek's office.

If she was surprised to see him, it didn't show. "Corwin," she nodded, closing the door behind him and ushering him to a seat. "Nice dilemma we have here, isn't it? What can I do for you?"

Corwin waited until she was seated again at her desk before speaking. "How do you see the vote?" he asked bluntly.

Again, she showed no surprise. "Myself, Brom, Dylan, and Howie for; you, Jor, and Olor against. Deadlock. You come here to try and change my mind?"

He shook his head. "You knew my father would be against the whole thing, didn't you? That's why you dragged Cally and Almo into it."

"Your father was one of the strongest opponents of the Cobra Academy when it was set up some twenty-five years ago," she reminded him. "It wasn't hard to guess he'd be against any proposal that would increase the number of Cobras."

Which made Jonny's philosophical objections to Cobras-for-hire sound like nothing more than camouflage for an old habitual reflex. Corwin swallowed hard against the rebuttal that wanted to come out. Now was not the time to defend his father's stand. "So what exactly do *you* want?" he asked instead. "A contractual commitment to handle whatever this threat is that Qasama poses?"

"Of course not," she snorted. "No one in their right mind would give a Troft a carte blanche like that. All I want is to commit us to a survey mission—at Troft expense."

"Won't that commit us to carrying out the rest of it, too?"

"Not if the agreement's drawn up carefully enough." She pursed her lips. "You're about to bring up the image question if we look Qasama over and then back out. I don't really have any better answer to that than the one I gave fifteen minutes ago. The risks of *not* knowing what kind of threat Qasama is are greater than the risks of looking weak to the Trofts."

Corwin took a deep breath. "Then I presume you'd like to have that as the official recommendation to the Council in a few hours?"

"I'd like that very much," she said cautiously. "What's it going to cost me?"

Corwin gestured toward the conference room down the hall. "Your proposed survey mission would include a maximum of twelve people plus ship's crew, as I recall. I want two of those twelve to be my father's choice."

"With his skeptic's attitude to keep the mission honest?" She smiled wryly. "As a matter of fact, that's probably a good idea ... but giving a governor emeritus sixteen percent of the package isn't likely to fly very smoothly."

"I can sweeten the deal considerably. How would you like to send an *undetectable* Cobra on the mission?"

He had the satisfaction of seeing her eyes widen with surprise. "I thought a careful deep-body scan would pick up even Cobra gear."

"It will," Corwin nodded. "But a scan of that type takes almost fifteen minutes to complete. How many times is a host likely to subject visiting dignitaries to that sort of thing?"

She frowned at him for several heartbeats. "My immediate reaction is that you're being anthropomorphic in the extreme. Suppose their deep-body stuff is more sensitive or just faster than ours, for example? But assuming you're right, then what?—cram a Cobra surgery team into the *Dewdrop* for some fast work?"

"Not at all. I propose sending a Cobra and a non-Cobra who

are virtually indistinguishable from each other. My twin brothers Joshua and Justin."

Telek's breath came out in a thoughtful hiss. "Cute. Very cute. So the Cobra stays aboard ship until the aliens have done all their studies on the landing party, and then they switch places? Interesting proposal. But suppose the Qasamans use something besides sight for identification? Sound or scent, for instance?"

Corwin shrugged, trying to make the gesture look casual. "Then we're out of luck. But most land predators we know of—including those on Troft and Dominion worlds—rely heavily on sight. I think it's a fair gamble, and if it doesn't work we haven't really lost anything."

"Except two places in the mission that could have gone to other people." Telek leaned back in her chair, her eyes focused somewhere behind Corwin's head. He waited, forcing himself to breathe normally . . . and abruptly her eyes returned to him and she nodded. "All right, it's a deal . . . on one further condition. You—or, rather, your father—must support *my* bid to go on the mission."

"You?" Corwin blurted. "But that's—"

"Ridiculous? Hardly. The mission's going to need both scientific and political experts aboard, and I'm the only governor who qualifies in both fields and is healthy enough to make the trip."

"Your biological degree is a long way behind you."

"I've kept up with the field. And we need *someone* of governor rank in case some major policy decision comes up. Unless you know any syndics you'd trust with that task."

But can I trust you with it? He pursed his lips tightly, unsure of what he should do.

"You've got time to think," she said calmly as the silence began to stretch. Glancing at her watch, she stood up. "The mission team's not likely to be determined for at least a week or two. Talk it over with Jonny, work through the logic—I think you'll agree I should be aboard. But it's time to go back in there and get a recommendation for the Council to chew on."

Corwin stood up, too. "All right . . . but if I vote with you now, I want you to support my getting Justin and Joshua aboard—whether my father ultimately backs your own bid or not."

She smiled wryly. "Realized you were giving away too much, did you? Well, that's how you learn. Sure, I'll support your brothers. It's a good idea . . . and to be perfectly honest, I don't expect I'll need Jonny's vote to get on the mission, anyway."

The vote was four to two in favor of Telek's proposal when it came to Corwin's turn. He avoided Hemner's and Roi's eyes as he made it six to two, but he could feel their astonished gazes on him as Stiggur recorded the vote into the record.

Three hours later, the full Council made it official.

Lying propped up in his hospital bed, Jonny listened silently to Corwin's report of the governors' session, the Council meeting, and the private deal he'd made. *I should be angry,* Jonny thought, peripherally aware of the IV tubes feeding clear fluids into his arms. *Some calming factor in the antibiotic voodoo mixture? Or did I really know all along my plan wouldn't make it?*

Corwin stopped speaking and waited, the tension lines visible in his face. "Have you spoken to Justin or Joshua about this?" Jonny asked. "Or your mother?"

Corwin actually winced. "No, to both questions. I came up with the basic idea last week, but I hoped I wouldn't have to suggest it to anyone. At least, not without talking to you first. I think they'd be willing, though."

"Oh, they'll be willing, all right—that's not the problem." Jonny turned his head to gaze out the window. Capitalia's streetlights were visible below, the cityscape superimposed on the reflection of the hospital room around him. "You boys have always been very precious to your mother, you know," he said. "You provided the extra family warmth that I often wasn't able to give her. Too often wasn't able to. As a Cobra . . . then a syndic . . . then a governor . . . it takes a lot of time to serve people, Corwin. Time taken away from your family. You came to work with me here, and Justin's becoming a Cobra . . . and now Joshua's going to be taken from her, too." He realized abruptly he was rambling and brought his eyes back to Corwin.

The other was looking pretty miserable. "I'm sorry. Maybe I shouldn't have done it. They *can* still back down."

Jonny shook his head. "No, you did the right thing, all the way down the line. Putting the twins aboard could give us a key tactical advantage, and the full council probably wouldn't have gone for my proposal any more than Brom and company did. Especially with the cost estimates Cally and Almo provided." He shook his head. "Pity Cally's too old to go along—a Cobra with military experience would be awfully nice to have on the scene. . . ." He trailed off thoughtfully as an idea suddenly occurred to him.

"You're not planning to go yourself, are you?" Corwin asked suspiciously into his train of thought.

"Hm? Oh, no. Not really. I was just trying to think of a way to make this all up to your mother." Taking a deep breath, he let it out in a controlled sigh. "Well. I'll be out of here in the morning, or so they say—soon enough for us to break this to her. Why don't you talk to Joshua tonight, get his reaction. If possible, I think we should all be together when we tell Chrys."

"All except Justin," Corwin reminded him. "He'll be in surgical isolation for another week."

"I know that," Jonny said, a touch of asperity making it through the emotional damper around him. "But the three of us should be there."

"Right," Corwin nodded, standing up. "I'll let you get back to resting now and see you in the morning. I can check on my way out when you'll be released and be here to drive you home."

"Fine. Oh, and while you're checking that, would you ask the doctor to drop by when he's got some time? There are some things I want to discuss with him."

"Sure," Corwin said. He held his father's eye another second, then turned and left.

Shifting to a more comfortable position, Jonny closed his eyes and let all tensions melt away. Had there been another touch of suspicion in Corwin's face as he left? Jonny wasn't sure. But it didn't really matter. Unlike his son, he had several other governors besides Telek with whom he could cut a deal . . . and by the time Corwin found out about it, it would all be arranged.

And the other would surely approve, anyway. Eventually.

Chapter 5

The room they'd taken him to was the first surprise—Justin had had the impression that the new trainees would be kept together for their first postoperative orientation session. A quick glance around the office as his escort left him alone was a second shock: no Cobra training instructor could possibly have an office this ornate. The desk—had he seen its carved cyprene wood in the Cobra lecture tapes he'd studied before applying? If so, this was the private office of Coordinator Sun himself. Whatever was going on, this was *not* part of the published schedule.

Behind the desk, a private door opened. Justin tensed; and as a man stepped into the room, he felt a relieved grin spread over his face. "Almo! I thought you were still out in Syzra District hunting down spine leopards."

"Hello, Justin—no, please stay seated." Pyre sat down behind the desk.

And Justin suddenly realized the other hadn't even smiled in greeting. "What's up, Almo?" he asked, his pleased surprise evaporating. "Is something wrong? Good Lord—is it Dad?"

"No, no, your family's fine," Pyre hastened to reassure him. "Although in a couple of months—" He broke off. "Let's start over. How much do you know about the Qasama thing?"

Justin hesitated. Admitting to Pyre that his father had given the family confidential information was no big deal in and of itself . . . but under *these* circumstances. . . . "Just the basics of the Troft offer," he said. "My father wanted to discuss the ethical aspects with us."

"Fine," Pyre nodded. "Then I won't need to go over that with you. In the past three weeks there've been some twists added—by the Council and, believe it or not, your own brother."

Justin listened in silence as Pyre explained the Council's expeditionary plan and Corwin's suggestion, his emotions turmoiling between shock and excitement with very little room left amid it all for rational thought. "The Council's voted to put you two aboard if you're both willing to go," Pyre concluded. "Any immediate reactions?"

Justin took a moment to find his tongue. "It sounds . . . interesting. Very interesting. What's Joshua had to say about it, and where do you fit in?"

"Joshua you can ask yourself—I'll send him in when I'm done. As for me—" Pyre's lip twitched in something between a smile and a grimace. "I'm going to be head of the shipboard Cobra contingent—four of us in all. And if you choose one of those slots, I'll be handling all your Cobra training for the next few weeks."

Justin was suddenly aware of the neckwrap computer nestling around his throat—the programmable training computer that would be replaced by the implanted Cobra nanocomputer if and when he graduated. "Specialized training, I gather? Stuff you don't need to fight spine leopards?"

"And special-function programmed reflexes that are built into the standard nanocomputer but never needed in forest work," Pyre nodded. "Ceiling flips, backspins; that sort of thing."

"Won't your other Cobras need that, too?"

"They'll be joining us once your basics are out of the way, three to four weeks from now." Pyre leaned his elbows on the desk, steepling his fingertips in front of him. "Look, Justin, I've got to be honest with you. I can tell you're seeing this as a big fat adventure, but you have to realize the chances are fair we'll all wind up dying on Qasama."

"Aw, come on, Almo," Justin grinned. "*You'll* be there, too, and you're too lucky to be killed."

"Stop that!" Pyre snapped. "Luck is statistical chance, with a weak coupling to skill and experience. Nothing more. I've got a little of both—you'll have practically none of either. If anyone dies, it's likely to be you."

Justin shrank into his chair, taken aback by Pyre's outburst. The older man had been one of Justin's most admired role models when he was younger, the one who—as much as his father—had catalyzed his decision to become a Cobra himself. To be chewed out by that role model was more of a shock than he'd ever dreamed such a thing could be.

His expression must have mirrored his feelings; but Pyre

nevertheless continued to glare for several more seconds before finally letting his eyes soften. "I know that hurt," he said softly, "but it didn't hurt nearly as much as a laser would. Get it into your head right now that this is a probe into *enemy* territory. Your father will tell you that fighting spine leopards is a picnic in comparison."

Justin licked his lips. "You don't want me along, do you?"

For the first time Pyre's gaze slipped away from Justin's face. "What I want personally is irrelevant. The Council made a decision, all the old war veterans concurred that it made good tactical sense, and Governor Telek persuaded them I was the man to lead the Cobra contingent. My job's been defined for me, and it's now up to me to carry it out. Period."

"And you're afraid I won't be able to handle it?" Justin asked, the first stirrings of anger starting to seep through the numbness.

"I'm afraid *none* of us will be able to," Pyre replied tartly. "And if the whole thing goes up, I don't like the fact that my attention will be split between the mission's safety and yours."

"Why should it be?" Justin retorted. "Because you've known me since I was in diapers? Because you've been Dad's friend even longer? I'm 22, Almo, old enough to take care of myself now— and if you want logic, how about the fact that I won't have to unlearn all the little tricks of fighting spine leopards that the rest of you will? You have any complaints about my youth, save them for after the training, all right? Then maybe we'll have some actual specifics to discuss."

Pyre's eyes were again locked with his and unconsciously Justin braced for a second outburst. But it didn't come. "Okay," Pyre said softly. "I just wanted to make sure you knew what you were getting into. Believe it or not, I *do* understand how you feel . . . though you'll find that others may not." He stood up, and a hint of the old Almo Pyre peeked through for an instant. "I'll let Joshua come and talk to you now. I'll be in the office across the hall; just come on over when you're finished. Take your time, but try not to make this one of those wide-ranging starvation sessions you two are famous for." With a glimmer of a smile he left the room.

Justin let out a shuddering sigh of relief. His heartbeat was heading back toward normal when his twin arrived a minute later. "Almo told me to keep this talk under six months," Joshua said, seating himself in the recently vacated desk chair. "Do we *really* talk that much?"

"Only together," Justin said.

"Probably true," the other conceded, running a critical eye over his brother. "So. How do you feel?"

"From the surgery, fine. From Almo's little talk, like someone just threw an oversized gantua at me. Accurately."

Joshua nodded his commiseration. "I know how you feel. So . . . what do you think?"

"Sounds like something I'd really like to do—or it did before Almo went into an amazingly deep discourage mode. I gather you also have reservations?"

Joshua frowned. "Not especially, aside from the obvious aversions to getting myself killed. Who said I did?"

"Almo implied someone was having problems with the plan."

Joshua's frown became a pained grimace. "Probably referring to Mom."

"Mom." Justin ground his left fist hard into his right palm with chagrin at having forgotten all about her in the excitement—and an instant later the stab of pain from both knuckles and palm reminded him that, even with the limitations imposed on it by the neckwrap computer, his new strength-enhancing servo network wasn't something he could afford to ignore. Fortunately, the skeletal laminae had made his bones virtually unbreakable, which meant that this time he'd get away with only bruises. On his pride, as well as on his skin. "Grumfick it, I didn't even think of what this would do to her," he admitted to Joshua. "She been told yet?"

"Oh, yeah—and believe me, you were having lots more fun in surgery." Joshua shook his head. "I don't know. Maybe we ought to pass this up."

"What did she say?"

"About what you'd expect," the other sighed. "Dead set against it emotionally, only marginally more for it intellectually, and feeling generally betrayed that Corwin would even suggest such a thing. We tried to convince her that you were getting off easier than if you'd been assigned to Caelian, or even to the spine leopard extermination squads, but I don't think she believed us."

"Almo doesn't believe that," Justin pointed out dryly. "Why should she?"

Joshua waved a hand in futility. "I didn't invent the art of wishful thinking; I just market it locally."

"Yeah." Justin found a vacant corner to stare at for a moment, then returned his gaze to this brother. "So you really think we should pass this up?"

"To be brutally honest, no." Joshua began ticking off fingers. "Corwin's basic idea sounds good, and it's obvious we're the only two in the Worlds who could pull it off. We're likely to also be the only ones aboard who share Dad's view that hiring ourselves out is a dangerous precedent. And finally—" He grinned suddenly, shyly. "Heck, Justin, you felt it in school, too. We're *Moreaus*—sons of the Cobra, Troft War veteran, governor emeritus, original Aventinian pioneer Jonny Moreau himself. People *expect* something great from us."

"That's a pretty blithering reason to do something."

"By itself, sure. But combined with reason number two, it means our report and recommendations will carry a hefty bit of inertia when we get back from Qasama . . . and given the current Council leaning, Dad may need that extra bit of weight to keep them from doing anything stupid."

And on the other hand, Justin thought grimly, *is what it'll do to Mom. Your basic no-win situation.* But Joshua was right . . . and if there was one thing they'd learned from *both* parents, it was that personal comfort and preference were never to stand in the way of service to the whole. "All right," he said at last. "If you're game, so am I. 'Gantuas, hell: charge!' and all that."

"Okay." Joshua stood up. "Well, then, we'd better get to it. Almo's got some serious sweat waiting for you, I don't doubt, and I've got a couple of surgeons down the hall warming up an operating table for me."

"Surgeons?" Justin frowned, getting—carefully—to his feet. "What do they want *you* for?"

Joshua winked slyly. "You'll find out. For now, suffice it to say that it's something that'll let you be the best me possible when we get to Qasama."

"The best *what?* Come on, Joshua—"

"See you in a couple of months," Joshua grinned and slipped out the door.

You and your stupid guessing games, Justin thought after him, and for a moment considered chasing him down and badgering whatever this was out of him. But Almo was waiting across the hall; *and we're not 16 years old anymore,* he reminded himself. Squaring his shoulders, he headed out to confront his new tutor.

Telephone screens had never in their long history come anywhere near the fine-detail resolution even the simplest computer displays required. It was a failing deliberately built in, Jonny had once heard, not for financial reasons but psychosocial ones. Wrinkles, worry lines, minor emotional perturbations—all were edited out, to the point that if the picture on the screen was happy, sad, or angry, it could be safely assumed the person himself was deep into the corresponding state.

It was a shock, therefore, to see how utterly *tired* Corwin appeared.

"As of ten minutes ago we were back to deadlock, Dad," his eldest son told him, shaking his head. "Of course, the Tlossies are really bargaining for the Baliu demesne, and Speaker One has only limited flexibility to work with. Especially on the survey mission budget. Every time we try to add something he has to take something else away. Or so he claims."

Jonny glanced over the screen. Chrys, seated at the dining room table, was pretending to be engrossed in the collection of electronics parts she'd spread out there, but he knew she was listening to the conversation. "Maybe I'd better come back down there, then," he told Corwin. "See if I can help."

"Not worth it," the other shook his head. "Governor Telek's bargaining at least as hard as you could, and everyone's keeping out of each other's way for a change. Besides, the temp's dropped ten degrees since sundown."

Jonny grimaced; but it was just one more environmental factor he'd had to learn to live with. Capitalia was in the middle of the first cold snap of autumn, and moving in and out of heated buildings was more than his arthritic joints could stand. The only alternatives to hiding indoors were heated suits or extra pain medication, neither of which especially appealed to him. "All right," he told his son. "But if you guys don't break for the evening soon, call me back and I'll relieve you. You look beat."

"I'll be all right. The main reason I called was to check a couple of things on this parallel survey mission request you put in. How much of that are you willing for the Worlds to finance?"

"Not a single quarter," Jonny told him flatly. "At the bottom line this is a trade deal, Corwin, and *no one* trades for merchandise he hasn't even seen, let alone inspected. Of course, since it's the Pua demesne that's actually offering the five planets, you can probably insist the Speaker charge *them* the survey costs. All that'll ultimately do is throw the issue back to Pua and Baliu to work out between themselves, but at least it should get it out of *our* hair."

"Yeah." Corwin shook his head in bemusement. "Hard to believe this collection of business cutthroats actually got together long enough to fight a war."

"They did. Believe me, they did. And there's nothing that says they couldn't do it again."

"Point taken. Well . . . are you willing for us to use the *Menssana* for the survey mission if the Trofts—whichever Trofts—pay all the other expenses?"

Jonny bit at his lip. "I'd rather they provide the ship, too. But okay—if you have to fall back to that position, go ahead and do so. They pay for the fuel, though."

"Okay. Actually, I'll probably wind up holding that option against something the Qasama mission needs. Talk to you later."

They signed off, and for a moment Jonny gazed at the screen as he tried to visualize all the various lines the negotiations could move along. But it was too much like an oversized game of trisec chess, with just too many possibilities to hang onto simultaneously. Getting to his feet—an easy enough operation in the overheated room—he went over to the table and sat down next to Chrys. "How's it coming?" he asked, eyeing the mass of wires, micro-components, and centipeds set into her circuit board.

"Slow," she said, fiddling with the controls on her diagnostic display. "I'm beginning to see why everyone prefers buying finished Troft electronics to just getting the components and building things themselves. These centipeds in particular have a lot of odd and not entirely obvious response characteristics outside their quote normal unquote usage range."

"You'll figure it all out," Jonny assured her. "You were once the best electronics tech in—"

"In Ariel?" She snorted. "Thanks a spangle. There were only two of us there—I *had* to be best or runner-up."

"Best, definitely," Jonny said firmly. A touch of the old Chrys, the sense of humor that had been so muted lately . . . perhaps she was finally getting a grip on the turmoil of the past few weeks.

Or perhaps she was simply retreating into her own past. It had been years since she'd done anything serious with her electronics training.

"You realize, of course," she cut quietly into his thoughts, "that if you let the *Menssana* go on this survey mission, there'll be no backup ship available if the *Dewdrop* gets in trouble on Qasama."

Jonny shook his head. "We weren't going to use the *Menssana* for that anyway. There'll be one or more Troft warships hanging back from Qasama in case some extra muscle is needed."

"I thought the Trofts didn't want to fight the Qasamans."

"If the mission has any trouble, they'll damn well have to," Jonny said grimly. "But they shouldn't have any real qualms—a local commando-type strike is hardly the same as committing to a full-scale war."

"Besides which, they'll want to protect their investment?"

"*Now* you're thinking like a Troft." Reaching over, he put an arm around her shoulders. "Just remember, Chrys," he added more seriously, "that the Baliuies had to have gotten at least one diplomatic team into and out of Qasama safely to have anything like the data we know they have. The third-level translator program they'll be giving us shows *that* much. Joshua and Justin will be all right. Really."

"I'd like to believe that," Chrys sighed. "But you know it's a mother's prerogative to worry."

"I seem to remember that being a *wife's* prerogative thirty years ago."

"Things change." Chrys toyed with a hex-shaped centiped. "Always do."

"Yes," Jonny agreed. "And not always for the better. I seem to also remember a time when the two of us went on trips together— *just* the two of us, with no kids along. What would you say to seeing if we can bring back those days?"

Chrys snorted faintly. "You think the Council could function without you that long?"

He winced at the implied criticism. "Sure they can," he said, choosing to take the question at face value. "Corwin knows the ropes well enough, and nothing important's likely to happen while the Qasama mission's gone, anyway. Perfect time for a vacation."

"Wait a second." She turned a frown his direction. "Are you talking about a vacation while your sons are out there in who knows *what* kind of danger?"

"Why not?" he asked. "Seriously. There's not a single thing we can do for them from here, even if we knew something had gone wrong, which we won't—sending shuttles back and forth has already been rejected as too possibly provocative. Giving your mind something besides worry to occupy it would be good for you."

She gestured minutely at the electronics in front of her. "If *this* can't keep my mind busy, I doubt a vacation will."

"That's only because you don't know the kind of vacation I have in mind," he told her, mentally crossing his fingers. If he presented this right she might just go for it . . . and he knew with a solid conviction that it was something they both needed. "I was thinking of a leisurely cruise sort of thing, with stops at various points for relaxing strolls through forests and grasslands, or maybe a swim through warm waters. Companionship with others when we want it, privacy when we want *that*, and all the comforts of home. How's it sound?"

Chrys smiled. "Like the coastline cruises they used to advertise when I was a child. Don't tell me some enterprising soul's bought a deep-sea liner from the Trofts?"

"Ah—not exactly. Would it help if I told you the cruise itinerary includes five planets?"

"Five pl—Jonny!" Chrys's eyes widened with shock. "You don't mean—the *survey mission?*"

"Sure—and why not?"

"What do you mean, why not? That's a scientific expedition, not a vacation service for the middle-aged."

"Ah, but I'm a governor emeritus, remember? If Liz Telek can talk her way aboard the Qasama trip on the grounds someone with authority should be present, I can certainly borrow her argument."

A muscle in Chrys's jaw twitched. "You've already arranged this, haven't you?" she asked suspiciously.

"Yes—but I'm going only if you do. I didn't misrepresent any of this, Chrys—I'll be there strictly to observe, make a policy decision should one come up, and otherwise just stay out of everyone else's way. It really *will* be just like an out-of-the-way vacation for the two of us."

Chrys dropped her eyes to the table. "It'd be dangerous, though, wouldn't it?"

Jonny shrugged. "So was life in Ariel when we were first married. You didn't seem to mind it so much."

"I was a lot younger then."

"So? Why should Justin and Joshua have all the fun?"

He'd hoped to spark a reaction of some kind, but was completely unprepared for the burst of laughter that escaped Chrys's lips. Genuine laughter, with genuine amusement behind it. "You're impossible," she accused, swiveling in her seat to give him a mock glare. "Didn't I just tell you I planned to be worried about them? What're we going to do—make this a Christmas exchange of worries?"

"Or we can deputize Corwin to do the worrying for all of us," Jonny suggested with a straight face. "Brothers in the morning, parents in the afternoon, and he can worry about the Council for me in the evenings. Come on, Chrys—it'll probably be our only chance to see the place our great-great-grandchildren may someday live." *At least our only chance together,* he added to himself, *in the three or four years I have left.*

Her face showed no hint of having followed that train of thought: but a minute later she sighed and nodded. "All right. Yes— let's do it."

"Thanks, Hon," he said quietly. It wouldn't, he knew, quite make up for losing her sons to the universe at large . . . but perhaps having a husband back for a while would be at least partial compensation.

He hoped so. Despite his assurances, it was quite possible two of those sons would soon be swallowed up by that same universe, never to return.

Chapter 6

The Council—along with an ever-expanding ring of agents/confidants—kept the secret of the Troft proposal remarkably well for nearly four weeks longer; but at that point Stiggur decided to release the news to the general population. From Corwin's point of view the timing couldn't have been worse. Still in the midst of detailed financial negotiations with the Trofts, he was abruptly thrust into the position of being answer man for what seemed sometimes to be all three hundred eighty thousand of Aventine's people. Theron Yutu and the rest of the staff were able to handle a lot of it on their own, but there were a fair number of policy-type questions that only he and Jonny could answer; and because of his private commitment to keeping his father's workload as light as possible, Corwin wound up spending an amazing amount of time on the phone and the public information net.

Fortunately, the reaction was generally positive. Most of the objections raised were along the ethical lines the Moreau family had discussed together in their own first pass by the issue, and even among those dissenters support for the Council ran high. Virtually no one raised the point Corwin had been most worried about: namely, why the Council had waited nearly two months before soliciting public feedback. That one he would have found hard to answer.

But all the public relations work took his attention away from the mission details being hammered out—took enough of it, in fact, that he completely missed the important part of the proposed survey mission team until the list was made public . . . and even then Joshua had to call and tell him about it.

"I wondered why you were taking it so calmly," Jonny said when

Corwin confronted him a few minutes later. "I suppose I should have mentioned it to you."

"Mentioned, my left eye," Corwin growled. "You should have at least *discussed* it with the rest of us before you went ahead and signed yourselves up."

"Why?" Jonny countered. "What your mother and I do with our lives is our business—we *are* old enough to make these decisions for ourselves. We decided we wanted a change of scenery, and this seemed a good way to get it." He cocked an eyebrow. "Or are you going to suggest neither of us would know how to handle an alien environment?"

Corwin clamped his teeth together. "You're a lot older than you were when you came to Aventine. You could die out there."

"Your brothers could die on Qasama," Jonny reminded him softly. "Should we all sit here in safety while they're out risking their lives? This way we're at least in a sense sharing their danger."

A cold shiver rippled up Corwin's back. "Only in the most far-fetched sense," he said. "Your danger won't diminish theirs."

"I know." Jonny's smile was wry but clear, without any trace of self-delusion in it. "That's one of the most fascinating things about the human psyche—a deep subconscious feeling can be very strong without making any logical sense whatsoever." He sobered. "I don't ask you to approve, Corwin; but grant that I know enough about myself and my wife to know what I'm doing on this."

Corwin sighed and waved a hand in defeat. "All right. But you'd both darn well better come back safely. I can't run the Council all by myself, you know."

Jonny chuckled. "We'll do our best." Reaching over to his phone, he tapped up something on the display. "Let's see . . . ah, good—Council's discussing Cobra contingent this afternoon. That one we can safely skip. How would you like to see some of your father's practical politics in action?"

"Sure," Corwin said, wondering what the other was talking about.

"Good." Jonny tapped a few more keys. "This is Jonny Moreau. Is the special aircar I ordered ready yet? . . . Good. Inform the pilot we'll be lifting in about twenty minutes: myself and two other passengers."

Signing off, he got to his feet and stepped over to the rack where his heated suit was hanging. "Go get your coat," he told Corwin. "We're about to give a customer the Aventine equivalent of a free sample . . . which, with any luck, won't turn out to be *exactly* free."

✧ ✧ ✧

The third passenger turned out to be Speaker One.

Corwin watched the Troft in a sort of surreptitious fascination as they flew high above the Aventinian landscape. He'd seen plenty of Trofts in his life, but never one so close and for so long a time. The back-jointed legs and splaytoed feet; the vaguely insectoid torso and abdomen; the arms with their flexible radiator membranes; the oversized head with its double throat bladder and strangely chicken-like face—all the gross anatomical features were as familiar to him as those of human beings or even spine leopards. But there were fine details which Corwin realized he'd never so much as noticed. The faint sheen of the alien's skin, for example, was a more muted version of the same shimmer shown by its leotard-like outfit. Even at a meter's distance he could see the tiny lines crisscrossing its skin and the slender hairs growing out of each intersection. Seated on its specially designed couch, the Troft moved only occasionally during the flight, but whenever it did Corwin caught a glimpse of wiry muscles working beneath the skin and—sometimes—a hint of its skeletal structure as well. The large main eyes were a different color than the three tiny compound eyes grouped around each one. The main eyes, he'd once read, were for good binocular vision; the compound eyes permitted both night vision and the detection of polarized sunlight for cloudy-day solar navigation. The alien's short beak remained closed during the trip, which Corwin regretted: he'd have liked to have seen what Troft tricuspid teeth really looked like.

Jonny said virtually nothing during the 20-minute flight, beyond giving the pilot their destination. Apparently he and Speaker One had worked this out in advance and neither felt the need to discuss anything further. Corwin considered pressing his father for information, but decided reluctantly that Jonny's silence was a cue to be followed. Splitting his attention between the Troft and the view out the window, he cultivated what patience he could muster.

They landed at last near a large, squarish building nestled inexplicably out in the snowy forest far from any village Corwin was familiar with. A two-man escort was waiting as Jonny led the way out of the aircar . . . and it was only then that Corwin began to get an inkling of what his father had in mind.

High on each man's chest was a patch with the words "Training Center"; beneath it was the stylized hooded-snake emblem of the Cobra Academy.

"Governor," one of them nodded at Jonny. "You and your guests are cleared for monitor room access. If you'll all follow me...."

Together they headed through an armored door and down an exceptionally drab and anonymous corridor, footsteps echoing oddly against the metallic walls. Their guide led them into an elevator; thirty seconds later they exited into a large, unevenly lit room and a scene of muted tension. In the darker areas along the wall at least thirty people sat before banks of small display screens, working away at keyboards and joysticks, while in the center a large semicircular console with larger displays was the focus of attention for a half-dozen men in the red and black diamond-patterned tunics of the Cobras. One of them headed over to meet the newcomers, and as he approached Corwin recognized him as Cobra Coordinator Sun himself. *The royal treatment, indeed,* he thought.

"Governor," Sun said, inclining his head briefly to Jonny as he neared the group. "Speaker One; Mr. Moreau," he added with similar nods to the Troft and Corwin. "If you'll step this way, the team has just penetrated the outer perimeter section."

"Is there an attack taking place?" Speaker One asked as they followed Sun back toward the crescent-shaped console.

"In a manner of speaking," Sun told it. "The Cobra team who'll be going to Qasama is practicing their building assault techniques. Let's see how they're doing."

The displays showed various degrees of activity, and Corwin scanned them quickly in an effort to make sense of it all. Despite the multiple camera angles shown, it was soon apparent that there were actually only a total of four Cobras involved: Almo Pyre, Justin, and two more Corwin knew only from pictures and Council reports, Michael Winward and Dorjay Link. The latter two were moving stealthily down a corridor, while Pyre and Justin huddled before a formidable-looking door.

"Those two," Sun explained, pointing at Pyre and Justin, "are blocked by a blast door with an electronic lock. They could probably force it open with their antiarmor lasers, but at this point there's been no general alarm and it's worth the time to see if they can get through more quietly. Looks like one of the Qasamans is about to surprise them, though." He tapped a display whose rolling image showed the gait of a mechanical remote—

The camera turned a corner and stopped, the blast door and Justin framed in its view. *Justin alone?* Corwin thought. *But Almo was there, too.*

The screen flared abruptly and went black. Corwin shifted his gaze to the fixed-camera monitors just in time to see Pyre drop from the ceiling to land in a crouch beside the disabled remote, hands curled into fingertip laser ready position. He checked around the corner, then lifted the remote and carried it back to the door. "All clear," he whispered to Justin.

"Just about ready here," Justin whispered back.

"Inside," Sun said, "is a key missile control tracking station." He leaned over to touch a switch, and a vacant display came to life with an overhead schematic of the entire test area. Corwin quickly located the dots representing his brother and Pyre . . . and with a stomach-wrenching shock saw that the room they were about to enter was far from unoccupied. "You'll note," Sun continued in the same emotionless voice, "that there are eight Qasamans on duty in there. All are armed, but the Cobras ought to have the advantage of surprise. Let's see. . . ."

Justin stood up and pulled on the door . . . and an instant before it began its swing the tense silence was shattered by the blare of alarm bells.

Corwin would later learn that Winward and Link had accidentally triggered the alarm, but for that first instant it seemed horribly obvious that Justin and Pyre had walked into a trap. The two Cobras seemed to believe that as well and, rather than charging through the open door, they hit the wall on either side. Beside him, Corwin heard Jonny mutter something vicious . . . but by the time it seemed to dawn on the Cobras that they'd make a mistake it was too late. The remotes in the tracking room were on guard, and when Pyre risked a glance around the door jamb he nearly caught a laser blast for his trouble.

Corwin's jaw was clenched hard enough to hurt; but the figures on the monitor wasted no time in recriminations. Pyre sent Justin a half dozen quick hand signals, got an acknowledging nod, and seemed to brace himself. Both men took a second to fire apparently random fingertip laser shots through the doorway . . . and then, gripping the jamb for leverage, Pyre hurled himself into the room.

Into *and* up. The tracking room monitors caught a perfect view of him arcing spinning into the air like an oddly shaped gyroscope coming off a jump board, the antiarmor laser in his left leg carving out a traveling cone of destruction. He'd just reached the peak of his jump when Justin came in behind him, the younger Cobra's flat dive and somersault landing him on his back in a sort of spinning fetal position . . . and his antiarmor laser, too, began its deadly sweep.

It was a classic high-low maneuver Corwin recognized from his father's stories of the war. Between Pyre's sensor-guided air attack and Justin's lower horizontal spray, effective cover simply ceased to exist, and in the space of maybe a second and a half all eight of the remotes' displays went dark.

Corwin suddenly realized he was holding his breath and risked a quick look to see what Winward and Link were up to. They'd split up since he'd last seen them, with Link at what was obviously an open outside door and Winward standing guard with fingertip lasers ready at the intersection of two hallways. Between them, the overhead schematic showed an impressive number of disabled remotes.

A flash and thunderclap jerked Corwin's attention back to the other displays, and he was just in time to watch as Justin aimed his right fingertip laser at one of the control panels in the tracking room and triggered his arcthrower. Corwin's hands curled into tight fists as the second flash and crash came; he had been burned once by a faulty electrical outlet as a child, and the arcthrower with its high-amperage current flowing along an ionized laser path made his skin crawl in a way the far more powerful antiarmor laser never did. But he forced himself to watch as Pyre and Justin worked methodically around the room, destroying every scrap of electronic equipment in sight. Pyre paused once before a large shielded display, and a low hum abruptly filled the room. "Sonic disrupter," Sun murmured, presumably for the Troft's benefit. A few seconds later Corwin thought he detected a muffled *crack*, and the hum disappeared as Pyre moved on.

Their escape from the room, two arcthrower blasts later, was so straightforward as to be anticlimactic. Link and Winward, it now became clear, had spent most of their time clearing the exit route, and Pyre had to take out only two more remotes. Winward joined them as they passed his crossroads guard post, and by the time all four headed into the woods through Link's door Corwin's heartbeat was almost back to normal.

"And that," Sun said, "is that. All remotes, shut down; signal the team to return."

Corwin glanced beyond the central console as, in the darkened areas around the room, displays went uniformly black and the remote operators began to stretch and stand up. Beside him, Corwin felt his father's hand grip his shoulder. "I'd forgotten what it was like to see Cobras in genuine combat situations," Jonny said, his voice showing lingering traces of his tension.

"Amazing how much adrenaline the human body can put out," another familiar voice said. Corwin looked past his father in surprise. So engrossed had he been in the displays that he'd never even noticed Jonny's old teammate Cally Halloran was among the group Sun had assembled. Halloran nodded a greeting in Corwin's direction and then shifted his attention to the Troft standing silently beside him. "I understand the Baliu'ckha'spmi demesne feels the cost of this initial expedition is too high, Speaker One," he said. "Having now seen Cobras in action, do you agree?"

Speaker One stirred, its arm membranes stretching out like bat wings for a moment before resettling against its upper arms. "The Tlos'khin'fahi demesne has always been aware of *koubrah*-warrior fighting skill," it said.

Which wasn't exactly an answer, Corwin realized. His father wasn't fooled by the evasion, either. "But not sufficiently impressed, I gather, to absorb the extra costs the Baliu demesne isn't willing to pay?" the elder Moreau suggested. "Perhaps your demesne-lord would like to see a tape of this exercise."

"It would be likely to interest him," the Troft agreed. "Presuming the price is reasonable."

"Quite reasonable," Jonny nodded. "Especially as you'll be able to recover some of the cost by selling a copy to the Baliu'ckha'spmi demesne. I think perhaps your two demesne-lords will be able to come to a new agreement afterwards on how much each is willing to spend to have our services."

"Yes," Speaker One said, and Corwin imagined he could hear a note of thoughtfulness in the flat translator voice. "Yes, I think that likely."

The prediction proved correct, and within two weeks the financial quibbles from the Troft side of the negotiation table suddenly ceased. It made little difference to the actual planning groups, which had already committed themselves to the twin goals of not scrimping on vital equipment while simultaneously keeping costs to a bare minimum. But emotionally, the tacit *carte blanche* was a big boost to all concerned; and politically Corwin found in the action a not-so-subtle enhancement of the Cobra Worlds' general reputation. A good thing, to a point . . . but he still had vivid memories of the days when the Trofts considered the Worlds a threat. The closing of their connection with the Dominion of Man had ended the Troft's fears in that direction, but it was easy to see how a rumor of power could wind up being as disquieting to the aliens as the real thing. For the first time he began to understand that part of his father's twin-edged reluctance to demonstrate the Cobras' true war-making capabilities. But it was far too late to back out now.

Three weeks later—barely eleven since the Council's approval of the project—the Cobra Worlds' two long-range spacecraft headed out from Aventine. On the *Dewdrop*, bound for Qasama, were Justin and Joshua Moreau; aboard the *Menssana*, destinations as yet not officially named, rode Jonny and Chrys Moreau.

Corwin watched the ships leave, and was left to wonder how a planet with nearly four hundred thousand people could suddenly feel so lonely.

Chapter 7

The *Dewdrop* had been Aventine's only interstellar craft in the days when the planet was first colonized, and since its sole purpose then had been to reconnoiter nearby systems for possible future habitation it made little sense to the Dominion planners to tie up anything larger than a long-range scout ship. With the normal complement of five crewers and four observers the *Dewdrop* had probably seemed adequately roomy; with a current load exactly twice that, it was pretty damned crowded.

Pyre didn't find it excruciatingly uncomfortable; but then, he'd grown up under conditions that were in their own way equally claustrophobic. The small village of Thanksgiving, ringed by spine leopard-infested forests, had by reasons of physical space been a very cozy place, and though Pyre had experienced both the greater anonymity of larger cities and the wide-open spaces of Aventine's frontier regions since then, he'd never lost his ability to create mental privacy where physical privacy didn't exist.

To varying degrees, most of the other ten passengers also seemed to adapt reasonably well. Justin and Joshua, of course, had shared a room for most of their lives, and even in a cramped stateroom got along together better than most other sets of brothers Pyre had known. The other two Cobras, Link and Winward, had survived both the academy's barracks arrangement and the intense training of the past few weeks, and Winward commented at least once that shipboard life was almost a vacation by comparison. The contact team members—who, besides Joshua, consisted of Yuri Cerenkov, Marck Rynstadt, and former Dominion Marine Decker York—had been screened for anything vaguely resembling a neurosis, and Pyre doubted much of *anything* would bother them, at least noticeably. And the two chief scientists, Drs. Bilman Christopher and Hersh Nnamdi, were so busy testing equipment, programs, and contingency branch schemes that it was unlikely they even noticed the lack of breathing space.

Which left Governor Telek.

To Pyre it was still a mystery why she was aboard this mission. Arguments about high Council representation notwithstanding, it seemed to him incredible that Governor-General Stiggur should allow a woman on what was looking more and more like a military mission. Pyre's attitudes were as healthy as anyone else's, and he had no qualms whatsoever about female doctors or engineers; but warfare *was* different, and Stigger with his roots back in the Dominion should feel that even more strongly than Pyre did. Which led immediately to the conclusion that the decision had been purely political . . . which led even faster to the question of why *he,* Pyre, was aboard.

And *that* was the really troublesome one. Pyre hadn't had as much access to closed-door information lately as he'd had when he'd been living near the Moreaus, but even so it was pretty obvious that Stiggur wouldn't have let Telek come unless he expected her report and recommendations on Qasama to fall more or less in line with his own expectations. Pyre was a good friend of Jonny Moreau, who had both as governor and governor emeritus locked horns regularly with Telek . . . and yet it was *Pyre's* team she'd asked to observe in the field back on Aventine; and it was *Pyre* whose cost/manpower estimates she'd solicited for presentation to the governors; and it was *Pyre* she'd sponsored to be Cobra team leader on this mission.

Why? Did she expect to flatter him into support for her more aggressive stance on the Qasama issue? To offer him one last chance at real Cobra action before the implant-related diseases began their slow but inevitable crippling of his body, in the hope that, in gratitude, he'd become a political ally when he retired to advisory positions on the sidelines? Or had she simply concluded he was the best man for the job and to hell just this once with politics?

He didn't know the answer . . . and it quickly became clear he wasn't going to figure it out en route. Telek's field biology background had left her little prepared for the *Dewdrop's* overcrowded zoo, and though she gamely tried to maintain both minimal sociability and her responsibilities as official head of the mission, it was obvious there weren't going to be any opportunities to sound her out properly on her thoughts and motivations. Perhaps when they reached Qasama and the contact team disembarked there'd be time for that. Assuming there was time for anything at all.

So he spent his time working out contingency plans with his team, renewing his friendship with the Moreau twins, and listening to the dull background drone of the *Dewdrop*'s engines as he tried to think of anything he'd forgotten. The nightmares of sudden, overwhelming disaster he did his best to ignore.

Taken at low-power, high-efficiency speeds, the forty-five light-years to Qasama would have run them a shade over a month; at the *Dewdrop*'s top speed, with frequent refueling stops at Troft systems, they could have made it in six days. Captain Reson F'ahl chose a reasonably conservative middle course, both out of fears for the *Dewdrop*'s aging systems and also—Pyre suspected—out of an old, lingering distrust of the Trofts.

So for fifteen days they were cooped up in the blackness of hyperspace, with only the deep-space refueling stops every five days to break the viewport's monotony . . . and on the sixteenth day they arrived at Qasama.

Purists had claimed for centuries that no photographic emulsion, holographic trace-record, or computerized visual reproduction ever made had quite the same range and power as the human eye. Intellectually, Joshua tended to agree; but on a more visceral level he discovered it for the first time in gazing out his stateroom viewport.

The poets were indeed right: there were few sights more majestic than that of an entire world spinning slowly and serenely beneath you.

Standing with his face practically welded to the small triple-plate plastic oval, he didn't even notice anyone had come into the room behind him until Justin said, "You going to build a nest there?"

He didn't bother to turn around. "Go find your own viewport. I've got land-use rights on this one."

"Come on—move," Justin said, tugging with token force on his arm. "Aren't you supposed to be with Yuri and the others anyway?"

Joshua waved a hand in the general direction of the intercom display. "There's no room up there for anyone bigger than a hamster—oh, all *right*." Snorting feigned exasperation, he stepped aside. Justin took his place at the viewport . . . and Joshua waited for the other's first awe-filled whistle before turning toward the intercom.

The display showed the room euphemistically called the lounge—

and "crowded" was far too mild a term for it. Packed in among the various displays and equipment monitors were Yuri Cerenkov, the scientists Christopher and Nnamdi, and Governor Telek. Back near the viewport, almost out of the intercom camera's range, Pyre and Decker York stood together, occasionally sharing inaudible comments. Joshua turned the volume up a bit, just in time to catch Nnamdi's thoughtful snort. "I'm sorry, but I simply don't see what in blazes the Trofts are so worried about," he said, apparently to the room at large. "How can a village-level society be a threat to anyone outside its own atmosphere?"

"Let's show a little patience, shall we?" Telek said, not looking up from her own bank of displays. "We haven't even finished a complete orbit yet. All the high-tech cities may be on the other side."

"It's not just the matter of technology, Governor," Nnamdi countered. "The population density is too low to be consistent with an advanced society."

"That's anthropomorphic thinking," Telek shook her head. "If their birth rate's low enough and they like lots of room around them they could still be high-tech. Bil, what're you getting?"

Christopher sat in silence another moment before answering. "Nothing conclusive one way or the other yet. I can see roads between some of the villages, but the tree cover's too thick to tell how extensive the network is. No satellite communications systems, though, and no broadcasts I can detect."

Joshua touched the intercom's talk switch. "Excuse me, but is there any way to see how much of the ground around the villages is being cultivated? That might be a clue."

Telek looked over at the intercom camera. "So far that's not conclusive, either," she said. "There are some good-sized candidates for crop fields, but the terrain and vegetation color scheme make real measurement iffy."

"Besides which," Christopher put in, "whether a given village is growing crops for local use or for export is something else we can't tell from up here."

"So let's go on down," Justin muttered from his place at the viewport.

Joshua looked back at his brother. Justin's face was thoughtful as he gazed at the planet below . . . but nowhere in expression or stance could Joshua detect the same hard knot that had taken up residence in his own stomach. "Let's be a little less anxious to throw the landing party outside, shall we?" he said tartly.

Justin blinked at him. "Sorry—did I sound callous?"

"You sounded overconfident, and that's worse. Your tendency toward optimism could be downright dangerous down there."

"Tiptoeing around up here like we've got some guilty secret to hide will be better?"

Joshua grimaced. Alike as two electrons, they'd often been called . . . but when the crunch came it was really very easy to tell them apart. Deep down, Justin had a strangely potent variety of fatalistic optimism that refused to let him believe the universe would really hurt him. A totally unrealistic philosophy, to Joshua's way of thinking—and all the more incomprehensible because Justin *wasn't* simply incapable of recognizing potential danger. He was as good at looking ahead and weighing odds as anyone else in the family; he just acted as if those odds didn't apply to him. It was this attitude, more than anything else, that had fueled Joshua's private reservations about Justin's Cobra ambitions . . . and had nearly persuaded him to back them out of this mission entirely.

"Aha!" Cerenkov's satisfied exclamation came from the intercom speaker into Joshua's musings. "There we go. You wanted a city, Hersh?—well, there it is."

"I'll be damned," Nnamdi murmured, fingertips skating across his display controls. "That's a city, all right. Let's see . . . electric power for sure . . . still no radio broadcasts detectable . . . looks like the tallest buildings are in the ten- to twenty-story range. Bil, can you find anything that looks like a power plant?"

"Hang on," Christopher said. "Got some odd neutrino emissions here—trying to get a spectrum analysis. . . ."

"Another city showing now—south and a little west of the first," Cerenkov reported.

Joshua let a breath hiss slowly between his teeth, caught between the desire to rush down to the lounge and see the cities for himself and the fear of missing something important en route. "I think I can see them," Justin said behind him. "Come take a look."

Joshua joined him at the viewport, glad to have found a compromise. The cities were just barely visible. "Your telescopic vision show anything interesting?" he asked his brother.

"At this range? Don't be silly. Wait a second, though—I've got an idea."

Stepping back to the intercom, Justin busied himself with the keyboard. A moment later the crowded lounge was replaced by a slightly fuzzy still picture. "Got the ultra-high-resolution-camera feed," he told Joshua with satisfaction.

Joshua craned his neck to look. The city seemed normal enough: buildings, streets, park-like areas . . . "Odd angle for a street pattern, isn't it?" he remarked. "I'd think it simpler to run their streets north-south and east-west instead of whatever angle that is."

He hadn't realized the voice link with the lounge was still open until Telek's voice came in reply. "The angle, in case you're interested, is twenty-four degrees, rotated counterclockwise from true north. And the southeast-northwest streets are considerably broader than the perpendicular set. Speculations as to why? Anyone?"

"Second city's the same way," Cerenkov grunted. "The streets are only skewed twenty-three point eight degrees, but the same wide/narrow pattern's there."

"Doesn't look like they're ringed, either, the way the villages are." Justin spoke up, leafing through the ultra-camera's other shots.

There was a short pause from the other end. "What do you mean, 'ringed'?" Nnamdi asked.

"There's a dark ring around each of the villages," Justin told him, backtracking a few photos. "I assumed it was shadow from the surrounding trees, but now I'm not so sure."

"Interesting," Telek grunted. "What's the number on that photo?"

"While you're doing that," Christopher put in, "we've got the neutrino spectrum identified now. Looks like they're using a tandem fission/fusion reactor system for their power supply."

Someone in the lounge gave a low whistle. "That's pretty advanced, isn't it?" another voice—Marck Rynstadt's, Joshua tentatively identified it—came in on the intercom hook-up.

"Yes and no," Christopher said. "They obviously haven't got anything as reliable as our fusion plant design or they wouldn't be fiddling with a tandem system. On the other hand, fission alone ought to be hundreds of years beyond a village society's capabilities."

"Dual cultures, then?" Joshua hazarded. "Cities and villages on separate development tracks?"

"More likely the cities are run by invading aliens," Nnamdi said bluntly, "while the villages are home to the original natives. I concede the technology issue—and it therefore becomes rather clear what the Trofts are worried about."

"That Qasama is the leading edge of someone else moving toward Troft territory," Telek said grimly. "Moreau—whichever of you asked—we've got an ID on those ring shadows now. They're walls, about a meter thick and two to three meters high."

The twins exchanged glances. "Primitive defenses," Justin said.

"Looks that way," Cerenkov said. "Governor, I think we'd do well to cut this part of the run to one or at most two more orbits. They're almost certainly aware by now that we're up here, and the longer we wait before landing, the less forthright and honest we look. Remember that we aren't going to be able to pretend we didn't know Qasama was here."

"At least not if we intend to use the Troft translator," Telek agreed—reluctantly, Joshua thought. Stealing a glance back at the intercom screen, he studied her face . . . but if she were feeling any fear at ordering them down into the snake pit, it wasn't visible. *Two of them,* he thought morosely, turning back to his brother and the viewport—*Or else it's* me *who's the odd one. Maybe I'm just overcautious . . .* or *even an out-and-out coward.*

Oddly enough, the possibility carried no sense of shame along with it. Justin and Telek, after all, wouldn't be leaving the relative safety of the *Dewdrop* the minute they landed; Joshua and the rest of the contact team would. An extra helping of native caution would likely be more an asset than a liability out there.

They came down on the next orbit over what Nnamdi had dubbed the "city belt," aiming for a set of runways at the north end of the northernmost of the five cities in the chain. There had been some excitement when the runways had first been noticed, Nnamdi pouncing on them as evidence that Qasama was indeed the forward base of a star-going people. Christopher, though, had suggested their width and length were more suitable for aircraft than robot glide-shuttles, and for a while a tension-sharpened argument had raged in the lounge. It was Decker York who eventually pointed out that the runway directions seemed oriented more along prevailing wind directions than along the most likely orbital launch/land vectors. Further study had failed to come up with anything else that could possibly be a starfield, and Telek had elected to use the airport as the next best site.

For Pyre, it was the most unnerving part of the mission thus far. Strapped into an emergency crash chair near the main exit hatchway, far from any viewports or intercom displays, he felt more helpless than a Cobra had any business feeling. If the Qasamans had any interest in shooting the *Dewdrop* down, the approach glide would be the ideal time to do so. More so than the aliens might think, in fact; they presumably had no way of knowing that the *Dewdrop* was a gravity-lift, VTOL craft and that her crew had little experience with the emergency runway landing procedure Telek had insisted they use.

But no one opened fire, and with only the mildest of lurches the ship touched down. Heaving an unabashed sigh of relief, Pyre nevertheless kept one eye firmly on the hatch's inner door as he unstrapped and got once more to his feet. The plan was to wait a few minutes and then send Cerenkov outside to wait for whatever reception committee the Qasamans might send. Through all of that Pyre and one of his Cobras would be the *Dewdrop*'s only real defense.

His auditory enhancers, still set on high power from the landing, picked up Nnamdi's gasp from down the hall in the lounge. "My God, Governor. Look! It's—oh, my *God!*"

"Almo!" Cerenkov's voice boomed from the other direction an instant later. "Get up here!"

Pyre was already moving, his hands automatically curving into fingertip laser firing position as he sprinted for the bridge, where Cerenkov had been for the landing.

The small gray-tone room was alive with color when he arrived, as virtually every screen displayed views of the city and surrounding forest outside the ship. Pyre hadn't realized before then just how colorful the city itself actually was, its buildings painted with the same wide range of shades as the forest, as if in deliberate mimicry. But for the moment the Qasamans' decorative sense was the last thing on his mind. "What's up?" he snapped.

Cerenkov, standing behind F'ahl's command chair, pointed a none too steady finger at a telescopic view of the nearest buildings a couple of hundred meters away. "The Qasamans," he said simply.

Pyre stared at the screen. Six figures were indeed heading in the *Dewdrop*'s direction, each with the bulge of a sidearm at one side and something that seemed to be a small bird perched on the opposite shoulder. Six figures—

As human as anyone aboard the *Dewdrop*.

Chapter 8

For a long minute Pyre just stood there, brain struggling mightily to reconcile what his eyes showed him with the sheer impossibility of it all. Humans *here?*—over a hundred and fifty light-years from the nearest world of the Dominion of Man? And past the Troft Assemblage, to boot?

Back in the lounge, someone cleared his throat, a raspy sound in the bridge intercom speaker. "So you say we've all been thinking too anthropomorphically, Governor?" Nnamdi said with exaggerated casualness.

For once, it seemed, Telek was at a loss for words. A moment later Nnamdi continued, "At least now we know for sure the Baliu demesne didn't have much to do with the Troft-Dominion War. They could hardly have failed to mention that the Qasamans were the same species as we were."

"This is impossible," York growled. "Humans can't be here. They just *can't.*"

"All right, they can't," Christopher spoke up. "Shall we go out and tell them that?"

"Maybe they're an illusion of some kind," Joshua suggested from the twins' room. "Controlled psychic hallucination or something."

"I don't believe in *that* sort of thing, either," York snapped.

"Besides," F'ahl added, touching some controls, "if they're an illusion they're a mighty substantial one. Short-radar's picking them up with no trouble and confirms shape."

"Maybe they're the slaves of the real Qasamans," Cerenkov suggested. "Descendants of people kidnapped from Earth centuries ago. Regardless, Governor, we've got to go out there and meet them."

Telek hissed between her teeth, finally seeming to find her voice. "Captain, what's the analyzer showing?"

"Nothing inimical so far," F'ahl reported, running a finger down one of the few displays not showing an outside view. "Oxygen, nitrogen, carbon dioxide, and other trace gasses in acceptable amounts. Uh . . . no evidence of unusual radioactive or heavy-metal contamination. Bacteria analysis has barely gotten started, but so far no problems—computer shows similar DNA and protein structures in the ones it's analyzed, but doesn't show any health hazards from them."

"Hmmm. Well, I'll want to check that data over myself later, but if the Aventine pattern holds here microbes probably won't be a big problem. All right, Yuri, I guess you can go out. But you'd better wear a filter bubble, to be on the safe side. The number two should be adequate unless Qasaman viruses come a *lot* smaller than ours."

"Right." Cerenkov hesitated. "Governor, as long as we've got a reception committee on its way, I'd like to take my whole team out with me."

The six Qasamans were almost to the ship now. Pyre watched the magnified view, his eyes shifting from the details of the faces to the silver-blue birds perched on each person's left shoulder to the pistols belted on each hip. "Governor, I'd recommend we let Yuri go alone first," he said.

"No, he's right—we ought to show good faith," Telek said with a sigh.

Cerenkov didn't wait any longer. "Marck, Decker, Joshua—meet me at the dock with full gear." He got three acknowledgments and hurried out of the bridge.

"Almo?" Telek called as Pyre turned to follow. "I want you back here for this."

Pyre grimaced, but there wasn't time to argue the order now. "Michael, Dorjay—back-up positions by the hatch," he called into the intercom. The two Cobras acknowledged and Pyre once again headed aft.

He passed the furious activity near the hatch without actually colliding with anyone; and by the time he skidded to a stop beside Telek, the lounge displays showed Cerenkov just emerging from the airlock.

If the Qasamans had been a shock to the *Dewdrop*'s passengers, the reverse was equally true. The welcoming committee jerked raggedly to a stop, and Pyre saw astonishment and disbelief sweep across their faces. He tensed; but the guns stayed firmly in their holsters. One of the birds squawked and flapped its wings, settling down only when its owner reached up to gently stroke its throat.

Pyre was aware of Telek leaning closer to him. "Do you buy Hersh's theory about the Baliuies?" she murmured.

"That ignorance was bliss?" he muttered back. "Not for a minute. The Baliuies knew we were the same species, all right—and if we were supposed to free human slaves from the Qasamans they sure as hell would have told us."

Telek grunted. Nnamdi and Christopher, Pyre noted, seemed to have missed the byplay. Shifting his own attention fully to the displays, the Cobra waited for the Qasamans to speak, wishing he knew what sort of game the Baliuies were playing.

The Qasaman delegation had shown a remarkably quick recovery to the contact team's appearance, a fact Cerenkov took to be a good sign. Whether the humans were slaves or masters, it was clear they weren't in the ignorant savage category. Which meant . . . what? Cerenkov wasn't sure, but he knew it was a good sign anyway.

The delegation had come to a halt now a couple of meters in front of the contact team. Cerenkov half-raised his right hand, freezing midway through the motion as one of the birds abruptly ruffled its wings and emitted a harsh caw. He waited until its owner had calmed it, then brought his hand chest high, palm outward. "I greet you in the name of the people of Aventine," he said. "We come to visit with peaceful intent. I am Yuri Cerenkov; my companions are Marck Rynstadt, Decker York, and Joshua Moreau. Whom do I have the honor of addressing?"

For another few seconds the translator pendant around his neck continued to talk, and Cerenkov sent a quick prayer skyward that the Trofts had indeed put together a decent translation program. All they would need now would be for him to have dropped an unintentional insult into his greeting. . . .

But if the translator had glitched it wasn't obvious. One of the Qasamans stepped a half pace forward, raising his hand in imitation of Cerenkov's gesture, and began speaking. "We greet you in turn," Cerenkov's earphone murmured seconds later. "I am Moff; I welcome you in the name of Mayor Kimmeron of Sollas and the people of Qasama. Your interpreter speaks our language well. Why does he rest aboard your craft?"

"Our translator is a machine," Cerenkov told him carefully,

wishing he knew just how technologically advanced these people were. Would they understand the word *computer,* or relegate the whole process to black magic? "Each word I speak is sent to it from this microphone, where it compares the word to those it knows of your language—"

"I understand translation devices," Moff interrupted him. "Other visitors here used such things, though we have no need of them on Qasama. Your machine uses many of the same inflections theirs did."

The hidden question was obvious, and Cerenkov had a split-second decision to make as to how to answer it. Honesty seemed the safest approach. "If you speak of the Trofts of the Baliu'ckha'spmi demesne, we did indeed purchase our translator from them. That's also how we knew you were here, though they failed to mention that we are of the same race. How did you arrive here, so far away from other human worlds, if I may ask?"

Moff ran his eyes over the *Dewdrop* for a moment before turning back to Cerenkov. "A large craft, though much smaller than the one of legends," he commented. "How many people does it usually carry?"

In other words, Cerenkov thought, *how many are still aboard?* Again, honesty would be best . . . honesty tempered with the fact that Justin Moreau was to be treated as nonexistent. "There are seven crewmen and six members of the diplomatic mission still aboard," he told Moff. "For various reasons they will remain there."

"During which time you four intend to do what?"

The question caught Cerenkov off guard. He'd expected to hold talks with the leadership and to be given a grand tour of the area—but he hadn't expected to have to make such requests out here beside the ship. "We'd like to visit with your people," he said. "Share information of mutual interest, perhaps open trade negotiations. We *do* share a common heritage, after all."

Moff's eyes bored into his. "*Our* heritage is one of struggle against both men and nature," he said bluntly. "Tell me, where is this world Aventine you come from?"

"It's about forty-five light-years from here," Cerenkov said, resisting the urge to point dramatically toward the sky. "I'm not sure of the actual direction or whether our sun is even visible at this distance."

"I see. What is your relationship with the Lords of *Rajan Putra* and the Agra Dynasty?"

Cerenkov felt his heartbeat pick up. At last, a clue of sorts as to when the Qasamans had left the Dominion of Man. He himself had only the vaguest idea when the Dynasties had existed—and no recollection at all of any *Rajan Putra*—but Nnamdi's sociologist training ought to cover at least some history as well.

But that wouldn't tell him what the Qasamans' own feelings toward the Dynasties had been . . . and if he didn't come up with a safely neutral answer the whole expedition could be shifted into the "enemies" column without any further warning. "I'm afraid that question doesn't mean anything to me," he told Moff. "We left the main group of human worlds ourselves some time ago, and at that time there wasn't any government calling itself a dynasty, at least not that I know of."

A slight frown creased Moff's forehead. "The Agra Dynasty claimed it was eternal."

Cerenkov remained silent, and after a moment Moff shrugged. "Perhaps a search through your records will show us what happened after we left," he said. "So. You wish to visit our world. For how long?"

Cerenkov shrugged. "That's entirely up to you—we wouldn't want to impose overmuch on your hospitality. We can also bring our own supplies if you'd like."

Moff's eyes seemed to focus on the clear bubble around Cerenkov's head. "You will have trouble eating like that, won't you? Or would you want to return to your craft for every meal?"

"That shouldn't be necessary," Cerenkov shook his head. "By the time we're likely to get hungry, our analysis of your air should be complete. I'm expecting it to show nothing dangerous, but we need to be cautious."

"Of course." Moff glanced to both sides, as if waiting for a protest from one of his party. But they remained silent. "Very well, Cerenkov, you and your companions may come with me into the city. But you must agree to obey my commands without question, for your own safety. Even in Sollas the many dangers of Qasama are not wholly absent."

"Very well, I agree," Cerenkov said with only the slightest hesitation. "We're well aware of how dangerous a planet can be for visitors."

"Good. Then my first order is for you to leave all weapons with your craft."

Beside Cerenkov, York stirred slightly. "Yet you just said Qasama could be dangerous," Cerenkov said, choosing his words carefully. He'd half expected this, but had no intention of giving in without at least trying to talk Moff out of it. "If you're afraid we might use our weapons against your citizens, let me assure you—"

"Our citizens have nothing to fear from your weapons," Moff interrupted. "It's *you* who would be in danger. The mojos—" he gestured to the bird resting on his shoulder—"are trained to attack when weapons are drawn or used, except for hunting or self-defense purposes."

Frowning, Cerenkov studied the bird. Silver-blue in color, built rather like a compact hawk, it returned his gaze with what seemed to be preternatural alertness. The talons clinging to the oversized epaulet were long and sharp, the feet themselves disproportionately large. A hunting bird, if he'd ever seen one . . . and he'd heard enough stories of professional falconers to have plenty of respect for such creatures. "All right," he said. "We'll—"

"By my instructions, and one at a time," Moff said, his hand curving up to stroke his mojo's throat again. "You first, Cerenkov. Rest your hand on your weapon, say 'clear,' and then draw it . . . slowly."

Cerenkov's laser was holstered across his belt, only its grip visible beneath his loose jacket. Reaching for it, he thumbed off the holster's safety strap. "Clear," he said, waiting for the translation before drawing it free.

The mojos' reaction was immediate. Practically in unison all six birds gave a single, harsh caw and snapped their wings out into flight position. Two of the birds even left their owners' shoulders, tracing a tight circle half a meter above Cerenkov's head before settling back onto their perches. Beside him, York spat something and dropped to a crouch; Cerenkov himself bit down hard on his tongue in an effort to remain absolutely motionless.

And as quickly as it had begun, the flurry of activity was over. The mojos, wings still poised at the ready, became living statues on the Qasamans' shoulders. Moving with infinite care, Cerenkov walked back to the *Dewdrop*'s hatchway and laid his laser in the airlock. As if on cue, the mojos relaxed again, and Cerenkov returned to the line. "Marck?" he said, striving to keep his voice steady. "Your turn."

"Right." Rynstadt cleared his throat. "Clear."

The mojos reacted a bit more calmly this time around; and their responses eased even further for York and Joshua. Clearly, they'd picked up rather quickly on the fact that hostilities were not being initiated. Just as clearly, they weren't taking chances, either.

"Thank you," Moff said when all four lasers were in the airlock.

He raised both hands over his head, and Cerenkov's peripheral vision caught movement at the edge of the colorful city. A large vehicle was approaching, an open car type of thing with two Qasamans in it. Both figures had bulging left shoulders; Cerenkov didn't have to see any more clearly to know the lumps would turn out to be mojos. "Mayor Kimmeron is waiting to meet you," Moff continued. "We'll be taken to his chambers now."

"Thank you," Cerenkov managed. "We're looking forward to meeting him.

He took a deep breath and tried not to stare at the mojos.

There were cultures in the Dominion of Man, Justin knew from his studies, that went in heavily for artistic expression on their buildings, and his first thought had been that the Qasamans were a branch of such a society. But as the contact team was driven slowly through the streets, he gradually began to question that assumption. There were no murals anywhere that he could see, nor were there any recognizable human or animal drawings, either realistic or stylized. The splashes of color seemed to have been thrown up more or less randomly, though in ways the Cobra found aesthetically pleasing enough. He wondered if Nnamdi would be able to find anything significant in the whole thing.

Cerenkov cleared his throat, and it was quickly obvious the contact leader had other things than the Qasamans' artistry on his mind. "Looks like a lot of your people have mojos with them," he commented. "Mojos *and* guns. Are conditions in Sollas *that* dangerous?"

"The weapons aren't often used, but when they are it's a matter of survival," Moff told him.

"I would think the mojos would be enough protection," York put in.

"From some things, yes, but not from everything. Perhaps while you're here you'll have the chance to see a bololin herd or even a hunting krisjaw enter the city."

"Well, if that happens, don't forget we're unarmed," Cerekov said. "Unless you plan to issue us weapons and mojos later on."

It was clear from his tone he wasn't exactly thrilled by that option, but Moff laid any such fears to rest. "As strangers I don't think the mayor would allow you to carry weapons," he said. "And the mojos seem too uncomfortable in your presence to serve as your protectors."

"Um," Cerenkov said and fell silent. Justin shifted his attention from the buildings to the people walking along the sidewalks. Sure enough, all of them had the ubiquitous mojos on their shoulders. A light breeze came up, ruffling human hair and mojo feathers and whistling gently in his ears. *Odd,* he thought, *to be able to hear the wind but not to feel it.*

Somehow, on a gut level, that seemed stranger even than the fact that he was possibly the first man in history to be almost literally walking in his brother's shoes.

From somewhere behind him a new voice spoke up. "Is that just an excuse?" Pyre asked.

"I don't think so," Telek's voice replied. "The nearest mojos *do* look a bit more nervous than those further away. I'd guess it has to do with the fact that we smell slightly different than the Qasamans."

Pyre grunted. "Genetic drift?"

"More likely dietary differences. Something, Hersh?"

"I think I've got their departure time bracketed," Nnamdi said. "The Agra Dynasty was the government that ruled Reginine from central Asia on Earth. It began in 2097 and ended when the Dominion of Man formally took over in 2180."

"What about the, uh, the Lords of *Rajan Putra*?" Telek asked.

"We'll have to check the full history records back on Aventine for that. But I know there was a major migration from Reginine when it was opened to general colonization, and I *think* the emigres founded the world Rajput."

"Hmmm. Ethnic separatists, basically?"

"No idea. My guess, though, is that the Qasamans were either one ship of that group or a separate emigration, in either case overshooting their target rather badly."

"Badly and a half," Telek snorted. "Where were the Trofts while they were wandering through Assemblage territory?"

"Probably never saw them coming," Christopher spoke up. "Really. The Dominion's early stardrives were nasty unstable things, and when they went supercritical they hit about ten times the speed we can get nowadays."

"Sounds rather handy, actually," Pyre said.

"Only if you didn't need to stop," Christopher said dryly. "Coming out of hyperspace in that condition would fry the drive and most other electronics on the ship. There are literally dozens of colony ships—*colony* ships, mind you, not just probes or scouts—that are listed as simply having disappeared. I guess Qasama was one of the lucky ones."

"Or else they were the unlucky ones who were kidnapped and brought here," Nnamdi put in. "You'll recall we haven't scrapped that possibility yet."

"We'll keep it in mind if we see any sign of another race," Telek assured him. "But it's hard to imagine slaves being allowed to carry guns."

Via the direct feed from Joshua's implanted optical sensors to his own, Justin saw that the car carrying the contact team had turned onto one of the broad streets they'd noted from orbit, and he waited for Cerenkov to ask about it. But the contact leader had apparently decided to hold off pumping the Qasamans for more information, at least for the moment. Probably just as well, Justin thought, since the lull enabled him to continue splitting his attention between the cityscape and the conversation in the lounge around him.

"Any indication in the translator program as to what bololins or krisjaws are?" Pyre asked.

Justin could almost see Telek's shrug. "Local fauna, I gather," she said. "Obviously pretty nasty—those guns of theirs don't look like target pistols."

"Agreed. So why didn't they put up a wall around the city, like they did around the villages?"

There was a short pause. "No idea. Hersh?"

"Maybe the village walls aren't there to keep the animals out," he suggested, not sounding particularly convinced. "Maybe both species fly or jump too high for walls to be effective."

"So why do the villages have them?" Pyre persisted.

"*I* don't know," Nnamdi snapped.

"All right, take it easy," Telek put in. "Finding out all of these things is Yuri's job. Let's just relax and leave it to him, okay?"

There was another pause. Back in Sollas Joshua turned his head to follow the passage of a particularly attractive woman. Justin admired the view himself, wondering whether it was her appearance or the fact that her mojo rode her *right* shoulder which had caught his brother's attention. He tried to see if her pistol was also strapped to the opposite side, but Joshua turned back to face forward before he could do so. *Left-handed?* he speculated, making a mental note to watch for others.

From the other reality Christopher spoke up. "Hersh, have you got anything like a population estimate for Qasama yet? Given that they're human, I mean, and that human personal space requirements are pretty well known."

"Oh, I'd guess somewhere between fifty and three hundred million," Nnamdi said. "That requires them to have bred like hamsters over the past three centuries, but you can get rates that high on new worlds. Why?"

"Would it be likely that you could keep track of that many people on a single-name basis?"

"Like *Moff*, for instance? Not hardly. Especially since they originally came from a multi-name background."

"Which means Moff wasn't giving his full name," Christopher said. "Which means in turn that the mojos aren't the only ones that are nervous about us."

"Yeah," Nnamdi said heavily. "Well . . . suspicion toward strangers is part of the heritage of lots of human cultures."

"Or else the Trofts who came here earlier started a new tradition," Telek growled. "I wish to hell we had a record of their visit. Either way, I suppose we ought to remind the team that they need to walk on eggs."

There was a faint click and Telek delivered a short message to the contact team along the translator carrier—a message that, for Justin, had a built-in echo as bone conduction carried part of the sound from Joshua's earphone to his implanted auditory pickups. The car seemed to be slowing now, and Justin scanned the buildings within view, wondering which one housed the mayor's office. Fortunately, the rest of the conversation in the lounge had ceased as the scientists returned to watching the same view on their more prosaic displays, so there was no risk of his missing anything while his primary attention was locked into Joshua's implants. There was a lot about this setup that annoyed him, but he had to admit it was doing its job well. Whenever he wound up replacing Joshua out there, he would have the same memories of Qasama that his brother did . . . and those memories could easily spell the difference between success and failure for such an impersonation.

The car had come to a halt by the curb. Resisting the urge to run his own muscles through the proper motions, Justin lay quietly on his couch as Joshua followed Cerenkov and the others up the three outside steps and into the building.

Decker York had been a Marine for twenty years before leaving the Dominion for Aventine eighteen years ago. During his hitch he'd served on eight different worlds and had seen literally dozens of officials, ranging in pomp and power from village councilor to full Dominion Committé. From all of it he'd developed a mental image of what human leaders and their surroundings should be like.

By those standards, Mayor Kimmeron of Sollas was a severe shock.

The room Moff led them to was hardly an office, for starters. The sounds of music reached them even before the liveried guards flanking the door pulled the heavy panels open, and the tendrils of smoke that drifted past as the group started in were evidence of either incense or drug use inside. York's nose wrinkled at the thought, but fortunately the filter bubble enclosing his head seemed to be keeping most or all of the smoke out. Inside, the room's lighting was muted and leaned to reds and oranges. The room itself seemed large, but free-hanging curtains all around gave it the feel of an elegant and soft-walled maze. Moff led them through two right angles to the room's center—

And a scene straight out of mankind's distant past. On a cushion-like throne lounged a large man who, while not fat, clearly hadn't seen strenuous exercise in quite some time. Facing him was a group of dancers, both male and female, in exotic dress; behind them was the semicircle of musicians—*live* musicians—who were providing the music. Seated on other cushions scattered around the room were a handful of other men and women, all seemingly splitting their attention between the dancers and low work tables set before them. York sent a studiously casual glance at one table as Moff led them toward the central throne, noting especially what seemed to be a portable computer or computer terminal among the papers there. Qasaman technology, it seemed, extended at least somewhat beyond guns and cars.

Everyone in the room, except the dancers, was accompanied by a mojo.

Moff stopped them a few meters to the side of the throne— and if its occupant was surprised by their appearance he didn't show it. He said something cheerful sounding, his voice clearly audible over the music; "Ah—welcome," York's earphone translated it. The big Qasaman raised a hand, bringing the musicians and dancers to an orderly halt a few notes later. "I am Mayor Kimmeron of the city of Sollas; I welcome you to Qasama. Please, sit down."

Moff indicated a group of cushions—four of them, York noted— placed in a row in front of the mayor. Cerenkov nodded and sat down, the others following suit. Moff and the rest of their escort remained standing.

"Now," Kimmeron said, rubbing his hands together in a curious gesture. "Your names are Cerenkov, Rynstadt, York, and Moreau, and you come from a world called Aventine. So. What exactly—exactly, mind you—do you wish from us?"

It seemed to take Cerenkov a moment to find his tongue. "You seem to know a great deal about us," he said at last. "You surely also know, then, that we're here to reopen communication with brothers we didn't know we had, and to explore ways of making such contact mutually profitable."

Kimmeron had a sly smile on his face even before the translator finished its version of the speech. "Yes, that is indeed what you have claimed. But why would you, who retain space flight, believe we would have anything worth your time?"

Careful, boy, York warned in Cerenkov's direction. *Primitive doesn't necessarily imply naive.* His eyes flicked to Moff and the rest of the escort, wishing he knew how to read this culture's body language.

But Cerenkov was on balance again and his answer was a masterpiece of pseudo-sincerity. "As anyone who's opened up a new world must surely know, sir, each planet is unique in its plants and animals, and to a lesser extent its minerals. Surely your foodstuffs and pharmaceuticals will be markedly different from ours, for a start." He gestured toward the musicians and dance troupe. "And for any people who respect artistic expression as much as you clearly do, there are the less tangible but equally rewarding possibilities of cultural exchange."

Kimmeron nodded, the half-smile still playing around his face. "Of course. But what if we came to Qasama for the express purpose of *avoiding* cultural contamination? Then what?"

"Then, Mr. Mayor," Cerenkov said quietly, "we would apologize for the intrusion and ask your permission to leave."

Kimmeron regarded him thoughtfully, and for a long moment the room rang with a brittle silence. Again York glanced toward Moff, his hand itching with the desire to have a weapon in it . . . and at last Kimmeron shifted on his cushion throne, breaking the spell. "Yes," he said, waving a hand casually. "Well, fortunately, I suppose, we're not quite that strict here on Qasama. Though some of us perhaps would prefer otherwise." In response to his gesture a new group of five men had moved forward from the edges of the room to stand behind the visitors, a group Moff now stepped over to join. "Moff, escort our guests to their quarters, if you would," the mayor addressed him. "See that their needs are taken care of and arrange a general tour for tomorrow. If you have no objections—" this to Cerenkov—"we'd like to run a general medical study of you this afternoon as well. For your protection as well as ours."

"No objections at all," Cerenkov replied. "Though if you're worried, our experience on Aventine indicates most disease organisms from one planet don't seem to bother much with creatures from another."

"That has been our experience, as well," Kimmeron said, nodding. "Still, it never hurts to be cautious. Until tomorrow, then."

Cerenkov got to his feet, York and the others following suit. "We look forward to seeing you again," Cerenkov said with a small bow to the mayor. Turning, they fell into step behind Moff and headed from the room.

And now straight to the hospital, York thought grimly as they emerged once more onto the sunlit street and were steered toward their car. The physical exam itself didn't particularly worry him; but he would bet goulash to garnets there'd be the Qasaman version of military ordnance experts assisting the doctors. And if they somehow managed to figure out exactly how his calculator watch, pen, and star sapphire ring fit together . . . and what they became in such a configuration. . . .

Cerenkov and Rynstadt were in the car, and it was his turn to get in. Trying not to grimace, he did so, telling himself there was no need for worry. The Marine palm-mate, after all, had been deliberately designed to be undetectable.

But he worried anyway as the crowded vehicle set off between the color-spattered buildings. Contingency worrying was part of a soldier's job.

The room Joshua and Rynstadt had been assigned to had been dark and quiet for nearly half an hour by the time Justin finally unhooked himself from the direct feed apparatus and rolled stiffly to a sitting position on his couch. The *Dewdrop*'s lounge, too, was quiet, its only other occupant a dozing Pyre. Justin moved carefully, working the kinks out of his muscles as he walked toward the door.

"There's food by the corner terminal if you're hungry."

Justin looked back to see Pyre stretch his arms out with a sigh and straighten up in his chair. "Didn't mean to wake you," he apologized, changing direction toward the tray the other had mentioned.

"S'okay. I'm not actually on duty, anyway—I just wanted to wait till you were up, make sure you were doing okay."

"I'm fine." Justin sat down beside the other Cobra, balancing the tray on his knees as he attacked the food. "So . . . what do you think?"

"Oh, hell, I don't know," Pyre sighed. "I'm not sure we can take anything they say or do at face value. That mayor, for instance. Is he *really* some throwback to the old despot tradition, or was all of that set up to confuse us? Or is that really the way they conduct business here?"

"Oh, come on," Justin growled around a mouthful of fried balis. "Who could concentrate in a din like that?"

"It was only a din because you're not used to it," Pyre said. "The music *could* actually have a calming effect on the brain's emotional activity, allowing the people in there to think more logically."

Justin replayed the scene in his mind. Possible, he decided—those hunched over the low tables had been doing *something*. And the smoke—? "Supplemented by tranquilizing drugs, maybe?"

"Could be. I wish we'd had some sampling equipment in there to run a quick analysis on the air." He snorted. "Though a lot of good it would have done."

Justin grimaced. Every bit of the contact team's recording and analysis equipment had been politely but firmly confiscated during their hospital examination. The best Cerenkov's protests had done was to elicit Moff's promise that the gear would be returned when they left. "I was locked into Joshua's sensors at the time, but I have the impression Governor Telek was pretty mad about that."

"That's putting it mildly. She was on the edge of a full-fledged tantrum." Pyre shook his head slowly. "But I think maybe she was right, that this is looking less and less like it's going to work. Yuri can't find out anything the Qasamans want to keep hidden, not with Moff steering them around like tame porongs and his equipment buried in some back room somewhere. And *we* sure can't do anything ourselves stuck out here."

Justin eyed him suspiciously. "Are you leading up to the suggestion that someone take a little midnight stroll in a day or two?"

"I don't know how else to find out their true threat potential," Pyre shrugged.

"And if we're caught at it?"

"Trouble, of course. Which is why the operation would have to be handled by someone who knew what he was doing."

"In other words, one of the Cobras or Decker. And since we're in plain view and Decker is both watched *and* unarmed, not getting caught starts sounding a bit unlikely."

Pyre shrugged. "At the moment, you're right. But maybe something will change." He gave Justin a long look. "And in that event . . . you weren't supposed to know this, but Decker *isn't* unarmed. He's carrying a breakapart palm-mate dart gun with him."

"He's *what?* Almo, they said *no weapons.* If they catch him with that—"

"He'll be in serious trouble," Pyre finished for him. "I know. But Decker didn't want the party completely helpless, and the gun *did* make it through the big inspection okay."

"As far as you know."

"He's still got it."

Justin sighed. "Great. I hope the Marines taught him patience as well as marksmanship."

"I'm sure they did," Pyre grunted, pushing himself to his feet with an ease that was probably due solely to his implanted servos. "I'm going to crash for a few hours—if you're smart you'll do likewise after your exercises."

"Yeah," Justin said with a yawn. "Before you do, though, has the governor said when she's going to call Joshua back in for our switch?"

Pyre paused halfway to the door, a look of chagrin flicking across his face. "Actually . . . her current plan is to go ahead and leave Joshua out there for the foreseeable future."

"What?" Justin stared at him. "That's not what we planned."

"I know," Pyre shrugged helplessly. "I pointed that out to her— rather strongly, in fact. But the situation seems pretty stable at the moment and. . . ."

"And she likes having Joshua's visual transmission too much to give it up. Is that it?"

Pyre sighed. "You can hardly blame her. She'd wanted the whole contact team implanted with those optical sensors, I understand, and been turned down on grounds of cost—split-frequency transmitters that small are expensive to make. And now with all our other eyes taken away, Joshua's all we've got left if we want to see what's going on." He held up a hand soothingly. "Look, I know how you feel, but try not to worry about him. The Qasamans are hardly going to attack them now without a good reason."

"I suppose you're right." Justin thought for a moment, but there didn't seem anything else to be said. "Well . . . good night."

"'Night."

Pyre left, and Justin flexed his arms experimentally. Thirteen hours in the couch had indeed left the muscles stiff, but he hardly noticed the twinges as his thoughts latched onto Pyre's last comment. *Without a good reason . . .* but what would constitute such a reason in the Qasamans' minds? An aggressive act or comment on Cerenkov's part? Discovery that the ostensibly voice-only radio link to the ship also had a split-freq channel that was carrying the visual images they'd obviously tried to suppress? Violent use of York's illegal gun?

Or perhaps even the outside reconnaissance Pyre had clearly already decided on?

Eyes on the darkened display, Justin settled into his exercises, pushing his body harder than he'd originally intended to.

Chapter 9

With less need for immediate debarkation—and more comfort and room aboard ship in which to wait—the *Menssana's* passengers didn't bother with filter helmets, but simply stayed inside until the atmospheric analyzers confirmed the air of Planet Chata was indeed safe for human use.

Long tradition gave Jonny, as senior official aboard, the honor of being the first human being to step out on the new world's surface; but Jonny had long since learned to put discretion before pomp, and the honor was claimed by one of the six Cobras who went out to set up a sensor/defense perimeter about the ship. Once again the passengers waited; but when an hour of Cobra work failed to entice any predators out of the nearby woods—or to flush out anything obviously dangerous within the perimeter itself—Team Leader Rey Banyon declared the *Menssana's* immediate area to be safe enough for the civilians.

Jonny and Chrys were near the end of the general exodus of scientists through the *Menssana's* main hatch. For Jonny it was a step into his own distant past. Chata looked nothing at all like Aventine, really; certainly not after even a cursory examination of plant life and landscape. Yet the simple fact of Chata's strangeness relative to Aventine's by-now familiarity gave the two experiences an identity. A new world, untouched by man—

"Brings back memories, doesn't it?" Chrys murmured at his side.

Jonny took a deep breath, savoring the almost spicy aromas wafting in along the light breeze. "Like Aventine when I first arrived," he said, shaking his head slowly. "A kid of twenty-five, just about overwhelmed by the sheer scope of what we were trying to do there.

I'd forgotten how it all felt . . . forgotten what all of us have really accomplished in the past forty years."

"It'll be harder to do it again," Chrys said. Dropping to one knee, she gently fingered the mat of interlaced vine-like plants that seemed to be the local version of grass. "Chata may only be thirty light-years from Aventine, but we don't have anything like the Dominion's transport capability. It hardly makes sense to spend our resources in this direction with so much of Aventine and Palatine still uninhabited. Especially—" She broke off abruptly.

"Especially when this whole group is only ten to fifteen light-years from Qasama?" Jonny finished for her.

She got to her feet with a sigh, brushing bits of greenery off her fingers as she did so. "I've heard all the arguments about buffer zones and two-front wars," she said, "but I don't have to like it. And I keep coming back to the fact that the *only* reason we consider Qasama a threat is because the Trofts say we should."

The beep of his phone preempted Jonny's reply. "Moreau," he said, lifting the device to his lips.

"Banyon, Governor," the Cobra team leader's voice came. "Got something off our satellite I think you should look at."

Chrys's presence beside him was a silent reminder of his promise to play passenger on this trip. "Can't you and Captain Shepherd handle it?" he said.

"Well . . . I suppose so, yes. I just thought that your advice would be helpful on this."

"Unless you're talking emergency—" Jonny broke off as a fluttering hand waved between him and the phone.

"What are you doing?" Chrys stage-whispered fiercely. "Let's go see what they've got."

If I live to be a thousand, the old line flashed through Jonny's head. "Never mind," he told Banyon. "I'll be right there."

They found Banyon and Shepherd on the *Menssana*'s bridge, their attention on a set of three displays. "It wasn't something that registered right off the blocks," Banyon began without preamble, indicating a dark mass now centered in the largest display. "Then we found out it was moving."

Jonny leaned close to the screen. The mass seemed to consist of hundreds or thousands of individual dots. "Enhancement all the way up on this?"

Shepherd nodded. "There's a lot of upper atmosphere turbulence over us at the moment, and that's limiting drastically what the computer has to work with."

"I'd say it's a herd or flock of some sort," Jonny said. "I gather it's headed this way?"

"Hard to tell—they're still a hundred kilometers away—but it looks right now like the flank will sweep across us," Shepherd said. He touched a switch and the infrared picture on one of the other screens was replaced by a schematic. The various extrapolation regions were done in different colors; and, sure enough, the edge of the red "90% probable" wedge just touched the *Menssana's* indicated position. The mass's average distance and speed were also given: 106 km, 8.1 km/hr.

"So we've got thirteen hours till they get here," Jonny murmured. "Well...we can break camp in one if necessary, but the scientists won't like all their *in situ* stuff being moved. I suppose the logical thing would be to send a squad of Cobras to check out this herd and see if they can be stopped or deflected."

"Yes, sir, that's what we thought." Banyon hesitated, and Jonny saw on his face the same expression that, on his sons, had usually signaled a favor request was coming. "Uh, Governor...would you be willing to fly out with the team? We'd all feel better with someone of your experience along."

Jonny looked back at Chrys, raised his eyebrows. She was still studying the displays, though, and when she finally met his gaze she seemed surprised he was even asking. "Of course," she said. "Just be careful."

If I live to be ten *thousand....* Turning back to Banyon, he nodded. "All right, then. Let's get cracking."

It was indeed a herd—a *big* herd—and to Jonny, who'd seen such things only on tape, the sight of so many wild animals together at once was both awesome and a little bit frightening. Even just jogging along, the mass of brown-furred quadrupeds made a thunder audible inside a sealed aircar two hundred meters overhead, and their wide hooves raised a dust cloud despite the damping effect of the webgrass underfoot.

"I think," Banyon commented as they all took in the sight, "we're going to have to rethink our basic plan."

One of the other Cobras snorted, and someone else let loose with a rather strained chuckle. Jonny let the tension-easing noises ripple around the crowded aircar and then gestured out the window. "Let's get a few kilometers ahead of them and see if we can come up with a way to shift them off their course."

Banyon nodded and turned the vehicle around, but as the roar faded behind them Jonny studied the landscape below with decreasing hope. The Cobras had already established that there weren't any natural obstacles between the herd and the *Menssana,* and now that he knew what they were up against it seemed very unlikely they could do *anything* to the terrain that would make any difference whatsoever. Something more drastic was likely to be necessary. Drastic *and* dangerous.

Banyon had apparently reached the same conclusion. "We're going to have to scare them, I'm afraid," he murmured, just loudly enough for Jonny to hear.

"There used to be herds this size all over parts of Earth and Blue Haven," Jonny said. "I wish I knew how they'd been hunted. Well. We don't have anything like real explosives aboard, and we don't yet know what this species' predators even look like. I suppose that leaves close-in work with lasers and sonics."

"Laser range isn't *that* short—oh. Right. If they don't *see* us, there's no guarantee they'll figure out which way to run."

"Or even notice they're being killed off." Jonny thought for a minute, but nothing else obvious came to mind. "Well . . . let's try buzzing them with the car first. Maybe that'll do the trick."

But the animals apparently had no enemies that were airborne. Completely oblivious to the darting craft above them, they continued stolidly on their way. "We do it the hard way now?" one of the others asked.

Banyon nodded. "Afraid so. But hopefully not *too* hard. Saving the biologists some work isn't worth anyone getting killed over."

"Or even hurt," Jonny put in. "We'll just—"

A ping from the car's phone interrupted him. "Governor, we've got something here that may or may not mean anything," Captain Shepherd said, his attention somewhere off-camera. "The satellite's been completing its large-scale geosurvey . . . and it looks very much like that herd is running along one of the planet's magnetic field lines."

Banyon looked at Jonny, eyebrows raised. "I thought the only things that used geomagnetic navigation were birds, insects, and tweenies."

"So did all the *Menssana*'s biologists," Shepherd returned dryly. "But they admit there's no reason something larger couldn't make use of the mechanism."

"If we assume they're indeed paralleling the field lines, is the camp still in danger?" Jonny asked.

"Yes. The probability actually goes up a couple of points."

Jonny looked questioningly at Banyon. "Worth a try," the other grunted. "Captain, is there anything aboard the ship that can generate a strong magnetic field?"

"Sure—the drive modulators. All we'll need to do is pull off some of the shielding and we'll get enough field leakage to overwhelm their direction finders. *If* that's what's really happening."

"It's worth trying," Banyon repeated. "How fast can you get that shielding off?"

"It's already being done. Say another hour at the most."

The gently rolling terrain could not by any stretch of the imagination be called hilly; but even so the flatfoot herd was audible long before it could be seen. Standing a few meters back from the main line of Cobras, Jonny wiped the perspiration off his palms as the thunder steadily grew, hoping this was going to work. In theory, the Cobra's antiarmor lasers should be able to make fungus feed out of the herd if something went wrong ... but Jonny couldn't help remembering how hard the equally herbivorous gantuas of Aventine were to kill.

"Get ready," his phone said. He glanced up to see the car as it hovered above and ahead of the Cobras. "You'll see them any minute now. Wait for the captain's signal. . . ."

And the leading edge of the herd came over a low rise, like a dark tsunami clearing a breakwater.

They weren't heading directly toward the Cobras, and in actual size were quite a bit smaller than gantuas, but the sheer numbers and ground-level view more than made up for it. Jonny clenched his jaw firmly, fighting hard against the urge to turn and run for cover ... and as the wave poured over the rise a new voice on the phone barked, "Now!"

The answer was a volley of Cobra antiarmor lasers—directed not at the flatfoots, but at the clusters of boulders the Cobras had wrestled into position fifty meters closer to the herd. Very special boulders ... and if the *Menssana*'s geologists had been right about that particular formation—

They had. The mix of high- and low-expansion minerals in each boulder could survive for only a second or less under a laser's glare before disintegrating with a crack that was audible even over the herd's rumble. Like a string of firecrackers the boulders blew up as the Cobras continued their sweep ... and like firecrackers, they actually produced little more than noise. But it was enough; and as the herd's headlong rush faltered in sudden confusion, Jonny could almost see them lose their internal sense of direction. An instant later the hesitation was gone and the herd had doubled its speed to a flat-out run . . . but in the slightly altered direction the *Menssana*'s additional magnetic field was defining for them from the ship's new position some ten kilometers away. The flank of the herd would now miss the line of Cobras; and when the *Menssana* lifted in an hour or so and the flatfoots resumed their original direction their path would be shifted at least a kilometer out of the way of the human encampment.

Theoretically. But there would be time to make sure.

The aircar was dropping toward the ground and the Cobras were beginning to converge on it. "Good job," Banyon's voice came from Jonny's phone. "Let's head back."

The last few clouds had cleared shortly before sunset, and the night sky was alive with stars. Walking hand in hand just inside the perimeter, Jonny and Chrys took turns naming the recognizable constellations and trying to match the more distorted ones with their Aventinian counterparts. Eventually, they ran out, and for a time they just walked in silence, enjoying the night air. Jonny, his audio enhancers activated, heard the faint roar before Chrys did; and by the time she took notice the steady volume level showed their plan had succeeded.

"The flatfoot herd?" she asked, peering off into the darkness.

"Right," he nodded. "And they're not getting any closer. At least a kilometer away—maybe two."

She shook her head. "Strange. I remember some biology class in school where the instructor took it upon himself to 'prove' that no land animal larger than a condorine could ever evolve with a magnetic sense unless there was some ridiculously high local field present. I wish he was here to see this."

Jonny chuckled. "*I* remember reading about the old theory that all the native plants and animals on the various Dominion worlds were mutated descendants of spores or bacteria that had ultimately been blown there by solar winds from Earth. The argument was still going strong when the Trofts and Minthisti were found, I understand, and I have no idea *what* its proponents made of Aventine. If there are still any of them around. I guess the possibility of making a public fool of yourself is just one of those risks scientists have to face."

"You know, that universal genetic code thing has always

bothered me, too," Chrys mused. "Why *should* all the life we find show the same DNA and protein forms? It doesn't seem reasonable."

"Even if that turns out to be the only workable structure?"

"I've never liked that theory. It seems arrogant, somehow."

Jonny shrugged. "I don't especially care for it either. I've heard the Troft theory is that some major disaster three or four billion years ago nearly sterilized this whole region of space, taking with it an early starfaring people. The algae and bacteria that survived on each world were therefore all from one common stock, though they've since evolved independently."

"That must've been one gantua of a disaster."

"I think it was supposed to be either a chain of supernovas or the final collapse of the galaxy's central black hole."

"Uh-*huh*. Almost simpler to believe God set it up this way deliberately."

"Certainly makes a colonist's life easier to be able to digest the local flora and fauna," Jonny agreed.

"Though the vice versa is occasionally a problem."

Jonny tensed; but Chrys's tone hadn't been one of accusation. "I appreciate your letting me go with the others today," he said, as long as they were now on the topic. "I know I promised to stay out of things on this trip—"

"You could hardly hold out when you were needed," she put in. "And it wasn't like you were in serious danger out there. Were you?"

"No, not with the aircar and *Menssana* as backup. Still, I'll try to behave myself the rest of the trip."

She chuckled and gave his hand a squeeze. "It's all right, Jonny. Really. I wouldn't want you to just sit on your hands when you're needed. Just be careful."

"Always," he assured her, wondering at her abrupt attitude change. This was the old Chrys back again, the one who'd been so supportive of his service when they were first married. What had happened to change her? Was she simply reacting to the new environment, slipping into old thought patterns with the reminder of their past struggles on Aventine?

He didn't know. But he liked the change ... and he had the rest of the trip to figure out how to keep her this way when they returned home.

Chapter 10

The clearance to remove their filter helmets had come from the *Dewdrop* just before the evening's medical exam, and in the hours between then and bedtime Joshua thought his nose had become thoroughly accustomed to the exotic scents of Qasama's air. But the group hadn't taken more than three steps outside their guest house in the morning before Joshua realized that belief had been a little premature.

The new odor seemed to be a mixture of baking aromas with some not-quite-aromatic smoke with something he couldn't begin to identify.

He apparently wasn't the only one. "What *is* that I smell?" Cerenkov asked Moff, sniffing the breeze.

Moff inhaled thoughtfully. "I smell the bakery one street down, the boron refinery, and the exhaust of vehicles. Nothing more."

"A boron refinery?" Rynstadt spoke up. "In the middle of the city?"

"Yes. Why not?" Moff asked.

"Well . . ." Rynstadt floundered a bit. "I would assume it would be safer to put industries like that away from populated centers. In case of an accident or something."

Moff shook his head. "We have no accidents of any consequence. And the equipment itself is safest right where it is."

"Interesting," Cerenkov murmured. "Could we see this refinery?"

Moff hesitated a second, then nodded. "I suppose that would be permissible. This way."

Bypassing the car waiting for them at the curb, he set off, the four Aventinians and five other Qasamans following. The refinery turned out to be less than a block away, located in an unremarkable building midway between two of Sollas's extra-wide avenues.

Joshua had never seen this kind of light industrial plant before, and the masses of tanks, pipes, and bustling Qasamans gave him more of a feeling of confusion than of productivity. But Rynstadt—and to a lesser extent York—seemed fascinated by the place. "Very nice setup," Rynstadt commented, gazing around the main room. "I've never heard of a boron extraction method using cold bubbled gas. What gas *is* that, if I may ask?"

"I'm really not sure," Moff said. "Some sort of catalyst, I expect. You are an expert in this sort of chemistry?"

"No, not really," Rynstadt shook his head. "I dabble in a lot of fields—my job as an educator requires me to know bits and pieces of almost every subject."

"A general scientific expert, then. I see."

There was something about the way Moff said that that Joshua didn't care for, as if Rynstadt's supposed expertise had added a point against the mission's peaceful image. "Would something like this method be marketable on Aventine, Marck, do you think?" he spoke up, hoping Rynstadt would pick up the cue.

He did. "Almost certainly," the other nodded at once. "Boron plays a major part in at least a dozen different industries, and while our methods aren't expensive something cheaper would always be welcome. Perhaps we can discuss this in more detail later, Moff, either with Mayor Kimmeron or someone in planetary authority."

"I'll pass on your request," Moff said. His tone was neutral, but to Joshua's eye he seemed to relax just a bit. *Like tiptoeing through a mine field with these people,* he thought.

"Well, I think we might as well move on, then," Cerenkov said briskly. "I'd still like to see the art gallery you mentioned yesterday, and perhaps one of your marketplaces."

"Of course," Moff agreed. "Back to the car, then, and we'll be off."

"Well?" Telek asked.

Christopher straightened up from his terminal. "I don't find any reference to this kind of boron refinement method," he said. "Again, these records are by no means complete—"

"Sure, sure. So have they got a new technique or were they lying about what that plant was doing?"

The intercom beeped and Pyre leaned toward it, tuning out the conversation beside him. "Yes?"

It was Captain F'ahl. "Just come up with a correlation that you people might like to know about," he said. "Those extra-wide streets in Sollas and the other cities? Well, it turns out that in each instance they run exactly parallel to Qasama's geomagnetic field."

The intricacies of boron refinement were abruptly forgotten. "Say again?" Christopher asked, turning toward the intercom.

F'ahl repeated his statement. "Any reason you can think of for that, Captain?" Telek asked.

"Nothing that makes sense," F'ahl replied. "You don't have to skew your whole city to use the field for navigation, and the field strength is far too weak to produce any effect on power lines or the like."

"Unless it periodically surges," Christopher mused. "No, even then the design doesn't make any sense."

"Maybe it has to do with their long-range communication system," Telek suggested. "Sending modulations along the lines of force or something."

From a corner of the lounge Nnamdi looked up in irritation. "I wish you'd all get off this idea that the Qasamans *have* to have broadcast communications," he growled. "We've already seen that Sollas is wired for both power and data transmission—that's really all they need."

"With nothing between the cities?—not to mention all those little villages out there?" Telek retorted. "Come on, Hersh—the isolated city-state concept may appeal to your sense of the exotic, but as a practicing politician I tell you it isn't stable. These people have calculators or even computers, as well as cars, machined weapons, and presumably something to use the runway we're sitting on. They *cannot* simply have forgotten the basics of electromagnetic waves or unified government."

"Oh? Then how do you explain the village walls?"

"How do *you* explain the cities' lack of them?" Telek shook her head irritably. "We can't assume the villages are primitive and fight among themselves and at the same time say the cities are advanced and don't."

"We can if there's no communication between city and village," Nnamdi said doggedly. "Or if the villagers are a different species altogether. I notice neither Moff nor Kimmeron has mentioned the villages at all."

Pyre caught Telek's eye. "It *might* be good to clear up that point."

She sighed. "Oh, all right." Picking up the translator-link mike, she dictated a short message to the contact team. Pyre switched his attention back to the displays and waited for Cerenkov to raise the subject with Moff.

The wait wasn't long. The car was approaching one of the narrower cross streets, and as they reached the corner Joshua's implanted cameras showed the street was lined on both sides by permanent-looking booths, each displaying the seller's goods on a waist-high ledge beneath an open window. Dozens of people were already milling about, inspecting the merchandise or engaged in animated conversation with the sellers. "This is the main market-place for this part of Sollas," Moff said as the car pulled up behind others parked along the wide avenue. "There are eight others like it elsewhere in the city."

"Seems an inefficient way of marketing," Rynstadt commented as they left the car and walked toward the bazaar. "Not to mention uncomfortable in the winter or on rainy days."

"The street can be sealed in bad weather," Moff said, pointing upwards. Joshua looked, and Pyre saw that at the third-floor level on the flanking buildings were two long roof sections, folded drawbridge-fashion against the walls. "As to inefficiency, we prefer to think of it as an expression of individual liberty and freedom. Lack of those qualities was the reason our ancestors came here originally. You've not said why *your* ancestors left the rule of the dynasties."

"Oh, hell," Telek growled, grabbing for the microphone. "Keep it non-political, Yuri," she instructed him. "Sense of adventure or something."

"We went to Aventine for various reasons," Cerenkov told the Qasaman. "The desire for adventure or to see a new world, dis-satisfaction with our lives—that sort of thing."

"Not political pressure?"

"Perhaps some came for that reason, but if so I'm not aware of it," Cerenkov answered cautiously.

"Tell that to the First Cobras," Pyre murmured.

"Quiet," Telek shushed him.

The contact team and its Qasaman escort was walking among the other shoppers now. A mojo on one of the buyers squawked, causing Rynstadt to jerk to the side. Pyre jumped in sympathetic response; he'd almost stopped noticing the ubiquitous damn birds. "Are all your goods from Sollas and the immediate area?" Cerenkov asked Moff as they passed a stand featuring neatly packaged loaves of bread.

"No, our commerce extends to the other cities and villages as well," the other told him. "Most of the fresh fruit and meat comes from the villages east of here."

"Ah," Cerenkov nodded, and continued walking.

"Satisfied?" Christopher asked Nnamdi.

The other glowered back. "Still doesn't prove the villagers are human," he pointed out stiffly. "Or are on an equal plane with the cities—"

"Almo?"

Pyre turned to the couch where Justin was lying. "What is it?"

"I . . . hear something . . . low rumble . . . from Joshua." The boy stopped, strain evident on his face as he fought to split enough of his attention from Joshua's sensors to speak. "Getting closer . . . I think."

Christopher was already at the controls, trying to find the sound Justin's Cobra enhancers had already gleaned form Joshua's signal. "Captain, we may have aircraft approaching," Pyre snapped toward the intercom.

"I'm on it," F'ahl replied calmly. "No sign of anything yet."

An instant later Pyre nearly went through the lounge's ceiling as a bellow erupted from the display speakers. "Yolp!" Christopher exclaimed, grabbing the volume control he'd just turned up. The roar subsided to a hooting sound . . . and as he looked at the screen, Pyre saw the Qasamans had abandoned their shopping and were beginning to move toward the wide avenues at each end of the bazaar. "What's going on?" Cerenkov asked Moff as the escort, too, joined the general flow. A second set of rumbles added to the first, and Pyre got a glimpse of cars being hurriedly moved off the avenue, presumably to the narrower cross streets.

"A bololin herd has entered Sollas," Moff told Cerenkov briefly. "Stay back—you're not armed."

Telek grabbed the mike. "Never mind that. Joshua—move up at least close enough to see what's going on. Decker, better go with him."

The two men began to move in Moff's wake. None of the Qasamans seemed particularly disturbed by whatever was about to happen . . . but as Pyre looked closer, he realized the same wasn't true of the mojos. Every bird in sight was fluffing its feathers, half opening its wings, and generally showing signs of agitation.

The rumble was clearly audible now as Joshua and York squeezed their way to the third rank of watchers. "Clear," a voice came faintly over Joshua's sensors, and someone off to the right in the front row drew his pistol, holding it muzzle upward in a ready position.

A dozen more calls and the entire front row had followed suit. Across the avenue, Pyre could just see that another group of people waited in the street there, weapons similarly drawn. "Crossfire situation, Decker," he called toward the mike Telek was still holding, drowning out whatever instructions she was giving the team. "Watch for trouble with that."

The rumble became a roar . . . and the animals appeared.

To Pyre it was instantly obvious why the Qasamans considered it worthwhile to walk around armed. The fact that there was an entire herd of beasts stampeding through their city was bad enough; but even *one* of these would have been cause for serious alarm. Each a good two meters long, the bololins were heavily muscled, with sets of hooves that looked as if they could break rock by running impact alone. A pair of wicked-looking horns sprouted from the massive heads, and running down the back was a dorsal strip of thirty-centimeter quills that even an Aventinian spine leopard would have been proud to possess. There were at least a hundred of the creatures in sight already, running shoulder to shoulder and head to tail, with more pouring in behind them . . . and as Pyre tensed in automatic combat reaction, the Qasamans opened fire.

Christopher spat something startled sounding, and even Pyre—who'd had an idea what to expect—jerked at the sound. The Dominion had given up simple explosive firearms long ago in favor of lasers and more sophisticated rocket cartridges, but such progress had apparently passed Qasama by. The guns ahead of Joshua roared like miniature grenades going off . . . and some of the bololins in the herd abruptly faltered and fell.

Pyre happened to be looking directly at one of the quadrupeds as it was hit; and he was thus the first one in the lounge to see the tan-colored bird that shot upward from the carcass.

It was at least half again as large as a mojo, that quick glance showed him as the bird arrowed off the screen, but seemed built along the same predacious lines. Its hiding place, as near as he could tell, had been the bololin's dorsal quill forest . . . an instant later Joshua reacted and the view shifted upward, and Pyre saw more of the birds already in the air, presumably having similarly deserted dying bololins.

Closing rapidly on them was a flock of mojos.

"They're crazy," Christopher said, barely audible over the gunfire. "Those birds are bigger than they are—"

"And *they* seem to be predators, too," Telek growled. "Something's wrong here—predators don't usually pick on other predators. Joshua!—keep tracking the birds."

The display steadied, and Pyre watched in morbid fascination as a mojo came in from above and behind one of the larger birds, swooping down with talons ready. It hit—got a grip—and for half a dozen heartbeats it clung there in piggyback position. The larger bird twisted violently, to no avail, leveled out once more—

And the mojo spread its wings and dropped off and back. Making no attempt to pursue, it turned in a lazy circle and headed back to the crowd of Qasamans.

"What the blooming *hell*?" Telek muttered.

Pyre couldn't have put it better himself.

Joshua's gaze returned to the street now. The herd was out of sight, and through the settling dust about twenty carcasses were visible, mangled to various degrees. One of the Qasamans—Moff, Pyre saw—stepped out into the avenue and looked carefully in both directions. Holstering his pistol, he stepped back; and as if on signal, the other guns likewise vanished and the crowds began to break up.

Telek squeezed the mike hard. "Yuri—everybody—find out everything you can about what just happened. Especially the thing with the birds."

Silently, Pyre seconded the order. Though he doubted the contact team really needed that prompting.

Joshua certainly hadn't needed Telek to state the obvious— bursting with curiosity, he could barely wait until Moff had pushed his way through the dispersing crowd to fire off his first question. "How did those animals get into the city so easily?" he asked.

Moff frowned, throwing a glance at York as well. "I told you to stay back."

"Sorry. What were those—bololins, you called them?—what were they doing here?"

Cerenkov and Rynstadt had joined the group now, as had most of Moff's associates. "The bololins migrate periodically," he said, almost reluctantly. "A herd like that always forms for a run, and you'll agree something like that would be almost impossible to stop. So we've built the city to pass them through with as little damage as possible."

York glanced at the carcasses in the avenue. "As little damage to *you*, anyway."

"Crews will be along momentarily to take them to a processing area," Moff said. "Both meat and hides will be saved."

"You'd do better to split a few off from the herd and stop them before you shoot," York persisted. "Letting them get trampled like that doesn't do hide *or* meat any good."

"What was all that with the mojos and those other birds?" Joshua asked as Moff started to reply. "Do mojos hunt like that even when they don't intend to eat?"

"To—? Oh, I see." Moff reached up to stroke his mojo's throat. "Tarbines aren't a food animal. Mojos seek them for reproduction. Cerenkov," he said, turning away from Joshua, "we will need to cut short our visit to the marketplace if we intend to reach the art gallery during the time it will be cleared for us. If you wish, we can return here another time."

"All right." Cerenkov sent a long look toward the bololin carcasses as Moff steered them down the avenue to the cross street where their car had been moved. "Does this sort of thing happen very often?"

"Occasionally. Perhaps more often in the next few days—there is a major migration underway. But there's no need for concern. The probability you will be near the affected streets is small, and even if you are the rooftop alarms always give adequate warning. Come now; we must hurry."

Conversation ceased. As they walked, Joshua nudged York and slowed his pace a bit. York matched his speed; and as Moff and the others pulled a few paces ahead, Joshua reached up to put his thumb over the microphone on his translator pendant. "You've lived on a lot of worlds," he murmured to the other. "You ever seen a male and female of the same species that look that different?"

York shrugged minutely, his hand similarly on his translator. "I've seen or heard of some that are even more mismatched than that . . . but I've never heard of a mating that looks that much like an out-and-out attack. Almost like—well, hell, I'll say it: like a rape."

Joshua felt a shiver run up his back. "It did, didn't it? The mojos were hitting them like condorines swooping down on rabbits."

"And the tarbines were trying like crazy to get away. Something really weird's happening here, Joshua."

Ahead, Moff glanced back. Casually, Joshua dropped his arm back to his side and increased his speed, York doing the same beside him. They'd have to find some private way to clue Cerenkov in on this and get him to start probing, Joshua knew, already trying to figure out a way to do that. He hoped the other's silver tongue would be up to the challenge . . . because if the mojo's mating behavior was evidence of some significant biological principle here, it could be vital to root such information out.

And it was sure as hell that the support team, stuck inside the *Dewdrop,* wouldn't be able to do anything in that direction.

"No," Telek shook her head. "Absolutely not. It's insane."

"It's *not* insane," Pyre retorted. "It's feasible, practical, and there's no other way to get hard data." He glanced at the displayed map of Sollas and the red mass that was the computer's estimate of the bololin herd's position. "And we've got maybe fifteen minutes to take advantage of that herd."

"You'll be outside—alone—in unknown and presumably hostile country," Telek growled, ticking off fingers with quick, almost vicious motions. "You'll have limited communication with us and none at all with the locals, should you stumble on any. And you probably wouldn't have a chance of sneaking back in unnoticed—which means that if you got hurt you'd be forcing me to choose between your life and anything further for the mission."

"And if I don't go you may never find out why male mojos rape their females," Pyre said quietly. "Not to mention why the tarbines ride bololins. Or for that matter, why the bololins are so hard to keep out of cities."

Telek looked at Christopher and Nnamdi. "Well?" she demanded. "Say something, you two. Tell him he's crazy."

The two scientists exchanged glances and Christopher shrugged uncomfortably. "Governor, we're here to learn everything we can about this place," he said, his eyes not meeting either Telek's or Pyre's. "I agree it's dangerous . . . but Almo's right about the bololins probably not getting this close again."

"And he *is* a Cobra," Nnamdi put in.

"A Cobra." Telek almost spat the word. "And so he's invulnerable to accidents and snake bites?" She dropped her eyes to the city display.

For a moment there was silence. "We have survival packs already made up," Pyre said quietly. "One would suffice for a week; I can take two. There are laser comm setups I could use to keep in touch from the woods without the Qasamans catching on. I've seen biological field analyzers being used; I'm sure I can set one up for you or even run it a little myself if necessary. And I could take a couple of small freeze boxes if you wanted a whole tarbine to study later."

She shook her head, eyes still on the screen. "You're Cobra team leader. Do what you like."

Which was not exactly enthusiastic support, but Pyre would have to take what he could get. The bololins were barely minutes away. "Michael, Dorjay—two survival packs and laser comm to the port cargo hatch; stat," he said into the intercom. The two Cobras acknowledged and Pyre left the lounge at a fast jog, heading for his stateroom for a quick change into more suitable clothing. There was a boxed bio field analyzer down in the cargo hold; he could grab it on his way out. The hatch itself, facing away from the city, should let him out into the ship's shadow unseen. At that point he would just have to hope the bololins were indeed running deliberately along magnetic field lines . . . and that the runways were as dusty as they looked.

He was in the cargo hold three minutes later. A minute after that, laden like a pack cart, he was crouching outside, hugging the *Dewdrop*'s hull as he moved toward the bow. The rumble of the bololins was audible without his enhancers now, and a quick glance under the *Dewdrop*'s nose showed they were indeed on the projected path, one that would take the herd's flank within fifty meters of the ship. Behind the first few ranks the dust was already beginning to obscure the city beyond, and it was getting thicker. Taking a deep breath, Pyre gave the edge of the forest a quick scan and got ready to run.

The leading edge of the herd thundered by. Pyre let the next few ranks pass as well; and then he was off, running bent over to present as low a profile as possible. Equipment banging against back and thighs with each step, he traced a curved path that ended with him pacing the snuffling herd barely a meter from its flank.

It was instantly obvious the nearest bololins didn't care for his presence. One or two veered at him as they ran, horns hooking toward his side; but even without his programmed reflexes he was more maneuverable than the massive beasts and evaded them without trouble. More troublesome—and unexpected—were the two-meter-long whiplash tails no one had noticed. If the first such blow hadn't landed across his backpack it would undoubtedly have left a painful welt or even torn muscle. As it was, his nanocomputer had to take over servo control briefly to restore his balance.

But it was only a few more seconds to the edge of the forest, and as the herd passed the first few trees Pyre parted company with them, angling off to the side and coming to a stop only when a glance behind showed nothing but greenery.

For a long moment he just stood there, turning slowly around as his auditory and optical enhancers probed as much of the surroundings as possible. Gradually the sound of the bololins faded into the distance, to be replaced by the chirps, clicks, and whistles of birds, insects, and God alone knew what else. Small animals moved in trees and undergrowth, and once he thought he heard something much heavier on the prowl.

It was just barely possible that this *hadn't* been the smartest idea he'd ever had.

But there was nothing for it now but to go ahead and do the job he'd promised Telek he would. Setting his equipment at the base of a tree, he made sure his auditory enhancers were on full and got to work.

Chapter 11

"If ever there was a world designed for colonization," Captain Shepherd said with satisfaction, "this is definitely it."

Gazing around the gray-brown landscape, Jonny had to agree. Whatever the mechanism that had scoured this region of space down to nucleic acids, it was clear Kubha had suffered more than most. Nothing but the most primitive life existed here: one-celled plants and animals, and perhaps a few hundred species of only slightly more complex organisms. A virtual blank slate, ready to accept whatever ecological pattern any future colony chose to set up on it.

Any pattern, that is, that could stand the heat.

A young biologist trudged up the knoll where Jonny and Shepherd were standing, a full rack of sample tubes held carefully to his chest. "Captain; Governor," he nodded, blowing a drop of sweat from the tip of his nose. "Thought you might be interested in seeing the preliminary compatibility test results before I file them."

Jonny hid a smile as he and Shepherd stooped to peer into the tubes at the various mixes of native and Aventinian cells. At Chata, at Fuson, and now at Kubha, the scientists had never ceased their efforts to persuade Shepherd to grant them more time for sample taking and general study, and getting him interested in the results was just one of the more subtle approaches. It wouldn't work, of course; the Council had made it very clear that this was to be a whirlwind tour, and Shepherd took his orders very seriously.

"Interesting," the captain nodded, straightening up from his brief examination. "Better get them to the freeze chamber, though, if you want time to gather any more. We're lifting in about two hours."

A hint of chagrin crossed the biologist's face before it could be suppressed. "Yes, sir," he said, and headed toward the *Menssana.*

"You're a cold-blooded taskmaster without a drop of scientific curiosity; did you know that?" Jonny asked blandly.

Shepherd's lip quirked. "So I've been told. But the Council said a fast prelim study, and that's exactly what they're going to get. Besides, I want to be back when the *Dewdrop* arrives, just in case—"

"Hi, Chrys," Jonny interrupted, turning as his wife came up to join them. His enhanced hearing had picked up the sound of her footsteps, and the last thing he wanted to remind her of was the *Dewdrop* sitting on alien soil with two of her sons aboard. "What do you think?" he added, waving a hand at the landscape.

"Too empty for my tastes," she said, shaking her head. "Seems spooky, somehow. *And* I'm not crazy about pan-frying my brain out here." She gave Jonny a careful look. "How are *you* feeling?"

"Fine," he told her, and meant it. "The heat's not only helping my arthritis, but also seems to be pushing my heart rate and circulation up enough to compensate a bit for my anemia."

"Which means you're going to trade anemia for a heart attack?" Shepherd grunted. "Great. Maybe you'd better get back inside until we're ready to lift, Governor."

"My heart's in no danger," Jonny protested. "It'll probably live two years longer than I do."

"Sure it will." Shepherd hooked a thumb in the *Menssana*'s direction. "Go on, Governor. Call it an order."

For a moment Jonny was tempted to unilaterally take himself out of the chain of command. He found it refreshing to be out in the open air—especially where there was no danger of anything sticking teeth, claws, mandibles, or stings into him—and very much wanted to enjoy the last hours he'd have here. But there was that promise to Chrys. . . . "Oh, all right," he grumbled. "But under protest."

Together, he and Chrys trotted down the knoll. "The Council sure named this one right," Chrys remarked as they reached level ground and slowed to a more sedate walk.

"Named what right? Kubha?"

"Uh-huh. You know—the five stars of the Southern Cross constellation of Asgard—"

"I know how the planets were code-named, yes," Jonny interrupted her.

"Well, it happens that Kubha's the hottest of those stars; and *this* Kubha's the hottest of these planets, at least so far. Must be an omen."

Jonny snorted. "Let's not give either the Council *or* the universe that much credit."

Chrys smiled. "Hey, cheer up," she said, taking his arm. "Everything's really going pretty well. The Jonny Moreau luck seems to hold up even when you're only along for the ride."

"Um. Aside from little things like snakele venom in the nucleic acid analyzer—"

"Fixed," she said. "We got it working again about ten minutes ago. Which was why I'd been released from my desk and could come out to drag you kicking and screaming back inside."

He shook his head in mock exasperation. "I swear, Chrys, you do a poorer imitation of a loafing passenger than *I* do."

"And you're delighted. Go on, admit it."

"Why? You're going to send me to my room anyway, aren't you?" he said, putting a well-remembered five-year-old's whine into his voice. "You always *want* me to play outside on nice days."

She poked him in the ribs. "Stop that—I had my fill of tantrums years ago."

He captured her attacking hand and wrapped the arm around his waist, and for a moment they walked like that in silence. "It *would* be an ideal planet for colonization, wouldn't it," she said quietly. "And that's going to make it all the harder to say no."

"No to the Trofts?"

She nodded. "The Council's going to want this world, and probably the others as well. And to get them they'll take on the Qasamans . . . whether that's the smart thing to do or not."

Jonny grimaced. The same thought had been lurking in the back of his own mind for at least two planets now. "We'll just have to hope the *Dewdrop*'s report is solid enough that it relegates ours to footnote status as far as that decision is concerned."

"With Lizabet Telek in charge of writing it?" Chrys snorted. "She wants these worlds so badly she can taste it. She'll make sure the Qasamans sound like crippled porongs as far as fighting ability is concerned."

"I don't know if she's *that* underhanded," Jonny demurred cautiously. "And with Almo, Justin, and Joshua aboard she'd have a hard time slanting things too far."

Still, he thought as they passed the Cobra guard at the *Menssana*'s airlock and stepped through to the cool shock of the ship's climate control, *it might not hurt to tone down our report a shade or two. Emphasize Chata's flatfoot herds, perhaps, and Fuson's spitting snakeles. Every world's got its drawbacks—all we have to do is find them and make them visible.*

And hope the Council doesn't take them too seriously. Already the ship's cooler air was affecting his arthritic joints, reminding him with each twinge that he'd been a bit lax with his medication schedule. He would hate to see a world like Kubha slip through mankind's fingers for no real reason.

Whether it was worth a war . . . well, that decision didn't yet need to be made.

Chapter 12

The complete tour of Sollas and its environs took six days; and for Cerenkov the most amazing part was how the Qasamans could keep them so busy while showing them so little.

So little of real importance, anyway. They spent a great many hours touring art galleries, cultural museums, and parks, while evenings were usually filled with dance and musical performances at their guest house and long discussions with Mayor Kimmeron or other high-ranking officials. At no time, despite Cerenkov's carefully phrased requests, was the contact team taken to anything resembling a communications or computing center; nor were they shown any of the city's industrial or manufacturing capability.

And yet such capability obviously existed. The glimpses they got of intercity roads and the relatively sparse traffic on them showed Sollas's goods weren't simply being shipped in from somewhere else.

"It's got to be underground," Rynstadt commented that evening as the four men relaxed in the lounge that connected their two sleeping rooms. "All of it: refining, manufacturing, waste processing—maybe there's even a tunnel network for product distribution."

"Except for smaller operations like the boron plant we saw the first day?" Cerenkov shrugged, "Possibly. Probably, even. Sure seems to be the hard way to do it, though."

"Depends on what they were after," Joshua put in. "Aesthetically, this is a clean, beautiful city, a good place to spend your leisure time even if you have to work underground all day."

"Or else," York said quietly, "they were simply worried about having everything out in the open."

Cerenkov felt his jaw tense up, forced it to relax. The unspoken

351

assumption was that the Qasamans were eavesdropping on these conversations, and to go anywhere near military concepts made him nervous. But on the other hand, ignoring such a normal aspect of human societies was likely to look even more suspicious. As long as York didn't let his professional interests run away with him— "What do you mean? They built underground to protect their manufacturing base from attack?"

"Or from detection," York replied. "Remember our assumed starting point: emigres—or exiles—from perceived repression, having gone way farther than they intended and now stuck on Qasama with a useless stardrive."

"Do you suppose they ran into some Troft ships on the way here?" Joshua suggested. "The Dominion probably hadn't met either them or the Minthisti when the Qasamans left. If *I'd* just seen a Troft for the first time, I think I'd probably have kept going until my tanks ran dry."

Nodding, York said, "I suspect that's exactly what they did. The distance seems right for a colony ship's full dry-tank range." He looked back at Cerenkov. "I'd guess they had their whole city underground to begin with, moving up only as they started to outgrow the space and no one showed up to stomp them."

"And they came up smack in the middle of the bololin migration pattern," Cerenkov sighed, shaking his head. "Definitely poor planning on someone's part."

"That doesn't explain where the villages came from," Rynstadt mused. "Though maybe we can get some of their history tomorrow. Assuming the trip is still on."

Cerenkov shrugged. "As far as I know Moff and company are driving us out there first thing tomorrow morning." He broke off as a familiar hooting sounded faintly in the distance.

York grimaced. "More bololins. I think I'd have stayed underground until I found a way to keep the damn things out."

At least, Cerenkov thought, *the streets ought to be pretty empty by now. I wonder how many people those things kill every year?* "I assume they had their reason. Maybe Moff will loosen up some day and talk about it."

First time in a week I'm close enough to make a grab, Pyre groused silently to himself, *and the damn herd decides to be nocturnal.*

From Pyre's end, of course, it wasn't all that bad. Locking in the light amplification capability of his optical enhancers gave him as good a view as he would have had on an overcast afternoon, and with magnification also on he'd be able to target any likely tarbines as soon as they emerged from the obscuring buildings. And once he had targeting lock established he could follow his chosen bird into the woods, where he could shoot it without anyone seeing the flash.

The problem was that with most good Qasamans tucked away in their beds there weren't likely to be many bololins running into bullets out there, and correspondingly few impregnated tarbines for him to hunt. Muttering under his breath, he mentally crossed his fingers and waited for the herd to appear.

It did; and his pleadings were answered from an entirely unexpected direction. Across the landing area—about half a kilometer away and somewhat northeast of his current position— a door suddenly opened in a tall building the *Dewdrop*'s crew had tentatively labeled the control tower, spilling light and people out onto the pavement. Flickers of fire erupted from outstretched hands, and even as their mojos took to the air the sound of gunfire reached Pyre's ears. Shifting his attention back to the herd, he waited. Within seconds the tarbines began to appear.

The multitarget capability hadn't been a part of Cobra optical enhancers since Jonny Moreau's war, but Pyre's team had trained with them prior to the Qasama mission and he'd developed a healthy respect for both their advantages and their dangers. Once he target-locked one or more tarbines, his nanocomputer and servos would make sure his next laser shots would be in that direction—whether or not he suddenly found a predator he needed to deal with first. He'd run into at least twenty such creatures since leaving the *Dewdrop*—dog- or monkey-sized, most of them, but none he'd care to give a free shot at his back regardless. But it was a chance he'd have to take. Keeping an ear cocked for suspicious sounds, he activated his multitarget lock and waited.

The wait wasn't long. As before, the mojos attacked swiftly, swooping in through the tarbines' attempts at evasion. With the larger birds' head start, though, most made it into the cover of the nearest trees before their mojos could disengage. Pyre targeted two of the tarbines just before they entered the forest and, on slightly reckless impulse, locked onto one of the riding mojos as well. The birds swept through the branches, disengaged . . . and, raising his hands, Pyre squeezed off three fingertip laser shots.

The birds dropped with a crunch of dead leaves into the undergrowth. Pyre sprinted over, scooped them up, and hastily got out of the way as the main herd caught up. Keeping well to the side, he paced them another hundred meters into the woods. Then, spinning on his right foot, he swung his left leg up and fired his antiarmor laser.

The trees flashed with reflected light as the targeted bololin crumpled to the ground. Its tarbine took off for the sky; it got maybe ten meters before Pyre's fingertip laser brought it down.

And as the rest of the herd continued on their way, silence returned. Retrieving his last tarbine, Pyre took his prizes to the bush where he'd cached his freeze boxes and stuffed them inside. Then, crouching with his back to a large tree within sight of the dead bololin, he settled down to wait.

It was an hour before the sounds of the Qasaman collection team faded from the area between forest and city. During that time Pyre had also heard someone else poking around the edges of the wood, whistling occasionally as he apparently searched for the mojo Pyre had killed. But he and the others clearly knew better than to go too deep into the forest at night, and no one came anywhere near Pyre's position.

Finally they were gone, and Pyre could address the task of moving the bololin carcass closer to the *Dewdrop*. With his servos the creature's weight wasn't a significant problem, but it took him four tries to find a grip that was reasonably balanced. Finding a wide enough path through the trees and bushes was another problem, and more than once he found himself wondering how in hell the beasts managed it on their own.

Eventually, though, he made it. Dumping the carcass beside his camouflaged laser comm, he activated the latter and slipped on the headphone. "Pyre to *Dewdrop*," he muttered. "Anyone home?"

"Lieutenant Collins," a voice came back promptly. "I believe Governor Telek and her people are still in the lounge, sir; let me switch you."

"Fine," Pyre said. A moment later Telek came on the circuit.

"Everything all right, Almo?" she said.

"Far as I can tell. Listen, I've got a bololin carcass for you and two freeze boxes' worth of tarbines and mojos. You want to warm up your equipment or wait until I can deliver them in person?"

"You got a tarbine? Wonderful! Impregnated or not?"

"Both types—which is why I've got a spare bololin."

"Uh-*huh*. I understand. Well . . . I suppose I ought to do the bololin first, before any scavengers get to it. Can you hook up the field analyzer to the laser comm for me?"

"Sure."

It took only a few minutes to set up the field analyzer and plug its control line into the laser comm's telemetry port, and by the time he'd finished Telek had the necessary control/display console hooked up at her end. "Okay," she said. "Now stand clear."

The analyzer remote, looking for all the world like a large double starfish with gripper treads, crawled up the bololin's flank to where the heart would be on most earthstock animals. A scalpel extended from one arm to slice a neat incision in the dark hide. Pyre paused long enough to make sure the analyzer's camera units were firmly mounted to nearby trees and then headed out to walk a sentry circle around the area. They couldn't afford to have either scavengers or Qasamans stumble onto the post-mortem now . . . and besides, it wasn't really something he wanted to watch.

It was three hours before the remote's return to the ground signaled the operation was at an end—and the bololin was no longer recognizable as such. Averting his eyes, Pyre again put on the headset. "Pyre."

"Ah, you're back." If Telek was at all tired, it wasn't evident from her voice. "You want to open up the freeze boxes and get me one of the tarbines? Better start with the unimpregnated one."

"You sure you want to do it out here?" he asked doubtfully.

"I've got as much sensitivity with the remote as I do with my hands," Telek assured him, "and I'd just as soon start getting some answers before we have to leave. Or at least have the questions I'll want Yuri to ask."

"You're the boss." Finding the proper box. Pyre opened it and set the chilly tarbine down on a patch of bare ground. The remote skittered over to it and Pyre resumed his walk.

He returned twice more, replacing the mess first with an impregnated tarbine and then with the mojo, wondering each time how long Telek could continue to handle delicate surgery without sleep. But she kept at it, and the eastern sky was starting to glow when the remote's operating light finally flicked out. "Well?" he asked into the headset as he started collecting the gear together.

"I'm not sure," Telek said slowly. "The data *seem* clear enough . . . but I'm not really sure if I believe it. Mojos and tarbines appear to be entirely different species . . . and the mojos don't seem to *impregnate* the tarbines as much as they *inoculate* them."

"They *what?*"

"Well . . . the mojo's only external sex organ is designed like an organic hypodermic needle. What it does is inject a seminal fluid that contains virus-like nuclei instead of more complete sperm cells.

The nuclei . . . well, this is still preliminary, but it *looks* like they invade some of the cells in the tarbine's back and turn them into embryo mojos."

Pyre stared down at the mutilated mojo on the ground, already beginning to crawl with insects in the growing light. "That's—*weird.*"

"That's what *I* said," Telek agreed with a sigh. "But the more I think about it the more sense it makes. This way the mojo relegates both the nourishment and protection of its young to another individual—an entirely different *species,* in fact—and therefore doesn't have to make that sacrifice itself."

"But what incentive does the tarbine have to live until the embryo kills it?" Pyre objected. "*And* what about the training most young have to receive from their parents?"

Christopher's voice came on the circuit. "You're thinking of the usual insectean pattern where one species lays eggs in the body of another, which becomes the larvae's food when they hatch. But the young mojo doesn't *have* to kill its host. If you look closely at the way the skin and muscle are arranged in the tarbine's back, it looks very much like the critical area could be split open and resealed with a minimum of damage and no real loss of flight capability."

"Assuming the mojo doesn't exceed a maximum size," Telek added. "And as to post-natal instruction, the mojo's brain seems to have a larger proportion of the high-neural-density 'primary programming' structure than earthstock or Aventinian animals I've studied. That's an assumption, of course; Qasaman biochemistry doesn't *have* to be strictly analogous to ours—"

"And you fried part of the brain shooting the thing down—" Christopher put in.

"Shut up, Bil. Anyway, it looks very possibly like the mojo young can simply poke through the tarbine's skin, fly its separate way and take up housekeeping in the forest."

"Or on somebody's shoulder." Pyre frowned as a sudden thought struck him. "On somebody's shoulder . . . the same way the tarbines ride bololins?"

"So you noticed the similarity, did you?" Christopher commented. "What makes it even more intriguing is that the tarbines have the same organic hypo organ the mojos do."

"As do the bololins themselves," Telek added, "though God only knows what species *they* use as embryo-hosts. Maybe each other; the top of the size chain has to do something different."

" 'Big fleas have little fleas upon their backs to bite 'em,' " Pyre quoted the old saying.

" '—and little fleas have lesser fleas, and so ad infinitum,' " Telek finished for him. "You're the third person who's brought that up tonight. Starting with me."

"Um. Well . . . the contact team still going sightseeing tomorrow?"

"Yes. I think I'll clue them in on all this as soon as they wake up—maybe Yuri will be able to worm out some more information from Moff." Telek paused and Pyre could hear, faintly, the sound of a jaw-cracking yawn. "You'd better get under cover and get some sleep, Almo," she said. "I think under the circumstances you can skip that riverside fauna survey we talked about yesterday—I've got enough data to keep me busy for quite a while."

"No argument," Pyre agreed. "I'll call in when I wake up."

"Just be careful you're not seen. Good night—or morning."

"Same to you." Shutting down the laser comm, Pyre spent a few moments rearranging its camouflage and hiding his other equipment. A dozen meters away was his shelter tree; tall and thick, its lowest branches a good five meters above the ground. A servopowered jump took him the necessary height, and a few branches higher he reached his "shelter," a waterproof one-man hammock bag slung under a particularly strong branch and surrounded by a glued-stick cage sort of arrangement. It made Pyre feel a little strange to sleep inside such a barrier, but it was the simplest way to make sure no carnivore could sneak up on him, no matter how quiet it was or how deeply asleep *he* was.

Entering, he sealed the cage and worked himself into the hammock with a sigh. For a minute he considered setting his alarm, ultimately decided against it. If anything came up, the *Dewdrop* had one-way communication with him via his emergency earphone, and if they were careful how they focused the beam, it was unlikely even a snooper set in the airport control tower could pick it up.

The control tower. His drift toward sleep slowed as he remembered the men who'd charged out of that dark and supposedly deserted building for bololin target practice. Certainly their presence didn't mesh with the building's assumed main function—no aircraft had so much as shown its nose since the *Dewdrop*'s arrival. But if they weren't in there to handle planes, then what *were* they doing there? Monitoring the visitors' ship? Probably. Still, as long as they were just watching they weren't likely to bother anyone.

Closing his eyes, Pyre put the image of silent watchers out of his mind and slid into oblivion.

Chapter 13

For the drive to the outer villages Moff exchanged their usual open-air car for a small enclosed bus. The reason wasn't hard to figure out; barely a kilometer out of Sollas the road began passing in and out of the patches of forest that had been visible from orbit. "Just a normal precaution," Moff explained about their vehicle at one point. "Cars are rarely attacked, even by krisjaws, but it does happen occasionally." Joshua shuddered a bit at the thought, wondering for the hundredth time what had possessed Pyre to go out into the forest alone—and what had possessed Telek to *let* him go. The *Dewdrop* had been maddeningly uninformative on everything dealing with Pyre's mission; and Joshua, for one, found it uncomfortably suspicious. He and Justin had discussed in some length the mystery behind Pyre's presence here during the trip from Aventine, though without finding any good answers. The possibility that Telek might have brought Pyre along solely because his political view made him expendable wasn't one that had occurred to Joshua before; but it was occurring to him now, and he didn't care for it at all.

But for the moment, at least, it was a low-priority worry. Pyre had demonstrated his ability to survive the Qasaman wilderness . . . and, besides, the biological breakthrough he and Telek had made last night was just too fascinating to ignore. Joshua's schooling had included only a bare minimum of the life sciences, but even he could see how radically different the Qasaman ecology was from anything known either in the Worlds or the Dominion and could guess at some of the implications. The contact team hadn't had a safe chance to discuss it among themselves yet, of course—as far as their hosts knew, they should have no inkling of any of this. But Joshua could see the same thoughts and speculations in their eyes. Watching the brightly colored foliage outside the bus, he waited impatiently for Cerenkov to start the gentle probing Telek had suggested.

Cerenkov's grip on his curiosity was apparently stronger than Joshua's, however, and he waited until the fifty-kilometer trip was nearly over before nudging the conversation in that direction. "I've noticed a fair sprinkling of smaller birds flying among the trees," he said, gesturing toward the window beside him, "but nothing that seems to be the size of the mojo or its female form of tarbine. Do they nest in trees in the wild, or do they raise their young in those quill forests on the bololins' backs?"

"There is no need of nests or the raising of young," Moff told him. "A mojo's young are born with all the necessary survival skills already present."

"Really? Doesn't the tarbine at least have to nest long enough to hatch the eggs?"

"There are no eggs—mojo young are born live. In this sense most of the bird-like Qasaman creatures are not true birds, by the old standards."

"Ah." Joshua could almost see Cerenkov casting about for a question that wouldn't reveal that he knew Moff was being deliberately misleading. "I'm also interested in the relationship between the tarbines and bololins. Is the tarbine merely a parasite, getting a free ride but not contributing anything?"

"No, the relationship is more equal than that. The tarbines often help defend their bololins against predator attack, and it's thought that they also help locate good grazing sites from the air."

"I thought the bololins liked to travel along magnetic field lines," Rynstadt put in. "Can they just get off that path any time they want to go foraging?"

Moff gave him an odd look. "Of course. They only use the magnetic lines as a guide to and from the northern breeding areas. How did you deduce the mechanism?"

"The layout of Sollas was the major clue," Cerenkov replied before Rynstadt could do so. "Those wide avenues all point along the field lines, with no real provision for bololin herds going any other direction. I think Marck's question refers to the fact that when the herd we saw was coming through the city the people stood just barely inside the cross streets, as if they knew the bololins wouldn't stray even slightly off their path. One of those still aboard the ship had wondered whether they were actually constrained to follow their individual lines pretty closely."

"No, of course not." Moff's quizzical look was edging toward suspicion. "Otherwise many would crash into buildings instead of finding their way into the streets. But how did your companion know where the people were standing?"

Joshua's heart skipped a beat. The Qasamans hadn't shown the slightest indication that they knew about his implanted sensors, but he still abruptly felt as if every eye in the bus had turned in his direction. It jump-kicked him back to childhood, to all the times his mother had easily penetrated his innocent expression to find the guilt bubbling up beneath it—

But Cerenkov was already well on top of things. "We told them about it, of course," he said, his tone one of genuine puzzlement. "We described the whole scene while you were up there shooting. They were interested in the odd mojo mating pattern, too— at least what I was able to tell them about it seemed odd to them. Was there some kind of ritual dance or pattern that I missed?"

"You seem excessively interested in the mojos," Moff said, his dark eyes boring into Cerenkov's.

Cerenkov shrugged. "Why not? You must admit your relationship with them is unique in human history. I know of no other culture where people have had such universal protection—*defensive* protection, I mean, not just a widespread carrying of weapons. It's bound to have reduced every form of aggression, from simple assault all the way to general warfare."

Joshua frowned as that fact suddenly hit him. So busy had he been observing the details and minutiae of Qasaman life that he'd missed the larger patterns. But Cerenkov obviously hadn't . . . and if he was right, perhaps the Trofts had cause to worry after all. A human culture that had had the willpower to break the pattern of strong preying on weak would be long on cooperation and short on competition . . . and a potential threat to its neighbors no matter what its technological level.

Moff was speaking again. "And you think our little mojos deserve the credit?" he asked, stroking his bird's throat. "You give no credit to our people and philosophy?"

"Of course we do," Rynstadt said. "But there've been countless cultures throughout history who've paid great lip service to the concepts of justice and freedom from fear without doing anything concrete for their citizens. You—and in particular the generation which first began taming the mojos—have proved humanity is capable of truly practical idealism. That achievement alone would make contact between our worlds worthwhile, certainly from our point of view."

"Your world has difficulties with war, then?" Moff's gaze shifted to Rynstadt.

"So far we've avoided that particular problem," Rynstadt answered cautiously. "But we have our share of normal human aggressions, and that occasionally causes trouble."

"I see." For a moment they rode in silence, and then Moff shrugged. "Well, you'll see that we aren't completely without aggression. The difference is that we've learned to direct our attention outward, toward the dangers of the wild, instead of inward toward each other."

Dangerous indeed, Joshua thought; and even Cerenkov's eyes seemed troubled as conversation in the bus drifted into silence.

A few minutes later, they reached the village of Huriseem.

Joshua could remember arguments aboard ship as to whether the rings around the villages were actually walls; but at ground level there was no doubt whatsoever. Made of huge stone or concrete blocks, painted a dead black, Huriseem's wall was a stark throwback to ancient Earth history and the continual regional warfare of those days. It seemed gratingly out of place here, especially after the discussion of only a few minutes earlier.

Beside him, York cleared his throat. "Only about three meters high," he muttered, "and no crenels or fire ports."

Moff apparently heard him. "As I said, there is no war here," he said—a bit tartly, Joshua thought. "The wall is to keep out bololins and the more deadly predators of the forests."

"Why not build along the same open lines as Sollas?" Cerenkov asked. "That works well enough for the bololins, and I didn't see any predators getting in there."

"Predators are rare in Sollas because there are many people and there is a wide gap between city and forest. Here such an approach would clearly not work."

So clear back the forest, Joshua thought. But perhaps that was more trouble than a single village was worth.

The bus followed the encircling road to the southwest side of the village, where they found a black gate set into the wall. Clearly they were both expected and observed; the gate was already opening as they came within sight of it. The bus turned in, and Joshua glanced back to see it close behind them.

The wall and the forest setting had somehow led Joshua's

subconscious to expect a relatively primitive, thatched-hut scene, and he was vaguely disappointed as he left the bus to find the buildings, streets, and people as modern as those they'd seen in Sollas. Three men waited off to the side, and as the last of the Qasaman escorts left the bus they stepped forward.

"Mayor Ingliss," Moff nodded in greeting, "may I present to you the visitors from Aventine: Cerenkov, Rynstadt, York, and Moreau."

Where Mayor Kimmeron of Sollas had been almost cheerful, Ingliss was gravely polite. "I welcome you to Huriseem," he said with a nod. "I understand you seek to learn about village life on Qasama. To what end, may I inquire?"

So Qasaman suspicion isn't limited to the big cities. Somehow, Joshua found that more of a disappointment than the lack of thatched huts.

Cerenkov went into his by-now familiar spiel about trade and cultural exchange, and Joshua allowed his gaze to drift around the area. Huriseem seemed to have none of the taller six-story-plus buildings of Sollas, and the colorful abstract wall paintings were also absent, but otherwise the village could have been a transplanted chunk of the larger city. Even the wall's presence was not intrusive, and it took him a moment to realize the structure's inside surface was painted with effectively camouflaging pictures of buildings and forest scenes. So *why is the outside painted black?* he wondered—and with a flash of inspiration it hit him. *Black— the same color as the tree trunks. A charging bololin must see the village as a giant tree and therefore goes around it.* And that meant—

Reaching to his neck, he covered the pendant's translator mike. "I've got it," he murmured. "The Sollas street paintings make the place look sort of like a clump of forest—same colors and everything. Keeps the bololins from shying away."

There was a long enough pause that he began to wonder if no one on the *Dewdrop* was monitoring the circuit. Then Nnamdi's voice came in over the earphone. "Interesting. Weird, but entirely possible. Depends partly on how good the bololins' eyesight is, I suppose. Governor Telek's still asleep, but I'll suggest this to her when she wakes up, see if she got any data on that last night."

"Fine," Joshua said, "but in the meantime can *you* find any sociological rationale for wanting those herds to come trampling through Sollas?"

"That *does* put into doubt Moff's assertion that they simply can't keep the bololins out, doesn't it?" Nnamdi agreed thoughtfully. "I'll work on it, but nothing comes immediately to mind. Wait a second—face left a bit, will you?"

Joshua obediently turned his head a few degrees in the requested direction. "What is it?"

"That red-bordered sign near the gate—haven't seen anything like it anywhere in Sollas. Let me get the visual translator going. . . ."

Joshua held his head steady for a moment to give the tape a good image, then turned back to face the others. "Okay," Nnamdi said after a moment. "It says, 'Krisjaw hunts this month: the 8th and 22nd at 10.' Today's the eighth, I think, if the numbers we've seen elsewhere are accurate. Wonder why they bother to post a sign with the other comm lines they have."

"Maybe a village this small doesn't have the same wiring as Sollas does," Joshua suggested. It looked like Cerenkov and the Qasamans had about finished the preliminaries; Mayor Ingliss was gesturing toward an open car of the sort they'd used in Sollas all week. "I'll try to find out," he added and let his hand fall to his side.

Its mike open again, the translator came back online. "—will be able to visit the farming areas later," Ingliss was saying. "At the moment many of the workers are out hunting, so there would be little to see."

"Is that the krisjaw hunt?" Joshua spoke up.

Ingliss focused on him. "Yes, of course. Only krisjaws and bololins are worthy of mass hunts, and you would have heard a warning siren if a bololin herd were approaching."

"Yes, Moff has mentioned krisjaws once or twice," Cerenkov said. "I get the impression they're dangerous, but we don't know anything more."

"Dangerous?" Ingliss barked a laugh. "Immensely so. Two meters or more in length, half that from paws to shoulder, with wavy teeth that can shred a man in seconds. Savage hunters, they threaten both our people and our livestock."

"Sounds a little like our spine leopards," Rynstadt commented grimly. "Native Aventinian predators that we've been fighting ever since we landed."

"It wasn't always that way here," Ingliss said, shaking his head. "The old legends say that krisjaws used to be relatively peaceful, avoiding our first settlements and willing to share the bololin herds with us. It was only later, perhaps as they realized we intended to stay, that they began to turn on us."

"Or as they found out humans were good to eat," York suggested. "Did this happen all at once or gradually?"

Ingliss exchanged glances with Moff, who shrugged. "I don't know," the latter said. "Records of those early years are spotty— the malfunction that stranded us here ruined much of our electronic recording equipment, and interim historical records did not always survive."

Nnamdi's voice clicked in on the circuit. "Pursue this point, Yuri; everyone," he said. "If the krisjaws are really showing signs of intelligence we need to know that."

"The reason I asked," Cerenkov said, "was that if they really did 'realize' you were settling here, they might be a sentient species."

"Our own biologists have studied that question," Moff said, "and they think that unlikely."

"They don't show any great ability to learn, for example," Ingliss offered. "All the villages—and some of the cities, too—hold periodic hunts in which often as many as fifty villagers and visitors participate. Yet the krisjaws haven't learned to stay away from civilized areas."

The light dawned. "Ah—so *that's* why you post a krisjaw hunt notice by the gate," Joshua said. "So anyone passing through will know about it, as well as just the local population."

Ingliss nodded. "Yes. It's an opportunity to practice the human predator's own hunting skill, and all who wish to come are welcome. Krisjaw hides are also very prestigious, and many people find the meat superior to that of bololins. If you'd arrived an hour sooner— but, no, you haven't got mojos, of course. Nor weapons, I see."

"Sounds like you should be close to wiping the things out by now," York grunted.

"Actually, we are," Ingliss nodded, "at least in the inhabited regions of Qasama. I speak of them as dangerous and numerous, but in fact a 50-man hunting group is fortunate to return with one or two trophies. In the days when Huriseem was first built a man could stand atop the wall and shoot one each hour."

"You're lucky any of you survived," York said.

Ingliss shrugged, a more deliberate gesture than the Aventinian version. "As I said, we were fairly well established before they began threatening us in earnest. And by then our adoption of the mojos as bodyguards was also well underway. Ironically enough, that program was stimulated in large part by concerns over the krisjaws."

"But that's enough about ancient history," Moff put in. "We have a limited amount of time; if you wish to observe the village we'll need to begin at once."

For just a second Joshua thought he saw something odd in Moff's face. But then the Qasaman had turned away toward the open car pulled up behind Ingliss and his companions, and Joshua decided he'd imagined the whole thing.

Looking around curiously, he followed the others to the car.

It had been literally decades since Telek had pulled the kind of all-night lab work she'd done the previous night—and *never* had she done it via the waldoes of a remote analyzer. Clumping into the *Dewdrop*'s lounge around noon, she felt like a good computer simulation of death. "What's happening?" she asked Nnamdi, heading immediately for the cahve dispenser in the corner.

"What're *you* doing here?" he frowned up from the displays at her. "You're supposed to be in bed doing some REMs."

"I'm *supposed* to be running a mission," she growled back, bringing her steaming mug over and dropping into the seat beside his. "I can sleep *next* year. Bil still down?"

"Yes. Left a call with the bridge for four o'clock."

And Christopher had done little except watch and make occasional suggestions. *Amazing how tiring it can be to kibitz,* she thought acidly, then put him from her mind. "Is this the village Moff promised us?"

"Yes; Huriseem. The stately fellow screen left is Ingliss, the mayor. This seems to be their version of the marketplace we saw in Sollas. Minus the bololins."

"Then the place *is* walled?"

"Solidly. And Joshua brought up an interesting point about Sollas's wild color scheme a while ago."

Telek listened with half an ear as Nnamdi described Joshua's idea about the cities seeming like clumps of forest to the bololins, the remainder of her attention on the scent and taste of her cahve and on the organized chaos on the displays. With the smaller marketplace of the village, she realized for the first time that services as well as goods were on display. One booth seemed to be manned by a builder, with wood and brick samples on a back table and what looked like a floor plan on a computer display screen set on the front counter. *So why don't they do the whole thing via computer?* she wondered. *They like the personal contact? Could be.*

Nnamdi finished his recitation and she shrugged. "Could very well be. I'll check later and see if the computer can make an estimate of the bololins' visual resolution. Sure seems stupid to help the bololins stampede your city, though."

"That's almost exactly what Joshua said," Nnamdi nodded. "Could there be something we're missing here? About the bololins and people, I mean?"

"I don't think we've got the whole society figured out after a week here, no," she said dryly. "What exactly did you have in mind?"

"Well . . ." He waved a hand vaguely. "I don't know. Some symbiotic relationship, like the people have with the mojos."

"I'd call the mojos more pets than symbionts, myself, but given the bololin-tarbine arrangement the point is well taken." Telek frowned into space, trying to remember all the forms of symbiosis that existed on the Worlds. "About the only possibility I can think of is that banging away at the bololins helps drain off the city-dwellers' aggressions. Keeps them peaceful."

"Oh, their aggressions aren't drained off, just rerouted," Nnamdi snorted, gesturing toward the display. "You missed the bargaining session at a jewelry store half a block back. These guys would put Troft businessmen to shame."

"Hmm. Probably a logical avenue to channel it into, given the mojo ban on fighting. That and politics, maybe. . . ."

She trailed off. "Something wrong?" Nnamdi asked.

"I'm not sure," she said, picking up the mike. "Joshua, do a slow three-sixty, would you?"

The scenery shifted as Joshua complied, pausing occasionally as he pretended to look at some booth or other . . , and by the time he'd completed his circle Telek's odd feeling had become a cold certainty. "Moff is missing," she told Nnamdi quietly.

"What?" He frowned, hunching his chair closer to the display as if that would do him any good. "Come on, now—Moff doesn't even go to the bathroom unless the contact team's off in some corner where they won't get into anything."

"I know. Yuri; everyone—Moff's gone. Anyone know where he went or notice him leave?"

There was a short pause. Then, at the edge of the display, Telek saw Cerenkov raise a hand to his pendant. "I hadn't even noticed. Governor," he said. "There're so many people around us here—"

"Which may be precisely why he picked this place," Telek cut him off with a grunt. "Has he said or done anything unusual this morning? Anyone?"

There were four quick negatives. "All right. Everyone keep an eye out for him, without being too conspicuous about it, and try to notice his expression when he shows up."

She turned off the mike and sat glaring for a moment at the noisy market scene. "What do you think it means?" Nnamdi broke into her thoughts.

"Maybe nothing. I hope nothing. But I think I'm going to replay this morning's tapes, see if I can spot anything in Moff's behavior myself. Keep an eye on things; let me know if anything happens." Picking up her cahve, she stepped to an unused display in the corner and keyed for the proper records.

"Should we alert Almo and the bridge?" Nnamdi asked.

"The bridge, yes—but don't make too big a deal of it." She hesitated. "And Almo . . . no, let's not bother him yet. There'll be plenty of time to talk to him when we've figured out what if anything is going on."

"Right."

Telek turned to her display. The semidarkness there was interrupted by a flickering light, the Qasamans' version of a wake-up alarm. Shifting one way and then the other, the picture changed as Joshua rolled over and then sat up. "Rise and glow, Marck," he said to Rynstadt in the other bed. "Busy day coming up."

"So what's new about that?" the other returned in a sleepy voice.

Groping blindly for her cahve mug, Telek settled down to watch.

Chapter 14

The blue skies of Tacta were just a shade redder than those of Chata and Fuson had been, Jonny thought idly as he paused from his contemplation of the bush forest that edged to within fifteen meters of the *Menssana*'s perimeter. More dust in the upper atmosphere, the experts had decided, probably spewed there by the dozens of active volcanos their pre-landing analysis had located. A potentially dangerous place to live, though that could probably be minimized by judicious choice of homestead. The weather and climate could be subject to rapid change, though, regardless of where one settled. All in all, he decided, a distinct fourth on their five-planet survey.

Or in other words, Junca would be keeping its dead-last spot.

Returning his gaze to the bushes, he found a large bird sitting on one of the thicker branches looking back at him.

His first thought was disbelief that neither his enhanced vision nor hearing had detected its approach; but hard on the heels of that came the realization that the bird had probably been sitting there quietly for as long as Jonny had been standing there, its protective coloring and motionlessness serving to hide it.

"You're in luck," Jonny murmured in its direction. "I'm not in charge of collecting fauna samples."

A footstep behind him made him turn. It was Chrys, a vaguely sour look on her face. "Feel like being a politician again?" she asked without preamble.

Jonny flicked a look past her at the bustling activity in the protected area between them and the ship. "What's up?" he asked, focusing on her again.

She waved a hand in disgust. "The same fight they've been

having since we hot-tailed it off Junca. The scientists want to take the time we didn't use there to go back for an additional look at Kubha or Fuson."

"And Shepherd wants to just drop the two days we saved out of the schedule and head back home as soon as we're done here," Jonny finished for her with an exasperated sigh. He was roundly sick of the whole issue, especially when Shepherd's first refusal should have settled things long ago. "So what do you want me to do?"

"*I* don't want you to do anything," she returned. "But Rey seems to think you might be able to inject a few well-chosen words into the debate."

Put another way, Banyon wanted him to thunder the scientists back into their labs. Jonny had no doubts which side of the issue the Cobras supported—having been saddled with both the defense of the expedition *and* its hardest work, they were quite ready to head home as soon as possible. The four who were still in sickbay with injuries from the mad scramble off Junca probably held triple batches of that opinion.

And it would certainly be the easiest way to settle the debate. Jonny Moreau the Cobra, Governor Emeritus, had more physical and legal authority than anyone else aboard, including Shepherd himself. He was opening his mouth to give in when he took a good look at Chrys's expression.

It was angry. She was trying to hide the emotion, but Jonny knew her too well to be fooled. The tension lines around her eyes, the slight pinch to her mouth, the tight muscles in cheeks and neck—anger, for sure. Anger and a smattering of frustration.

It was the same expression he'd seen on her far too often these past few years.

And with that sudden connection came the *truly* proper response to the *Messana*'s intramural squabbles. "Well, Rey and the others can just forget it," he told her. "If Shepherd's too polite to chew the scientists' ears off he can just put up with their yammering. I'm on vacation out here."

Chrys's eyes widened momentarily; but even as a faint smile flickered across her lips the tension was leaving her face and body. "I'll quote you exactly," she said.

"Do that. But first take a look here," he added as she started to turn back toward the encampment. "It looks like we're starting to attract the local sightseers."

The bird was indeed still sitting quietly on its branch. "Odd," Chrys said, studying it through a pair of folding binoculars. "That beak looks more suited to a predator than to a seed or insect eater. The feet, too."

Jonny bumped his optical enhancers up a notch. They *did* rather look like condorine talons, now that she mentioned it. "What's odd about it? We've catalogued birds and rodentoids here small enough for it to prey on."

"I know . . . but why is it just *sitting* there? Why isn't it out hunting or something?"

Jonny frowned. Sitting motionlessly amid the low bushes . . . as if afraid of losing what little cover its position provided. "Maybe it's hurt," he suggested slowly. "Or hiding from a larger predator."

They looked at each other, and he saw in her eyes that she was following the same train of logic and reaching the same conclusion. And liking it no better than he did. "Like . . . us?" she eventually voiced the common thought.

"I don't see anything else it could be afraid of," he admitted, giving the sky a quick sweep.

"A ground animal—? No. Anything the size of a cat could get it in those low bushes." Chrys's eyes shifted to the bird. "But . . . how could it know—?"

"It's intelligent." Jonny didn't realize until he'd said the words just how strongly he was starting to believe them. "It recognizes we're tool-makers and aliens and is being properly cautious. Or is waiting for us to communicate."

"How?"

"Well . . . maybe I should go over to it."

Chrys's grip on his arm was surprisingly strong. "You think that'd be safe?"

"I *am* a Cobra—remember?" he growled with tension of his own. Contact with the unknown . . . his old combat training came surging back. *Rule One: Have a backup.* Carefully, keeping the movements fluid, he pulled his field phone from his belt. "Dr. Hanford?" he said, naming the only zoologist he knew to be close by, the only one he remembered seeing near the ship when Chrys came up a few minutes ago.

"Hanford."

"Jonny Moreau. I'm at the southeast part of the perimeter. Get over here, quietly. And bring any Cobras nearby with you."

"Got it."

Jonny replaced the phone and waited. The bird waited too, but seemed to be getting a little restless. Though perhaps that was his imagination.

Hanford arrived a couple of minutes later, running with an awkward-looking waddle that made for a fair compromise between speed and stealth. Banyon and a Cobra named Porris were with him. "What is it?" the zoologist stage-whispered, coming to a stop at Jonny's side.

Jonny nodded toward the bird. "Tell me what you make of that."

"You mean the bushes—?"

"No, the bird there," Chrys said, pointing it out.

"The—? Ah." Hanford got his own binoculars out. "Ah. Yes, we've seen others of the species. Always at a distance, though—I don't think anyone's ever gotten this close to one before."

"They're rather skittish, then?" Jonny prompted. "Normally, that is?"

"Um," Hanford grunted thoughtfully. "Yes. He *does* seem unusually brave, doesn't he?"

"Maybe he's staying put *because* he's afraid of us," Banyon said.

"If he's afraid then he should take off," Hanford shook his head.

"No, sir. We're too close to him for that." Banyon pointed. "The instant he leaves that bush he'll be silhouetted against the sky—*and* he'll be in motion. Either one would be more than enough for most predators. He's in lousy position where he is, but it's the best option he's got."

"Except that he's a bird and we're obviously not," Hanford said. "Once he's aloft he shouldn't have anything to fear from us."

"Unless," Jonny suggested quietly, "he understands what weapons are."

There was a short silence. "No," Hanford said at last. "No, I can't believe that. Look at that cranium size, for starters—there's just not enough room in there for a massive brain."

"Size isn't all-important—" Porris began.

"But cell number is," Hanford shot back. "And Tactan cell sizes and biochemistry are close enough to ours to make the comparison valid. No, he's not a sentient lifeform—he's just frozen with fear and doesn't realize he can escape any time he wants to."

"'Ladybird, ladybird, fly away home,'" Chrys murmured.

"Yes, well, he's missed his chance now," Hanford said briskly. "Porris, you know where the flash nets are stored?" He half-turned toward the *Menssana*—

And the bird shot off its perch.

Chrys gasped with the suddenness of it, as beside her Banyon reflexively snapped his hands into firing position. "Hold it!" Jonny barked to him. "Let it go."

"What?" Hanford yelped. "*Shoot* it, man—*shoot* it!"

But Banyon lowered his hands.

The bird went. Not straight up into the sky, as Jonny would have thought most likely, but horizontally along the tops of the bushes. And . . . zigzagging. Zigzagging like. . . .

It disappeared beyond a gentle rise and Jonny turned to find Banyon's eyes on him. "Evasive maneuvers," the other almost whispered.

"Why didn't you shoot it?" Hanford barked, gripping Jonny's arm, his other hand clenched into a frustrated fist. "I gave you Cobras a direct order—"

"Doctor," Jonny interjected, "the bird didn't move *until* you suggested we try and capture it."

"I don't care. You should—" Hanford stopped abruptly as it suddenly seemed to penetrate. "You mean—? No. No. I don't believe it. How could it have known what we were saying? It *couldn't* have."

"Of course not." Banyon's voice was dark. "But it knew it had to leave; and it took a low, evasive route when it did. The sort of pattern you'd use against enemy fire."

"*And* it waited until you, Doctor, had your back turned," Chrys added, shuddering. "The one who gave the capture order. Jonny . . . this sounds too much to be coincidence."

"Maybe they've seen tool-makers before," Jonny said slowly. "Maybe the Trofts landed when they were surveying the area. That way they could know about weapons."

"They could all be part of a hive mind, perhaps," Porris suggested suddenly. "Each individual wouldn't have to be independently intelligent that way."

"The hive mind theory's been in disrepute for twenty years," Hanford said. But he didn't sound all that confident. "And anyway, that doesn't explain how they knew our language well enough to realize I was sending you for a flash net."

Abruptly, Jonny realized he was still staring at the spot where the bird had vanished. He looked around quickly; but no vast clouds of attacking birds were sweeping down from the sky, as he'd half expected. Only occasional and far-distant specks marred the red-tinged blue. Still . . . "I think it might be a good idea to get everything packed up early," he said to the others. "Be ready to leave at a moment's notice if . . . it becomes necessary."

Hanford looked as if he would object, seemed to think better of it, and turned to Banyon instead. "Would it be possible to get a couple of Cobras to come on a hunting run with me? I want one of those birds—alive if possible, but I'm no longer that fussy."

"I'll see what I can do," Banyon said grimly. "I think finding out more about them would be an excellent idea."

In the end. Captain Shepherd accepted all the recommendations put before him. The quick-lift preparations were made, the perimeter Cobra guard was doubled, and the scientists shifted into an almost frantic high speed. Two separate hunting parties failed to make so much as visual contact with any of the mysterious birds. The facts, the speculations, and the rumors circulated widely . . . and the *Menssana* lifted a full twelve hours ahead of schedule. For once, there were no complaints.

Chapter 15

They spent a great deal of time wandering around the Huriseem marketplace—more time, York thought, than they'd spent at any other single place during their entire Qasaman tour—and he breathed a private sigh of relief when the end was finally in sight. The presence of so many mojos virtually eye to eye with him was something he found particularly unnerving, and Moff's continued absence wasn't helping a bit. He wondered how Mayor Ingliss would explain the latter, something he would have no choice but to do as soon as they left the marketplace mob. Alone with their escort, the team would *have* to "notice" that Moff was missing, and Ingliss would then have to spin some story.

York didn't want to hear it. It would be a packet of lies; worse yet, a packet of obvious lies. Moff's exit had been too smooth, the timing of it too well chosen, to have been accidental. Clearly, the team hadn't been intended to miss him at all. York's gut instincts told him that having to admit Moff had been away would be almost as bad in the Qasaman's minds as actually telling where and why he'd gone. The more York saw of the Qasamans—the more he listened to Moff's evasive answers to their questions, the more he saw of what they were and were not being shown—through all of that the descriptions *overcautious* and *suspicious* were gradually giving way to the word *paranoid*. Whether their history had given them a right to be that way was irrelevant; what mattered at the moment was that York had seen paranoid minds at work before, and he knew how they worked. The simple fact of Moff's absence gave him not a single byte of useful information, but the Qasamans might not recognize that. They were just as likely to assume that their entire plot—or plan, or scheme, or damn

374

surprise party, for all *he* knew—had been totally compromised, and that they would have to spring things prematurely.

York didn't want that. If Moff were planning something—*any-thing*—it would be safer for all involved if it went off smoothly and on schedule. *Damn it, Moff, get back here,* he thought furiously into the air. *Get back here and keep your illusion that you're in control.*

So engrossed was he in watching surreptitiously for Moff that he completely missed whatever it was that started the fight.

His first rude notice, in fact, was a sudden grip on his shoulder by one of Moff's assistants, hauling him up short at the very edge of a ring of people that had formed just past the marketplace boundary. The open area so encircled was perhaps twenty meters wide; inside, barely five meters apart, two men without mojos faced each other. Their expressions were just short of murderous.

"What's going on?" York asked the Qasaman still holding his arm.

It was Ingliss, two people down the circle, who answered. "A duel," he said. "Insult has been made; challenge offered and accepted."

York's mouth went dry as his eyes found first the opponents' belted pistols and then the two hundred or more people gathered to watch. Surely they wouldn't start shooting *here*—

A man with a blue-and-silver headband appeared halfway around the circle and stepped to the two men. From a large shoulder pouch he took a thirty-centimeter rattan-like stick and a set of two small balls connected together by fifty centimeters of milky-white cord. Handing the stick and balls to one of the combatants, he went to the other man and gave him a second set from the bag. He stepped back to the edge of the circle, raised his right hand, and then brought it down in a chopping motion—

And the combatant to York's right, who'd been swinging the balls lazily over his head by their cord, abruptly hurled them at his opponent.

Hurled them well, too, with power and accuracy. But the other was ready. Holding his stick vertically in front of him, he deftly caught the spinning projectile on it, letting the balls wrap themselves up. An instant later his own set of balls were whirling back toward the first man, who similarly caught them on his stick. A momentary pause for each to disentangle his opponent's captured weapon and they were ready to begin again.

"What's going on?" York whispered again.

"A duel, as I said," Ingliss murmured back. "Each man takes turns casting his curse ball bola at the other until both weapons have been lost to the crowd or one opponent has conceded. The curse balls will leave impressive bruises, but seldom do more physical damage."

"Lost to the crowd?"

"If a throw goes wide or is otherwise not caught, the observers will not return it. Two such misses, clearly, and the duel must end."

"What keeps one of them from charging his opponent between throws and beating his brains out?"

"The same thing that keeps them from using their guns," Ingliss replied calmly. "Their mojos—there and there." He pointed to two of the spectators, each of whom had an extra bird on his shoulder.

York frowned. "You mean they guard against *all* attacks, even unarmed ones? I thought they only reacted to the drawing of guns."

"Oh, of course they can't defend against *all* attacks," the mayor shrugged. "You could hit me now, suddenly, before my mojo could stop you. Though it would keep you from continuing the attack." He nodded to the duelists, now beginning to show sweat sheens from their efforts. "But they are so obviously fighting that their mojos will keep them apart."

"I see." York thought about the implications of that for the Cobras, should they eventually need to go into action. Would the mojos recognize them as the source of the lethal laser flashes in a battle? There was no way to know. "At least," he commented out loud, "that explains why no one's tried to come up with a gun or weapon the mojos wouldn't recognize as such. You'd get one free shot at your target, but that's about all."

"You Aventinians seem to think a great deal in terms of interpersonal conflict," Ingliss said in a voice that seemed oddly tight. "Your planet must be a frightening one to live on. Perhaps if you had mojos of your own. . . . At any rate, you're correct about alternative weapons. In the early days of mojo domestication many people tried making them, with the result you've already deduced."

"Uh-huh," York nodded and settled down to watch.

It seemed to take a long time, but in actual fact the duel was over in just a few minutes. York couldn't tell offhand what it solved; but as the crowd closed in on the fighters, separating them as secondary masses of seemingly happy well-wishers and friends formed around each, he decided that *they* all considered it to have been worthwhile. Maybe Nnamdi could sort out the sociology and psychology of it aboard ship; for York, it was a low-priority worry indeed. Glancing around through the dispersing crowd, he located the islands of stability that were the rest of the contact team, Mayor Ingliss and the escorts—

And Moff.

York blinked, trying hard to keep any hint of surprise or chagrin out of his face. Despite his best efforts, the Qasaman had slipped back into the group unnoticed, just as he'd left it. It suddenly made the duel's timing suspicious . . . and if the duel was a fake it automatically raised the importance of Moff's secret errand; raised it uncomfortably high. Throwing together such a diversion required either a lot of people ready on a moment's notice, or else a smaller group capable of fooling the locals as well as the Aventinian visitors. Either one implied a great deal of effort and—perhaps—a fair amount of advance planning.

Were the Qasamans on to them? And if so, for how long?

"I'm sorry you had to see that," Moff said as the team and escort drew back together. "It's a form of aggression we've been unable to eliminate completely."

"It seems pretty mild compared to some I've seen," Cerenkov assured him. Neither he nor the others showed any reaction to Moff's reappearance, and York quietly let out the breath he'd been holding.

"It's still more than a truly civilized society should have," Moff said stiffly. "Our strength of will should be turned outward, toward the conquering of this world."

"And beyond?" Rynstadt murmured.

Moff looked at him, an intense look on his face. "The stars are mankind's future," he said. "We won't always be confined to this one world."

"Mankind will never be confined again," Cerenkov agreed solemnly. "Tell me, does this sort of duel happen very often? The whoever it was with the headband seemed to be right on top of things."

"Each village and city has one or more judges, depending on its population," Moff said. "They have many other duties besides overseeing duels. But come—we have a great many more places to visit here. Mayor Ingliss has yet to show you the local government center, and we should also have time to see a typical residential neighborhood before the krisjaw hunters return. At that point we'll be able to visit the farming areas."

Cerenkov smiled. "Point taken, Moff—we *do* have a busy schedule. Please, lead on."

They turned a corner and headed for the cars Ingliss's people had driven around the marketplace area for them, and York decided to be cautiously optimistic. Sticking to the tour at this point meant Moff believed his absence hadn't been noticed. Which meant whatever the Qasamans had planned would be going off on their original schedule.

Abruptly, he was aware of the gentle pressure of the calculator watch on his wrist, and of the similar feel of the star sapphire on his hand. Together with his pen, they were the sections of his palm-mate . . . a weapon neither the Qasamans nor the mojos had ever seen before. *One free shot,* the words echoed in his brain. *One free shot before the mojos can stop me. I'd damn well better make that shot count.*

It happened as they were driving back toward Sollas that evening, and their first warning was the sudden burst of static that replaced the hum of the *Dewdrop*'s radio link. At the front of the bus Moff stood up, steadying himself with his left hand. In his right hand was his pistol.

"You are under confinement," a voice boomed from the man sitting beside him—or, rather, from the phone-sized box in the Qasaman's hand. "You are suspected of spying on the people of Qasama. You will make no aggressive move until the final destination is reached. If you disobey your ship will be destroyed."

"What?" Cerenkov barked, his voice a blend of shock, bewilderment, and outrage. "What's all this about?"

But there was no sound from his translator pendant and the words fell on effectively deaf ears. "Moff—" Cerenkov began, half rising.

"Don't bother," Rynstadt advised quietly. "That's just a recorder, not a translator. We'll have to wait until we get back to Sollas to clear this up."

Cerenkov opened his mouth, apparently thought better of it, and dropped back into his seat. Moff's gun hadn't so much as twitched, York noted uncomfortably. A steady man, with nerves not easily rattled—which severely limited the range of ploys that could be used against him. And his mojo . . .

His mojo hadn't so much as squawked at the sight of his owner with a gun drawn on another human being. None of the birds had. For whatever reason—appearance, odor, speech—the Aventinians apparently had been exempted from the automatic protection the mojos gave their Qasaman masters. York had almost dared to hope that any Qasaman action against the team would be at least hindered a bit by the mojos' presence. But that was obviously not going to happen.

Across the aisle, Joshua shifted in his seat. "They must have one gantua of a computer capability to get even that much of a translation this fast," he muttered.

"They presumably *have* been recording both our words and their translation, though," Rynstadt pointed out. He seemed relaxed, almost unconcerned, and for a moment York stared at him in utter incomprehension. Didn't the idiot *realize* just how much trouble they were in? *This isn't some game*, the snarl welled up in his throat. *These people are serious, and they're scared.*

He choked the words down unsaid. Of *course* Rynstadt wasn't worried—weren't there four Cobras aboard the *Dewdrop* ready to burst out and rescue them in a blaze of laser fire?

Except it wasn't going to be that easy; and if none of the others realized that, York certainly did. Shifting his gaze to the window, he studied the darkening sky and the even darker forest flanking the road. *Moff's timed this well*, he thought, a touch of professional respect adding counterpoint to the pounding of his heart. Far from the *Dewdrop*, in dangerous and unfamiliar territory with night coming on, only a lunatic would attempt an escape. The sun glinted through a gap in the trees, and he realized suddenly that sometime in the past few minutes they'd turned to the southwest, off of the direct east-west route between Huriseem and Sollas. South, to the next city in the chain? Probably. Keep the hostages away from the temptation of a rescue, while to the potential rescuers themselves you did . . . what? What did the Qasamans intend to do to the *Dewdrop*?

He looked at Joshua, saw his own fears and uncertainties reflected in the younger man's taut face. Son of a Cobra, brother of a Cobra, he understood far better than Rynstadt the limits of the *Dewdrop*'s defenses.

A measure of fear prepares the body; panic paralyzes it, his old Marine instructor's favorite aphorism echoed through York's mind. Consciously slowing his breathing, he blocked the panic and let the fear remain. When the opportunity came, he would have to be ready.

✧　　✧　　✧

The announcement that briefly penetrated the roar of static in the *Dewdrop*'s lounge was short and excruciatingly to the point: "You are suspected of spying on the people of Qasama. You will make no aggressive move or try to escape. If you disobey you will be destroyed."

The static resumed at full intensity, and Christopher spat something blasphemous. "How the *hell* did they figure it out—?"

"Shut up!" Telek snapped, her own heart a painful thudding in her ears. It had happened—her worst nightmare—and she'd failed to get the team out before the hammer fell. She'd failed. *Oh, God. What am I going to* do—?

A voice from the intercom cut into her thoughts. "Governor, I'm picking up motion and hot-spots on top of the airfield tower," Captain F'ahl said. "No clear view of any weapons or people yet; they may have something like mortars or lob-rockets that'll avoid line-of-sight exposure."

With a wrench Telek shoved the rising panic out of her way. "I understand, Captain. Can our lasers take down the entire tower?"

"Probably not—and I wouldn't even want to try until we'd gotten everyone we could back on board."

"I wasn't suggesting we start now," she said icily. So F'ahl was already preparing himself to accept team casualties. Well, she was damned if *she* was going to give up that easily. "Anything on the computer screening? Joshua's split-frequency signal is supposed to be jam-proof by ordinary—"

Without warning, the field of snow on the displays abruptly cleared, and they were back in the Qasaman bus.

Telek leaned forward, hands tightening painfully . . . but the carnage she'd half expected wasn't there. The scene was almost exactly as it had been when the signal had been cut off a scant few minutes ago . . . except that Moff was sitting facing the Aventinians with his gun drawn.

Telek groped for the mike. "Joshua, let me see the rest of the team," she called.

The scene remained unchanged. "He can't hear you," Christopher murmured. "We can clean up the signal at this end, but there's no computer equipment out there to do the same."

"Great," Telek gritted. "Which means we can't contact Almo, either. Damn it all." She stared at the display another moment, then turned to the two men standing quietly just inside the lounge door. "Well, gentlemen, it looks very much like your paid vacation is over. Suggestions?"

Michael Winward gestured toward one of the displays showing the nearby forest. "The Qasamans presumably don't know Almo's out there, which is theoretically an advantage for our side. But if we can't tell him what's going on the advantage is pretty useless. Somehow, we've got to get his attention so that he'll set up the comm laser."

"In other words, you think you should try and sneak out to him." Telek hesitated, shook her head. "No. Too risky. Even if we could come up with a diversion for you you'd probably be spotted before you could get to cover. Let's see if we can wait until the usual check-in time."

The other Cobra, Dorjay Link, glanced at Winward and shook his head minutely. "The Qasamans may be moving people and weapons into the forest to cover the *Dewdrop* from that side," he told Telek. "Almo could come down from his nest right into the middle of them."

"He'd hear or see them, though, wouldn't he?" Nnamdi spoke up.

"Cobras are human, too," Winward said tartly. "And if he doesn't even wake up until they're in position they won't be making much noise."

Telek stared at the forest display. *I'm out of my depth*, she admitted to herself. *We've gone to a military situation without a scrap of warning—*

No. They *had* had their warning; and that was what really hurt. The purpose of Moff's mysterious disappearance a few hours ago was now clear: he'd been setting up this operation, coordinating things via the still unknown, triple-damned long-range communication system of theirs. In which case—"The soldiers and guns are probably already in place out there," she said out loud. "The only way to wake Almo up and simultaneously let him know there's trouble . . ." She stopped and looked back at the two Cobras.

Winward nodded—understanding or agreement, she didn't know which. "A quick sortie. Gunfire and all that. Let me get into my camouflage suit—be back in a minute. Dorjay, start looking for my best approach, will you?"

"Sure," Link said as Winward vanished out the lounge door. "Any chance, Governor, that we can wait until full dark?"

"No," Christopher spoke up before Telek could say anything. "Governor, we've got a new problem—the contact team's not being brought back to Sollas."

"Damn." Telek stepped to his side, looked at the display that was now showing an aerial photo of the area between Sollas and Huriseem. "How do you know?"

"Joshua's been looking around a little—I saw the sun out of the side window. Looks to me like they're taking this road—" he traced it with a finger—"down to the next city southwest of here."

Telek checked the scale. "Damn. Closest approach doesn't get them under twenty kilometers from the *Dewdrop*. Where's the next connecting road?—oh, there it is. Three kilometers past that point. Any idea where on the road they are?"

Christopher spread his hands helplessly. "The range finder doesn't seem to work when the computer's mucking with the signal like this. About all I can do is estimate their speed and extrapolate from Huriseem. Looks like they're about *here*, maybe fifteen or twenty minutes from that crossroads."

Telek looked over at Justin, immobile on his coach. If she'd just let him replace his brother as they'd planned . . . but, no, she'd wanted to have her damned window to the world. "We've got to intercept that car," she said to the room in general. "Either free the team outright or try to replace Joshua. Somehow."

"With Moff on the alert I somehow doubt the latter option's open," Link said from in front of the display he'd appropriated from Nnamdi.

"I know." Telek gritted her teeth, then turned toward the intercom. "Captain, I want a pulse-laser message to the Troft backup ships right away. Tell them to get in here as fast as they can."

"Yes, Governor."

And it'll do no good at all. She knew it, and everyone aboard knew it. The Troft ships were too far away even to make orbit before dawn. The *Dewdrop* was on her own.

Which meant that Winward would have to make his suicide sortie in a few minutes . . . and Almo still had an even chance of getting caught before he knew what was happening . . . and it was all futility anyway, because there was no way a Cobra or even two could ambush that bus without killing or injuring everyone aboard in the ensuing firefight.

The inescapable conclusion was that it would be better to lift off now, hoping the *Dewdrop* would have the necessary speed to escape the Qasamans' shells or rockets.

To cut their losses. And if that was to be the decision, it had to be made before Winward went outside to sacrifice his life. Which meant within the next ninety seconds.

A no-win situation . . . and even as she wondered what she was going to do, there was a slight movement in the forest far to the south of them, and an invisible laser beam lanced out, catching the *Dewdrop* squarely in the nose.

Chapter 16

For a long moment Pyre lay quietly in his hammock bag, wondering what had awakened him. The level of sunlight filtering through the trees indicated sundown was approaching. He'd slept the whole day away, he realized, guilt twinging at him. Probably woke up simply because his body had had all the rest it needed; he must have been a lot more tired than he'd thought.

He was just starting to pull his arms out of the bag when he heard the muffled cough.

He froze, notching his auditory enhancers to full power. The normal rustlings of the forest roared in his ears . . . the normal rustlings, and the fainter sound of quiet human voices. Ten or more of them, at the least.

Hunting party? was his first, hopeful thought. But he heard no footsteps accompanying the voices, just the occasional sounds of someone easing from one position to another. Even stalking hunters moved around more . . . which implied that his unexpected guests were less akin to hunters than to fishermen.

And there were only two fish out here worth such a concerted effort, at least as far as he knew: the *Dewdrop* and himself.

Damn.

Slowly, moving with infinite care and silence, he began disentangling himself from the hammock bag and the defense cage. If they were looking for him the activity could well be a mistake; but whether it brought them down on him or not, he had no intention of getting caught wrapped up like yesterday's leftovers. The cage creaked like a tacnuke explosion as he opened it, but no one seemed to notice, and a minute later he was standing above the hammock bag with his back pressed against the tree trunk.

And the prey was now ready to become the hunter. The voices had come from the strip of forest between him and the *Dewdrop*; moving to the far side of the trunk he started down, pausing at each branch to look and listen.

He reached the ground without seeing any of the hidden Qasamans, but further noises had given him a better idea of their arrangement and he wasn't surprised to have avoided drawing fire. They seemed to be paralleling the edge of the forest nearest the *Dewdrop*, their attention and weaponry almost certainly focused on the ship. And to have been set up *now*, an entire week after the landing, implied something had gone wrong. Whether the contact team had gumfricked up or the exaggerated Qasaman paranoia had finally asserted itself hardly mattered at this point. What mattered—

What mattered was that Joshua Moreau was out there in the middle of it. And if he'd been killed while Pyre overslept—

The Cobra bit down hard on the inside of his cheek. *Stop it!* he snarled. *Settle down and* think *instead of panicking.* The fact that the Qasamans had not yet openly attacked the *Dewdrop* implied they were still in the planning stages here . . . and if so, then chances were Joshua and the others were still okay. Moving against the contact team would tip off the *Dewdrop*, and the Qasamans were surely smart enough to avoid doing that.

And with the ship and Cerenkov both unaware that anything was wrong, it was all up to Pyre now.

He didn't have a lot of options. His emergency earphone was a one-way device, with no provision for talking to the ship. His comm laser was well hidden and probably undiscovered, but if the Qasaman cordon line wasn't sitting on top of it they weren't far off. Take out the whole bunch of them? Risky, possibly suicidal, and almost certain to run the timer to zero right there and then.

But if the members of the cordon weren't in actual visual contact with each other, it might be possible to quietly take out the one or two closest to his laser without alerting all the others. Grab the laser, back off to somewhere safe—the top of a tree, if necessary— and call the ship. Together they might be able to figure out a way to snatch the contact team from under Moff's nose.

Mindful of the crunchy forest mat underfoot, Pyre set off cautiously toward the laser's hiding place, trying to watch all directions at once. He was, he estimated, only five meters from his goal when a sudden roar erupted from beside him.

He was halfway through his sideways leap before his brain caught

up with his reflexes and identified the sound: his emergency earphone was screaming with static. He twisted it out and thumbed
it off in a single motion, and as the echo of it bounced for another
second around his head he realized with a sinking feeling that he
was too late. Static at that intensity could mean only that the
Qasamans were attempting to jam all radio communications in
the area. They were making their move—

"*Gif!*" a voice hissed.

Pyre froze, his eyes shifting between the two Qasamans crouched
facing him from half-concealed positions. The pistols pointed his
way seemed larger than those he'd seen others wearing; the mojos
with their wings poised for flight were certainly more alert. One
of the men muttered something to his companion and stepped
toward Pyre, gun steady on the Cobra's chest.

There was no time to consider the full implications of his
actions, no consideration beyond getting out of this without
bringing the rest of the troops down on him. Clearly, his captors
still hoped to keep their presence secret from the *Dewdrop*; just
as clearly, they'd lose that preference once he made his own move.
His first attack would have to be fast and clean.

Pyre had never killed a human being before. His closest brush
with such a thing had been on that awful day long ago when Jonny
Moreau and a man apparently returned from the dead shot down
Challinor's fledgling Cobra warlords in two or three seconds of
the most terrifying display of laser fire he'd ever seen, then or since.
For a teenaged boy on a struggling colony world such a slaughter had been the stuff of nightmares—particularly as the knowledge of his own early support of Challinor carried with it a small
but leaden piece of the responsibility for the deaths. The last thing
he wanted to do was to add more deaths to that weight between
his shoulders.

But he had no choice. None at all. His sonic weapons could stun
men at this range, but not for long enough . . . and the necessary
frequencies were unlikely to be effective on the two mojos. All of
them had to be silenced before any of them—human or mojo—
could screech out a warning.

The leading man was barely two meters away now, properly staying out of his partner's line of fire. Four instants of eye contact to
give his nanocomputer its targets; the gentle pressure of tongue
against the roof of his mouth to key automatic fire control . . . and
as the Qasaman opened his mouth to speak Pyre fired.

His little fingers spat laser bursts, arms and wrists shifting in response to the computer-directed servos within them. Like all his Cobra reflexes, this one was incredibly fast, and it was all over almost before he had a chance to wince.

That wasn't so hard, he thought, dropping to a crouch as he waited to see if the quiet crash of falling bodies would draw attention. *Not too hard at all.* And his eyes strayed to the corpse which had landed almost beside him and the head where the laser burn would be, though the undergrowth was hiding it, and the mojo who had died so quickly its talons still gripped its epaulet perch, and he began to tremble violently and tried hard not to throw up.

He waited for nearly half a minute, until the worst of the muscle spasms had subsided and the taste of bile had left his mouth, before resuming his cautious move forward. With no buzzing earphone to startle him this time, he made it the rest of the way to his laser without attracting attention. Once, as he was pulling the device from concealment, he saw another Qasaman; but the other was looking another way and Pyre was able to complete his task without being spotted.

Moving deeper into the forest, he headed south, hoping the Qasamans hadn't lined the whole damned forest with soldiers. If they had, he might have to climb a tree to contact the ship, after all.

But their exaggerated caution hadn't carried them to quite that length. A hundred meters from his laser's hiding place the silent cordon line ended; Pyre went another fifty and then pushed his way cautiously to the edge. A convenient bush allowed him to get a clear shot at the *Dewdrop*'s nose without exposing himself to direct view of the airfield control tower. Flat on his stomach, he set up the laser as quickly as he could and aimed it toward where he thought the bow sensor cluster was located. Crossing his fingers, he flipped it on. "Pyre here," he murmured into the mike. "Come in; anyone."

There was no response. He waited a few seconds, then shifted his aim fractionally and tried again. Still nothing. *My God—have they somehow taken everyone out already?* He searched the hull for signs of damage. Gas, perhaps, or sonics that could have penetrated without harming the ship itself? The taste of fear starting to well up into his throat, he again adjusted his aim—

"—*in,* Almo; are you there? *Almo?*"

Pyre's body sagged with relief. "I'm here, Governor. Phew. I thought something had happened to all of you."

"Yeah, well, it's about to," Telek said grimly. "Somehow they've tumbled to the fact that we're a spy mission, and it's probably a tossup as to whether they try and board us or take the safer way out and just blow us up."

"Any word from the contact team?" Pyre asked, forcing his voice to remain steady.

"Moff still has them on the bus, and so far they seem okay. They're being taken somewhere besides Sollas, though, probably the next city down. We were hoping you'd have a chance of intercepting them before they got too far away, assuming we could contact you in time."

"And?"

Telek hesitated. "Well . . . we estimate the bus will be passing the main road heading south from Sollas in ten or fifteen minutes. But that's twenty-plus kilometers from us—"

"How many Qasamans aboard?" he cut her off harshly.

"The usual six-man escort," she told him. "Plus their mojos. But even if you could get there in time I don't know how you'd get them out safely."

"I'll find a way. Just don't lift until I get back here with them . . . or until it's clear I'm not going to make it back at all."

He broke the connection without waiting to hear her reply and began crawling backwards from his concealing bush toward the protection of the forest, leaving the comm laser deployed for possible future use. Twenty kilometers in ten minutes. Hopeless even if he'd had clean ground to run on instead of a forest . . . but maybe the Qasamans would outsmart themselves on this one. Six guards in an ordinary bus was a fairly loose setup, even with the mojos and against four unarmed prisoners. In their place Pyre would transfer the Aventinians to a safer vehicle at the first opportunity . . . and to his way of thinking the crossroads to the south would be the ideal spot for such a switch.

And if his guess proved correct the whole party would be there for a few extra minutes. Long enough, perhaps, for Pyre to get there too.

At which point he'd have to face not only the busload of Qasamans but also whatever troops they'd assembled for the transfer. But there was nothing he could do about that. It was time for Almo Pyre, Cobra, to become what his implanted equipment had always intended him to be. Not a hunter, spy, nor even a killer of Aventinian spine leopards.

But a warrior.

Setting off at the fastest run the forest permitted, he headed south. It was all up to him now.

It was all up to him now.

York took a quiet breath, using his Marine biofeedback techniques to relax his muscles and nerves and to prepare him for action. To the right and slightly ahead he could see the buildings of Sollas silhouetted against the darkening sky, and if he remembered the aerial maps correctly they were now about as close to the city as this road got. It was time to make his attempt . . . and to find out just how deadly these mojos were.

His pen and ring were already resting casually in his left hand. Easing his calculator-watch off his left wrist, he fit the pen through its band, making sure the contacts were wedged solidly together. The ring slid onto the pen's clip to its own slot, and the palm-mate was ready. The arming sequence was three keystrokes on the calculator.

Wrapping the watchband into position around his right palm, he raised his hand over the back of the seat in front of him. Moff had given up his guard duty to one of the others a few kilometers back, but the Qasaman's attention was on Rynstadt and Joshua at the moment. *I get one free shot,* York reminded himself distantly; and bringing the pen to bear on the guard, he squeezed the trigger.

The Qasaman jerked as the tiny dart buried itself deep in his cheek, his gun swinging wildly in reflexive search for a target. Reflexive but useless; already his eyes were beginning to glaze as the potent mix of neurotoxins took effect. York shifted his aim to the mojo on the dying man's shoulder and a second dart found its target . . . but as he brought the palm-mate to bear on Moff's mojo all hell broke loose.

They were smart all right, those birds. The dead Qasaman hadn't even fallen to the floor before the remaining five mojos were in the air, sweeping toward him like silver-blue Furies. He got off two more shots, but neither connected—and then they were on him, talons digging into his face and gun arm and slamming him hard into the seat. Through the haze of agony he could dimly hear screams from Rynstadt and the incomprehensible shouts of the Qasamans. Mojo wings slapped at his eyes, blinding him, but he didn't need his sight to know that his right forearm was being flayed, his right hand torn by beaks and talons as the mojos fought single-mindedly to get the palm-mate away from him. But it was wrapped firmly around his open hand, caught there though the will to hold it had long since vanished. His arm was on fire—wave after wave of agony screaming into his brain—and then suddenly the birds were gone, fluttering away to squawk at him from seat backs and Qasaman shoulders, and he saw what they'd done to his arm—

And the emotional shock combined with the physical shock . . . and Decker York, who had seen men injured and killed on five other worlds, dropped like a stone into the temporary sanctuary of unconsciousness.

His last thought before the blackness took him was that he would never wake up.

"Oh, my God," Christopher whispered. "My *God.*"

Telek bit hard into the knuckles of her right hand, curled into an impotent fist at her mouth. York's arm. . . . She willed her eyes to turn away, but they were as tightly frozen to the scene as Joshua's own eyes were. Like a violent, haphazard dissection of York's arm—except that York was still alive. For now.

Beside her, Nnamdi gagged and fled the room. She hardly noticed.

It seemed like forever, but it was probably only a few seconds before Rynstadt was at York's side, a small can of seal-spray from his landing kit clutched in his shaking hand. He sprayed it on York's arm, sloppily and with an amateur's lack of uniformity; but by the time the can hissed itself dry Cerenkov had broken his own paralysis and moved in with a fresh can. Together they managed to seal off the worst of the blood flow.

Through it all Joshua never budged. *Terrified out of his mind,* Telek thought. *What a thing for a kid to see!*

"Governor?" F'ahl's voice from the intercom made her jump. "Will he live?"

She hesitated, With the blood loss stopped and the seal-spray's anti-shock factors supporting York's system . . . but she knew better than to give even herself false hope. "Not a chance," she told F'ahl quietly. "He needs the *Dewdrop*'s medical facilities within an hour or less."

"Almo—"

"Might be able to get him here in time. But he won't. If he tries he'll just get himself killed, too." The words burned in her mouth, but she knew they were true. With the Qasamans and their birds jarred out of any overconfidence they might have had, Pyre wouldn't get within ten meters of the bus. But he would try anyway. . . .

And now there *was* no other choice. "Captain, prepare the *Dewdrop* for lift," she said, her eyes straying at last from the display, only to stop on Justin lying in his couch. His fists, too, were clenched, but if he recognized she had just condemned his brother to death he didn't show it. "We'll try to take out as much of the tower and forest weaponry before we go and hope the ship can absorb whatever we don't destroy."

"Understood, Governor."

Telek turned to the lounge doorway, where Winward and Link were standing, their faces pale and grim. "We won't be able to get it all from here," she told them quietly.

"Already figured that out," Winward grunted. "When do you want us to head out?"

The pre-launch sequence would take at least ten minutes. "About fifteen minutes," she said.

Winward nodded. "We'll get geared up." Together the two Cobras turned and left.

"Full survival packs," Telek called after them.

"Sure," the reply drifted back along the corridor.

But she wasn't fooling anyone, and they all knew it. Even if the two Cobras lived through the coming battle, there was virtually no chance the *Dewdrop* would be able to come back and pick them up. Assuming the *Dewdrop* survived its own gauntlet.

Well, they'd find out about that in half an hour or less. Until then—

Until then, there'd be enough time to watch Pyre die in his rescue attempt.

Because it was her duty to do so, Telek turned her attention back to the displays. But the taste of defeat was bitter in her throat, and she felt very, very old.

Chapter 17

Joshua's heart was a painful thundering in his throat, his eyes blurred by tears of fear and sympathetic pain. Hidden from sight by the white crust of the seal-spray, York's terrible arm injuries were burned into Joshua's memory as if the vision would be there forever. *Oh, God, Decker,* he mouthed. *Decker!*

And he'd done nothing to help. Not during York's escape attempt nor even afterwards. Rynstadt and Cerenkov had jumped in with their medical kits; but Joshua, terrified of the Qasamans and mojos, hadn't twitched a muscle to assist them. If it'd been up to him, York would've quietly bled to death.

People expect great things from us. He felt like a child. A cowardly child.

"We've got to get him back to the ship," Cerenkov murmured, raising a blood-stained arm to wipe at his cheek. "He's going to need transfusions and God only knows what else."

Rynstadt muttered something in response, too low for Joshua to hear. Lifting his gaze finally from the carnage, Joshua looked up toward the front of the bus to see Moff watching them, his gun braced and ready on the nearest seat back. The bus had sped up, Joshua noted mechanically, and ahead in the gloom he could see a cluster of dim lights. An unwalled village or crossroads checkpoint? Joshua guessed the latter. A half dozen vehicles were faintly visible, as was a small shed-like building.

And milling among them a *lot* of Qasamans.

The bus came to a halt among the cluster of vehicles. It had barely stopped before a burly Qasaman had the door open and had bounded inside. He exchanged a half-dozen rapid-fire sentences with Moff, then looked at the Aventinians. "*Bachuts!*" he snapped, hand jabbing emphatically toward the door.

"Yuri?" Rynstadt murmured.

"Of course," Cerenkov said bitterly. "What choice do we have?"

Leaving York propped up against the seat, they stepped past the newcomer and out the door. Joshua followed, his stomach a churning cauldron of painful emotions.

Four more heavily armed men were waiting in a semicircle around the bus door. With them was a wizened old man with stooped shoulders and the last remnants of white hair plastered down over his balding head. But his eyes were bright—disturbingly bright—and it was he who addressed the three prisoners. "You are accused of spying on the world Qasama," he said, his words heavily accented but clear enough. "Your companion York is also accused of killing a Qasaman and a mojo. Any further attempts at violence will be punished by immediate death. You will now come with your escort to a place for questions."

"What about our friend?" Cerenkov nodded back toward the bus. "He needs medical attention immediately if he's to live."

The old man spoke to the apparent leader of the new escort, was answered in biting tones. "He will be treated here," the old man told Cerenkov. "If he dies, that is merely his just punishment for his crime. You will come now."

Joshua took a deep breath. "No," he said firmly. "Our friend will be taken back to our ship. Now. Otherwise we will all die without answering a single question."

The old man translated, and the escort leader's brow darkened as he spat a reply. "You are not in a position to make any demands," the old man said.

"You are wrong," Joshua said as calmly as his tongue could manage, the vision of York's flaying superimposed on the scene around him. If his bluff was called . . . and even as he slowly raised his left fist he knew he was indeed a coward. The thought of such a fate made his stomach violently ill . . . but this had to be tried. "This device on my wrist is a self-destruct—a one-man bomb," he told the old man. "If I unclench my fist without turning it off I will be blown to dust. Along with all of you. I will give you the device only when I have personally escorted Decker into our ship."

A long, brittle silence followed the translation. "You continue to think us fools," the leader said at last through the old man. "You enter the ship and you will not return."

Joshua shook his head minutely. "No. I *will* return."

The leader spat; but before he could speak again Moff stepped to his side and whispered into his ear. The leader frowned at him for a moment; then, pursing his lips, he gave a brisk nod and spoke to one of his men. The other disappeared into the darkness, and Moff turned to the old man, again speaking too quietly for Joshua to hear. The other nodded. "Moff has agreed to your request, as a gesture of goodwill, on one condition: you will wear an explosive device around your neck until you emerge from the ship. Should you remain inside for more than three minutes it will be allowed to explode."

Joshua's throat tightened involuntarily, and for a handful of heartbeats thoughts of betrayal and treachery swirled like a dark liquid through the cautious hope rising in his brain. Surely there were simpler ways of killing him if the Qasamans so chose . . . but if they wanted to make sure the *Dewdrop* never lifted again, there would be no easier way to penetrate the outer hull. But that might lose them the secret of the stardrive—but they might not care—but if he didn't take the risk York was dead—but why would they have any interest in a good-faith gesture when they held all the cards—

He focused at last on Cerenkov and Rynstadt, who were watching him in turn. "What do I do?" he whispered from amid the turmoil.

Cerenkov shrugged fractionally. "It's *your* life that's at stake. You'll have to use your own best judgment."

His life . . . except that it wasn't, Joshua suddenly realized. Together, the three of them had no chance at all of being rescued . . . but Cerenkov and Rynstadt plus Justin might just be able to break the odds.

It was *all* of their lives at stake here. Corwin's plan—the reason the Moreaus were here at all—and the whole thing was in Joshua's trembling hands. "All right," he said to the old man. "It's a deal."

The old man translated; and the leader began to give orders.

The next few minutes went quickly. Cerenkov and Rynstadt were taken to another, obviously armored, bus and were driven off into the darkness along their original southwest road. York, still unconscious, was transferred by hand stretcher to a second armored vehicle. Joshua, Moff, and the translator joined him. As they rumbled northward toward Sollas and the *Dewdrop* one of the escort carefully fitted Joshua with his explosive collar.

It was a simple device, consisting of two squat cylinders at the sides of his neck fastened together by a soft but tough-feeling plastic band about three centimeters wide and a couple of millimeters thick. It seemed to make breathing difficult . . . but perhaps that was just his imagination. Licking his lips frequently, he tried not to swallow too often and forced his mind to concentrate instead on York's condition and chances.

All too soon, they had arrived.

The bus coasted to a halt some fifty or sixty meters from the *Dewdrop*'s main hatch. Two Qasamans unloaded a rolling table and placed York's stretcher on top of it, returning then to the vehicle. Moff motioned Joshua to stand and held a small box up to each of the cylinders around the Aventinian's neck. Joshua heard two faint clicks; felt, rather than heard, the faint vibration from within. "Three minutes only—remember," Moff said in passable Anglic, looking the younger man in the eye.

Joshua licked his lips and nodded. "I'll be back."

The trip to the ship seemed to take a lifetime, torn as he was between the need for haste and the opposite need to give York as smooth a ride as possible. He settled for a slow jog, praying fervently that someone would be watching and be ready to pop the hatch for him . . . and that he could explain all of this fast enough . . . and that they'd be able to switch the collar in the time allotted. . . .

He was two steps from the hatch when it opened, one of F'ahl's crewers stepping out to grip the front stretcher handles. Seconds later they were inside, with Christopher, Winward, and Link waiting for them in the ready room.

"Sit down," Christopher snapped tightly as someone took Joshua's half of the stretcher.

Joshua's knees needed no urging, dropping him like a lump of clay into the indicated chair. "This thing on my neck—"

"Is a bomb," Christopher finished for him. Already the other was tracing the strap with a small sensor, his forehead shiny with perspiration. "We know—they weren't able to jam your signal. Now sit tight and we'll see if we can get the damn thing off without triggering it."

Joshua gritted his teeth and fell silent; and as he did so Justin entered the room, clad only in his underwear. For a moment the twins gazed at each other . . . and the expression on Justin's face sent half the weight resting on Joshua's shoulders spinning away into oblivion. They weren't in the clear yet—not by a long shot—but there was a satisfaction in Justin's eyes that said Joshua had done his job well, had made the decisions that gave them all a chance.

Justin was proud of him . . . and, ultimately, that was what really mattered.

The moment passed; and, kneeling before his brother, Justin began to remove Joshua's boots. Joshua unfastened his own belt and slid off his pants, and he was beginning to work on his tunic when Christopher gave a little snort. "All right, here it is. Let's see . . . bypass *here* and *here*. Dorjay?"

Joshua felt something cool slide between the collar and his neck. "Hold still," Link muttered from behind him. There was the soft crackle of heat-stressed plastic . . . and suddenly the pressure on his throat eased, and Winward lifted the broken ring over his head. "Out of the chair," Link said tersely. "Justin?"

Joshua's place was taken by his brother, and the collar lowered carefully around Justin's neck. "Time?" Christopher asked as the Cobras eased the two broken ends back together and began the ticklish job of reconnecting them.

"Ninety seconds," F'ahl's voice came over the room intercom. "Plenty of time."

"Sure," Link growled under his breath. "Come down *here* and say that. *Easy,* Michael."

Joshua got his tunic and watch off and waited, heart thudding full blast again as he watched Christopher and the Cobras work. If they weren't able to do it in time—

"Okay," Christopher announced suddenly. "Looks good. Here go the bypasses. . . ."

The wires came off, and the cylinders remained solid. Cautiously, Justin stood up and reached for Joshua's tunic, and by the time Christopher had eased the protective ring out from under the collar he was nearly dressed. "I don't know where Yuri and Marck were taken," Joshua told him as he fastened on the other's watch.

"I know that," Justin nodded. "I *was* you, remember."

"Yeah. I just meant—be careful, okay?"

Justin gave him a tight smile. "I'll be fine, Joshua—don't worry about me. The Moreau luck goes with me."

He slipped out the hatch, and Joshua collapsed back into the chair as the shock of all that had happened finally caught up with him and his legs turned to rubber. *The Moreau luck. Great. Just great.* And the worst part of it was that Justin really *believed* in his imaginary immunity. Believed in it, acted on it . . . and while Joshua sat idly by in the *Dewdrop*'s relative safety, his brother's superstition could easily get him killed.

"Damn them," he hissed at the universe in general—at Moff and the Qasamans; the Cobra Worlds' Council, who'd sent them; even his own brother Corwin, whose idea this had ultimately been. "Damn all of them."

A hand fell on his shoulder. Looking up through eyes suddenly tear-blurred, he saw Link standing over him. "Come on," the Cobra said. "Captain F'ahl and Governor Telek are going to want to hear your analysis of the situation out there."

Sure they are, Joshua thought bitterly. The sole value such a report could have would be to keep his mind too busy to dwell on Justin. But he merely nodded and got to his feet. He was too tired to argue . . . and, actually, some distraction might not be a bad idea right now.

He took a moment to stop by his stateroom first and get dressed, letting Link go on ahead without him. York was nowhere in sight when he finally reached the lounge, but Telek allayed his worst fears before he was able to voice them. "Decker's stable, at least for now," she said, glancing up at him before returning her gaze to the outside monitor display. "Monitors and I.V.s are all hooked up; he'll be all right until we can figure out what to do about his arm."

Translation: where exactly it'll need to be amputated. Swallowing the thought, Joshua stepped behind Telek and looked over her shoulder. Moff and Justin were just getting back into the armored bus. The explosive collar, he noted with marginal easing of tension, had been removed, as had the "self-destruct" watch with which he'd bluffed the Qasamans. "What's he supposed to do now?" he asked Telek. "I mean, you *did* give him some sort of plan to follow, didn't you?"

"As much of a plan as we could come up with," Winward grunted from another display. "We're assuming he'll be taken to wherever they've got Yuri and Marck. Once he's inside—well, we're hoping Almo will have followed the other two when they headed south. With Cobras inside and outside, they should be able to break out of wherever the Qasamans put them."

"Almo was going to follow us?"

"He was going to try. If he didn't get down to the crossroads in time—" Winward shrugged fractionally. "We'll hope he'll follow the road and try to catch up. It's the only logical thing for him to do."

Follow the road . . . except that he wouldn't know Moff would be bringing a second vehicle up from behind. Joshua shivered at the vision of Pyre caught, alone, between two carloads of armed Qasamans and mojos. And with the radios still jammed there was no way to alert him to the potential pincer closing on him.

Telek leaned back in her seat, exhaling a hissing sigh. "Well, that's it, gentlemen," she said. "We've done everything we can for the moment for Yuri and Marck. Next job, then, is to figure out how to deactivate the defenses around the *Dewdrop* so that they've got a ship to come back to. Let's get busy on that one, shall we?"

The armored bus sped past Pyre's place of concealment. Though the windows were small and dark his enhanced vision enabled him to identify two of its occupants: Moff, and the same driver who'd earlier taken the vehicle toward Sollas with Joshua and an apparently injured Decker York aboard. It was back now, following the same road Cerenkov and Rynstadt had taken a half hour or so ago. And the major question of the hour: who exactly was in there?

Pyre rubbed a hand across his forehead, smearing the sweat and dirt there as he tried to think. *York, Joshua,* and *Moff head toward Sollas; Moff, at least, heads away shortly thereafter.* Had they decided to split up the contact team, with Cerenkov and Rynstadt stashed away down south while York and Joshua were hidden in Sollas? Possible; but given the lengths the Qasamans had gone to to keep their prisoners as far away as possible from the *Dewdrop* it didn't seem likely. Had they taken York to the nearest hospital to treat what had looked to be one double hell of an arm injury? But then why take Joshua along?

The sounds of the bus were fading away down the road. If he was going to follow it, he had to make that decision fast.

When he'd first dashed off through the forest on this crazy rescue attempt the question hadn't even been a debatable one. But since then he'd had time to think it all through . . . and though it wrenched his soul to admit it, he knew he'd gotten his priorities scrambled.

The contact team was, at least from a purely military standpoint, expendable. The *Dewdrop,* with all the data they'd collected about Qasama, was not.

The *Dewdrop* had to be freed . . . and three-quarters of her Cobra fighting force was still trapped inside.

To the southwest, the sounds of the bus had vanished into the forest. Notching his optical sensors up against the darkness, Pyre began circling cautiously around the vehicles and men that still straddled the crossroads. He could stay within the relative cover of the forest for a few kilometers, but long before he got to the airfield area he would have to move into the city proper if he wanted any chance of approaching the Qasamans' tower defenses undetected. The contact team had spent little time on the streets of Sollas at night—and none of it near the edges of the city. Pyre had no idea what sort of crowd level he'd have to get through once he left the forest. If he could steal some Qasaman clothing... but he couldn't speak word one of their language; and he would at any rate be instantly conspicuous by his lack of a mojo companion.

The crossroads, he judged, were far enough behind him now to risk a little noise. Senses alert for forest predators as well as wandering Qasamans, he broke into a brisk jog. Whatever he came up with, the inspiration had better come fast. In five minutes, ten at the most, Sollas was going to play host to its first Cobra.

Chapter 18

Joshua's implanted sensors were reputed to be the best the Cobra Worlds had available; but sitting in a bouncing vehicle across from a man he'd seen almost constantly for a week, Justin recognized with an unpleasant shock just how limited his piggybacked experience of Qasama had really been. The texture of the seat where his hands rested on it—the odd paving of the road as transmitted by the bus's vibration—above all the tangy and exotic scents filling the air around him—it was as if he'd stepped into a painting and found that the world it depicted was real.

And the whole effect made him nervous. He was supposed to be an undetectable substitute for his brother, and instead was feeling like the new kid on the block. All he needed now was for Moff to pick up that something was off-color here and bury him a hundred kilometers from Cerenkov and Rynstadt while the Qasamans figured out what was going on.

When your defense stinks, attack. "I must say, Moff," he remarked, "that you people are nothing short of astonishing at learning new languages. How long have you been able to speak Anglic?"

Moff's eyes flicked to the old man two seats down, who let loose with a stream of Qasaman. Moff replied in kind, and the translator turned back to Justin. "*We* will ask the questions today," he said. "It will be *your* position to answer them."

Justin snorted. "Come on, Moff—it's hardly a secret anymore. Not with your friend here speaking as well as I do. And you said something to me yourself, right after you switched on the little insurance policy you had around my neck. So come on—how did all of you learn it so fast?"

He kept a surreptitious eye on the old man as he spoke, watching for hesitations with words or grammar. But if the other had any trouble, it wasn't obvious. Moff eyed Justin for a moment after the translator finished, then said something in a thoughtful tone that the Cobra didn't care for even before he heard the old man's version: "You seem to have regained some of your courage. What did those aboard your ship say to strengthen you so?"

"They reminded me of what your planetary superiors will say when they're informed how you have threatened a peaceful diplomatic mission," Justin shot back.

"Oh?" Moff said through the translator. "Perhaps. We shall soon see if that, too, is one of your lies. By the time we have reached Purma, or perhaps even before."

"I resent the implication I would lie to you."

"Resent it if you wish. But the cylinders you wore into your ship will show the truth of the matter."

Justin felt his mouth go dry. "What do you mean?" he asked, hoping his sudden horrible suspicion was wrong.

It wasn't. "The cylinders contained cameras and sound recording devices," the translator said. "We hoped to get a first approximation of the situation and number of personnel aboard."

And smack dab in the middle of the tape would be that free and unexpected bonus, the Moreau twin switch. And when they saw *that*—"A fat lot of good it'll do you," he snorted, putting as much scorn into his voice as he could scrape together. "We told no lies about our ship or people. What are you expecting— hundreds of armored soldiers squeezed into that little thing?"

Moff waited for the translation and then shrugged. *Apparently really* doesn't *understand Anglic*, Justin decided as the two Qasamans held a brief discussion. *Just learned that one phrase to emphasize the three-minute limit, probably. And we fell for it like primitives. Stupid, stupid, stupid.*

"We shall see what is there," the old man said. "Perhaps it will help us decide what should be done with all of you."

I'll just bet it will, Justin thought, but remained silent. Moff settled back in his seat, indicating the conversation was over for the moment . . . and Justin tried to get his brain on-line.

All right. First off, the spy cameras probably weren't transmitting a live picture from the *Dewdrop*—the Qasamans would've had to open up part of their radio jamming, and an action of that sort might have been detected. So Moff and company didn't yet know about the Moreau switch, an ignorance they would keep until those back in Sollas found out themselves and were able to blow the whistle. The jamming meant Justin was safe enough while the bus was still on the road. If he made his move before they reached the next city—Purma, had Moff called it?—he'd take them totally by surprise . . .

And would then have to search the whole city for Cerenkov and Rynstadt.

Justin grimaced. He *could* afford not knowing where the others were being kept, but only if Pyre had followed their bus instead of waiting for Justin's. There was no way of knowing which option the other Cobra had taken, and Justin didn't dare gamble on it. He would just have to let them take him to the other prisoners, hope he could take out all the additional guards and mojos that would undoubtedly be present—

And pray the bus didn't stop outside of town at a checkpoint with long-range communications capability.

Damn. If they did *that* then all bets were instantly off. Moff was being pretty casual about his prisoner, but that was surely based on a week's worth of observation of Joshua's character and reactions. If he found out he had someone else he was bound to react with a tighter leash . . . and there were ways to render even a Cobra helpless.

Through the window ahead the bus's headlights showed nothing but road and flanking forest. No city lights yet . . . Carefully, methodically, Justin activated his multiple-targeting lock and sequentially locked onto all the mojos in the vehicle. Just in case.

Easing back into his seat, he watched the road ahead and kept his hands well clear of any possible obstructions. And tried to relax.

"What do you suppose is keeping them?" Rynstadt asked quietly from the lightweight table in the middle of their cell.

Standing at the barred window, Cerenkov automatically glanced at his bare wrist, dropping it back to his side with an embarrassed snort. All jewelry had been taken from them immediately after they left the Sollas crossroads—fallout, obviously, from York's gun and Joshua's "self-destruct" bluff. For Cerenkov, not knowing the time could be a major annoyance at the best of times; under the present circumstances, it was an excruciating form of subtle torture. "It may not mean anything yet," he told Rynstadt. "We haven't been here all that long ourselves, and if transferring Decker to the ship took longer than expected Moff and Joshua may still not be overdue."

"And if—" Rynstadt let the sentence die. "Yeah, maybe you're right," he said instead. "Moff would undoubtedly want to be here before they start this silly questioning."

Cerenkov nodded, feeling frustration welling up within him at having to stifle the thoughts clearly uppermost in both their minds. Such as whether York had really been allowed back into the *Dewdrop* ... and whether it would be Joshua or Justin who would soon be joining them in their cell. But after the old man at the crossroads Cerenkov had no intention of assuming none of the guards lined up against the cell wall understood Anglic.

And so he kept his thoughts and speculations to himself. But time *was* dragging on ... and as the minutes slowly added up he began to feel as if he and Rynstadt were standing on a sheet of rapidly thawing ice. If Justin had been forced to take premature action, that would also explain the delay ... and it would leave the two of them in a dead-end position here.

Outside, a flicker of light caught Cerenkov's eye, off toward the right. Pressing the side of his face to the glass, he could just see what appeared to be another of the armored vehicles he and Rynstadt had arrived in. A handful of figures stepped to the door. "Looks like they're here," he announced over his shoulder, striving for calm. Now the *real* fun would begin ... especially since they wouldn't know themselves which twin they had until he took some sort of action. That would be tricky; he didn't want to get caught flatfooted in a crossfire, but neither did he want to be poised on tiptoe waiting expectantly for the order to hit the floor. Moff or one of the guards might pick up on something like that—

The thought froze in place. The bus was pulling away from the building, its welcoming committee heading back inside ... but no one else was with them.

An empty bus? was his first, hopeful guess ... but he didn't believe it for even a moment. The vehicle was speeding up now, heading further into the city ... and deep within him, Cerenkov knew Moff and Justin were aboard it. Something had gone wrong. Badly enough wrong that the prisoners were being split up, apparently on the spur of the moment.

And Cerenkov and Rynstadt were in their own private hole. A very deep private hole.

Slowly, he turned away from the window. "Well?" Rynstadt demanded.

"False alarm," Cerenkov murmured. "It wasn't them."

✧　　✧　　✧

Justin watched the tall building disappear from view through the window as the bus picked up speed, muscles tight with adrenaline and the sinking certainty that the game was, in one sense or another, over. Moff could pretend all he liked that they'd stopped only for information from Sollas; but Justin had been watching the driver as Moff consulted with the men from the building, and it was clear that he'd been taken by surprise by the order to move on. Almost certainly Cerenkov and Rynstadt were somewhere in that structure behind them. Moff's studied casualness merely underscored the fact that they wanted Justin to attach no special significance to the place.

So they knew. The films had been seen, word had been flashed south from Sollas, and Moff was taking him somewhere high-security for a long talk and probably some careful study as well. Justin had to act fast, to kill or disable everyone aboard and escape before the Qasamans figured out exactly what to do with him.

He had his omnidirectional sonic tuned to the optimum human stun frequency and was on the verge of triggering it when a sudden, sobering thought struck him.

No matter how he did this, it was going to be obvious to whoever examined the bus afterwards that the attack had come from inside the vehicle. From *inside* . . . from a man who'd already been searched and stripped of anything that could possibly be a weapon.

A cold sweat broke out on Justin's forehead. What would the Qasamans make of such a conclusion? Could they possibly deduce the truth?—or even get close enough as made no difference? The question had little relevance to the immediate situation, of course— the *Dewdrop* would hopefully be long gone by the time the local experts began sifting through the debris. But if the Council decided to take on the Trofts' mercenary job here, such forewarning could give Qasama an edge against the arriving Cobras.

But what were his options? Shoot up the bus thoroughly from the outside after escaping, hoping he could do a convincing enough job of it? Or wait until he was taken some place where the existence of an armed infiltrator would at least be possible? Or even probable—Pyre was out here somewhere, and he clearly hadn't taken out the other prison building. Perhaps he'd arrived late at the crossroads and was even now tailing Justin's bus.

Moff was saying something. Justin turned to look at him as the old man translated: "At least I now understand your changed attitude when you emerged from your ship."

For a second Justin considered playing dumb, decided it wasn't worth the effort. "That three-minute limit was the key," he said calmly. "Any longer than that and we might have picked up on what those cylinders really were."

Moff nodded at the translation. "Our experts felt two and a half minutes safer, but I didn't want to have to take you close enough for that limit to seem reasonable. I didn't know then that your people were still monitoring you and wouldn't misunderstand our approach." His eyes bored into Justin's face. "We are very interested in your conversation with your double."

"I'll just bet you are," Justin said.

"I should also tell you that some in authority feel you are an as-yet unknown danger and should be eliminated quickly."

Abruptly, Justin realized that half of the eight Qasaman guards had their pistols drawn, two of them going so far as to point them in the Cobra's direction. "And how do *you* feel?" he asked Moff carefully.

For a long moment the other studied him. The mojo on his shoulder, sensing perhaps the general tension level, twitched its wings nervously. "I agree that you are dangerous," Moff said at last through the old man. "It is perhaps foolish to keep you alive in hopes of learning your secrets. But unless we discover your intentions toward us we cannot know how to properly defend ourselves. You will therefore be taken to a place where you may be properly questioned."

"And *then* be eliminated?"

Moff didn't reply . . . but the conversation had already made up Justin's mind. Qasama was already tacitly assuming a war was likely, and to give them anything he didn't absolutely have to would be a betrayal of those who'd come after him. Besides which, it might be interesting to see what sort of place they'd consider safe enough to hold an unknown threat. And besides *that* . . .

He caught Moff's eye again. "Just out of curiosity, how did you come to the conclusion that we were spying on you?"

Moff pursed his lips thoughtfully. Then, with a slight shrug, he began to speak. "Your double correctly interpreted a sign in the village of Huriseem this morning," the translator said. "It showed that, despite our efforts, you still had a visual connection with your ship. A device you had not told us about, and which was clearly designed to be undetectable."

Justin frowned. "*That* was all you had?"

"It was enough to justify questioning you. York's similarly

undetectable weapon—and his use of it—proved our guess was correct."

"You were the one who picked up on our hidden camera, I suppose?"

Moff nodded once, a simple gesture that admitted the fact without the trappings of pride or false modesty. Justin nodded in return and settled down to wait, the last piece of his rationalization complete. He had no desire to kill any more people than absolutely necessary when he made his break, and leaving someone with Moff's observational skills behind as witness would be a poor idea. No, he would wait until they reached their destination and Pyre had made his appearance. Together, the two Cobras would leave the Qasamans wondering for a long time just how the escape had been managed.

So he settled back in his seat and tried to keep track of the bus's path through the wide streets of Purma. And thought about his father's stories of his own war.

The strip of clear land that would, farther north, open up to become the airfield was barely sixty meters wide here at Sollas's southwest edge; but Pyre found little comfort in that fact as he raced across it toward the darkened building that was his target. None of the structures at the city's edge seemed to be showing many lights—another concession to the wandering bololins, perhaps?—but he felt as if a thousand pairs of eyes were watching him the whole way. Two thousand eyes, one thousand guns. . . .

But he reached the building without challenge, and for a minute he stood in relative shadow considering his next move. The four-story structure beside him was made of brick, and in the weeks before the mission the First Cobras had taught him how to scale such things. Once on top, he could theoretically leap from rooftop to rooftop until he reached the more open areas near the airfield.

Pyre looked up the flat side of the building, grimacing. *Theoretically.* Most of the streets in his path were the wider bololin-speedway type, and while jumping one of them would be reasonably within his servos' range, he wasn't at all sure he wanted to try it a dozen or more times.

Around the corner of the building, a faint scrape reached his ears. Notched up to full power, his audio enhancers pulled in the sound of several sets of footsteps.

Sidling to the corner, Pyre took a cautious look down the street.

Barely two hundred meters away, at the next intersection, a group of six Qasamans were standing in a loose circle, conversing in low tones. As he watched, three of them split off and began striding purposefully down the street directly toward him.

Pyre eased back. Sealing the city's edge with a sentry net was a precaution he hadn't expected even the Qasamans to bother with, given they thought they had everyone under lock and key.

Unless...

Of course. They'd found the men he'd killed in the forest.

He mouthed a silent curse. With all that had happened he'd completely forgotten that glaring evidence of his presence. And with the sentry patrols alert and in visual contact with each other, he'd now run out of choices. Locking his fingers around the bricks facing him, he began to climb.

It was a long way to go, and Pyre had had very little practice in this sort of thing, but the Qasaman patrol was apparently in no special rush to take up its post and he was nearly to the top before they emerged from the street. He froze, holding his breath... but neither the men nor their mojos looked up, and after a few seconds he continued his climb, taking care not to make even the slightest sound.

Which probably saved his life. Reaching the low parapet surrounding the roof, he raised his head over it—and found himself eye to eye with a kneeling Qasaman not three meters away, his hands in a small cloth bag in front of him.

The man's eyes and mouth went wide with surprise. But his hand was still scrambling for his gun when Pyre's arm swung over the parapet and a flicker of laser light caught his spread-winged mojo in the breast. He was still trying to draw the weapon from its holster when the second flicker caught him in the same place and he fell gently to the side, his astonishment still unvoiced.

Pyre was over the parapet in a second, trembling with the hair's-breadth closeness of the call and the cold knowledge that he was by no means safe yet. If the ground sentries had heard anything—or if an observer on the next roof over had witnessed the incident—

Activating his optical enhancers, he raised his head cautiously and checked the nearest buildings. The roof to the south was vacant. The one to the north held another figure, some sort of light-amp binoculars at his eyes as he gazed out toward the forest. A quick glance over the parapet showed the sentries below were undisturbed. Crawling to the dead Qasaman, Pyre reached into the other's bag, found a set of the same light-amp glasses and what looked like a water container and some sort of vegetable cake.

So the rooftop guards, like those on the ground, had apparently just now taken up their positions, which explained how he'd made it safely from the forest. So he was in, and behind their first lines, and temporarily undetected. So . . . now what?

Pyre found himself gazing at the dead mojo. Whatever he did, he was going to need a certain amount of camouflage. . . . Carefully, trying not to wince, he rolled the dead man over and eased off his jacket. Beneath it the man had worn a knitted sweater-like garment; cutting and unraveling a piece of it, Pyre used the yarn to tie the mojo's talons to the jacket's epaulet. Smoothing the wings back in place, he tied them together with more yarn. The whole effect would never hold up even under moderately close scrutiny, but with luck it wouldn't have to. Keeping close to the roof, he struggled into the jacket which was, thankfully, too large rather than too small. The dead man's gun belt came next; and, almost as an afterthought, he scooped up the light-amp binoculars as well. Then, mentally crossing his fingers, he headed for the cityside edge of the roof.

He made it, again without raising any obvious alarm. Below him was one of the narrower, northeast-southwest streets; across it, the building roof facing him appeared deserted. At both of the closest street intersections he could see triads of sentries, their attention apparently ground level and outward. Giving all the rooftops in the immediate area one last scan, he gathered his feet beneath him, got a good grip on his mojo, and jumped.

His leg servos were more than equal to the task. A second later he hit the far rooftop, rolling on his right shoulder to soften the sound of his impact. Coming up on one knee, he lifted the light amps to his eyes and, trying hard to look like a Qasaman sentry, waited for a reaction.

It didn't come, and a minute later he eased across the roof and repeated the procedure. One more building and he had left both the rooftop and the groundside sentries far behind him. Two more, and he began to breathe again.

And finally he had to make a decision. Each move in this direction angled him a little farther from the *Dewdrop,* and with the perimeter penetrated it was time to head north. But straight north now would take him near the center of the city, and while the streets immediately below were deserted, he had no real hope that things would be that easy for long. The city's center was where the mayor's office and, presumably, the rest of Sollas officialdom were located, and if the place wasn't crawling with people he would be very surprised. He would have to work his way around it, threading the region between that activity and the sentry line—

Or else run smack through the middle of it.

Pyre paused at roof's edge, rolling the sudden thought through his mind as if tasting it. Hitting the Qasamans' political stronghold would be a grand gesture, a message of Cobra courage and power the leaders here couldn't possibly miss. Tactically, it would serve to split the Qasamans' attention, drawing firepower away from the *Dewdrop* and perhaps from Cerenkov and the other prisoners as well.

And speaking of them, if he could manage to take the mayor captive or hold some critical nerve center, he might even be able to wangle their freedom without the dangers a brute-force approach would entail.

All in all, he decided, it was worth trying.

Scanning the street one last time, he lowered himself quickly over the parapet and dropped to the ground, bouncing off a convenient window ledge halfway down to ease the final shock of landing. Checking the cross street, he started northeast toward the center of town at a deceptively easy-looking lope, enhanced vision and hearing alert for the Qasamans who would inevitably appear.

The static crackle of the Qasamans' radio jamming blanket dominated the *Dewdrop*'s lounge, its monotony matching perfectly the unchanging still-life on the ship's outside monitors. For all the evidence offered, the entire population of Qasama could have fallen off the planet immediately after Justin had been taken away nearly an hour ago. Telek glanced at her watch, sloshing the untasted cahve in her mug as she did so. Three minutes gone, and not even a hint the Qasamans intended to reply. "Try it again," she told Nnamdi.

He nodded and raised the mike to his lips. "This is Dr. Hersh Nnamdi aboard the Aventinian ship *Dewdrop*," he said. "We urgently request communication with Mayor Kimmeron or other Qasaman leaders. Please respond."

He lowered the mike into his lap and Telek strained her ears, listening. The *Dewdrop*'s most powerful tight-beam transmitter was spitting Nnamdi's translated words directly at the nearby tower.

Jamming or no jamming, *some* of that signal should be getting through. If the Qasamans were listening.

If they weren't, this was a complete waste of effort. If they were, even if they didn't care to reply, Winward might have a chance.

Might.

"Stage two," Telek said to Nnamdi. "Put some emotion into it."

The other's cheek twitched, but he lifted the mike. "This is Dr. Hersh Nnamdi aboard the *Dewdrop*. I would like to send an unarmed representative out to negotiate our companions' release with you. Will you grant him safe-conduct to someone in authority?"

Static. Beside Nnamdi, Christopher stirred and looked at Telek. "You realize, of course, that if Justin and Almo have made their move down south, Kimmeron will know we've got super-warriors aboard and will be waiting for Michael with all the guns they've got."

Telek nodded wordlessly. Winward knew it too, of course. She stole a glance at the Cobra as he sat in quiet conversation with Link at one of the other displays. They would be discussing tactics and strategy, she knew—and what good it would do she couldn't imagine. Shots or shells fired from a distance by an unseen gunner weren't something that could be fought. Not even by Cobras.

"Someone—*anyone*—answer me, *please*." Nnamdi's voice cracked a bit, and Telek shifted her attention back to him. The strain was beginning to get to him, she realized uneasily. A little of that would add believability to the whole scheme, but too much could be trouble. "Look, I'm going to send out my second-in-command, Mr. Michael Winward," Nnamdi continued. "*Please* talk to him, all right? There's no need for any more bloodshed than we've all already suffered. I'm sure we can make a deal if you'll only agree to negotiate."

Nnamdi paused, looking to Telek. Steeling herself, she nodded. He licked his lips and turned back to the mike. "I'm sending him out now. Okay?"

The static remained unbroken. Putting down the mike, Nnamdi slumped in his seat and closed his eyes. Across the room, Winward got easily to his feet. "That's my cue, I believe," he remarked, picking up his formal tunic from the back of a chair and slipping it on over his black nightfighter combat suit.

"Comm set," Link murmured.

"Got it," Winward nodded, scooping up the translator-link

pendant/earphone set laying on the table in front of Nnamdi. "Governor, I'll try to find and hit the jammer first, but if I can't find it I'll go straight for the tower's defenses. If you pick up gunfire and explosions from back there, sweep the forest with comm laser fire and send Dorjay out."

"Right," Telek said, trying to match his calm tone. "Good luck, and don't take any stupid chances."

He twitched a smile at her and left. Sinking into the seat next to Nnamdi, Telek watched the screen ... and a minute later the outside monitors showed the Cobra walking slowly toward the tower, a half-meter-square white flag held prominently in front of him.

No shells arced out of the sky as he made his slow way across the airfield. Telek's heart thudded painfully, her emotions flip-flopping between hope and the fear that too much hope would automatically bring about disaster. Link, who had moved to watch over her shoulder, twice reached down to jump the magnification. The second time he did so they saw that a force of eight Qasamans had gathered at the foot of the tower to await Winward's arrival. Eight Qasamans, and of course eight mojos.

Two stepped forward as Winward neared the group, their drawn guns glinting in the faint backwash of Sollas's lights. They relieved him of his flag and frisked him for weapons. The entire force then formed a box around him and led him away, not into the tower but around toward the building's side. *Taking him to someone in authority?* Telek wondered. *Maybe even to the officer in charge of their antiaircraft weapons?*

They all disappeared around the corner ... and a minute later the breeze carried with it the sound of a single gunshot.

Chapter 19

The bus pulled finally to a stop beside a darkened building and Moff motioned toward the door with his pistol. "Out," the old man added unnecessarily. Keeping his movements smooth and non-threatening, Justin stood up and let the Qasamans escort him outside.

The building was a shock of déjà vu, and it took Justin only a second to realize what it reminded him of. "Looks like a stunted version of the Sollas airfield tower," he remarked as Moff led him toward a guard-flanked door. "Oddly out of place here in the middle of a city."

Moff didn't answer. *Two separate doors at least,* Justin noted, scanning the structure casually, *and three floors with windows. Lots of ways in. Come on, Almo—hit these guys and let's see what's in there.*

But no flashes of laser light interrupted them as they walked to the building door. There Moff stopped and turned, leveling his gun at Justin's chest. "You will put your hands behind your back now," the old man said from behind the ring of Qasamans.

Justin complied, and cold metal bands clamped around his wrists. *Almo, where are you?* he thought fiercely, flicking glances at the surrounding buildings.

Moff led them between the guards and into the building. The high-security building where the Qasamans felt it safe to bring an unknown danger.

The sweat was beginning to break out on Justin's forehead. *It's all right,* he told himself. *It's all right. So you're on your own; but you've been trained for this sort of thing. Two doors, and three floors of windows, remember? Getting away will be a snap.* Carefully he let his fingers explore the cuffs holding him. The wrist rings were dauntingly thick . . . but it was a short chain, not a solid bar, that connected them. A moment's experimentation showed he could curl either of his fingertip lasers to rest against one of the links. While he might get burned in the process, it should only take a few seconds to cut himself free. Though not if the targeting lock wanted to hit the mojos first. . . . Shivering at what could have been a nasty mistake, he canceled the lock. *Take it* easy, *Justin—you're letting yourself get flustered.*

Moff led them down a hallway to an elevator. A car was waiting for them. "Where are we going?" Justin asked, just to break the silence.

But no one answered. Three of the guards herded Justin into the car; Moff and the old man joined them. *Steady, kid, steady.* Justin bit down on his rising fear. *Just see where they're taking you, then knock 'em against the walls and out a window.*

Moff pushed the bottom of a *long* row of buttons . . . and the elevator started *down.*

Down. Into the ground—*deep* into the ground, if the buttons were each a full floor—where there were no doors or windows to escape through. And for perhaps the first time in his life Justin realized he was terrified. The universe, which had always seemed to protect him, was a long way up, far above his little elevator car. He was surrounded by the armed guards and hairtrigger killer birds of a frightened and angry society . . . and it dawned on him with a sharpness like the smell of ozone that the men he would soon be facing intended him to die in this deep hole. They didn't know he was a Moreau, didn't care that he was a Cobra, and when they were through with him they would kill him.

And Justin panicked.

All thoughts of finding out what this place was, all considerations of not revealing his Cobra equipment, all thoughts even of mercy—all of it simply fled his mind before the bubbling wave of panic that welled suffocatingly up into his throat. The men, guns, and mojos surrounding him were a claustrophobic pillow across his face . . . and without making a conscious decision to do so, he exploded into action.

His fingertip lasers and sonic fired first, the former at the chain binding his wrists, the latter in a stunning wavefront in all directions. An instant later his head slammed into an invisible wall and he recognized with a fresh surge of panic the folly of using a sonic in such an enclosed space. His arms tugged convulsively against the handcuffs as the lasers fired again, and abruptly the metal snapped and his arms swung free.

But the brief sonic blast and flash of light had alerted the Qasamans. Even as Justin's arms came loose they were grabbed by hard hands. Grabbed tightly—and the servos beneath the skin and muscle twisted the arms up and forward, slamming the two men head to head. Their grips slipped and he pulled free—and then there was no time for anything but terror as the five mojos screamed to the attack.

Justin's mind blanked completely then, and the only memory he had of what happened next was the sounds of the birds and the horrible thunderstorm dazzle of a hundred laser flashes. . . .

The stench brought him back to reality a few seconds later; the stench of burned meat and of his own vomit. Unsteadily, he got to his feet and looked around at the carnage. The mojos—all of them—were dead. The five Qasamans . . . Justin couldn't tell. Two of them definitely were, with prominent laser burns over vital spots, but the others—Moff included—were less certain. But whether burn shock, the sonic, or his flailing arms had put them out of action wasn't important. They could not hurt him, and he had no desire to inquire further.

The elevator was still going down. The whole thing had clearly taken less time than it'd seemed to, and it penetrated dimly into Justin's rattled consciousness that unless the elevator contained monitors the Qasamans waiting below for him would be unaware of what had just happened. He might still be able to escape.

He jabbed at his best guess for the ground floor button . . . and then at a second and a third before he realized that, unlike those on Aventine, this elevator design didn't allow for cancellation. The car would keep going down until it reached the floor Moff had signaled. Where more Qasamans would be waiting for him.

He had flipped over on his back on the unmoving bodies and his antiarmor laser was already tracing an off-center square in the ceiling before he recognized on a conscious level that he would not, *could* not, face whatever awaited him at the bottom of the elevator shaft. The false ceiling and relatively thin metal behind it were no match for the laser, and as the charred square fell practically into his lap Justin scrambled to his feet. He took a bare second to gain his balance and jumped.

Never before, not even in training, had he pushed his leg servos to their limit, and he actually gasped in shock as he shot through the opening like a misshapen missile. All around him, only dimly visible even with the aid of his enhancers, were cables and guy lines. A flicker of light from a door crack washed over him— then another, and another—he was slowing down—stopping in midair—

Instinctively, he grabbed; and a second later he was again moving downward, his arms wrapped solidly around the main elevator cable.

So he was out of the car, and out of the direct line of fire from the Qasamans below . . . but he was still deep within their stronghold and had left a trail a child could follow. He had to figure out a way to escape, and he had to do so fast.

Oddly enough, though—or so it seemed to him—the suffocating panic had dissipated far enough for him to be able to think again. His incredible jump had been a sledge-hammer reminder both of the power his Cobra equipment gave him and of the fact that his father, too, had once been imprisoned like this and had survived.

A sheet of light swept by: one of the landing doors he'd jumped past seconds ago. On a hunch, he shoved off the cable toward it, fingers and feet finding holds on framework and opening-mechanism bars. He found a narrow ledge to stand on and regained his balance as, a meter away, the cable continued its way down.

Carefully, he took a shuddering breath. *I am Justin Moreau,* he reminded himself firmly. *A Cobra, following in my father's footsteps. I will—I will—survive this. Fine. So how do I start?*

One thing was for sure: he had several floors to go before he even got to the surface. Shifting his grip, he leaned out as far as he safely could. The position of the door directly above could be inferred from reflected light, but there were too many bars and other metallic junk in the way for it to be visible. So jumping floor to floor was out; ditto for climbing through stuff that questionable. A service ladder? But a quick survey of the shaft showed nothing that would serve such a function.

A meter away, the cable abruptly slowed and stopped . . . and from below came the faint sound of elevator doors opening.

Again Justin shifted position, swinging his left leg to point directly toward the hole he'd cut in the car's ceiling and simultaneously bringing up his optical enhancers' magnification capabilities. The sight of the bodies on the floor sent a fresh wave of revulsion through him; but before he had time for more than a quick shiver there was an explosion of Qasaman voices from below, and someone stepped into the car.

Damn. Justin mouthed the word, caught once more in indecision. Should he try and get out of the shaft before the Qasamans below came to the obvious conclusion as to his whereabouts, or should he stay and try to discourage pursuit?

The decision was made for him. Abruptly, the figure below became a face and a pistol, and the shaft thundered with the echo of his shot.

A wild shot, of course; he couldn't have any idea where Justin actually was. The Cobra's response was considerably more accurate, and even at this range the antiarmor laser was perfectly adequate for such a purpose. The gunner fell in a heap onto the bodies beneath him. A second face appeared, and Justin shot that one, too—

And from below came the sound of the car's doors closing. A second later, the cable beside him started *upwards.*

Justin gaped for a couple of heartbeats before his mental wheels caught and he jumped over to again cling to the cable. What had happened was now obvious: having reached the floor Moff had sent it to, the elevator was now responding to the buttons Justin had pushed on the way down.

For the moment, at least, Justin seemed to be one step ahead of them.

After the flurry of activity preceding it, the ride toward ground level seemed to drag on and on, and it gave him the chance to assess his own injuries. Both hands, particularly the little fingers, were speckled with tiny molten-metal burns from his blasting of the handcuff chain an eternity earlier. The rings themselves were biting hard into his wrists as he pressed against the greasy cable. Something, presumably blood, was dripping slowly down his cheek from a cut over his left eye that hurt like blazes. He hadn't realized before that any of the mojos had gotten so close . . . and the thought of what might have happened—or could yet happen—

Reality broke into the uncomfortable speculation: the elevator was slowing down. The car, he estimated, was about three floors below him. When the doors opened he would begin sliding down the cable toward it, keeping his antiarmor laser aimed and ready. If the Qasamans still hadn't caught on he would drop through the ceiling hole, out the door, and make a mad dash for the exit, relying on his speed and computerized reflexes to get him through.

Below him the car doors opened—and as they did, the top of the car was abruptly flooded with light and the roar of sustained gunfire exploded into the shaft.

Justin jerked violently, nearly losing his grip. The car was already being obscured by a haze of smoke. Through it the staccato flashing of the guns lit up the shaft with an unearthly glow. Splinters of shattered steel scythed the air in counterpoint to the invisible battering of the bullets that were demolishing everything in range.

And Justin's brief respite from panic was over.

Across from him another of the landing doors was visible in the flickering light. As the barrage below reached its peak his leg swung convulsively around, the laser within it tracing a distorted ellipse across the doors. For that heart-rending second it didn't matter that the Qasamans might have a dozen gunmen ringing each elevator door; didn't even matter that a moment's study probably would have revealed an emergency mechanism that might have given them far less warning of his presence. All that mattered was that the guns below could be turned upwards at any second, and that he wanted out of the deathtrap *now*. Twisting his legs to the horizontal, he shoved hard against the cable with his hands. The charred ellipse broke like foil as he hit it, and he flew helplessly into the hallway beyond, slamming into the far wall and bouncing off into a barely balanced crouch.

The hallway was empty.

For a long moment he sat there trembling on his haunches, his brain struggling to pierce the unreality of the situation to figure out what had happened. They *knew* he was in the shaft—the roar of gunfire still coming from below more than proved that. So why weren't all the exits from the shaft being guarded?

Because they thought he was still on the elevator roof?

Probably. A concealed weapon would likely not have been powerful enough to kill the two men from any further away than the roof. And they wouldn't have any idea just how high his servos let him jump.

Getting to his feet, he gulped a ragged breath and took stock of the situation. The hallway stretched for thirty meters or so in both directions, its walls lined with incomprehensibly labeled doors. At the far ends small windows reflected his image.

Small, but probably large enough to get through. Picking the closest of the two ends, Justin headed for it at a dead run.

And he almost made it. But if guarding all exits from the elevator shaft hadn't been the Qasamans' first priority, neither had it been forgotten. His own footsteps masking the sound of their approach, Justin's first warning was the blood-chilling scream of a mojo directly behind him. He twisted around, getting just the briefest glimpse of talons arcing for his face before his nano-computer took over.

The servos in his legs wrenched him to the side, out of the mojo's line of flight. Its wingtips brushed his face as it overshot him, screaming again in what sounded uncannily like rage. At the far end of the hall, five Qasamans had come from somewhere, their guns aimed and ready; and four more mojos were sweeping to the attack.

And for the second time that night the sight of the birds drove all reason and nerve from his mind. Falling backwards to slam against the wall, he snapped his burned hands up . . . and as his brain fogged over with terror, his nanocomputer turned them into fountains of laser fire.

He came to a few seconds later to find all five mojos dead. At the end of the hallway, he could see at least three Qasaman bodies, as well. The survivors—if there'd been any—had vanished.

Witnesses to his Cobra firepower; but that thought didn't occur to Justin until a long time afterwards. Back on his feet, he headed again for his target window, sonic disrupter focused on it. The weapon found and locked onto the window's primary resonance, increased its amplitude . . . and with Justin two steps from it, the glass shattered, taking much of the sash framework with it in its violent demise. Increasing his speed, Justin put down his head and dove through the hole.

Three floors below him, the edge of the tower was a blaze of floodlights and the crazy-quilt shadow pattern of running men. Justin saw just enough to realize he would most likely land outside the lit area before his nanocomputer pulled his arms and legs tightly in toward his torso. He tensed; but a second later when the limbs snapped out to normal position again he was relieved to find the computer's calculation had been correct. Properly vertical once more, he hit the ground on his feet, servos taking the impact as they fought against his forward momentum to regain his balance before he ran full tilt into the building immediately across from his former prison. The effort was a success; turning to run parallel to the building, he sprinted to the nearest corner and rounded it.

He'd not had a chance yet to really focus on his surroundings, but as he picked up speed now he realized the universe had betrayed him one final time. Directly ahead the buildings and street abruptly gave way to the sort of open grassland that surrounded

Sollas as well. The bus had taken him through several kilometers of city before reaching the tower; ergo, what he faced now was Purma's southwestern edge.

He was running directly *away* from Rynstadt and Cerenkov . . . directly away from the *Dewdrop*.

I should turn around, he thought. *Or at least circle around a block or two and head back along a different street.* But his feet kept running; and as he crossed the sharp line between city and grassland he finally recognized that no intentions in the world were going to make his body turn around. Behind him were the mojos, and the paralyzing fear their talons induced in him was far more terrifying than the talons themselves.

His father had faced the might of whole Troft armies and won through without flinching . . . and his only Cobra son had turned out to be a coward.

The city was far behind him now, but as Justin keyed in his optical enhancers he saw the forest that had flanked the road into Purma had receded sharply this far south. The nearest edge, his enhancers' range finder told him, was over a kilometer away—much too far to reach in time if the Qasamans had taken up the chase. Throwing a glance over his shoulder, Justin skidded to a halt and dropped down on his stomach in the knee-high grass, turning to face the city with all senses alert.

But so far there was no sign of pursuit. Did they think he'd headed north, as he should have? Or were they perhaps not even aware yet that he'd escaped from the building?

There was no way to tell . . . and with emotional fatigue washing over him, Justin almost didn't even care. Whatever he did now, Cerenkov and Rynstadt were as good as dead unless Pyre had already managed to free them. No matter how fast Justin got to their prison, he would find the place hip-deep in guards.

His burns and bruises throbbed with aches both sharp and dull, but they were no match for his fatigue. Slowly but inexorably his eyelids dragged themselves closed, his head sank down to rest pillowed on his arms, his shame found the only oblivion available.

He slept.

Chapter 20

For the third time in five minutes a vehicle approached from ahead, and for the third time Pyre tensed and forced himself to maintain a steady walk. The vehicle passed without slowing, and the Cobra sighed quietly with relief.

Momentary relief, at best. If his memory of Sollas's layout was correct, he was only two or three blocks from the building where Joshua and the others had been taken a week ago to meet Mayor Kimmeron. The trip so far had indicated that no one was considering the possibility that any of the Aventinians could have made it this deep into the city, but it was equally clear that the bubble could burst any time now. There were bound to be sentries surrounding the mayoral office, as well as various people scurrying around with errands as these supposedly peaceful people continued their war against the *Dewdrop*. A straight-in penetration, Cobra firepower or no, was likely to be pretty bloody. On both sides.

But so far he'd been unable to come up with anything better. He'd passed a handful of parked cars, but a quick check had shown their drive mechanisms were locked and he had no idea how to bypass the system. Rooftop jumping was possible, but its usefulness decreased in direct proportion to the number of nearby ears that might hear the thud of the landing and eyes that might see the leap itself. If he had some timed bombs he could set up a diversion a few blocks from his goal; but none of his meager supply of equipment could be adapted to such a purpose. The propellant in the bullets, perhaps? Surely there was a goodly amount of it—you didn't take down an animal the size of a bololin without a lot of punch behind the projectile.

Bololins. . . .

The ghost of an idea brushed his mind. Looking around quickly to make sure he was unobserved, Pyre found a dark section of wall and began to climb.

The rooftop, when he reached it, didn't have what he was looking for; but a careful study showed a likely candidate two buildings away. Two jumps later he was squatting next to a square yellow box mounted with a large-mouthed horn.

A bololin alarm.

Fingertip lasers made quick work of the box's access panel, and Pyre was soon poking gingerly around the wires and components inside. The reasonable way to set such a device up was to run it off the building's own power supply, with the on/off switch several floors down and inaccessible . . . but if the Qasamans had been as cautious here as they seemed to be everywhere else. . . .

And they had. The horn's emergency battery took up nearly a quarter of the box's volume.

A few minutes' work tracing wires and Pyre had the system figured out. Cutting the main power line *here* would allow the battery—and, more importantly, the emergency trigger switch—into the circuit. The battery's switch seemed to be designed for radio control, though. He would have to come up with some other way to trigger the thing.

By the time the preliminary cutting and adjustments were complete he'd thought of one. Maybe.

It took nearly fifteen minutes more to complete the jury-rig trigger. Then, wiping the sweat off his forehead, he took a moment to study the landscape. The mayor's office . . . that one there, probably. Circle cautiously and find a roof past it to wait on . . . that one.

Glancing at his watch, Pyre grimaced. Time was slipping away from him, and with each lost minute the chances increased that the Qasamans would kill one of their hostages or take some action against the *Dewdrop*. Dropping down the side of the building, he began to run silently through the deserted streets.

Luck was with him. Fifteen minutes later he was on his chosen rooftop, ready to go. Two buildings away, the mayoral building was, from the muted sounds reaching his ears, indeed surrounded by milling groups of people. Four blocks beyond it Pyre's optical enhancers located the bololin alarm and the stolen light-amp binoculars resting atop the box there. Taking a deep breath, Pyre locked onto the binoculars, raised his left leg, and sent a low-power antiarmor shot toward it.

The light triggered a pulse through the light-amp's electronics, a pulse which Pyre's rewiring sent not to the lenses but around the alarm's emergency switch system—

And the hoot of the horn tore into the darkness.

Pyre was ready. Stray eyes were still a danger, but for the moment there was no way anyone in the street below was going to hear the impact of his landings. He reached the edge of his building and jumped, getting a glimpse of running people below. He hit the next roof, crossed it in a dead run, and with a quick prayer to the patron of fools, jumped again.

Not to the mayoral building roof, but to a spot midway down the side—and that only to provide a slight braking impact before he hit the street. The building was seven stories high, its lit windows testifying to activity inside, and Pyre knew he was taking a big gamble going in at ground level. But the mayor's office itself had been on the first floor, and the Cobra was betting that Qasaman paranoia would bury the most important facilities underground.

And then he hit the street and there was no time left for planning and thought. Most of the thirty or so people in sight were hurrying away from him in the direction of the hooting alarm, but the two who flanked the ornate door were standing fast . . . and their frozen astonishment didn't extend to their mojos.

But the birds saw no drawn weapon, and their movements were the slow ones of surprised study instead of the swifter ones of attack. Pyre targeted and shot both out of the air; and then, as the guards belatedly reacted, he shot them as well. He took the three outside steps in a single bound and slipped inside.

He hadn't been paying all that much attention to the route the one time Cerenkov's team had been in this place, but fortunately the layout seemed straightforward. Pyre followed the main corridor to the first junction and branched right. At the next cross corridor he turned left, aiming toward the center of the building— and there, barely ten meters away, were the two liveried guards he remembered seeing at the mayor's door.

They looked at him in frowning surprise, hands dropping to their guns. Pyre shot both of them out from under their mojos, then killed the birds as they tried to disengage their talons from their epaulet perches and become airborne. Mentally bracing himself, he shoved the doors open and stepped inside, hands held at the ready.

It was almost a repeat of the scene he'd seen through Joshua's sensors the last time, with two important exceptions. The fumes that both he and the contact team had missed out on before were an almost literal sledgehammer to the nose, bringing him to an abrupt halt and nearly gagging him. And this time the mayor's cushiony throne was vacant.

It took Pyre a handful of heartbeats to get his breath and voice back. For the people seated at the low tables around the throne, those few seconds turned out to be their salvation. Whether the fumes enhanced their mental processes or whether they were simply naturally observant he didn't know, but by the time he was able to function again all of them had apparently deduced who he was and were making mad dashes from the room. Within seconds the scene was deserted.

"Damn," Pyre murmured under his breath. The smoke, he discovered, tasted odd, too. Clicking up his audio enhancers, he held his breath . . . and from somewhere out of sight among the free-hanging curtains he heard the faint sound of shallow breathing.

So they *hadn't* all made it out of boltholes. Was the straggler armed? Probably . . . though none of the others had tried to use their guns, and that carried some interesting implications. But even if the skulker was afraid to shoot, Pyre had no desire to hunt him down in this maze, with only the diffuse sounds of breathing to guide him. But there might be another way. If the mojos were really as touchy about weapons as they'd seemed when the contact team first stepped outside the *Dewdrop*'s lock . . .

Left hand ready for trouble, he reached down with his right and drew his stolen pistol.

The sound of steel on leather was loud in the silent room— and the single flap of bird wings that followed gave direction enough. Ahead and to the left . . . he sprinted around the curtains there and came face to face with a crouching, terror-eyed man.

For a second they gazed at each other in silence. Pyre's main attention was on the Qasaman's mojo, but the bird seemed to realize that an attack would be suicide, and it stayed put on its shoulder perch. Shifting his full attention to the man, Pyre said the only Qasaman word he knew: "Kimmeron."

The other, apparently misunderstanding, shook his head wildly. "Sibbio," he choked, slapping his chest with an open palm, eyes dropping to the gun still in Pyre's hand. "*Sibbio.*"

Pyre grimaced and tried again. "Kimmeron. Kimmeron?" He waved his free hand vaguely around the room.

The Qasaman got it then. Even through the haze of fumes

Pyre saw his face visibly pale. *Doesn't know where the mayor is? Or* does *know and the place is top-secret?* The latter, he suspected; Sibbio's clothes seemed too ornate for a mere servitor. Taking a long step forward, the Cobra glared as hard as he could at the man. "Kimmeron," he bit out harshly.

The other gazed into Pyre's eyes and silently got to his feet.

The bolthole was right where, in retrospect, Pyre should have expected to find it: directly in front of the cushiony throne. Sibbio showed him the hidden lever that released the trap door; looking down the hole, Pyre saw the meter-square shaft change a few meters down into a curving ramp that presumably dumped the passengers into the safety of a heavily guarded room somewhere down the line.

Unfortunately, the trap's position implied it was also useful for getting undesirables out of the mayor's sight, which meant the guards below would be trained to handle potential nuisances. But there was nothing Pyre could do about that on his time budget . . . and now that the trap was open, there was no point in further hesitation. Giving Sibbio's mojo one last glance, the Cobra stepped into the pit.

It was a smooth enough ride, the curved section of tunnel beginning early enough and gradually enough to ease him onto his back for the final thirty-degree slope. It was also a much shorter trip than he'd planned on, and he had barely registered the dim square outline rushing toward him when he shot through the light-blocking curtain and landed flat on his back on a giant foam pad, the gun slipping from his grip as he hit. His eyes adjusted—

To find a ring of guns surrounding him.

Five of them, he counted as he lay motionless. The guard nearest his fallen weapon scooped it up, jamming it into his own empty holster. "You will make no move," said a man standing at Pyre's feet in the middle of the semicircle, in harshly accented Anglic.

Pyre locked eyes with him, then sent his gaze leisurely around the ring of guards. "I want to talk to Mayor Kimmeron," he said to the spokesman.

"You will not move until you are judged to be weaponless," the Qasaman told him.

"*Is* Kimmeron here?"

The other ignored his question. He spoke instead to his men, two of whom handed their weapons to the others. They knelt down on either side of Pyre . . . and the Cobra kicked his heels hard into the pad.

The pad was spongy, but the kick had servo strength behind it and an instant later Pyre was flipping rigidly around the pivot point of his head. One of the guns barked, too late—and then it was too late for any further response as Pyre triggered the laser salvo he'd set up while looking around the guard ring. For an instant the room blazed with laser fire . . . and by the time Pyre's body had completed its flip the five Qasamans were kneeling or lying on the floor in various stages of shock, their flash-heated guns scattered among the dead mojos.

Pyre got to his feet, eyes seeking the spokesman. "I could as easily have killed all of you," he said calmly. "I'm not here to kill Mayor Kimmeron—"

Without warning, the other four Qasamans leaped to their feet and rushed him.

He let them come; and as the first one got within range, he snapped out his arm to catch the other in the chest with his palm. There was a *wumph* of expelled air, the sharper *crack* of snapped ribs, and the Qasaman flew two meters backwards to crash to the floor.

The other three skidded to a halt, and Pyre saw an abrupt swelling of fear and respect in their faces. It was one thing, he reflected, to be disarmed by effectively magical bursts of light; it was quite another to see brute physical force in action. Or to feel it, for that matter. The temporary numbness in his palm was wearing off and the skin there was aching like fury. The Qasaman would feel a lot worse when he woke up. If he ever did.

Pyre's eyes caught the spokesman's again. "I'm not here to kill Mayor Kimmeron, but merely to talk with him," he said as calmly as his tingling hand permitted. "Take me to him. Now."

The other licked his lips, glancing over to where one of his men was ministering to his injured colleague. Then, looking back at Pyre, he nodded. "Follow me this way." He said something else to his men, then turned and headed for a door in the far end of the room. Pyre followed, the two remaining Qasamans falling into step behind him.

They passed through the door, and Pyre felt a split second of déjà vu. The same cushiony throne and low tables as in the office upstairs were here as well. But this room was smaller, and the hanging curtains had been replaced by banks of visual displays.

And glaring darkly at one of the displays was Mayor Kimmeron.

He looked up as Pyre and his escort approached, and the Cobra waited for the inevitable reaction. Kimmeron's gaze swept Pyre's matted hair and growth of beard; his borrowed jacket over camouflage survival suit; the dead mojo now hanging over his shoulder by a single thread. But his expression didn't change, and when he looked up again at Pyre's face the Cobra was struck by the brightness of the other's eyes. "You are from the ship," Kimmeron said calmly. "You left it before our cordon was set up. How?"

"Magic," Pyre said shortly. He glanced around the room. Another fifteen or so Qasamans were present, nearly all of them staring in his direction. All had the usual sidearm and mojo, but no one looked like he was interested in making any move for his weapon. "Your underground command post?" he asked Kimmeron.

"One of them," the other nodded. "There are many more. You will gain little by destroying it."

"I'm not really interested in destroying anything," Pyre told him. "I'm here mainly to arrange our companions' release."

Kimmeron's lip curled. "You are remarkably slow to learn," he spat. "Didn't the death of your other messenger teach you a lesson?"

Pyre felt his mouth go dry. "What other messenger? You mean the contact team?"

For a moment the other frowned. Then his face cleared in understanding. "Ah. The jamming of your radio signals was effective against *you*, at least. I see. So you do not know the man Winward left your ship without permission and was shot."

Winward? Had Telek started her breakout attempt already? "Why did you shoot him?" he snapped. "You just said he was a messenger—"

"For the unprovoked deaths of eight men in Purma and six here you are *all* responsible. You have spied and you have murdered, and your punishment will be that of death."

Pyre stared at him, mental wheels unable to catch. Winward . . . shot down like a spine leopard, probably without so much as a warning. *Then, why aren't they shooting at me? Simple fear?—he* wouldn't be taken by surprise, after all. Or was it something more practical? With Winward gone and whatever the hell had happened in Purma—whatever *that* was—all over, did they want a live Cobra to study?

His gaze drifted to the particular bank of displays Kimmeron had been studying. Rooms, corridors, outside views . . . three showed the *Dewdrop*. *Must be from the airfield tower,* he realized. *Live picture?* If so, there was still a chance for some of them to escape; the ship seemed undamaged.

"We would prefer to keep you alive at present," Kimmeron broke into his thoughts. "You, and the ones named Cerenkov and Rynstadt, have no possibility of escaping. I tell you this so that you will not try and thereby force us to kill you prematurely."

"Our ship might escape," Pyre pointed out. "And it will tell our people of our imprisonment."

"Your ship, too, cannot escape." Kimmeron was quietly certain. "The weapons set against it will destroy it before it reaches the end of the field."

But the Dewdrop *can lift straight up.* Would that make enough of a difference? There was no way to know . . . but given the national paranoia, Pyre tended to doubt it. "I'd still like to talk to you about release of our companions," he told the mayor, just for something to say.

Kimmeron arched his eyebrows. "You speak foolishness," he bit out. "We have you and the body of Winward, from which your so-named 'magic' powers can surely be learned."

"Our magic cannot be learned from a corpse," Pyre lied.

"*You* are still alive," the other said pointedly. "From Cerenkov and Rynstadt we will obtain information about your culture and technology which will prepare us for any attack your world launches against us in the future. And from your ship—intact or in pieces—we will learn even more, perhaps enough to finally regain star travel. All that is within our hands; what could you offer of greater value for allowing your departure?"

There was no answer Pyre could give to that . . . and it occurred to him that a method which allowed its users to learn Anglic in a week might indeed let them reconstruct the *Dewdrop* and its systems from whatever wreckage remained after its destruction.

Which meant that his gallant rescue attempt was now, and always had been, doomed to failure. Cerenkov and Rynstadt were beyond help, and Pyre's own last minutes would be spent right here in the mayor's underground nerve center. If he could somehow find the communications panel—and then find a way to shut off or broadcast through the jamming—and then figure out how to signal the *Dewdrop* to get the hell away—and all before sheer weight of numbers overwhelmed him—

And as the impossibilities of each step lined up before him like mountains the universe presented him a gift. A small gift, hardly more than a sign . . . but he saw it, and Kimmeron did not, and he had the satisfaction of giving the mayor a genuine smile. "What do I have to offer, Mr. Mayor?" he said calmly. "A great deal, actually . . . because all that was in your hands a moment ago is even now slipping through your fingers."

Kimmeron frowned . . . and as he started to speak Pyre heard a sharp intake of breath from the guard spokesman beside him. Kimmeron twisted to look behind him . . . and when he turned back his face was pale. "How—?"

"How?" Pyre shifted his eyes over Kimmeron's shoulder, to the displays that showed the airfield tower and environs.

—Or that had done so a few minutes earlier. Now, the entire bank showed a uniform gray.

How? "Very simple, Mr. Mayor," Pyre said . . . and suppressed the shiver of that boyhood memory. Like MacDonald before him on that awful day of vengeance against Challinor. . . . "Winward, it appears, has returned from the dead."

Chapter 21

It was so unexpected—so totally unexpected—that Winward never even had a chance to react. One minute he was walking around the tower with his Qasaman escort, surreptitiously searching the building and immediate area for weapons and additional guards and trying to work out exactly what he would say when they reached whoever he was being taken to. Just walking peacefully . . . and then the leader muttered something and turned around . . . and before Winward could do more than focus on the other the night lit up with a thunderous flash and a sledgehammer slammed into the center of his chest, blowing him backwards into nothingness as the crack of the lethal shot echoed in his ears. . . .

The blackness in his brain faded slowly, and for what seemed like hours he drifted slowly toward the reality he could faintly sense above him. The pain came first—dull, throbbing pain in his chest; sharp, stinging pain in his eyes and face—and with that breakthrough the rest of his senses began to function again. Sounds filtered in: footsteps, doors opening and closing, occasional incomprehensible voices. He discovered he was on his back, bouncing rhythmically as if being carried, and every so often he felt a trickle of something run down his ribs under his tunic.

And slowly, he realized what had happened.

He'd been shot. Deliberately and maliciously shot. And was probably dying.

The only general rule he could recall from his first-aid training was that injury victims should not be unnecessarily moved. And so he remained still, eyes closed against the pain there, as he waited for loss of blood to dim his consciousness back into darkness.

But it wasn't happening. On the contrary, with each passing

heartbeat he felt his mind sharpening, with strength and sensation rapidly returning to his limbs. Far from dying, he was actually coming back to life.

What the hell?

And it was only then, as his body and brain finally meshed enough to localize his wound, that he realized what had happened.

The Qasaman had shot him in the center of his chest. Directly over the breastbone. The breastbone which, coated with ceramic laminae, was functionally unbreakable.

The aftermath was less clear, but its main points weren't hard to figure out. The bullet's impact had knocked the air out of him, possibly even temporarily stopped his heart, and for the past few seconds or minutes he'd been fighting to get oxygen back into his system. His face and eyes must have taken the impact of burning propellant to sting as they did, and for a painful heartbeat he recognized that he might have been permanently blinded.

But somehow even that didn't seem important at the moment. He was alive, he was reasonably functional—

And the Qasamans thought he was dead.

They would pay for that mistake. Pay in blood.

Starting right now. Winward's eyes might be unusable, but the optical enhancers set into the skin around them were harder to damage and fed into the optic nerves further back inside the skull's protection. They weren't really designed to replace normal vision, but a minute's experimentation showed that a zero-magnification setting combined with the lowest light-amp level provided an adequate picture.

Between the four head-and-upper-torsos bobbing at the edges of the view, he could see a ceiling passing overhead. Carefully, keeping the motion slow, he eased his head a few degrees to the side. A couple of doors went by, the party turned a corner, and abruptly they were through open double doors and into a white-walled room with bright steel fixtures extending to the ceiling in various places. The four stretcher-bearers set him down on a hard table, and he let his head loll so to leave it turned to his right, toward the exit. The men left, closing the doors behind them, and he was alone.

Though probably not for long. The room he was in was very obviously a sick bay or surgery, and in the Qasamans' place Winward would want a preliminary dissection started on a dead Cobra as quickly as possible. The doctors were probably prepping in another room, and could arrive at any time.

Forcing himself to again move slowly, Winward eased his head up and down until he located the glassy eye of a fisheye monitor camera. It was in a back upper corner, out of direct line of any of his lasers or his sonic disrupter. He could lift his hands and fire, of course, but if someone was watching the monitor closely the alarm would be raised before he even got through the double doors into the hall. Using his omnidirectional sonic to shake up the picture before shooting wouldn't help appreciably, either. What he really needed was a diversion.

Behind him there was the sound of a door opening, and a second later four white-gowned people came around the maze of support equipment and into view.

And a diversion abruptly became vital. The soldiers and stretcher-carriers outside might miss his slow breathing or the fact that the skin of his chest was still bleeding, but the approaching doctors hadn't a chance in hell of doing so. He had to keep them away before they found out he was still alive.

The leader was within a meter of him now. Activating his omnidirectional, Winward ran it to its lowest frequency setting and held his breath.

Their reaction was all he could have hoped for. The leader jerked to a stop as the inaudible waves hit him, the second in line stumbling into him as she staggered slightly. For a minute they all stood together in a little knot just beyond the most uncomfortable zone, conversing in voices that sounded both concerned and irritated. Winward waited, gritting his teeth himself against the gut-rattling sound as he waited for their next move.

It came quickly, and was one more indication of how much the high command wanted the Cobra dissected *immediately.* Waving the others back, the leader picked up a sharp-looking instrument from a nearby tray and stepped to the table. He reached down to pull back Winward's tunic—

And jumped back with a strangled gasp as the Cobra's sonic disrupter flash-heated the skin of his hand. Followed by one of the others, he dashed around the table to the back door, shouting as he ran.

The door opened and closed, and for a moment the last two Qasamans huddled together, whispering in fear or awe or both to each other. Winward tried to guess what they'd try next, but the grinding of his sonic combined with the throbbing pain in his chest and face was fogging his mind too much for him to hold a coherent train of thought.

Again, he didn't have long to wait. One of the two disappeared toward the back of the room, returning a minute later with a coil of insulated electrical cable. Snaring a knife from the instrument tray, he began stripping the insulation from one end . . . and as the other Qasaman plugged the wire's other end into what appeared to be a ground socket beneath a wall outlet, Winward realized with growing excitement that the break he'd hoped for was here.

Clearly, the Qasamans had jumped to the conclusion that their colleague had suffered an electrical burn from Winward's body and were preparing to try and drain the excess charge away.

Another minute and they were ready. The first Qasaman replaced the knife in the tray and swung the bare copper wire gently as he prepared to loft it over the Cobra's chest. Moving his right hand fractionally, Winward lined up his fingertip laser on the socket where the cable had been grounded. It was going to be a bit of a stretch, but he had no choice but to try it. The copper snake flew through the air, draped itself across his chest . . . and Winward fired his arcthrower.

A bit of a stretch indeed, and for a heart-stopping fraction of a second he watched the clean light of the laser burning its solitary way through the air without any response from the capacitors deep within his body cavity. Then the split second was past, and the ionized path reached the required conductance and a lightning bolt shattered the air. And even as the thunderclap seemed to split open Winward's head, the sudden current flow overloaded the circuit breakers—

And the room was plunged into darkness.

Winward was off the table before the echoes had faded away; was out through the double doors a second later. If the monitor camera hadn't been taken out with the room's lights, it was almost guaranteed that the afterimage of that flash would mask the brief flicker of hall light as the Cobra escaped.

For a wonder, the hall was deserted. Presumably the medical area had no command stations within it and, hence, little traffic under normal conditions. He headed down the hall to look for a stairway; and as he did so, he carefully pried open his eyelids.

Nothing. The Qasaman's gunshot had blinded him. Perhaps beyond even Aventine's surgical abilities.

The cold fury simmering within him began to heat up again. Along with York's arm, it was one more score to be settled with this world.

He changed hallways twice before spotting anyone; and when he finally did, he hit the entire jackpot at once. Rounding a corner, he was just in time to see the elevator he'd been seeking disgorge a half dozen Qasamans barely ten meters away from him. One of them was the man who'd shot him.

The whole group froze in shock, and even the limited quality of his enhancer image gave Winward the grim satisfaction of watching sheer unbelieving terror flood into his former assailant's face. Three seconds they all stood there; four seconds, five—and, abruptly, they all went madly for their weapons.

Winward pirouetted on his right foot and cut a blaze of death across them with his antiarmor laser.

The mojos escaped that first shot, but even as they swept toward him in impotent rage his fingertip lasers shot them to the floor. Winward didn't waste a backward glance as he jumped over the charred bodies and between the closing elevator doors. The selector panel gave him momentary pause—there were at least three times as many buttons as the tower ought to need. But he knew where he needed to go. Pushing the top button, he listened to the faint hum of the elevator's motor and prepared himself for combat.

The door opened, and he stepped out into a dimly-lit room to face a dozen drawn pistols.

They barked as one . . . but Winward was no longer in the line of fire. Leg servos snapped him upwards, flipped him over in time to hit the ceiling feet first, crashing shin-deep through the tiles there to bounce off the stronger ceiling above; pushed him back toward the floor behind the line of gunmen, again flipping him over in midflight. He hit the floor with fingertip lasers blazing . . . and it was doubtful that any of the Qasamans realized what had happened before they died.

Again the mojos outlived their masters, and again Winward made that escape momentary. But this time one of them got through before dying, its talons opening up a ten-centimeter gash in his left arm.

"Damn it all," Winward snarled aloud, tearing off the bloody tunic sleeve and wrapping it awkwardly around the wound. The ambush meant the alarm had gone out, though he hadn't heard any sirens . . . and as he focused for the first time on the room around him, he realized why they hadn't needed any such warning.

Ringing the room at eye level were large windows—presumably one-way since he hadn't noticed any windows this high from the outside—through which he could see the *Dewdrop* lying so painfully vulnerable out on the darkened landing field. Below the windows was a ring of monitor displays.

So he'd found the situation room, or at least an auxiliary one. On some of the displays armed men were rushing about madly, and Winward stepped back to the elevator doors to listen. The car was on its way up—filled, no doubt, with suicidal soldiers. Looking around the room, he found the three monitor cameras and put laser bolts into each. Blinder now than he was, they'd just have to guess what he was up to . . . and while they sweated that one, he had a couple more surprises in store for them.

Moving to the side away from the *Dewdrop,* he put his face to the windows there and looked down. He hadn't had much of a look out back before he was shot, but he'd seen *something* . . . and, sure enough, from above he could pick out the heavy guns waiting in the tower's shadow. Ready to be pushed from cover and throw explosives at the ship . . . but only if there was someone there to do the pushing.

The nearest monitor cabinet displayed duplicates of a dozen other screens around the room, as if it was the feeder nexus for another monitor station elsewhere in the building. Winward sent an arcthrower charge into the mechanism to trip out any power lines; then, gripping it firmly, he pulled it out of its wall fastenings and raised it to a precarious balance over his head. The glass—or whatever—of the window was tough: it took nearly fifteen seconds of the Cobra's sonic disruptor. Winward wondered what those below would make of the sudden rain of glass as he stepped to the opening and hurled the cabinet at one of the guns with all the accuracy and strength his Cobra gear could give him.

The startled yelps began the instant before the cabinet smashed into the gun crew; and, simultaneously, the elevator doors across the room slid open. But Winward didn't stay to count the reinforcements. Stepping into the shattered window frame, he turned and jumped in a single motion. His hands grabbed the window's upper edge as he flew past it, changing his direction and angular velocity just enough to pinwheel him neatly onto the tower roof.

And right into the middle of a small crowd who'd apparently rushed over to investigate the commotion below.

Winward didn't bother with lasers or sonics for this group, and they *still* didn't have a chance. Swinging his arms like a servo-powered threshing machine, he hurled them in all directions, bleeding or stunned. The mojos were a different story; but he was getting used to their arch-winged attack, and took a perverse pleasure in burning them out of the air.

And that flicker of overconfidence nearly killed him . . . because four of the Qasaman contingent had stayed by their weapons across the roof, and as Winward looked up from his latest carnage, he found their four mojos arrowing in bare meters away.

His computerized reflexes saved him in that first instant, recognizing the projectile threat and hurling him down and to the side in a flat dive and roll. It was a maneuver he'd experienced innumerable times while fighting spine leopards . . . but neither spine leopards nor the antipersonnel missiles the system had been designed for had the mojos' hairpin maneuverability. Winward had barely rolled back to his feet when the first two birds reached him . . . and this time they got through his defenses.

He gasped with shock and pain as talons dug deep into his left forearm, a beak shredding at the makeshift bandage he'd wrapped around the gash there. He twisted his head aside barely in time to avoid the second mojo's slashing attack at his face, but even so its wing caught him full across the eyes, smashing the tip of his nose with stunning force. The last two mojos reached him then, one swooping down to a grip on his right forearm, the other landing on his right shoulder and digging its beak into his cheek.

And Winward went berserk.

He dropped onto his back and slammed both forearms hard onto the rooftop, feeling mojo bones crack under the crushing impact. He smashed them down again and again until the bloodied pulps loosened their grips and fell off. Reaching up with his right hand, he grabbed another mojo by the neck and twisted hard. He heard it snap; and then the last bird was back, diving toward his face. He grabbed for its feet, missed, caught the wings instead, and pulled sideways. One wing tore off, and Winward hurled both pieces from him. Across the roof there was the flash-boom of a gunshot and a bullet whistled past him. Winward swept his antiarmor laser across the crouching gunmen, then leaped to his feet and ran to them.

All four were dead. Winward glared down at them, gasping for air . . . and as his rage subsided into the rivers of new pain coming from arms, cheek, and shoulder, his brain began to function again and his eyes searched out the weapons his enemies had been manning.

Mortars, or something very much like them. Simple tubes with a firing mechanism at the bottom, the shells stacked nearby. By inference, they were designed with an equally simple impact detonator. Scooping up an armful, he trotted back to the rear of the roof.

A couple of faces were peering upwards from the window he'd smashed, and his first shell therefore went in there. The explosion blew out a couple more windows, and Winward followed it with one aimed more toward the monitor room's center. Then he turned his attention to the guns and ground crews shooting uselessly at him from below. By the time his arms were empty it was abundantly clear that those cannons wouldn't be firing again for a long time.

Behind him, the roof stairway door slammed open. Winward didn't even bother to look, but grabbed the parapet edge and swung down into the room below. His nanocomputer compensated for a slight overbalance, and he landed among the glass shards on his feet.

The place was a mess. Where the two mortar shells had hit, floor and ceiling were torn and blackened. Dozens of the monitor screens had been smashed by flying debris; the rest were blank. At least six bodies were visible.

I did all this. The thought hit him with unexpected force, sending a queasy shiver through his body. For the first time in his life, he truly understood why the Dominion of Man had won its war against the Trofts . . . and why its citizens had rejected their returning protectors.

Gingerly, he picked his way through the rubble to the elevator and pushed the call button. Risky, perhaps, if the Qasamans hadn't learned yet not to send piles of people against him. But the emotional reaction combined with loss of blood was making him feel light-headed, and for the moment the elevator seemed safer than trying to handle stairs.

An instant later a flash of light from the side caught his eye, and he turned to find the woods beyond the *Dewdrop* on fire.

Involuntarily, he hissed with the fear that he'd been too late, that the ship was being attacked. But on the heels of that came the memory of his instructions to Telek before he left. F'ahl had heard the explosions and obediently swept the forest with laser fire. What it had done to the soldiers waiting there was uncertain; but it had sure as hell not done much for the foliage, and if any surviving Qasamans were still at their posts they were probably thinking more of escape than attack.

Speaking of which. . . .

The elevator car arrived—empty—and he punched the second button from the top. For a wonder, the elevator performed as directed—perhaps the override controls had been on the top floor?—and he bounded out into a small, deserted room.

Deserted, but not quiet. Like the floor above, this one was filled with electronic gear, and from a panel near the middle two voices were speaking.

Propping open the elevator doors, Winward stepped over to the talkative board. Communications, probably, left running when the people on duty heard the ruckus overhead and wisely cut out. He wondered whether the mike at this end was still open, decided there was a simple way to find out. "Can you hear me?" he called.

The voices stopped abruptly. "Who are you?" one of them asked a moment later in passable Anglic.

"Michael Winward, currently in charge of this tower," he said. If he was lucky, they'd tell him why he wasn't really in control yet, and he'd know where he needed to attack next. Link should already be on his way over from the *Dewdrop;* together the two of them should be able to make a respectable showing—

"Michael, this is Almo," Pyre's voice cut unexpectedly into the line. "What's your situation?"

Winward had to try twice to get any words out. "Almo! Where *are* you?"

"In the mayor's underground command center," Pyre replied. "Your return from the dead seems to have rattled him somewhat."

Despite his pain and weakness, Winward felt a grim smile spread across his face. Rattled, indeed. Out-and-out terrified, if the man had any sense at all.

Pyre was speaking again. "Now, Mr. Mayor, the situation seems to have changed. I have you, Winward has the tower—"

"He does not control the tower," Kimmeron put in. "I have been speaking to the tower commander—"

"I can take control whenever I wish," Winward interrupted harshly. Pyre was clearly attempting to negotiate with the Qasamans; the stronger the hand Winward could give him, the better the chances he could get back to the ship before he passed out from loss of blood. "And the weapons trained on the *Dewdrop* have been neutralized. F'ahl can lift any time he wants to."

Kimmeron's voice was low, but his words were precise. "You seek to trade your lives for more of ours. I have said that that is an unacceptable bargain. You know too much about us; at whatever additional cost, you must not be allowed to leave."

Winward didn't wait for Pyre's reply, but stepped quickly back into the elevator. In Kimmeron's place he would probably have made the same decision, and before Pyre's negotiations officially broke down he wanted to be on his way back to the *Dewdrop*. The long floor-selection panel gleamed at him as he reached toward it—

And paused.

All those those buttons . . . *far* more than a building this size needed. . . .

Blocking the doors open again, he stepped back into the communications room. Pyre was saying something about mass destruction; Winward didn't bother to let him finish. "Almo?" he called. "Listen—remember the idea someone had that a lot of the Qasaman industry was underground? I think this tower is an entrance to the place. Shall I go out and get Dorjay and head down to take a look?"

He waited, heart pounding, hoping Pyre would know how to use the opening he'd just given him. Winward had a dim idea, but his mind was beginning to fog over, and he knew instinctively he couldn't trust it to follow any straight logical lines. He hoped Pyre was in better shape.

"You seem upset, Mr. Mayor," Pyre's voice came through the fog. "May I assume your underground facilities are something you'd rather we not see?" There was no response, and after a moment Pyre went on, "We *can* get down there, you know. You've seen what we can do, and how little effect your guns have on us. With our ship free and clear, we can go down the tower, take a good look, and still get off Qasama alive."

"We will kill you all," Kimmeron said.

"You know better than that. So I'll offer you a deal: release all our people unharmed and we'll leave without seeing what you've got down there."

Kimmeron's laugh was a harsh bark. "You seek to trade something for a lack of something. Even if I wanted to agree, how could I persuade others to do so?"

"You explain that we take home details of city and village life, or we take home every secret you've got," Pyre told him coldly. "And your time is running out. Winward will start down the tower in three minutes, and I can't guarantee Link won't find his way underground even sooner."

It took the full three minutes and a little more, but in the end Kimmeron agreed.

Chapter 22

It took another fifteen minutes for Kimmeron to get the agreement of the Purma officials who were holding Cerenkov and Rynstadt. The radio jamming wasn't lifted for five minutes longer, but Pyre had already been allowed to send Link a message via the tower's outside speakers, warning the other Cobra to lie low and hold off on any attack. Telek, when Pyre was finally allowed through to her, agreed to the arrangement and directed Link to wait in the tower with Winward until Pyre made it back. Then, with Kimmeron his reluctant companion, Pyre got into a car and headed down the broad avenues toward the airfield . . . and waited with lasers ready for the inevitable ambush.

It didn't come. The car passed through several sets of sentries, none of whom even raised a weapon; passed beneath tall buildings without so much as a brick being thrown; passed even among the grim mass of Qasamans at the base of the airfield tower. Nothing. They pulled up to the *Dewdrop*'s main hatch, and Pyre waited with Kimmeron close beside him until Winward and Link returned.

The two Cobras entered the ship, and Pyre turned to Kimmeron. "We've completed our part of the deal," he said, putting as much quiet steel as he could into the words. "You've done half of yours. I trust you won't be tempted to back out."

"Your two companions will be waiting when you land at Purma," Kimmeron said coldly.

"Good. Now take the car and get clear before we lift." Pyre stepped into the hatchway, and the airlock door closed.

The inner door slid open, and in that same moment the *Dewdrop* lurched slightly and they were airborne.

Link was waiting as Pyre stepped into the ready room. "Looks like we might actually pull this off," the younger Cobra said quietly.

"Heavy emphasis on the *might*," Pyre nodded. "How's Michael? He looked in pretty bad shape when you passed me out there."

"I don't know—the governor's looking at him now. Probably in better shape than Decker."

"Yes, what happened to him? I saw him carried away from the bus on a stretcher, but I couldn't tell anything more."

Link's lip twitched in a grimace. "He tried to break the contact team out of the bus at the beginning of all this. The mojos flayed his arm, practically down to the bone."

Pyre felt his neck muscles tighten. "Oh, God. Is he—?"

"Too soon to tell anything, except that he'll probably live." Link licked his lips. "Listen . . . did Kimmeron say anything about Justin? He switched with Joshua when they brought Decker in and was taken off toward Purma."

For the unprovoked deaths in Purma, Kimmeron had said, sentencing the *Dewdrop* to death. Justin's work? Undoubtedly. But Kimmeron hadn't mentioned him in negotiating the other prisoners' release. Was he, then, free somewhere out in the Qasaman night?

Or was he dead?

"Kimmeron didn't say," he told Link slowly. It had happened, his mind told him vaguely; the danger to Justin he'd worried about all the way back at the beginning of this mission. "Well. First things first, I suppose. We'll land at Purma, get Yuri and Marck safely aboard . . . and then try to find out what we can about him."

"Yeah." Link searched his face another moment, then nodded. "Yeah. Come on, let's get back to the lounge, find out what's happening."

"Sure." Back to the lounge, where Joshua would be waiting. . . . But Pyre wouldn't have to tell him his brother might be dead. Not yet, anyway.

Strapped tightly into the highly uncomfortable interrogation chair, Rynstadt stared at the door through which his questioners had left, trying to keep his expression neutral for the cameras he could see focused on him.

It wasn't an easy task. The questioning had been loud and brutal, and it'd been a relief when the four Qasamans abruptly switched off the painful strobe lights and left the room. But as the minutes had dragged on and he'd had time to pull himself together, their continued absence began to seem increasingly ominous. What were they preparing for him that took a half hour to set up? Shock treatments? Sonics? Maybe even something as crude—and horrible—as slow dismemberment? His stomach churned at the thought. Death—fast death—he'd been willing to risk for the opportunity of coming to Qasama. Slow torture was something else entirely . . . and he knew far more about Aventinian technology than he really wanted to tell them.

Without warning the door swung open, causing Rynstadt to jerk against his restraints. Two of the four interrogators entered and stepped over to him. For a moment they stared down at him, Rynstadt forcing himself to return their gaze. Then, still wordlessly, they bent down and began unstrapping him.

Here it comes, Rynstadt thought, steeling himself. The torture chamber had been readied, and he was about to find out what they'd come up with.

The Qasamans finished their task; but even as Rynstadt uncramped his legs and got them under him the men turned and left. The door banged shut, and he was left standing there, alone.

It made no sense to his befuddled mind, but they didn't give him time to wonder. "Rynstadt," a hidden speaker boomed, "your companions have bargained for your release. You will be allowed to eat and drink and then be taken to city's edge."

The speaker went off with a loud click, and simultaneously a slot in the base of the door opened and a steaming tray was pushed through.

None of this made any sense, either. What did the *Dewdrop* have to bargain with that the Qasamans would consider worth Rynstadt's life? But at the sight of the food, one clear thought cut through the confusion in his mind.

Poison.

The stew and hot berry juice were poisoned . . . and he would soon tell them anything they wanted to know in exchange for the antidote. Or else he really *was* being released, in which case he'd be dead before the *Dewdrop* cleared the system, in a final act of Qasaman vengeance.

His stomach rumbled, reminding him he hadn't eaten since lunch in Huriseem, a medium-sized eternity ago . . . and on closer examination, poisoning him *did* seem a little melodramatic.

Again his stomach growled. Suppose he simply refused to eat? If the food was indeed safe, probably nothing, except that he'd go hungry. If it was poisoned . . . presumably they'd come and hypospray the stuff into him.

Walking over to the tray, he picked it up and sniffed cautiously at the bowl and mug. He'd had the stew and juice several times before during the contact team's tour, and both smelled just the way he remembered. For a long moment he was tempted . . . but if there was really a chance for freedom, he'd be foolish to take even slim risks. "Thanks," he called to the hidden mike as he set the tray back on the floor by the slot, "but I'm not hungry right now."

He held his breath. If the Qasaman voice sounded angry or annoyed . . . "Very well," the other said simply. The slot opened again, and Rynstadt glanced down to see a hand snare the tray and pull it back out of sight.

A *shiny* hand.

A hand encased in a surgeon's glove.

The slot cover slid back in place, and Rynstadt walked back to the chair, feeling cold all over. Poison, for sure—but not in the food. On the tray. Mixed with a contact absorption enhancer and spread on the tray.

And now it was on his hands . . . and in his blood.

He sat down, legs trembling with reaction. He was, then, being released—there was no need for such an elaborate subterfuge if the poison was just part of his interrogation. Released—and simultaneously murdered. Melodramatic or not—barbaric or not—they had opted for vengeance.

Was there any chance at all of coming through this alive? Perhaps, but only if the Qasamans had timed their dosage so as to let the *Dewdrop* get a good distance away before their treachery became known. How long? One hour? Two? Twelve?

There was no way to know. But the fact that he knew he'd been poisoned gave Telek and the medical analyzers aboard ship the maximum time to identify and counteract the specific toxin used on him.

Come on, he urged the *Dewdrop* silently. *Get me the hell out of here.* In the meantime . . . letting his body slump in the chair, he consciously slowed his breathing. The slower the metabolism, in theory, the slower the poison would be absorbed into his tissues.

And he settled back to wait.

The distinctive whine of gravity lifts, faint even in his enhanced hearing, finally dragged Justin from his sleep. For a moment he lay quietly in the tall grass, reorienting himself, allowing the bitter memories to return. Then, carefully, he raised his head.

The motion drew an involuntary hiss between his teeth; he'd forgotten all the places his body ached. But the sight in the northern sky drove all such considerations into the background. Against the blazing stars of Qasama's night a hazy reddish oval was drifting.

The *Dewdrop* was making a break for it.

He watched the haze for a long minute, teeth clamped together as he tried not to cry. They were leaving. Without him. Without Cerenkov and Rynstadt, as well? Probably. There was no way to know for sure; but Telek had counted on him to rescue them, and his failure probably meant they were all marooned.

Marooned.

Automatically, as if trying to insulate itself from the emotional shock, his mind began tracing out his options. He could escape into the forest, living off the wild game there, and hope he could hold out until the military expedition that would surely follow. Or he could try to find a village that would trade his Cobra skills for sanctuary from the central authorities. Or—

Or he could just stay here in the grass until he died. It all amounted to that in the end.

It was only then that the realization broke through to him that the *Dewdrop* was moving too slowly.

Much too slowly. *They crippled it,* was his first, awful thought . . . but if the grav lifts had been damaged F'ahl should have kicked in the main drive by now to assist. No, something else was happening . . . and abruptly, he understood.

They were flying low and slow on purpose. Looking for *him.*

He'd rolled over on his back in an instant, glancing toward the city as he lifted his left leg, but not really caring if anyone there spotted his signal. In a few minutes the *Dewdrop* would be here . . . and after his moments of despair the promise of rescue was flooding his mind and body with adrenaline-fueled determination. Let the Qasamans come for him now—let the whole *city* get in his way if they wanted to.

Targeting the *Dewdrop,* he fired his antiarmor laser three times.

Thirty kilometers away, the ship's hull would barely register the heat of those shots; but for the watchers aboard, the flashes of light should be impossible to miss. Assuming someone was watching.

And apparently they were. From the front-inside of the red oval the *Dewdrop*'s landing lights flicked twice in acknowledgment.

Shifting to a crouch, Justin got ready to move, keeping alert for trouble from the city.

It took the *Dewdrop* a few minutes to come to ground—and it did so, inexplicably a good kilometer north. Justin briefly considered signaling again, decided it would be safer to just go to it, and set off in a crouching run.

No one opened fire before he reached the ship. Link was waiting by the open hatchway as he came up, and favored the younger man with a tight smile. "Welcome back," he said, gripping Justin's hand briefly. He gave the other a fast once-over before returning his eyes to the city. "You've never seen a group of people so happy as when we saw your signal."

"I was happy enough for all of you put together," Justin told him, following Link's gaze. A half-dozen cars and a bus could be seen approaching from city's edge. "Looks like a good time to get out of here."

Link shook his head. "They're bringing Yuri and Marck—Almo struck a deal for their release."

"What kind of deal?" Justin frowned.

"A sort of promise not to tear up their industrial base before we go." Link glanced at the other. "Why don't you go inside, get any injuries seen to. I can handle this."

"Well . . . all right." Something about this felt wrong, but for the moment Justin couldn't figure out what. Turning, he stepped into the hatch and sprung the inner door—and walked straight into his brother's arms.

For a minute they just held each other—the man who'd done his job, Justin thought bitterly, and the man who hadn't.

But for the moment his shame was swallowed up in the relief of being safe again.

Joshua released him and stepped back, still gripping his brother's shoulders. "You hurt anywhere?"

"I'm fine," Justin shook his head. "What's happened since I left?"

Joshua glanced toward the hatch. "Let's get to the lounge where we can watch that convoy," he suggested. "I can give you a fast rundown on the way."

They reached the lounge a minute later to find Nnamdi and Christopher gazing at the outside monitors, the scientists' greetings muted by their attention being elsewhere. That suited Justin; he'd already had more of a hero's welcome than he properly deserved. "Where's the governor?" he asked Joshua as they took seats in front of another screen.

"Back in sick bay with Michael. She should be back by the time the others get here. And Almo's outside, behind the front landing spotlights, where he can back up Dorjay if the Qasamans make any trouble."

"But they won't," Nnamdi spoke up. "They've made their deal, and it's a fair one. And we've already seen they follow through on their promises."

Justin snorted. "Like with that fake explosive collar?"

All eyes turned to him. "What do you mean, fake?" Christopher asked.

"I mean they suckered us royally. Those cylinders held cameras and recorders, not explosives. They let Joshua come in so that they could get a quick look inside the *Dewdrop*."

Christopher swore under his breath. "But then they must have seen you two switch places. My *God*—you're lucky you got out alive after that."

Some of the burden seemed to lift from Justin's conscience. Seen in *that* light, perhaps he hadn't done such a bad job, after all.

The convoy outside had halted a hundred meters from the *Dewdrop* and a crowd of Qasamans was forming around the vehicles when Telek reappeared in the lounge. "Justin; glad you made it," she said distractedly as she leaned over Christopher's shoulder. "Any sign of them yet?"

"I don't see them," he replied. "They're probably in the bus off to one side, there." He pointed; and as if on cue, two figures emerged from the vehicle, struggling a bit as they plowed through the knee-high grass.

Cerenkov and Rynstadt.

The edge of the crowd withdrew a bit as the two men passed on their way to the *Dewdrop*. "Watch for drawn weapons," Telek said to the room in general. "We don't want them pulling a last-minute suicide rush or some such trick."

"If they were going to pull something, wouldn't they have done it while they still had Almo, Michael, and Dorjay under the gun?" Nnamdi suggested.

"Maybe," Telek grunted. "But we were hair-trigger alert then. Maybe they expect us to be lulled now. Anyway, I don't trust them—they accepted this deal too easily for my taste."

"Like they accepted my ultimatum to bring Decker back," Joshua muttered. Justin looked at his brother, found him staring at the approaching men with a look of intense concentration on his face.

Telek glanced in the twins' direction. "Something?"

"Tell her, Justin," Joshua said, eyes and frown still on the display.

Justin explained again about the spy collar. "Um," Telek grunted when he'd finished. "You think they've planted a bomb or something on one of them, Joshua?"

"I don't know," Joshua said slowly. "But I suddenly don't like this."

"Me, neither." Telek hesitated, then picked up the mike and punched for the outside speakers. "Yuri, Marck? Hold it there a second, would you?"

The two men came to a hesitant looking halt about twenty meters from the hatch. "Governor? What's wrong?" Cerenkov called.

"I want you both to strip to your underwear," she told them. "Safety precaution."

Rynstadt glanced back over his shoulder at the silent Qasamans. "Can't we skip that?" he called, his voice almost breaking with strain. "They didn't put anything in our clothes—I'm sure of that. Please—let us get aboard."

"Something's wrong," Christopher muttered. Grabbing the mike from Telek, he punched a new button. "Dorjay, signal them to tell you—*quietly*—what's going on." Without waiting for an acknowledgment he switched back to the outside speaker. "Come on, guys— you heard the governor. Strip."

Flicking off the speaker, he handed the mike silently back to Telek, who accepted it the same way. On the screen, the two men were pulling off their tunics; and because he knew to watch for it, Justin could see Rynstadt's lips moving. They were working on their boots when Link's voice came quietly into the circuit. "Marck says they've both been poisoned—some sort of toxin on a meal tray that the server wore gloves to avoid touching."

"No wonder they were so willing to let them go," Nnamdi growled. "We've got to get them aboard right away and into the analyzer, Governor."

But Telek was staring through the screen, her face frozen into a mask of horror. "They're not poisoned," she whispered. "They're *infected*. They've dosed them with something to kill all of us."

For a long moment shock hung thickly in the air. Telek recovered first. "Almo, get back in here—use the cargo hatch you went out by. Dorjay . . . come inside and seal the outer door. Now."

"What?" Christopher and Joshua yelped in unison.

"No choice," Telek snapped back. Her hand was white-knuckled where she clutched the mike, and her face looked very old. "We haven't got isolation facilities aboard—you all know that."

"The medical analyzer—"

"Has an even chance of not even figuring out what they've been given," she cut Christopher off, "let alone knowing how to cure it."

Beneath his feet, Justin felt the deck vibrate slightly as Pyre closed the cargo hatch; an instant later it was echoed as Link sealed the main hatchway.

And on the outer display, Rynstadt and Cerenkov froze in horrified disbelief. "Hey!" Cerenkov yelled.

"I'm sorry," Telek said, the words almost a sigh. She seemed to remember the mike, lifted it to her lips. "I'm sorry," she repeated. "You've been infected. We can't risk taking you aboard."

"Guns being drawn!" Nnamdi said abruptly. "They know we've figured it out."

"Captain—comm laser on the Qasamans," Telek snapped toward the intercom. "Dazzle them. Then . . . then prepare to lift."

"You can't leave them here."

Justin hadn't even noticed Pyre's entry into the lounge, but his voice made it clear he'd been there long enough to know what was happening.

And that he wasn't going to accept it.

Telek turned to face him, but there was no fight in her eyes. "Give me an alternative," she said quietly. "Put them in spacesuits for two weeks?—and watch them die there because we can't get to them to even attempt treatment?"

"The rest of us could stay in suits," Pyre said.

"Oxygen wouldn't last long enough," F'ahl said from the bridge. "And recharging in a contaminated atmosphere would be damned risky."

The display screens lit up briefly as comm laser fire swept the Qasamans. Rynstadt and Cerenkov broke their paralysis as the sound of gunshots and mojo screams became audible, the two men dashing for the *Dewdrop*'s tail. Heading for what cover the ship would provide, Justin guessed . . . until it lifted into space away from them.

And suddenly he had it.

"Almo!" he shouted, interrupting Telek but not caring. "Two spacesuits—out the cargo hatch. Hurry."

"Justin, I just got done saying—" Telek began.

"We can lift with them in the hold," Justin continued, the words tripping over each other as he tried to get them out as fast as possible. "The hold's got an airseal—we can evacuate it and set up UVs to sterilize the outsides of the suits."

"And watch them die in there?" Telek snarled. "The hold hasn't even got a true airlock, and we haven't got the facilities—"

"_But the Troft ships out there do!_" Justin shouted back.

And the lounge was abruptly quiet, save for the deep hum of the idling gravity lifts and the fading sounds of Pyre's running footsteps down the hall.

Three minutes later, in a highly inaccurate rain of bullets from the Qasamans, the _Dewdrop_ lifted and made for the starry sky. An hour after that, Cerenkov and Rynstadt were inside a Troft warship's isolation facility, prognosis uncertain.

An hour after that, the _Dewdrop_ was in hyperspace, heading for home.

Chapter 23

The *Menssana* had returned from its survey mission to Aventine to the sort of welcome explorers throughout the ages must have received. Its personnel were received with an official vote of congratulations by the Council, its magdisks of data copied and disseminated to hundreds of eager scientists around the planet.

The *Dewdrop*'s reception, two days later, was considerably more subdued.

The last page of Telek's preliminary report vanished from the comboard screen, and Corwin put the instrument aside with a sigh.

"Reaction?"

Corwin looked up to meet his father's eyes. "They were lucky," he said bluntly. "They should all have been killed out there."

Jonny nodded. "Yes. The Qasamans' only error was that they wanted as much information as they could get before destroying the mission. If they hadn't cared they could have blown up the *Dewdrop* any of a dozen different times."

Corwin grimaced. York's arm gone, Winward's eyes only slowly coming back, Cerenkov and Rynstadt still in critical condition aboard an orbiting Troft ship—and with all of that, he could still consider the mission *lucky*. "What in heaven's name have we gotten ourselves into?" he muttered.

"A real mess." Jonny sighed. "How long before Sun and company finish with their debriefing? Any idea?"

"Uh . . ." Corwin retrieved his comboard, punched up a request. "Not before this evening. And they're not releasing anyone to the public until morning."

"That's okay; we're not public." The elder Moreau stared into space a moment. "I want you to call your mother and arrange with her to go to the Cobra Academy tonight—use my name to get in, and if they give you any interference quote 'em some next-of-kin prerogatives—I'm sure you can find *something* applicable on the books. Don't talk politics with your brothers, and don't keep them up too late; life'll get hectic again for them when the Council gets its turn tomorrow."

Corwin nodded. "Will you be there, too?"

"Yes, but don't wait for me. I've got a couple of errands to do first."

"Alone?"

Jonny gave his eldest a lopsided smile. "My joints just had a nice vacation on sunny worlds. I can face Aventine's winter on my own for a few hours, thank you."

Corwin shrugged. "Just asking."

But he lingered in the outer office long enough to hear Yutu make arrangements with the starfield for a ground-to-orbit shuttle. His father, it appeared, would not have to worry much about Aventine's winter tonight.

Winter, as such, didn't exist aboard Troft warships.

For the fourth time in almost that many minutes the comboard screen seemed to blur in front of Telek's eyes; and for the fourth time she shook her head stubbornly and swallowed a mouthful of cahve. It was late, she was tired, and she would need to be at least marginally coherent for the Council meeting in the morning. But this was the first chance she'd had to see the *Menssana*'s report, and she was determined to have at least a passing acquaintance with what they'd found before she checked out for the night.

There was a light tap at the door. "Come," she called.

It wasn't, as she'd expected, one of the Academy medical staff. "The nurses at the monitor station are annoyed you haven't gone to sleep yet," Jonny commented as he walked into the room.

She blinked, then snorted. "They brought you all the way from Capitalia to tell me that?"

"Hardly. I was in the neighborhood and thought I'd drop in." Pulling up a chair, he sat down.

Telek nodded. "They did good. You can be damn proud of them."

"I know. Though Justin doesn't think so."

"Well, he's wrong," Telek growled. "If he'd tried to get to Purma's underground stuff, he wouldn't have made it out alive. Period. And if he hadn't made it out, we might have taken Yuri and Marck aboard before we knew how the Qasamans like to stack their deals."

"I understand that. He will too, eventually. I hope." Jonny waved toward her comboard. "The *Menssana's* report?"

"Uh-huh. You people did pretty well yourselves."

Jonny nodded. "They all look promising," he agreed. "At least two are better even than that."

Telek looked him in the eye. "I want those worlds, Jonny."

He returned the gaze without flinching. "Badly enough to fight a war for?"

"Badly enough to do whatever we have to," she said bluntly.

He sighed. "I'd rather hoped that what happened on Qasama would have blunted your eagerness a bit."

"It's made me aware of what it'll cost. But the option is the loss of the last nineteen thousand people on Caelian."

"Or so goes the argument. They *can* always move back here, you know."

"But they won't. Anyone who was willing to lose that much face by admitting defeat has already done so. We can't move the rest of them back to civilization—their pride won't take it."

"Whereas *your* pride won't let you turn tail on the Qasamans?" he countered.

"Pride has nothing to do with it."

"Sure." Reaching into his tunic, Jonny produced a magdisk and handed it to her. "Well, whatever your motives, as long as you're solidly hell-bent on smashing Qasama, you might as well know as much about the place as possible."

Telek frowned at the disk. "What's this?"

"The official Baliu'ckha'spmi report on Qasama."

She looked up at him, feeling her mouth fall open. "It's *what?* Where did you get it?"

"From the Troft ship out there," he replied. "Clearly, any ship sent to back up our mission would have their own world's report aboard for emergency reference. So I went up this afternoon and got a copy."

"Just like that?"

"More or less. A combination of bluff, bluster, and legal footwork." He smiled faintly. "Plus a healthy new respect for us on their part."

"God knows we earned *that* much," she said quietly. York and Winward alone had earned them at least that much. . . . She shook off the sudden resurgence of guilt for her failures on the trip. "So why give it to me?"

"Oh, the whole Council will get copies in the morning," he shrugged. "As I said, I was in the neighborhood."

"Yeah. Well . . . thanks."

"No charge." Jonny got to his feet—wincing with the effort, she noticed—and walked to the door. There he paused and looked back at her. "Lizabet . . . I'm not going to let the Worlds go to war for your new planets," he told her quietly. "Not after what we've seen of Qasama. A surgical strike against their technological base, perhaps, if feasible; aerial bombings, probably, if it'll actually do any good. But no land war. Not even for Caelian."

She nodded slightly. "I understand. And I'm as willing to look for middle ground as you are."

"Let's hope we can find it. Good night."

He left, and Telek found herself staring at the Troft magdisk in her hand. Suddenly she was very, very tired. . . .

Ejecting the *Menssana*'s report, she inserted the Trofts' into her comboard, keying to run it through the Academy's central translator. Then, sighing wearily, she splashed more cahve into her mug and began to read.

Chapter 24

The Council meeting was postponed two days, to give the members a chance to read both the Qasama Mission debriefing and the Troft data package Jonny had obtained. But when the debate finally began it was quickly and abundantly clear that the cautious approval that had existed for the original mission had flipped solidly in the opposite direction.

And it wasn't hard to figure out why.

"If the damn planet wasn't a lost human colony no one would be nearly this emotional about the whole thing," Dylan Fairleigh growled afterward as the governors gathered for their own meeting.

"Neither of the Caelian syndics was complaining," Vartanson pointed out quietly. "We know what the trade-off is here."

"Us or them?" Jonny asked. "Is that it? Come on, now—we don't even know why the Trofts are so worried about Qasama."

"Don't we?" Roi shot back. "A thriving, highly cooperative, highly *paranoid* human culture? That's not something to be afraid of?"

"A culture without starflight, without even system space travel?" Hemner quavered.

"We don't *know* they don't have spaceflight capability," Fairleigh reminded him tartly. His eyes flicked to Jonny. "There's a *lot* we don't know about their industrial and technological base. That we *should* have found out."

Jonny bristled; but Telek got her word in first. "If that's a slur on my team in general and Justin Moreau in particular, you're invited to withdraw it," she said coldly.

"I only meant—"

"If you'd like, *you* can head the next trip to Qasama," she cut him off. "We'll see then how well *you* do."

Stiggur chose that moment to make his own belated entrance, his presence stifling the budding argument. "Good afternoon; sorry I'm late," he said with an air of harried distraction as he sat down at his place and pushed a pile of magdisks into the center of the table. "Preliminary biological data analysis—just came in. Summary in the front. Take a quick look and we'll discuss it."

It was, as Jonny had expected, an analysis of the *Dewdrop* and Troft data, concentrating on the mojos. He skimmed the summary and was halfway through a more careful study when Vartanson harrumphed. "Nasty. Reminds me of some of the feathered killing machines we have on Caelian."

"Aside from the weird reproductive setup, I presume," Roi said. "The whole arrangement looks pretty fragile to me. Kill off enough of their embryo-hosts—these whatyoucallem, these tarbines—and you could wipe out the species overnight."

"Most ecosystems look that unstable at first glance," Telek put in dryly. "In practice, you'd find you'd need to kill a *hell* of a lot of tarbines to make any real dent. I take it, though, that you feel the mojos to be the major threat to any Cobra forces we put down there?"

"No question," Roi said. "Look at the record. No one except Winward suffered any appreciable damage from the Qasamans' guns, and that single case was a surprise attack. But the mojos got him *and* York and came close with Pyre and Moreau."

"They really *are* the first line of defense," Fairleigh agreed. "And the Qasamans know it. Hell, they design their *cities* to keep the things happy."

"Makes sense, of course," Stiggur said with a shrug. "Why risk human deaths in a battle when you've got animals to take the brunt of the attack?"

"That's not how the arrangement began," said Telek. "It was originally for defense against predators and evolved into a personal bodyguard system."

"And now shows itself easily adapted to warfare," Stiggur said. "The history doesn't concern us as much as the current situation does." He turned to Jonny. "Is there any way you know of to make the Cobra equipment better able to deal with the mojos? Some change in the targeting mechanism, for instance?"

Jonny shrugged. "The targeting procedure is designed to allow fast target acquisition while minimizing accidental lock-ons. Make it any easier and faster and you'll automatically get more misfires."

"Then how about reprogramming the nanocomputer to identify

mojos as hostile?" Fairleigh suggested. "That way at least the next generation of Cobras could handle them."

Vartanson snorted. "If that could be done, don't you think we'd already have something like that for the Caelian Cobras? Shape recognition just takes up too much computer memory."

"It's actually more basic than that," Jonny shook his head. "The minute you put some kind of automatic recognition targeting into the Cobras, you rob them of their versatility and, ultimately, their effectiveness. Once the Qasamans figured it out, they could throw birds by the hundreds at us, and while we're helplessly shooting down ones who couldn't even get near us for three minutes, the Qasaman gunners shoot us at their leisure. Automatic single-purpose weapons are fine in their place—and you're using them quite effectively on Caelian—but don't try to make them out of Cobras."

There was a moment's silence. "Sorry," Jonny muttered. "Didn't mean to lecture."

Stiggur waved the apology aside. "The point was reasonable and well taken. I don't think anyone wants to have specialized cadres of Cobras. So. Is there some other way to reduce the mojos' effectiveness?"

"Excuse me for changing the subject," Hemner spoke up hesitantly, "but there are still some points about Qasama generally that bother me. History, Brom, you implied wasn't important, but I'd like to know a little about the colony's background. Specifically, how and when it came to be."

"I didn't mean history wasn't *important*." Stiggur poked at his comboard. "Only that—oh, never mind. Let's see. The historians' report indicates the original Qasamans left the Dominion circa 2160, probably as colonists bound from Reginine for Rajput. The direction vector is about right, and the various historical references and language—not to mention the name Qasama itself— all point to one of Reginine's basic subcultures."

"The *name* Qasama?" Vartanson frowned.

"You've *got* this report yourselves," Stiggur said, a bit tartly. " 'Qasama' is an Old Arabic word meaning 'to divide.' It's come into Anglic through a couple of different languages and changes to become 'kismet,' meaning 'fate' or 'destiny.' "

"Divided by destiny," Roi murmured. "Some linguist aboard the original ship had a strange sense of humor."

"Or sense of manifest destiny," Telek said, half to herself. "I never saw a scrap of evidence the Qasamans had any humor whatsoever. They took themselves incredibly seriously."

"Fine," Hemner said. "So Qasama's been in existence for something under three hundred years, and in that time the mojos and humans have become symbiotically entwined. Correct?"

"Correct," Stiggur nodded. "Though 'symbiosis' might be too strong a word."

"Oh?" Hemner raised an eyebrow. "The people kill the tarbines' protector bololins so that the mojos can breed more easily; in turn the mojos protect their owners from attack. What's that if not symbiosis? But my real question is what did the mojos do before humans came along?"

All eyes shifted to Telek. "Lizabet?" Stiggur prompted. "Any ideas?"

"Not offhand," she answered slowly, a frown creasing her forehead. "Huh. Never even occurred to me to wonder about that. Have to be a predator, certainly—a *big* one, to deal with the bololins. I'll have to check the Troft records, see how many likely candidates there are."

"If you'll forgive me," Roi put in, "I don't see that this is a vital part of figuring out how to stop the mojos now that they *are* riding around on the Qasamans' shoulders."

"If you'll forgive *me*," Telek shot back, "one never knows in this business where a key fact will show up."

She launched into a mini-lecture abut the interdependence of biological structure and function with ecological position, but Jonny missed most of it. Skimming the Qasaman biological data, he hit a small sentence that brought his eyes and mind to a screeching halt. He backed up and read the section carefully . . . and a not-quite-understood shiver went up his spine.

Stiggur was saying something mollifying when Jonny's attention returned to the group. He waited until the governor-general was finished and then spoke up before anyone else could do so. "Lizabet, have you had time to study the fauna records the *Menssana* brought back? Specifically, the ones from the planet Chata?"

"I glanced through them." Her expression said *you know I did,* but the thought remained unsaid. "You driving at anything specific?"

"Yes." Jonny tapped keys to send the two pages he'd been looking at to the others' displays. "On the left is our profile of the flat-foot quadruped of Chata; on the right, yours of the Qasaman bololin. If you'd all take a moment to scan the two pages, I think you'll see what I mean."

"Interesting," Vartanson nodded a minute later. "A lot of similarity there."

"In particular the use of magnetic field lines for navigation," Telek agreed. "Highly unusual for large land animals. Probably a classic example of the Trofts' so-called common-stock theory—you know, the same argument as to why we get similar flora and fauna on Aventine, Palatine, and Caelian."

"Uh-huh," Jonny said. He'd found the other two pages he needed and now put them on the displays. "Okay, then, how about the mojo on the right and *this* bird on the left?"

Fairleigh snorted. "From a binocular photo and computer-generated views? Even *I* know you need more than that for a similarity study."

Jonny kept his eyes on Telek. "Lizabet?"

"Both predators," she said slowly. "Beaks and wing coverts very similar. Feet . . . not enough detail, but . . . interesting. Those short filaments coming off the crown and lore—here and here? The mojo's got some sort of vibrissae there, too; tied somehow into its auditory system, we think. Unless that's a false construct generated by the computer. Where did you spot this—oh, there it is. Tacta. The last planet on your survey, right?"

"Right," Jonny said absently. So the mojos were apparently close cousins to the strange bird whose behavior had spooked them off its world. Which meant . . . what?

"For the moment, at least," Stiggur said, "Lizabet is right that the mojo data needs more detailed study before we can discuss a counter to them. So I'd like to move on to a strategic discussion of the society itself, particularly the structural aspects that we already know. Uh . . . let's see . . . right: page 162 is where it starts."

The discussion lasted nearly an hour, and despite the relatively raw state of the data a picture emerged which Jonny found as depressing from a military standpoint as it possibly could have been. "Let's see if I've got all this straight," he said at the end, trying to go as easy as he could on the heavy sarcasm. "We have a society whose members all regularly carry firearms, whose population is largely spread out in small villages, whose light industry is also solidly decentralized and whose heavy industry is buried deep underground, and whose exact technological level is still unknown. Does that pretty well cover it?"

"Don't forget their willingness to use brain-boosting drugs and to hell with the personal consequences," Roi growled. "And all of them hellbent paranoids on top of it. You know, Brom, the more we get into this, the less I like the idea of them sitting out there ready to explode across space as soon as they reinvent the stardrive."

"You sound as if they'll be orbiting us the next morning," Hemner said. He coughed, twice, the spasms shaking his thin shoulders, but when he continued his voice was firm enough. "Qasama is forty-five light-years away, remember—it'll take them *years* to find us, even if they're specifically looking. Long before that they'll run into the Trofts, and whether they begin trade or warfare they'll be tied up with them for generations. By then they'll have forgotten this little fiasco and we'll be able to start fresh with our brother humans as if this had never happened."

"A nice speech, Jor," Telek said tartly, "but you're missing a few rather vital points. One: What if they hit Chata and the other worlds out there *before* they find the Trofts?"

"What of it?" Hemner replied. "If we quit the job now our people won't be out there, anyway."

Telek's lip might have twitched, but her voice was even enough as she continued. "Second is your assumption the Qasamans will forget us. Wrong. They'll remember, all right, and whether it's a year or a century they'll brace for war the minute they run into us again. You may not believe that," she added, glancing around the table, "but it's true. *I* was there; *I* saw and heard the way they talk. You wait until Hersh Nnamdi's final report is in, see if he doesn't agree with me on that. And third: We let them get off Qasama and we're in for a long and very bloody war indeed. Our current technological edge is meaningless with brain-boosters in the picture—a few months or years of warfare and they'll be at our level, whatever it is at the time. And if you think they're decentralized *now* wait'll they're dug in on Kubha and Tacta and God knows where else."

"Your points are certainly valid," Stiggur said as Telek paused. "But all your tactical arguments miss the one big emotional stumbling block we're going to face here. Namely, are the Cobra Worlds *really* going to fight as Troft mercenaries against other human beings?"

"That's a rather inflammatory way of putting it," Vartanson accused.

"Of course it is. But it's the way that side of the issue is going to present their case. And in all honesty, I have to admit it's a valid point. We started this whole affair worrying about looking weak in the Trofts' eyes, if you'll recall, and a world's ethics are certainly part of its total strength. Besides, wouldn't we actually be adding to our position to have other human allies on the Troft border?"

"You're ignoring history, Brom," Jonny put in quietly. "Having two human groups on their borders is precisely what got the Troft demesnes worried enough to jointly prepare for war fourteen years ago."

Fairleigh snorted. "There's a good-sized difference between the Dominion of Man and Qasama as far as border threats go."

"Only in magnitude. And remember that Trofts don't go in for mass destruction from starships. They make war by going in and physically occupying territory . . . and Qasama would *not* be a fun place to go in and occupy."

"Agreed," Telek murmured with a slight shudder.

"Or in other words," Hemner said, "the Trofts can't bring themselves to slaughter, so they're hiring *us* to do it for them."

Several voices tried to answer; Vartanson's was the one that got through. "*Forget* the Trofts for a minute—just forget them. We're talking about a threat to *us*, damn it. Lizabet is right—we've got to deal with them, and we've got to deal with them *now*."

For a long moment the small room was quiet. Jonny glanced at Hemner, but the old man was staring down at his hands, clenched together on the table. Stiggur eventually broke the silence. "I think we've done about as much as we can with the data at hand," he said, looking at each of the others in slow, measured turn. "The final geological, biological, and sociological studies are due in ten days; we'll meet then—prior to a full Council meeting—and try to come to a decision." Reaching to the side of his display, he shut off the sealed recorder. "This meeting is adjourned."

Chapter 25

Stiggur's prediction of the opposition's tactical methods took only a few days to be borne out; and as he had when the Qasaman story first broke weeks earlier, Corwin abruptly found himself in the middle of the whole public debate.

But with a difference. Before, Qasama had been seen as little more than a mathematical equation: an abstract challenge on one hand, with the very concrete hope of more than doubling the Cobra Worlds' land holdings on the other. Now the comfortable fog was gone. As details of Qasama's people and dangers were released, a growing emotional fire began to simmer within even the most logical and rational arguments, both pro and anti. Most of the antis Corwin talked to were only marginally mollified by the assurance that Jonny was also against a massive war with other humans, their attitude usually being that he should be doing more to bring the Council over to that point of view. The pros tended simply to ignore such sticky ethical questions while claiming that the Cobra Worlds' own safety should be Jonny's first priority. It made for a verbal no-win situation, and within three days Corwin was heartily sick of it.

But it wasn't until he got a call from Joshua that he realized just how much the phone and public information net had again taken over his life.

"Have you had a chance to see Justin lately?" Joshua asked after the amenities were out of the way.

"Not since the evening after your debriefing." Corwin winced at that sudden revelation. Four days, it had been now, without talking to *anyone* in his family except his father. He wasn't used to getting so far out of touch. "I haven't had much time lately."

"Well, I think you'd better find the time for this. Soon."

Corwin frowned. "Why? Something wrong?"

Joshua's phone screen image hesitated, shook its head minutely. "I don't know. It's nothing I can put my finger on, but . . . well, he hasn't come back from the Academy yet, you know."

Corwin didn't. "Medical observation?"

"No, but he's spending almost all his time alone in the room they've given him out there. And he's doing a lot of computer library searches."

Corwin thought back to Justin's report, which he'd hurriedly skimmed and filed away two days ago. His brother had gone through hell's own porch out there . . . "Maybe he's just killing time while the emotional wounds heal over a bit," he suggested. But even as he said them the words rang false in his ears. Justin simply wasn't the type to lick his wounds in private.

Joshua might have been reading his mind. "Then those wounds must be a lot deeper than he's letting on, because he's never holed up like this before. And the library search stuff bothers me, too. Any way for you to get a list of what he's been researching?"

"Possibly." Corwin scratched his cheek. "Well . . . did you remind him we're having a Moreau Family war council this evening?"

"Yes," the other nodded. "He said he'd try to make it."

"Okay," Corwin said slowly. "Okay. I haven't talked to you, so of course I don't know he's been reminded. I'll call him up like a good big brother should, and while I'm at it I'll see what else I can get out of him. All right?"

"Fine. Thanks, Corwin—this has been driving me just barely south of frantic."

"No problem. See you tonight."

Joshua disappeared from the screen. Scowling, Corwin punched up the Cobra Academy and asked for Justin. A moment later his brother's face came on. "Hello?—oh, hi, Corwin. What can I do for you?"

It took Corwin a second to find his tongue. Seldom if ever had he known Justin to be so coolly polite, so—the term *businesslike* leapt to mind. "Uh, I was just calling to see if you'd be coming to the family round table tonight," he said at last. "I presume Dad told you about it?"

"Yes, a couple days ago, and Joshua again today. I understand Aunt Gwen's going to be there too."

Nuts, Corwin thought with a mental grimace. He'd been planning to drop that tidbit on Justin himself as a surprise bonus incentive to attend. Aunt Gwen—Jonny's younger sister—had been Justin's favorite relative since childhood, but her visits had been few and far between since her move to Palatine six years earlier. "That's right," he told Justin. "She's one of the geologists working on the Qasama data."

Justin's lip might have twitched at the name *Qasama*; Corwin wasn't sure. "Yes, Dad mentioned that. Well, as I told Joshua, I'll try to make it."

"What's to keep you away?" Corwin asked, studiously casual. "You're still off-duty, aren't you?"

"Officially, yes. But there's something I've been working on lately that I'm trying to finish up."

"What sort of something?"

Justin's face didn't change. "You'll find out when it's done. Until then I'd rather not say."

Corwin exhaled quietly and admitted defeat. "All right, *be* mysterious; see if I care. But let me know if you need transport and I'll send a car for you."

"Thanks. Talk to you later."

"'Bye." The screen blanked, and Corwin leaned back in his seat. The trip to Qasama had definitely changed his younger brother— and not necessarily for the better. Still, as he'd told Joshua, some things simply took time to work out.

His intercom buzzed: Yutu with something new on the public net that needed an official response. Sighing, Corwin turned on the net and, pushing his worries about Justin into the background, got back to work.

For Pyre, it was just like old times. Almost.

An invitation to the Moreau family dinners had always ranked at the very top of his list, not only because he enjoyed their company but also because their tacit acceptance of him as part of the family was an honor bestowed on few other outsiders. Over the years he'd had the privilege of watching the three boys move from high chairs to boosters to full adult participation; had learned by osmosis some of the intricacies of Cobra World politics; had even gotten to know Gwen Moreau, barely three years his senior, well enough to seriously consider marriage to her. Tonight as he looked around the table, listening and contributing to the chitchat, he felt the memories of those happier times drifting like the scent of good cahve through his mind.

But tonight the warmth was chilled, and all their efforts could not dispel the cloud that Justin's empty chair cast over the proceedings. Jonny had assured them that Justin would be there in time for the discussion, but as dinner wore down to dessert and then cahve Pyre began to doubt it.

And worse than Justin's voluntary exile was the cold certainty in Pyre's gut that ultimately it was his fault.

Not just the fact that he'd been Justin's Cobra trainer, the one responsible for making sure the boy was ready for the mission. Pyre had trained Cobras before, and if Justin had failed to develop that touch of defensive paranoia a man in danger needed, that was simply the other's basic personality. Too, he *could* have forbidden Justin's participation on the mission; but the Council wanted the twins aboard and there was nothing Pyre could have pointed to to justify dropping them out.

But if he'd followed the armored bus when Moff had taken Justin from Sollas to Purma. . . .

It was a scenario Pyre had played over and over in infinite variation on the trip back to Aventine, and it still haunted the quiet times of his day. If he'd followed the bus he could have broken Justin out at that first stop, the two of them then freeing Cerenkov and Rynstadt. Or even have waited until the high-security building and then backtracked to the others' rescue. Justin would never have had to face the situation of being deep in enemy territory, abandoned by the outside assistance he'd counted on.

And he wouldn't have had to learn quite so hard the fact that even Cobras were allowed to be afraid. Allowed to panic.

Allowed to remain human.

Dinner ended, and the group moved into the living room. But Jonny had barely begun when there was a quiet knock on the door and Justin let himself in.

There was a brief, awkward moment as everyone tried for the right balance of greeting, interest, casualness, and solicitude. But then Joshua managed to break the ice. "About time," he growled, mock-seriously. "*You* were supposed to be bringing the main course."

Justin smiled, and the tension eased. "Sorry I'm late," he apologized, also mock-seriously, to his brother. "The gantua steaks will be along in a minute—and as partial compensation for the delay, the meat is *exceptionally* fresh."

He sat down beside Joshua, nodded to the others, and then turned his eyes expectantly to his father. "How much have I missed?"

"As a matter of fact, we were just starting." Jonny hesitated. "What I'm about to say—about to suggest—is going to sound pretty strange," he said, glancing around at the others. "What's worse is that I haven't got any solid evidence whatsoever for it. That's the main reason you're all here: to help me decide whether I'm actually on to something or just hallucinating." His eyes shifted to Chrys, seated on the couch between Corwin and Gwen, and stayed there as if seeking strength. "I asked you to read the report on the planet Tacta that the *Menssana* brought back, in particular the section on the bird we've nicknamed the *spookie*. What was in there wasn't much—mainly just a brief encounter we had with one near the ship's perimeter. What *wasn't* there was the strong suspicion I've had ever since then that the spookie is in some degree telepathic."

The word seemed to hang like smoke in the air. Pyre flicked his eyes around the room: at Chrys, who looked troubled; Corwin, Gwen, and Joshua, whose faces appeared to register astonished skepticism; at Justin, whose expression was closed but . . . interested.

"All my evidence is subjective," Jonny continued, "but let me describe exactly what happened and see what you think."

Carefully, almost as if giving evidence in court, he went on to tell of the spookie watching him from the low bushes; of its agitation when he called others over to see; of its deftly timed, deftly executed break for freedom; and of the mission's failure to locate any more of the species. When he finished there was a long silence.

"Anyone else come to this conclusion?" Gwen asked at last.

"Two or three others are wondering about it," Jonny told her. "Understandably, none of us put it in our official reports, but Chrys and I weren't imagining things out there."

"Um. Doesn't have to be a complete, mind-reading telepathy, does it?" Gwen mused. "With a spookie's brain capacity it shouldn't have the intelligence to handle input like that."

"Dr. Hanford made a similar comment at the time," Chrys said. "We've talked about the possibility the spookies might form some kind of group mind, or that the sense boils down more to a feeling for danger than actual mind-reading."

"I'd vote for the latter," Corwin put in. "A group mind, even if such a thing could exist, shouldn't worry too much about losing one of its cells. In fact, it might deliberately sacrifice a spookie or two to get a look at your weaponry in action."

"Good point," Jonny nodded. "I lean toward the danger-recognition theory myself, though it requires a pretty fine scale to have timed things that well."

"The fine-tuning, at least, could have been coincidental," Corwin suggested.

"Or the whole thing could have been coincidence," Joshua said hesitantly. "Sorry, Dad, but I don't see anything here that can't be explained away."

"Oh, I agree," Jonny said without rancor. "And if I hadn't been there I'd be treating it with the same healthy skepticism. As a matter of fact, I hope you're right. But one way or the other, we've got to pin this down, and we've got to pin it down fast."

"Why?" Pyre asked. "It seems to me Tacta's fauna is pretty far down the priority stack. What's the big rush for?"

Jonny opened his mouth—but it was Justin who spoke. "Because the Council's about to make a decision on war with Qasama," he said evenly, "and the mojos are related to these spookies. Aren't they."

Jonny nodded, and Pyre felt the blood draining out of his face. "You mean to say we were fighting *telepathic birds* down there?"

"I don't know," Jonny said. "You were there. You tell me."

Pyre licked his lips briefly, eyes shifting to Justin. The immediate shock was fading and he was able to think. . . . "No," he said after a minute. "No, they weren't strictly telepathic. They never recognized that we were Cobras, for one thing—never reacted as if I was armed until I started shooting."

"Did you ever *see* how they reacted to a conventional weapon, though?" Gwen asked.

Pyre nodded, "Outside the ship, the first contact. The team had to leave their lasers in the airlock."

"And Decker," Joshua murmured.

"And Decker," Pyre acknowledged, swallowing with the memory of York's sacrifice. "In fact, I'd go so far as to say the mojos don't even sense the presence of danger, at least not the way you claim your spookie does. When I climbed up a building at the edge of Sollas that last night I surprised both a Qasaman sentry *and* his mojo. The bird should at least have been in the air if it felt me coming." He cocked an eyebrow at Justin. "You notice anything, one way or the other?"

The young Cobra shrugged. "Only that the group mind thing goes out the window with at least the mojos—none of them learned anything about us no matter how many of their friends we slaughtered." He paused, and a haze of emotional pain seemed to settle over his face. "And . . . there may be one other thing."

The others sensed it as well, and a silence rich in sympathy descended on the room. It took Justin a couple of tries to get started, but when he finally spoke his voice was steady and flat with suppressed emotion. "You've all read my report, I expect. You know I—well, I panicked while I was being taken underground in Purma. I killed all the mojos and some of the Qasamans in the elevator, and a few minutes later I killed another group in the hallway upstairs. What . . . what some of you don't know is that I didn't just panic. I literally lost my head when each set of mojos attacked. I don't even remember fighting them off, just sort of coming to with them dead around me."

He stopped, fighting for control . . . and it was Joshua who spotted the key first. "It was *only* when the mojos were attacking you?" he asked. "The Qasamans themselves didn't bother you?"

Justin shook his head. "Not to the same extent. At least not those in the elevator. The others . . . well, I don't remember killing them, either, I guess. I don't know—maybe I'm just rationalizing for my failure."

"Or maybe you're not," Jonny said grimly. "Almo, did *you* experience anything like that when you were fighting the mojos?"

Pyre hesitated, thinking back. He wished he could admit to such a thing, for the sake of Justin's self-esteem. If the mojos actually *had* been fueling the younger man's reaction. . . .

But he had to shake his head. "Sorry, but I'm afraid not," he told Jonny. "On the other hand, I never faced mojos who'd already seen I was dangerous, either. I was always in a position to target and eliminate them in the first salvo. Perhaps we could talk to Michael Winward, see what he went through."

Joshua was gazing into space. "The cities. They're *designed* for the mojos' benefit. You suppose there's more significance to that than we thought?"

Gwen stirred. "I have to admit I don't understand this 'designed city' bit, especially the lunacy of letting herds of bololins charge up your streets. Wouldn't it have been simpler to just go out on hunting trips when you wanted to let your mojo breed?"

"Or else set up tarbine aviaries in the cities," Chrys suggested. "I would think it harder to go out and trap wild mojos than to breed tame ones, anyway."

"That would certainly make the most sense," Pyre said.

"Assuming," Corwin said quietly, "that the Qasamans were the ones making those decisions."

And there it is, Pyre thought. *What all the rest of us are skating around, out in the open at last.* He looked around the circle, but superimposed on the view was an unsettling image: a Qasaman as marionette, its strings in the beak of its mojo. . . .

It was Justin who eventually broke the silence. "It's not as simple as the mojos being able to take control of people," he said. "We had mojos all around us that last night and still were able to escape."

Pyre thought back. "Yes," he agreed slowly. "Both outside of Purma and in Kimmeron's office in Sollas the mojos should have been able to influence me. If they could."

"Maybe they need a longer association with a person," Corwin said. "Or there's a distance or stress factor that inhibits them."

"You're talking degrees now," Chrys spoke up, her voice low. "Does that mean we're all agreed that somehow, on some level, the mojos are influencing events on Qasama?"

There was a brief silence; and, one by one, they nodded. "The cities," Joshua said. "That's the key indicator. They've gone to enormous trouble to duplicate the mojos' natural breeding patterns, even when simpler ways exist. Funny none of us picked up on that before."

"Maybe not," Pyre told him grimly. "Maybe the mojos were able to dampen our curiosity that much, at least."

"Or maybe not," Joshua retorted. "Let's not start giving these birds *too* many superhuman abilities, all right? They're not even intelligent, remember. I think we humans are all perfectly capable of missing the obvious without any outside help."

The discussion went back and forth for a while before turning to other matters . . . and so engrossed did they all become that Pyre alone noticed Justin's quiet departure.

The desk in his temporary Cobra Academy room was small and several centimeters shorter than he liked; but it was equipped with a computer terminal, and that was all Justin really cared about. He'd just punched in a new search command and was waiting for the results when there was a tap at the door. "Come in," he said absently. Probably someone here to complain about his late hours again—

"No one ever tell you it was impolite to leave without saying good-bye?"

Justin spun his chair around, surprise and chagrin flooding his face with heat. "Oh . . . hi, Aunt Gwen," he managed to say without stuttering. "Uh—well, you were all busy discussing the mojos, and I had work to do here. . . ."

He trailed off under her steady, no-nonsense gaze, the look that since childhood had been more effective on him than any amount of brimstone or lecture. "Uh-*huh*," she said. "Well, it's too bad you took off when you did. You missed *my* report."

"The one on the Qasaman strategic material situation?"

"That's the one. *And* the surprise bonus: the Qasamans' long-range communication method."

Justin blinked, his heartbeat speeding up. "You've figured it out? Well, come on—how do they do it?"

"I'll trade you," she said, waving at the desk and its scattering of papers and maps. "You tell me *your* secret first."

He felt his mouth twist into a grimace . . . but he'd have to tell someone soon, anyway. Aunt Gwen he could at least hope to be sympathetic. "All right," he sighed. "I'm trying to work up a tactical plan for the next intelligence raid on Qasama."

Gwen's eyes remained steady on his. "What makes you think there'll *be* another mission?"

"There *has* to be," he said. "The first mission ended with too many critical facts still unknown. Those underground manufacturing centers, at the very least, and if Dad's right the mojos as well."

"Uh-huh. I presume you plan on leading this expedition?"

Justin's lip quirked. "Of course not . . . but I *will* be one of the team."

"Um." Gwen glanced around the room, snared a chair from beside the door and pulled it over to face her nephew's. "You know, Justin," she said, sitting down, "if I didn't know better, I'd think you were running away from something."

He snorted. "Heading to Qasama hardly qualifies as running away, in my opinion."

"Depends on what you have here to face. Staying put when you feel real or imagined public animosity isn't easy. But sometimes any other option is the coward's way out."

Justin took a deep breath. "Aunt Gwen . . . you can't possibly know what this situation is like. I failed on Qasama—pure and simple—and it's my job now to make up for it if I can."

"You're not listening. Failure or not isn't the issue. Rushing ahead with a premature course of action qualifies as running away, period.

And yes, I *do* know what you're facing. When your father came back from the war he—" She stopped, lips compressed, then quietly continued. "There was an accident in town one night, and he . . . killed a couple of teenagers."

Justin felt his mouth go dry. "I've never heard this," he said carefully.

"It's nothing we're anxious to talk about," she sighed. "Basically, the kids pretended they were going to run him over with their car and his Cobra reflexes countered in a way that wound up indirectly killing them. But the details don't matter. He wanted to run away afterwards—had a whole bunch of off-world university applications filled out and ready to go. But he stayed. He stayed, and along with helping the rest of us cope with the ostracism, he just happened incidentally to save a few men from a fire."

"So he stayed . . . until he left for good and came here to Aventine?"

Gwen blinked. "Well . . . yes, but that's not the same. The Dominion government wanted the Cobras to come help open up the colony—"

"Could he have refused?"

"I—can't say. But he wouldn't have, because his skills and abilities were needed out here."

Justin spread his hands. "But don't you see?—you're giving my own argument back at me. Dad's Cobra abilities were needed, so he came; my Cobra abilities are needed on Qasama, so I'm going. It's the exact same thing."

"But it's *not*," Gwen said, her voice and eyes almost pleading. "You don't have the training and experience to be a warrior. You're just trying to cleanse your conscience through an act of revenge."

Justin sighed and shook his head. "I'm not out for revenge, really I'm not. Between the ride back and my time here I've had two weeks to work through my emotions on the matter, and . . . I think I understand myself and my motives. Qasama has to be stopped, we need more information to do that—" he took a deep breath— "and if I'm not a real warrior, I'm probably the closest thing to one left on Aventine."

"Jonny has worked hard to make the Cobras a force for peace and development in the Worlds."

"But he had to go through his war first," Justin told her quietly. "And I have to go through mine."

For a long minute the room was silent. Then Justin gave his aunt a passable attempt at a smile. "Your turn now. What's *your* secret?"

Gwen sighed, a long hissing sound of defeat. "If you look at a topographical map of Qasama, you'll see that all the cities and villages are scattered along a low, roughly boomerang-shaped ridge four thousand kilometers or so in total length and maybe six hundred at its largest diameter. There's evidence that it was caused by an upwelling of basaltic magma in the fairly recent geological past."

"That's a *lot* of magma," Justin murmured.

"Granted, though there are even larger examples of this sort of thing back on some of the Dominion worlds. Anyway, I've done some computer modeling, and it looks very possible that the basalt intruded into some highly metallic rock layers. If that's the case the Qasamans have a ready-made waveguide for low-frequency radio waves a hundred meters below them, ready to dig antennas into. That sort of system's been used before, but with the metallic ore around it the basalt would keep nearly all of the signal inside it, leaking very little of it out for anyone to pick up."

Justin whistled under his breath. "Cute. Very cute. A planet already wired for sound." And if true, it would eliminate the last lingering doubts he had about mojo long-distance telepathic abilities. That was worth a lot right there. "When will you know for sure if you're right?"

She sighed again. "I suppose it won't be certain until your intelligence raid finds the antennas." She gazed at him another moment, then got to her feet. "I'd better be going," she said, backing toward the door. "Almo's waiting to take me back to my hotel. I'll . . . talk to you later."

"Thanks for coming by," Justin said. "Don't worry—this'll be done in a day or two, and after it's submitted I'll have more time to spend with the family."

"Sure. Well . . . good night."

"'Night, Aunt Gwen."

For a long minute after she left he stayed where he was, eyes on the closed door. A hundred meters down to the Qasamans' basaltic waveguide. Thirty stories, more or less . . . approximately the depth of the Purma building he'd escaped from. Had *that* been all the place was?—the local communications center, not the industrial complex that he'd thought? If so—

If so, he'd missed little of truly vital importance by his premature break for freedom.

He was, perhaps, not a failure, after all. Or at least not as much of one as he'd thought.

It was nice to know. But, ultimately, it made little practical difference. There was still the job on Qasama to do, and he and his fellow Cobras the only ones who could do it.

Turning to his desk once more, he got back to work.

Chapter 26

Stiggur was neither impressed nor convinced by Jonny's arguments. Neither, very obviously, were most of the others.

"A telepathic bird," Vartanson snorted. "Come *on*, now—don't you think you're reaching just a little too far for this one?"

Jonny kept his temper with an effort. "What about the design of the cities?" he asked.

"What about it?" Vartanson shot back. "There are any of a hundred explanations for that. Maybe the mojos get sick if they don't breed regularly and the city dwellers don't want to take trips into the woods for the purpose. Maybe they can't wall out the bololin herds and this was the best compromise available."

"Then why *build* cities?" Jonny said. "They like being decentralized—why not just stick with villages?"

"Because there are social and economic advantages to a certain amount of population concentration," Fairleigh spoke up. "Masking any trace of their underground industry would be a good reason all by itself."

"And before you bring up the Tactan spookies," Roi said, "your correlation between those and the mojos is tentative at best—and the conclusions you come to about the spookies is ridiculous. I'm sorry, but it is."

"That's a rather blanket assessment for someone who doesn't know a thing about biology," Jonny told him tartly.

"Oh, is it? Well, perhaps we ought to ask our resident biologist, then." Roi turned to Telek. "Lizabet, what do *you* think?"

Telek favored him with a cool look, which she sent slowly around the table. "I think," she said at last, "that we'd damn well better find out for sure. And that we'd better do it fast."

There was a stunned silence. Jonny stared at Telek, her unexpected support throwing his brain off-line. "You agree the mojos are influencing the Qasamans' actions?" he asked.

"I agree they're more than they seem," she said. "How *much* more is what we've got to find out."

Stiggur cleared his throat. "Lizabet . . . I understand that your professional interests here are naturally directed more toward the mojos than the Qasaman technological base. But—"

"Then let me put it another way," Telek interrupted him. "I've known about Jonny's theory since yesterday—never mind how—and I've used that time to do a couple of new studies on the visual record the team brought back." She looked at Roi. "Olor, I would say that the Palatinian glow-nose is probably the most popular pet anywhere in the Worlds—you agree? Good. How many people on Palatine own one?"

Roi blinked. "I don't know, off hand. Eighty percent, I'd guess."

"I looked up the numbers," Telek said. "Assuming only one per customer the figure is actually under sixty percent. If you include all other pets the number of owners is still only about eighty-seven percent."

"What's your point?" Stiggur asked.

Telek focused on him. "Thirteen percent of an admittedly pet-crazy people don't own pets. But *every single damn Qasaman has a mojo.*"

Jonny frowned into the thoughtful silence, trying to visualize the scenes he'd seen from the records. It was possible, he decided with some surprise. "No exceptions?" he asked Telek.

"Only three the computer scan came up with, and two don't really count: children under ten or so, and dancers and duelists. The duelists get their birds back after their curse ball game, though, and I suspect the dancers have them waiting backstage, too. At which point we're back to one hundred percent of the adult population with mojos. The floor is open for speculation."

"They're living in a dangerous environment," Vartanson shrugged.

"Not really," Telek shook her head. "The villages ought to be safe enough, with the walls and the scarcity of the krisjaw predators that were mentioned. And with the bololin alarms even Sollas and the other cities aren't all that hazardous any more. The big 'danger' argument strikes me as a convenient but flimsy rationale."

"What about all their fellow humans running around with guns?" Roi snorted.

"Yes, what *about* that?" Jonny put in. Across the table Hemner muttered something and began fiddling with his display. Jonny waited a second, but he didn't say anything, so Jonny turned to Vartanson. "Howie, do you allow your people to carry their weapons inside the fortified compounds?"

Vartanson shook his head slowly. "The Cobras are armed, of course, but all hand weapons are checked inside the inner doors."

"The Qasamans have grown up with a tradition of carrying their guns, though," Fairleigh argued. "You couldn't get them to just give them up overnight."

"Why not?" Telek asked. "They've also got a tradition of not attacking each other, remember."

"Besides which," Hemner added without looking up, "banning in-city weapons has been done successfully in dozens of places in the Dominion."

"The Qasamans wouldn't put up with that, in my opinion," Roi shook his head.

"Let's get back to the point, shall we?" Telek said. "The question is why the Qasamans are still bothering to carry these birds around with them when it's not necessary to do so."

"But we've answered that question," Stiggur said with a sigh. "As long as *anyone* carries a gun and a mojo, *everyone* has to do so. Otherwise they won't feel safe."

"The cultural conditioning—"

"Will be adequate for most of them," Stiggur said. "But not for all. And if I were a Qasaman, I'd want protection against even that small group of dangerous people."

Telek grimaced, clearly hunting for a new approach. "Brom—"

"All right, we've talked long enough," Hemner said firmly. "We're going to vote on Lizabet's proposal. Now."

All eyes shifted to the frail old man. "Jor, you're out of order," Stiggur said quietly. "I know emotions are running high on all this—"

"You do, do you?" Hemner smiled thinly. His hands, Jonny noted with a vague twinge of uneasiness, had left their usual place on top of the table and were hidden from view in his lap. "And you prefer words to actions, I suppose. It's so much easier to manipulate people's emotions. Well, the time has come for action. We're going to vote, and we're going to pass Lizabet's mojo study. Or else."

"Or else what?" Stiggur snapped, irritation finally breaking through.

"Or else the nay votes will be eliminated," Hemner said harshly. "Beginning with *him*."

And his right hand came up over the edge of the table, the small flat handgun clutched in it swiveling to point at Roi.

Someone gasped in shock . . . but even before the pistol had steadied on its target, Jonny was in motion. Both fingertip lasers spat fire, one into the pistol, the other tracing a line directly in front of Hemner's eyes. The old man jerked back with a cry as the heat and light reached his hand and face, the pistol swinging away from the others. Gripping the table edge with both hands, Jonny kicked back and up with his feet, sending his chair spinning across the room and flipping his body to slam onto his back on the table. His legs caught Hemner's arm full force, eliciting a second yelp from the other and sending the gun sailing into the far wall.

"Get the gun!" Jonny snapped through the agony the sudden violence had ignited in his arthritic joints. He swung up to a sitting position, grabbed both of Hemner's wrists. "Jor, what the *hell* was *that* supposed to accomplish?"

"Just proving a point," Hemner said calmly, the harshness of a minute earlier gone without a trace. "My wrists—*easy*—"

"You were *what?*"

"I'll be damned." The voice was Roi's and Jonny turned to look. Roi was standing by the far wall, holding Hemner's "gun."

Which was nothing more than a pen and an intricately folded magcard.

Jonny looked down at Hemner. "Jor . . . what's going on?"

"As I said, I was proving a point," the other said. "Uh—if you wouldn't mind . . . ?"

Releasing his grip, Jonny climbed carefully off the table and walked around back to his seat. Roi sat down, too, and Stiggur cleared his throat. "This had better be good," he warned Hemner.

The other nodded. "Olor, were you armed just now when I pretended to pull a weapon on you?" he asked.

"Of course not," Roi snorted.

"Yet even with a real gun I wouldn't have been able to shoot you. True? Why not?"

"Because Jonny was here and he's faster than you are."

Hemner nodded and turned to Stiggur. "Security, Brom. You *don't* need everyone carrying mojos for your citizens to be protected. The mojos attack *anyone* drawing a gun, whether their own masters are specifically threatened or not." He waved at his display. "The records of the bus attack on York clearly show that—I've just checked. Even if everyone wants to carry a gun, you still don't need that many mojos. Twenty percent, or even less, combined with the cultural bias against fighting would be more than adequate."

"Assuming they're that peaceful without that taloned reminder on their shoulders," Fairleigh growled. "Maybe they're more violent without mojos nearby."

Vartanson laughed abruptly. "Dylan, did you hear what you just *said?* Almost exactly what Jonny's been suggesting." He nodded at Jonny. "All right; I'm convinced the mojos need more study. But we need to learn about the Qasaman technological base, too, and I'm not sure which is more important."

"Then let's do both," Telek spoke up. Reaching to the stack of magdisks in front of her, she selected one and slid it into her reader. "This is a complete tactical plan that was submitted to my office yesterday via Almo Pyre. I'd like us all to read it through and seriously consider it as a basis for the next mission to Qasama. Brom?"

"Any comments or objections?" Stiggur asked, his eyes sweeping the table. "All right, then. Let's take a look."

Telek sent the report to the other displays and they all settled down to read. Jonny felt memories of his own tactical training rising to the surface as he studied the plan . . . memories, and a growing respect for Pyre's work. Granted that there *were* some military manuals and histories in the computer library, it still took a great deal of raw talent to put together a scheme this comprehensive, especially with only the limited training the First Cobras had been able to give Pyre and his team.

It wasn't until he reached the end that he found the author's name . . . and he stared at it for nearly a minute before he finally could believe it.

Justin Moreau.

The wait in Telek's office had stretched into nearly two hours, but Pyre had been almost too busy to notice. Justin's plan was highly detailed, but the boy naturally had not done any actual personnel assignments, a task that would fall to Coordinator Sun and the Cobra upper echelon if the plan was accepted. Nothing said Pyre couldn't submit his own roster for their approval, though. He'd finished the main group and was working on the first of the three outrider teams when Telek returned.

"Well?" he asked as she closed the door and sank into her desk chair.

"They bought it," she said with tired satisfaction. "Brom wants to submit it to a review board of First Cobras, but I doubt they'll change it too much. You still hold with two weeks to equip and train the task force?"

Pyre nodded. "All they'll need is the multiple-targeting enhancers and some tactical training. For a change, all the experience we've logged hunting down spine leopards is going to do some of us some good."

"Um. You . . . ah . . . plan to be out in the forest, then?"

"I had, yes. Unless you wanted me on the village force."

Telek pursed her lips. "Might be better for you to stay aboard the ship, actually. To coordinate things."

"Oh?" Pyre eyed her. "You'd rather I not be down on Qasama?"

"I'd rather you not risk your life, if you must know," she said grudgingly. "You've done your bit."

"Ah. You feel the same way about Justin, Michael, and Dorjay? Or is it different because you specifically asked that *I* be aboard the *Dewdrop* the last time around?"

Her lip curled. "So you *did* know. I'd hoped I'd hid my tracks a bit better than that."

"I have friends among the elite, too. Which is why I was surprised you'd requested me."

Telek exhaled loudly. "Well, it *wasn't* because you were a good friend of the Moreaus," she said. "Though that *was* why I asked you and Halloran for the initial cost study. But for the trip itself. . . ." She paused, eyes drifting to the window and the Capitalia cityscape beyond. "It bothered me all the way from the beginning why the Baliu demesne should think Cobras would have a better shot at the Qasamans than they did."

"They already knew the mojos attack drawn weapons," Pyre suggested.

"True. And there was the whole question of whether this was a test. But it occurred to me that there was one other possibility."

Pyre frowned in thought . . . and suddenly it hit him. "You think they *knew* we were the same species as the Qasamans?"

"I think it highly probable," Telek nodded. "Cobras *would* have an advantage in a war against other humans. And being the connivers they are, of course, they wouldn't want us to know who we were facing until we'd committed to some course of action."

"Yeah," Pyre said slowly. "We nearly got killed on Qasama and we're *still* barely holding our own with public opinion. Imagine the furor if we'd known in advance we were being asked to exterminate another human society." He cocked an eyebrow at her. "That doesn't explain my presence aboard, though."

She took a deep breath. "I didn't like the fact that I might be called upon to betray another human colony out there. You were there to make sure I kept my priorities straight. Did you know, Almo, that I was married once?"

He shook his head, taking the abrupt subject change in stride. "Divorced?"

"Widowed. Since before I became a governor. He was a Cobra . . . and he died on Caelian."

She paused, memories flicking visibly across her face. Pyre waited, sensing what would come next. "You remind me a great deal of him," she continued at last. "In appearance; even more in spirit. I wanted you there as a constant reminder that we *need* a new world for the Caelians to move to."

"Even if that world is bought with the Qasamans' lives?" he snarled.

The words came out harsher than he'd intended them to, but Telek never flinched. "Yes," she said quietly. "Even then. My duty is to the Cobra Worlds, first and foremost . . . and it's going to stay that way."

Pyre looked at her, a sudden chill sending a shiver up his back. All the time together on the *Dewdrop* . . . and he hadn't really known her at all.

"I'm sorry if that makes you hate me," she said after a moment. "But in my opinion I had no choice."

He nodded, though to which part of her statement he wasn't sure. "If you'll excuse me," he said, hearing the stiffness in his voice, "I need to get back to work. I have a roster to complete for the team I'll be taking to Qasama."

She nodded. "All right. I'll talk to you later."

He turned and left . . . and wondered that he didn't hate her for her ruthlessness.

The Cobra board took Justin's plan apart, examined it, debated it, and—in places—changed it; and then they put it together again and pronounced it sound. The forty-eight Cobras and fourteen scientists who would be landing on Qasama were chosen and trained. The Baliu demesne expressed their displeasure at funding a second mission on what still amounted to speculation, but well before the training period was over Jonny and Stiggur were able to change the aliens' minds.

And less than a month after the *Dewdrop* had returned from Qasama, both it and the *Menssana* lifted quietly from the Capitalia starport and headed back.

Chapter 27

Night on Qasama.

The villages along the eastern arm of what was now referred to as the Fertile Crescent were dark as the *Menssana* drifted down on its gravity lifts. Dark, but visible enough in infrared scanners. The roads connecting the towns were visible, too, the network narrowing like a filigree arrowhead to point at the most southerly village at the end of the crescent ... with but a single road northward connecting it to the rest of Qasaman civilization.

The *Menssana* stopped first along that road, some twenty kilometers north of town; and when it lifted again it had left twenty-two people and the two aircars behind. The aircars themselves lifted before the ship was out of sight, bound on missions of their own; and, almost lazily, the *Menssana* swung southward toward the sleeping target village, its sensors taking in great gulps of electromagnetic radiation, sound, and particulate matter and spitting out maps and lists in return. The ship circled the village once, maintaining a discreet distance to avoid detection. When it finally set down in the forest some fifty meters from the wall, the forty passengers who emerged had a fair idea what they were getting into.

Within half an hour, though no one else yet knew it, they had taken the town.

The mayor got a full two steps into his office before his face registered the fact that someone else was sitting on his cushions—and he managed another step and a half before he was able to stop. His eyes widened, then narrowed as surprise turned to anger. He snapped something; "Who are you?" the *Menssana*'s computer translated it.

"Good morning, Mr. Mayor," Winward said gravely from the cushions, his newly reconstructed eyes steady on the other's mojo. "Forgive the intrusion, but we need some information from you and your people."

The mayor seemed to freeze at the first words from the pendant around Winward's neck . . . and as his eyes searched the Cobra's face the blood abruptly drained from his cheeks. "You!" he whispered.

Winward nodded understanding. "Ah, so Kimmeron circulated our pictures, did he? Good. Then you know who I am . . . and you know the foolishness of resistance."

The mayor's gun hand was trembling as if in indecision. "I wouldn't advise it," Winward told him. "I can kill both you and your mojo before you can draw. Besides, there are others with me— *lots* of others—and if you start shooting the rest of your people probably will, too, and we'll just have to kill a bunch of you to prove we can do it." He cocked his head. "We *don't* have to prove that, do we?"

A muscle in the other's cheek twitched. "I've seen the reports of your carnage," he said grimly.

"Good," Winward said, matching the other's tone. "I hate having to cover the same ground twice. So. Are you going to cooperate?"

The mayor was silent for a moment. "What do you want from us?"

Quietly, Winward let out the breath he'd been holding. "We want only to ask your people some questions and do a few painless and harmless studies on them and their mojos."

He watched the mayor's face closely, but he could see no obvious reaction. "Very well," the Qasaman said. "Only to prevent unnecessary bloodshed, I will give in. But be warned: if your tests aren't as harmless as you claim you'll soon have more bloodshed than you have taste for."

"Agreed." Winward stood and gestured to the cushions and the low switch-covered console beside it. "Call your people and tell them to leave their homes and come into the streets. They may bring their mojos but must leave their guns inside."

"The women and children, too?"

"They must come out, and some will need to be tested. If it'll make you feel better, I can allow a close relative to be present while any woman or child is being questioned."

"That . . . would be appreciated." The mayor's eyes held

Winward's for a moment. "To what demon have you sold your soul, that you are able to return from the dead?"

Winward shook his head minutely. "You wouldn't believe it if I told you," he said. "Now call your people."

The Qasaman pursed his lips and sat down. Flipping a handful of switches on the console, he began speaking, his voice echoing faintly from the streets. Winward listened for a moment, then reached to his pendant and covered the translator mike. "Dorjay: report."

"Situation quiet at the long-range transmitter," Link's voice came promptly through his earphone. "Uh . . . looks like the mayor's message is starting to stir up things out there now."

"Look sharp—we don't want anyone sneaking in there to send an SOS off to Sollas."

"Particularly as they'd catch us dismantling and studying all the nice equipment in here," Link added dryly. "We'll be careful. You want me to continue managing the gate and motor patrols, too?"

"Yes. It'll get pretty hectic here once the psych people get their business going."

"Okay. Keep me posted."

Winward tapped the mike once to break the private connection and then covered it again. "Governor Telek? How're the pickups coming over?"

"Perfectly," Telek's voice said in his ear. "Got some good baseline readings on the mayor while he was heading through the building, and the high-stress ones there in the office look even better."

"Good. We'll get things started here as soon as we can. Any word yet from the outrider teams?"

"Just routine check-ins. *Dewdrop*'s not reporting any obvious troop movements, either. Looks like we sneaked in undetected."

Which should mean they'd have a few hours or even a day or two before the rest of the planet realized they'd been invaded. After which things could get sticky. "Okay. Dorjay says the tech assessors are already pulling things apart, so you'll get some data coming in on that front soon. Out."

The mayor leaned back from his console to look up balefully at Winward. "They will comply with your demands," he said. "For now, at any rate."

Getting his courage back? That was fine with Winward—the more mood swings the Qasamans went through, the more useful the data the hidden sensors would get. Provided the mayor didn't get *too* courageous. "Fine," the Cobra nodded. "Then let's go out and join them while our people get things organized. After you give me your gun, of course."

The Qasaman hesitated a split second before sliding the weapon out of its holster and laying it atop the console. "Okay; let's go," Winward said, leaving the gun where it was. If Telek's theory was right, chances were he could pick up the weapon without drawing a mojo attack . . . but he wasn't ready to make a test case out of it, not yet.

Silently the Qasaman rose to his feet, and together the two men left the office.

The section of forest the outrider-two team had put their aircar down into was reasonably sparse, as such things went, reminding Rey Banyon more of the woods they'd seen on Chata than the denser forests of Aventine's far west region where he'd grown up. The good news was that the openness aided visibility; the bad was that it allowed for larger animals to live here. By and large, a fairly even trade.

But for the moment the forest's denizens, large *and* small, were keeping their distance. Eyes sweeping the vicinity of the aircar, he listened with half an ear to the conversation between Dr. Hanford and the *Dewdrop* in orbit above them.

"Well, *we* didn't spot anything when we swept the area," Hanford was saying. "Are you still showing something nearby?"

"Negative," the voice came back. "I think it went back under the trees and we lost it."

Hanford exhaled loudly. Banyon understood his irritation perfectly: this was the third time in the six hours they'd been on Qasama that they'd made a mad dash to the possible location of a krisjaw, only to come up empty.

And to make it worse, they weren't even sure that a krisjaw was what they needed to find.

"Any idea even which way it *went?*" the zoologist asked at last.

"Dr. Hanford, you have to understand the *Dewdrop*'s infrareds weren't designed for such pin-point work, at least not from this distance. Let me see . . . if I had to guess, I'd say to try northwest."

"Thanks," Hanford said dryly. "Call if you spot another target."

"Northwest," one of the other two zoologists muttered as Hanford broke the connection. "*I'd* guess northwest, too, if I had to. That's the direction animals run on this crazy planet."

"I doubt the predators do." Hanford sighed. "Well, Rey? On foot or by air?"

"By air, I suppose," Banyon said. "We'll try spotting on our own for awhile. See if we can do any better."

"Can't possibly do any worse. Well, let's go."

The three zoologists climbed back into the aircar, followed by Banyon and his three Cobra teammates. Rising to just over tree-top level, they headed slowly northwest.

Christopher flipped off the mike with a snort and settled back to glaring at the infrared display, muttering under his breath. Eyeing him over his own screen, York chuckled. "Having trouble, Bil?"

"This isn't even my job," Christopher growled without looking up. "How am I supposed to find krisjaw hot spots when I don't even know what they're supposed to look like?"

"You find a large hot spot that's moving—"

"Yes, I know all that. Eisner just better hurry up and get back here, that's all I've got to say."

"He still at the main display looking for a bololin herd for outrider-three?"

"Yeah." Christopher visibly shivered. "Those guys must be nuts. You sure wouldn't catch *me* chasing bololins around."

"You wouldn't catch *me* down there at all," York murmured.

Christopher sent him a quick look. "Yeah. I, uh . . . I understand you were asked to be on the *Menssana* with Lizabet, Yuri, Marck, and the others."

"That's right," York told him evenly. "I refused."

"Oh." Christopher's eyes strayed to York's new right arm—his new *mechanical* right arm—then slipped guiltily away.

"You think it's because of this, don't you?" York asked, raising his arm and opening his hand. The fingers twitched once as he did so, mute reminder of the fact that his brain hadn't totally adapted to the neural/electronic interfaces yet. "You think I'm afraid to go down there again?"

"Of course not—"

"Then you're wrong," York told him flatly. "I'm afraid, all right, and for damn good reasons."

Christopher's face was taking on an increasingly uncomfortable expression, and it occurred to York that the other had probably never heard anyone speak quite this way before. "You want to know why Yuri and Marck and the others are down there and I'm up here?" he asked.

"Well . . . all right, why?"

"Because they're trying to prove they're brave," York said. "Partly to others, but mainly to themselves. They're demonstrating that they can stick their heads in the spine leopard's mouth a second time if they have to, without flinching."

"Whereas you feel no such need?"

"Exactly," York nodded. "I've had my courage tested many times. Both before I came to Aventine and since then. I *know* I'm brave, and I'm damn well not going to take unnecessary chances to prove it to the universe at large." He waved at his display. "If and when the Qasamans make their move I can assess their military level just as well from up here as I could on the surface. Ergo, here's where I stay."

"I see," Christopher nodded. But his eyes still looked troubled. "Makes sense, certainly. I'm—well, I'm glad that's cleared up."

He turned back to his display, and York suppressed a sigh. Christopher hadn't understood, any more than the rest of them had. They still thought it was all just a complicated way of not saying he was a coward.

The hell with all of them.

Turning back to his own screen, he resumed his watch for military activity. In his lap his mechanical hand curled into a fist.

It was shortly after noon when the *Dewdrop* finally located a bololin herd within the specified distance of the village, and it was another hour before outrider-three's aircar reached it. The herd had paused among the trees to graze, and as the aircar drifted by overhead Rem Parker whistled under his breath. "Nasty-looking things," he commented.

One of the other three Cobras muttered an agreement. "I think I can see the tarbines—those tan spots behind the heads, inside the quills."

"Yeah. Great place for a summer home." Parker glanced at the tech huddled over his instruments in the next seat. "Well, Dan? Possible?"

Dan Rostin shrugged. "Marginal. We're pretty far south of the direct route here—it'll take a large deviation to get them on track. But if they cooperate as well as the flatfoots on Chata it ought to work okay. Hang on a second and I'll have the details for you."

It turned out not to be quite as bad as Parker had feared. Nowhere would the magnetic field they would be superimposing change the overall field line direction by more than twenty degrees, and the amplitudes necessary were well within their equipment's capabilities.

Of course, they would occasionally need to get within a hundred meters of the herd's center, with the risk to the aircar from the flanks that such a close approach would entail. But then, that was why the Cobras were along in the first place.

"Well, let's get started," Parker told the others. "And let's hope they're as much like their flatfoot cousins as the bio people say they are." Otherwise—he didn't add—the Cobras might just wind up herding them, rancher style, all the way to the village.

And *that* was a trick he wasn't anxious to try.

It was almost sundown when Winward returned from a tour of his Cobras' positions to the mayoral office building, where Dr. McKinley and the rest of the psych people had set up shop. One of the Qasamans was being escorted out of McKinley's room as Winward arrived, and he took the opportunity to take a quick look inside. "Hello," he nodded to the two men as he poked his head around the door. "How's it going?"

McKinley looked about as tired as Winward had ever seen a man; but his voice was brisk enough. "Pretty good, overall. Even without the computer analysis I can see the stress levels changing pretty much as predicted."

"Good. You about to close down this phase for the evening?"

"Got one more to do. If you'd like, you could stay and watch."

Winward eyed the Cobra guard standing silently against the wall. He, too, looked tired, though just as far from admitting it as McKinley was. "Alek, why don't you go ahead and get some dinner," he told the other. "I'll stay here while Dr. McKinley finishes up."

"I'd appreciate that," Alek nodded, heading for the door. "Thanks."

McKinley waited until he was gone, then touched a button on his translator pendant. "Okay; send in number forty-two."

A moment later Winward's enhanced hearing picked up two sets of footsteps approaching; and the door opened to admit another Cobra and a tense-looking Qasaman male. The Cobra left, and McKinley gestured to the low chair facing his appropriated desk. "Sit down, please."

The Qasaman complied, throwing a suspicious glance at Winward. His mojo, Winward noted, was almost calm by comparison, although it seemed to be rippling its feathers rather frequently.

"Let's begin with your name and occupation," McKinley said. "Just speak clearly toward the recorder here," he added, waving at the rectangular box perched on a corner of the desk.

The man answered, and McKinley moved on to general questions concerning his interests and life in the village. Gradually the tone and direction of the questioning shifted, though, and within a few minutes McKinley was asking about the man's relationships with friends, his frequency of intercourse with his wife, and other highly personal matters. Winward watched the Qasaman closely, but to his untrained eye the other seemed to be taking McKinley's prying with reasonable grace. The stress indicators built into the recorder and the man's chair, of course, would deliver a more scientific assessment.

McKinley was halfway through a question about the man's childhood when he broke off and, as he'd done forty-one times already that day, pretended to listen with annoyance to something coming through his earphone. "I'm sorry," he told the Qasaman, "but apparently your mojo's flapping noises are interfering with the recording. Uh—" He glanced around the room, pointed to a large cushion in the far corner. "Would you mind putting him over there?"

The other grimaced, glancing again at Winward. Then, body language eloquent with protest, he complied. "Good," McKinley said briskly as the Qasaman seated himself again. "Let's see; I guess I should backtrack a bit."

He launched into a repeat of an earlier question, and Winward shifted his attention to the mojo sitting in its corner. Sitting; but clearly not happy with its banishment. The head movements and feather ruffling Winward had noted earlier had increased dramatically, both in frequency and magnitude. *Nervous at being separated from its protector?* the Cobra wondered. *Or upset because it can't influence things as well at this distance?* The whole idea of the mojos having some subliminal power over the Qasamans made Winward feel decidedly twitchy. Alone among all he'd talked to, he still hoped Jonny Moreau's theory was wrong.

"Damn."

Winward turned his attention back to the interrogation to find McKinley scowling into space. "I'm sorry, but the recorder's *still* picking up too much noise. I guess we're going to have to put your mojo out of the room entirely. Kreel?—would you come in here a minute. Bring something talon-proof with you."

"Wait," the Qasaman said, half rising from his seat. "You cannot take my mojo away from here."

"Why not?" McKinley asked. "We won't hurt it, and you'll have it back in a few minutes." The door opened and the Cobra who'd earlier escorted the Qasaman in stepped into the room, a thick cloth bunched in his hand.

"You must not take him," the Qasaman repeated, the first hint of anger beginning to show through his stoicism. "I have cooperated fully—you have no right to treat me this way."

"Seven more questions—that's all," McKinley said soothingly. "Five minutes or less, and you'll have it back. Look, there's an empty office across the hall; Kreel can just stand there in the middle of the room with your mojo on his arm, and when we're done you can open the door and get it back. No harm will come to it—I promise."

Provided it behaves itself, Winward added silently. Kreel would have another Cobra in the room with him, lasers targeted on the bird the whole time, but Winward didn't envy him the job of standing there with mojo talons less than half a meter from his face. The Qasaman was still protesting, but it was clear from his voice that he knew it was futile. Kreel meanwhile had wrapped the cloth around his left forearm and stooped to present it to the mojo. With obvious hesitation the bird climbed aboard. Kreel left, closing the door behind them, and McKinley resumed his questioning.

It was all over, as he'd promised, in less than five minutes; but well before it ended Winward came to the conclusion that he was seeing just how angry a Qasaman could become without physically attacking something. The man's earlier grudging cooperation became an almost palpable bitterness as he spat his answers at the recorder. Twice he refused to answer at all. Winward found his own muscles tensing in anticipation of the moment when the Qasaman's control broke completely and sent him diving across the desk in a strangulation attempt.

That moment, fortunately, never came. McKinley finished his list, and thirty seconds later the man and mojo were reunited across the hall. "One more thing and you can go," McKinley told him as he stroked the bird's throat soothingly. "Kreel's going to put a numbered ribbon around your neck so we'll know we've already talked to you. I presume you won't want to go through this again."

The Qasaman snorted, but otherwise ignored everyone except his mojo as Kreel wrapped the red ribbon snugly around his neck and sealed the ends together. Then, still wordlessly, he stalked down the hall toward the exit, Kreel a step behind him.

McKinley took a deep breath, let it out in a long sigh. "And if you thought *that* was rough," he told Winward wryly, "wait'll you see what's on-line for tomorrow."

"I can hardly wait," Winward said as they walked back to the testing room. "You really getting anything worthwhile from all of this?"

"Oh, sure." Swiveling the recorder box around, McKinley opened a panel to reveal a compact display and keyboard. He busied himself with the latter and a set of curves appeared on the screen. "Composite of the three hundred sixty Qasamans we tested today," he told Winward. "Compared to a data base-line we took on Aventine the week before we left. The Qasamans maintain a much lower stress level, despite the obnoxious content of the questions, as long as their mojos are on their shoulders. It rises some when we put the birds across the room, but it doesn't really shoot up until the birds are out of sight. Then it actually goes *above* our baseline levels—right here—*and* it drops off much faster when they get the mojos back."

Winward pursed his lips. "Some of that could be irritation from having to go over the same questions twice," he suggested.

"And some of it could be differences between our cultures, though we've tried to minimize both effects," McKinley nodded. "Sure. We haven't got any proof yet, but the indications are certainly there."

"Yeah." Subliminal control . . . "So what are you doing tomorrow that'll be worse?"

"We're going to let them keep their mojos throughout the questioning, but we're going to irritate the birds with ultrasonics and see how much if any of the tension transfers."

"Sounds like great fun. You know enough about mojo senses to know what'll do the trick?"

"We think so. I guess we'll find out."

"Um. Then day three is when you try mixing the mojos and owners up?"

"Right. And we'll also do the hunt-stress test some time in there, whenever outrider-three is able to get their bololin herd here. I only hope we'll have enough people with sensor-ribbons on by then to get us some good numbers—it's for sure we won't be able to repeat *that* experiment." McKinley cocked an eyebrow. "You look pensive. Trouble?"

Winward pursed his lips. "You really think it'll take the rest of the planet two more days to figure out something's wrong and make some major response?"

"I thought we *wanted* them to react."

"We want them to react sufficiently for us to see their heavy weaponry, if any," Winward said. "We *don't* want them to put together something powerful enough to roll over us."

"Ouch. Yes; I concede the difference. Well . . . if they move faster, I guess we'll just have to speed things up. And you Cobras will have to start earning your room and board here the hard way."

Winward grimaced. Heavily armed Qasamans . . . and clouds of mojos. "Yes. I guess we will."

Chapter 28

York had put in a long day aboard ship and had looked forward to at least one good night's sleep before things heated up below. But he'd been asleep barely four hours when the intercom's *pinging* dragged him awake. "Yes—York," he mumbled. "What is it?"

"Something happening on Qasama," the duty officer's voice said. "I think you'll want to see this."

"On my way."

Robed and barefoot, he was seated before one of the big displays in two minutes flat . . . and the image there was indeed worth waking him for.

"Helicopters," he identified them to the two spotters on duty. "Possibly with auxiliary thrusters—they're making pretty good speed. Where'd they come from?"

"We first picked them up a few kilometers east of Sollas," the duty officer told him. "Could have come a fair distance, though, if they'd been going slower; it was the movement we noticed first."

"Uh-huh." York tapped keys, watched the results appear at the bottom of the screen. Six units, flying just a bit subsonic—which didn't prove anything about their actual capabilities—heading southeast toward the *Menssana*'s village. ETA, roughly two hours. "Get me Governor Telek," he said over his shoulder.

Telek had also been asleep, and by the time the *Menssana*'s duty officer rousted her out of bed York had a bit more information. "Two of them are fairly big, possibly implying troop carriers," he told her. "The other four are smaller; I'd guess reconnaissance or attack. Odds are probably good that they're converted civilian craft, instead of specifically military ones, which should be to our advantage."

"Well, at least they don't have gravity lifts," Telek mused. "That's one technological edge we know we've got."

"Not necessarily." York shook his head. "No one puts grav lifts on attack helicopters, whether they've got 'em or not—the things are wildly inefficient for tight, high-speed maneuvering. Besides, for nighttime applications a grav lift's glow makes you a flying bull's-eye."

"So these *are* something we should worry about?"

York snorted. "Worry and a half. We used a lot of helicopters back in the Marines, and I've seen them chew up areas twice the size of your village."

Telek's intercom image went tight-lipped. "Except that they'd kill three thousand of their own people if they try that."

"Right, and I doubt they're quite that desperate yet," York agreed. "*And* they're unlikely to hang around overhead sniping at the Cobras until they have an idea of what *we've* got to shoot back with."

"So the gleaner-team stays put," Telek said. "But the outrider teams go to ground?"

"They certainly make themselves inconspicuous. *And* the *Menssana* gets the hell out of there."

"Damn." Telek bit at her lip. "Yeah, you're right. You think going to ground a hundred kilometers away will be safe enough?"

"The farther the better. But you've got to move fast, before they're close enough to spot your grav lifts. I don't want to find out the hard way what sort of air-to-air capability they have."

"Good point. Captain Shepherd?"

"Three minutes to lift," the other's voice came into the circuit. "We've picked a tentative hiding place three hundred kilometers northwest of here, subject to your approval."

"What, right in the path of the helicopters?" York frowned.

"No, several kilometers off their approach. There's a large section of good rock cover under a crevasse overhang there—and it's certainly the last direction the Qasamans would expect us to run."

"Fine," Telek put in impatiently. "Just get us moving; I'll look the maps over when I have time. Decker, keep an eye on those helicopters and let us know if anything else shows up."

"Will do," York said. "And *you* people sit on your screens, too—they could have sneaked antiaircraft or spotters out there under the trees earlier today."

"You're a comfort in my old age," Telek returned dryly. "I've got to go now, get Michael on the line. Talk to you later."

Telek's image vanished from the screen. "At least they can't block or trace our communications this time around," the duty officer said.

"Unless they've learned about split-frequency radio in the past six weeks," York told him heavily. "And I wouldn't put it past them." Taking a deep breath, he chased the last of the sleep from his mind. "All right, gentlemen, let's get busy. Complete sweep of the village and everything for a thousand kilometers around it. If anything's moving out there, I want to know about it."

The helicopter formation broke up about fifty kilometers west of the village, two of the smaller ones heading straight in while the others circled to the north and south. Winward's Cobras braced for an attack . . . but the craft made only a single pass overhead before regrouping to the east and swinging around to head north. For awhile they tracked along the road, and Pyre and his outrider-one team braced in turn. But if they were spotted there was no sign. Continuing north, the helicopters faded into the background somewhere near the next village, disappearing from the *Dewdrop*'s screens.

"You think they picked us up?" Justin asked Pyre as the ten Cobras of outrider-one returned cautiously to their roadside positions.

"Hard to tell," the other sighed, checking his watch. About an hour and a half to local sunrise—plenty of time for the craft to refuel, rearm, even sit around for awhile and discuss strategy, and *still* get back in time for a predawn attack if they wanted to. "Depends really on how good their infrareds are. Radar and motion sensors would have been pretty useless with the tree canopy this thick."

"I would have thought they'd have attacked if they'd spotted us," one of the others commented.

"Unless they still think we didn't notice them in the darkness," Pyre pointed out. "In that case they might prefer not to tip off the gleaner-team by incinerating a section of forest twenty kilometers north."

"They'll leave *that* for the ground troops in the morning, I suppose," someone else put in dryly.

Pyre grimaced; the news of the convoy moving south along the roads had come from the *Dewdrop* only fifteen minutes earlier. "Probably," he admitted. "Though if I were them I'd bring the helicopters back for the party, too. Not much point in subtlety by that time."

"What fun," Justin said. "Any other good news?"

Pyre shrugged. "Only that the convoy's not due for a few more hours at the least—which means some of us should get reasonably caught up on our sleep before then."

"Only some of us?"

"We've got to have sentries," Pyre pointed out. "Can't count on the Qasamans not to sneak something past the *Dewdrop*—and the helicopters *might* come back. Hey, get used to it, friends—this is what warfare is all about: worry and lack of sleep."

Plus, of course, a lot of dying. Pyre hoped they wouldn't have to find out too much about that part.

The helicopters' early morning flyby hadn't gone unnoticed by the gleaner-team, of course. But it wasn't until the day's testing began that they discovered the villagers, too, had heard the overhead activity.

"You can see it in their faces and body language as clearly as if they were wearing wraparound displays," McKinley told Winward tightly an hour into the interviews. "They know the government's on to us and they're fully expecting some kind of move soon, probably within a day."

Winward nodded; York and the others aboard the *Dewdrop* had come to the same conclusion. "Well, we certainly can't sit put for a full-scale military operation here. What's the earliest time you can be finished?"

"Depends on how much data you want to take back," the other shrugged. "We're already combining the original day two and day three schedules, taking half the data points we'd originally planned for each—"

From one of the rooms down the hall came a muffled shriek and the crash of a falling object. "What—?" McKinley snapped, spinning around.

Winward was already moving at a dead run, auditory enhancers keyed for follow-up noises. The sounds of a struggle . . . muffled curses . . . *that* door—

He slammed it open to see one of the Cobras pulling a struggling Qasaman from the desk he'd apparently thrown himself across. The experimenter, picking himself up shakily from the floor behind his overturned chair, was white-faced with shock, the pale skin in sharp contrast to the oozing blood on his cheek. Beside him on the floor lay a dead mojo.

The Cobra looked up as Winward strode in. "The mojo tried

to attack, and I had to kill it. I was a little too slow to stop this one."

Winward nodded as McKinley skidded into the room behind him. "Get him out of here," he told the Cobra.

"Killers," the Qasaman spat toward Winward as the other Cobra hauled him toward the door. "Foulspring excrement vermin—"

The door slammed on his tirade. "Loses a lot in translation, I'll bet." Winward and McKinley moved to the tester's side. "You okay?"

"Yeah," the other nodded, dabbing with a handkerchief at his cheek. "Took me completely by surprise—his control just seemed to snap, and there he was on top of me."

Winward exchanged glances with McKinley. "When was that? When his mojo was killed?"

"Oddly enough, no. As a matter of fact, I think they both jumped me at the same time. Though I couldn't swear to that."

"Um," McKinley nodded. "Well, the tapes will show the details. You'd better go to HQ, get those scratches looked at. No point taking any chances."

"Yes, sir. Sorry."

"Not your fault. And don't come back until you're sure you feel ready to continue. We're not in *that* much of a hurry."

The tester nodded and left. "If he's too obviously nervous it could skew his results," McKinley explained.

Winward nodded. He had the recorder box back on the table now and popped the rear panel. "Let's see what really happened."

The tester, it turned out, had been correct. Bird and man had attacked at precisely the same moment.

"You can see signs of agitation in both of them," McKinley pointed out, running the tape again. "The rippling feathers and snapping motions of the beak here; the shifting muscle lines in his face, here, and the hand movements."

"This is all in response to ultrasonics that humans can't hear?" Something prickled on the back of Winward's neck.

"Right. Just look at the tester here—he's in the same ultrasonic beam and isn't so much as sweating hard." McKinley bit at his lip. "But I wasn't expecting this *much* of a common reaction."

"They're getting some of their courage back, maybe, knowing troops are on the way."

"But the birds aren't supposed to be intelligent enough to pick up on things like that," McKinley growled.

"Maybe they pick it up via body language from their humans. Maybe that's the way the mojos' agitation transmits in reverse, too."

"Possible." McKinley sighed. "Unfortunately, the body language and telepathic theories are going to be very hard to distinguish between without long-term studies."

"Which we don't have time for." Winward grimaced. "Well, do the best you can—maybe you and the bio people will be able to pull useful results out of the raw data. In the meantime, try to avoid pushing any more of your subjects over the brink."

"Yeah."

Banyon took a deep breath, exhaled it carefully. At long last, paydirt.

The three creatures eyeing the humans from the undergrowth were krisjaws, all right—surely no two creatures on Qasama could have those wavy, flame-shaped canine teeth. Nearly two meters long, with the lean musculature and stealth of predators, they eased toward the four humans, eyes fixed on their prey.

And Governor Telek's theory had been correct. On the shoulder of each sat an equally attentive mojo.

"Now what?" Hanford murmured, a bit nervously, at Banyon's side.

"You have the recorders running?" The Cobra sensed rather than saw Hanford's nod. "Everyone else in position?"

Three acknowledgments came through his earphone. The other Cobras had the krisjaws boxed up . . . and it was time to test the predators' reactions. "Get ready," he muttered to the zoologists grouped behind him. "Here goes." Raising his hands, he fired a salvo from fingertip lasers into the brush at either side of the stalking animals.

The krisjaws weren't stupid. All three froze in place for a long minute and then began backing away as cautiously as they'd been advancing. They got barely a meter, though, before a second burst of laser fire from one of Banyon's hidden flankers traced a line of smoldering vegetation behind them. Again they froze, heads turning slowly as if to seek out their hidden assailant. "Well," Banyon said after a few seconds, "it looks like they'll be staying put for a bit. How close did you want to examine them?"

"No closer than necessary," one of the zoologists muttered. "I don't trust a flash net to hold anything that size."

"Nonsense," Hanford said—though not all that confidently,

Banyon thought. "Let me take a shot at the one on the right. Everyone watch for trouble."

There was a soft *chuff* of compressed air from behind Banyon's shoulder, a glimpse of a tiny cylinder arrowing toward the target krisjaw—and with an explosive crack the flash net blew out to tangle the krisjaw's head and forelegs. Screeching, the mojo on its back shot clear . . . and the krisjaw went berserk.

Banyon had used flash nets against spine leopards on Aventine on numerous occasion—had trapped bigger and meaner-looking animals on the *Menssana*'s five-world tour a couple of months ago—but never in all that had he seen such a violent reaction. The krisjaw screamed in rage, slashing as best it could with teeth and claws at the fine mesh clinging to its body, rolling around in the underbrush and occasionally even twisting itself entirely off the ground in its frenzy.

And within seconds it had opened up tears in the net.

Hanford stepped a pace forward, raising his air gun again, but Banyon had already made his decision. "Forget it," he called to the zoologist over the noise, pressing the gun barrel down. Targeting, he swung his leg up and fired his antiarmor laser.

The landscape lit up briefly, and with one final scream the krisjaw collapsed among the ruins of the net.

Someone swore feelingly under his breath. "No wonder the Qasamans organize hunts against these things."

"Yeah." Banyon shifted his attention to the other two krisjaws, still waiting quietly. Waiting, but several meters further to the side than they'd been a minute earlier. A new line of blackened vegetation smoldered beside them. "What happened?—they try to slip away in the confusion?"

"They thought about it," one of the Cobras replied dryly. "I think we've convinced them to cooperate for the moment."

"Cooperate," Hanford mused. "I seem to remember the mayor of Huriseem mentioning the krisjaws were pretty peaceful when the Qasamans first got here."

"He said it was a legend," one of the others reminded him. "I find it hard to swallow that an animal's behavior would change that drastically."

"What do you think we're looking at right now?" Hanford snorted. "Those two krisjaws are being about as peaceable as they come."

"Only because they see they'll be cut to ribbons if they try anything."

"Which in itself is highly suggestive," Banyon put in. "Remember the gleaner-team report this morning about the apparent transfer of aggression between mojos and humans?"

"You think the mojo made the krisjaw fight back against the net?" Hanford shaded his eyes as he searched the trees for the escaped bird.

"Just the opposite," Banyon told him. "I'm wondering if perhaps the mojo was sitting on the krisjaw's natural aggression, holding it in check until it was forced too far away."

"That's crazy," one of the Cobras scoffed. "The krisjaws are sitting targets out there—their best survival tactic right now is to run or attack."

"Except that we've demonstrated we can kill them if they try either," Hanford said thoughtfully. "Remember the spookies on Tacta? If the mojos have a similar sense for relative danger they may recognize that their best bet really *is* to sit and wait."

There was a long moment of silence as the others digested that. "I suppose it's reasonably self-consistent, as theories go," one of the zoologists said at last. "Hard to see how a system like that would get started, though. Not to mention how you'd prove it."

"Given a telepathic ability, it seems pretty straightforward to me," Banyon said. "The mojos need some predator strong enough to take on a bololin in order to get access to their embryo-hosts. Maybe the mojo acts as long-range spotter for the krisjaw in return or something."

"Though with the mojo's control the relationship doesn't have to be particularly mutual," Hanford murmured. "The birds may be out-and-out parasites."

"Yeah," Banyon said. "And as for proving it . . . Dale, target the mojo nearest you, all right? Head shot; fast and clean, without affecting the krisjaw directly."

"Okay," the voice came in his ear. "Ready."

Banyon targeted the appropriate krisjaw and eased his weight onto his right leg. If this worked he wanted his antiarmor laser ready to fire. "Okay: *now.*"

A flicker of light from beside and behind the krisjaw caught the mojo—and an instant later the krisjaw screamed and charged. Banyon leaned back as he activated the automatic fire control, his leg swinging up to fire point blank at the creature's face. There was a blaze of reflected light, and the krisjaw's fur blackened as the laser flash-burned it. The animal slammed heavily to the ground—

And Banyon looked up just in time to see the remaining krisjaw's mojo streaking for his face.

The landscape tilted crazily as his nanocomputer threw him out of the way of the bird's attack—but not before he saw the the krisjaw, too, was in motion. He hit the ground, rolling awkwardly on his left shoulder as someone screamed . . . and he came up into a crouch to see the krisjaw spring toward Hanford.

Banyon snapped his hands up in a fast dual shot at the predator, but what saved the zoologist's life in that first half second was his own reflexive shot with his flash net gun. The krisjaw hit, slamming Hanford to the ground, but with claws and teeth temporarily blocked by the netting it could do little except gouge at its victim. Banyon scrambled to get his legs clear of the undergrowth . . . but before he could bring his antiarmor laser to bear two brilliant spears of light lit up the forest and the krisjaw collapsed in a charred heap.

Banyon got to his feet, looking quickly around. The mojo was still unaccounted for . . .

But not for long. The bird was perched atop one of the other zoologist's crossed forearms, wings beating at the man's head and shoulders as it tried to work its beak in to the face.

Banyon was on it in a second, grabbing its neck with both hands and squeezing. The mojo released its grip, fluttering wildly as it tried to get at its new attacker. But Banyon's grip had Cobra servos behind it . . . and within a few seconds the bird lay limp in his hands. "You okay?" he asked the zoologist, wincing at the blood oozing through the other's sleeves.

"Arms and head hurt like crazy," the other grunted, lowering his guard hesitantly. "Otherwise . . . okay, I think."

His face, at least, was unmarked. "We'll get you right back to the aircar," Banyon told him, turning back to Hanford. The other Cobras had the krisjaw carcass off him now, and Dale was kneeling beside him. "How is he?" Banyon asked.

"Might have a cracked rib or two," Dale said, getting to his feet. "Not a good idea to carry him far; I'll go bring the aircar here."

Banyon nodded and knelt beside Hanford as Dale set off at a fast trot. "How are you feeling?" he asked.

"Scientifically vindicated," Hanford murmured, managing a weak smile. "We've now proved that mojos in the wild serve the same role they do for the Qasamans. They help the krisjaws fight."

"And apparently help decide when fighting's the best approach," Banyon nodded.

"As opposed to simply getting out of the way?"

Banyon looked up to meet the angry glare of the team's unin-jured zoologist. "I wasn't running out on you," he said quietly.

"Of course not," the other snorted. "Just getting to a place where you could line up a clear shot, right? While it was busy with the rest of us. Fine job—really fine." He turned his back.

Banyon sighed, closing his eyes briefly. They would never learn—neither the people who assigned Cobras as bodyguards, nor the bodyguarded people themselves. In a pinch a Cobra's computer-ized reflexes were designed to protect him and him alone. There was no provision for heroic self-sacrifice in the nanocomputer's programming . . . and the civilians would never understand that, no matter how many times they were told.

There was a quiet click in his earphone: a relay from the split-freq equipment in their aircar. "Banyon? This is Telek; come in."

"Yes, Governor. What's up?"

"Any results on your hunt yet?"

"As a matter of fact, yes. We can send them to you as soon as we get the recorders tied into the transmitter."

"Don't bother," Telek said, and Banyon could hear a new undertone of tension in her voice. "Just get yourselves and the data back to the *Menssana*—you've got our current location?"

"If you haven't moved since last night, yes. What's gone wrong?"

"Nothing, really," she sighed. "At least nothing unexpected. But I want to be able to pull out quickly if we need to."

Banyon grimaced as something tight took hold of his stomach. "The Qasaman convoy has reached outrider-one?"

"Ten minutes ago. And the team's under attack."

Chapter 29

The forest was alive with the stutter of rapid-fire guns and the furious sleet of bullets tearing at leaves and undergrowth and blasting great sprays of splinters from tree trunks all around. Flat on his belly behind the largest tree he could find near his station, Justin hugged the ground and waited for the barrage to ease up or shift direction. It did, and he took a cautious peek around the bole. A hundred meters away six Qasamans were running back toward the convoy from the tree trunk the Cobras had felled across the road. They'd been placing explosives, Pyre had guessed . . . and even as Justin watched, the barrier erupted with yellow fire. The smoke cleared to show a section of the trunk had disintegrated.

"Barrier down," one of the Cobras reported in Justin's ear. "Convoy starting up again."

The hail of lead intensified, almost covering the sound of car engines, but little of the fire was coming in Justin's direction. "I'm on it," he said into his mike. Twenty meters closer to him was the next of the trees along the road they'd prepared so carefully last night. Raising his hand out of the matted leaves, he targeted carefully and fired.

The rope holding the precut tree snapped; and with a crack of breaking wood audible even over the gunshots it toppled gracefully across the road. "Barrier replaced," he reported.

"Stand by to pull back," Pyre said tersely. "Smoke . . . ?"

In response, the forest on both sides of the road erupted with black smoke. "Lead team, pull back," Pyre ordered.

Justin began backing away from his tree, balancing the need for speed with the need to remain low. The smoke would block visual and infrared targeting, but there were always lucky shots to worry about. So far the Qasamans' lack of experience with warfare had showed up clearly in their unimaginative tactics; but they more than made up for that with enthusiasm.

He was midway to his new cover, smack in the middle of nowhere, when a new stutter opened up from above. He froze, muffling a curse.

The helicopters were back.

Or at least one of them was. It was off to the east a ways, he estimated from the sound, probably blowing up some of the hundred or so "warm-body" infrared decoys they'd spent the morning setting up. But the machine was drifting closer. Making a quick decision, Justin leaped to his feet and dashed for cover. The pitch of the helicopter's drone shifted as he did so, and a second later he got a glimpse of the craft through the trees ... and a rain of bullets abruptly splattered at his heels.

He put on a burst of speed, and was behind his target tree before the Qasaman gunner could correct his aim. "I'm okay," he called into his mike before anyone had to ask. "But I'm pinned down."

"I'm on it," someone grunted. "Someone give me covering fire?"

"Got it," Pyre said. "On three. One, two, *three.*"

The helicopter had swung around, trying for a clear shot at Justin, and was framed almost perfectly between tree branches as Pyre's antiarmor laser flashed squarely into the cockpit windows.

The craft jerked, nearly destabilizing enough to slide into the treetops bare meters below. But the pilot was good, and within seconds the craft was nearly steady again ... and from directly beneath, a figure shot upward through the leafy canopy to grab the helicopter's side door handle. Twisting his legs upward, the Cobra turned himself around his precarious grip to what was in effect a one-armed handstand along the helicopter's side ... and with his feet barely a meter from the main rotor hub, his antiarmor laser blazed forth.

The pilot did his best. Almost instantly the craft banked hard to the side, throwing the Cobra off in an action that should have killed him. But with the nanocomputer's cat-landing programming even that small satisfaction would be denied the Qasaman ... and as he carefully righted the helicopter the stressed rotor metal gave way. Two seconds later the forest shook with the thunder of the crash.

"Report," Pyre snapped as the explosion died into the dull crackle of burning fuel.

"No problem," the Cobra assured them all. "Watch the branches if any of you have to try that—the damn things scratch like hell."

Justin let out a relieved sigh . . . and suddenly became aware of the relative silence. "They've stopped shooting—"

"Almo, we've got a Qasaman on the road," one of the others interrupted. "He's alone—well, with a mojo—and he's holding a white flag."

A white flag. Winward had gone out under a white flag the last trip here and had been shot for his trouble. Justin's jaw tightened as he wondered if Pyre remembered that . . . wondered what the other's response would be.

"Okay," Pyre said after a moment. "Everyone keep looking sharp—they may be using him as a diversion while they sneak around to encircle us on foot. I'm going to call him over and see what he wants."

"Target the mojo right away," someone said dryly.

"No kidding. Here goes."

Pyre's voice continued normally in Justin's ear as, bullhorn amplified, the Qasaman translation echoed among the trees: "Continue forward. Keep your hands visible and your mojo on your shoulder. I'll tell you where to leave the road."

Quiet returned to the forest. Notching up his auditory enhancers, Justin settled down beside his tree to wait.

Telek rubbed her eyes with the heels of both hands. "The problem," she told Pyre wearily, "is the same one we've had ever since the convoy first appeared: namely, we simply don't have enough data yet to pull out."

"What you mean is that you haven't proved yet that the mojos are directly controlling the Qasamans," he retorted.

Probably true, she admitted to herself. "What I mean is that the gleaner-team hasn't finished its agenda."

"It may not get the chance," Pyre growled. "I don't think they're bluffing when they say this is our last chance to pull out before they turn up the fire. And if they don't mind how much it costs them we really aren't going to be able to hold them very long."

And that short reprieve would cost them ten good Cobras—*and* probably give the Qasamans reasonably undamaged Cobra equipment to study. "The last thing I want is a full battle with you on the losing end," Telek told him. "But I don't see the hook yet, and past experience tells me there's one somewhere in this offer."

"Maybe there isn't. Maybe Moff just wants to avoid bloodshed."

Telek's lip twitched at the name. Moff. Escort for off-world visitors, sharp-eyed observer who'd pulled the whole thing down on them last time, and now one of the leaders of this thrown-together task force. A man of many talents . . . and a man of luck, too, to have survived Justin's Purma rampage. She wondered how Justin was feeling about Moff's presence out there, chased the thought irritably from her mind. Moff. What did she know about him that might give her a clue as to what he was up to with this? Did he want to chase the invaders away from the village into an ambush where the Qasamans wouldn't be risking civilian lives? Was there something in the village they didn't want found? *Could* it really be as simple as an attempt to drag the two cultures back from an otherwise almost inevitable war?

But the gleaner-team needed more *time.*

"Governor?"

"Still here, Almo," she sighed. "All right, let's try an experiment. Tell them we'll pull out as soon as we've shown a representative that we haven't hurt or killed anyone in the village."

"Will that give outrider-three enough time to bring their bololin herd by the village?"

Telek checked her projections. "It might, if we take things slow enough. But we probably wouldn't have time after the hunt-stress test to remove the neck sensors the gleaner-team's got on the subjects."

"The Council was pretty firm on the point of not leaving any electronics behind," Pyre reminded her.

"I know, I know. Well, if we have to scrap that test, we scrap it, that's all. Look, just see if they'll buy the idea of a tour. I'll talk to Michael and McKinley while you do that, see if they have any ideas."

"All right." Pyre hesitated. "If it'll really help . . . we *are* prepared to die out here."

Telek blinked away sudden moisture. "I appreciate that," she managed. "But you also qualify as electronics I'd rather not leave behind. Talk to the Qasamans and call me back."

"Yes, I *do* have an idea," Winward told Telek with grim satisfaction. "I've been thinking about it ever since the psych people first started complaining that we needed to do long-term studies."

"And?"

"*And* if you can't do the studies themselves, the next best thing is to get the results," he said. "And I think I know just where to find them."

✧   ✧   ✧

"We want it to be someone in authority, whose word the Qasaman leadership trusts," Pyre warned the messenger, watching his words carefully. "We want to prove our people have acted humanely."

"You invade our world and terrorize an entire village and then expect to earn a reputation as gentlemen?" the Qasaman spat. "You're in no position to make demands of us; but as it happens Moff is willing to accompany your escort to the village. As a gesture of good faith only, of course."

"Of course," Pyre nodded. Winward had called it correctly . . . and whatever Moff's own reasons for accepting the offer, he would soon be in their hands.

And at that point it would be up to McKinley and Winward. Pyre hoped they could pull it off.

"Two . . . one . . . *mark.*" Dan Rostin flipped the aircar's huge electromagnet off as, in perfect synch, Parker swung the little craft into the air. Just in time: the flankers of the bololin herd thundering by grazed the aircar's underside with their dorsal quills. Parker grabbed some more altitude and blew a drop of sweat from the tip of his nose. "Outrider-three to Telek," he called toward the long-range mike. "Last course change complete. Can you confirm the direction is right?"

"Telek here," the governor's voice came back promptly. "Just a second—we're getting a reading from the *Dewdrop.*" There was a short pause. "Yes; confirmed. Have they picked up speed for some reason?"

"They sure have," Parker told her. "I think all these direction changes and field strength fluctuations are starting to get to them. If they keep it up they'll pass the village in about fifty minutes."

"*Dewdrop* gives us essentially the same number. All right, I'll let gleaner-team know. I hope it doesn't ruin their schedule."

"So do I," Parker snorted. "There's no way we're going to slow them down, that's for sure."

Telek sighed. "Yeah. Well . . . get back here, preferably without drawing attention to yourselves. Don't worry about making good speed; it doesn't look like we'll be moving from here for quite some time."

Moff drove his car through the open village gate and then said his first words since leaving the Cobras' blockade: "Where now?"

"The mayoral building," Justin told him. "It's ahead down the street and to the left."

The other nodded, and Justin sent a sidelong look at the Qasaman's face. Moff hadn't seemed surprised to have Justin assigned as his escort; but then, little ever seemed to surprise him. Even now, entering an enemy-held village, his face was impassive, only his darting eyes giving any indication of concern or worry. "Where are all the villagers?"

Justin glanced around. Except for a Cobra at each end of the block they were approaching, the streets were indeed deserted. He put the question via communicator to Winward. "They're all outside in the north and central parts of town," he relayed the answer.

"I'd like to see them before I speak to your leaders."

Justin shrugged, striving for unconcern. They were on a tight schedule, but he couldn't tell Moff that. "Okay with me," he said. "Just don't take too long. I want the talks to get underway before anyone starts shooting out there again."

"Our people won't start more fighting if yours don't."

Justin shrugged again and settled back to endure the detour. He was supposed to try and get an inkling of what Moff was up to, but aside from spotting a likely recording device built into the Qasaman's mojo perch he hadn't seen any sort of equipment that could give him any hints. The thought of the bacteriological attack on Cerenkov and Rynstadt on the last trip made his skin creep, despite the assurances by Telek and Winward that Moff was unlikely to risk his own life with such stuff when safer delivery methods existed. The Aventinians' logic, he kept remembering, was required by no law of nature to be the same as the Qasamans'.

Moff drove them around a couple of corners—and there, indeed, were the villagers.

It looked like a giant in-town picnic, to Justin's eyes, with most of the adults sitting around in small groups while children played games around and among them. At the edges of the square Cobras stood on guard.

"The remainder are through the archway there?" Moff asked, pointing.

"I think so, yes."

Without asking permission the Qasaman turned a corner and headed that way. The rest of the villagers were in a smaller open area a couple of blocks further north, and Moff stopped as they came within sight of the crowd. For a moment he looked them over, as if searching for mistreatment, and Justin noticed his shoulders turning slowly as he gave the recorder in his epaulet a sweep of the area. Allowing the troops back at the blockade to see the villagers were all right, if the recorder was transmitting a live picture—

Justin felt his body stiffen. No, *not* the villagers. He watched the other's eyes, noted where they paused. Moff was looking at the guards.

He was counting the Cobras.

Of course. It was the same trick, turned inside-out, that he'd used to view the *Dewdrop*'s interior when Joshua and York were allowed back inside. Of the thirty Cobras in the village, Justin guessed about twenty were guarding the two groups of civilians—an absurdly small number for three thousand people, even given Cobra abilities. Moff had surely noticed that, and would just as surely conclude that the total number of Cobras wasn't much higher than the number visible.

Or, in other words, that the gleaner-team was a sitting target. Which implied . . . what?

Justin didn't know; but the others needed this information right away. Pressing his mike surreptitiously against his lips, he began to whisper.

York shook his head, eyes hard on the display before him. "No helicopter movement I can see," he told Telek. "You sure Moff's gadget isn't just recording?"

"We've found the transmission band it's using," she said tightly. "What about other aircraft? You said some fixed-wing craft had appeared on the Sollas airfield."

"They're still there. Almo still says no trouble at outrider-one's blockade?"

"Not unless they're sneaking troops in a *wide* circle around the area to head south on foot." Telek's image shook its head. "You think they're just waiting until we're clear of the village?"

York opened his mouth . . . and paused as a new thought struck him. "Tell me, does Moff seem to know his way around the village?"

"I'm sure they've got maps of the place in Sollas, yes," she said dryly.

"Right. Now tell me where there's enough room in the village for a landing shuttle."

"Why—" Telek broke off. "The area by the gate, and the two areas where we've got the villagers."

"And Moff's seen all three," York nodded grimly. "So he's now just confirmed what the helicopters last night probably reported: the gleaner-team has no ship standing close enough for a quick escape."

Telek let out a long, shuddering breath. "Damn. Damn, and damn again. No wonder he's not in any hurry to attack. He wants another crack at a starship, and he wants his task force in reasonable combat shape when it shows up. Hence the cease-fire. Captain, what's our best possible time to the village?"

"From here, no less than thirty minutes," Shepherd's voice came on. "The ship's not designed for extended high-speed atmospheric flight."

"Half an hour," York snorted. "*We* could drop down and reach them faster than that."

"Except that there's no way you could stuff the fifty people from gleaner and outrider-one aboard and still lift," Telek growled. "Well, gentlemen, we'd better figure something out, and fast. Our best chance at a diversion's due to hit the village in just under forty minutes now. Gleaner-team *has* to get out then."

Or, York added silently, *they might not get out at all.* Gnawing at the inside of his cheek, he stared at the display and tried to think.

The Cobra at the mayoral building's entrance stepped aside as Moff and Justin came up. "They're waiting in the first office on your left," he said, pulling open the door for them. Out of Moff's sight as the Qasaman passed, his hand made a quick brushing motion: the code sign for *stay back.* Justin nodded and drifted an extra half step behind Moff as they went to the office the guard had indicated. The door was open, and as they walked in Justin saw there were two men waiting for them: Winward and gleaner-team's head psychologist, Dr. McKinley. Both were standing in front of the room's low desk, and both looked vaguely tense.

"Good day, Moff," Winward nodded. "We've never actually met, but I've heard a great deal about you."

"And I you," Moff replied coolly. "You're the demon warrior who couldn't be killed. Or so it's said."

"Not by treachery, at any rate," Winward said, his tone chilling to match Moff's. "You'll note we treated *your* flag of truce more honorably."

"You speak of honor—"

"I speak of many things," Winward cut him off. "But before I do, I'd like to ask you to put your mojo in the next room."

Moff's back stiffened visibly. "So that I'll be totally defenseless before you?"

"Don't be ridiculous. If I wanted to harm you, both you *and* your damned bird would be stretched out on the floor there. You know that as well as I do. I'll ask you only once more."

"My mojo stays with me."

Winward sighed. "All right, have it your way." Reaching to the desk behind him, he scooped up a short-barreled, stockless rifle lying there and brought it to bear. With a screech the mojo leaped—

And shrieked again as the flash net caught it square across the beak.

"Here, Justin, put these in the next office," Winward said tiredly, handing the younger Cobra the immobilized bird and the net gun. "They don't show much capacity for learning, do they?" he remarked to Moff.

Moff's reply was lost to Justin as he deposited his charges next door; but by the time he returned Winward was speaking again. "Well, no matter. We have a pretty good idea of what the mojos do for you, and it's clear enough that if it comes to a full-fledged war we'll win easily."

"Because you cannot die?" Moff snorted. "Some may believe that; I don't. No demon protects you—or splits one mind into two men—" he added, throwing a baleful glare at Justin. "Your magic is simply science we have forgotten, and it will work as well for us when we've learned how it's done."

"Possibly," Winward shrugged. "But it's rather academic, because to learn how our magic works you'll need to kill some of us . . . and I doubt very much that your mojos will let you fight us face to face anymore."

Moff's mouth opened, but whatever he'd been planning to say apparently died on his lips. "What do you mean, won't *let us* fight?" he asked cautiously.

McKinley shook his head. "It's no use pretending, Moff. We've been taking data for less than two days and we already know how the mojos dangle you around like puppets. You've had three hundred years to study them—surely you know at least as much as we do."

"Puppets, you say." Moff's lip curled. "You understand *nothing*."

"Oh?" Winward said. "Then enlighten us."

Moff glared at him but remained silent. "The details don't matter," McKinley shrugged. "What matters is that the mojos have a vested interest in keeping their hunters—that's you—alive, and that they possess enough telepathic ability to back up their wishes. If they think you don't have a chance against us, they won't let you fight." He waved a hand. "The reactions toward us here in the village are all the proof we need."

"Oh, are they?" Moff spat. He seemed to be rapidly losing control, Justin noted uneasily. Were McKinley's assertions really so hard for him to take? Or was this perhaps simply the first waking moment Moff had had in years without a mojo by his side? A mojo keeping his human aggression under control. . . . "Then what do you say about the fighters waiting to sweep down on you twenty kilometers north of here? Are *they* unable to fight?" He jabbed a finger at McKinley. "The villagers have a fear of you based on superstition—our fighters aren't so handicapped. And once we've proved you can be beaten—as we will within hours—the fear the mojos sense and are paralyzing them with will be gone. The next time you return, you'll find a world united to oppose you."

"You don't think the mojos will try and save your lives?" McKinley asked.

Moff smiled thinly. "They will protect us, certainly—by tearing the flesh from your bones in battle. This conversation is at an end."

Winward and McKinley exchanged glances, and the latter nodded fractionally. "All right, if that's the way you want it," Winward said. "We'll be out of your way within those few hours you mentioned; and if we're lucky, we won't have to come back."

"It doesn't matter if you do or not," Moff said quietly . . . and to Justin his voice had the feel of an open grave about it. "We *will* rediscover the secret of star travel someday. And *we* will then come and find *you.*"

Winward's lips compressed and his eyes sought Justin's. "Return his mojo and escort him outside. He can stay with the rest of the villagers until we're ready to leave."

Justin nodded and indicated the door. Wordlessly, Moff strode past him and out into the hall, where he waited until Justin had brought him his mojo, still entangled in its net. "Just unwrap it carefully and the bird won't be hurt," he told the Qasaman, handing the creature into the other's arms.

Moff nodded, once, and stalked to the door. Justin watched him walk down the street toward the civilian holding area, then returned to the office. "He's on his way to the square," he told Winward.

The older Cobra nodded, his attention clearly elsewhere. " . . . All right. If you're ready, so are we," he said toward his pendant. "You'll get outrider-one moving? . . . Good. Justin's here; I'll just go ahead and take charge of him. ETAs? . . . Fifteen and twenty; got it. Good luck."

"Well?" McKinley asked.

"The *Dewdrop*'s on its way," Winward said tightly. "It'll drop into the central square in about fifteen minutes."

"The *Dewdrop*?" Justin frowned. "Why's *it* coming down?"

"Because the *Menssana* would take longer to get here and be subject to attack the whole way." Winward turned to McKinley. "All the sensor collars off?"

"And packed for loading, along with the rest of the gear." The other picked up a small box that had been resting on the low table. "This is the last of it right here."

"Okay. Get your people to the square." Winward tapped his pendant as McKinley headed for the door. "Dorjay? It's a go. . . . Right; fifteen minutes. Get the people out and set up a perimeter to protect it. Watch out for Moff particularly—he's not nearly as impressed as the rest of them, and there are guns lying around he might pick up. . . . Good. Diversion's due in just under twenty— we'll need to be ready to go then. . . . Okay. Out."

Dropping his hand, he looked at Justin. "Let's get moving—you and I are going to be part of the helicopter defense, and we need to be at the wall when they figure out what's going on."

"And then what?" Justin asked quietly. "The *Dewdrop* can't possibly carry all of us."

Winward gave him a tight smile. "That's sometimes what rearguards are for, you know: to stay behind. Come on, let's hit the wall and find some good positions to shoot from."

"Okay, start easing back," Pyre murmured into his mike. "No noise, and be sure you're out of sight of the Qasamans before hitting the road."

There were answering murmurs in his ear, and Pyre shifted his attention to the knot of troops facing him twenty meters away. He'd agreed to stay within sight as a sort of exchange hostage while Moff was in the village . . . which meant that when the timer ran down on this one he would have to be gone before the Qasamans decided to start shooting. Activating his auditory enhancers, he tried to listen for the excited voices that would mean the *Dewdrop* had been spotted.

The shouts, centered on the Qasamans' lead car, erupted barely two minutes later; and Pyre was racing through the trees before anyone thought to take a shot at him. With the need for stealth gone, he made straight for the road, where better footing would let him use his leg servos to best advantage. From behind came an explosion as the Qasamans destroyed the tree that blocked their path. Slowing as he passed the last of their prepared trees, Pyre sent it crashing down behind him, a move that should put the ground troops out of the game for good. Pushing his pace to the limit, he watched the sky for both the descending *Dewdrop* and the Qasamans' inevitable aerial response.

From his vantage point the events occurred simultaneously. Far ahead the glittering shape of the small starship dropped rapidly against the blue sky as, overhead, three small helicopters screamed southward to the attack. A hard lump rose into Pyre's throat as he watched them disappear behind the treetops. They were, as York had predicted, modified civilian craft . . . but the Cobras' brief tangle with them had showed them well worth taking seriously.

He kept running. Far ahead the roar of the helicopters' engines changed pitch as they reached the village. Small explosions came faintly over the wind in his ears and, once, the sort of blast he remembered from the helicopter they'd shot down over the barricade. He wondered who had pulled it off this time, and whether the Cobra had lived through it. Blinking the tears from his eyes, he squinted against the wind and kept going.

And suddenly it was all over. A great roiling pillar of black smoke rose above the trees; and seconds later the *Dewdrop* shot out of it like a missile from its launcher. The two remaining helicopters climbed after it, but their weapons weren't designed to fire straight up and the *Dewdrop*'s gravity lifts were more than adequate to maintain the starship's lead. The three craft became points of reflected light in the sky . . . and then were just two spots.

The *Dewdrop*, gleaner-team's scientists aboard, had escaped. Leaving the Cobras behind.

Ahead, someone stepped from the trees along the road and gave Pyre a quick wave before retreating to cover again. Pyre slowed and joined him. "Any trouble?" the other Cobra asked.

Pyre shook his head. "They're at least ten minutes behind me. Any sign of our escort yet?"

The other grinned. "Sure. Just listen."

Pyre notched up his enhancers. In the distance he could hear a low rumble, accompanied by a well-remembered snuffling. "Right on schedule. Everyone ready?"

"This end is, anyway. I presume gleaner-team's Cobras made it out while everyone was blinded by the smokescreen."

"And were all busy assuming the Cobras were going inward instead of *outward*," Pyre nodded. This would be a whole lot easier if the Qasamans thought *everyone* had escaped in the *Dewdrop*.

The rumbling was getting closer. . . .

And then, across the road, they burst out of the woods: a bololin herd, running for all it was worth. A *big* herd, Pyre saw, the far end of its leading edge lost beyond a curve in the road and the dust of its own passage. Maybe a thousand animals in all . . . and among all those warm bodies, hidden from sight by all that dust, forty Cobras would hardly be noticeable. Even if someone thought to look.

The leading edge had passed, the herd's flanks perhaps twenty meters away. Turning, Pyre and the other Cobra began to pace them, drifting closer to the herd as they ran until they were perhaps four meters away. Glances ahead and behind showed the rest of outrider-one joining the flow. At the herd's opposite flank, if all had gone well, the gleaner-team Cobras were doing likewise.

And for the next few hours, they should all be reasonably safe. After that—

After that, the *Menssana* lay three hundred kilometers almost dead ahead, presumably still unnoticed by the planetary authorities. If it could stay that way for the next six hours, the Cobras would be aboard and the ship in orbit long before any aircraft could be scrambled to intercept it.

Theoretically, anyway. Pyre settled his legs into a rhythmic pace, letting his servos take as much of the load as possible. Personally, he would be happy if things even came close.

And in this case, they did.

Chapter 30

They listened in silence as McKinley went through his presentation, and when he was finished Stiggur sighed. "No chance of an error, I don't suppose."

McKinley shook his head. "Nothing significant, certainly. We had enough test subjects to get good statistics."

Across the table from him, Jonny pursed his lips, the bittersweet taste of Pyrrhic victory in his mouth. He'd been vindicated, his "crazy" theory about the mojos more or less confirmed.

But the price of that victory was going to be war.

He could see that in the faces around the table. The other governors were *scared*—more than they'd ever been after the *Dewdrop*'s first mission. And even though some of them might not know how they'd respond to that fear, he understood human nature enough to know which way most would eventually go. Fight and flight were the only basic options . . . and the Cobra Worlds had no place to run.

Fairleigh cleared his throat. "I still don't understand how the mojos can be doing all this. I mean, you've established their brain capacity is too small for intelligence, haven't you?"

"There's no particular need for intelligence in this," McKinley said. "It's the mojo's symbiont—either human or krisjaw—who actually assesses the situation. The mojo simply picks up that evaluation and pushes for the response that is in the mojo's best interests."

"But that takes judgment, and *that* implies intelligence," Fairleigh persisted.

"Not necessarily," Telek shook her head. "Straight extrapolative logic could simply be part of the mojo's instinct package. I've seen instincts in other animals that appear to take as much or more

514

intelligence than that would require. You'll notice that the Chata spookie seems to manage the same trick with only a slightly larger cranial capacity."

"It could be even easier, at least for the mojo," McKinley added. "Presumably the human comes up with his own list of possible responses, including—on some level—how each response would affect the mojo. Choosing among those takes no more intelligence than *any* animal needs to survive in the wild."

"Could you be reading the data wrong, somehow, then?" Stiggur asked. "We need to be absolutely sure of what's going on."

"I don't think we are, sir," McKinley shook his head. "We didn't get as many details out of Moff as Winward was hoping we would, but I think what he *did* say pretty well confirms this interpretation."

"Not to mention the krisjaw incident," Roi murmured. "There's no rational explanation for their behavior if the mojos weren't in at least partial control."

The room fell silent. Stiggur glanced around the table, then nodded at McKinley. "Thank you, Doctor, for your time. We'll get in touch if we have any more questions. You'll be able to give this presentation to the full Council tomorrow?"

McKinley nodded. "Two o'clock, right?"

"Right. We'll see you then."

McKinley went out, and Stiggur turned back to the table. "Any discussion before we vote on our recommendation?"

"How could something like this have happened?" Vartanson asked, his tone almost petulant. "Symbionts don't just swap partners whenever they feel like it."

"Why not?" Roi shrugged. "I'm sure Lizabet could come up with dozens of other examples."

"Nothing like that many, but there are some," Telek nodded. "In this case, I think, you just have to look at the krisjaw's characteristics to see why humans look so attractive as partners. First off, the mojos need good hunters to kill bololins for them; but the viciousness that makes krisjaws good hunters also means a returning mojo probably has half a chance of being eaten itself until it reestablishes control. You saw the films of the attack—the mojos were barely off their krisjaws' backs before the animals went berserk."

"And their range is longer with humans?" Hemner asked.

"It seems to be, yes, but that may be only incidental," Telek said. "The real point is that humans with guns are simultaneously safer hunters *and* better hunters. That also means the humans seldom if ever lose the fight and get killed, by the way, which saves the mojo the trouble of finding and getting used to someone new."

"The training period being especially dangerous if it's breaking in a new krisjaw instead," Vartanson said, nodding heavily. "Yeah, I see now. What you're saying is that the Qasamans have made the planet a little slice of mojo-heaven."

Telek snorted softly. "Hardly. It may have been so once, but the mojos are rapidly heading down a dead-end street." She keyed her display, and an aerial map of the Fertile Crescent region appeared. "Down here," she said, tapping white spots onto the image with a pointer. "Here, here, and here. The Qasamans are adding on to their chain of cities."

"So?" Vartanson frowned.

"Don't you see? Cities are lousy places for a predator bird to live. They've got to fly long distances to do their own hunting or accept the equivalent of pet food from their masters. But the human population is increasing, and their cute little underground communication system requires them to stay in the same reasonably limited area of the planet. And *that* means cities."

"But I thought the cities were laid out expressly for the mojos' benefit," Roi growled. "That was your whole argument for the second study trip, remember?"

"For their reproductive benefit, yes," Telek nodded. "But not for their feeding benefit. I don't think we ever actually got to see a mojo hunting, but their usual prey is probably small birds or large insects; and no matter what the bololins and tarbines do, small birds are *not* going to venture into the cities in great numbers. The city design is essentially a compromise, and if I were a mojo I think I'd be feeling definitely cheated by it."

"Then why don't they switch back?" Vartanson demanded. "They did so once—why not do it again?"

"Switch back to what? Practically since they landed the Qasamans have been shooting every krisjaw that poked its head out of the grass. They must have the entire Fertile Crescent nearly cleared out by now, and they *still* pull people off work to go hunt the things every month or so. It's crazy."

"Maybe not," Jonny put in. "As you said, the Qasaman leadership knows what's going on. What better way to insure their bodyguards' continued loyalty than to make sure there's nowhere else for them to go?"

Telek shrugged. "Could be. They're certainly devious enough to come up with something like that."

"Which would imply, in turn," Jonny continued, "that they recognize the benefits of having mojos around to keep down interpersonal friction. If they consider that factor to be *that* important, perhaps instead of considering war we should instead be concentrating on getting rid of the mojos."

"How?" Telek snorted. "Kill them all off?"

"Why not? Whole species have been exterminated before, back in the Dominion. Species-specific pesticides can be made for *any* animal, can't they?"

"Theoretically, once enough is known about the animal's hormone sequence during breeding. We haven't got anything like that much data on mojos."

"We've *got* the time, though," Jonny persisted. "The tech assessment puts them at least fifteen years away from a stardrive."

"Won't help," Roi murmured. "The cities, Jonny. Any animal that would prefer a good breeding setup to a good feeding setup is going to be incredibly hard to kill off."

"Especially when the Qasamans will be on their side," Telek said. "Remember, whatever input the mojos had on the design of the cities, it was the humans who put them up. Could be that they actually didn't need much prompting after all—this arrangement encourages a steady supply of mojos for their growing population while at the same time keeps them on a short enough food leash that they won't just give up and go look for a krisjaw to team up with."

"And unlike the aviary approach, this looks more natural to the mojos," Roi mused. "Suckers them into thinking things are going their way while the Qasamans kill off every krisjaw for a thousand kilometers around."

Stiggur tapped his fingers gently on the tabletop. "The ultimate, crowning irony: the puppets conspire to keep the puppeteers with them."

"The crowning irony?" Hemner shook his head. "No. The crowning irony is Moff's last warning . . . and the fact that, given their cultural paranoia, they might very well have cowered there on their one little world forever, afraid to venture into space where they might run into something they didn't like. If the Trofts hadn't poked at them, and persuaded us to do likewise, they might never have become even the smallest threat to either of us. Consider that when you're tempted to congratulate yourselves on how well we've handled this."

A long, painful silence settled on the table. Jonny shifted quietly in his chair, the dull ache in his joints echoed by the bitterness in his mind. Hemner was right; had been right, in fact, all the way from the beginning. And now the threat they'd worried and argued about was on its way to becoming a self-fulfilling prophesy.

And it was far too late to go back.

Stiggur broke the silence first, and with the words Jonny knew he would use. "Does anyone have a recommendation to make?"

Vartanson looked around the table, compressed his lips, and nodded heavily. "I do, Brom." He took a deep breath. "I recommend we accept the Baliu demesne's offer of five new worlds in exchange for eliminating the Qasaman threat."

Stiggur nodded. "Anyone else?"

Jonny licked his lips . . . but in his mind's eye he saw the Qasamans and their mojos moving on Chata, Kubha, and Tacta . . . and from there to the Cobra Worlds themselves. *We will come and find you*, Moff had said, and Jonny knew he'd meant it . . . and the objection he'd been about to raise died in his throat.

The others may have seen similar visions. Certainly, none of them spoke.

Three minutes later, Vartanson's recommendation became official.

It had been a long time since Justin had been in his Capitalia apartment. Standing at the living room window, gazing out at the city lights, he tried to count how many times he'd been back here since beginning his Cobra training . . . four months ago? Five?

The train of thought petered out from lack of interest. Sighing, he stepped back to his desk and sat down. The clean paper and magdisks he'd put there an hour ago were still untouched, and down deep he knew they were going to remain that way for a while longer. Tonight he could see nothing but the faces of the three men who'd been buried this morning, the Cobras who'd died getting the *Dewdrop* off Qasama. He hadn't even known there'd been casualties in the confusion of that time; hadn't known until they all arrived at the *Menssana* and he saw the bodies being carried by their friends.

Tonight was not the night to begin preparations for war.

The doorbell twittered. Governor Telek, most likely, come to check on his progress. "Come in," he called.

The door unlocked and opened. "Hello, Justin," Jonny said.

Justin felt his stomach tighten. "Hi, Dad. What're you doing out this late?"

"In the cold rain?" Jonny added with a half smile, shaking the last few drops off his coat before stepping into the apartment and letting the door close behind him. "I wanted you to come by the house tonight and your phone was off. This seemed the logical alternative."

Justin dropped his eyes to his desk. "I'm sorry, but I'm supposed to be working on . . . something."

"A battle plan?" Jonny asked gently.

Justin grimaced. "Governor Telek told you?"

"Not in so many words, but it wasn't hard to figure out. You've already shown yourself to have a surprisingly good tactical ability, and she was bound to want something to show the full Council tomorrow."

"Tactical ability," Justin said bitterly. "Oh, sure. A great plan, wasn't it?—except for the minor fact that Decker and Michael had to improvise an ending just to get us out. And even at that we lost three men."

Jonny was silent for a moment. "Most military plans wind up being changed somewhere along the line," he said at last. "I wish I could offer some words of comfort about the casualties, too, but only the inadequate line about them sacrificing themselves to save everyone else comes to mind. That one never satisfied me, either."

"So they sacrifice themselves for the mission, and the next thousand sacrifice *themselves* for the Worlds. Is that how it goes?" Justin shook his head. "Where do you draw the line?"

"Anywhere you can," Jonny said. "And the sooner the better. Which is why I want you to come back to the house tonight."

"A family round table?"

"You got it. We have until the Council meeting to come up with an alternative to war."

"Like a blockade or something?" Justin sighed. "It's no good, Dad—I've tried already to come up with a way to do that. But a planet's just too *big* to surround." He stared down at his hands. His Cobra-strong, Cobra-deadly hands. "We just don't have any other choice."

"We don't, huh?" Jonny said, and Justin looked up at the unexpected fire in his father's voice. "People have been saying that ever since the Trofts first suggested this mess. As a matter of fact, people have been telling me that for most of my life."

Carefully, Jonny got to his feet and walked to the window. "They told me the Trofts *had* to be thrown bodily off Adirondack and

Silvern. Maybe they were right that time, I don't know. Then they said we Cobras *had* to stay in the Army because we wouldn't fit into Dominion society. Instead, we came to Aventine and built a society that could live with us. *Then* they said we had to fight the Trofts again or Aventine would be destroyed . . . and with a little work we proved them wrong *that* time, too. Don't ever accept that something bad *has* to be done, Justin; not until you've explored all the possibilities yourself." He coughed, twice, and seemed to slump as he turned back to face his son. "That's what I want you to help me do tonight."

Justin exhaled quietly. "What about Mom?"

"What about her? She doesn't want war, either."

"You know what I mean." Justin tried to get the words out, but his tongue seemed unwilling to move.

"You mean volunteering for the second mission without consulting with the family?" Jonny walked back to his chair and sank into it. "She was hurt by that, yes. We all were, though I think I understand why you did it. But watching her children go their own way has been one of the silent aches of being a mother since the beginning of time." He sighed. "If it helps any, I can tell you her fears and worries about you aren't entirely based on what you yourself have done. She's been . . . well, *haunted,* I guess, by the memories and bitterness of the path *I* took after I'd done my service as a Cobra."

Justin frowned. "You mean politics? I know Mom doesn't care that much for politics, but—"

"You understate the case badly." Jonny shook his head. "She hates politics. Hates the time it's taken from us these past couple of decades. Hates what she sees as a wastefully high work-to-result ratio."

"But you were needed. She's told me herself you helped integrate the Cobras into the political system."

"Maybe I was needed once, but not any more. And with you seemingly determined sometimes to be a replay of me—well, it's brought things to a head."

"Well, she doesn't have to worry about me in *that* area," Justin said emphatically. "Corwin can *have* Aventinian politics, as far as I'm concerned. I'd rather hunt spine leopards any day."

Jonny smiled slightly. "Good. Why don't you come with me and tell her that yourself?"

"And while I'm there, come up with a way to stop a war?"

"As long as you're there anyway, why not?"

Justin shook his head in mock exasperation and got to his feet. "Dad, you have *definitely* been in politics too long."

"So I've been told. Let's go; it's likely to be a long night."

The transfer module beeped its indication that the magdisk copying was complete. Stifling a yawn, Telek turned back to the phone and Jonny's waiting image. "Okay, I've got it," she told him. "Now you want to tell me why you had to wake me at—uh—"

"Four-forty," Jonny supplied.

"—at four-forty in the morning to receive a magdisk you could have sent to my office four hours from now?"

"Certainly. I wanted you to have those four extra hours to see if we've come up with an alternative to war."

Telek's eyes focused hard on his. "You've got a viable counter-proposal?"

"That's what you're going to tell me. And the Council, if the answer is yes."

She licked her lips. "Jonny . . ."

"If it works, we *will* get the new worlds," he added quietly. "Corwin and I have already worked out how to sell the whole thing to the Baliu demesne as a reasonable fulfillment of their contract."

"I see. Thank you, Jonny. I'll get on it right away."

The Moreau Proposal, as the plan came to be called, eventually was given an eighty percent chance of success by the experts who studied it. Lower by several points than a properly managed war . . . but with vast savings in human and economic costs. After two weeks of public and private debate, it was accepted.

And two months later, the *Menssana* and *Dewdrop*, accompanied by two Troft troop carriers, once again headed for Qasama.

Chapter 31

Night on Qasama.

Again they dropped down silently, with only gravity lifts visible; but this time there were three ships instead of just one. The Troft transports set down in two widely separated wilderness areas along the inner curve of the Fertile Crescent, while the *Menssana* landed near the top of the Crescent's arc. For York, aboard the latter ship, it was a significant location: barely ten kilometers from the road connecting Sollas and Huriseem. A suitable place indeed for him to repay the Qasamans for his lost arm.

There was a crackle of split-frequency static from the bridge speaker. "*Dewdrop* to *Menssana*; hurry it up. We've got some very nasty-looking supersonic aircraft coming your way. ETA no more than fifteen minutes."

"Acknowledged," Captain Shepherd said calmly. "The Trofts drawing similar attention?"

"Not specifically, but we've got other aircraft scrambling in what looks like a search pattern toward their general location. They've been alerted."

"Better anti-radar equipment," York grunted.

"There they go," someone said from the bridge's left viewport.

York stepped to his side. The *Menssana*'s outer floods had been dimmed to a soft glow, but there was enough light for him to see the silent exodus from the ship's cargo holds.

The mass exodus of spine leopards.

Most of the animals paused a moment as they stepped out onto the unfamiliar soil, looking around or visibly fighting for balance as the effects of their long sleep dissipated. But none lingered long by the ship. They loped off into the darkness of the forest, the mass already beginning to spread out as they vanished from view, and York could almost sense the eagerness with which they set out to study their new home. However they knew such things, they must surely know this was a world literally *full* of unclaimed territory. How large would their first litters here be, he wondered. Fifteen cubs? Twenty? No matter. An ecological niche existed, and the spine leopards would do what was necessary to fill the gap.

And with luck, the mojos would soon find they again had a choice of partners. York hoped to hell Telek was right about the birds' distaste for cities.

"All out," a voice came from the intercom. "Hatches sealed, Captain."

"Prepare to lift," Shepherd said. "Let's head home."

A moment later the ship was floating toward the stars. Peering out into the darkness, York sought one final glimpse of the almost literal seeds of discord they'd just sown on an unsuspecting world. *Be fruitful and multiply,* he thought the ancient command toward the spine leopards below, *and replenish the land. And subdue it.*

Chapter 32

"I understand," Joshua remarked, "that the Baliu Trofts weren't exactly overwhelmed by our solution to the Qasaman problem."

Corwin shrugged, his eyes lingering on the starfield for another second before turning to face his brothers. The *Menssana* was due to load at any minute and he didn't want to miss seeing that. "They weren't at all sure it was going to work, if that's what you mean," he told Joshua. "We had to pull out disks and disks of data that showed how really uncooperative humans normally were and how any progress toward space would be dramatically slowed or even halted altogether once the mojos deserted them."

"If they do," Justin murmured, his own attention still directed out the window.

"There *is* that," Corwin admitted. "Actually, the Trofts were more convinced that would happen than we were—it was the *results* of the change they weren't sure of. I get the feeling their biopredictor methods are a bit ahead of ours."

"Like everything else," Joshua agreed wryly. "Hey—here come Almo and Aunt Gwen."

"*There* you are," Gwen said as they came up through the milling crowd to the others. "I thought you'd be watching from around the other corridor."

"You get a better view of the passengers here," Corwin explained. "I was starting to think you were going to miss the event entirely."

Pyre shook his head. "We just came from saying goodbye. Everyone else had been shooed out already, but they made an exception for us. Amazing what being a hero will do for you."

The others chuckled—all except Justin, Corwin noted, who merely smiled slightly. Still, that was progress of a sort. The scars of his failings—real or perceived—were still visible, but at least they weren't bleeding any more. For his brother's sake alone Corwin could hope the Moreau Proposal succeeded.

"Jonny tells me you persuaded the Trofts to lend some troop carriers for the Caelian evacuation," Pyre continued. "How'd you sell them *that* one?"

Corwin shrugged. "Wasn't really hard. If the Qasamans *do* manage to get into space the Baliuies would just as soon they were as immediate a threat to us as to them. It's to their advantage to let us have the new worlds and help us a bit in settling them. Especially considering they've just saved themselves the cost of financing a war."

"There they go," Justin said suddenly.

Everyone turned to look. The line of passengers for the trip to Kubha—or Esquiline, as it'd now been officially renamed—were crossing the short distance from the old entrypoint building to the waiting ship. Near the front of the column Corwin spotted his parents, Chrys supporting Jonny with an arm around his waist but both walking with a firm tread. Bound for a new world. . . .

Behind him, Gwen sighed. "This really is crazy, you know," she said to no one in particular. "Emigrating in his condition—and to an untested world, yet."

"Not *entirely* untested," Pyre reminded her. "Besides, the hot climate there will be better for him than anything the civilized areas of Aventine have to offer."

"And there're no politics there, either," Justin murmured.

Corwin looked at the other, wondering how much he knew of that old parental sore spot. But Justin's face was giving nothing away. *Doesn't really matter,* Corwin thought with a mental shrug. What mattered was that his parents would have their last two or three years together away from the worst of Aventine's memories. Away from Aventine—and in precisely the same sort of culturally uncluttered world in which they'd first fallen in love. It was, Corwin thought, perhaps their best shot at happiness. He hoped it worked.

Together, the five of them watched Chrys and Jonny board the *Menssana.* Then Joshua let out a quiet breath and craned his neck to look down the hall. "I think we'll get a better view of the launch path from the gallery over there," he said, pointing. "Anyone want to come?"

"Sure," Gwen said. "Come on, Almo."

"I've seen enough lifting ships to last me both this life and the next," Pyre grumbled. But he nevertheless allowed her to steer him away.

Justin remained gazing out the window as the three left, and for a few heartbeats Corwin wondered if the other hadn't realized that he, too, had stayed behind. Then Justin stirred and glanced down the hallway. "You think they'll ever get together?" he asked.

"Who—Almo and Aunt Gwen?" Corwin shrugged. "Don't know. I guess it depends on whether Almo ever allows himself to give up the responsibilities of being a Cobra long enough to accept someone else into his life. You know better than I do how seriously he takes his job."

"Yeah." Justin was silent a long moment. "You realize if it doesn't work . . . well, Dad will be dead before the Qasamans can find the new worlds, but Mom might not be."

Corwin understood. "I don't know, Justin. But if the mojos really *do* leave them there'll be nothing in particular to unite them into a common front, warlike or otherwise. Especially since they'll probably flounder around for a while just getting used to the new competition. And if they're broken up into smaller states or factions they're as likely to open trade as to take shots at us."

Justin shook his head. "You're forgetting what they're like. I've seen them, Corwin, and I know they'll hold the grudge they have against us until their sun burns out. That kind of hate and fear will keep them working together against us, no matter what other competition arises."

"Perhaps," Corwin nodded. "But only if their paranoia level stays as high as it is now."

"Why would it change—?" Justin broke off as a look of disbelief crossed his face. "You mean . . . the *mojos* might have been behind that?"

"Why not? We know they can amplify human emotions when they want to."

"But what does it gain them to have their hunters jumping at shadows?"

"Well . . ." Corwin's lips twitched in a secret smile. "If *you* were convinced the universe was out to get you, where would you rather live? A city on a plain, or a village in the middle of a forest?"

Justin opened his mouth, blinked . . . and abruptly laughed. "I don't *believe* it."

"Well, maybe I'm wrong," Corwin shrugged. "But maybe in a couple of generations we'll find the Qasamans have become a perfectly reasonable society, ripe for trade and diplomacy."

"We can hope so, anyway." Justin sobered and turned again to the window. "It's so hard when the old folks leave the nest."

Corwin laid a hand on his brother's shoulder. "We'll all miss them," he said quietly. "But . . . well, they're old enough to make these decisions for themselves. Come on, let's get over to the others. Traumatic times like this are what families were made for." Together, they headed down the hallway.

COBRA BARGAIN

Chapter 1

"Governor Moreau?"

Deep in personal combat with the official bafflegab staring out at him from his reader, Governor Corwin Jame Moreau switched mental gears with an effort and turned his attention to his intercom. It made for a pleasant change; Thena MiGraw's face was a lot nicer to look at than Directorate papers. "Yes, Thena?"

"Sir, Justin is here. Shall I have him wait a few minutes?"

Corwin grimaced. *Shall I have him wait.* Translation: should she give Corwin a few minutes to prepare himself. Typically perceptive of Thena . . . but Corwin had already stalled this confrontation off a couple of days, and if he wasn't ready now, he never would be. "No, go ahead and send him in," he instructed her.

"Yes, sir."

Corwin took a deep breath, straightening himself in his chair and reaching over to shut off the reader. A moment later the door opened and Justin Moreau strode briskly into the room.

Strode briskly; but to Corwin's experienced eye the subtle beginnings of Cobra Syndrome were already starting to show in his brother's movements. The ceramic laminae coating Justin's bones, the implanted weaponry, servos, and joint strengtheners—after twenty-eight years his body was beginning to react to all of it, precipitating the arthritis and anemia that would, a decade or two from now, bring his life to a premature end. Corwin winced in sympathetic pain, wishing for the millionth time that there was something he could do to alter the inevitable. But there wasn't. Like his father before him, Justin had chosen this path willingly.

And like the late Jonny Moreau, he had also chosen to accept his fate with quiet dignity, keeping his pain to himself whenever possible and quietly deflecting any offers of sympathy. In Corwin's opinion, it was a counterproductive approach, serving mainly to increase the Moreau family's collective sense of frustration and helplessness. But he understood his brother well enough to know they had to grant him his choice of how to face the long and painful path ahead.

"Justin," Corwin nodded in greeting, reaching across the desk to offer his brother his hand. "You're looking good. How are you feeling?"

"Pretty good," Justin said. "Actually, I suspect that at the moment you're suffering more from Cobra Syndrome than I am."

Corwin felt his lip twist. "Caught the debate on the pub/info net last night, I see."

Justin made a disgusted sound in the back of his throat. "All of it I could stomach, anyway. Which wasn't very much. Is Priesly as much of a phrijpicker in private as he is in public?"

"I almost wish he was. I'd actually be happier if he and the rest of the Jects were simply the frothing idiots they look like on the net—if they were we'd have found their strings years ago." Corwin sighed. "No, unfortunately Priesly is as sharp as he is gantua-headed, and now that he's finally hammered the Jects into a real political force he sees himself as holding the balance of power in both the Council and Directorate. That's heavy stuff for someone who considers himself an outcast, and he sometimes goes a little overboard."

"Does he?" Justin asked bluntly. "Hold the balance of power, I mean?"

Corwin shrugged. "I don't know," he admitted. "With his pack of sore losers trying to stir up a full-fledged crisis none of the Syndics or Governors seem quite sure of how to handle him. If Priesly offers them a deal that would henceforth keep him quiet..." He shook his head. "It's conceivable they might go for it."

"We still need the Cobras," Justin interjected with some heat. "Need them more than ever, in fact. With Esquiline and the other New Worlds expanding like crazy, they need a steady supply of Cobras. Not to mention the need to keep a credible Cobra force here in case some group of Trofts decide to—"

"Easy, brother," Corwin cut him off, hands held palm outward. "You're preaching to the converted, remember?"

"Sorry," Justin growled. "Priesly's pack has a way of getting under my skin. I wish someone had realized sooner that the Jects were a political powder keg waiting for a flicker to come along. *That* should have been obvious as soon as we found out about Cobra Syndrome."

"Hindsight is wonderful, isn't it?" Corwin said dryly. "What would *you* have done, then?"

"Given them the regular nanocomputer and made them full Cobras in the first place," Justin growled. "It's just a waste of time, energy, and expensive equipment to have them running around with bone laminae and servos their computer won't let them use."

Corwin cocked an eyebrow. He'd heard variants of that argument before, but never from Justin. "You don't really mean that."

"Why not?" Justin countered. "Okay, so the training period uncovered psychological problems the pre-screening had missed. So what? Most of the glitches weren't all that severe; given time, they'd probably have worked things out eventually by themselves."

"And what about the harder cases?" Corwin asked. "Would you really have taken the risk of turning potentially unstable Cobras loose on the general population?"

"We could have handled that," Justin said doggedly. "They could have been assigned out of the way somewhere—permanent spine leopard hunting duty, maybe, or the really tricky cases could have been sent to Caelian. If they didn't work out their problems, eventually they'd have done something stupid and gotten themselves killed."

"And if they weren't so cooperative?" Corwin asked quietly. "If they decided instead that they were being dumped on and went after revenge?"

Some of the energy went out of Justin's face. "Yeah," he sighed. "And then it would be Challinor all over again."

A shiver went up Corwin's back. Tors Challinor's attempted treason had occurred well over half a century ago, before he'd even been born . . . but he remembered the stories his parents had told him about that time. Remembered them as vividly as if he'd been there himself. Jonny had made sure of that; the incident had carried some vital truths, and he hadn't wanted them to ever get lost. "Challinor, or worse," he told Justin soberly. "Remember that this time it wouldn't have been basically stable Cobras pushed by idiot bureaucracy to take matters into their own hands. It would have been flawed Cobras, and a hell of a lot more of them." He took a deep breath, willing the memories away. "Agreed, Priesly is a nuisance; but at least as a Ject all he can go for is political power."

"I suppose you're right," Justin sighed. "It's just that . . . never mind. As long as we're on the subject, though—" Digging into his tunic pocket, he pulled a magcard out and tossed it onto the desk. "Here's our latest proposal for how to close the remaining gaps in the prelim psych tests. I figured as long as I was coming over here anyway I'd give you an advance copy."

Corwin took the magcard, trying not to grimace. A perfectly reasonable thing for Justin to do, and under normal circumstances nothing for anyone to complain about. But things in the Council and Directorate weren't exactly normal at the moment. *Advance notice.* Corwin could just hear what Priesly and his allies would say about this. "Thanks," he told Justin, placing the magcard over by his reader. "Though I may not get time to look at it until after the rest of the Council get their copies, anyway."

Justin's forehead furrowed slightly. "Oh? Well, it's hardly going to make a big splash, I'm afraid. We're projecting to go from a seven-percent post-surgery rejection rate to maybe a four, four and a half percent rate."

Corwin nodded heavily. "About what we expected. No chance of getting things any tighter?"

Justin shook his head. "The psych people aren't even sure we can get it this tight. The problem is that having Cobra gear implanted in people sometimes . . . changes them."

"I know. It's better than nothing, I suppose."

For a moment there was silence. Corwin's gaze drifted out his window, to the Capitalia skyline. That skyline had changed a lot in the twenty-six years since he'd struck out on his own into the maze that was Cobra Worlds politics. Unfortunately, other things had changed even more than the skyline. Lately he found himself spending a lot of time staring out that window, trying to recapture the sense of challenge and excitement he'd once felt about his profession. But the bootstrapping seldom worked. Somewhere along the line, pushed perhaps by Priesly's public bitterness, Cobra Worlds politics had taken on a hard edge Corwin had never before experienced. In many ways it had soured the game for him—turned both his victories and defeats a uniform bittersweet gray—and made the governorship a form of combat instead of a means for aiding the progress of his worlds.

It brought to mind thoughts about his father, who had similarly soured on politics late in life, and more and more often these days he found himself fantasizing about chucking the whole business and escaping to Esquiline or one of the other New Worlds.

But he couldn't, and he knew it. As long as the Jects' sour grapes were threatening the foundation of the Cobra Worlds' security and survival, someone had to stay and fight. And he'd long ago realized that he was one of those someones.

Across the desk from him Justin shifted slightly in his chair, breaking the train of Corwin's musings. "I assume you had a specific reason for asking me here?" he probed gently.

Corwin took a deep breath and braced himself. "Yes, I did. I heard from Coordinator Maung Kha three days ago about Jin's application to the Academy. He was . . ." He hesitated, trying one last time to find a painless way to say this.

"Summarily rejecting it?" Justin offered.

Corwin gave up. "She never had a chance," he said bluntly, forcing himself to look his brother straight in the eye. "You should have realized that right from the start and not let her file it."

Justin didn't flinch. "You mean there's no reason to try and change an unfair policy simply because it is policy?"

"Come on, Justin—you *teach* out there, for heaven's sake. You know how traditions hang on. Especially military traditions."

"I also know that those traditions started back in the Old Dominion of Man," Justin countered. "We haven't exactly been noted for blindly adopting their methods in anything else. Why should the military be immune?"

Corwin sighed. Various combinations of Moreau family members had hashed through all this in one form or another dozens of times over the past few years, ever since Justin's youngest daughter had first decided she wanted to follow in her father's Cobra footsteps. Like Justin's father before him . . . and Corwin was well aware that, for the Moreaus at least, family tradition wasn't something to be treated lightly.

Unfortunately, most of the others on the Council didn't see it that way. "Military tradition is always particularly hidebound," he told Justin. "You know it, I know it, the worlds know it. It comes of having conservative old people like you at the top running things."

Justin ignored the attempt at levity. "But Jin would be a *good* Cobra, possibly even a great Cobra—and that's not just my opinion. I've given her the standard screening tests—"

"You've *what?*" Corwin cut him off, aghast. "Justin—damn it all, you know better than that. Those tests are *exclusively* for the use of the Academy."

"Spare me the lecture, please. The point is that she scored in the top five percent of the acceptance range. She's better equipped, mentally and emotionally, than ninety-five percent of the people we've accepted."

"Even granting all that," Corwin sighed, "the point remains that she's a woman, and women have never been Cobras."

"Up till *now* they haven't—"

"Governor!" Thena MiGraw's voice on the intercom cut him off. "There's a man coming—"

And behind Justin the door slammed open and a stranger leaped into the office.

"Destroy the Cobras!" he shrieked.

Corwin froze, the sheer unexpectedness of it holding him in place for those first crucial seconds. The intruder took a few rapid steps into the room, arms waving, raving just short of incomprehensibility. Out of the corner of his eye Corwin saw that Justin had dropped out of his chair, spinning on his heels into a crouch facing the intruder. "All right, hold it!" the Cobra snapped. His hands were up, the little fingers with their implanted lasers tracking the man.

But if the other heard Justin's command, he ignored it. "The Cobras are the destruction of freedom and liberty," he screamed, taking yet another step toward Corwin. "They must be *destroyed*!" His right hand swung in a wide circle toward Corwin's face and then dipped into his tunic pocket—

And Justin's outstretched fingers spat needles of light directly into his chest.

The man shrieked, an oddly gurgling sound. His knees buckled, slamming him to the floor. With an effort, Corwin shook off his stunned paralysis and jabbed at the intercom. "Thena! Security and a med team, fast."

"Already called them, Governor," she said, her own voice trembling with shock.

Justin had stepped to the intruder's side and knelt down beside him. "Alive?" Corwin asked, holding his breath as his brother's fingers touched the other's neck.

"Yeah. At least for the moment. Any idea what the hell that was all about?"

"None. Let's let Security sort it out." Corwin took a deep breath, let it out carefully. "Glad you were here. Thanks."

"No charge. Let's find out what kind of gun he was carrying..." Justin reached into the intruder's tunic pocket . . . and an odd expression settled onto his face. "Hell," he said, very softly.

"What?" Corwin snapped, getting to his feet.

Still kneeling beside the wounded man, Justin gazed down at him. "He's unarmed."

Chapter 2

Cari Moreau slouched back in her lounge chair, a seventeen-year-old's version of a martyr's expression plastered across her face. "Aw, come on, Jin," she complained. "*Again?*"

Jasmine Moreau—"Jin" to her family and everyone else she could persuade to use the nickname—gazed at her younger cousin with a combination of patience, affection, and rock-solidness. "Again," she said firmly. "You want to pass this test or don't you?"

Cari sighed theatrically. "Oh, all *right*. Slavemaker. *Misk'rhe'ha solf' owp'smeaf, pierec'eay'kartoh—*"

"That's '*khartoh*,' " Jin interrupted. "Kh-sound, not k. And the initial 'p' in '*pierec'eay'khartoh*' is aspirated." She demonstrated. "The difference between p-sounds in 'pin' and 'spin.' "

"*I* don't hear any difference," Cari grumbled. "And I'll bet Ms. Halverson won't, either."

"Maybe *she* won't, no," Jin agreed. "But if you ever plan to use your catertalk on any Trofts, you'd better be sure to get it right."

"So who says I'm planning to use it on any Trofts?" Cari grumbled. "Any Trofts *I* run into are gonna understand Anglic."

"You don't know that," Jin shook her head. "Traders or demesne representatives assigned to the Worlds will, sure. But who says you're never going to wind up somewhere out in space with only Trofts who snargled off in *their* language lessons, too?"

That got her a snort from her cousin. "That's easy for *you* to say. You're gonna be the Cobra zipping around out there, not me. Of *course* you're gonna need to know catertalk and Qasaman and all."

Jin felt a lump rise to her throat. Of all her relatives, Cari was the only one who was truly enthusiastic about her Cobra ambitions . . . and the only one who took for granted that she would achieve them. On that latter point even Jin's father had trouble, and Jin could remember times when only a long private talk with Cari had kept those hopes and dreams alive . . .

And with a jolt she realized that the younger girl had neatly deflected the conversation into a right angle. "Never mind what *I'm* going to need," she growled with mock irritation. "At the moment it's *you* who needs to know this stuff, because *you're* the one who's going to be tested on it tomorrow. Again—and remember the aspirated-p in *pierec'eay'khartoh* this time. You pronounce it the wrong way to a Troft and he's either going to fall over laughing or else challenge you to a duel."

Cari perked up a bit. "Why?—is it something dirty the way I said it?" she asked eagerly.

"Never mind," Jin told her. The error was, in fact, a fairly innocuous one, but she had no intention of telling her cousin that. She could remember back three years to when she'd been seventeen herself, and a slight hint of wickedness might help spice up a course Cari clearly considered to be deathly dull. "Let's try it again," she said. "From the top."

Can took a deep breath and closed her eyes. "*Misk'rhe—*"

Across the room the phone warbled. "I'll get it," Cari interrupted herself, bounding with clear relief out of her chair and racing toward the instrument. " . . . Hello? . . . Oh, hi, Fay. Jin!—it's your sister."

Jin unfolded her legs from beneath her and walked over to Cari's side. Three steps from the phone screen the expression on Fay's face suddenly registered, and she took the remaining distance in two quick strides. "What's wrong?" she asked.

"Thena MiGraw just called from Uncle Corwin's office," Fay said grimly. "There was some kind of crazy incident there a few minutes ago, and Dad wound up shooting someone."

Beside Jin, Cari gasped. "He *what?*" Jin asked. "Did he kill him?"

"No idea yet. The guy's been rushed to the hospital, and Dad and Uncle Corwin are there now. Thena said she'd call again and let us know if and when they learned anything."

Jin licked suddenly dry lips. "Which hospital are they at?"

Fay shook her head. "She said specifically *not* to go there. Uncle Corwin told her he didn't want anybody else underfoot while they sorted this out."

Jin gritted her teeth. Understandable, but she didn't have to like it. "Did she say how Dad was doing? Or give any other details?"

Fay shrugged uncomfortably. "Dad was pretty shaken up, I guess, but he wasn't falling apart. If there were any other details Thena wasn't giving them out."

Even through the surreal numbness in Jin's mind, she felt a brief flicker of pride. No, of course her father wouldn't fall apart. A Cobra who'd survived both Qasaman missions wouldn't break over something like this. Besides which, she would bet large sums that whatever had happened had been the other guy's fault. "Have you talked to Gwena yet?"

Fay shook her head. "I was hoping to have more details before I did that. She's got all she needs on her mind already, and I'd hate for her to drop everything and fly in unnecessarily."

"Better let her decide how necessary it is," Jin advised. "They can always reschedule her thesis defense, and she'll be pretty hurt if she has to learn about this from the net. Anything on the net yet, speaking of which?"

"This early? Shouldn't be. Anyway, I just wanted you to know what had happened, make sure you were here when Dad gets home."

"Yeah, thanks," Jin nodded. "I'll come now."

"Okay. See you soon." Fay's face vanished from the screen.

Beside Jin, Cari took a shuddering breath. "I'd better call Mom and Dad," she said. "They'll want to know about this."

"Thena's probably already done that," Jin told her, eyes focused on the empty phone screen. Something was nagging, premonition-like, at the back of her mind . . . Reaching out, she tapped the phone's numberpad, keying it into Capitalia's major public/info net. *Search/ proper name: Moreau, Justin,* she instructed it.

"What are you doing?" Cari asked. "Fay said there wouldn't be anything on it yet."

Jin clenched her teeth. "Fay was wrong. Take a look."

There was no sign on the driveway leading to the squat, square building nestled back from the street a few blocks from Capitalia's main business district. Not that a sign would have made much difference; the small plaque beside the windowless front door proclaiming the place to be the Kennet MacDonald Memorial Center would mean little to the average Capitalian citizen.

To the city's Cobra population, the name meant a great deal more. As did the building itself.

The door was locked, but Jin knew the code. The center's softly lit social areas were largely deserted, she noted as she padded quietly past them, with only a relative handful of Cobras sitting together in twos or threes. Attendance had been dwindling, she knew, ever since Priesly and his loud-faced Jects had started harping on what they liked to call "Cobra elitism." Gazing across the empty chairs and tables, Jin's mind flashed back to her childhood, to the hours she'd spent here with her father and the other Cobras. The men who were the true heroes of the Cobra Worlds.

And now those men avoided the center, hesitant to add fuel to Priesly's fires by congregating together. For that alone, Jin thought bitterly, she could wish the Jects to drown in their own saliva.

Her father was where she'd expected to find him: downstairs, alone, in the large practice area the Cobras had dubbed the Danger Room.

For a few minutes she stood above him in the observation gallery, watching and remembering. The target robots the room's computer controlled weren't especially smart, but they were fast and numerous. As a child, Jin had also thought their low-power lasers were dangerous, and she could still remember the terror she'd felt watching from up here as her father went head-to-head against them. In actuality, as she'd finally learned years later, the robots' lasers were dangerous only to a Cobra's pride; but that knowledge couldn't entirely suppress her adrenaline-fueled gut reaction as she watched her father fight.

It wasn't exactly an even fight, for one thing. Arrayed against Justin at any given time were between four and seven of the target robots, all taking pot shots at him, often with little concern for their own welfare. Cover in the Danger Room had been deliberately kept to a minimum, leaving the Cobra no choice but to keep moving if he was to survive.

And Justin kept moving. Superbly, to Jin's admittedly biased way of thinking. Using walls, floor, and ceiling as backstops, his computer-driven servos had him bouncing all around the room, flashes of light flickering almost continuously from the little fingers of both hands as his metalwork lasers combined with his optical-enhancement targeting system to make impossible midair hits on his attackers. Half a dozen times the observation gallery's windows vibrated as reflections from one or the other of Justin's sonic weapons hit them, and once the brilliant spear of his antiarmor laser flashed out from the heel of his left leg to take out a persistent enemy right through the low covering wall it was hiding behind. Jin found herself gritting her teeth as she watched, hands clenched into fists at her sides as her body half crouched in sympathetic readiness. *Someday,* the thought came dimly through her tension, *that could be me in there.* Will *be me in there.*

At last the lopsided duel was over; and it was with mild surprise that Jin discovered she'd been watching for less than five minutes. Taking a deep breath, she blew at the drop of sweat on the tip of her nose and tapped on the window.

Below, her father looked up, surprise creasing his face as he saw her. *Can I come down?* she hand-signed to him.

Sure, he signed back. *Main door.*

She took the stairway down, and by the time she pushed open the heavy door he had a towel wrapped around his neck and was dabbing at his face with it. "Hi, Jin," he greeted her, coming forward for a quick hug. His expression, she noted, was the flat-neutral one he always used when he was trying to bury some strong emotion. "This is a surprise."

"Thena called an hour ago and said you were on your way home from the hospital," she explained. "When you didn't show up, I decided to come and find you."

He grunted. "I hope you didn't drive all over Capitalia looking for me."

"Of course not. Where else would you be?"

"Visiting my past?" He glanced around the room.

"Working out tension," she corrected him. "Come on, Dad—I know you better than *that.*"

He gave her a half-hearted smile, the mask sliding from his face as he did so to reveal the hidden ache behind it. "You do indeed, my little Jasmine," he said quietly. "You always have."

She put her hand on his arm. "It's a mess, isn't it?"

He nodded. "Yeah. How are you and your sisters holding up?"

"Oh, we're doing all right. The real question is how are *you* doing?"

He shrugged. "As well as can be expected. Better, after this," he added, waving a hand to take in the Danger Room. "How much did Thena tell you?"

"The condensed version only. What happened, Dad?"

His eyes held hers for a minute, then slipped away to look around the room. "It was the stupidest slop-headed thing you've ever seen," he sighed. "On *my* part, I mean. This guy—Baram Monse, the hospital ID'd him—just burst in and started yelling and cursing—anti-Cobra stuff, mainly. I tried stunning him, but he was moving and I turned too slowly to get the sonic lined up properly." He shook his head. "Anyway, he reached into his pocket and I figured he was going for a weapon. It was too late to physically jump him . . . so I used my lasers."

Across the room a maintenance robot trundled in through an access door and began picking up one of the "dead" target robots. "And he didn't have a gun?" Jin ventured at last.

"You got it," Justin said, a touch of bitterness seeping into his tone. "No gun, no spray, not even a tangler reel. Just a simple, harmless, unarmed crank. And I shot him."

Jin looked past him at the maintenance robot. "Was it a setup?" she asked.

From the corner of her eye she caught her father's frown. "What do you mean?" he asked carefully.

"Was Monse trying to goad you or Uncle Corwin into attacking him? Trying to make you look bad?" She turned back to face him. "I don't know if you've seen the net yet, but an absolute flood of condemnation hit the thing practically from the minute Monse was taken off to the hospital. That wasn't reaction—those people had their rhetoric primed and ready to go."

Justin hissed through his teeth. "The thought *has* crossed my mind, I'll admit. And you haven't even heard the best part yet: the fact that Monse is going to live despite taking a pair of setting-two fingertip laser blasts square in the center of his chest. Want to hazard a guess as to how he managed that?"

She frowned. Body armor was the obvious answer . . . but it was clear from her father's tone that it was something more interesting than that. Monse would have needed *some* kind of protection, though—at short range, a twin laser burst at number-two setting would have been perfectly adequate to cut through bones the thickness of ribs or breastbone and take out the lungs or heart beneath them.

Adequate, at least, to cut through normal bones . . . "The same reason Winward lived?" she asked hesitantly.

Justin nodded. "You got it."

A shiver went up Jin's spine. Michael Winward, shot in the chest by a projectile gun during the first Qasaman mission twenty-eight years ago . . . surviving that attack solely because the bullet was deflected by the ceramic laminae coating his breastbone and ribcage. "A Ject," she murmured. "That little phrijpicker Monse is a lousy *Ject*."

"Bull's-eye," Justin sighed. "Unfortunately, that doesn't change the fact that he was unarmed when I shot him."

"Why not?" Jin demanded. "It means I was right—that the whole thing was a setup—*and* it means that Priesly is behind it."

"Whoa, girl," Justin said, putting a hand on each of her shoulders. "What may look obvious to you or me or Corwin isn't necessarily provable."

"But—"

"And until and unless we *can* prove any such connection," he continued warningly, "I'll thank you to keep your allegations to yourself. At this stage it would hurt us far more than it would hurt Priesly."

Jin closed her eyes briefly, fighting back sudden tears. "But why? Why is he picking on you?"

Justin stepped to her side, slipping his arm tightly around her shoulders. Even full-grown, she was a few centimeters shorter than he was—the ideal height, she'd always felt, to nestle in under his arm. "Priesly's not after me in particular," Justin sighed. "I doubt he's even especially after Corwin, except as he's an obstacle that's in Priesly's way. No, what really after is nothing less than the elimination of Cobras from the Cobra Worlds."

Jin hugged him a little closer. She'd heard all the rumors, arguments, and speculations . . . but to hear it said in such a straightforward, cold-blooded way by someone in a position to know the truth sent a chill up her back. "That's insane," she whispered. "Totally insane. How does he expect Esquiline to expand without Cobras leading the way into the wilderness?—Esquiline or the other New Worlds? Not to mention the Caelian Remnant—what's he going to do, just throw them to the peledari and let them get eaten alive?"

She felt his sigh against her side. "Jin, as you grow older you're going to run into a surprising number of otherwise intelligent people who get themselves trapped into some single-rail goal or point of view and never get out of it. Caelian is a perfect example—the people still living there have been fighting that crazy ecology for so long they can't break the habit long enough to back out and accept resettlement somewhere else. Some of the Jects—not all, certainly, but some—are equally single-minded. They wanted to be Cobras—wanted it very badly, most of them—but were deemed unfit, for one reason or another . . . and the love they had has been twisted into hatred. Hatred that demands revenge."

"No matter what the consequences are for the rest of the Cobra Worlds?"

He shrugged. "Apparently not. I don't know—maybe some of

them genuinely think the need for Cobras has passed, that everything the Cobras do can be done more efficiently by ordinary men
with machines or enhancement exoskeletons. And I'll even admit
that some of Priesly's complaints may not be entirely unreasonable—maybe we *have* picked up a little too much elitist attitude
than is good for us."

A maintenance robot passed them, heading toward another of
the target robots. Jin's eyes followed it, came to rest on the
target . . . and somewhere in the back of her mind a synapse clicked,
and for the first time in her life she suddenly realized what those
hulking machines she'd been watching all these years really were.
"My God," she whispered. "They're Trofts. Those target robots are
supposed to be *Trofts.*"

"Don't be silly," Justin said; and his voice made her look sharply
up at him. On his face—

The expression was blank. Like someone playing poker . . . or
someone denying all knowledge of a secret he wasn't allowed to
divulge. "I just meant—" she began awkwardly.

"Of course it's not a Troft," Justin cut her off. "Look at the shape,
the size and contours. It's nothing but a generic practice target."
But even as she looked at him his face seemed to harden a fraction. "Besides, the Trofts are our trading partners and political
allies," he said. "Our friends, Jin, not our enemies. There's no reason
for us to know how to fight them."

"Of course not," she said, trying hard to match his same neutral tone as she belatedly caught on. No, certainly the robots didn't
look much like Trofts . . . but the shape and positioning of their
target areas were too accurate to be accidental. "And I don't suppose
anyone really wants to be reminded that they were once our
enemies," she added with a touch of bitterness. "Or that it was
the Cobras who kept that war from even starting."

He squeezed her shoulders. "The Cobras remember," he said
quietly. "And so do the Trofts. That's what really matters . . . and
that's why we'll find a way to stop Priesly and his lunatic gang."
He took a deep breath. "Come on; let's go home."

Chapter 3

Tamris Chandler, Governor-General of the Cobra Worlds, had come into politics from a successful legal career, and Corwin had noted more than once at Council and Directorate meetings that Chandler seemed to relish his occasional opportunities to play at being prosecuting attorney. He was doing so now...but for once, he didn't seem to be enjoying it very much.

"I hope you realize," he said, glaring out from Corwin's phone screen, "how much of a mess your brother has gotten all of us into."

"I understand the mess, sir," Corwin said, keeping a tight rein on his temper. "I contest, however, the assumption that it's Justin's fault."

Chandler waved aside the objection. "Motivational guilt aside, it was he who fired on an unarmed man."

"Who was technically trespassing in my office and threatening me—"

"Threatening *you?*" Chandler cut in, raising his eyebrows. "Did he say anything specifically that applied to you?"

Corwin sighed. "No, sir, not specifically. But he *was* vehemently denouncing the Cobras, and my pro-Cobra views are well known. It may not technically be assault, but any jury would agree that I had cause to fear for my safety."

Chandler glared a moment longer. Then his lip twitched and he shrugged. "It'll never reach a jury, of course—we both know that. And just between us, I think your scenario here is probably correct. Priesly's had you in his sights ever since he joined the Directorate, and to get both you and the Cobras in trouble with a single move is just the sort of sophistication I'd expect from him."

Corwin gritted his teeth against the sarcastic retort that wanted to come out. Sniping at Chandler's thinly disguised admiration of Priesly the Bastard would feel good, but Corwin needed the governor-general's support too much to risk that. "So we both agree the Monse affair was deliberately staged," he said instead. "The question remains, what is the Directorate going to do about it?"

Chandler's eyes drifted away from Corwin's gaze. "Frankly, Moreau, I'm not sure there's anything we *can* do about it," he said slowly. "If you can prove—not allege, *prove*—that Monse came in there trying to goad your brother into opening fire, and if you can *prove* that Priesly was involved in it, then we'll have something we can hook onto. Otherwise—" He shrugged. "I'm afraid he's got too much of a power base for us to throw unsubstantiated accusations at him. You've seen what his people are doing to your brother on the net—he'd flay all the rest of us, too, if we moved against him at this stage."

Or in other words, the governor-general was going to react to this blatant power bid by simply ignoring it. By letting Priesly play out his gambit and hoping he wouldn't bother Chandler himself in the process. "I see," Corwin said, not trying to hide his bitterness. "I presume that if I *am* able to get some of this proof before the Directorate meeting tomorrow that you'll be more supportive of my position?"

"Of course," Chandler said immediately. "But bear in mind that, whatever happens, we won't be spending a lot of time on this incident. There are more important matters awaiting our discussion."

Corwin took a deep breath. *Translation: he'll do what he can to cut Priesly's tirade to a minimum.* It was, he supposed, better than nothing. "Understood, sir."

"Well. If that's all . . . ?"

"Yes, sir. Goodnight, sir."

The screen blanked. Corwin leaned back in his chair, stretching muscles aching with tension and fatigue. That was it: he'd talked to all the members of the Directorate that he had a chance of bringing onto his side in this. Should he move on to the Council and the lower-ranking syndics there? He glanced at his watch, saw to his mild shock that it was already after ten. Far too late to call anyone else now. No wonder, in retrospect, that Chandler had been a little on the frosty side.

A motion off to his side caught his eye, and he looked up as

Thena MiGraw put a steaming cup of cahve on his desk. "You about finished for the night?" she asked.

"I don't know if *I* am, but *you* sure should be," he told her tiredly. "Seems to me I told you to go home a couple of hours ago."

She shrugged. "There was some busywork I had to do, anyway," she said, seating herself with her usual grace in a chair at the corner of the desk.

"Besides which, you thought I might need some moral support?"

"That and maybe some help screening out crank calls," she said. "I see that wasn't necessary."

Corwin lifted the cup she'd brought him, savoring for a moment the delicate aroma of the cahve. "The Moreau name's been an important one on Aventine for a long time," he reminded her, taking a sip. "Maybe even the more predatory of the newswriters figure the family's earned a little respect."

"And maybe a little rest, too?" Thena suggested quietly.

Corwin gazed at her, eyes tracing her delicate features and slender figure. A pang of melancholy and loss touched his heart, a pang that seemed to be coming more and more often these days. *I should have married,* he thought tiredly. *Should have had a family.*

He shook off the thought with an effort. There had been good and proper reasons behind his decision all those years ago, and none of those reasons had changed. His father's long immersion in Cobra Worlds' politics had nearly destroyed his mother, and he had sworn that he would never do such a thing to any other human being. Even if he could find a woman who was willing to put up with that kind of life . . .

Again, he forced his mind away from that often-traveled and futile path of thought. "The Moreaus have never been famous for resting when there was work to be done," he told Thena. "Besides, I can rest *next* year. You ought to get on home, though."

"Perhaps in a few minutes." Thena nodded at the phone. "How did the calls go?"

"About as expected. Everyone's a little uncertain of how to handle it, at least from the perspective of practical politics. My guess is that for the time being they'll all keep their heads down and wait for more information."

"Giving Priesly free rein to plant his version in their minds tomorrow." She snorted gently. "Uncommonly nice timing for him, having all this happen just before a full Directorate meeting."

Corwin nodded. "Yeah, I noticed that myself. As did, I'm sure, the other governors. Unfortunately, it doesn't exactly count as evidence."

"Unless you can use it to find a connecting thread—" She broke off, head cocked in concentration. "Was that a knock?"

Frowning, Corwin hunched forward and keyed his intercom to a security camera view of the outer corridor. "If it's a newswriter—" Thena began ominously.

"It's Jin," Corwin sighed, tapping the intercom and door release. Probably the last person he felt up to facing at the moment . . . "Jin? Door's unlocked—come on in."

"You want me to leave?" Thena asked as he switched the intercom off.

"Not really," he admitted, "but it'd probably be better if you did."

A faint smile flickered across Thena's face as she stood up. "I understand. I'll be in the outer office if you need me." Touching him on the shoulder as she passed, she headed toward the door.

"Uncle Corwin?"

"Come in," Corwin called, waving to the girl—*no; she's a young woman now*—standing in the doorway.

Jin did so, exchanging quiet greetings with Thena as the two women passed each other at the doorway. "Sit down," Corwin invited, gesturing to the chair Thena had just vacated. "How's your dad doing?"

"About as you'd expect," she said, sinking into the chair. "Uncle Joshua came over a while ago and they spent a lot of time talking about other problems the family's had in the past."

Corwin nodded. "I remember similar trips down memory lane. Pretty depressing to listen to?"

She pursed her lips. "A little."

"Try not to let it bother you. It's one of the methods we Moreaus have traditionally used to remind ourselves that things usually wind up working out for the best."

Jin took a deep breath. "Dad told me my application for the Cobra Academy's been rejected."

Corwin's jaw tightened; with a conscious effort he relaxed it. "Did he explain why?" he asked.

She shook her head. "We didn't really discuss it—he had other things on his mind. That's one reason I came to see you."

"Yeah. Well . . . to put it bluntly, you were rejected because you're a woman."

He hadn't really expected her to looked surprised, and she didn't. "That's illegal, you know," she said calmly. "I've studied the

Academy's charter, the official Cobra Statement of Purpose, and even the original Dominion of Man documents. There's nothing in any of them that specifically excludes women from the Cobras."

"Of course there isn't," he sighed. "There isn't anything that excludes women from the governorship, either, but you'll notice that there aren't very many women who make it to that office. It's a matter of tradition."

"Whose tradition?" Jin countered. "Neither of those unspoken rules started with the Cobra Worlds. We inherited them from the Old Dominion of Man."

"Sure," he nodded. "But these things take time to change. You have to remember that we're barely two generations removed from the Dominion and its influence."

"It took less than *one* generation for us to give the Cobras their double vote," she pointed out.

"That was different. Tors Challinor's attempted rebellion forced an immediate political acknowledgment of the Cobras' physical power. Your case, unfortunately, doesn't have that kind of urgency to it."

For a long moment Jin just looked at him. "You're not going to fight the Council for me on this, are you?" she asked at last.

He spread his hands helplessly. "It's not a matter of fighting them, Jin. The whole weight of military history is against you. Women just haven't as a rule been welcomed into special military forces. Not *official* military forces, anyway," he corrected himself. "There've always been women rebels and guerrilla fighters, but I don't think that argument'll go over very well on either the Council or the Academy."

"You have a lot of influence, though. The Moreau name alone—"

"May still have some force out among Aventine's people," he grunted, "but the aura doesn't carry over into the upper echelons. It never did, really—in many ways your grandfather was a more popular figure than I am, and even in his time we had to fight and scrap and trade for everything we got."

Jin licked her lips. "Uncle Corwin . . . I have to get into the Academy. I *have* to. It's Dad's last chance to have one of the family carry on the Cobra tradition. Now, more than ever, he needs that to hang onto."

Corwin closed his eyes briefly. "Jin, look . . . I know how much that tradition means to Justin. Every time one of you girls was born—" He broke off. "The point is that the universe doesn't always work the way we want it to. If he and your mother had had a son—"

"But they didn't," Jin interrupted with a vehemence that startled him. "They *didn't;* and Mom's gone, and I'm Dad's last chance. His *last chance*—don't you understand?"

"Jin—" Corwin stopped, mind searching uselessly for something to say . . . and as he hesitated, he found his eyes probing the face of the young woman before him.

There was a lot of Justin in her face, in her features and her expressions. But as he thought back over the twenty years since her birth he found he could see even more of her father in her manner and personality. How much of that, he wondered vaguely, was due to genes alone and how much was due to the fact that Justin had been her only parent since she was nine years old? Thoughts of Justin sent a new kaleidoscope of images flurrying past his mind's eye: Justin fresh out of the Cobra Academy, excited by the upcoming mission to what was then the totally mysterious world of Qasama; an older and more sober Justin at his wedding to Aimee Partae, telling Corwin and Joshua about the son he would have someday to carry on the Moreau family's Cobra tradition; Justin and his three daughters, fifteen years later, at Aimee's funeral . . .

With an effort, he forced his thoughts back to the present. Jin was still sitting before him, the intensity of purpose in her expression balanced by a self-control rarely found among twenty-year-olds. One of the primary factors looked for in all Cobra applicants, he remembered distantly . . . "Look, Jin," he sighed. "Odds are very high that there's nothing at all I can do to influence the Academy's decision. But . . . I'll do what I can."

A ghost of a smile brushed Jin's lips. "Thank you," she said quietly. "I wouldn't be asking you to do this if it weren't for Dad."

He looked her straight in the eye. "Yes, you would," he said. "Don't try to con an old politician, girl."

She had the grace to blush. "You're right," she admitted "I *want* to be a Cobra, Uncle Corwin. More than anything else I've ever wanted."

"I know," he said softly. "Well. You'd better get back home. Tell your father . . . just tell him hi for me, and that I'll be in touch on this thing."

"Okay. Goodnight . . . and thank you."

"Sure."

She left and Corwin sighed to himself. Your *basic chicken-egg problem,* he thought. *Which came first: her desire to be a Cobra, or her love for her father?*

And did it really make any difference?

Thena reappeared in the doorway. "Everything all right?" she asked.

"Oh, sure," he growled. "I've just promised to take a running leap at a stone wall, that's all. How do I get myself into these things?"

She smiled. "Must be because you love your family."

He tried to glare at her, just on general principles, but it was too much effort. "Must be," he admitted, returning her smile. "Go on, get out of here."

"If you're sure . . . ?"

"I am. I'm only going to be a few more minutes myself."

"Okay. See you in the morning."

He waited until he heard the outer door close behind her. Then, with a sigh, he leaned back to his reader, keying for the government info net and his own private correlation program. Somewhere, somehow, there had to be a connection between Baram Monse and Governor Harper Priesly.

And he was going to find it.

Chapter 4

The Directorate meeting started at ten sharp the next morning ...
and it was as bad as Corwin had expected.

Priesly was in fine form, his tirade all the more impressive for
being brief. A less gifted politician might have overdone it and
wound up boring his audience, but Priesly avoided that trap with
ease. In front of the entire Council, where the sheer number of
members lent itself to the generation and manipulation of
emotional/political winds, the longer-winded speeches were often
effective; in front of the nine-member Directorate such ploys were
dangerous, not to mention occasionally coming off as downright
silly. But Corwin had hoped Priesly would try anyway and hang
himself in the process.

He should have known better.

" ... and I therefore feel that this body has the *duty* to reexam-
ine the entire concept of elitism that the Cobras and the Cobra
Academy represent," Priesly concluded. "Not only for the sake of
the people of Aventine and the other worlds, but even for the Cobras
themselves. Before another tragedy like this one occurs. Thank you."

He sat down. Corwin glanced around the table, noting the
expressions of the others with the frustration he was feeling more
and more these days. They were falling into the standard and
predictable pattern: Rolf Atterberry of Palatine firmly on Priesly's
side, Fenris Vartanson of Caelian—himself a Cobra—and
Governor Emeritus Lizabet Telek just as firmly against him, the
others leaning one way or the other but not yet willing to commit
themselves.

At the head of the table Governor-General Chandler cleared his
throat. "Mr. Moreau: any rebuttal?"

Or in other words, had Corwin found any positive link between Priesly and Monse. "Not specifically, sir," he said, getting briefly to his feet. "I would, though, like to remind the other members of this body of the testimony Justin and I have already put on record . . . and also to remind them that my brother has spoken here many times in the past in his capacity as an instructor of the Cobra Academy. A position, I'll mention, that requires him to submit to frequent psychological, physical, and emotional testing."

"If I may just insert here, sir," Priesly put in smoothly, "I have no quarrel at all with Cobra Justin Moreau. I agree with Governor Moreau that he is an outstanding and completely stable member of the Aventinian community. It is, in fact, the very fact that such a fine example of Cobra screening could still attack an unarmed man that worries me so."

Chandler grunted. "Mr. Moreau . . . ?"

"No further comments, sir," Corwin said, and sat back down. Priesly had taken a chance with that interruption, he knew, and with a little luck it would wind up working against him. The thrust of his arguments, serious though they were, were still a far cry from the result he and Monse had almost certainly been trying for. If Monse had succeeded in triggering the combat reflexes programmed into Justin's implanted nanocomputer, Priesly would have had a far stronger bogy to wave in front of both the Directorate and the populace as a whole.

Across the table, Ezer Gavin stirred. "May I ask, Mr. Chandler, what Cobra Moreau's status is at the moment? I presume he's been suspended from his Academy duties?"

"He has," Chandler nodded. "The investigation is proceeding—much of it at this point into Mr. Monse's background, I may add."

Corwin glanced at Priesly, read no reaction there. Hardly surprising—he already knew that whatever Priesly's connection was with Monse, it was well buried.

"I'd like to also point out, if I may," Lizabet Telek spoke up with an air of impatience, "that for all the fuss we're generating—both here and on the nets," she added with a glance at Priesly, "this Monse character wasn't killed or even seriously injured."

"If he hadn't had that ceramic laminae on his bones he would have been," Atterberry put in.

"If he hadn't been trespassing in the first place he wouldn't have been hurt at all," Telek retorted. "Mr. Governor-General, could we possibly move on to some other topic? This whole discussion is turning my stomach."

"As it happens, we do have another topic to tackle today—one which is far more serious," Chandler nodded. "All further discussion on the Monse case to be tabled until further investigations are complete . . . now, then." He tapped a button next to his reader; a moment later the door across the room opened and a dress-uniformed Cobra ushered a thin academic type into the chamber. "Mr. Pash Barynson, of the Qasaman Monitor Center," Chandler introduced the newcomer as he walked over to the guest chair at the governor-general's left. "He's here to brief us on a disturbing pattern that may or may not be—Well, I'll let him sort it all out for you. Mr. Barynson . . . ?"

"Thank you, Governor-General Chandler," Barynson said with a self-conscious bob of his head. Setting a handful of magcards down on the table, he picked one up and inserted it into his reader. "Governors; governors emeritus," he said, glancing around at them all, "I'm going to admit right up front that I'm rather . . . uncomfortable, shall we say, about being here. As Mr. Chandler has just indicated, there are hints of a pattern emerging on Qasama that we don't like. On the other hand, what that pattern really means—or even if it really exists—are questions we still can't answer."

Well, that's *certainly clear,* Corwin thought. He glanced across the table at Telek, saw a sour expression flicker across her face. As a former academician herself, Corwin knew, she had even less patience with flowery fence-straddling than he did. "Suppose you elaborate and let us judge," she invited.

That got her a frown from Chandler, but Barynson didn't seem insulted. "Of course, Governor Emeritus," he nodded. "First, since all of you may not be familiar with the background here—" he glanced at Priesly—"I'd like to briefly run through the basics for you.

"As most of you know, in 2454 the Council had a series of six spy satellites placed into high orbit over the world of Qasama for the purpose of monitoring their technological and societal development following the introduction of Aventinian spine leopards into their ecological structure. In the twenty years since then the program has met with only limited success. We've noted that the village system has expanded beyond the so-called Fertile Crescent region, indicating either that the Qasamans' cultural paranoia has eased somewhat or that they've given up on keeping their long-range communications immune from interception. We've spotted evidence of some improvement in their aircraft and ground vehicles, as well as various minor changes you've had full reports on over the years. Nothing, so far, that would give us any reason to believe the Qasaman threat vis-a-vis the Cobra Worlds has in any way changed for the worse."

He cleared his throat and tapped a button on the reader. A series of perhaps fifty dates and times appeared on Corwin's reader—the earliest nearly thirty months ago, he noted, the most recent only three weeks old—under the heading *Satellite Downtimes*. A quick scan of the numbers showed that, for each downtime listed, the affected satellite had lost between three and twelve hours of its record. "As you can see," Barynson continued, "over the last thirty months we've lost something on the order of four hundred hours of data covering various parts of Qasama. Up until recently we didn't think too much about it—"

"Why not?" Urbanic Bailar of the newly colonized world Esquiline cut in. "I was under the impression that the main duty of your Monitor Center was to keep the planet under constant surveillance. I wasn't aware that leaving twelve-hour gaps qualified as *constant*."

"I understand your concern," Barynson said soothingly, "but I assure you that Esquiline was—is—in no danger whatsoever. Even if the Qasamans knew your world's location—which they don't—there's simply no way they could create an attack fleet without our knowing it. Remember that they lost all their interstellar capability shortly after they reached Qasama—they'd be starting from literal step zero." Something flicked across his eyes, too fast for Corwin to read. "No, none of us are in any immediate danger from the Qasamans—that much we're certain of."

"Well, I for one don't see what the fuss is," Atterberry snorted. "Self-repairing machinery like satellites are *supposed* to fail occasionally, aren't they?"

"Yes, but not this often," Governor Emeritus David Nguyen put in.

"Both of you are correct, actually," Barynson nodded, licking briefly at his lips. "Which is why we hadn't paid the gaps any real attention. However, a week ago one of our people, more on a hunch than anything else, tried running location and vector correlations on them. It turned out—well, here, you can see for yourselves," he said, pushing another series of keys.

A map of the Fertile Crescent region of Qasama, home to virtually all the humans on that world, appeared on Corwin's reader. A series of colored ovals and arrows had been superimposed on the landscape.

"Interesting," Telek growled. "How many of these gaps are missing that same chunk of the Crescent's western arm?"

"Thirty-seven of the fifty-two," Barynson said. "All but two of the others—"

"Lose some of the territory directly to the east of that section," Priesly interrupted him.

Corwin felt something cold crawl up his back. "You have any small-scales of that place?" he asked.

A slightly grainy picture replaced the map. "This is a photo taken three years ago, before the rash of malfunctions," Barynson said. "For those familiar with the Qasaman landscape, the city in the left-center of the picture is Azras; the one northeast of it, near top-center, is Purma."

Involuntarily, Corwin glanced up at Telek, to find her eyes likewise on him. *Purma*—the city where the Qasamans had tried their damnedest to kill three members of Telek's original spy mission . . . one of those three being Justin.

"Now *here*—" the photo changed "—is that same area as of the last satellite collection two weeks ago."

Azras and Purma were essentially unchanged. But in the center of the screen—"What's that thing in the middle?" Gavin asked.

"It appears to be a large compound or encampment or something." Barynson took a deep breath. "And from all indications, it's not only encircled by the standard Qasaman defensive wall, but is also completely covered on top."

Protected from overhead surveillance . . . "And those areas on either side of it?" Corwin asked.

"Those could have been blanked out by accident," Barynson said carefully. "But if they're not . . . we think it significant that east— parallel to the planet's rotation—is the obvious direction for practice in firing large, long-range rockets."

There was a long moment of silence. "Are you telling us," Bailar said at last, "that that covered compound is the center of a Qasaman missile base?"

Barynson nodded grimly. "The probability seems high that the Qasamans are attempting to rediscover space travel. And that they may be succeeding."

Chapter 5

For a long minute there was silence in the room. Then Atterberry stirred. "Well," he said to no one in particular, "so much for *that* one."

"So much for that one *what?*" Telek growled at him.

"That attempt to keep the Qasamans down," Atterberry amplified. "Trying to break their intersocial cooperation by tricking the mojos off the people and onto spine leopards—the whole Moreau Proposal, in other words."

"Who says it's been a failure?" Corwin put in, not bothering to keep the annoyance out of his voice. He and his family had sweat blood over that proposal . . . and in the process had saved the Cobra Worlds a long and costly and possibly losing war. "All we have here is an inference from a possible assumption based on questionable data. With that underground communications system of theirs we have no way of really knowing what's going on down there."

"All right," Atterberry snorted. "Let's hear *your* idea of what that compound is for, then."

"There could be hundreds of explanations," Corwin shot back. "Ninety percent of which would have nothing to do with any spaceward expansion."

"Such as a new test facility for the air-to-air missiles they've already got, for instance," Telek said. "Or longer-range ones for use against each other."

Chandler cleared his throat. "I think you're both missing the point," he said. "Whatever they're doing down there, the fact is that *if* Dr. Barynson and his colleagues are correct about the satellite malfunctions, then we're already talking a serious threat. Am I correct, Dr. Barynson, in the assumption that those satellites aren't easily knocked out?"

"Without our realizing that they *had* been deliberately hit?" Barynson nodded. "Most definitely. That's one of the reasons we were so slow to notice the pattern of the downtimes, in fact—with no obvious physical damage anywhere, there was no reason to assume the Qasamans were responsible."

"Have we established the Qasamans *were* responsible?" Vartanson spoke up. "You haven't yet suggested a mechanism for this purported sabotage, Doctor, and until you do I don't see how this can be treated as anything but an admittedly odd coincidence."

Barynson scratched at his cheek. "That's the dilemma we're in, all right, Governor," he admitted. "As I said, there hasn't been any obvious physical damage to any of the satellites. We've checked into some of the other possibilities—high-powered lasers blinding the lenses from the surface, for example—but so far none of the simulations give us the right kind of damage profile."

"How about ionizing radiation?" Vartanson persisted. "And I don't necessarily mean radiation from Qasama."

"Solar flares?" Barynson shrugged. "It's certainly one possibility. But if we assume random flares or ionosphere shifts we're still left with the question of why only that one area was so often left unmonitored."

"It seems to me," Nguyen spoke up quietly, "that we could argue about this forever without getting anywhere. Mr. Moreau is correct: we have insufficient data for any solid conclusions. The only way we're going to get the kind of information we need will be to go back down there."

"In other words, send in another spy mission," Atterberry said with undisguised distaste. "The last one we sent in—"

"Wound up buying us nearly thirty years of peace," Telek put in tartly.

"Postponing a war that's going to have to be fought anyway, you mean—"

"Who said it's going to have to be fought?" Telek snapped. "For all we know, that compound has nothing to do with us—it could just as well be part of the preparations for an all-out internecine war that'll blow the Qasamans back to a pre-metal culture."

"I hope," Priesly said quietly, "that you aren't as eager for that result as you sound."

Telek's jaw tightened visibly. "I don't particularly want to see the Qasamans destroy themselves, no," she growled. "But if it comes down to a choice between them and us, I want us to be the ones who survive."

Chandler cleared his throat. "It should be obvious that, whatever reservations we might have, Mr. Nguyen is correct. Another mission to Qasama is called for, and the sooner we get it underway, the sooner we'll find out what's going on." He tapped a key on his reader, and the telephoto on Corwin's reader was replaced by a list of nine names. "Given the experience of the first Qasaman mission," Chandler continued, "it would appear to make more sense to start primarily with new Cobra recruits than to try and retrain older frontier-duty Cobras for the different kind of action they might face on Qasama. I've taken the liberty of running a preliminary sort-through of the latest acceptance list; these are the names that fell out."

"Sorted how?" Gavin asked.

"Particular emotional stability, ability to mix well and comfortably socially—that sort of thing," Chandler replied. "It's just a preliminary sorting, of course."

Vartanson straightened up from his reader. "How many Cobras were you planning to send on the mission?" he asked Chandler.

"The initial plan is calling for one experienced Cobra and four fresh recruits—"

"You can't have them," Vartanson said flatly.

All eyes turned to the Cobra. "What in the worlds are you talking about?" Bailar asked, frowning.

Vartanson gestured at his reader. "Six of these recruits are from Caelian. We need them back there."

Chandler took a deep breath. "Mr. Vartanson . . . I understand the close community feeling the people of Caelian have—"

"There are barely three thousand of us left, Mr. Chandler," Vartanson said, his tone icy. "Twenty-five hundred civilians, five hundred Cobras—all of us fighting for our lives against Hell's Own Blender. We can't afford to let you take even one of those Cobras away from us . . . and you're not going to."

An uncomfortable silence filled the room. Caelian was a dead-end world, in every sense of the word—a planet abandoned after years of struggle against its incredibly fluid ecology had bought the colonists nothing but a stalemate. Most of the population, when offered transport to the new world of Esquiline a quarter-century ago, had jumped at the chance . . . but for a small fraction of that populace, the mindless Caelian ecology had taken on the status of a powerful and almost sentient enemy, and to run from that enemy had seemed to them to be an acceptance of defeat and dishonor. Corwin had visited Caelian once since that remnant had dug in for the battle, and had come away with the uncomfortable picture of the people of Hell's Blender as rafters on a raging river. Drifting away not only from the rest of the Cobra Worlds community, but possibly even from their own basic humanity.

All of which made Vartanson a very wild card indeed . . . and a man no one else in the Directorate ever really liked to cross.

Not even the governor-general. "I understand," Chandler said again to Vartanson. Soothingly. "Actually, I think that even if we don't find another good candidate, these three new Cobras plus the experienced one ought to be adequate for the mission's needs."

Corwin took a deep breath. "Perhaps," he said carefully, "we ought to see this lack of a fifth Cobra not as a problem but as an opportunity. A chance to throw the Qasamans a curve."

He looked over to see Telek's eyes on him. "You mean like that switch your brothers pulled back on the first mission?" she asked. "Good idea, that—may even have saved the entire mission."

Silently, Corwin blessed her. She couldn't know what he was about to propose, but by reminding the others of how well that other scheme had worked out she'd weakened the automatic resistance his enemies would almost certainly come up with. "Something like that," he nodded, unconsciously bracing himself. "I'd like to suggest that we create, solely for this mission, the first woman Cobra. Now, before you voice any objections—"

"A *woman* Cobra?" Atterberry snorted. "Oh, for—Moreau, that is the most *ridiculous* idea I've ever heard."

"Why?" Corwin countered. "Just because it hasn't ever been done?"

"Why do you suppose it *has* never been done?" Priesly put in. "Because there are good reasons for it, that's why."

Corwin looked over at Chandler. "Mr. Chandler?"

There was a slightly sour look on Chandler's face, but he nodded. "You may continue," he said.

"Thank you." Corwin's gaze swept the table, settled on Priesly and Atterberry as the two most hostile-looking. "One reason that the idea of women Cobras sounds so outlandish is that the Old Dominion of Man had a fairly strong patriarchal orientation. Women simply weren't considered for elite military troops—though I'll point out that during the Troft War there were a large number of female resistance fighters on both Adirondack and Silvern."

"We all know our history," Nguyen put in gruffly. "Get to the point."

"The point is that even what little we know of Qasaman society paints it as even more patriarchal than the Dominion was,"

Corwin told him. "If the thought of female warriors strikes *you* as ridiculous, think of how they'll see it."

"In other words," Telek said slowly, "they're not likely to even *consider* the possibility that a woman along on the mission could be a demon warrior."

"A demon *what?*" Priesly frowned.

"It's the Qasaman term for Cobras," Chandler told him.

"Appropriate," Priesly grunted.

Vartanson threw him a cold look. "Being borderline demonic is often part of our job," he said icily.

Priesly's lip twitched, and he turned abruptly back to Corwin. "Your assumption, of course, is that the mission will be caught," he said. "Isn't that being a little pessimistic?"

"It's called being prepared," Corwin said tartly. "But assuming they *won't* get caught brings me to my second point: we want people who can fit in well enough with the Qasamans to poke around for answers without being immediately branded as foreigners. Correct?" He looked at Chandler. "Can you tell me, Mr. Chandler, how many of the Cobra candidates on your list can speak Qasaman?"

"All of them," the governor-general said stiffly. "Give me a little credit, Mr. Moreau—Qasaman may not be an especially popular language course to take, but there's a reasonable pool of proficient people out there to choose from."

"Especially since most young men with Cobra ambitions try and learn it," Gavin pointed out.

"I understand that," Corwin nodded. "How many of this pool can speak it without an Aventinian accent?"

Chandler's brow darkened. "Everyone who learns a foreign language speaks with an accent," he growled.

Corwin looked him straight in the eye. "I know someone who doesn't," he said flatly. "My niece, Jasmine Moreau."

"Ah—well, there it is, everyone," Atterberry put in sardonically. "*That's* what all this is about—just another blatant grab for power by the Moreau family."

"How does this qualify as a grab for power?" Corwin snorted. "By sending my niece out to possibly get herself killed?"

"Enough." Chandler hadn't raised his voice, but something in his tone sliced cleanly through the burgeoning argument. "I've worked up a preliminary cost analysis for the proposed Qasaman mission—we'll take a short recess now for you to examine it. Mr. Moreau, I'd like to see you in my office, if I may."

❖   ❖   ❖

"You realize, I presume, what you're asking the Directorate to do," Chandler said, gaze locked on Corwin's face. "Not to mention what you're asking me, personally, to do."

Corwin forced himself to meet the other's gaze. "I'm doing nothing but trying to give this mission of yours a better chance of success."

Chandler's lip twitched. "So it's 'my' mission now, is it?"

"Isn't it?" Corwin countered. "You clearly set it up privately, without the assistance or even the knowledge of the Academy board. Not to mention the knowledge of the Directorate itself."

Chandler's expression didn't change. "You have any proof of that?"

"If Justin had known this was in the works, he would have told me about it."

"That's hardly proof. I could have sworn all of the Academy directors to secrecy."

Corwin didn't answer, and after a moment Chandler sighed. "Let's be honest, here, shall we, Moreau? Logic and social goals notwithstanding, the real reason you want your niece in the Cobras is because your brother wants her there."

"She wants it herself, too," Corwin told him. "And, yes, I'll admit that there's part of me that wants to keep the family tradition alive. That doesn't negate the reasons I gave the Directorate a few minutes ago."

"No, but it muddies the politics considerably," Chandler grunted. "Okay, then—run the scenario. Tell me how the votes would fall if we went back and called a showdown."

"Telek and I would vote yes," Corwin said slowly. "Priesly and Atterberry would of course vote no, whether they agreed with me or not. Vartanson and Bailar . . . probably yes. Vartanson because if women were allowed in, it would effectively double Caelian's pool of Cobra candidates; Bailar because the Qasamans are only a few light-years from Esquiline's doorstep and he'll be more concerned with the logic of Jin's case than in history. With Vartanson's double vote, that would give me five votes."

"Which means you need one more vote for a clear majority," Chandler said. "Mine, for instance."

Corwin looked him square in the eye. "Yours was always the only vote I really needed."

For a moment Chandler gazed back at him in silence. "Politics goes in cycles," he said at last. "If the governor-general's office has more power now than it has had in the past, I make no apologies for it." He pursed his lips, slowly shook his head. "But you're wrong if you think I can push this through on my own, against all opposition. Priesly alone would be too much to buck."

Corwin turned away from him, eyes drifting to the governor-general's floor-to-ceiling window and the panoramic view of Capitalia that it opened onto. In his mind's eye, he could see Jin's face, last night, as she pleaded with him . . . could see Justin's expression at the hospital as the enormity of what he'd inadvertently done slowly became apparent. *What price power?* he thought dimly to himself. *What use is this office, anyway, if it's not to do what needs to be done?* "All right, then," he said slowly. "If Priesly needs incentive, I'll give it to him." He turned back to Chandler. "We'll let Jin into the Cobras, ostensibly for the reasons I listed as to her usefulness on a Qasaman spy mission. But we'll also bill it as a grand experiment into whether or not women can successfully be integrated into the entire Cobra program. If it doesn't work—if the experiment's a failure—" he took a deep breath "—then I'll resign my governorship."

It was perhaps the first time he'd ever seen genuine shock on Chandler's face. "You'll—*what?*" the other all but sputtered. "Moreau, that's—it's *crazy.*"

"It's what I want to do," Corwin told him evenly. "I know what Jin's capable of. She'll handle the job, and she'll handle it well."

"That's practically irrelevant. Whatever happens, Priesly will claim the experiment was a failure, just to get you out. You know that."

"He'll *try* to claim that, certainly," Corwin nodded. "Whether or not the claim sticks will depend on how Jin does, won't it?"

Chandler pursed his lips, his eyes searching Corwin's face. "It'll need the approval of the entire Council, of course."

"We all have our supporters and allies there," Corwin said. "Between yours, mine, and Priesly's, we ought to have enough. Especially if we use the secrecy of the Qasaman mission to keep the experiment on closed-access. Less of a possibility for political flak from the general populace that way."

A lopsided smile creased Chandler's face. "You're getting cynical in your old age."

Corwin looked back out the window again. "No," he said with a sigh. "Just getting political."

And wondered why that should sound so like a curse in his ears.

Chapter 6

Late spring in Syzra District, Jin had once heard, was the most enjoyable time of the year in that particular part of Aventine . . . if you happened to be a duck. Supposedly, for the better part of three months straight, the sky over Syzra was either heavily overcast or pouring its guts out in torrents of cold rain.

But if those stories were true, this day was a pleasant exception. The rising sun, peeking through the dense forest surrounding them at a distance on three sides, shone clear and bright through a sky that had only a few high cirrus clouds to add counterpoint to its brilliant blue. What wind there was came in short, mild gusts; and the air temperature, while chilly, was more bracing than uncomfortable. It was the kind of day Jin had always loved.

And she felt absolutely terrible. Squinting her eyes slightly against the sunlight, she clenched her fists at her sides, tried to stand as tall as the three young men to her right, and fought hard to keep from throwing up.

"All right, recruits, let's bend your ears forward," the man standing facing them bellowed, and Jin clamped down a little more on her rebellious gastrointestinal tract. Instructor Mistra Layn's voice, unusually rich in deep tones, wasn't helping things a bit. So *much for my celebrated cast-iron gut,* she thought wryly to herself, remembering the warnings everyone had given her about the normal physiological reaction to Cobra surgery. Clearly, she'd been too quick to dismiss them; now all she could hope for was that the reaction was as short-term as they'd all said it would be.

"You already know," Layn continued, "that we've been selected for a special mission to Qasama. So I won't bore you with that harangue again. What you're probably wondering instead is why we're out here in the middle of nowhere instead of at one of the main Academy centers. Well?"

It took a second for Jin to realize that he was asking them a question. It took a few seconds longer to realize that none of her fellow trainees were going to respond. "Sir?" she said tentatively.

A flicker of something crossed Layn's face, but his voice was neutral enough. "Trainee Moreau?"

"Sir, are we here because the mission will involve travel through forested areas of Qasama?"

Layn cocked an eyebrow and threw a leisurely look behind him. "Why, yes—there *is* forest here, isn't there? There's forest at the training center in Pindaric District, too, as I recall. So why aren't we there instead of here?"

Jin gritted her teeth. "I don't know, sir."

The young man at Jin's right stirred. "Sir?"

"Trainee Sun?"

"Sir, the Pindaric center concentrates on teaching new Cobras how to hunt and kill spine leopards," Mander Sun said. "Our mission won't involve hunting so much as it will evasion and simply staying alive."

"Don't the Cobras at Pindaric need to learn how to stay alive?" Layn countered.

Her eyes locked on Layn, Jin couldn't see if Sun flushed. But from the tone of his voice she rather thought he had. "The methods of training for attack versus defense are entirely different, sir," he said. "More than that, they would be *obviously* different to the other trainees there. I understood this *was* supposed to be a secret mission."

For a long moment Layn merely looked at Sun. "More or less correct, Trainee Sun. The secrecy part, that is. But who says attack and defense training are different?"

"My grandfather, sir. He was Coordinator of the Academy for twenty years."

"Does that give you the right to stiff-neck your instructor?" Layn said coldly.

This time there was no doubt that Sun flushed. "No, sir," he said stiffly.

"Glad to hear it." Layn let his gaze drift to all four of them. "Because I have no intention of going to Qasama without the absolute best people available backing me up. If I don't think one or more of you measures up, I can and will bounce you—and I don't much care whether it's on the first day of training or while you're being wheeled in to have your nanocomputers implanted. All of you got that?"

Jin swallowed, suddenly conscious of the neck-wrap computer nestling up under her jaw. If she failed her training—was deemed unsuitable, for whatever reason—the nanocomputer that would eventually be implanted beneath her brain would be a mere shadow of the true Cobra computer, disconnecting all of her newly acquired weaponry and severely limiting the power available to the servos augmenting her muscles. She would be, in short, a Ject.

"All right, then," Layn said. "Now. I know you're all eager to find out just what those aching bodies of yours can do. For the moment, actually, that's not a hell of a lot. Those computers around your necks will give you limited servos and no weapons whatsoever. In four days—assuming adequate progress—you'll be given new neckwraps that let you activate your optical and auditory enhancers. After that, over a period of about four weeks, you'll get the use of your fingertip lasers, the lasers plus enhancers, the sonic weapons and arcthrower, the antiarmor laser alone, antiarmor plus everything else, and finally your preprogrammed reflexes. The purpose, you'll note, is to give you the best possible chance of learning to use your new bodies without killing yourselves or anyone else in the process."

"Question, sir?" the trainee at the far end of the line spoke up tentatively.

"Trainee Hariman?"

"Sir, I was under the impression that the normal training period was six to eight weeks, not four."

"Weren't you told this wasn't going to be normal training?" Layn countered.

"Ah, yes, sir, I was. It just seemed to me . . . a little quick, that's all. Especially with the new weapons being introduced with this group."

Layn cocked an eyebrow. "What new weapons are those, Trainee?"

"Ah . . . I was under the impression, sir, that the Council had approved the use of short-range voltage generators for use through the arcthrower circuits."

"You're referring, I take it, to the so-called stun-guns? You're well informed, Trainee Hariman."

"Much of the weapons debate has been public knowledge, sir."

"So it has. As it happens, though, that won't be a consideration. For the simple reason that none of you will be participating in that experiment. The Council decided you were going to be experimental enough as it was—" Layn's eyes flicked to Jin "—and there was no need to give you untried equipment as well."

"Yes, sir," Hariman said. "That doesn't explain how we're going to learn how to be Cobras in four weeks instead of six, sir."

"You questioning your ability as a trainee, or my ability as an instructor?"

"Uh . . . neither, sir."

"Good. Did you say something a moment ago, Trainee Todor?"

"Sir?" The trainee standing between Hariman and Sun sounded startled.

"The question was simple enough, Trainee. Did you say something to Trainee Sun while I was explaining why you hadn't had stun-guns installed?"

"Uh . . . it was nothing, sir."

"Repeat it."

"I, uh . . ." Todor audibly took a breath. "I was just thinking that, as far as extra weaponry was concerned . . . uh, that Trainee Moreau could be easily implanted with a pair of turret guns."

Layn's expression didn't change, but it seemed to Jin that his eyes flicked briefly to her breasts before rising to her face. "Trainee Moreau? Any comment?"

A truly scathing retort had already come to mind, but it seemed better not to use it. At least not here and now. "No, sir," she said.

"No. Well, then, I've got one." Layn's eyes flicked to the other three trainees . . . and abruptly his face hardened. "It's pretty clear that none of you is exactly thrilled at having a woman in the unit. Now, you've all heard the Council's reasons as to why they think this is worth trying, so I won't hash that over again. But I will say this.

"To tell you the absolute truth, I don't much like it either. Special military units have always been men-only, from the Dominion of Man's old Alpha Command all the way on up to the Cobras. I don't like breaking tradition like this; I especially don't like the idea that this is a test to see if the Cobras should be opened up in the future to more women. In fact, I'll go so far as to say that I hope Trainee Moreau will fail. *But.*" His gaze hardened even more. "*If* she fails, she is going to do it on *her own.* Understood? Specifically, she is *not* going to fail because you or I or anyone else pushed her harder than she should have been pushed. Considerations of fairness aside, I don't want anyone claiming that the test was unfair. You got all that?"

There were three murmurs. "I asked if you got all that," Layn snapped.

"Yes, sir," the others said in unison.

"Good." Layn took a deep breath. "All right, then, let's get to work. That tree over there—" he pointed to their right "—is about three kilometers away. You've got six minutes to get there."

Sun moved first, stepping behind Todor and Hariman to take the lead. Jin was right behind him, the other two trainees falling in belatedly after her. *Pace yourself, girl,* she warned herself, trying as best she could to let the servo motors in her legs do most of the work. Around her, the thudding of the others' footsteps filled her ears, almost drowning out the faint whine from above . . .

Abruptly, the sound clicked with her consciousness, and she glanced up, eyes searching the sky. There it was, just coming into sight over the treetops to her right: a Troft-built aircar, bearing toward the complex that was serving as their training center. She twisted her head further around, seeking out Layn, but if the instructor was surprised by the craft's arrival it didn't show in his stance. *Probably someone here to observe from the Directorate,* she decided, shifting her attention back to the race.

To her annoyance, she found that while she'd let the aircar's presence distract her both Todor and Hariman had managed to pass her by. *It's okay,* she reminded herself, picking up her speed a little. *They're more concerned with making sure they don't come in last than they are with pacing themselves. That'll probably work against them.* Todor, she noted, was already breathing harder than he should—either hyperventilating or else not letting his servos take as much of the load as he ought to. Either way, he should find himself in trouble before the run was over.

Involuntarily, Jin's jaw clenched. She didn't like having to play tactical games like this, least of all against the men who were going to be her teammates on Qasama. But she didn't have much choice in the matter. Layn had put it very clearly: her performance here on the training field was going to determine not only whether or not she herself became a full Cobra, but also whether or not any other woman in the Cobra Worlds would ever have that same chance.

She'd never before been much of a one to fight for universal causes; but whether she liked it or not, she was smack square in the middle of this one. In the middle, with nothing but her own stamina and determination going for her.

And—maybe—the legacy of the Moreau family. *Pace yourself,* she repeated over and over to herself, using the words as a running cadence. *Pace yourself...*

She was second, behind only Sun, when they at last reached the tree.

The Troft lying on his couch by the aircar's starboard window stirred as the four trainees far below reached the tree. [The second-place human,] he said, his high-pitched catertalk almost swallowed up by the whine of the aircar's thrusters. [It was a female?]

Beside Corwin, Governor-General Chandler harrumphed. "You're very perceptive," he said reluctantly, throwing a glare in Corwin's direction.

"It's just an experiment," Priesly added sourly. "Pushed through by certain elements in our government—"

[Of the four, she is the best,] the Troft said.

Priesly's eyes narrowed. "Why do you say that?" he demanded.

The Troft's arm membranes flexed, then relaxed back against his upper arms. [Our approach, she was the only one who noticed it,] he explained. [Her face, it sought out the sound and confirmed our identity as non-hostile before resuming her running. That sort of alertness, it is a preferred attribute for a Cobra warrior?]

"It is indeed," Chandler admitted. "Well. At any rate, now that you've seen the trainees—at least from a distance—we'll be heading over to the special camp where this proposed mission is being headquartered. You'll be able to examine all the Qasaman data there, see why it is we think there's something happening that we ought to investigate."

The Troft seemed to consider that. [This information, you would not be giving it to me without need. What is it you want?]

Chandler took a deep breath. "In a nutshell: transport. We can use one of our own starships to get the team from here to Qasama, of course, but we haven't yet got a safe way for them to get from orbit to ground. We would like to borrow a Troft military shuttle for that purpose."

"We don't want to land a full starship," Priesly put in. "Not only because of the danger of detection—"

[A vehicle with a stardrive, you do not want it to fall into

Qasaman hands,] Speaker One cut him off. [My intelligence, do not insult it, Governor Priesly.]

Priesly shut up, a pained look on his face, and for a moment Corwin could almost feel sorry for him. There'd been no anger in Speaker One's comment—merely a desire to save time—but Priesly hadn't dealt with this particular representative of the Tlos'khin'fohi demesne long enough to know his personality. Speaker One had been an interdemesne trader before being given the Cobra Worlds liaison post four years ago, and Corwin had long since noted that such Trofts had an almost supernatural control over their tempers. Not surprising, given the loose and often combative relationships that existed between the hundreds of demesnes that made up the Troft Assemblage. A trader who got into verbal fights with his customers every third time he was out of his home demesne wouldn't be a trader for long.

"Governor Priesly meant no harm, Speaker One," Chandler spoke up into the conversational void, looking pleased himself at Priesly's discomfiture. "The tactical reasons for borrowing such a landing craft are of course obvious. The financial reasons, I imagine, are also obvious to you."

[Such a shuttle, you cannot afford to buy.]

Chandler nodded. "That's it exactly. Though we're in far better shape now than we were thirty years ago when this whole Qasaman mess began, even now our budget will only support the cost of the mission itself—that is, the personnel, basic equipment, and specialized training. You'll remember we're still paying off the last full starship we bought from you; we can't afford to buy a shuttle, too."

[The Tlos'khin'fahi demesne, why should it lend you this craft? We are far from Qasama, with little at stake should they escape their world.]

Translation: the bargaining had begun. "We don't necessarily want the Tlos'khin'fahi demesne itself to provide the shuttle," Corwin put in before Chandler could answer. "However, as our main trading partner, the health of our economy should be of some concern to you . . . and if our buying a shuttle would hurt that economy, it would have at least a minor effect on you."

[The Baliu'ckha'spmi demesne, would it not have more of a reason to provide you a shuttle?]

Chandler threw a glance at Corwin. "Probably," he conceded. "The problem is that . . . the Baliu'ckha'spmi demesne might infer the wrong thing from such a request."

[You refer to the trade by which you obtained the New Worlds?]

"Basically," Chandler said heavily. "The agreement *was* that we would neutralize the Qasaman threat for them, after all. If they decide this means that Qasama wasn't properly neutralized . . . well, we don't really want to open that can of snakes."

The Troft's arm membranes fluttered again as he sorted through the idiom. [The reason for bringing me out here in secret, it is also because of this concern?]

"You don't miss much," Chandler admitted. "Yes, we didn't want any word of this leaking out to other demesne representatives if we could possibly avoid it."

For a moment Speaker One was silent. The aircar began a leisurely turn, and Corwin glanced out the window. Below them, nestled in an artificial clearing, was the small logging complex that had been temporarily taken over by the Cobra Academy for the special training course. [The question, I will bring it to my demesne-lord's attention,] Speaker One said as the aircar dipped toward a scarred landing square near the main building's entrance. [Some sort of trade, it will of course be necessary.]

"Of course," Chandler nodded, sounding relieved. "We'll be happy to consider any request he suggests."

[My demesne-lord, he will also remember that the original pacification plan was created by the late Governor Jonny Moreau,] the Troft continued. [If I could inform him that one of Governor Jonny Moreau's line would be planning this mission as well, it would give more weight to my arguments.]

Chandler threw Corwin a surprised look. "Why?" he asked.

[Continuity in the affairs of war, it is as valued as in the affairs of business,] the Troft said—rather coolly, Corwin thought. [Such a thing, Governor-General Chandler, it is possible?]

Chandler took a deep breath. From the expression on his face, he was clearly envisioning the political flap were he to reinstate Justin to the Academy while still under a cloud from the Monse shooting . . . "I'm afraid, Speaker One," Priesly spoke up tartly, "the Moreau family is no longer directly involved with such military planning—"

"Fortunately, that won't be a problem," Corwin interrupted him. "The human female you saw in the clearing a few minutes ago— the one you thought was the best of the trainees? She is Jasmine Moreau, daughter of Cobra Justin Moreau and Governor Jonny Moreau's granddaughter."

Priesly sputtered; Chandler cut him off with a hand signal. "Will that be adequate, Speaker One?" the governor-general asked.

There was a slight bump as the aircar touched down. [It will indeed,] the Troft said. [Your data, I will now be pleased to study it.]

Chandler exhaled quietly. "Certainly. Follow me."

Chapter 7

"All right, Cobras, move it out," Mistra Layn growled. "Remember this is a forest—watch your feet *and* your heads."

Keying her auditory enhancers up a notch, Jin fell into her usual leftguard position in the loose diamond formation around Layn and crossed with the others under the trees at the edge of the clearing. It was an operation they'd practiced several times in the past few days: walking through the fenced-off part of the forest around their camp, using their optical and auditory enhancers to try and spot the various animal-cue simulators and moving-head targets the instructors had planted around them. Spotting a squawker or target first earned the trainee a point; nailing it cleanly with fingertip lasers before the group got within the animal's theoretical attack range was worth two more points.

It was just one more of the silly competitions Layn was continually using to pit his trainees against each other. One more needless opportunity, Jin thought bitterly, for the other three trainees to hate her.

It was hardly her fault that she was better than they were at these games. It was certainly not her fault that they couldn't accept that.

Her innocence in the matter was cold comfort, though, and thinking about it brought an ache to her throat. She hadn't expected instant acceptance by the others—she'd known full well that Uncle Corwin's lectures about military traditions hadn't merely been scare tactics. But she had thought that by now, eleven days into the training, some of the hostility would surely have faded away.

But it hadn't. Oh, they were polite enough to her—Layn's big

speech the first day of training about letting her fail on her own
had been backed up by action, and both he and the others were
clearly bending over backwards to avoid any kind of overtly preju-
dicial behavior. But the whispered comments and secret smiles were
still there, lurking most outwardly in the quiet times when the
trainees were alone.

Or rather, when Jin was alone. The other three spent a lot of
that time together.

It hurt. In many ways, it hurt worse than the worst physical
aftereffects of her surgery. She'd always been something of a misfit
as she was growing up—either too quiet or too aggressive for the
other girls and even most of the boys her age. Only with her family
had she ever felt truly at home, truly accepted. With her family,
and to a lesser extent with the Cobra friends of her father's . . .

A faint chirping from ahead penetrated her brooding. A tarbine
squawker, she identified it, head automatically turning back and
forth to pinpoint the sound. There?—*there.* Activating her optical sensors' targeting capability, she locked onto the small black
cube nestled in the crook of a branch and fired her right fingertip laser.

A needle of light lanced out, and the box abruptly stopped
chirping.

"A tarbine?" Sun called softly to her from the rear point of the
diamond.

"Yeah," she said over her shoulder.

"Why'd you kill it?" Layn asked from the center. "Tarbines aren't
dangerous."

"No, sir," she said, recognizing that she'd made the right decision and that Layn simply wanted her to explain it for the
others. "But where tarbines are, there's a good chance you'll find
mojos, too."

"With their accompanying spine leopards or krisjaws," Layn
nodded. "Right. Besides which . . . ? Anyone?"

"Their chirping might mask the sound of something more
dangerous?" Todor hazarded from in front of Layn.

"Good enough," the instructor grunted. "Enough conversation.
Look sharp."

And a bare second later, the exercise abruptly ceased to be
routine. Dead ahead, the bushes suddenly parted and a huge
cat-like animal stepped out to face them.

A spine leopard.

It's impossible, a small fraction of Jin's mind insisted. The fence surrounding this part of the forest was five meters high, a theoretically impossible barrier even for a spine leopard.

And then the animal snarled, and theory was abruptly forgotten as four sets of fingertip lasers flashed out to converge on the spine leopard's head.

Uselessly, of course, and Jin silently cursed herself for letting her reflexes waste precious time that way. The decentralized spine leopard nervous system was functionally invulnerable to the kind of localized damage the fingertip lasers could inflict. The only known way of dealing with the animals was to get in a clean shot with the antiarmor laser running lengthwise down her left calf—

She was actually starting to shift her weight onto her right foot when the crucial fact caught up with her conscious mind: the trainees' current neckwrap computers didn't allow the antiarmor laser to be activated.

The others' fingertip lasers were still slicing uselessly at the spine leopard, leaving blackened tracks in the fur where they passed. And the look that was growing in the creature's eyes . . . "Stop it!" Jin snapped. "Can't you see you're just making it mad?"

"Then what the hell do you want—?" Todor barked back.

"Try your disruptors!" Sun cut him off. An instant later a backwash of half audible, half felt sound washed over Jin as the others obeyed, playing tight cones of ultrasound over the spine leopard. *Another waste of time,* Jin thought tightly. Sonic weapons could throw the predators off-balance, but only temporarily; and like the fingertip lasers, their use seemed to enrage the beasts. As soon as this one got its balance back—

And then it struck her. Layn, fully equipped with both antiarmor laser *and* the nanocomputer needed to use it, had yet to fire a shot.

Another test. Of course—and with that all the pieces fell together. A single spine leopard, captured and released into the enclosure, to see if their first response would be to scatter or to continue their assigned mission of protecting Layn. Doubtless the Cobra already had his antiarmor laser target-locked on the animal, ready to fire the second it looked like things were getting out of control.

Phrijpicker mousfin, she snarled mentally at him. It was a particularly stupid trick—under target-lock or not, spine leopards were far too dangerous to fool around with this way, especially on inexperienced trainees. Somehow, they had to stop the thing before it shrugged off the effects of the sonics and charged. And maybe wound up killing someone.

And whatever they were going to do, they had better do it fast, The spine leopard was rolling its weight slightly from side to side now, the spines along its forelegs beginning to bristle outward— a sign that it was starting to feel endangered. Which would make it that much more vicious when it finally attacked . . .

Her eyes flicked around the area, came to rest on the cyprene trees and the thick gluevines running up many of their trunks . . . and a small chapter of family history bobbed to the surface. "Sun!" she snapped, leaping with servo-enhanced strength into the lower branches of a gluevine-wrapped tree midway from her to the spine leopard. Her muscles tensed, but the sudden motion didn't trigger an attack. "Cut the gluevine at the base of the tree," she called back over her shoulder as she got her own lasers going on the top part of the nearest vine. "Rip it free of the trunk—*don't* touch the cut end."

Sun moved to obey, and three seconds later a five-meter section of gluevine hung free in Jin's hand. Glancing down, she saw that the spine leopard was still holding its ground . . . but even as she watched, it leaned back on its back haunches. Preparing to spring . . .

"Hariman—split the vine lengthwise," Sun called. "Moreau?— I've got this end. You ready?"

Which meant he'd figured out what she had in mind. "Ready," she called back, clenching her teeth in anticipation. "Hariman?"

Her answer was a burst of laser fire that cracked the gluevine's thick outer coating, letting the incredibly sticky stuff inside ooze out. "Go!" Sun snapped; and Jin leaped.

Her target was another cyprene just beyond where the spine leopard was coiling itself for its spring. A spring that would carry it to Todor, still doggedly playing his sonic over the predator . . . and as time seemed to slow down for her, Jin saw for the first time that, in moving over to cut the gluevine, Hariman had unwittingly put himself directly in the line of fire between Layn and the spine leopard. Which meant that if this didn't work, either Hariman or Todor would probably die.

The outer twigs of her target tree scratched at her face and hands as she came in through them . . . and with all her strength she hurled the vine to the ground.

Directly across the spine leopard's back.

The creature screamed, a blood-chilling sound Jin had never before heard one make. It almost made her miss grabbing the cyprene's trunk; as it was, she tore a gash in the back of her left hand scrambling for a grip. Twisting around, heart thudding in her ears, she looked down.

The spine leopard went ahead and leaped anyway . . . but even as its feet left the ground, Sun tugged on his end of the gluevine with Cobra servo strength, and an instant later the predator was flying past Todor on a tightly curved course. It landed on its feet, gluevine still draped solidly across its back, foreleg spines spread out in full defensive position—

And twisted to face Sun.

"Stick the vine somewhere and get out of there!" Jin shouted to him.

Sun needed no prompting. In a single motion, he jammed the cut end of the gluevine against the tree he'd cut it from and leaped straight up into the cyprene's branches. Barely pausing to catch his balance, he changed direction and pushed off toward Jin's tree, half a second ahead of the now leashed spine leopard's own leap toward his ankles.

He caught the trunk just above her, sending a rain of twigs and leaves down around her head. "Now what?" he muttered.

"I assume Layn's eventually going to laser it," she told him . . . but the Cobra was still standing there with Todor and Hariman, watching with them as the spine leopard thrashed about trying to free itself from the gluevine. Todor took a step toward the animal, and it paused in its efforts to make a short leap and slash with its front claws.

"Doesn't seem interested in doing so, does he?" Sun grunted as Todor made a hasty leap back. "Maybe they're going to tranq it and use it on the next batch of trainees."

So Sun had tracked the same line of thought she had. "Pretty damn fool game, if you ask me," she growled to him. "They could at least have waited until we had our antiarmor lasers activated."

"So maybe they want us to be creative."

Jin twisted up her head to look at him. "Meaning . . . ?"

"Well . . . how long do you suppose it could live with its pseudospine broken?"

She looked down at the animal. Already it had worried a few centimeters of the gluevine free, sacrificing a narrow line of its fur in the process. Left on its own another minute of two . . . "What say we find out," she suggested grimly.

"Sounds good. You take the rear, I'll take just back of the head. On three; one, two, *three*."

And Jin pushed off from the tree, arcing into the air as high as she dared. Sun's leap paralleled hers . . . and as they passed the top of their arcs and started down—

"No!" Layn bellowed; but it was far too late. Jin hit the spine leopard full in the back, keeping her knees stiff until the last second in order to transfer as much impact to the spine leopard's body as she could. Sun hit a fraction of a second behind her, and she both heard and felt the twin *cracks*—

"No, damn it, no!" Layn yelled again, leaping belatedly forward to kneel down at the limp spine leopard's side . . . but this time Jin could hear a strange note of resignation in his voice. "*Damn it all*—"

The look on his face when he got to his feet effectively silenced any comments Jin might have had. But Sun wasn't so reticent. "Is there a problem, sir?" he asked blandly. "You *did* want us to kill it, didn't you?"

Layn impaled him with a laser-strength glare. "You were merely supposed to get me clear of it," he bit out. "Not—" He took a deep breath. "For your information, *trainee,* you two idiots have just broken the central mobility transmain of an extremely *expensive* robot. I trust you're satisfied."

Sun's jaw fell, and Jin felt her eyes go wide as she looked down at the spine leopard. "I suppose that explains," she heard herself say, "why you didn't laser it."

Layn looked like he was ready to chew rocks. "Return to your quarters, all of you," he snarled. "Evening classes are as usual; you're free until then. Get out of my sight."

The tap on her door was gentle, almost diffident. "Yes?" Jin called, looking up from her reader.

"It's me, Mander Sun," a familiar voice answered. "Can I come in?"

"Sure," Jin called back, frowning as she keyed the door open.

He looked almost shy as he stepped hesitantly a couple of paces into the room. "It occurred to me that someone ought to check up on that cut you got out there this afternoon," he said.

She looked down with a little surprise at the heal-quick bandage on her left hand. "Oh, no problem. The cut wasn't deep, just a little messy."

"Ah," he nodded. "Well, then . . . sorry to have bothered you . . ." He hesitated, looking a little lost.

Jin licked her lips. *Say something!* she told herself as her mind went perversely blank. "Uh—by the way," she managed as he started to turn back toward the door, "do you think Layn's going to make trouble for us because of what we did to that robot?"

"He'd better not try," Sun said, turning back again. "If they're going to drop pop tests like that on us, they'd better not complain when we don't do what they expect." He hesitated just a fraction. "That was, uh . . . a pretty good trick you came up with out there, incidentally. The thing with the gluevine."

She shrugged. "Wasn't all that original, really," she admitted. "My grandfather did something similar once against a berserk gantua. And as long as we're handing out compliments, you were pretty fast on the uptake yourself."

"I didn't have much choice," he said wryly. "It didn't look at the time like you were going to have a chance to explain it to anyone."

"Stupid robot," she muttered, shaking her head. "Almost a shame we didn't figure that part out. Layn would probably have had a stroke if one of us had gone up and petted the thing."

Sun grinned. "I think he came close enough to a stroke as it was." His grin changed into a tight, almost embarrassed smile. "You know, Moreau—Jin . . . I have to admit that I didn't think much at the beginning of having you in the squad. Not for the tradition reasons Layn trotted out, but because none of the women I've ever known has had the kind of—oh, I don't know; the killer instinct, I guess, that a warrior has to have."

Jin shrugged, forcing herself to meet his gaze. "You might be surprised," she said. "Besides, a lot of what Cobras do these days is more like patrol officer work than full-fledged war, certainly in the more settled areas of the Worlds."

"Hold it right there," Sun growled in mock annoyance, holding his hands up palm-outward. "I don't mind having *you* here, but I'm not getting drawn into any theoretical discussions on the merits of women in the Cobras, thank you. Not with a test on surveillance techniques breathing down our necks." He glanced at his watch. "Like in half an hour. Phrij—and I still need to study for it some more."

"Me, too," Jin licked her lips. "Thanks for coming by, Mander. I—uh—"

"Mandy," he said, pulling open the door. "That's what everyone else calls me. See you in class."

"Right. Bye."

For a long minute after he was gone she stared at the closed door, not entirely sure whether or not to trust the warm glow beginning to form deep within her. Could her long isolation from the group really be ending? As quickly and easily as that? Just because she'd unwittingly helped give their rough and demanding instructor something of a black eye?

Abruptly, she smiled. Of course it could. If there was one military tradition that superseded every other, it was the "us versus them" feeling of trainees toward everyone else . . . and *especially* toward instructors. In helping Sun ruin Layn's robot spine leopard, she'd suddenly become one of the "us."

Or at least, she warned herself, *I've got my foot in the door.* But for now, at least, that was enough. The first barrier, her father had often reminded her, was always the hardest to break.

For just a moment she frowned as an odd thought flickered across her mind. Surely Layn hadn't *deliberately* let her destroy that robot . . . had he? No—of course not. The very idea was absurd. He'd already said he didn't *want* her to succeed.

And speaking of succeeding . . . Turning back to her reader, she keyed for a fast scan of the lessons on surveillance methods. As Sun had pointed out, there was a test breathing down their necks.

Chapter 8

The reminder clock on his desk pinged, and Corwin looked up at it with mild surprise. Somehow, while he hadn't been looking, the afternoon had disappeared. It was four fifty, and in just forty minutes the celebration was scheduled to start over at Justin's house. The celebration for his daughter's graduation from the Cobra Academy.

For a moment Corwin gazed unseeingly at the clock, his mind jumping back almost thirty years to the similar celebration his parents had thrown for Justin himself. It had been a strained evening, with everyone trying to ignore the fact that the new Cobra and his twin brother would be heading off in a few days to the mysterious world of Qasama, possibly never to return.

And now it would be Jin who'd be going off in a week. To the same world. Under almost identical circumstances.

To try and fix the same problem.

Corwin could remember a time, far back in the dim haze of his youth, when it had seemed to him that if you fixed a problem right the first time it would stay fixed. When he believed there were problems that *could* be permanently fixed.

The memories made him feel very old.

"Corwin?"

With a jolt, he brought himself back to the real world. "Yes, Thena, what is it?"

"The governor-general's on the line. Says it's important."

Corwin flicked another glance at his clock. "He always does," he growled. "Oh, all right." He stabbed at the proper button, and Thena's image was replaced by Chandler's. "Yes?"

Chandler's face looked like he'd been chewing on something not quite ripe. "I've got some bad news for you, Moreau," he said without preamble. "I have here on my desk a petition calling for your brother Justin to be confined until the matter of the Monse shooting can be definitively cleared up. It's been endorsed by seventy-one members of the Cobra Worlds Council."

Corwin felt his face go rigid. Seventy-one members was something like sixty percent—an utterly incredible number. "That's ridiculous," he said. "The whole thing—"

"The whole thing," Chandler cut him off grimly, "has been pulling far more net space than any seven-week-old issue has any right to be getting. In case you haven't noticed, the public rumblings over the whole mess never completely vanished; and in the past week or so they've started getting louder again."

Corwin gritted his teeth hard enough to hurt. Preoccupied with arrangements and details for the Qasama mission, he hadn't had time to keep up with the ebb and flow of Aventinian public opinion. But then why hadn't Justin or Joshua or someone else pointed it out to him—?

Because they hadn't wanted him to worry, of course. And so, while he'd been busy looking the other way, Priesly's gang had been busy weaving an encirclement.

But maybe it still wasn't too late to fight back. A petition, even one from the Cobra Worlds Council, wasn't legally binding on the governor-general's actions. If he could get Chandler on his side . . . or at least onto neutral . . . "Since you're calling me about it," he said carefully, "do I presume you intend to comply with their demand?"

Chandler's eyes flashed. "It's hardly a *demand*, Moreau—I can ignore the thing entirely if I choose to do so. The question really boils down to whether or not you're worth bucking this kind of public opinion for."

"Or in other words, why risk political fallout over a governor who's on his way out anyway?" Corwin asked softly.

Chandler at least had the grace to look uncomfortable. "It's not like that," he muttered. "Whatever happens with your niece on Qasama doesn't change the fact that you *are* at present a full Aventinian governor."

"True," Corwin nodded. "Not to mention the possibility that Jin may actually do so well out there that I won't have to resign in the first place."

"I suppose that's possible," Chandler conceded. "Hardly likely, though."

Corwin shrugged. Despite his words, it was clear from Chandler's manner that he felt awkward about writing Corwin off without cause. It gave Corwin a psychological lever—a weak one, but the best he was likely to get. "I presume you'll be ordering Justin into house arrest, then?" he asked. "Surely there's no need to put him in an actual prison."

Chandler's eyes bored into his. "It might be enough to satisfy them," he said evenly. "Suppose someone suggests that he's potentially a threat to the community and ought to be somewhere more secure?"

"You could counter by asking this person where the hell he thinks would be a safe place to incarcerate a Cobra who doesn't want to stay put," Corwin told him. "Or point out the obvious fact that Justin's not a danger to anyone who isn't threatening him. Alternatively, if this person's on the Directorate and privy to such information, you could just point out that the use of that Troft shuttle for the Qasaman mission might be in jeopardy if Speaker One finds out you've locked up a Moreau."

Chandler's eyebrows lifted a fraction. "I find it hard to believe you and the Tlossies are that friendly."

"Of course we aren't," Corwin shook his head. "But you'll recall this unnamed someone of yours *was* on the aircar when Speaker One asked that a Moreau help plan the Qasama mission. Reminding him of that ought to make him a little cautious about pushing too hard for public incarceration."

Chandler snorted, gently. "Perhaps. Perhaps." He took a deep breath. "All right. House arrest it is, with as little publicity as we can get away with."

"Thank you, sir." Corwin hesitated. "If I could ask one more favor, though . . . we're having the graduation party for Jin this evening. Could you postpone the order until tomorrow morning? It would make things a lot easier on all of us."

"I hardly think Justin's going to sneak off and leave the planet," Chandler said, almost offhandedly. Having already made up his mind to buck Priesly on one point, bucking him on another one as well apparently didn't cost any extra effort. "The house arrest will officially begin tomorrow morning at eight, then. You realize, of course, that Priesly is likely to consider this a favor you owe him. Whether you look at it that way or not."

"I've already put my career on his block over Jin's Cobra appointment," Corwin said coldly. "If Priesly thinks he can squeeze blood out of me beyond that, he's going to be sorely disappointed."

"I suppose." Chandler sighed. "Though I wouldn't underestimate his skills at manipulating the nets if I were you. Resigning quietly from a governorship and resigning in public disgrace are two very different ends. I think he'd take a great deal of pleasure in the chance to drag the Moreau name out for the gantuas to walk on."

Corwin felt his stomach tighten. The Moreau name. It was a noble part of the Cobra Worlds' young history, one of the few names virtually everyone on Aventine had grown up knowing. Protecting it had been a deciding factor in his father's fight against the Challinor rebellion so many years ago, and his subsequent work in reshaping Aventinian politics; and it was one of the few gifts of real value Corwin himself had to give to his nieces and—if he ever had any—to his own children. The thought of Priesly with his grubby hands on it . . . "If he tries it, he'll be sorry," he told Chandler softly. "Call it a threat, or call it a statement of fact; but make sure he understands."

Chandler nodded. "I'll try. I just wanted *you* to understand what we were dealing with here. Anyway . . . I expect I ought to let you go. You'll of course want to tell your brother about this tonight."

"I will," Corwin sighed. "Goodnight, sir . . . and thank you."

The governor-general threw him a grim smile and vanished from the screen.

For a long moment Corwin just sat there, staring blankly at the empty screen. So Priesly hadn't been content with merely embarrassing Corwin's family; instead, he was out for real blood. *Well, if it's a fight he wants,* he thought bitterly, *it's a fight he's going to get.* And Corwin had been in politics considerably longer than Priesly had. Somehow, he'd find a way to turn all this back on the Ject.

Somehow.

Taking a deep breath, he pushed the thought back as far as he could and got to his feet. He was going to a party, after all, and ought to at least try to project an image of happiness. Whether he felt that way or not.

The red streaks of sunset were fading into the early-evening darkness of the springtime Capitalia sky as Jin drove up to the curb and stepped out onto the walk. For a moment she just stood there in the dusk, gazing at the house and wondering why the home of her childhood should look so different to her now. Surely it wasn't just that she'd been away for four weeks—she'd been away that long many times before. No, the house hadn't changed; it was she who was different. The home of her childhood . . . but she was no longer a child. She was an adult.

An adult; and a Cobra.

Almost automatically, she keyed through a series of settings on her optical enhancers as she walked up toward the house, spotting things about the building and grounds that she'd never known before. The infrared setting showed what seemed to be a minor heat leak in the corner by her bedroom—no wonder that room had always felt colder than the rest of the house in the winter. Telescopic enhancement showed that the allegedly permanent siding was beginning to crack near the guttering; and a telescopic/light-amplified study of a hole in the tall sideyard borlash tree won her a glimpse of bright animal eyes hiding there. Memories of the past, thoughts of the future—all of it mingled together with the reality of the present. The reality that, against all odds, she'd achieved her life's ambition.

She was a Cobra.

The sound of a decelerating car behind her registered on her consciousness and she turned, expecting to see one of her uncles driving up.

It was Mander Sun.

"Hey! Jin!" he called, leaning his head out the window. "Hold up a minute."

She retraced her steps and crossed the street as he pulled to a halt against the opposite curb. "What is it?" she asked, belatedly noticing the hard set of his mouth. "Is anything wrong?"

"I don't know." His eyes probed her face. "Maybe it's just rumors . . . look, I heard something this afternoon from a friend of my dad's who does datawork for the Directorate. Do you know why you were approved for the Academy?"

The obvious reasons—the official reasons—came to Jin's mind, faded unsaid. "I know what I was told. What did *you* hear?"

"That it was a quiet deal," he growled. "That your uncle—the governor—put himself on the line for you. If this mission succeeds he gets to keep his position. Otherwise . . . he has to resign."

Jin felt her mouth go dry. The memory of that horrible night so many weeks ago flashed back to mind: the night her father had shot Monse . . . the night she'd gone and pleaded with Uncle Corwin to get her—somehow—into the Cobras. "No," she whispered. "No. He wouldn't do that. Politics is his *life*."

Sun shrugged helplessly. "I don't know if it's true or not, Jin.

I just thought . . . well, that maybe you didn't know. And that maybe you should."

"Why?—so that I can be more nervous about the mission than I already am?" she snarled, the numbness suddenly flashing into anger.

"No," Sun said quietly. "So that you could hear it from a friend. And so I could tell you that the rest of the team is behind you."

She opened her mouth, closed it again as the anger vanished. "So that . . . what?"

He held her gaze. "I talked to Rafe and Peter before coming over here," he said. "We all agreed that you were a good teammate who didn't deserve this kind of extra pack on her shoulders." He snorted gently. "We also agreed that anyone who would pull a scummy move like that on Governor Moreau was a full-blooded phrijpicker, and that a guy like that might arrange to leak the the word to you just before we left—little extra squeeze value, you know. And like I said . . . I thought you'd do better to hear it from friends."

She looked back toward the house so that he wouldn't see the moisture in her eyes. It was true, of course—in retrospect it had to have been something like that. *Oh, Uncle Corwin . . .* "Yes," she said. "I . . . yes. Thank you."

A tentative hand touched hers where it rested on the car. "We'll do it, Jin," Sun said. "All of us together—we'll do such a bang-up job on Qasama that they'll be lucky if they don't have to give us a full-city parade *and* canonize Governor Moreau in the bargain."

Jin blinked the tears back and tried a smile. "You're right," she said, squeezing his hand briefly. "We'll make them sorry they tried to pick on a Moreau."

"And even sorrier that they tried to use a Sun to do it," Sun added with grim pride in his voice. "Anyway. I've got to get moving—my family's waiting for me. You going to be okay?"

"Sure," she nodded. "Mandy . . . thanks."

"No charge. Partner." Reluctantly, she thought, he pulled his hand away from hers. "Well. Look, you take care of yourself—try not to get into any trouble—and I'll see you at the starfield in a week."

"Right. Bye."

"Bye."

She watched until his car turned a corner and vanished from sight. Then, taking a deep breath, she straightened her shoulders and started back toward the house. Not all the nuances of this mess were clear to her, but one of them was clear enough. The family didn't intend for her to know about Uncle Corwin's bargain; and so, as far as they were concerned, she wouldn't. She'd never had any formal acting experience, but she'd grown up with two older sisters and had long since learned how to bend the truth with a straight face.

Or even with a smiling face. She was going to a party, after all, and ought to at least try to project an image of excitement. Whether she felt that way or not.

Chapter 9

The new Cobras had a week of liberty before they were due to leave. For Jin, at least, the week went by very quickly.

"...and whatever you do, listen to Layn, okay?" Justin told his daughter as they walked arm in arm up the long ramp leading to the *Southern Cross*'s entryway. "I know he's a pain in the butt as an instructor, but he's a smart tactician and a crackling fighter. Stick with him and you'll be all right."

"Okay, Dad," Jin nodded. "Hey, don't worry—we'll be fine."

Justin looked down at his daughter's face as, for a brief second, an intense feeling of déjà vu washed over him. "Qasama is the last place in the world to be overconfident about, Jin," he said quietly. "Everything about the planet is dangerous, from the krisjaws and spine leopards to the mojos to the Qasaman people. They're all dangerous, and they all hate you. Especially you."

Jin squeezed him a little tighter. "Don't worry, Dad, I know what I'm getting into."

"No, you don't. No one ever does. You have to—well, never mind." He took a deep breath, fighting back the urge to lecture her. "Just be careful, and come back safely. Okay?"

"Good advice," she said solemnly. "You be careful, too, huh? At least *I'll* be with a group of Cobras and other competent people. *You'll* be stuck here with Priesly and his mob."

And under Priesly's trumped-up house arrest... Justin's jaw tightened momentarily with a freshly renewed awareness of the two guards standing a few paces behind them. "Yeah, well, it's not all *that* bad," he told his daughter, forcing a smile. "As long as Corwin's in there fighting for me Priesly hasn't got a chance of making this thing stick."

Something passed, too quickly to identify, across Jin's face. "Yeah," she said. "Yeah. Well . . . walk me up the ramp?"

He did. At the entryway they exchanged one last hug . . . and as Jin's arms tightened, Cobra-strong, around him, Justin's vision blurred with moisture. A quarter century of hope and frustration was finally over. His child had succeeded him as a Cobra.

A triple tone sounded from the entryway. "I'd better get inside," Jin said into his chest. "I'll see you in a few weeks, Dad. Take care of yourself, okay?"

"Sure." Reluctantly, he released her and took half a step back. She smiled at him, blinking back tears of her own, then turned to wave one last time down the ramp to where her sisters and cousins were waiting for the *Southern Cross*'s takeoff.

Then she was gone, and Justin found himself walking away from the ship. *She'll be all right,* he thought over and over to himself. *She'll be all right. Really she will. She's my daughter—she* has *to come through it all right.*

And for the first time he truly knew how his own parents must have felt on that day, so long ago, when he and Joshua had themselves lifted off for Qasama. The realization brought a half-bitter smile to his lips.

Whether there was justice in the universe he didn't know. But there did appear to be a certain symmetry.

Chapter 10

It was a two-week trip to Qasama; two weeks that went by very quickly. It was, for one thing, the first time the new Cobras had had a chance to interact with each other on anything approaching a social level. With each other, and also with the two men who would actually be leading the mission.

They were, to her mind, a study in contrasts. Both were top experts at Aventine's Qasama Monitor Center, but at that point all similarity ended. Pash Barynson was middle-aged and thin and short, a few centimeters shorter even than Jin, with sparse black hair and an excruciatingly academic manner that was so stiff that it bordered on caricature. His associate, Como Raines, was almost exactly the opposite, in both manner and appearance. Tall and chubby, aged somewhere in his mid-thirties, he had red-blond hair, a perpetual smile, and an outgoing manner that enabled him to become friends with everyone on board almost before the *Southern Cross* had cleared Aventine's atmosphere.

It was an unlikely pairing, and it took Jin nearly a week to realize that the mission's planners hadn't simply pulled their names out of the grab-bag. Raines, with his easy friendliness, would presumably be the main contact man with the Qasamans, while Barynson's job would be to stay in the background and analyze the data as Raines and the others pulled it in.

From the briefings, too, it was quickly clear that Barynson was the man in charge.

"We'll be making our approach along here—from the uninhabited west—making our landing about here," Barynson said, leaning over the photomap and jabbing a finger at a section of forest.

"Timing the touchdown for about an hour before dawn, local time. The nearest of the villages bordering the Fertile Crescent area are about fifteen kilometers to the east and southeast—" he touched each in turn "—with what looks to be lumbering operations to the northeast here on the river at about the same distance. You'll note that the site is—theoretically, at least—a fair compromise between distance and seclusion. Whether it'll turn out that way in practice, of course, we won't know until we get there."

"Any idea what kind of undergrowth we'll have to go through?" Todor asked.

"Unfortunately, no," Barynson admitted. "Most of the data we've got on Qasaman forests comes from far to the east of this site, and infrared studies indicate that the canopy here, at any rate, is different in composition from that area."

"Of course," Raines put in, "if travel turns out to be impractical, we can always take the shuttle up to treetop height and move it closer to the villages."

"Only if things are pretty *damn* difficult," Layn muttered. "We have only the Trofts' word for it that the Qasaman observation systems won't be able to track our approach. The more we move the shuttle around, the higher the risk we'll be spotted."

"Agreed," Barynson nodded. "Though the more immediate danger will probably be the Qasaman fauna. I hope you Cobras will be up to the challenge."

"We're ready," Layn told him. "My men—people—know what they're doing."

Baryson's eyes flicked to Jin, turned quickly away. "Yes, I'm sure they do," he said, almost as if he believed it. "Well, anyway . . . we'll all be equipped with the best simulations of Qasaman clothing that the Center's analysis of telephotos could provide. The landing is timed so that we can get through the forest in daylight and reach one of these villages by nightfall. That'll give us the chance to make a close check of our clothing and get a first approximation of the culture before we have to tackle Azras and the main Fertile Crescent civilization. So; questions?"

Jin glanced across the table, caught Sun's eye. The other shrugged fractionally, echoing Jin's own thoughts: there wasn't a lot of point in asking questions to which there were as yet no answers.

"Very well, then." Barynson threw a look around the table. "We have three days left before planetfall, and for those three days I want all of you to do your best to become Qasamans. You'll wear our ersatz Qasaman clothing, eat our nearest approximations to the food the Qasamans were eating thirty years ago, and—most important of all—speak only Qasaman among yourselves. That rule is absolute—you aren't to speak Anglic to *anyone*, not even to one of the *Southern Cross*'s crew. If any of them talks to you, you aren't to understand them. Is that clear?"

"Isn't that carrying things just a little far?" Hariman asked with a frown.

"The Qasmans had ample opportunity to study Anglic the last time we were here," Jin put in quietly. "Some of them were even able to force-learn it well enough to speak it. If they suspect us, they might throw one of those people at us."

"Right," Barynson nodded, looking impressed despite himself. "The old trick of getting a spy to speak in his native language. I'd just as soon none of us falls for it."

"We understand," Sun said in Qasaman. "We demon warriors, at least, won't fall for it."

"I hope not." Barynson looked him straight in the eye. "Because if you ever do, you'll probably wind up earning your pay the hard way."

Qasama was a dark mass against the stars, a fuzzy new-moon sliver of light at one edge showing the dawn line, as the shuttle fell free of the *Southern Cross* and began its leisurely drift toward the world below. Gazing down through the tiny porthole to her left, Jin licked dry lips and tried to quiet her thudding heart. *Almost there,* she told herself. *Almost there.* Her first mission as a Cobra— a goal she'd dreamed about and fantasized about for probably half her life. And now, with it almost close enough to taste, she could feel nothing but quiet terror.

So much, she thought half bitterly, *for the heroic Cobra warrior.*

"You ever fly before this trip?" Sun, sitting on the aisle seat next to her, asked quietly.

"Aircraft, sure, but never any spacecraft," Jin told him, thankfully turning her attention away from the porthole. "Hardly ever into enemy territory, either."

He chuckled, a sound that almost masked the nervousness she could see around his eyes. "We'll do fine," he assured her. "Parades and canonization, remember?"

A smile broke of its own accord through her tension. "Sure." Reaching across the armrest, she took his hand. It was almost as cold as her own.

"Hitting atmosphere," she heard the pilot say from the red-lit cockpit at the front of the passenger compartment. "Injection angle . . . right on the mark."

Jin gritted her teeth. She understood all the reasons behind coming in as far as they could on an unpowered glide approach—the light from a ship's gravity lifts was extremely visible, especially against a night sky—but the eerie silence from the engines wasn't helping her nervousness a bit. Looking back out the porthole, she tried not to imagine the planet rushing up to hit them—

"Uh-oh," the pilot muttered.

"What?" Barynson snapped from the seat beside him.

"A radar scan just went over us."

Jin's mouth went a little drier, and Sun's grip on her hand tightened. "But they can't pick us up, can they?" Barynson asked. "The Trofts told us—"

"No, no, we're okay," the pilot assured him. "I was just surprised they're scanning this far from the Fertile Crescent, that's all."

"They're paranoid," Layn muttered from the seat across the narrow aisle from Sun. "So what else is new?"

But they aren't supposed to be that way any more, Jin thought morosely. *They were supposed to lose that when we got the mojos off their shoulders.* That had been the whole point of seeding the planet with Aventinian spine leopards thirty years ago, after all. If it hadn't worked—

She shook her head to clear it. If it hadn't worked, they would find out soon enough. There wasn't any point in worrying about it until then.

"Parades and canonization," Sun murmured, misreading her thoughts. It helped, anyway, and she threw him a grateful smile.

The minutes dragged on. An oddly distant scream of air against the shuttle's hull increased and then faded, and slowly all but the brightest of the stars overhead began to be swallowed up by the thickening atmosphere around them. Straining upward against her restraints, Jin could make out the gross details of the ground beneath them now, and in the distance the horizon had lost all of its curve. Five minutes, she estimated—ten at the most—and they would be down. Setting her nanocomputer's clock circuit, she leaned back in her seat, closed her eyes, took a deep breath—

And through the closed lids she still saw the right-hand side of the passenger compartment abruptly blaze up like a fireball, and a smashing wall of thunder slammed her against her seat and into total blackness.

Chapter 11

The pain came first. Not localized pain, not even particularly bad at first; more like a vague and unpleasant realization that somewhere in the darkness something was hurting. Hurting a *lot*...

A large part of her didn't care. The blackness was quiet and uncomplicated, and it would have been pleasant to stay hidden there forever. But the pain was a continual nagging at the roots of the nothingness, and even as she was forced to accept and notice its existence she found herself being forced slowly up out of the blackness. Grudgingly, resentfully, she passed through the black, to a dark gray, to a lighter gray—

And with a gasp as the pain suddenly sharpened and focused itself into arms, chest, and knee, she came fully awake.

She was in an awkward and thoroughly uncomfortable position, half-sitting and half-lying on her left side, the safety harness digging painfully into her chest and upper thighs. Blinking the wetness— *blood?* she wondered vaguely—from her eyes, she looked around the tilted and darkened interior of the shuttle. Nothing could be seen clearly; only after several seconds of straining her eyes did it occur to her befuddled mind to key in her optical enhancers.

The sight made her gasp.

The shuttle was a disaster area. Across the aisle the far hull had been literally blown in, leaving a ragged-edged hole a meter or more across. Strands of twisted and blackened metal curled inward from the gap like frozen ribbons; bits and pieces of plastic, cloth, and glass littered everything she could see. The twin seats that had been by the hole had been ripped from their bracings and were nowhere to be seen.

The twin seats that Layn and Raines had been sitting in.

594

Oh, God. For a moment Jin gazed in horror at the ruined struts where the seats had been. They were gone, gone totally from the shuttle . . . from thirty or forty kilometers up.

Somewhere, someone groaned. "Peter?" she croaked. Todor and Hariman had been in the seats just behind the missing men . . . "Peter?" she tried again. "Rafe?"

There was no answer. Reaching up with a hand that was streaked with blood, she groped for her safety harness release. It was jammed; gritting her teeth, she put servo-motor strength into her squeeze and got it free. Shakily, she climbed to her feet, stumbling off-balance on the canted floor. She grabbed onto what was left of her seat's emergency crashbag to steady herself, jamming her left knee against the bulkhead in the process. A dazzling burst of pain stabbed through the joint, jolting her further out of her fogginess. Shaking her head—sparking more pain—she raised her eyes to look over the seat back to where Todor and Hariman should be.

It was only then that she saw what had happened to Sun.

She gasped, her stomach suddenly wanting to be sick. The explosion had apparently sent shrapnel into his crashbag, tearing through the tough plastic and leaving him defenseless against the impact of the shuttle's final crash. Still strapped to his seat, blood staining his landing coveralls where the harness had dug into his skin, his head lolled against his chest at an impossible angle.

He was very clearly dead.

Jin stared at him for a long minute. *This isn't real,* she told herself wildly, striving to believe it. If she believed it hard enough, maybe it wouldn't have happened . . . *This isn't real. This is our first mission—just our first mission. This can't happen. Not now. Oh, God, please not now.*

The scene began to swim before her eyes, and as it did so a red border appeared superimposed across her optically enhanced vision. The sensors built into her Cobra gear, warning her of approaching unconsciousness. *Who cares?* she thought savagely at the red border. *He's dead—so are Layn and Raines and who knows who else. What do I need to be conscious for?*

And as if in answer, the groan came again.

The sound tore her eyes away from Sun's broken body. Clawing her way past him, she stumbled out into the littered aisle, eyes focusing with an effort on the seats where Hariman and Todor dangled limply in their harnesses. One look at Hariman was all she could handle—it was clear he'd died in the explosion, even more violently and terribly than Sun. But Todor, beside him in the aisle seat, was still alive, twitching like a child in a nightmare.

Jin was there in seconds, pausing only to grab the emergency medical kit from the passenger compartment's front bulkhead. Kneeling down beside him, ignoring the pain from her injured knee, she got to work.

But it was quickly clear that both the kit's equipment and her own first-aid training were hopelessly inadequate. Surface-wound treatment would be of no use against the massive internal bleeding the sensors registered from Todor's chest; anti-shock drugs would do nothing against the severe concussion that was already squeezing Todor's brain against the ceramic-reinforced bones of his skull.

But Jin wouldn't—couldn't—give up. Sweating, swearing, she worked over him, trying everything she could think of.

"Jin."

The husky whisper startled her so badly she dropped the hypospray she'd been loading. "Peter?" she asked, looking up at his face. "Can you hear me?"

"Don't waste . . . time . . ." He coughed, a wracking sound that brought blood to his lips.

"Don't try to talk," Jin told him, fighting hard to keep the horror out of her voice. "Just try and relax. Please."

"No . . . use . . ." he whispered. "Go . . . get out . . . of here . . . someone . . . coming. Has to . . . be some . . . one . . ."

"Peter, please stop talking," she begged him. "The others—Mandy and Rafe—they're all dead. I've got to keep you alive—"

"No . . . chance. Hurt too . . . badly. The mish . . . mission, Jin . . . you got . . . got to . . ." He coughed again, weaker this time. "Get out . . . get to . . . some . . . where hid . . . hidden."

His voice faded into silence, and for a moment she continued to kneel beside him, torn between conflicting commitments. He was right, of course, and the more her brain unfroze itself from the shock the more she realized how tight the deadline facing her really was. The shuttle had been deliberately shot down . . . and whoever had done the job would eventually come by to examine his handiwork.

But to run now would be to leave Todor here. Alone. To die.

"I can't go, Peter," she said, the last word turning midway into a sob. "I *can't*."

There was no answer . . . and even as she watched helplessly, the twitching in his limbs ceased. She waited another moment, then reached over and touched fingertips to his neck.

He was dead.

Carefully, Jin withdrew her hand and took a long, shuddering breath, blinking back tears. A soft glow from Todor's fingertip lasers caught her eye: the new self-destruct system incorporated into their gear had activated itself, shunting current from the arcthrower capacitors inward onto the nanocomputer and servo systems. Automatically destroying his electronics and weaponry beyond any hope of reconstruction should the Qasamans find and examine his body.

No. Not *if* the Qasamans found him; *when* they found him. Closing her eyes and mind to the carnage around her, Jin tried to think. It had been—how long since the crash? She checked her clock circuit, set just before the initial explosion.

Nearly seventy minutes had passed since then.

Jin gritted her teeth. *Seventy minutes?* God—it was worse than she'd realized. The aircraft the Qasamans would have scrambled to check out their target practice could be overhead at any minute, and the last thing she was ready for was a fight. Clutching at Todor's seat, she pulled herself to her feet and made her way forward.

The cockpit was in worse shape even than the passenger compartment, having apparently survived the explosion only to take the full brunt of what must have been a hellish crash landing. One look dashed any hope she might have had of calling the *Southern Cross* for advice or help—the shuttle's radio and laser communicator would have been mangled beyond repair.

Which meant that unless and until the *Southern Cross* figured out on its own that something was wrong, she was going to be on her own. Totally.

Barynson and the pilot—she realized with a distant twinge of guilt that she'd never even known that latter's full name—were both dead, of course, crushed beyond the protective capabilities of harness and crashbag. She barely gave them a second look, her mind increasingly frantic with the need to get out as quickly as possible. Behind Barynson's chair—thrown from its rack by the impact—was what was left of the team's "contact pack," containing aerial maps, close-range scanning equipment, trade goods, and base communicator. Scooping it up, Jin headed aft to the rear of the passenger compartment where the rest of the gear was stored. Her survival pack seemed to be as intact as any of the others; grabbing Sun's pack as well for insurance, she stepped to the exit hatch and yanked on the emergency release handle.

Nothing happened.

"Damn," she snarled, tension coming out in a snap of fury. Swiveling on her right foot, she swung her left leg around and sent a searing burst of antiarmor laser fire into the buckled metal.

The action gained her purple afterimage blobs in front of her eyes and a hundred tiny sizzleburns from molten metal droplets, but not much more. *All right,* she grimaced to herself as she blinked away the sudden tears. *Enough of the hysterics, girl. Calm down and try thinking for a change.* Studying the warped door, she located the most likely sticking points and sent antiarmor shots into them. Then, wincing as she took her full weight onto her weak left knee, she gave the center of the panel a kick. It popped open about a centimeter. More kicks and a handful of additional shots from the antiarmor laser forced it open enough for her to finally squeeze outside.

They'd been scheduled to land an hour before local sunrise, and with the extra delay the forest had grown bright enough for her to shut off her light-amps. Leaning on the hatch, she managed to close it more or less shut again. Then, taking a deep breath of surprisingly aromatic air, she looked around her.

The shuttle looked even worse on the outside than it had on the inside. Every hullplate seemed to be warped in some way, with the nose of the ship so crumpled as to be almost unrecognizable. All the protruding sensors and most of the radar-absorbing overlay were gone, too, torn away in a criss-cross pattern that looked as if a thousand spine leopards had tried to claw it to death. The reason for the pattern wasn't hard to find: for a hundred meters back along the shuttle's approach the trees had been torn and shattered by the doomed craft's mad rush to the ground.

Gritting her teeth, she took a quick look upward. The blue-tinged sky was still clear, but that wouldn't last long ... and when they came, that torn-up path through the trees would be a guidepost they couldn't miss. Keying her auditory enhancers, she stood still and listened for the sound of approaching engines.

And heard instead a faint and all-too-familiar purring growl.

Slowly, careful not to make any sudden moves, she eased her packs to the ground and turned around. It was a spine leopard, all right, under cover of a bush barely ten meters away.

Stalking her.

For a moment Jin locked gazes with the creature, feeling eerily as if she were meeting the species for the first time. Physically, it looked exactly like those she'd trained against on Aventine ...

and yet, there was something in its face, especially about the eyes, that was unlike anything she'd ever seen in a spine leopard before. A strange, almost preternatural alertness and intelligence, perhaps? Licking dry lips, she broke her eyes away from the gaze, raising them to focus on the silver-blue bird perched on the spine leopard's back.

A mojo, without a doubt. It matched all the descriptions, fitted all the stories she'd heard from her father and his fellow Cobras . . . and it was clear that none of them had done the birds proper credit. Hawklike, with oversized feet and wickedly curved talons, the mojo was as perfect a hunting bird as she'd ever seen. And in its eyes . . .

In the eyes was the same alertness she'd already seen in its companion spine leopard.

Again Jin licked her lips. Standing before her was living proof that the plan her father had worked out all those years ago had actually worked, at least to some degree, and under other circumstances she should probably have taken some time to observe the interaction. But time was in short supply just now, and academic curiosity low on her priorities list. Two twitches of her eyes put targeting locks on both creatures' heads. Easing onto her right foot, she swung her left leg up—

And as the mojo shrieked and shot into the sky, the spine leopard sprang.

The first blast from her antiarmor laser caught the predator square in the face, vaporizing most of its head. But even as Jin turned her attention toward the sky the mojo struck.

Her computerized reflexes took over as the optical sensors implanted in the skin around her eyes registered the airborne threat, throwing her sideways in a flat dive. But the action came a fraction of a second too late. The hooked talons caught her left cheek and shoulder as the bird shot past, burning lines of fire across the skin. Jin gasped in pain and anger as she fought against the entangling undergrowth, her eyes searching frantically to locate her attacker. There it was—coming around for a second diving pass. Praying that her targeting lock hadn't been disengaged by that roll, she triggered her fingertip lasers.

Her arms moved of their own accord, the implanted servos swinging them up at the nanocomputer's direction, and the bird's shimmering plumage lit up as the lasers struck it. The mojo gave one final shriek, and its blackened remains fell past Jin's head and slammed harmlessly to the ground.

For a moment she just knelt there among the vines and dead leaves, gasping for breath, her whole body trembling with reaction and adrenaline shock. The scratches across her face burned like fire, adding to the aches and throbs of her other injuries. Up until now she'd been too preoccupied with other things to pay much attention to herself; now, it was clearly time to take inventory.

It wasn't encouraging. Her back and neck ached, and a little experimentation showed both were beginning to stiffen up. Her chest was bruised where the safety harness had dug into the skin during the crash, and her left elbow had the tenderness of a joint that had been partially dislocated and then popped back into place. Her left knee was the worst; she didn't know what exactly had happened to it, but it hurt fiercely. "At least," she said aloud, "I don't have to worry about broken bones. I suppose that's something."

The sound of her voice seemed to help her morale. "Okay, then," she continued, getting to her feet. "First step is to get out of here and find civilization. Fine. So . . ." She glanced up at the sky, keying her auditory enhancers again as she did so. No sounds of aircraft; no sounds of predators. The sun was . . . there. "Okay, so that's east. If we crashed anywhere near our landing site, that's the direction we want to go."

And if the shuttle had instead overshot the Fertile Crescent . . . ? Firmly, she put that thought out of her mind. If she was going the wrong direction, the next village would be roughly a thousand kilometers of forest away. Collecting her three packs, she settled them as comfortably as she could around her shoulders and, taking a deep breath, fixed her direction and headed off into the forest.

Chapter 12

It started easily enough, as forest travel went. Within a few meters of the crash site she ran into a patch of mutually interlocking fern-like plants that lasted most of the first kilometer, giving her the feeling of wading through knee-deep water; and she'd barely left the ferns behind when she found herself having to use fingertip lasers to cut through a maze of tree-clinging vines that reminded her of Aventinian gluevines with five-centimeter thorns. But physical obstacles were the least of her worries, and even as she used lasers and servo strength to good advantage against the forest's best efforts, she tried to keep as much of her attention as possible on the subtle sounds filtering in through her audio enhancers.

The first attack came, in retrospect, right where she should have expected it: at the spot where the forest undergrowth abruptly vanished into a wide path of trampled earth bearing northwest. The path of a bololin herd . . . and where there were bololins, there were bound to be krisjaws, too.

She didn't identify the attacker as a krisjaw at first, of course. It wasn't until after the brief battle was over, and she was able to turn over the laser-blackened corpse and get a clear look at the wavy, flame-shaped canines that she could positively identify the beast. Vicious, cunning, and dangerous was how krisjaws has been described to her; and even with only this one interaction to go on she could well understand why the first generation of humans to reach Qasama had done their damnedest to try and wipe the things out. Wrapping a field bandage from her kit around the gash the predator's claws had torn in her left forearm, she continued on her way. Krisjaws were as nasty as Layn had warned, but now that she knew what to listen for she should be able to avoid being sneaked up on. If the forest didn't get any worse, she decided, she should be able to get through all right.

The forest, unfortunately, got worse.

The line of trampled undergrowth marking the bololins' route turned out to be nearly three kilometers wide, and within that cleared area an astonishing number of ground animals and their ecological hangers-on had set up shop. Insects buzzed around her in large numbers, attracted perhaps by the blood from her injuries. Most of them were merely annoying, but at least one large type was equipped with stingers and showed little compunction about using them. It was as she was swatting at a group of those that she found out that krisjaws weren't Qasama's only predator species.

This kind—vaguely monkey-like except for their six clawed limbs—hunted in packs, and it cost her another clawing before she found the best way to deal with them. Her omnidirectional sonic, designed originally to foul up nearby electronic gear, turned out to be equally effective in disrupting the monkeys' intergroup communication, and the arcthrower with its thundering flash of current scattered them yipping back into the cover of the surrounding trees.

Unfortunately, the sonic had an unexpected side effect, that of attracting a species of gliding lizard that, like the monkeys, launched their attacks in groups from the trees above her. Smaller and less dangerous than the larger predators, they were also too stupid to be frightened by the arcthrower's flash. She wound up having to kill all of them, collecting several small needle-toothed bites in the process.

It seemed like forever before she finally reached the road cutting across her path.

Captain Rivero Koja gazed down at the high-resolution photo on his viewing screen, a cold hand clenched around his heart. The line of destruction through the Qasaman forest could mean only one thing. "Hell," he said softly.

For a long moment the *Southern Cross*'s bridge was silent, save for the quiet clicking of keys from the scanner chief's station. "What happened?" Koja asked at last.

First Officer LuCass shrugged helplessly. "Impossible to tell, sir," he said. "Some malfunction, perhaps, that knocked them too far off their glide path—"

"Or else maybe someone shot them down?" Koja snapped, his simmering frustration and helplessness boiling out as anger.

"The Trofts claimed that wouldn't happen," LuCass reminded him.

"Yeah. Right." Koja took a deep breath, fought the rage back down to a cold anger. If only the *Southern Cross* had been overhead when the shuttle went down, instead of in their own orbit half a world away. If only they'd *been* there; had seen the crash as it happened, instead of finding out about it an hour afterward...

And if they had, it wouldn't have made any difference. None at all. Even if the *Southern Cross* had the capability of landing down there—which it didn't—they would still have been too late to save anyone. A crash like that would have killed everyone on board on impact.

Koja closed his eyes briefly. *At least,* he thought, *it would have been quick.* It wasn't much consolation.

"I'll be damned," the scanner chief muttered abruptly into his thoughts. "Captain, you'd better take a look at this."

Koja turned back to his display. A closer view of the crash site had replaced the first photo on his display. "Lovely," he growled.

"Maybe it is," the chief said, picking up his lightpen. A circle appeared briefly in the photo's lower right-hand corner. "Take a look and tell me if I'm seeing what I think I am."

It was an animal—that much was obvious even to Koja's relatively untrained eye. A quadruped, with the build of a hunting feline, lying prone on the leafy ground cover in the clearing the shuttle's passage had torn through the tree canopy. "A spine leopard?" he hazarded.

"That's what I thought, too," the other nodded. "Notice anything unusual about its head?"

Frowning, Koja leaned closer. The head...

Was gone. "Must have gotten caught in the crash," he said, feeling suddenly queasy. If something outside the shuttle had been torn up that badly...

"Maybe, maybe not," the chief muttered, an odd note in his voice. "Let me see if I can get us in a little closer—"

A new, tighter photo replaced the one on the display, the normal atmospheric blurring fading away as the computer worked to clean up the image. The spine leopard's head...

"Oh, my God," LuCass whispered from his side. "Captain—that's not crash damage."

Koja nodded, the cold hand on his heart tightening its grip. Not crash damage; laser damage. *Cobra* laser damage.

Someone had survived the crash.

"Complete scan," Koja ordered the scanner chief through dry lips. "We've got to find him."

"I've already done a check of the area we can penetrate—"

"Then do it again," Koja snapped.

"Yes, sir." The chief got busy.

LuCass took a step closer to Koja's chair. "What are we going to do if we do locate him?" he asked softly. "There isn't any place down there we could possibly set this monster down."

"Even if there was, I doubt the Qasamans would sit back and let us do it." Koja clenched his teeth until they ached. He'd asked the Directorate—*begged* the Directorate—to rent a second shuttle from the Trofts as an emergency backup. But no; the damned governor-general had deemed it an expensive and unnecessary luxury and vetoed the request. "Any chance we could get some food and medical supplies down to him? It would at least give him a fighting chance."

LuCass was already typing on Koja's computer keyboard. "Let's see what we've got on board . . . well, we could foam some ablator onto a mini cargo pod. A parachute . . . yes, we could rig a chute. Pressure sensor to tell it when to pop . . . ? Hmm. Nothing . . . wait a second, we could put it on a simple timer and have it pop at a prefigured time. Looks feasible, Captain."

"At which point the question arises of where to send it so that he can actually find it." Koja looked over at the scanner chief. "Anything?"

The other shook his head. "No, sir. The canopy's just too thick for short-wave or infrared penetration. His only shot at civilization is to the east, though—we could try dropping the supplies where the road ahead of him intersects an eastward path." He hesitated. "Of course, there's no guarantee he's lucid," he added. "He could be going in *any* direction, in that case, or even walking around in circles. Or his brain could be functioning fine but his body too badly injured to get all the way to the road."

"In either case he's dead," Koja said tightly. "He may be dead even if he *does* get to a village—the Qasaman leaders are hardly going to keep the shuttle crash an official secret." He looked at LuCass. "Get a crew busy on that pod," he ordered. "Include a tight-beam split-freq radio with the other supplies. We'll have a spot picked out to aim for by the time you're ready."

"Yes, sir." LuCass turned back to his own board, keyed the intercom, and began issuing orders.

Exhaling in a silent sigh, Koja looked back at the dead spine leopard still on his display. *And it's all just so much wasted effort,* he thought blackly. Because as long as the Cobra was alone in enemy territory the time clock would be ticking down toward zero. Eventually, the Qasamans would identify him; or else a wandering krisjaw or spine leopard would find him; or else something completely unknown would get him.

Qasama was a deathtrap . . . and the only people who had any chance at all of pulling him out of it were back on Aventine. Eight days and forty-five light-years away.

Eight days. Koja cringed, trying desperately to find a closer alternative. The New Worlds, perhaps—Esquiline and the other fledgling colonies—or even the nearby Troft demesne of Baliu'ckha'spmi. But Esquiline would have no spacecraft capable of making groundfall, either; and with neither an official credit authorization nor a supply of trade goods on board, trying to deal through an unfamiliar Troft bureaucracy for the rent of another shuttle could take literally months.

Eight days. A minimum of fourteen days for the round trip, even if the faster *Dewdrop* was available. Add the time needed to choose and equip a search and rescue team, and it could easily be twenty days before they could even begin to look for him.

And with or without a supply pod, twenty days alone on Qasama was a death sentence. Pure and simple.

But that didn't mean they had to give up without a fight . . . and if the fight in this case consisted of hoping for a miracle, then so be it. The fact that one of the Cobras had survived the crash was a miracle in and of itself; perhaps the angel in charge of this area would be feeling generous.

Eventually, they would find out. In the meantime . . .

Reaching to his keyboard, Koja began plotting out the route and fueling stops for a least-time course back to Aventine. It had been his experience that miracles, when they happened, tended to favor those who had laid the proper groundwork for them.

Chapter 13

Jin stood at the road for a long time, trying to figure out what to do next.

It was, at any rate, confirmation that the shuttle had indeed crashed to the west of the Fertile Crescent. Roads always led to civilization; all she had to do was follow it.

The question was, which way?

For a moment the landscape seemed to swim before her eyes, and the red warning border appeared superimposed on the scenery. She twisted her head, sending a jolt of pain through the stiffness in her neck. There had been no fewer than five such warnings in the past half hour, a sure sign that she was losing it. Combat fatigue, shock from her injuries, some slow poison in the animal bites and scratches she'd suffered—it didn't much matter the cause. What mattered now was finding somewhere safe to collapse before she did so on her feet.

So . . . which way?

Blinking hard against a sudden moisture in her eyes, she studied the road. Two lanes wide, probably, paved with some kind of black rocktop—hardly a major thoroughfare. Running almost due north-south, at least at this point, it was probably one of the connecting roads between the small forest villages west and northwest of the major Fertile Crescent city of Azras. The maps in her pack showed those villages to be anywhere from ten to fifteen kilometers apart. A trivial distance for a Cobra in good condition, but her present condition was anything but good.

The red circle appeared around her vision again. Biting hard on her lower lip, she again managed to force it away.

Thoughts of the maps had reminded her of something.

Something important . . . Concentrating hard, she tried to force her brain awake enough to think of what it might be. Her packs— that was it. Her packs, with their Aventinian maps and packaged survival food and Qasaman clothing—

Qasaman clothing.

With an effort, Jin keyed her auditory enhancers. Nothing but insect and bird twitterings. Stepping off the road, she walked back to the line of trees and dropped her packs to the ground behind a bush that seemed to be half leaves and half thorns. Locating her personal pack among the three, she fumbled the catches open and pulled out a set of Qasaman clothing.

Changing clothes was an ordeal. Between the oozing cuts on her arms and face and the ache and throbbing of her crash injuries, every movement seemed to have its own distinctive pain. But with the pain came a slight clearing of her mind, and when she was done she even had the presence of mind to stuff her torn Aventinian garb away and to push all three packs into at least marginal concealment under the thorn bush. A minute later she was trudging along the road, heading north for no particular reason.

She never heard the car's approach. The voices, when they called to her, seemed to come from a great distance, echoing out of a wavering mist that filled her ears as much as it did her eyes.

"—matter with you? Huh?"

Bringing her feet to a halt, she tried to turn around, but she'd made it only halfway when a pair of hands suddenly were gripping her shoulders. "—God in heaven, Master Sammon! Look at her face—!"

"Get her into the car," a second, calmer voice cut the first off. "Ende—give him a hand."

And in a dizzying flurry Jin was picked up by shoulders and thighs and carried bouncing to a dimly seen red box shape. . . .

The air sensor strapped to his right wrist beeped twice, and Daulo Sammon raised it close to his face, rubbing some of the dust off his goggles for a better view. The readout confirmed what his lungs and the beep had already told him: that the air in this part of the mine was beginning to get stale. Raising his other wrist, Daulo consulted his watch. Officially, the workers had fifteen minutes to go before their shift was over. If he had the air exchangers started now, running them for perhaps three minutes . . .

Not worth it. "Foreman?" he called into his headset microphone.

"This is Daulo Sammon. The shift is hereby declared over; you may begin moving the men back to the shaft now."

"Yes, Master Sammon," the other's voice came back, hissing with static from the ore veins' metallic interference. Daulo strained his ears, but if the foreman was pleased or surprised by such uncommon leniency, his voice didn't show it. "All workers, begin moving back to the central core."

Daulo clicked his headset off the general frequency and turned back himself, his light throwing sharp shadows across the crisscrossing of shoring that half covered the rough tunnel walls. His grandfather had expected the mine to play out in his own lifetime, and had neglected its safety accordingly, and it had taken Daulo's father nearly ten years to reverse the deterioration that had ensued. *Will it all be gone before it becomes mine?* Daulo wondered, sweeping his light across the star-sparkling rock peeking out between the bracings. A small part of his mind rather hoped it would; the thought of being responsible for all the lives that toiled daily down here had always made him a little uneasy. He'd seen his grandfather neglect that responsibility, and had seen what the burden had done to his father. To have that weight on his own shoulders . . .

But if the mine went, then so did the Sammon family's wealth and prestige . . . and very likely its place in the village, as well. Without the mine, only lumber processing would remain as a major industry, and it was for certain the Sammon family wouldn't be involved in that.

And as for the dangers of the mine, outside Milika's wall the miners would have to risk the krisjaws and razorarms and all the rest of Qasama's deadly animal life. Behind his filter mask, Daulo's lip twisted as the old proverb came to mind: on Qasama there were no safe places, only choices between dangerous ones.

He reached the central shaft a few minutes later to find a growing line of men waiting for their turns at the mine's three elevators. Bypassing them, he stepped to the car that was currently loading and motioned the men already in it to get off. They did so, making the sign of respect as they passed him. Stepping into the elevator, Daulo slid the gate closed and punched for the top.

The ride up was a long one—though not as long as the trip the opposite direction always seemed—and as the car shook around him he pulled off headset, goggles, and mask and gingerly rubbed the bridge of his nose. A hot shower was what was needed now— a shower, followed by a good meal. No; the meal would be third—

after the shower he would presumably be summoned by his father for a report on his trip down the mine. That was all right; he would have time to organize his observations and conclusions while he scrubbed the mine's grit and chill from his body.

The sudden stream of light as the car reached ground level made Daulo blink. Shifting the equipment around in his hands, he surreptitiously wiped away the sudden tears as the operators outside opened the gates and stepped back, making the sign of respect as they did so. Daulo stepped out, nodding at the mine chief as the latter also made the sign of respect. "I trust, Master Sammon," the chief said, "that your inspection found nothing wanting?"

"Your service to my father seems adequate," Daulo told him, keeping his face and voice neutral. He had, in fact, found things down there to be excellent, but he had no intention of saying so on the spur of the moment. Aside from the danger of swelling the mine chief's ego with unnecessary public praise, Daulo's father had always warned him against rendering hasty judgments. "I shall report to my father what I have seen."

The other bowed. Passing him, Daulo walked out from under the elevator canopy and headed past the storage and preparation buildings toward the access road where Walare was waiting with his car.

"Master Sammon," Walare said, making the sign of respect as Daulo came up to him. Daulo climbed in, and a moment later Walare was guiding the car off the mine grounds and onto Milika's public streets.

"What news is there?" Daulo asked as they turned toward the center of town and the Sammon family house.

"Public news or private?" Walare asked.

"Private, of course," Daulo said. "Though you can skip past the backlife gossip."

In the car's mirror, Walare's eyes were briefly surrounded by smile lines. "Ah, how times have changed," he said with mock sadness. "I remember a time—no more than three years ago—when the backlife news was the first thing you would ask for—"

"The news, Walare; the news?" Daulo interrupted with equally mock exasperation. He'd known Walare ever since the two were boys; and while the public relationship between driver and Sammon family heir were rigidly defined, in the privacy of Daulo's car things could be considerably freer. "You can reminisce about the lost golden age later."

Walare chuckled. "Actually, it's been a very quiet day. The Yithtra family trucks are mobilizing—someone there must have found a rich section of forest. Perhaps because of that, the mayor's trying again to talk your father into supporting his efforts to have the top of the wall rebuilt."

"Waste of money and effort," Daulo snorted, glancing behind him. Part of the village wall was visible past the village's buildings, the forest-like paintings on the lower part in sharp contrast with the stark metal mesh extension atop it. "The razorarms can't get over what we've got now."

Walare shrugged. "Mayors exist largely to make noise. What else is there for him to make noise about these days?"

Daulo grinned tightly. "Besides our trouble with the Yithtra family, you mean?"

"What can he say about that that he hasn't already said?"

"Not much," Daulo admitted. There were times he wished the competition between his family and the Yithtra family didn't exist; but it was a fact of life, and disliking it didn't change that. "Anything else?"

"Your brother Perto brought in that shipment of spare motor parts from Azras," Walare said, his voice abruptly taking on a grim tone. "Along with a passenger: an injured woman they found on the road."

Daulo sat up a bit straighter. "A woman? Who?"

"No one at the house recognized her."

"Identification?"

"None." Walare hesitated. "Perhaps it was lost in . . . the trouble she had."

Daulo frowned. "What sort of trouble?"

Walare took a deep breath. "According to the driver who helped bring her in, she'd been clawed at least once by a krisjaw . . . as well as clawed by a baelcra and bitten by one or more monota."

Daulo felt his stomach tighten. "God above," he muttered. "And she was still alive?"

"She was when they brought her to the house," Walare said. "Though who knows how long she'll stay that way?"

"God alone," Daulo sighed.

Chapter 14

They reached the house a few minutes later, Walare guiding the car expertly through the filigreed doors and over to the wide garage nestled behind a pair of fruit trees in one corner of the large central courtyard. Stomach tightening against what he knew would be a horrible sight, Daulo headed for the women's section of the house.

Only to discover that his worst fears had been for nothing.

"Is that the worst of it?" he asked, frowning across the room at the woman on the bed. Surrounded by three other women and a doctor, with a blanket pulled up to her neck, it was nevertheless clear that the injured woman wasn't the horribly mauled victim he'd expected to find. There was a bad set of scratches on her cheek, visible beneath the healing salve that had been applied, and a rather worse set on her arm that was still being treated. But aside from that . . .

From her seat across the bed Daulo's mother glanced up at him. "Please stay back," Ivria Sammon said softly. "The dust on your clothing—"

"I understand," Daulo nodded. His eyes searched the visible wounds again, then settled for the first time on her face. About his age, he judged, with the soft-looking skin of someone who had spent little time out in the sun and wind. His eyes drifted down her left arm, past the wounds, to her hand.

No ring of marriage.

He frowned, looking at her face again. No mistake—she was at least as old as he was. And still unmarried—?

"She must have come from a far way," Ivria said quietly, almost as if to herself. "See her face, the way her features are formed."

Daulo glanced at his mother, then back at the mysterious woman

611

again. Yes; now that he was looking for it he could see it, too. There was a strangeness in the face, a trace of the exotic that he'd never seen before. "Perhaps she's from one of the cities to the north," he suggested. "Or even from somewhere in the Eastern Arm."

"Perhaps," the doctor grunted. "She certainly hasn't built up much resistance to monote bites."

"Is that what the problem is?" Daulo asked.

The doctor nodded. "On the arms and hands—here, and here," he added, pointing them out. "It looks like she had to fend them off with her bare hands."

"After her ammunition ran out?" Daulo suggested. She surely hadn't fended off that krisjaw with her bare hands, after all.

"Perhaps," the doctor said. "Though if she had a gun it was gone by the time she was found. As was the holster."

Daulo gnawed at his inner cheek, glancing around the room. A pile of clothing had been tossed into the corner; keeping well back from the bed, he stepped over to it. The injured woman's clothes, of course—the bloodstains alone would have attested to that, even without the odd feel of the cloth that branded it as from someplace far away. And the doctor was right: there *was* no holster with the ensemble. Nor any markings on the belt where one might once have hung.

"Maybe she had some companions," he suggested, dropping the clothing back on the floor. That would certainly make more sense than a single woman wandering alone out in the forest. "Was any effort made to see if there were others in the area where she was found?"

It was Ivria who answered. "Not at the time, but I believe Perto has now gone back to continue the search."

Stepping to the room's intercom, Daulo keyed the private family circuit. "This is Daulo Sammon," he identified himself to the servant who answered. "Has Perto returned from the forest?"

"One moment, Master Sammon," the voice answered. " . . . He is not answering."

Daulo nodded. Out of the house, away from all the Sammon family holdings in Milika, Perto would be out of touch with the buried fiber-optic communications network which was the only safe way to send messages in Milika. "Leave a message for him to contact me as soon as possible," he instructed the other.

"Yes, Master Sammon."

Daulo keyed the intercom off and turned back for one last look at the woman. *Where could she be from?* he wondered. *And why is she here?* There were no answers as yet . . . but that lack would eventually be corrected. For the moment the important fact was that the Sammon family had matters under control. Whether this mysterious woman represented a totally neutral happenstance, or a chance opportunity granted them by God, or part of some strange plot by one of their rivals, the Sammons were now in position to use her presence to their own advantage.

Which reminded him, he still had to clean up before his meeting with his father. Opening the door quietly, he slipped out of the room.

"Come in," the familiar grating voice came from the opposite side of the carved door; and, steeling himself, Daulo opened the door and went in.

He could still remember a time, not all that long ago, when he'd been absolutely terrified of his father. Terrified not so much by Kruin Sammon's strength and stature, nor even by the man's cold voice and piercing black eyes; but by the fact that Kruin Sammon *was,* to all intents and purposes, the Sammon family. His was the power that ran this immense house and the mine and nearly a third of the village; his the influence that stretched beyond Milika to touch the nearby villages and logging camps and even the city of Azras, whose people normally treated villagers like themselves with barely concealed contempt. Kruin Sammon was *power* . . . and even after the fear of that power had abated somewhat, Daulo had never forgotten the emotions it had aroused in him.

It was only much later that he had realized it was probably a lesson his father had deliberately set for him to learn.

"Ah; Daulo," the older man nodded from his cushion-like throne in solemn greeting to his eldest son. "I trust your trip down the mine went well?"

"Yes, my father," Daulo said, making the sign of respect as he stepped to the cushion before Kruin's low work table and seated himself before it. "The necessity for extra shoring is keeping progress slow in the new tunnel, but not as slow as we feared it would."

"And the job is being done properly?"

"It appeared to be, yes, at least to the best of my knowledge."

"The job is being done properly?" Kruin repeated.

Daulo fought to keep his emotions from his face and voice. That had been a thoughtless qualification—if there was one thing his father hated, it was equivocation. "Yes, my father. The shoring was being done properly."

"Good," Kruin nodded, picking up a stylus from the table and making note on a pad. "And the workers?"

"Content. In my presence, at any rate."

"The mine chief?"

Daulo thought back to the other's face as he'd left the elevator. "Impressed by his own importance," he said. "Eager that others know of it, as well."

That brought a faint smile to Kruin's lips. "He is all of that," he agreed. "But he's also capable and conscientious, and the combination is one that can be put up with." Tossing the stylus back on the table, he leaned back against the cushions and gazed at his son. "And now: what is your impression of our visitor?"

"Our—? Oh. The woman." Daulo frowned. "There are things about her I don't understand. For one thing, she's well within marriageable age and yet is unmarried—"

"Or is widowed," Kruin put in.

"Oh. True, she could be a widow. She's also not from anywhere around here—her clothing is made of a cloth I'm unfamiliar with, and the doctor said she had a low tolerance to monote bites."

"And what of her rather dramatic entrance to Milika?—found alone on the road after some unspecified accident or such?"

Daulo shrugged. "I've heard of people getting stranded on roads before, my father. And even of surviving krisjaw attacks."

The elder Sammon smiled. "Very good—you anticipated my next question. But have you ever heard of someone who was close enough to a krisjaw to be clawed *and* still survived the experience?"

"There are cases," Daulo said, a small part of his mind wondering why he was being so stubborn. He certainly had no reason to take the mysterious woman's part in this debate. "If she had one or more armed companions during the attack one could have shot the creature off of her, even at that late moment."

Kruin nodded, lips tightening together. "Yes, there's that possibility. Unfortunately, it leads immediately to another question: these alleged defenders of hers seem to have vanished, djinn-like, into thin air. Why?"

Daulo thought about it for a long minute, painfully aware that his father must have already thought all this through and was merely testing him to see if he came up with similar answers. "There are only three possibilities," he said at last. "They are dead, incapacitated, or in hiding."

"I agree," Kruin said. "If they are dead or incapacitated, Perto will find them—I've sent him to search the road now for just that purpose. If they are hiding . . . again, why?"

"Afraid, or part of a plot," Daulo said promptly. "If afraid, they will reveal themselves once their companion is proved to have come to no harm. If part of a plot—" he hesitated "—then the woman is here either to infiltrate and spy on our house or else to distract our attention from her companions' task."

Kruin took a deep breath, his eyes focused somewhere beyond Daulo's face. "Yes. Unfortunately, that is my reasoning, as well. Have you any thoughts as to who would plot against us?"

The snort escaped Daulo's lips before he could stop it. "Need we look farther than the Yithtra family?"

"It could be that obvious," Kruin shrugged. "And yet, I generally credit Yithtra with more subtlety than that. And more intelligence, too—with a new shipment of lumber due in, he'll have more than enough legitimate work to keep him occupied. Why launch a plot to discredit us at the same time?"

"Perhaps that's how he expects us to think," Daulo suggested.

"Perhaps. Still, it would be good to remember that there are others on Qasama who might find profit in stirring up mischief in Western Arm villages."

Daulo nodded thoughtfully. Yes; and foremost among them were the enemies of Mayor Capparis of Azras. Capparis's unlikely friendship with the Sammon family—and the easy access that relationship gave the mayor to the mine's output—had been a thorn in the side of Capparis's enemies for a long time. Perhaps one of them was finally going to try and break the Sammon family's power, to replace them with someone more malleable.

Especially with that strange self-contained Mangus operation east of Azras gobbling up so much of the mine's output lately. Azras and the other cities in the Western Arm were enough of a headache to Milika and its fellow villages; Mangus and its slimy purchasing agents were as bad in their way as all the cities combined. If someone in Azras thought Mangus's mineral needs would go still higher—and thought that someone other than the Sammon family should profit by those needs . . . "What shall we do, then, my father?" he asked. "Send this woman out of our house, perhaps allow her to recuperate in the mayor's house?"

Kruin was silent a moment before answering. "No," he said at last. "If our enemies believe we consider her harmless, it gives us a slight advantage in this game. No, we will keep her here, at least for now. If Perto fails to find any companions for her—well, by then we may be able to question her directly about how she survived her journey."

And if that story was patently false . . .? "I understand. Shall I assign a guard to her recovery room?"

"No, we don't want to be that obvious. As long as she's ill and confined to the women's section the normal contingent of guards there will be adequate. You will alert them to be prepared for possible trouble from her, of course."

"Yes, my father. And once she's recovered?"

Kruin smiled. "Why, then, as a proper and dutiful host, it will be your responsibility to act as escort to her."

And to learn just what she's up to. "Yes, my father," Daulo nodded. The elder Sammon's posture indicated the audience was at an end; getting to his feet, Daulo made the sign of respect and bowed. "I will attend to the guards, and then await Perto's return."

"Goodbye, my eldest son," Kruin said with an acknowledging nod. "Make me proud of you."

"I will." *As long as breath is in me,* Daulo added silently.

Pulling open the heavy door, he slipped quietly out of the chamber.

Chapter 15

The first thing Jin noticed as she drifted back to consciousness was that something furry was tickling the underside of her chin. The second thing she noticed was that she didn't seem to hurt anywhere.

She opened her eyes to slits, squinting against the light streaming in from somewhere to her right and trying to orient herself. If her memory was correct—and there might be some doubt about that—it had been past noon when she finally made it through the forest and found the road. Could it still be afternoon on that same day? No, she felt far too rested for that. Besides which . . . Gently, she tried turning her neck. Still a little stiff, but not nearly as bad as it had been. At least a day had passed, then, probably more.

And she'd been unconscious through the whole thing. Naturally unconscious? Or had she been deliberately drugged?

Drugged *and* interrogated?

From her right came the squeak of wood on wood. Keeping her movements small, Jin turned her head. Seated in a heavy looking chair beside the window was a young girl, perhaps seven or eight years old, seated crosslegged with an open book across her lap. "Hello," Jin croaked.

The girl looked up, startled. "Hello," she said, closing her book and laying it on the floor beside her chair. "I didn't realize you were awake. How are you feeling?"

Jin forced some moisture into her mouth. "Pretty good," she said, the words coming out better this time. "Hungry, though. How long was I asleep?"

"Oh, a long time—almost five days—though you were awake and feverish for part of—"

"Five *days?*" Jin felt her mouth fall open in astonishment . . . and then the rest of the girl's comment caught up with her. "I was feverish, you said?" she asked carefully. "I hope I didn't say or do anything too outlandish."

"Oh, no, though my aunt said you're very strong."

Jin grimaced. "Yes, I've been told that." She just hoped her Cobra-enhanced strength hadn't hurt anyone . . . or given her away. "Did anyone—I'm sorry; what is your name?"

The girl looked stricken. "Oh—forgive me." She ducked her head, raising her right hand to touch bunched fingers to her forehead. "I am Gissella; second daughter of Namid Sammon, younger brother of Kruin Sammon."

Jin tried the hand gesture, watching Gissella's face closely as she did so. If she botched the maneuver the younger girl didn't seem to notice. "I am Jasmine," Jin introduced herself. "Third daughter of Justin Alventin."

"Honored," Gissella nodded, getting to her feet and walking around the foot of the bed. "Excuse me, but I was to let my Aunt Ivria know if you awakened in your right mind."

She stepped to the door and what looked like an intercom set into the wall next to it, and as she got her connection and delivered her news Jin took a quick inventory of her injuries.

It was astonishing. The deep gashes on arm and cheek were already covered with pink skin, and the deep bruises left across her chest by the shuttle safety harness were completely gone. Her left knee and elbow were still tender, but even they were in better shape than she would have expected from the way they'd felt right after the crash. Either the injuries had been more transient than she'd thought at the time, or else—

No. No *or else* about it. Qasaman medicine was as advanced as that of the Cobra Worlds, pure and simple. Possibly more so.

Gissella finished her conversation and stepped to a wardrobe cabinet on the opposite side of the door. "They'll be here shortly," she said, withdrawing a pale blue outfit and holding it out for Jin's approval. "Aunt Ivria suggested you might like to get dressed before they arrive."

"Yes, I would," Jin nodded, pulling back the furry blanket and swinging her legs out of bed.

The material, she quickly discovered, was markedly different from that of the best-guess Qasaman clothing the team had landed with, but the design was similar. Still, Jin took no chances, feigning trouble with her left arm in order to let Gissella do as much of the actual fastening and arranging as possible. Fortunately, there were no major surprises. *Which means I ought to be able to dress myself adequately from now on,* Jin thought as she straightened the hem of the short robe/tunic. *At least until they switch styles on me.* Trying to relax, she listened for the others to arrive.

She didn't have to wait very long. Within a few minutes her enhanced hearing picked up the sound of three sets of footsteps approaching. Taking a deep breath, she faced the door . . . and a moment later the panel swung open to reveal two women and a man.

The first woman was the one in charge of the party—that much was abundantly clear from both her rich clothing and her almost regal bearing. She was a woman, Jin recognized instinctively, who commanded the respect of those around her and would demand nothing less from a stranger in her household. The second woman was in sharp contrast: young and plainly dressed, with the air of one whose role was to go unnoticed about her duties. A *servant,* Jin thought to herself. *Or a slave.* And the man—

His eyes were captivating. Literally; it took Jin a long second to free her gaze from those dark traps and give the rest of him a quick once-over. He was young—her age, perhaps a year or two younger—but with the same regal air as the older woman. And some of the same features, as well. *Related?* she wondered. Very possibly.

The older woman stopped a meter away from Jin and ducked her head a few degrees in an abbreviated bow. "In the name of the Sammon family," she said in a cool, controlled voice, "I bid you greeting and welcome."

Something expectant in her face . . . on impulse, Jin repeated the fingertips-to-forehead gesture Gissella had already shown her. It seemed to work. "Thank you," she told the older woman. "I am honored by your hospitality." The verbal response wasn't the prescribed one—that much was quickly apparent from the others' faces. But they seemed surprised, rather than outraged, and Jin crossed her mental fingers that the story she'd concocted would cover these slips well enough. "I am Jasmine, daughter of Justin Alventin."

"I am Ivria Sammon," the older woman identified herself. "Wife of Kruin Sammon and mother of his heirs." She gestured to the youth, now standing beside her. "Daulo, first son and heir of Kruin Sammon."

"I am honored by your hospitality," Jin repeated, again touching fingers to forehead.

Daulo nodded in return. "Your customs and manners mark you as a stranger to this part of Qasama," Ivria continued, eyes holding unblinkingly on her. "Where is your home, Jasmine Alventin?"

"I have spent time in many different places," Jin said, working hard at controlling her face and voice. This was the stickiest part; no matter what she said now, the lie could be eventually run to ground if they were persistent enough. Given that, her best chance lay with one of the half-dozen cities dotting the western curve of the Crescent, where the higher population density should make any investigation at least a little harder. "My current home is in the city of Sollas."

For a single, awful moment she thought she'd made a mistake, that perhaps something unknown had happened to Sollas in the years following her father's first visit to Qasama. The hard look that flicked across Ivria's face—

"A city dweller," Daulo said sourly.

"City dweller or not, she is our guest now," Ivria replied, and Jin started breathing again. Whatever they had against cities, at least it wasn't something that immediately branded her as an offworlder. "Tell me, Jasmine Alventin, what has brought you to Milika?"

"Is that where I am, then?" Jin asked. "Milika? I didn't know where it was I was brought—the accident that wrecked our car . . ." She shivered involuntarily as images from the shuttle wreck rose unbidden before her eyes.

"Where did this accident happen?" Ivria asked. "On the road from Shaga?"

Jin waved her hands helplessly. "I don't really know *where* we were. My companions—my brother Mander and two others—were searching the forest for insects to take back to their laboratory."

"You were in the forest on foot?" Daulo put in.

"No," Jin told him. "Mander studies insects, trying to learn their secrets and put them to use. He has—or had; I suppose it's ruined now—a specially built car that can maneuver between trees and through a forest's undergrowth. I was just along for the trip— I wanted to see how he worked." She let a note of puzzlement creep into voice and face. "But I'm sure he knows much more about where the accident happened. Can't you just ask *him* about it when he awakens?"

Ivria and Daulo exchanged glances. "Your companions are not here, Jasmine Alventin," Daulo said. "You were alone when my brother found you on the road."

Jin stared at him a long moment, letting her mouth sag in what she hoped was a reasonable semblance of shock. "Not ... but they were *there*. With me. We—we all walked to the road together—Mander killed a krisjaw that attacked me—no, they *have* to be here."

"I'm sorry," Ivria said gently. "Do you remember if they were still with you when you reached the road?"

"Of course they were," Jin said, letting her voice drift toward the frantic. "They were still with me when I was carried into the truck. Surely they saw—it was your brother, Daulo, who found us? Didn't he *see* them?"

Daulo's cheek twitched. "Jasmine Alventin ... you were suffering the effects of several monote bites when Perto found you. Hallucinations are sometimes among these effects. My brother wouldn't have left your companions if they'd been anywhere nearby—you must believe that. And after you were safe here he took several men and went back to do an even more thorough search, covering both the road and the forest areas flanking them, all the way back to Shaga."

Thorough enough to find the packs I hid? Jin's stomach tightened; and immediately relaxed. No, of course the packs were still hidden. If anyone had found them she'd have awakened in a maximum-security prison ... if she'd been allowed to awaken at all. "Oh, Mander," she whispered. "But then ... where is he?"

"He may still be alive," Daulo said, his voice steady with forced optimism. "We can send more people to look for him."

Slowly, Jin shook her head, gazing past Daulo into space. "No. Five days ... If he's not out by now ... he's not coming out, is he?"

Daulo took a deep breath. "I'll send more searchers, anyway," he said quietly. "Look ... you've had a bad time, and I doubt that you're fully recovered. Why don't you have a warm bath and something to eat and then rest for a few more hours."

Jin closed her eyes briefly. "Yes. Thank you. I'm ... sorry. Sorry for everything."

"It's our honor and our pleasure to offer you our hospitality," Ivria said. "Is there someone elsewhere on Qasama to whom a message should be sent?"

Jin shook her head. "No. My family is ... gone. My brother was all I had left."

"We grieve with you," Ivria said softly. For a moment she was silent; then, she made a gesture and the young Qasaman woman behind her stepped forward. "This is Asya; she will be your servant for as long as you are under our roof. Command her as you will."

"Thank you," Jin nodded. The thought of having a private servant grated against her sensibilities—especially a servant whose manner seemed more fitting to a slave—but it would undoubtedly be out of character to refuse.

"When you feel up to joining us, let Asya know, and she'll find me," Daulo added. "It will be my privilege to be your guide and escort while you are in Milika."

"I will be most honored," Jin said, trying to ignore the warning bells clanging in the back of her mind. First a live-in servant, then the owner's son to walk her around the place. Common hospitality . . . or the first indications of suspicion?

But for the next couple of days, at least, it hardly mattered. Until her elbow and knee were fully functional again, she had little choice but to stay in Milika and recuperate; and if the Sammons wanted to keep her under a microscope, she could handle that. "I look forward to seeing your house and village," she added.

And for a second the compassion seemed to leave Daulo's eyes. "Yes," he said, almost stiffly. "I'm sure you do."

Chapter 16

It turned out to be surprisingly easy for Jin to get used to having a servant around.

The exception was the bath. Jin hadn't had company in the bathroom during baths since she was ten, and to have someone standing quietly ready with cloth, soap, and towel was both strange and not a little discomfiting. The hot water itself felt wonderfully good—and the bathroom more luxurious than any she'd ever seen, let alone been in—but she nevertheless cut the operation as short as she reasonably could.

Once past that, though, things improved considerably. Asya ordered her a large dinner, setting it out at a small window seat table overlooking a magnificently landscaped courtyard. *Sort of like the way your family fusses over you when you're sick,* Jin decided as Asya seated her and began serving. *Or like having an obedient little sister available to boss around.* That role she remembered all too well.

The food itself wasn't as strange-tasting as she'd feared it would be, and she astonished herself by eating everything Asya had had sent up. The trauma of the crash and trek through the forest, combined with five days of fasting, had given her more appetite than she'd realized.

And apparently more fatigue, too. She'd barely finished the meal when she began to feel sleep tugging again at her eyelids. Leaving Asya to clean up, she made her way back to her bed and got undressed. *I wonder,* the thought occurred to her as she slid under the furry blanket, *if the food might have been drugged.*

But if it had there was nothing she could do about it. As long as she was in Milika and the Sammon household, she was in their power. Best to look as innocent and guileless as possible . . . and concentrate on getting her strength back.

When she awoke again, the room was dark, with only a bare hint of light coming in around heavy curtains covering the room's window. "Asya?" she whispered, keying her optical enhancers to light-amplification. There was no response, and a quick visual survey of the room showed she was alone. Activating her auditory enhancers, she picked up the sounds of slow breathing from the doorway leading to the bathroom/dressing area, and Jin remembered now noticing that one of the couches there had seemed to be of a daybed design. Sliding out of bed, she padded to the doorway and looked in.

Asya was there, all right, snuggled under a blanket on the daybed, oblivious to the world. For a long moment Jin stood watching her, pondering what she should do . . . and as she stood there, it suddenly occurred to her that of the four members of the Sammon household she'd seen so far, none of them had been accompanied by a mojo. Or had worn clothing adapted to carrying one.

She frowned into the darkness. Had the plan, then, worked? Had they truly succeeded in splitting the Qasamans away from their bodyguard birds? *If so, that might explain their reaction to my telling them I was from Sollas,* she realized. *General hostility between villages and cities may have begun.*

Unfortunately, it could just as easily be that Ivria and Daulo had left their mojos behind when they came to see her, for whatever reason. She needed to find out for sure . . . and the sooner the better.

Gnawing thoughtfully at her lip, she looked back at the door where her visitors had entered that afternoon. Somehow, she doubted that Daulo's offer of hospitality had included midnight tours; but on the other hand, no one had suggested that she was a prisoner here, either. Stepping back over to the wardrobe, she located the clothing she'd worn earlier and quietly put it on. Then, senses fully alert, she opened the door and stepped out.

She was in the approximate center of a long hallway, its dim indirect lighting bright enough for her to see without the aid of her enhancers. Halfway to the end in either direction were archways that led off opposite to the courtyard, perhaps to larger suites than hers. The decor was elaborate, with delicate tracings and filigrees of gold and purple everywhere.

All this she noted only peripherally. Her primary attention was on the end of the hallway, and the pair of uniformed men standing there.

Each with the silver-blue plumage of a mojo glinting on his shoulder.

For a second Jin hesitated; but it was too late to back out now. The guards had seen her, and while she didn't yet seem to have provoked anything but mild interest in them, ducking back into her room could hardly fail to pique their interest. The other direction . . . ? But a glance behind her showed another pair of men standing at that end of the hall, too. Gritting her teeth, she turned back and started down the corridor, walking as casually as she could manage.

The guards watched her approach, one of them taking a step away from the far wall as she neared them. "Greetings to you, Jasmine Alventin," he said, touching his fingers to his forehead. "We stand at your service. Where do you go at this time of the evening?"

"I woke up a short while ago," Jin told him, "and as I couldn't fall back asleep I thought a walk would help."

If that sounded odd to the guard it didn't show in his expression. "Few in the household are still awake," he said, glancing down the hall and making a quick series of hand signals. Jin looked around the corner, saw that the hallway bent around to that direction, probably following the perimeter of the courtyard she could see from her window. At the far end of that hallway were another pair of guards, one of them signaling to someone around the corner from him. These guards, too, came equipped with mojos. "I'll see if there is any of the Sammon family who can receive you," Jin's guard explained.

"That's really not necessary—" Jin started to say.

But it was too late. The guard in the distance was already gesturing back their way. "There is a light on in Kruin Sammon's private office," Jin's guard informed her. "The guard down there will escort you."

"That's really not necessary," Jin protested, heart loud in her ears. If this was the same Kruin Sammon who'd already been identified as patriarch of this family—"I don't want to cause unnecessary trouble."

"Kruin Sammon will wish to be informed that you need entertainment," the guard admonished gently; and Jin swallowed any further argument. The guards clearly had orders concerning her . . . and again, a sudden backing out at this stage would attract the wrong kind of attention.

"Thank you," she told him through stiff lips. Forcing herself to walk steadily, she started down the long hallway ahead toward the men and mojos waiting there . . .

Kruin Sammon leaned back into his cushions, a mixture of irritation and deep thought on his face. "How far did you go?"

"All the way down the road to Shaga, and then out to Tabris," Daulo told him. "We found absolutely nothing. No car, no bodies, no marks where a car might have bololined its way into the forest."

Kruin sighed and nodded. "So. Your conclusion?"

Daulo hesitated a second. "She's lying," he said reluctantly. "She faked the accident, perhaps deliberately inflicting her injuries on herself, in order to gain entrance to our house."

"I find no grounds to argue with you," Kruin agreed. "But it still seems so much effort for so little gain. Surely there are many simpler paths that would have gained her the same end."

Daulo pursed his lips. That was the same knot that had steadfastly refused to come apart for him, as well. "I know, my father. But who knows what convoluted scheme our enemies may have come up with? Perhaps they wish us to spend so much time trying to unravel her secrets that we fail to anticipate their main thrust."

"True. I take it, then, that you would counsel against my sending word to Azras and asking Mayor Capparis to contact the authorities in Sollas?"

"Since it seems clear enough already that she's a plant," Daulo said, "I don't see that it would gain us very much. It would merely confirm that she lied about her home, and in the meantime might alert her friends that we suspect her."

"Yes." For a moment Kruin was silent. Then, with a sigh, he shook his head. "I feel my age tugging at me, my son. In days gone by I would have relished the challenge of such a battle of wits as this. Now, all I can see before me is the danger this woman represents to my family and house."

Daulo licked his lips. Seldom in his life had he been given this kind of unobstructed view into his father's soul, and it was both embarrassing and a little unnerving. "It's the duty of a family leader to consider the well-being of his household," he said, a little stiffly.

Kruin smiled. "And as such you see your own future. Does the thought of so much responsibility frighten you?"

Daulo was saved from the need to answer such an awkward

question by a soft ping from Kruin's low desk. "Enter," the elder Sammon said into the inlaid speaker.

Daulo turned to look as the door behind him opened. Two of the guards from the women's wing entered; and sandwiched in between them—

"Jasmine Alventin," Kruin said calmly, as if her presence was no surprise at all. "You are awake late."

"Forgive me if I've overstepped the bounds of your hospitality," the woman said, matching Kruin's tone as she made the sign of respect in that odd way of hers. "I awoke and thought I would walk about until I felt ready to sleep again."

"There are few entertainments available in Milika at night, I'm afraid," Kruin told her. "Unlike, I presume, the larger cities you're accustomed to. Shall I call for food or drink for you?"

"No, thank you," she shook her head. If the reference to her claimed home city startled her, Daulo couldn't see any sign of it in her face. "I'm embarrassed enough already for disrupting your work—please don't let me be any further trouble."

Daulo finally got his tongue unstuck. "Perhaps you'd like to continue your walk out in the courtyard," he suggested. "My father and I are finished here, and I'd be honored to accompany you."

He watched her face closely, saw the brief surprise flicker across her eyes. "Why—I would also be honored," she said. "But only if it's truly no trouble for you."

"None at all," he said, getting to his feet. He'd rather expected her to make some excuse to turn him down—if she was prowling around on some nefarious errand, she'd hardly want to have the Sammon family heir along to watch. But now that he'd made the offer, he couldn't back out. "It *will* have to be a short tour, though," he added.

"That would be fine," she agreed. "I'm not especially sleepy, but I realize I'm not fully recovered yet."

Daulo turned back to his father. "With your permission . . . ?"

"Certainly," Kruin nodded. "Don't be too late; I want you to be at the mine with the first diggers in the morning."

"Yes, my father," Daulo bowed, making the sign of respect. Turning back, he caught the guards' eyes. "You may return to your posts," he told them. "Come," he added to Jasmine, gesturing toward the door. "I'll show you our courtyard. And as we walk you can tell me how our home differs from yours."

Chapter 17

Great, Jin groused at herself as they left Kruin's chambers and headed down the hall toward an ornate stairway. *Just great. A moonlight walk with the local top man's son, discussing a home town you've never been to. Terrific way to start a mission, girl.*

Though as the initial panic began to fade she realized it wasn't quite as bad as it sounded. She'd studied hundreds of satellite photos of Qasaman cities; more importantly, she'd seen all the tapes that had been made at ground level through her Uncle Joshua's extra "eyes" when he and her father were in Sollas thirty years ago. Whatever had changed since then, she at least wouldn't have to build her story up from ground level.

Though it would certainly be safer to steer the conversation away from Sollas entirely . . . and perhaps, in the process, get started on her own research.

Twisting her head as they walked, she looked back at the departing guards and forced a small shiver. "Is something wrong?" Daulo asked.

"Oh, no," she assured him, taking a deep breath. "Just . . . the mojos. They scare me a little."

Daulo glanced back himself. "Mojos are available," he said tartly. "Or would you prefer we not protect our household as best we can?"

"No, I didn't mean that," she shook her head. "I understand why you need them, this deep in the forest and all. I'm just not used to having dangerous animals that close to me."

Daulo snorted. "Those bololin herds you let trample through Sollas don't qualify as dangerous?"

"The more intelligent among us stay as far back from them as possible," she retorted.

"Which makes Mayor Capparis and his people doubly stupid, I suppose?"

Jin's mouth went a little dry. Who in blazes was Mayor Capparis? Someone she should be expected to know? "How do you mean?" she asked cautiously.

"I mean because he has a mojo *and* also participates with his people in the bololin shootings when they come through," Daulo ground out. "Or doesn't Azras even count as a city, being down here at the end of the Eastern Arm with us provincials?"

Jin began to breathe again. Azras was a name she knew: the Fertile Crescent city just southeast of here, fifty kilometers or so southwest of the mysterious roofed compound she was here to take a look at.

And with that useful tidbit of information in hand it would be wise to back off a little. "Forgive me," she said to Daulo. "I didn't mean to sound overbearing or prejudiced."

"It's all right," he muttered, sounding a bit embarrassed. They reached the bottom of the staircase and he steered her toward a large double door. "I shouldn't have reacted so strongly, either. I just get tired of the cities and their infernal harping on the mojo question. Maybe in Sollas they're more trouble and danger than they're worth, but you don't have to worry about razorarms and krisjaws there, either."

"Of course," Jin murmured. So in at least some of the cities the mojo presence had gone from practically universal to practically nonexistent over the past thirty years. How much had that trend affected the villages? "Do you mostly just take them along when you go outside, then?" she asked.

The double door leading outside, she noted, wasn't guarded like the hallways upstairs had been. Daulo pulled it open himself, giving her a somewhat odd look as he did so. "People who choose to own mojos carry them however and wherever they choose," he said. "Some only outside the walls, others at all times. Do all the people of Sollas have this same fascination for birds?"

Jin stepped out into the darkness of the courtyard, thankful that the gloom hid her blush. "Sorry—I didn't mean to bore you. I was merely curious. As I said, I haven't had much experience with them."

Daulo said nothing for a moment, and Jin took advantage of the silence to look around her. The courtyard, impressive enough when seen from an upper window, was even more so at ground level. Fruit trees, bushes, and small sculptures were visible in the dim light of small glowing globes set into a second-floor over-hang. Off to the right, she could hear what sounded like the steady splashing of water from a small fountain, and the light breeze carried with it the scents of several different kinds of flowers. "It's beautiful," she murmured, almost unconsciously.

"My great-grandfather created it when he built the house," Daulo said, and there was no mistaking the pride in his voice. "My grandfather and father have changed it somewhat, but there's still much of the ancient Qasama in it. Does your house have anything like this?"

"Our house is but one of several facing onto a common court-yard," Jin said, remembering the tapes she'd studied. "It's not as large as this one, though. Certainly not as lovely."

The words were hardly out of her mouth when a faint scream abruptly wafted through the night air.

Jin jerked, thoughts snapping back to Aventine and the forest where her team had fought against spine leopards—

"It's all right," Daulo said into her ear, and she suddenly real-ized he'd moved close to her. "Just a rogue razorarm trying to get over the wall, that's all."

"That's *all*?" Jin asked, fighting to calm her stomach. The thought of a spine leopard running loose in the sleeping village . . . "Shouldn't we do something?"

"It's all right, Jasmine Alventin," Daulo repeated. "The mesh is high enough to keep it out. It'll either eventually give up or else get its paws or quills stuck, in which case the night guardians will kill it."

The scream came again, sounding angrier this time. "Shouldn't we at least go and make sure things are under control?" she per-sisted. "I've seen what—razorarms—can do when they get crazy."

Daulo hissed between his teeth. "Oh, all right. From the sound it is in our section of town. You can wait here; I'll be back in a few minutes." Stepping away from her, he headed across the court-yard toward a long outbuilding nestled in one corner.

"Wait a minute," Jin called after him. "I want to go with you."

He threw an odd look over his shoulder. "Don't be absurd," he snorted, disappearing into the outbuilding through a side door. A few seconds passed; and then, with a gentle hum, a large door in the building's front swung up. A low-slung vehicle emerged, gliding across the drive with the utter silence only a very advanced electrical motor could provide. A second door, richly filigreed, opened to provide exit from the courtyard.

And a second later Jin was alone.

Well, that's just terrific, she fumed, glaring at the courtyard door as it swung closed again. *What does he think I am, some useless bit of—?*

Of course he does, she reminded herself with a grimace. *Severely paternalistic society, remember? You knew that coming in. So relax, girl, and try and take it easy, okay?*

Easier advice to give than to take. The whole idea of being a secondary citizen, even temporarily, rankled more than she ever would have imagined it could. But if she was going to maintain her cover, she had no choice but to stay within that character.

Or at least to not get caught stepping outside of it....

The sounds of activity were growing louder now, centering somewhere toward the west. Keying in her optical enhancers, Jin made a careful sweep of both the courtyard and the windows and doors looking out onto it. No one was visible. Trotting to the western edge of the courtyard, she did a second sweep, this time adding in her infrared sensors as well. Same result: she was alone and unobserved. Gritting her teeth, she looked at the three-story wall towering above her, made a quick estimate of its height, and jumped.

She was, if anything, a bit long on her guess, and a second later she found herself gazing down from midair at the roof of the Sammon house. Fortunately, Daulo's great-grandfather had gone in heavily for ornamental stonework when he'd built the place, and it was no effort to find hand and foot grips as her upward momentum peaked and she started the downward trip. Taking care not to make noise, she clambered up and across the slightly slanted roof to its peak. From that vantage point she could see across much of the village; and there, perhaps a kilometer away to the west, was the wall.

It looked about as she would have expected it, given the pictures brought back from Qasaman villages further north and east. The main part was a three-meter height of tough ceramic, hard and thick enough to withstand a charging bololin, with its inner surface painted to blend in with the forest just beyond it. Unlike the others she'd seen, however, this one had a bonus: an extension of some kind of metal mesh that added another two meters to its original height.

Midway up that fence, holding on with all four feet, was the spine leopard she'd heard.

Jin chewed at her lip. Below the animal, moving around in a

purposeful manner, were a handful of figures armed with large handguns. She strained, but even with optical enhancers at full magnification, she couldn't tell if Daulo was among them. *Probably not,* she assured herself. *He couldn't have gotten there that fast.*

And even as she watched, a car pulled up beside the wall and Daulo got out.

For a few seconds he and the men already there conversed. Then, two of the men set up ladders and climbed to the top of the main wall, staying well to either side of the spine leopard. Below them, Daulo and one other raised their guns in two-handed marksman's grips. Apparently they were hoping to kill the predator and grab the carcass before it fell to the ground outside.

Idiots, Jin thought, heart pounding in her ears. If stray bullets or ricochets didn't get the men up there, there was a good chance the spine leopard's death throes would. With their decentralized nervous systems spine leopards weren't easy to kill, certainly not quickly.

The multiple flashes from the guns were like sunglints off rippling water in her enhanced vision. She bit at her lip . . . and by the time the quickfire stutter of the shots reached her it was all over. Before the spine leopard had even sagged completely against the mesh the men on the wall were in front of it, hands poked through to grip the animal's forelegs. Two more men—Jin hadn't even noticed them get up on the wall—grabbed the top of the mesh and pulled themselves up and over to the spine leopard's side. Another second and they'd each taken a hind leg in one hand; hanging onto the mesh with the other hand, they heaved the carcass over the top to flop onto the ground inside the wall.

Carefully, Jin let her breath out, an odd shiver running up her back as the two men climbed the mesh again to safety. Of course these people knew what they were doing—they'd had a whole generation, after all, to figure out how to deal with the spine leopard legacy the Cobra Worlds had given them. There was little need for her to worry about the Qasamans on that account.

Which meant she could concentrate all of her worrying on herself.

Daulo was getting back into his car now. Carefully, Jin retraced her steps to the edge of the roof. With her leg servos and ceramic-coated bones there to take the impact, the fastest way down would be to simply drop straight back into the courtyard. But the noise of the impact might be loud enough for someone to hear, and after seeing that display of firepower she wasn't in the mood to risk drawing unwelcome attention. Licking her lips, she hooked her fingers into servo-strength talons and started the long climb down the stonework.

She'd decreased the distance by nearly a full story by the time her auditory enhancers picked up the hum of the outer door opening. Clenching her teeth, she let go and dropped the rest of the way to the ground. By the time Daulo came looking for her she was seated on a low bench beneath a fragrant tree, waiting for him.

"Are you all right?" she asked.

"Oh, sure," he nodded. "It was just a razorarm stuck in the wall. We got it without any trouble."

"Good," Jin told him, standing up. "Well, then, I suppose—"

She broke off abruptly as the courtyard did a mild *tilt* around her. "Are you all right?" Daulo asked sharply, stepping to her side and taking her arm.

"Sudden flash of dizziness," Jin said, swallowing hard. Even with her servos doing most of the work, her rooftop sightseeing trip had apparently taken more out of her than she'd realized. "I guess I'm not as recovered as I thought I was."

"Shall I call for a litter?"

"No, no, I'll be all right," she assured him. "Thank you very much for bringing me out here—I hope I didn't take up too much of your time."

"It was my pleasure, Jasmine Alventin. Come on, now..."

He insisted on walking her all the way back to her suite, despite her protestations that she really *was* all right. Once there, he also wanted to awaken Asya, and it took the best part of Jin's verbal skills and several minutes of whispered debate out in the hall before she convinced him that she would make it from doorway to bed without further assistance.

For a long time after his footsteps had faded down the hall she stared at the ceiling above her bed, listening to the pounding of her heart and thinking about those quickfire weapons. For a while there she'd actually started to relax in the comfort and luxury of the Sammon house...but that warm feeling was gone now. *The entire planet of Qasama is one big fat enemy camp,* Layn had told them again and again.

Now, for the first time, she really believed it.

Chapter 18

She awoke to the delicate aroma of hot food, and opened her eyes to find a truly massive breakfast set out by the window seat. "Asya?" she called, climbing out of bed and padding over to the table.

"I am here, mistress," Asya said, appearing from the other room and touching her fingertips to her forehead. "How may I serve you?"

"Are we expecting company for breakfast?" Jin asked her, indicating the size of the meal.

"It was sent up on the order of Master Daulo Sammon," Asya told her. "Perhaps he felt you were in need of extra nourishment, after your illness. May I remind you that your meal yesterday was as large as this?"

"My meal yesterday followed a five-day fast," Jin growled, staring in dismay at the spread. "How am I supposed to eat all this?"

"I am sorry if you are displeased," Asya said, moving toward the intercom. "If you'd like, I can have it removed and a smaller portion brought up."

"No, that's okay," Jin sighed. She'd been taught since childhood not to waste food, and the sinking feeling that she was about to do exactly that was sending reflexive guilt feelings rippling through her stomach. But there was nothing that could be done about it now. Sitting down, she took a deep breath and dug in.

She managed to make a considerable dent in the meal before finally calling it quits. Along the way she noticed something that hadn't registered the day before: each variety of food, whether served cold or hot, remained at its original temperature throughout the course of the meal. A classy trick; and her eventual conclusion that there were miniature heat pumps or microwave systems built into each of the serving dishes didn't detract a bit from its charm.

Charming or not, though, it was also a sobering reminder of something she still had a dangerous tendency to forget: that for all their colorful customs and cultural differences, the Qasamans were emphatically *not* a primitive society.

"What would you do next, mistress?" Asya asked when Jin finally pushed herself away from the table.

"I'd like you to choose an outfit for me," Jin told her, still uncertain as to how all the clothing in her closet went together. "Then I'd like to walk around Milika for awhile, if that would be all right."

"Of course, mistress. Master Daulo Sammon suggested that you might want to do that; he left instructions that I was to call him when you were ready to go out."

Jin swallowed. The busy heir again taking valuable time out of his schedule to play escort for a simple accident victim . . . "I would be honored," she said between stiff lips.

It turned out that Daulo was still out on some unspecified family business when Asya called for him. Jin tried suggesting that Asya escort her instead, but whoever was on the other end of the intercom politely informed her she would wait for Daulo.

The wait turned out to be nearly an hour. Jin chafed at the delay, but there was really nothing she could do about it if she was to stay in character. Finally, though, Daulo appeared, and the two of them headed out into the bustle of Milika.

The tour proved well worth the wait. Towns and villages on Aventine and the other Cobra Worlds, Jin had long ago learned, basically grew on their own, with no more attention given to design and structure than was absolutely necessary. Milika, clearly planned in detail from the ground up, was a striking contrast to that laissez-faire attitude. What was even more impressive was the fact that whoever had done the planning had actually put some intelligence into the job.

The village was basically a giant circle, some two and a half kilometers across, with five major roads radiating like spokes between an inner traffic circle and a much larger outer circular drive. Inside the Small Ring Road was a well-groomed public park called the Inner Green; circling the village between the Great Ring Road and the wall, Daulo informed her, was a larger belt of parkland called the Outer Green.

"The Greens were designed to be public lands, common meeting and recreational places for the five families who founded Milika," Daulo told her as they passed through the crowds of pedestrians on the Small Ring Road and crossed over onto the Inner Green. "Like your home in the city, most of the minor family members and workers live in group houses bordering on small common courtyards, and this allows them more space than they would otherwise have."

"A good idea," Jin nodded. "The children especially must like it."

Daulo smiled. "They do indeed. Specific play areas have been built for them—there, and over there. There are others on the Outer Green, as well." He waved around at the residential areas outside the park. "Originally, you see, each of the five wedge-shaped main sections of the village was to be the property of one family. Over the years, unfortunately, three of the founding families have become split or diluted; these three," he added, indicating the directions. "Only the Sammon family and the Yithtra family remain as sole possessors of their sections."

Jin nodded. Something bitter in his voice . . . "It sounds like you would prefer there to be only one such family," she commented without thinking.

"Would that be your choice, as well?" he countered.

She looked at him, startled by the question, to find his face had become a neutral mask. "The way your village chooses to live is hardly my business," she told him, choosing her words carefully. What kind of local politics had she stumbled into? "If it were all up to me, I would choose peace and harmony between all peoples."

He eyed her in silence another moment before turning away. "Peace isn't always possible," he said tightly. "There are always some whose primary goal is the destruction of others."

Jin licked her lips. *Don't say it, girl*, she warned herself. "Is that the Sammon family's goal?" she asked softly.

He sent her a razor-edged look. "If you believe such a thing—" He broke off, looking annoyed with himself. "No, that is *not* our goal," he ground out. "There's far too much petty conflict between us—and I, for one, am tired of wasting my energy that way. Our true enemy lies out there, Jasmine Alventin; not in the cities or across village greens." He pointed at the sky.

The true enemy: us. Me. Jin swallowed. "Yes," she murmured. "There are no real enemies here."

Daulo took a deep breath. "Come," he said, starting back across the Small Ring Road. "I'll take you to the main marketplace in our section of the village. After that, perhaps you'd like to see the Outer Green and our lake."

The marketplace was situated along one edge of the Sammon family's wedge, its placement clearly designed to get business from both its own section and the one across the spoke-road from it. It was also the most familiar thing Jin had yet found in Milika, an almost direct photocopy of the marketplaces her uncle had visited thirty years earlier. A maze of small booths where everything from food and animal pelts to building services and small electronic devices were available, the marketplace was crowded and noisy and just barely on the civilized side of pandemonium. Jin had never understood how anyone could actually shop in such a madhouse day after day without going insane; now that she was actually here, she understood it even less.

And as they made their way through the crowds she kept an eye out for mojos.

They were there, all right, silvery-blue hunting birds riding patiently on the special epaulet/perches she'd seen in the Qasaman films. Thirty years ago, virtually every adult had been accompanied by one of the birds; here and now, a quick estimate put the proportion with mojos no higher than twenty-five percent. *So in the cities the mojos have largely disappeared,* she decided, remembering her conversation with Daulo the previous night, *while in the villages they're still a major force. Is that the "mojo question" Daulo mentioned?*

And was the mojo question one of the driving forces behind the village-city hostility she kept hearing about? If Qasama's city-based leaders had finally decided that having mojos around was dangerous, it would make sense for them to press the whole planet to get rid of them.

Except that the villages couldn't do that. Whatever the long-term effects caused by mojos, it was an undeniable fact that they made uncommonly good bodyguards . . . and people out in the Qasaman forest definitely needed all the protection they could get. Jin could attest to that personally.

So what it seemed to boil down to was that the Moreau Proposal to seed Qasama with spine leopards had indeed undermined the universal cooperation the Cobra Worlds had found so frightening . . . at a price of making the world even more dangerous for its inhabitants.

There are always some whose primary goal is the destruction of all others, Daulo had said. Had the Cobra Worlds been guilty of that kind of arrogance? The thought made her stomach churn.

Someone nearby was calling for a Jasmine Alventin . . . *Oof— that's me,* she realized abruptly. "I'm sorry, Daulo Sammon—what did you say?" she asked, feeling her cheeks redden with embarrassed anger at the slip.

"I asked if there was anything you'd like to buy," Daulo repeated. "You lost everything in that car wreck, after all."

Another test? Jin wondered, feeling her pulse pick up its pace. She had no idea what a normal Qasaman woman might have been carrying into the forest on a bug-hunting expedition. *No, he's probably just being polite,* she reminded herself. *Don't get paranoid, girl . . . but don't get sloppy, either.* "No, thank you," she told him. "I had nothing of real importance except clothing; if I may take some of the clothing your family has lent me when I go, I will be sufficiently in your debt."

Daulo nodded. "Well, if something should occur to you, don't hesitate to let me know. Since you mention it, have you given any thought to when you might wish to leave?"

Jin shrugged. "I don't wish to impose on your hospitality any longer than necessary," she said. "I could leave today, if I'm becoming a burden."

Something flicked across his face. "If that's what you'd like, it can be arranged, of course," he said. "You're certainly no burden, though. And I'd counsel, moreover, that you stay until you're fully recovered from your ordeal."

"There's that," she admitted. "I'd hate to collapse somewhere between Azras and Sollas—to find assistance elsewhere as caring as the Sammon family has been would be too much to ask."

He snorted. "You've been taught the fine art of flattery, I see." Still, the statement seemed to please him.

"Not really—just the fine art of truth," she countered lightly. *Except for the grand lie I'm currently feeding you about myself.* The thought brought heat to her cheeks; quickly, she looked around for something to change the subject. Beyond the market to the northwest was an oddly shaped building. "What's that?" she asked, indicating it.

"Just the housing for the mine elevators," he told her. "It's not very attractive, I'm afraid, but my father decided it had to be replaced too often to justify proper ornamentation."

"Oh, that's right—your father mentioned a mine last night," Jin nodded. "What kind of mine is it?"

Daulo threw her a very odd look. "You don't know?"

Jin felt sweat breaking out on her forehead. "No. Should I?"

"I'd have thought that anyone planning a trip would at least have learned something about the area to be visited," he said, a bit huffily.

"My brother Mander did all the studying," she improvised. "He always took care of . . . the details." Unbidden, Mander Sun's face rose before her eyes. A face she'd never see again . . .

"You cared a great deal for your brother, didn't you?" he asked, his tone a little softer.

"Yes," she whispered, moisture blurring her vision. "I cared very much for Mander."

For a moment they stood there in silence as the bustling marketplace crowds broke like noisy surf around them. "What's past cannot be changed," Daulo said at last, reaching down to briefly squeeze her hand. "Come; let me show you our lake."

Given the overall size of Milika, Jin had envisioned the "lake" as a medium-sized duck pond sandwiched between road and houses; and it was a shock, therefore, to find a rippling body of water fully three-quarters of a kilometer long cutting across the Sammon section of Milika. "It's . . . big," she managed to say as they stood on the spoke-road bridge arching over the water.

Daulo chuckled. "It is that," he agreed. "You'll notice it goes under the Great Ring Road over there and extends a way into the Outer Green. It's the source of all the water used in Milika, not to mention the obvious recreational benefits."

"Where does the water come from?" Jin asked. "I haven't seen any rivers or creeks anywhere."

"No, it's fed by an underwater spring. Or possibly an underwater river, tributary perhaps of the Somilarai River that passes north of here. No one really knows for sure."

Jin nodded. "How important, if I may ask, is a nearby source of water to the operation of your mine?"

Looking at the lake, she could still feel his eyes on her. "Not particularly," he said. "The mining itself doesn't use any, and the refining process is purely catalytic. Why do you ask?"

She hesitated; but it was too late to back out now. "Earlier, you mentioned people who sought others' downfall," she said carefully. "Now I see that, along with the mine, your part of Milika also controls the village's water supply. Your family indeed has great power . . . and that sort of power often inspires others to envy."

She counted ten heartbeats before he spoke again. "Why are you interested in the Sammon family?" he asked. "Or in Milika, for that matter?"

It was a fair question. She'd already learned about all she really needed to about Qasama's village culture, and would at any rate be moving on within a day or two to scout out the cities. The political wranglings of a small village buried out in the forest ought to be low on her priority list. And yet . . . "I don't know," she said honestly. "Perhaps it's out of gratitude for your help; perhaps because I'm growing to feel a friendship for your family. For whatever reason, I care about you, and if there's any way I can help you I want to do so."

She wasn't sure just what reaction she was expecting—acceptance, gratitude, even suspicion. But the snort of derision that exploded behind her ear took her completely by surprise. "You help *us?*" he said scornfully. "Wonderful. A woman with no family?—just what help do you propose to give?"

Jin felt her cheeks burning. *Count to ten, girl,* she ordered herself, clamping down hard on her tongue. *You're sliding way out of character.* "I'm sorry," she said humbly through clenched teeth. "I didn't mean it that way. I just thought—well, even though my family's gone, I *do* have friends."

"*City* friends?" he asked pointedly.

"Well . . . yes."

"Uh-huh." Daulo snorted again, gently, then sighed. "Let's just forget it, Jasmine Alventin. I appreciate the gesture, but we both know that's all it is."

"I . . . suppose we do."

"All right. Come, I'll take you across to the Outer Green."

Gritting her teeth, she lowered her eyes like a good little Qasaman woman ought to and followed Daulo across the bridge.

Chapter 19

The courtyard outside Daulo's suite was dark, his late supper over and the dishes cleared away; and with the stillness and privacy came thoughts of Jasmine Alventin.

He didn't want to think about her. In fact, he'd gone to great pains to immerse himself in work over the past few hours in order to *avoid* thinking about her. He'd ended their walking tour of Milika early in the afternoon, professing concern over her weakened condition, and gone directly back to the mine to watch the work on the shoring. After that, he'd come back to the house and spent a couple of hours poring over the stacks of paperwork that the mine seemed to generate in the same volume as its waste tailings. Now, having postponed eating so that he wouldn't have to face her over a common family meal, he'd hoped the fullness of his stomach would conspire with the pace of the day to bring sleep upon him.

But it hadn't worked that way. Even while his body slumped on its cushions, numbed with food and fatigue, his mind raced ahead like a crazed bololin. With, of course, only one topic at its forefront.

Jasmine Alventin.

As a young boy the fable of the Gordian Knot had always been one of his favorites; as a young man one of his chief delights was the solving of problems that, like the Knot, had driven other men to despair. Jasmine Alventin was truly such a problem, a Gordian Knot in human guise.

Unfortunately, it was a Knot that refused to unravel.

With a sigh, he rolled off his cushions and got to his feet. He'd been putting this off for almost a day now, hoping in his pride that he could get a grip on this phantom without artificial assistance. But it wasn't working that way . . . and if there were even a slight chance that Jasmine Alventin was a danger to the Sammon family, it was his duty to do whatever was necessary to protect his household.

His private drug cabinet was built into the wall as part of his bathroom vanity, a reinforced drawer with a lock strong enough to discourage even the most persistent of children. It had been barely a year now since his acceptance into this part of adult society, and he still felt a twinge of reflex nervousness every time he opened the drawer. It would pass with time, he'd been told.

For a long moment he gazed in at the contents, considering which would be the best one to use. The four red-labeled ones— the different types of mental stimulants—drew his eye temptingly, but he left them where they were. As a general rule, the stronger the drug, the stronger the reaction afterward would be, and he had no particular desire to suffer a night of hellish dreams or to spend the coming day flat on his back with vertigo. Instead, he selected a simple self-hypnotic which would help him organize the known facts into a rational order. With luck, his own mind would be able to take it from there. If not . . . well, he would still have the mental stimulants in reserve.

Returning to his cushions, he emptied the capsule into his incense burner and lit it. The smoke rose into the air, at first thin and fragrant, then increasingly heavy and oily smelling. And as it enveloped him, he took one more try at untying the Gordian Knot that was Jasmine Alventin.

Jasmine Alventin. A mysterious young woman, survivor of an "accident" which no one had witnessed and which therefore no one could confirm. A suspiciously timed arrival at Milika, coincident with a flurry of activity by the Yithtra family's lumber business and fresh metals orders from the Mangus operation. Her speech that of a city-educated business mediator, yet her manners more befitting some ignorant outcast from polite society. And the things she said in that cultured voice—

Even with the artificial calmness of the hypnotic wrapped like a smoky cocoon around him, Daulo still gave muttered vent to his feelings about this one. *I want to go with you,* she'd said—as if going out in the dead of night to take care of a razorarm was the sort of thing women did all the time. *Let me help you—* totally laughable coming from a lone woman with neither family nor estate. It was as if she lived in her own private world. A private world with its own private rules.

And yet she couldn't be dismissed simply as that sort of feeblebrained scatterhead. Every time he'd tried to do so she'd casually done or said something that painted an exact opposite side of her. A half-dozen examples came to mind, the most obvious being her casual understanding of the consequences of having Milika's lake on Sammon family territory. Even more disturbing, she had a distinct talent for deflecting questions that she didn't want to answer . . . and a talent like that required intelligence.

So what was she? Innocent victim as she claimed? Or agent sent in by someone to cause trouble? The facts fell almost visually into neat organization in front of Daulo's eyes . . . without doing any good at all. The Knot remained tightly tied; and the only fresh conclusion he could find at all was that, totally against both his will and his common sense, he was growing to like her.

Ridiculous. He snorted, the sudden change in his steady respiration pattern bringing on a short fit of coughing. It was ridiculous—totally, completely ridiculous. Without position, she was at the very least beneath his own social status; at the very worst, she might be coldly using him to try and destroy everything he held dear.

And yet, even as he gazed mentally at the list of points against her, he had to admit there was still something about her that he found irresistible.

Just what I needed, he groused silently. *Something else about Jasmine Alventin that won't unknot.* So what could it be? Not her features or body; they were pleasant enough, but he'd seen far better without this kind of threat to his emotional equilibrium. It certainly wasn't her upbringing; she couldn't even make a simple sign of respect properly.

"Good evening, Daulo."

Startled, Daulo twisted around on his cushions, blinking through the haze to see his father walk quietly between the hanging curtain dividers. "Oh—my father," he said, starting to get up.

Kruin stopped him with a gesture. "You weren't at your customary place at evening meal tonight," he said, pulling a cushion toward his son and sinking cross-legged onto it. "I came to see if there were some trouble." He sniffed at the air. "A hypnotic, my son? I'd have thought that after a full day a sleep-inducer would be more appropriate."

Daulo looked at his father sharply, the last remnants of the hypnotic's effects evaporating from his mind. He'd hoped he could rid himself of this obsession with Jasmine Alventin before any-one else noticed. "I've been rather . . . preoccupied today," he said cautiously. "I didn't feel up to a common meal with the rest of the family."

"You may feel worse tomorrow," Kruin warned, waving a finger through one last tendril of smoke and watching it curl around in the eddy breezes thus created. "Even these mild drugs usually have unpleasant side effects." His eyes shifted back from the smoke to Daulo's face. "Jasmine Alventin asked about you."

A grimace passed across Daulo's face before he could stifle it. "I trust her recovery is proceeding properly?"

"It seems to be. She's a very unusual woman, wouldn't you say?"

Daulo sighed, quietly admitting defeat. "I don't know *what* to think about her, my father," he confessed. "All I know is that I'm . . . in danger of losing my objectivity with her." He waved at the incense burner. "I've been trying to put my thoughts in order."

"And did you?"

"I'm . . . not sure."

For a long moment Kruin was silent. "Do you know why you're living in this house, my son? Amid this luxury and prestige?"

Here it comes, Daulo thought, stomach tightening within him. *A stern reminder of where the family's wealth comes from—and the reminder that it's my duty to defend it.* "It's because you, your father, and his father before him have toiled and sweated in the mine," he said.

To his surprise, the elder Sammon shook his head. "No. The mine has made things easier, certainly, but that's not where our true power lies. It lies here—" he indicated his eyes "—and here—" he touched his forehead. "Material wealth is all very good, but no man keeps such wealth unless he can learn how to read the people around him. To know which are his friends and which his enemies . . . and to sense the moment when some of those loyalties change. Do you understand?"

Daulo swallowed. "I think so."

"Good. So, then: tell me what form this lack of objectivity takes."

Daulo waved his hands helplessly. "I don't know. She's just so . . . different. Somehow. There's a . . . perhaps it's some kind of mental strength to her, something I've never before seen in a woman."

Kruin nodded thoughtfully. "Almost as if she were a man instead of a woman?"

"Yes. That's—" Daulo broke off abruptly as a horrible thought occurred to him. "You aren't suggesting—?"

"No, no, of course not," Kruin hastened to assure him. "The doctor examined her when she was brought in, remember? No, she's a woman, all right. But perhaps not one from a normal Qasaman culture."

Daulo thought that over. It *would* go a long ways toward explaining some of the oddities he'd observed in her. "But I thought everyone on Qasama lived in the Great Arc. And besides, she claimed to be from Sollas."

"*We* don't live strictly inside the Great Arc," Kruin shrugged. "Only a short ways outside it, true, but outside nonetheless. Who's to say that others don't live even further? As to her claimed city, it's possible that she was afraid to tell us her true home. For reasons I can't guess at," he added as Daulo opened his mouth to ask.

"An interesting theory," Daulo admitted. "I'm not sure how it would stand up to Occam's Razor, however."

"Perhaps an additional bit of new information would save it from that blade," Kruin said. "I've been thinking about the accident Jasmine Alventin claimed to have been in, and it occurred to me that if it happened near Tabris someone there might have either heard the crash or found one of her companions."

"She couldn't possibly have come that far," Daulo objected. "Besides, we checked all the way along that road."

"I know," Kruin nodded. "And I trust your findings. But in such a case as this I thought extra confirmation might be a good idea, so I sent a message there this morning. Someone *did* hear a sound like a large and violent crash . . . but not near the road or village. It was far to the north, several kilometers away at the least. In deep forest."

Daulo felt his mouth go dry. Several kilometers due north of Tabris would put the accident anywhere from five to ten kilometers from the place where Perto had found her on the road. The suggestion that she might have made it from Tabris proper—a full twenty kilometers of forest road—had been ludicrous enough, but *this*—" She couldn't have survived such a trek," he said flatly. "I don't care *how* many companions she started out with, she couldn't have made it."

"I'm afraid that would be my assessment, as well," Kruin nodded reluctantly. "Especially through the heightened activity the bololin migration a few days ago probably stirred up. But even if we allow God one miracle to get her out alive, there's an even worse impossibility staring at us: that of getting a car so far into the forest in the first place."

Daulo licked his lips. This one, unfortunately, was obvious. "So it wasn't a car that crashed. It was an aircraft."

"It's beginning to look that way," Kruin agreed heavily.

Which meant she'd lied to them. Pure and simple; no conceivable misinterpretation about it. Anger and shame welled up within Daulo's stomach, the emotions fighting each other for supremacy. The Sammon family had saved her life and taken her in, and she'd repaid their hospitality by lying to them . . . and by playing *him* for a fool.

Kruin's voice cut into his private turmoil. "There are many reasons why she might lie about that," he said gently. "Not all of them having anything to do with you or our family. So my question for you, my son, is this: is she, in your judgment, an enemy of ours?"

"My judgment doesn't seem to be worth a great deal at this point," Daulo retorted, tasting bitterness.

"Do you question *my* judgment in asking for yours?" Kruin asked, his tone suddenly cold. "You will answer my question, Daulo Sammon."

Daulo swallowed hard. "Forgive me, my father—I didn't mean impertinence. It was just that—"

"Don't make excuses, Daulo Sammon. I wish an answer to my question."

"Yes, my father." Daulo took a deep breath, trying desperately to sort it all out. Facts, emotions, impressions . . . "No," he said at last. "No, I don't believe she came here for the purpose of harming us. I don't know why I think that, but I do."

"It's as I said," Kruin said, his cold manner giving way again to a gentler tone. "The Sammon family survives because we have the ability to read others' purposes. I've tried since childhood to nurture that talent in you; the future will show whether I've succeeded." Moving with grace, he got to his feet. "At the meal tonight Jasmine Alventin announced that it was her belief she'd recovered sufficiently from her injuries to return to her home. She'll be leaving tomorrow morning."

Daulo stared up at him. "She's leaving *tomorrow*? Then why all this fuss about whether or not we can trust her?"

Kruin gazed down at him. "The fuss," he said coolly, "was over whether or not it would be wise to let her out of our sight and control."

Daulo clenched his teeth. "Yes, of course. I'm sorry."

A faint smile touched Kruin's lips. "I told her we would give her transportation as far as Azras. If you'd like, you may accompany her there."

"Thank you, my father," Daulo said steadily. "It would also give me the opportunity to discuss future purchases with some of our buyers there."

"Of course," Kruin nodded, and Daulo thought he saw approval on the elder Sammon's face. "I'll leave you to your sleep, then. Goodnight, my son."

"Goodnight, my father."

And that's that, Daulo thought when he was once again alone. *Tomorrow she'll be gone, and that'll be the end of it. She'll return to whatever mysterious village she really comes from, and I'll never see her again.* There was some hurt in that; perhaps even a little bit of anger. But he had to admit his primary reaction was relief.

If a Gordian Knot couldn't be unraveled, after all, the next best thing was to send it out of sight.

Chapter 20

An hour, Daulo had thought as he and Jasmine drove off down the winding forest road toward Azras. *We'll have one more hour together, and then I'll never see her again.*

But he was wrong. They were on the road together considerably less than an hour.

"This is insane," he fumed as the gatekeepers swung the heavy north gate of Shaga village closed behind them and he let the car coast to a halt at the side of the road. "There's nothing here you can possibly want."

"How do you know?" she countered, fumbling for a moment before she was able to get the door open. "I thank you for the ride, Daulo Sammon—"

"Would you for one minute listen to me?" he snarled, getting out on his side to glare at her across the car roof. "You're a stranger in this part of Qasama, Jasmine Alventin—you've admitted that yourself. I *assure* you that Shaga is no closer to your home than Milika was."

"Sure it is—ten kilometers closer," she retorted.

It was a long time since anyone had talked to Daulo like that, and for a moment he was speechless. Jasmine took advantage of the pause to retrieve from the back seat the small shoulder bag Daulo's mother had given her. "All right, fine," Daulo managed at last as she closed the door and slipped the bag's strap over her shoulder. "So you're ten kilometers closer to Azras. What does that gain you?— especially since no one here is likely to offer you a free ride even as far as Azras? So enough of this nonsense. Get back in the car."

She gazed across the roof at him . . . and again, it wasn't the kind of look he was accustomed to receiving from a woman. "Look,

Daulo Sammon," she said in a quiet voice. "There's something I have to do—by myself—and I have to do it *here*. Please don't ask me any more. Just believe me when I tell you that the less you have to do with me, the better."

Daulo gritted his teeth. "All right, then," he bit out. "If that's how you want it. Goodbye." Feeling his face burning, he got back in the car and started off, continuing on toward the center of the village.

But only for a short way. Unlike Milika, Shaga had been haphazardly constructed, its roads curving and twisting all over the place, and Daulo hadn't gone more than a hundred meters before the woman's image in his mirror disappeared behind a turn in the road. Another hundred meters brought him to a cross road, which he took; and less than two minutes later he'd circled his way back to where he'd dropped her off.

There was no reason why she should suddenly decide to stay in Shaga; which could only mean that it was what she'd intended all along. Either she was planning to double back to Milika by unknown means—and for equally unknown purposes—or else she was meeting someone here. Whichever it turned out to be, he had every intention of keeping track of her while she did it.

But whatever her purpose, it didn't seem to involve the center of town. Even as he drove cautiously to within sight of the north gate he spotted her walking briskly away from him, paralleling the wall. He eased the car forward a bit, taking care to stay well back of her. There were few buildings in this part of Shaga, and while that meant he could keep watch on her from a reasonable distance away, it also meant he would be easier for her to spot.

But she apparently had no inkling that anyone might be watching. She never once looked over her shoulder . . . and as she continued on, Daulo noticed she was angling toward the wall.

Was she going to try and climb out? Ridiculous. It would get her out of Shaga without being seen, perhaps, but then where would she be? *Out on a forest road, that's where,* he thought sourly, *with razorarms and krisjaws all around her. And ten solid kilometers to anywhere safe.*

And yet she clearly *was* headed for the wall. Daulo gnawed at his lip, wondering if perhaps his original assessment had been right, after all. Perhaps she *was* simply a feeblebrained scatterhead.

Right by the wall, now, she paused and glanced around her. Looking for a ladder, probably. Daulo tensed, wondering if she would notice him sitting in this parked car—

And an instant later she was standing on top of the wall.

Daulo gasped. *God above!* No climbing, no running start, no leaping up to grab hold of the top with fingers—she'd simply bent her knees *and jumped.*

To the top of a wall over a meter taller than she was.

She took the anti-razorarm mesh just as casually, grabbing the top with one hand as she jumped to deflect her body into a tight-moving arc that dropped her onto her feet on the other side. An instant later she was gone.

For another five heartbeats Daulo just sat there, dumbfounded. She *was* insane, all right . . . insane, but with an athletic ability that was totally unheard of.

And she's getting away.

With a jerk, Daulo broke his paralysis and swung the car back toward the gate.

She was already out of sight by the time he was back on the road, but with forest hemming them in on both sides there were only two directions she could have gone. And since she'd already turned down a free ride on to Azras . . . Trying to keep an eye on both sides of the road at once, Daulo started back toward Milika.

For several painful minutes he wondered if he'd guessed wrong. With no more than a three-minute head start, there was simply no way she could have gotten this far ahead of him, even at the deliberately slow speed he was making. He was just wondering if he should turn around when he caught a glimpse of someone just around a curve ahead.

It took another few minutes of experimentation to find the speed that would let him get a glimpse of her every couple of minutes but yet not get him too close. It turned out she was every bit as phenomenal a runner as she was a high jumper.

Hang with her, he told himself grimly, teeth clenched with tension at this unaccustomed trick driving. *She can't keep up this kind of pace for very long. Just hang with her.*

She *did* hold the pace, though, and for considerably longer than he would have guessed possible. It was only as they passed the halfway point back to Milika that she began to slow down; and it was pure luck on his part that he happened to get a glimpse of her heading off toward the tree line paralleling the road a dozen meters to the west.

He pulled over quickly, wincing at the sounds of crunching

vegetation beneath his wheels as he eased off the road and stopped. But presumably she was making at least as much noise wading through the undergrowth of the forest. At any rate, she didn't turn around, but merely dropped her shoulder bag behind a large thaurnni bush and kept going.

Straight into the forest.

No, was his immediate thought. *She's not really going into the forest. She's cutting through a bit to throw me off her track. Or—*

But even as a part of his brain tried to think up safer alternatives he was digging under the seat for the quickfire pistol holstered there and climbing quietly out of the car. There was only one thing out there that could possibly be worth risking the razorarms and krisjaws for.

Her wrecked aircraft. The aircraft whose existence she'd taken great pains to conceal . . . and which therefore was very probably worth seeing.

Besides which—he was honest enough to admit—his pride wouldn't let him lose track of her now. Taking a deep breath, he cradled the barrel of his gun with his left hand and stepped in under the tree canopy.

Daulo had been out in the raw Qasaman forest before, of course, but never under conditions like this; and it only gradually dawned on him just how different this was. Always before he'd been part of a squad of village hunters, shielded from danger by their guns and experience. Now, however, he was alone. Worse, he was trying to follow another person without being spotted in turn, a chore that took far more concentration than he liked.

And no one knew he was here. Or would even miss him for several hours.

If he was killed, would they ever even find his body?

He fought the growing fear for nearly fifteen minutes . . . and then, all at once, something seemed to snap within him. The sounds of animals and insects buzzing and scurrying all around him mingled with the rapid thud of his heartbeat in his ears, and suddenly it didn't seem quite so important anymore that he, personally, find out what Jasmine Alventin was up to. *This is crazy,* he told himself, wiping sweat from his forehead with the back of a trembling hand. *She wants something from her aircraft?—fine. She can have it.* Whatever it was, it was no longer worth risking his life over—especially when he could have a squad of armed men waiting for her by the time she came back to retrieve her bag.

Checking one last time to make sure she wasn't looking back, he turned around—

The purring growl came from off to his left, and his heart skipped a beat as he nearly tripped over his feet spinning around to face it. A razorarm stood there, crouched ready to spring.

It was one thing to face a razorarm caught in a village wall's upper mesh; it was something else entirely to encounter one on its own home ground. Daulo didn't even realize he'd pulled the trigger until the gun abruptly jerked in his hand and a stutter of thunderclaps shattered the quiet of the forest. Dimly, through the gun's roar, he heard the razorarm's purr become a scream—saw the clawed front paws coming at him like twin missiles—

And with a flash like a lightning bolt from God, the razorarm blazed with light and flame.

It slammed into him, flooding his nostrils with the nauseating stench of seared meat and fur. He staggered back, gagging, trying to shove the dead weight off his shoulders and chest—

"Daulo—duck!"

The warning did no good. Daulo's horror-numbed muscles had no chance to react before a flash of silver-blue exploded in his face—

And to the stench was added pain.

Pain like nothing he'd ever felt before—a dozen nails jabbing and twisting and ripping through his flesh. He was aware in a distant way that he was screaming; aware that his efforts to tear his tormentor away merely made the pain worse. One eye was closed against something slapping at it; with the other he saw Jasmine running toward him, the look of an avenging angel on her face. Her hands reached out—no, he tried to scream, *don't try to tear it off*—

And then her hands seemed to flicker with light . . . and the claws digging into his face were suddenly stilled.

"Daulo!" Jasmine said tautly, her hands gently yet firmly pulling the tormentor off him. "Oh, my God—are you all right?"

"I'm—yes, I think so," he managed, struggling to regain his dignity in front of this woman. "It—what happened?"

"You tried to shoot a razorarm," she said grimly, holding his hands firmly away from the throbbing in his cheek as she examined the wounds with eyes and fingertips. "It wasn't a complete success."

"It—?" Turning away from her probing fingers, he looked down at the carcass lying limply beside him.

Its head was gone. Burned away.

"God be praised," he sighed. "That lightning bolt was . . ." He paused, an eerie feeling crawling up his back. The second attacker . . . his eyes found where Jasmine had tossed it. The razorarm's mojo, of course. Also burned.

Slowly, he looked back at Jasmine Alventin. Jasmine Alventin, the uncultured woman who'd appeared from nowhere . . . and who'd made it through raw forest alone . . . and whose hands had spat fire deadly enough to kill.

And it all finally fell together.

"God above," he groaned.

And to his everlasting shame, he fainted.

Chapter 21

Daulo wasn't unconscious for more than about ten minutes. It was still plenty of time for Jin to dress his injuries as best she could, move the spine leopard and mojo carcasses away before they could attract scavengers, and call herself every synonym for idiot that she could think of.

The worst part was the knowledge that her detractors had been right. Totally. She simply didn't have what it took to be a Cobra; not the emotional toughness, not even the ability to keep her focus on her mission. Certainly not the basic intelligence.

She looked down at Daulo for a moment, gritting her teeth hard enough to hurt. That was it, then—the mission was scrubbed. An hour after he got home half the planet would be out here looking for her. Nothing left to do now but to strike out into deep forest and wait in the vain hope that she might somehow connect up with the next team the Cobra Worlds sent. Whenever in the distant future that might be.

Not that it mattered. At this point it would be better for everyone concerned if she died here, anyway.

Daub groaned, and his hands twitched against his chest. Another minute and he'd be fully conscious, and for a moment Jin debated whether or not it would be safe for her to leave him here alone. The road wasn't more than fifteen minutes away, and his injuries wouldn't slow him down all that much. And he *did* have a gun.

Sighing, Jin stayed where she was, giving the area a quick visual sweep. There wasn't much point, after all, in shooting spine leopards and mojos off a man and then turning him loose for the forest to take another crack at.

When she looked down again, his eyes were open. Staring up at her.

For several heartbeats neither spoke. Then Daulo took a shuddering breath. "You're a demon warrior," he croaked. There was no question in his voice.

Nor anything that required a verbal answer. Jin merely nodded once and waited. Daulo's hand went to his cheek, gingerly touched the handkerchief Jin had tied there with a strip of cloth. "How . . . badly am I hurt?"

He was clearly fighting to sound and act natural. "It's not too bad," Jin assured him. "Deep gouges in places, but I don't think there's any major muscle or nerve damage. Probably hurts like blazes, though."

A ghost of a smile touched his lips for a second. "That's for sure," he admitted. "I don't suppose you'd happen to have any painkillers with you."

She shook her head. "There are some near here, though. If you feel up to a little travel we could go get them."

"Where are they?—at your wrecked spacecraft?"

Jin hissed between her teeth. So they *had* found the shuttle, after all. "You're a good actor," she said bitterly. "I would have sworn that none of you knew about the crash. No, the painkiller's in my pack, hidden near the road. Unless your people have grabbed that by now, of course."

She took his arm, preparing to lift him upright, but he stopped her. "Why?" he asked.

"Why what?" she growled. "Why am I here?"

"Why did you save my life?"

"That's a stupid question. Come on—I've got to retrieve those packs before the rest of your army starts beating the bushes for me. You at least owe me a little head start."

Again she started to lift him; again he stopped her. "You don't need a head start," he said, his voice trembling slightly. "No one else knows about you. I followed you in alone."

She stared at him. Truth? Or some kind of test?

Or a ploy to keep her in one place while they encircled her?

It doesn't really matter, she realized wearily. As long as Daulo was alive, the clock was already ticking down. "Well . . ." she said at last. "We still need to go and get you that painkiller. Come on."

She'd expected to have to support him most of the way back, and was mildly surprised that he made it the whole way under his own power. Either the physical shock to his system wasn't as bad as she'd feared or else the boneheaded male arrogance she'd already seen too much of on Qasama *did* have its useful side. They made it back to the road in just over fifteen minutes . . . and there was indeed no army waiting for them.

"So," Daulo said with elaborate casualness after she'd treated his cuts with a disinfectant/analgesic spray and replaced the handkerchief with a proper heal-quick bandage. "I suppose the next question is where we go from here."

"I don't see much of a question," Jin growled. "I'd guess you're going back to Milika to sound the alarm, and I'm going to start running."

He stared silently at her . . . and, oddly enough, behind the tight mask she could see there was a genuine battle of emotions underway. "I see you don't know very much about Qasama, Demon Warrior," he said after a moment.

It was a second before she realized he expected a response. "No, not really," she told him. "Not much more than I learned from you over the past couple of days. That's one of the reasons we came, to find out more."

He licked his lips. "We put a high premium on honor here, Demon Warrior. Honor and the repayment of debts."

And she'd just saved his life . . . Slowly, it dawned on Jin that it might not yet be over. "I see your dilemma," she nodded. "Would it help to tell you I'm not here to make war on Qasama?"

"It might—if I could believe you." He took a deep breath. "Is your spacecraft really wrecked?"

Jin shivered at the memory. "Totally."

"Why were you going back there, then?"

And there was no longer any way out of it. She was going to have to admit, in public, just what an emotional idiot she was being. "I had to leave the wreck in a hurry," she said, the words tearing at her gut. "I thought it would be found right away, and that there would be a manhunt started—" She broke off, blinking angrily at a tear that had appeared in one eye. "Anyway, I left . . . but it seemed to me that if you'd found it the authorities would certainly have checked all nearby villages for strangers. Wouldn't they?"

Daulo nodded silently.

"Well, don't you see?" she snapped suddenly. "You *haven't* found it . . . and I ran off and left my friends there. I can't just . . . I have to—"

"I understand," Daulo said softly, getting to his feet. "Come. We'll go together to bury them."

It took them only a few minutes to get the car off the road and into concealment behind a pair of trees. Then, together, they headed back into the forest.

"How far will we need to go, Demon Warrior?" Daulo asked, peering up at the leafy canopy overhead and trying not to feel like he'd just made a bad mistake.

"Five or six kilometers, I think," the woman told him. "We should be able to get through it a lot faster than I did the first time. Thanks to your people's medical skill."

"It's the kind of skill that comes from living on a hostile world," he ground out. "Of course, it's been considerably more hostile lately—say, in the past twenty or thirty years?"

She didn't answer. "Did you hear me, Demon Warrior?" he demanded. "I said—"

"Stop calling me that," she snapped. "You know my name—use it."

"Do I?" he countered. "Know your name, I mean?"

She sighed. "No, not really. My name is Jasmine Moreau, of the world Aventine. You can also call me Jin."

"Djinn?" he said, startled. All the childhood scare-stories of djinns came flooding back in a rush . . . "Given to you when you became a demon warrior, I assume?"

She glanced a frown over at him. "No. Why?—oh, I see. Huh. You know, I never noticed that before. No, it has nothing to do with the djinns of folklore—it's just pronounced the same. It's a name my father gave me when I was very young."

"Um. Well, then, Jin Moreau, I'd still like an answer to my question—"

"Freeze!"

For a single, awful second he thought he'd pushed her too far and that she'd decided to kill him after all. She dropped onto her side, left leg hooking up beneath her skirt—

There was a brilliant thunderbolt flash, and a smoking krisjaw slammed into the dead leaves.

"You okay?" she asked, rolling to her feet and peering around them.

Daulo found his tongue. "Yes. That's . . . quite a weapon," he managed, blinking at the purple afterimage.

"It comes in handy sometimes. Let's get moving—and if I yell, you hit the ground fast, understand? If there are as many animals out here today as there were my first time through it could be a busy trip."

"There shouldn't be," he shook his head. "You came in right after a major bololin herd went through, and that always stirs up lots of animal activity."

It pleased him to see that that knowledge was completely new to her. "Well, that's a relief. In that case it should only take us a couple of hours to get to the shuttle."

"Good," he nodded. "And maybe to pass the time you could explain to me just why your world declared war on ours."

Watching her out of the corner of his eye, he saw her grimace. "We didn't declare war on you," she said quietly. "We were told by others that Qasama was a potential threat. We came to see if that was true."

"What threat?" he scoffed. "A world without even primitive spaceflight capability? How could we possibly be a threat to a world light-years away?—especially one protected by demon warriors?"

She was silent for a moment. "You won't remember it, Daulo, but for much of Qasama's history all of you lived together in a state of extreme noncompetition."

"I know that," he growled. "We aren't ignorant savages who don't keep records, you know."

She actually blushed. "I know. Sorry. Anyway, it seemed odd to us that a human society could be so—well, so cooperative. We tried to find a reason—"

"And while you were looking you became jealous?" Daulo bit out. "Is that it? You envied us the society we'd created, and so you sent these razorarm killing machines in to kill and destroy—"

"Did you know that mojos can control the actions of their owners?"

He stopped in mid-sentence. "What?"

She sighed. "They affect the way their owners think. Cause them to make decisions that benefit the mojo first and the owner only second."

Daulo opened his mouth, closed it again. "That's absurd," he said at last. "They're bodyguards, that's all."

"Really? Does your father have a mojo? I never saw him with one."

"No—"

"How about the head of the Yithtra family? Or any of the major leaders of Milika or Azras."

"Cities like Azras have hardly any mojos at all," he said mechanically, brain spinning. No; it had to be a lie. A lie spun by Aventine's rulers to justify what they'd done to Qasama.

And yet . . . he had to admit that he *had* always sensed a difference in the few mojo owners he knew well. A sort of . . . placidity, perhaps. "It doesn't make sense, though," he said at last.

"Sure it does," she said. "Out in the wild mojos pair up with krisjaws for hunting purposes—hunting and, for the mojos, access to embryo hosts."

"Yes, I know about the native reproduction cycle," Daulo said hastily, obscurely embarrassed at discussing such things with a woman. "That's why cities were designed to let bololin herds charge on through, so that the mojos there could get to the tarbines riding the bololins."

"Right," she nodded. "You could have walled the cities like you did the villages, you know, and kept the bololins out completely. It would have saved a lot of grief all around . . . except that it was in the mojo's best interest to keep the bololins nearby, so that's how you built them. And because they didn't want to risk their own feathers with any more bodyguarding than they could get away with, they made sure you cooperated with each other in every facet of life."

"And so we had no warfare, and no village-city rivalry," Daulo growled. He understood, now . . . and the cold-bloodedness of Aventine's scheme turned his stomach. "So you decided to interfere . . . and with krisjaws all but gone from the Great Arc, you had to give the mojos somewhere else to go. So you gave them razorarms."

"Daulo—"

"Have you seen enough of what Qasama has become since then?" he cut her off harshly. "Okay, fine—so perhaps we used to bend our own lives a little to accommodate other creatures. Was that too high a price to pay for peace?"

"Was it?" she countered softly.

The obvious answer came to his lips . . . and faded away unsaid. If what she said was the truth, *had* it really been worth the price? "I don't know," he said at last.

"Neither do I," she whispered.

Chapter 22

They made the trip in just under two hours . . . and for Jin, the whole thing was in sharp contrast with the ordeal a week earlier.

There was no way to tell, of course, how much of the difference was due to the abatement of the bololin coattail effect Daulo had described and how much was due to her own recovery. Certainly there was less fighting; only one other predator besides the krisjaw tried its luck with them, compared with the half-dozen single and multiple attacks she'd had to fight off on her last trip through. On the other hand, with her alertness and concentration again at full capability, it could have been simply that she was spotting potential trouble early enough for evasive methods to be effective.

Ultimately, though, the real reason didn't matter. She'd brought both herself *and* an untrained civilian safely through some of the most dangerous territory Qasama had to offer . . . and it brought a welcome measure of self-confidence back to her bruised ego.

"Here we are," she said, gesturing to the battered hulk of the shuttle as they finally cleared the edge of the interweaving-fern patch and stepped out from the trees into view of the crash site.

Daulo muttered something under his breath, gazing first at the shuttle and then at the long death-scar it had torn into the landscape. "I was never truly sure . . ." His voice trailed off into silence, and he shook his head. "And you *survived* this?"

"I was lucky," she said quietly.

"God was with you," he corrected. He took a deep breath. "Forgive me for doubting your story. Your companions . . . ?"

Jin gritted her teeth. "Inside. This way."

The hatch door was as she'd left it, stuck a couple of

centimeters open, and she had to put one foot against the hull to get the necessary leverage to pull it open. *At least,* she thought grimly, *that means none of the larger scavengers have gotten to them. Grateful for small favors, I suppose.* Taking one last clean breath, she braced herself and stepped inside.

The smell wasn't quite as bad as she'd feared it would be. The bodies themselves looked perhaps a bit worse.

"The door wouldn't have kept out insects," Daulo commented from right behind her. His voice sounded only slightly less strained than she felt, and it was clear he was breathing through his mouth. "Are there any shovels on board?"

"There's supposed to be at least one. Let's try back here."

They found it almost at once, in with the emergency shelter equipment. It was sturdy but small, clearly designed for only minor entrenchment work. But Jin had had no intention of digging very deeply anyway, and the extra strength her Cobra servos provided more than made up for the awkwardness of the short handle. Half an hour later, the five graves near the edge of the crash site were ready.

Daulo was waiting for her near the shuttle, and she found that while she'd been digging he'd improvised a stretcher from some piping and seat cushions and had hacked loose five of the expended crashbags to use as body bags. *They might as well be useful for something,* she thought bitterly at the thick plastic as she and Daulo worked the bodies into them. *They sure didn't do much good while we were all alive.*

And a few minutes later she and Daulo stood side by side in front of the graves. "I . . . don't really know a proper burial service," Jin confessed, partly to Daulo, partly to the bodies in their graves before her. "But if its purpose is to remember and mourn . . . that much I can do."

She didn't remember afterward just what she said or how long she spoke; only that her cheeks were wet when she was finished. A quiet goodbye to each in turn; and she was picking up the shovel when Daulo touched her arm. "They were your friends, not mine," he said in a quiet voice. "But if you will permit me . . . ?"

She nodded, and he took a step forward. "In the name of God, the compassionate, the merciful . . ."

He spoke only a few minutes; and yet, in that short time Jin found herself touched deeply. Though the phrasing of the words showed them to be a standard recitation, there was at the same time something in Daulo's delivery that struck her as being intensely personal. Whatever his feelings toward Jin or the Cobra Worlds generally, he clearly felt no animosity toward her dead teammates.

" . . . We belong to God, and to Him we return. May your souls find peace."

The litany came to an end, and for a moment they stood together in silence. "Thank you," Jin said softly.

"The dead are enemies of no one," he replied. "Only God can approve or condemn their actions now." He took a deep breath, threw Jin a hesitant glance. "One of them—you called him Mander?"

"Mander Sun, yes," she nodded. "One of my fellow . . . demon warriors."

"Was he truly your brother, as you named him in the story you told my family?"

Jin licked her lips. "In all except blood he was truly my brother. Perhaps the only one I will ever have."

"I understand." Daulo looked back at the graves, then glanced up at the sun. "We'd best be leaving soon. I'll be missed eventually, and if a search finds my car it'll probably find your packs, too."

Jin nodded and again picked up the shovel.

Filling in the graves took only a few more minutes, and when she was done she took the shovel back to the shuttle. "No point in letting it lie around out here and rust," she commented.

"No."

Something in his voice made her turn and look at him. "Something?"

He was frowning at the blast damage in the shuttle's side. "You're certain it couldn't have been an internal malfunction that made this?"

"Reasonably certain," she nodded. "Why?"

"When you expressed your surprise earlier that it hadn't been discovered, I assumed the crash had somehow concealed it. But *this*—" he waved at the shattered trees "—couldn't possibly be missed by any aircraft looking for it."

"I agree. It's *your* world—any ideas why no one's shown up yet?"

He shook his head slowly. "This area is well off normal air routes, which would explain why it hasn't been found by accident. But I don't understand why our defense forces wouldn't follow up on a successful hit."

Jin took a deep breath. She'd wondered long and hard about

that same question . . . and had come up with only one reasonable answer. "Unless it wasn't your defense forces that did it in the first place."

Daulo frowned at her. "Who else *could* it have been?"

"I don't know. But there've been some odd things happening here, Daulo. That's why we came, looking for some answers."

"And to change any of them you didn't like?" he said pointedly.

She felt her face warming. "I don't know. I hope not."

He stared at her for several seconds more. "I think," he said at last, "that the rest of this conversation ought to wait until my father can be included."

Jin's mouth went dry. "Wait a minute, Daulo—"

"You have a choice of three paths before you now, Jasmine Moreau." Daulo's face had again become an emotionless mask, his voice hard and almost cold. "You can come with me and accept the decision of my family as to what we should do with you. Or you can refuse to confess your true identity and purpose before my father and leave right now, in which case the alarm will be out all over Qasama by nightfall."

"Assuming you can make it back through the forest alone," Jin pointed out softly.

"Assuming that, yes." A muscle in Daulo's cheek twitched, but otherwise his face didn't change. "Which is of course your third choice: to allow the forest to kill me. Or even to do that job yourself."

Jin let her breath out in a hiss of defeat. "If your father elects to turn me over to the authorities, I won't go passively," she told him. "And if I'm forced to fight, many people will be hurt or killed. Given that, do you still want me to come back to your household?"

"Yes," he said promptly.

And at that, Jin realized, the choice was indeed clear. She could take it or leave it. "All right," she sighed. "Let's get going."

Chapter 23

"My son knew from the beginning that you were different," Kruin Sammon said, staring unblinkingly at Jin as he fingered an emergency ration stick from her pack, spread open on the low table beside him. "I see he erred only in degree."

Jin forced herself to meet the elder Sammon's gaze. There was no point now in continuing to pretend she was a good little submissive Qasaman woman. Her only chance was to persuade them that she was an equal, one with whom bargains could be struck.

Persuading them to make any such bargains, of course, would be something else entirely.

"I'm sorry it was necessary to lie to you," she told him. "You have to realize that at the time I was helpless and feared for my life."

"A demon warrior, helpless?" Kruin snorted. "The history of your attacks on Qasama doesn't mention such failings."

"I've explained our side of all that—"

"Yes—your side," Kruin cut her off harshly. "You hear from these—these—"

"Trofts," Daulo supplied quietly from his place beside his father's cushions.

"Thank you. You hear from these Troft monsters—who also visited us professing peace, I'll point out—you hear from them that we're dangerous, and without even considering the possibility that they may be wrong you prepare to make war on us. And don't claim it was the fault of others—if my son hasn't yet recognized your name, I do."

"Her name?" Daulo frowned.

Jin licked her lips. "My father's name is Justin Moreau," she said evenly. "His brother's name is Joshua."

Daulo's face went a little pale. "The demon warrior and his shadow," he whispered.

So the ghost stories about her father and uncle hadn't faded with time. Jin fought back a grimace. "You have to understand, Kruin Sammon, that in our judgment the mojos were as much a threat to your people as they were to ours. We were considering your welfare, too, when we made our decision."

"Your kindness has clearly gone unrewarded," Kruin growled, heavily sarcastic. "Perhaps the Shahni will offer you some honor for your actions."

"The option was full warfare," Jin told him quietly. "And don't scoff—there were those who thought that would be necessary. Many among us were terrified of what a planet of people under mojo control could do to us when they escaped the confines of this one world. Do your histories record that it was *your* people who threatened to come out someday and destroy us?"

"And *this* is your justification for such a devastating preemptive strike?" Kruin demanded. "A threat made in the heat of self-defense?"

"I'm justifying nothing," Jin said. "I'm trying to show that we didn't act out of hatred or animosity."

"Perhaps we'd have preferred a more heated emotion to such icy calculation," Kruin retorted. "To send animal predators to fight us instead of doing the job yourselves—"

"But don't you see?" Jin pleaded. "The whole razorarm approach was the only one that would get the mojos away from you without causing any truly permanent damage to your safety and well-being."

"Permanent damage?" Daulo cut in. "What do you think the extra mesh above the wall is for—?"

Kruin stopped him with a gesture. "Explain."

Jin took a deep breath. "Once the majority of razorarms are accompanied by mojos, most of their attacks on people should stop."

"Why?" Kruin snorted. "Because the mojos have fond memories of us?"

"No," Jin shook her head. "Because you can kill the razorarms."

A frown creased Kruin's forehead. "That makes no sense. We can't possibly destroy enough of them to make a difference."

"We don't have to," Daulo said, his voice abruptly thoughtful. "If Jasmine Moreau is right about the mojos, simply having the capability to kill them will be enough."

Kruin cocked an eyebrow at his son. "Explain, Daulo Sammon."

Daulo's eyes were on Jin. "The mojos are intelligent enough to understand the power of our weapons; is that correct?" She nodded, and he turned to face his father. "So then the mojos have a strong interest in making sure there's as little fighting as possible between us and their razorarms."

"And what of the one in the forest this morning?" Kruin scoffed. "It had a mojo, and yet attacked you."

Daulo shook his head. "I've been thinking about that, my father. It didn't attack until I first fired on it."

"Speculation," Kruin shook his head. But the frown remained on his face.

"Remember your history," Jin urged him. "Your own people told us that the krisjaws, too, were once relatively harmless to the Qasaman people. It was only after the mojos began deserting them for you that they became so dangerous."

Kruin's gaze drifted to the offworld supplies and equipment spread out on his table. "You said the Shahni were aware of the mojos' effect on us. Why then would they have risked their internal harmony by purging the cities of their mojos?"

Jin shook her head. "I don't know. Perhaps the mojos simply deserted the cities more quickly once an alternative came along."

"Or perhaps the cities realized that the main conflict would be not with their own citizens but with those of us in the villages," Daulo muttered.

"Perhaps." Kruin looked hard at Jin. "But whatever the reasons or motivations, what ultimately matters is that the people of Aventine interfered with our society. And in doing so brought hardship and death upon us."

Jin looked him straight in the eye, trying to shake off the feeling that she personally was on trial here. "What matters," she corrected quietly, "is that you were slaves. Would you rather we have left you as you were, less than truly human?"

"It's always possible to claim love as a motive for one's actions," Kruin said, a bitter smile on his face. "Tell me, Jasmine Moreau: if our positions were reversed, would you honestly thank us for doing to you what you have done to us?"

Jin bit at her lip. It would be so easy to lie . . . and so pointless. "At the place in your history where you now live . . . no. I can only hope that future generations will recognize that what we did truly *had* to be done. And will accept that our motives were honorable even if they can't honestly thank us."

Kruin sighed and fell silent, his eyes drifting away from her and to his table. Jin glanced at Daulo, then turned to look out the window. The afternoon shadows were starting to stretch across Milika, and in a short while it would be time for the evening meal.

A perfect time to drug or poison her if they decided she was too dangerous to bargain with . . .

"What is it you want from us?" Kruin cut abruptly into her thoughts.

Jin turned her attention back to him, bracing herself. The question was an inevitable one, and she'd put a great deal of thought into considering just how much she should tell them. But each time she'd turned the problem over in her mind she'd come to the same conclusion: complete honesty was the only way. Whatever trust they had in her now—and she didn't flatter herself that it was much—would evaporate instantly if they ever caught her in another lie. And without their trust she had no chance at all of completing her mission. Or even of staying alive. "First of all," she said, "I have to tell you that for the past thirty years we've been keeping tabs on you through spy satellites orbiting your world."

She braced herself for an explosion, but Kruin merely nodded. "That's hardly a secret. Everyone on Qasama has seen them—dim specks moving across the night sky. It's said that a favorite topic of conversation when the Shahni meet is how we might go about destroying them."

"I can't blame them," Jin admitted. "Well, anyway, it seems that someone's finally come up with a way to do it."

Kruin cocked an eyebrow. "Interesting. I take it you came here to stop that person?"

Jin shook her had. "Actually, no. Our group came to gather information, and that alone. It's not quite as simple as it sounds, you see: the satellites aren't being physically destroyed, just temporarily disabled . . . and we're so far unable to figure out how it's being done."

She described as best she could the gaps that had been made in the satellites' records. "What eventually tipped them off was the discovery that there was a definite pattern in the blank regions. Most of them fell over that roofed complex northeast of Azras."

"You must mean Mangus?" Daulo said.

"Is that what it's called?" Jin frowned. The word sounded vaguely familiar . . . "Is Mangus someone's name?"

Daulo shook his head. "It's the ancient root of the word *mongoose*. I don't know why they call the place that."

Jin felt her mouth go dry. *Mongoose.* A legendary Old Earth animal . . . whose fame lay in their ability to kill cobras. *I could probably tell you,* she thought morosely, *why they named it that.* "Any idea what exactly they're doing in there?"

Kruin's eyes were hard on her face; but, surprisingly, he didn't ask about whatever it was he saw there. "Electronics research and manufacture," he said. "Quite a lot of it, apparently, judging by the quantities of refined metals they buy from us."

"Quantities that seem excessive for that kind of electronics manufacture?" Jin asked.

"How much metal would be excessive?" Kruin countered. "I'd need to know their output before making any comparison."

"Well, what exactly do they make? Do you have any examples here?"

Kruin shook his head. "Their goods go mainly to the cities."

Or at least that's what they tell the villages, anyway, Jin thought. "Any way to check on what their output actually is?"

Kruin and Daulo eyed each other. "We could probably get the appropriate figures for Azras," Kruin told her. "For the other cities . . . unlikely. It might help if we knew what it is you're looking for."

Jin took a deep breath. "The analysis group on Aventine seemed to think Mangus might be a site for missile testing."

Kruin's face went suddenly hard. "Missile testing? What kind of missiles?"

Jin held out her hands, palm upward. "That's one of the things I have to find out. But I can only think of two uses for missiles: as vehicles for space travel . . . or as weapons."

For a long moment Kruin stared at her in silence. "So if it's the first, you'll report that we're again a threat to you?" he said abruptly, his voice harsh. "And the demon warriors will come here again and destroy Mangus as a warning? Whereas if it's merely the cities planning blackmail or open warfare on the villages, you'll all smile and leave us alone?"

Jin met his gaze without flinching. "If all we wanted was to destroy you, we could do it in a hundred different ways. That's not a threat, that's simple reality. You came originally from the Dominion of Man—you must have some memories of the horrible weapons a technological world can create."

Kruin grimaced. "We do," he admitted. "It was one of the reasons our ancestors left."

"All right, then. We aren't going to try and destroy you—whether you believe that or not, it's true. It's also true that we have absolutely no interest in fighting an unnecessary war with you. We don't have the time or money or lives to waste on one, for starters. If Qasama is developing space flight . . . well, we ought to be able to live with that. *If*, that is, we can be reasonably certain that the whole planet isn't going to rise, en masse, and attack us."

Daulo hissed derisively. "Who on Qasama would be foolish enough to lead such a suicidal attack? And who would be foolish enough to follow them?"

Jin shook her head. "I don't know. That's another of the things I have to find out."

"And if Mangus is building missiles for internecine war?" Kruin persisted. "Will your people, having revived in us this ability to destroy, simply turn their backs on us?"

Jin clenched her teeth. Again there was no point in lying. "It's possible. I hope not, but our leaders *could* decide that way. Bear in mind, though, that with my companions dead I *am* this mission. If my report states that you're not a threat, and that we stand more to gain by establishing political and trade relations with your culture than by letting that culture destroy itself . . ." She shrugged. "Who knows what they'll do? And with my uncle on the Directorate, my voice will at least have a chance to be heard."

"This is your uncle who barely escaped from Qasama with his life?" Kruin reminded her pointedly.

She shook her head. "Different uncle. His brother, Corwin Moreau, is a governor on Aventine."

Kruin frowned. "Your family has such status and power in your world?"

A shiver ran up Jin's back. Her father under house arrest; Uncle Corwin's political power balanced precariously across her own shoulders . . . "For the moment, at least, it does," she sighed. "There are forces trying to change that."

"With the decision dependent on the report you bring back?" Kruin asked.

"More on how I personally do on the mission." Jin shook her head. "But never mind that. I've told you why I'm here, answered all your questions as well as I could. I need to know—now— whether you're going to allow me to complete my mission."

Kruin pursed his lips. "Keeping your identity within our family would be highly dangerous—I'm sure you realize that. If you were discovered by some other means the repercussions would be disastrous. What do you offer in exchange for this risk on our part?"

"What do you suggest?" Jin asked, trying to keep her voice steady. *I did it,* she thought, not quite sure she believed it. *He's actually bargaining with me.*

Now if only he wanted something she could deliver.

"As you're now well aware," Kruin said, "your plan to split our society into conflicting factions has succeeded only too well. Whatever Mangus turns out to be, you also know that there's already a certain amount of trouble between the cities as a group and the villages as a group. Besides the mojo question, the tension is fueled by the fact that heavy industry is concentrated in the cities, while control of resources lies mainly with the villages."

Jin nodded. It was a classical enough situation, probably played out hundreds of times throughout mankind's early days. Fleetingly, she wished she knew how those various Old Earth cultures had handled it. "I hope you don't want me to try and defuse the situation—"

"Grant me more intelligence than that," Kruin cut her off coldly. "This is *our* world—*our* politics, *our* culture, *our* people—and any advice you as an outlander could give would be less than useless."

Jin swallowed. "Excuse me. Please continue."

Kruin glared at her a moment before continuing. "We're already preparing to stand together against attempts to dominate us—the village leaders in this part of Qasama meet periodically to discuss the situation and coordinate any activities that seem called for. But there are some who see turmoil as a chance for advancement . . . and if there is indeed turmoil in Qasama's immediate future, I want the Sammon family able to face it without such dangerous distractions at our backs."

Jin grimaced. "Distractions such as the Yithtra family across the Inner Green?"

"I see Daulo has told you of them," Kruin growled. "Then you'll understand that their obsession with dragging us down is something that must be dealt with. Now would seem to be a good time to do so."

"Are you asking me to murder one or more of them?" Jin asked quietly. "Because if you are, I'll tell you right now that I can't do that."

"You're a warrior, aren't you?" Daulo put in.

"Killing in warfare isn't the same as murder," she countered.

"I don't ask you to murder," Kruin shook his head. "I ask merely that you find a way to diminish the Yithtra family's influence in this village. That's the bargain I offer you, Jasmine Moreau:

destruction of the Yithtra family's power in exchange for sanctuary in our household."

Jin licked her lips. It ought to be possible, surely, though at the moment she didn't have the vaguest idea how she would pull off such a trick. *But then what happens?* she wondered. *What would that kind of power loss mean in this culture?—loss of homes, maybe, the whole family even turned out of the village? Could it even lead directly to wholesale death, either suicide or murder?*

The moral implications were bad enough . . . but the possible political ramifications were even worse. It would set a clear precedent of Cobra-World meddling in Qasaman affairs, with all that that would mean from both sides' perspectives. The Directorate would probably welcome the idea of rewarding cooperative Qasamans; but from the Qasaman side, Kruin's bargain smacked of high treason. Could she ethically allow herself to be a part of such a thing?

Or did she really have any choice? "I offer you a counter proposal," she said at last. "I won't destroy the Yithtra family's power directly; but I will so enhance your own prestige and standing that they won't dare oppose you."

Kruin gazed at her, his eyes measuring. "And how do you propose to do that?" he asked.

"I don't know," she confessed. "But I'll find a way."

For a long minute the room was silent. Then, taking a deep breath, Kruin nodded gravely. "The bargain is sealed. You, Jasmine Moreau, are now under the protection of my family. Our household is yours; we shield you with our lives."

Jin swallowed. "Thank you, Kruin Sammon. I will betray neither your hospitality nor our bargain."

Kruin nodded again and rose from his cushions, Daulo following suit. "Tomorrow representatives from Mangus will be arriving at Milika to receive a shipment of our metals. You may wish to begin your investigation by observing them."

"I will do so," Jin said.

"And now—" Kruin leaned back down to his desk and touched a button "—it's time for the evening meal. Come, let us join the others."

Jin kept her expression neutral. Drugs or poison at the evening meal . . . "Yes," she agreed. "Let us."

Chapter 24

The insistent warble of his bedside phone snapped Corwin wide awake. *Must be some trouble,* was his first thought, focusing with an effort on his clock. But it wasn't the middle of the night, after all; it was only a little after six and almost time to get up anyway. *Probably just Thena with some latebreaking appointment change or something,* he decided, reaching to the phone and jabbing the instrument on. "Hello?"

But it wasn't Thena's face that appeared on the screen. It was Governor-General Chandler's ... and it was as grim as Corwin had ever seen the man. "You'd better get over to the starfield right away," he said without preamble. "The *Southern Cross*'ll be landing in about fifteen minutes, and you'll want to see what they've got."

"The *Southern Cross?*" Corwin frowned, a knot starting to form in his stomach. "What's gone wrong?"

"Everything," Chandler snarled. "Just get down here."

Corwin gritted his teeth. "Yes, sir."

The phone screen went black. "Damn," Corwin muttered under his breath. Swinging his legs out of bed, he grabbed his clothes and started pulling them on. There was only one conceivable reason why the *Southern Cross* would be back so soon: the Qasaman mission had met with some kind of disaster.

He paused, half dressed, heart pounding in his throat. A disaster. An emergency, perhaps, requiring swift action ... and long experience had showed him that committees and councils weren't built for speed.

Most jobs are done, the old couplet came back to him, *by committees of one.*

Gritting his teeth, he reached back to the phone and punched a number.

He arrived at the starfield twenty minutes later to find that Chandler had sealed off one of the conference rooms in the entrypoint building. Two other Directorate members—Telek and Priesly—had arrived before him . . . and one look at their faces told him that the situation was even worse than he'd feared.

He was right.

Captain Koja's report was short, partly because there wasn't much to say and partly because the enhanced telephoto on the wall display behind him said it all anyway. "We elected not to wait and see if he found the survival pod," the captain concluded, "under the assumption that we could serve him better by getting back and sounding the alarm." He looked at Chandler. "That's really all I have, sir. Do you have any questions?"

Chandler asked something and was answered, but Corwin didn't really hear any of it. A horrible shimmer of unreality seemed to have fallen between him and the rest of the room. Between him and the rest of the universe. That last image of Jin as she'd waved to them from the *Southern Cross*'s entryway hovered ghost-like in front of his face . . . in front of the computer-enhanced image of the shuttle's death still displayed on the conference-room wall. *I sent her there*, the thought swirled like a bitterly cold tornado through his mind. *I pushed it through. I forced them to make her a Cobra. And then I sent her off to Qasama . . . all in the name of thwarting political enemies.*

In the name of politics.

Someone was calling his name. He looked over to see Chandler eyeing him. "Yes?"

"I asked if you had any comments or suggestions," the governor-general repeated evenly.

For a moment Corwin locked eyes with him. Chandler returned the gaze steadily, without so much as flinching. It was the statesman look that Corwin had seen on him so often . . . and always hated. It inevitably appeared at those times when Chandler wanted to appear above politics, or to disclaim all responsibility for something he'd had a hand in. *So that's how it's going to be here, too, is it?* Corwin thought silently toward that look. *Not going to accept any more responsibility than you absolutely have to? Well, we'll just see about that.*

But first there was a question he had to ask. Shifting his eyes to Koja, he took a deep breath. "Captain, is there . . . ?" He licked his lips and tried again. "Is there any indication as to . . . which of the Cobras might have survived?"

A muscle in Koja's cheek twitched. "I'm sorry, Governor, but there isn't," he said, almost gently. "We've gone over the data a hundred times in the past eight days. There just isn't any way to tell."

Corwin nodded, feeling the others' eyes on him. "Then it *could* be Jin who's still alive down there, couldn't it?"

Koja shrugged fractionally. "It could be her, yes. Could be *all* the Cobras, for all we can tell."

No false hope, Corwin warned himself. But the admonition wasn't serious, and he knew it. Without hope, he could already feel his mind turning inward again, away from the wave of guilt threatening to overwhelm him. But *with* hope . . . that same wave could be turned outward. Turned outward to claim vengeance for what had happened to his niece. Alive or dead, he owed her that much. "For the moment," he said, looking back at Chandler, "we can skip over any recriminations as to why the *Southern Cross* wasn't carrying any emergency equipment for just such a disaster as this. Right now our first priority is to get a rescue team together and out to Qasama as quickly as possible. What steps have you taken toward that end?"

"I've spoken to Coordinator Maung Kha," Chandler replied. "The Academy directors are going to assemble a list for us."

"Which will be ready when?" Corwin asked.

Priesly shifted in his seat. "You want it fast or you want it good?" he asked Corwin.

"We want it both," Telek snapped before Corwin could respond.

"I'm sure you do, Governor—" Priesly began.

"Mr. Chandler," Telek cut him off, "do I assume I've been included in this council of war because of my first-hand expertise on Qasaman matters? Fine. Then kindly pay attention to that expertise when I tell you that Moreau's right. If you want your Cobra back alive, minutes could literally count. The Qasamans are fast and smart, and once they make their move they don't leave a whole hell of a lot of room to maneuver in."

"I understand," Chandler said with clearly forced patience. "But as Governor Priesly points out, to do the job properly takes a certain amount of time."

"That depends on how far into complicated channels you insist on dragging the process," Corwin told him.

"Channels exist for a reason," Priesly growled. "The Academy has the computers and lists you'd need to find the best people for the job. Unless you'd rather just toss some ragtag collection of Cobras together on your own?"

"I won't have to," Corwin said calmly. "It's already being done."

All eyes turned to him. "What's that supposed to mean?" Chandler asked cautiously.

"It means that before I left home this morning I called Justin and told him something had gone wrong with the mission."

"You *what?*" Priesly snarled. "Moreau—"

"Shut up," Chandler cut him off. "And . . . ?"

"And I told him to organize a rescue mission," Corwin said calmly. "He should have a list ready in an hour or so."

For a long moment the room was filled with a brittle silence. "You've overstepped your bounds rather badly," Chandler said at last. "I could have you removed from office for that."

"I realize that," Corwin nodded. "One other thing: Justin will also be leading the team."

Priesly's mouth fell open. "Justin Moreau is under house arrest," he bit out. "In case you've forgotten, there are charges of assault pending against him."

"Then those charges will have to be summarily dropped, won't they?"

"Oh, of course," Priesly snarled. "What, you expect us to just roll over—?"

"Justin's been to Qasama," Corwin said, his gaze on Chandler. "He's seen the Qasamans up close, both in combat and non-combat situations. There's no one else anywhere in the Worlds who has those same qualifications."

"There were forty-eight Cobras who participated in the second Qasaman mission," Chandler pointed out. His face was a mask, but Corwin could sense the anger behind it . . . and perhaps a growing resignation, as well. "One of them could lead the mission."

"Except that none of them have anything near Justin's experience with Qasaman society," Telek shook her head. "He's right, Mr. Chandler. The best choice for team leader is someone from our first spy mission. And there's only one other person young enough even to be considered."

"Well, let's get him, then," Priesly demanded.

Telek turned glacial eyes on him. "Help yourself. His name's *Joshua* Moreau."

A second silence fell over the room. "I don't have to let you get away with this, you know," Chandler told Corwin at last, very softly. "I can ignore your brother's unauthorized recommendations and take those of the Academy directors instead. And Mr. Priesly's correct—we *can* get someone else to lead the mission."

"And can you also hear what the people of Aventine will say," Corwin returned, just as softly, "when they learn that their leaders wasted time wrangling over fine details. And then settled for second best."

"That's blackmail," Priesly snapped.

Corwin looked him straight in the eye. "That's politics," he corrected. Getting to his feet, he looked back at Chandler. "If we're done here, sir, I'll be going to my office—Justin'll be contacting me there when he's finished. I'm sure he'll want to personally organize the team as the members arrive in the Capitalia; can I assume you'll have his release papers filed by noon or so?"

Chandler gritted his teeth. "It can be managed. I suppose you'll want a full pardon?"

"That or a formal dropping of the charges. Whichever you and Mr. Priesly decide to work out."

He started for the door, but Chandler stopped him. "You realize, of course," the governor-general said darkly, "that as of right now you've taken this entire rescue mission onto your own head. If it fails—for any reason—it'll be *you* who bears the brunt of that failure."

"I understand," Corwin said between tight lips. "I also understand that if it succeeds Mr. Priesly and his associates will do their best to make sure I get as little of the credit as possible."

"You understand politics very well," Telek murmured. "I'm almost sorry for you."

Corwin looked at her. "Fortunately, I understand family loyalty, too. And know which one's more important."

He nodded to Chandler and left.

Corwin had seen Justin's organizational skills many times in the past; but even so he was astonished by the speed with which his brother got the rescue team assembled in Capitalia. By eight that evening—barely fifteen hours after the *Southern Cross* had reentered Aventine's system—the *Dewdrop* was loaded and ready to lift.

"You sure you've got everything you'll need?" Corwin asked as he and Justin stood together a little way from the *Dewdrop*, watching the last load of equipment disappear into the cargo hatch.

"We'll make do," Justin replied, his voice glacially calm.

Corwin threw him a sideways glance. For a man who'd just lost a daughter—either dead or captive—Justin was far too calm, and it was making Corwin more than a little nervous. Whatever the other was feeling about his daughter's fate, it wasn't healthy to keep it bottled up forever. Somehow, it was going to have to come out . . . and if Justin was saving up the anger to dump on the Qasamans, it would be a very bloody purging indeed.

"Something?" Justin asked, his eyes still on the loading.

Corwin pursed his lips. "Just wondering about your people," he improvised. "You put the list together pretty quickly—you still sure they're the ones you want?"

"You've seen the profiles," Justin said. "Four vets of the last Qasaman mission, eight young but experienced Cobras with impressive spine leopard hunting records."

"But without any military training," Corwin pointed out.

"We've got six days to change that," his brother reminded him.

"Yeah." Corwin took a deep breath; but Justin got in the next word.

"I don't think I thanked you yet for getting Chandler to let me off those trumped-up charges," he said calmly.

"No problem," Corwin shrugged. "They didn't have a lot of choice, actually."

Justin nodded, agreement or simple acknowledgment. "I also appreciate what you've done in putting your neck on this fresh block for me. If I'd had to sit around for the next two weeks . . . it would've been pretty hard. At least this way there's something I can do."

"Yeah. Well . . . I expect you know that if Jin's—if she didn't make it, I mean . . . that extracting vengeance from the Qasamans isn't going to help any."

"That depends on what happened to her, doesn't it?" Justin countered. "If she died in the crash . . . well, I'll hold the Trofts partly to blame for that. They're the ones who claimed their shuttle would get through the Qasamans' detectors. But if Jin was captured—" His face hardened. "Teaching the Qasamans a lesson won't bring Jin back, no. But it might prevent someone else's child from dying at their hands."

Corwin bit at his lip. "Just remember that you have two other daughters," he reminded Justin quietly. "Make sure you come back to them, all right?"

Justin nodded solemnly, and his lip twitched in a faint smile.

"Don't worry, Corwin; the Qasamans won't even know what hit them." Across the way, the *Dewdrop*'s cargo hatch swung shut with a muffled thud. "Well, that's it—time to go. Hold the fort here, okay?"

He gave Corwin a brief, almost perfunctory hug, and a moment later had vanished up the ramp into the *Dewdrop*'s main entryway.

They won't even know what hit them. Justin's statement echoed through his mind . . . and standing there alone, Corwin shivered at the lie in those words. Justin would make sure the Qasamans knew what had hit them, all right. What had hit them, and why.

And he wondered if he'd now sent his brother to die on Qasama. Just as he'd done his niece.

Chapter 25

Jin had never been one to make snap judgments of people. But in the case of Radig Nardin she was severely tempted to make an exception.

"Overbearing sort, isn't he?" she murmured to Daulo as they stood a short distance from where Nardin was loudly supervising the loading of his metals.

"Yes," Daulo said tightly. His eyes and most of his attention, she saw, were on Nardin; his arms, at his sides, were rigid.

Jin licked her lips. The tension in the air around them seemed almost thick enough to cast a shadow, and her stomach was beginning to tighten in sympathetic reaction. Whatever it was that was happening here, things seemed to be rapidly building up to a head, and she found herself easing away from Daulo just in case she suddenly needed room to maneuver. Nardin's two drivers and aides were somewhere off to the side . . . there. Nowhere near cover, should Nardin decide to pick a fight—

"Stop!" Daulo snapped.

Jin whipped her eyes back to Nardin. Almost leisurely, he turned around to face them, his hand raised in striking pose above one of the sweating Sammon workers. His gaze flicked measuringly across Daulo's clothing, returned to his face. "You tolerate insubordinate attitudes in your workers, Master Sammon?" he called.

"If and when such insubordination is seen," Daulo said evenly, "it will be punished. And *I* will do the punishing."

For a moment the two young men locked eyes. Then, breathing something inaudible, Nardin lowered his arm. Turning his back on Daulo, he stalked a few meters away from the loading area.

Jurisdictional dispute? Jin wondered. Apparently. Or else Nardin just liked going out of his way to irritate people. "You all right?" Jin asked Daulo quietly.

The other took a deep breath, seemed to relax a bit. "Yes," he said, exhaling in a hiss. "Some people just can't handle power this young."

Jin glanced at him, wondering if he noticed the irony of those words coming from a nineteen-year-old heir. "Radig Nardin is high in the Mangus hierarchy?" he asked.

"His father, Obolo Nardin, runs the place."

"Ah. Then Mangus is a family-run operation like yours?"

"Of course." Daulo seemed puzzled that she'd even have to ask such a question.

Across the way, the last few crates were being loaded onto the trunk. "How often does Mangus need these shipments?" she asked Daulo.

He considered. "About every three weeks. Why?"

She nodded at the truck. "Riding inside a crate might be the simplest way for me to get inside Mangus."

Daulo hissed thoughtfully between his teeth. "Only if you had time to get out before they locked all the crates away somewhere."

"Do they do that?"

"I don't know—I've never been there. Mangus always sends someone to pick up their shipments."

"Is that normal?"

"It is for Mangus. Though if you're right about what they're doing in there, it makes sense for them not to let villagers in."

The qualifier caught Jin's attention. "Only villagers? Can city people get in?"

"Regularly," Daulo nodded. "Mangus brings in work parties from Azras every two to three weeks for one-week periods. Simple assembly work, I gather."

"I don't understand," Jin frowned. "You mean they import their entire labor force?"

"Not the entire force, no. They have some permanent workers, most of them probably Nardin family members. I assume their assembly work comes in spurts and they'd rather not keep people there when they're not needed."

"Seems inefficient. What if some of those workers take other jobs in the meantime and aren't available when they need them?"

"I don't know. But as I said, it's simple assembly work. Training newcomers wouldn't be hard."

Jin nodded. "Do you know anyone personally who's been in one of the work parties?"

Daulo shook his head. "For city people only, remember? We only know about it through my father's relationship with Mayor Capparis of Azras."

"Right—you've mentioned him before. He keeps you informed on what Azras and the other cities are doing?"

"Somewhat. For a price, of course."

That price being preferential access to the Sammon family mine, no doubt. "Do the rest of Azras's political leaders share in this tradeoff?"

"Some." Daulo shrugged, a bit uncomfortably. "Like everyone else, Mayor Capparis has enemies."

"Um." Jin focused on Nardin's arrogant expression again; and, unbidden, an image popped into her mind. Peter Todor, early in their Cobra training, visibly and eagerly awaiting the moment when Jin would finally give up and quit. The moment when he'd be able to gloat over her defeat. "Is there any reason," she asked carefully, "why Mangus or Mayor Capparis's enemies should resent Milika in particular?"

Daulo frowned at her. "Why would they?"

She braced herself. "Could you be charging more for your goods than they consider fair?"

Daulo's eyes hardened. "We don't overcharge for what we sell," he said coldly. "Our mine produces rare and valuable metals, which we purify to a high degree. They'd be costly no matter who sold them."

"What about the Yithtra family, then?" Jin asked.

"What about them?"

"They sell lumber products, right? Do *they* overcharge the cities?"

Daulo's lip twisted. "No, not really," he admitted. "Actually, most of the lumber business out there bypasses Milika entirely. The Somilarai River, which cuts through the main logging area to the north, passes directly by Azras, so much of the lumber is simply floated downriver to processing areas there. What the Yithtra family has done has been to specialize in exotic types of wood products like rhella paper—things the more wholesale lumbering places can't do properly. You probably saw a few rhella trees on your way in from your ship: short, black-trunked things with diamond-shaped leaves?"

Jin shook her head. "Afraid I was looking more at what might be crouching up there than I was at the trees themselves. These rhellas are rare?"

"Not all that much, but the paper made from the inner pulp is the preferred medium for legal contracts, and that creates a high demand. Writing or printing on fresh rhella paper indents the surface, you see," he added, "and that indentation is permanent. So if the writing is altered in any way, it can be detected instantly."

"Handy," Jin agreed. "Expensive, too, I take it?"

"It's worth the cost. Why are you asking all this?"

Jin nodded toward Nardin. "He has the air about him of someone who's getting all ready to gloat," she said. "I was wondering if he's looking forward to gloating over the villages in general or Milika in particular."

"Well . . ." Daulo hesitated. "I'd have to say that even among Qasama's villages, we're considered somewhat . . . not renegades, exactly, but not quite part of the whole community, either."

"Because you're not tied into the central underground communications network?"

He looked at her in surprise. "How—? Oh, that's right; you learned all about that when you took over that Eastern Arm village your last time through. Yes, that's a large part of it. And even though other villages are now starting to sprout up outside the Great Arc, we were one of the first." He eyed her. "This is all part of your research on us?"

Jin felt her face warming. "Some," she admitted. "It's also related to the problem of Mangus, though."

He was silent for a long moment. Shifting her eyes from the loading dock, Jin looked around her. It was a beautiful day, with gentle breezes coming from the southwest adding contrast to the warmth of the sunlight. The sounds of village activity all around her melded into a pleasant hum; the occasional clinking of chains and cables from the mine entrance nearby added to the voices of the workers.

It was almost a shock to shift her eyes westward and see the wall. The wall, and the metal mesh addition the village had had to erect against the high-jumping spine leopards . . . the spine leopards her people had sent to them.

On the recommendation of her own grandfather.

A sudden shiver of guilt ran up her back. What would Daulo and Kruin think, she wondered bleakly, if they knew her family's role in bringing this burden onto them? *Maybe that's why I was marooned here in the first place,* the thought occurred to her. *Maybe it's part of a divine retribution on my family.*

"You all right?" Daulo asked.

She shook off the train of thought. "Sure. Just . . . thinking about home."

He nodded. "My father and I were wondering last night about what plans your people might be making to get you back."

She shrugged uncomfortably. "They're not likely to be planning anything except my memorial service. The way the crash destroyed the shuttle's transmitters, there wasn't any way I could signal our mother ship; and between that and what they would have seen from orbit they'd have assumed that everyone was dead. So they'll go on back, and everyone will mourn us for awhile, and then the Directorate will start debating what to do next. Maybe in a few months they'll try this again. Maybe it won't be for a couple of years."

"You sound bitter."

Jin blinked away tears. "No, not bitter. Just . . . afraid of how my father's gong to take this. He wanted so much for me to be a Cobra—"

"A what?"

"A Cobra. It's the proper name for what you call a demon warrior. He wanted so much for me to follow in the family tradition . . . and now he'll wonder if he pushed me where I didn't want to go."

"Did he?" Daulo asked quietly.

Oddly enough, Jin felt no resentment at the question. "No. I love him a lot, Daulo, and I might have been willing to become a Cobra just from that love. But, no—I wanted this as much as he did."

Daulo snorted gently. "A warrior woman. Seems almost a contradiction in terms."

"Only by your history. And on our own worlds Cobras are more like civilian peacekeepers than fighters."

"Almost like what the mojos were to us," Daulo pointed out.

Jin considered. "Interesting analogy," she admitted.

He gave a sound that was half snort, half chuckle. "Just think of the sort of peacekeeper force we could have if we combined the two."

"Cobras and mojos?" She shook her head. "No chance. In fact, it's occurred to me more than once that that may be exactly the thought that scared our leaders the most: the idea that your mojos might spread to Aventine, that we might wind up having our Cobras controlled by alien minds."

"But if it would make them less dangerous—"

"The mojos have their own priorities and purposes," Jin reminded him. "I'd just as soon not find out what one might do with a Cobra."

Daulo sighed. "You're probably right," he conceded. "Still—"

"Master Sammon?" a voice called from behind them. They turned, and Jin saw Daulo's chauffeur waving to them from the doorway of the mine's business center. "A call for you. Important, he says."

Daulo nodded and set off at a brisk trot. Jin watched him take the chauffeur's place at the phone, then turned back to watch Nardin. *Mangus. Mongoose.* The name alone gave the lie to all her talk about city versus village warfare. A compound called Mongoose could have only one possible focus, and that was outward from Qasama. In the back of her mind, her conscience twinged: should she continue to let Daulo and his father believe that Mangus was a plot against the villages? Especially since they might withdraw their support from her if they knew the truth?

"Jasmine Alventin!"

She started and twisted around. Daulo was beckoning urgently to her as he opened the car's left-hand rear door; the chauffeur was already in the front seat. Heart thudding in her throat, Jin jogged over to join them. "What is it?" she asked, pulling open the right-hand door and sliding in the back beside Daulo.

"One of our people noticed a Yithtra family truck coming in by the south gate," Daulo said, his voice tight. "It had something like a tree trunk sticking from the back, covered with some kind of cloth so that it couldn't be seen.

Jin frowned. "An unusual tree they don't want anyone to see?"

"That's what our spotter thought. It occurred to me that there's something else of that shape that they might be even more anxious to hide from sight."

Jin's mouth went dry. *A missile?* "That's . . . crazy," she managed. "Where would they have gotten something like that?"

Daulo's eyes flicked to the chauffeur. "Whatever it is, I want to try and get a look at it."

The chauffer sped them down the spoke road to the Small Ring, turning counterclockwise onto it. "The simplest route would be to take the spoke road directly from the south gate to the Small Ring," Daulo muttered. "But in this case . . . I'm going to guess they'll turn instead onto the Great Ring and take it to the Yithtra section, then come down that spoke road to the house. What do you think, Walare?"

"Sounds reasonable, Master Daulo," the chauffeur nodded. "Shall I run that in reverse and see if we can catch them?"

"Right."

Guiding the vehicle expertly through the pedestrian crowds, Walare curved around the Inner Green, passed the spoke road from the south gate, and continued on toward the grand house Daulo had identified some days earlier as that of the Yithtra family. Another spoke road angled off just before it, and Walare turned down it. Jin looked back at the house as they headed away, noting the liveried guards at all the visible entrances—

"There," Daulo snapped, pointing at a small truck far ahead down the spoke road. Jin keyed in her optical enhancers for a look at the truck's three occupants. All three looked oddly tense, but none seemed especially suspicious of the car approaching them. A minute later the two vehicles passed each other, and Daulo and Jin both spun around in their places.

There was indeed something cylindrical poking awkwardly out from between the truck's rear doors; and it was indeed swathed heavily in some kind of silky white cloth. "Follow it," Daulo ordered Walare. "Well, Jasmine Alventin?" he added as the car swung into a tight U-turn.

Jin pursed her lips, trying to estimate the object's length and circumference. "It's not very big, if it's what we think it is," she told him. "Rather obvious, too."

"Point," Daulo admitted. "Especially since they've got regular log carriers they could have used to bring something like that in without it being seen at all. You think perhaps it is nothing but a tree trunk brought in to stir us up?"

Jin chewed at her lip. It might be possible to glean something even through all that cloth. "Let me try something," she said. Leaning her head out the side window, she keyed in her optical enhancers' infrared capability.

The reflection/radiation profile was strong and dramatic; and even with the background clutter from the truck and pavement around it, there was no room for doubt. "It's metal," she told Daulo.

He nodded grimly. "I'm sure you realize what this means. The Yithtra family's made a deal with Mangus."

"Or else they stole it. Which could get the whole village in trouble."

Daulo hissed between his teeth. "Trouble from agents seeking to retrieve it?"

Or straightforward retaliation, Jin thought. But there was no point in worrying Daulo with that one. "Basically," she told him. "On the other hand, we've now got a chance to pick up some information without having to go all the way to Mangus for it."

He stared at her. "Are you *serious?* We can't break into the Yithtra family house."

"I didn't think we could," Jin told him tightly. "That's why I'm going to have to do this here and now."

He said something incredulous sounding, but she was too busy thinking to pay attention. There were a dozen ways to take out a vehicle, but all of them would instantly brand her as a demon warrior. To their right, another of Milika's marketplaces stretched alongside the street, teeming with potential witnesses to anything she tried.

Potential witnesses . . . but also potential diversions. "Pull up closer to the truck," she ordered the chauffeur. "In a minute I'll want you to pass it."

"Master Daulo . . . ?" the other asked.

"Do it," Daulo confirmed. "Jin—?"

"I'm going to jump out as you start to pass and get into the truck," she told him, eyes searching across the marketplace booths ahead as she lowered the window. Somewhere out there had to be what she was looking for . . .

There—right beside the street fifty meters ahead: a group of six customers holding an animated discussion beside a vendor of food and drink . . . and four of the six carried mojos on their shoulders. "Pull up," she ordered Walare. "Daulo Sammon, I'll meet you back at the house." From the corner of her eye she saw them closing on the truck ahead; activating her target system, she locked onto the bellies of three of the mojos. Even in the glare of full daylight, she knew, it was going to be a calculated risk to fire even low-power shots from her fingertip lasers. But there wasn't anything she could do about that except cross her fingers and pray that no one noticed them. Walare had them directly behind the truck now, and was starting to pull around; and as the food booth shot past, Jin fired three shots in rapid succession.

It was all she could have hoped for. The birds' screams pierced the air like a triple siren, followed immediately by an equal number of human bellows. Jin got a quick glimpse of the scorched mojos tearing furiously around through the air as everyone nearby scrambled for safety from the birds' unexpected behavior; and as the sudden ruckus audibly spread behind her she wrenched the car door open and flipped her legs out onto the pavement. For a second she held onto the door for balance as her feet caught the stride; then, shoving the door shut, she surged forward. Her timing was perfect: with Walare halfway into his passing maneuver, her side of the car had been directly behind the truck, out of view of any rear-facing mirror. A two-second quick-sprint put her beside the cylinder's bouncing nose; grabbing the edge of one of the open doors, she pulled herself up and through the gap and into the welcome shadows inside the truck.

She took a shuddering breath, acutely aware of the time limit now counting down. In five minutes or less the truck would reach the Yithtra house, and if she didn't get out before then, she might very well have to shoot her way out. Crouching down beside the cylinder, she tore away its silky covering . . . and froze.

The cloth wasn't just cloth. It was light and tight-woven, with cords tied between it and the cylinder.

A parachute.

And the cylinder beneath it was smooth and white, with black scorch marks liberally splattered over its surface. Marks that nevertheless didn't obscure the lettering on the loosely fastened access panel:

TYPE 6-KX TRANSFER CONTAINER: FOR GOVERNMENTAL SHIPPING USE ONLY.

God above, she thought numbly. The Yithtra family hadn't bought or stolen a missile, after all. They'd found something far worse: a goodbye present from the *Southern Cross.*

A present for her.

Chapter 26

For a long second her mind seemed to be on ice, skidding along without control. The pod's existence was bad enough; but its existence in the hands of Qasamans was even worse. The minute the Yithtra family realized what it was they'd found and turned it over to the authorities—

And she had maybe three minutes to figure out a way to stop that. Gritting her teeth, she dug her fingers under the access panel's edge and pried it open.

The contents were no surprise: packaged emergency rations, lightweight blankets, medical packs, a backpack and water carrier— all the things a castaway in hostile territory might need to survive. All of them clearly labeled with Anglic words.

Which meant obscuring the writing on the outside of the pod wouldn't gain her anything. Unless she could also completely destroy the pod's contents . . .

A trickle of sweat ran down her cheek. She jabbed and probed her fingers through the packages, trying desperately to think of something. Her lasers weren't designed for starting this kind of fire, but if they'd sent her some cooking fuel—

Her roving fingers struck something that rustled: a tightly folded piece of paper. Frowning, she dug it out and opened it. The message was short:

Can't get down to you. If you can hang on, we'll be back with help as quickly as we can. We'll listen for your call at local sunrise, noon, sunset, and midnight—if you can't signal, we'll come down and find you.
Courage!
Captain Rivero Koja

Jin bit down hard on her lip. *We'll come down and find you.* In her mind's eye she saw a full Cobra assault force descend on Milika, shooting indiscriminately as they tried to find her . . . Swearing under her breath, she dug into the packages with renewed energy, searching now for the transmitter Koja's note implied had been packed in with the supplies. But either it was buried too deeply among the groceries . . .

Or else the Yithtra workers who'd found and opened the pod had already taken it out.

Damn. It was right there, a few meters away from her in the cab of the truck . . . and yet it might as well be in orbit. For one wild second she had the image of herself blasting through to the cab with her antiarmor laser, using her sonic to stun the cab's occupants and retrieve the transmitter—

And then taking what refuge she could in deep forest. While the Sammon family went up on treason charges.

Angrily, she shook the train of thought from her mind. The transmitter was gone, period. Crumpling Koja's note into her pocket, she jammed the access panel back in place and stepped to the rear doors, grabbing for balance as the truck made a sharp right-hand turn. Between the doors, the Small Ring Road appeared.

Which meant the truck had left the spoke road and would be reaching the gate of the Yithtra house any moment now. Licking her lips, Jin peered through the gap, trying to find something she could use to create a diversion. But nothing obvious presented itself. There were as many pedestrians out there as usual, and once out of the truck she ought to have enough cover to blend into. But there was nothing she could do to cover the jump itself. Clenching her teeth, she got ready; and as the truck abruptly decelerated, she swung down out the rear and dropped to the pavement below. A couple of braking steps brought her to a halt; turning quickly, she started walking down the road away from the Yithtra house.

No shouts of discovery followed her. Behind her, she heard the truck come to a brief halt and then start up again, vanishing behind the background hum of closing gateway doors. Fighting a trembling in her hands, she kept walking.

Eventually, after a wandering route, she reached the Sammon house.

Kruin Sammon laid the crumpled paper down on his desk and looked up at her. "So," he said. "It seems your anonymity is about to come to an end."

Jin nodded. "So it seems," she agreed tightly.

"I don't see why," Daulo objected from his usual place beside his father. "The Yithtra family can't really make trouble for you unless they can offer the Shahni some physical proof. Why can't you simply break into the Yithtra household tonight and destroy or steal the pod?"

Jin shook her head. "It wouldn't work. First of all, there's a fair chance they'll have odds and ends from the pod scattered around throughout the house by then, and there's no guarantee I'd be able to retrieve all of it. More importantly, the very fact that I got in and out of a guarded house without being caught will be pretty strong evidence that I'm not just an offworlder, but an offworld demon warrior. I don't think we want to cause that kind of panic just yet."

"So the Yithtra family informs the Shihni that an offworlder has landed secretly among us." Kruin's eyes were steady on Jin's face. "And for their patriotism and alertness the Yithtra family gains new prestige. Is this how you help us bring them down?"

A wisp of anger curled like smoke in Jin's throat. "I realize you have your own priorities, Kruin Sammon," she said as calmly as she could, "but it seems to me you'd do better to forget about the Yithtra family earning a pat on the head and concentrate instead on the problems this might cause Milika as a whole."

"The problems it might cause *you*, you mean," Kruin countered. "We of Milika are blameless, Jasmine Moreau, if we are duped by a cunning offworlder into extending our hospitality."

Jin looked hard at him. "Are you abrogating our bargain, then?" she asked softly.

He shook his head. "Not if it can be helped. But if it should become clear that your capture is certain, I will not allow my household to be destroyed in the process." He hesitated. "If that happens . . . I'll at least give you warning."

So *that any major firefights will take place away from Sammon territory*? Still, it was as much as she could expect under the circumstances . . . and probably more than she would have gotten elsewhere. "I thank you for being honest with me," she said.

"Which is more than you have been with us," the elder Sammon said.

Jin's stomach began to tighten into a knot. "What do you mean?"

"I mean your true name," he said evenly. "And the connection of that name to Mangus."

Jin's eyes flicked to Daulo, feeling a sudden chill in the room.

The younger man looked back at her steadily, his face as masked as Kruin's. "I never lied to you," she said, eyes still on Daulo. "To either of you."

"Is the withholding of truth not a lie?" Daulo asked quietly. "You understood the significance of the name *mongoose*, yet didn't share that knowledge."

"If I'd wanted to keep it to myself, why did I tell you at all that we were called Cobras?" she countered, "The fact is that I didn't think it was all that important."

"Not *important?*" Kruin spat. "*Mongoose* is hardly a name of a place seeking only to dominate Qasaman villages. And if Mangus is truly an attempt to fight back at our common enemies, how can the Sammon family help you destroy it?"

"I don't seek to destroy it—"

"More half-truths," Kruin shot back. "Perhaps *you* don't but others will surely follow you."

Jin took a deep breath. *Steady, girl,* she warned herself. *Concentrate, and be rational.* "I've already told you I don't know what my people will do with my report—*and* pointed out that a non-threatening Qasama is perfectly welcome to advance back into space. But if the Shahni are truly bent on attacking us, do you really think they'll do so without the full weight of Qasama behind them? Or to put it another way, won't they demand that both cities and villages supply their full shares of the resources *and* manpower—" her eyes flicked to Daulo "—that a full-scale war requires? Whether you want to or not?"

For a moment Kruin sat in silence, gazing at Jin. She forced herself to return the gaze; and after a moment he shifted on his cushions. "You again try to prove that Mangus threatens us directly. Yet without any proof."

"Whatever proof exists will only be found inside Mangus itself," Jin pointed out, feeling the knots in her stomach starting to unravel again. Whatever his apprehensions, it was clear that Kruin was smart enough to see that the scenario Jin painted made too much sense to ignore. "The only way to find out for sure will be to get inside and take a look for ourselves."

"Ourselves?" A faint and slightly bitter smile touched Kruin's lips. "How quickly you change between offworlder and Qasaman, Jasmine Moreau. Or don't you think we know that once inside Mangus it will be *your* priorities, not ours, that you will address?"

Jin's hands curled into fists. "You insult me, Kruin Sammon," she bit out. "I don't play games with people's lives—not those of

my own people, not those of yours. If Mangus threatens *anyone*—
Aventinian *or* Qasaman—I want to know about it. *That's* my
priority."

For a moment Kruin didn't answer. Then, to her astonishment,
he inclined his head toward her. "I had assumed you were a warrior,
Jasmine Moreau," he said. "I see I was mistaken."

She blinked. "I don't understand."

"Warriors," he said softly, "don't care about the people they are
told to kill."

Jin licked her lips, a cold shiver replacing the fading indignation in her muscles. She hadn't meant to blast Kruin that
strongly—certainly hadn't meant to imply that Milika's welfare was
truly any of her concern. She was here for only one purpose, she
reminded herself firmly: to find out if the Cobra Worlds were being
threatened. If it was merely one group of Qasamans preparing to
slaughter another, that was none of her business.

Except that it was.

And for the first time her conscious mind was forced to acknowl-
edge that fact. She'd *lived* with these people; lived with them, eaten
their food, accepted their help and hospitality . . . and there was
no way she could simply turn her back on them and walk away.
Kruin was right; she *was* no warrior.

Which was to say, no Cobra.

A sudden moisture obscured her vision; furiously, she blinked
it away. It didn't really matter—she'd already fouled things up so
badly that one more failure wouldn't make much of a difference.
"Never mind what I am or am not," she growled. "The only issue
here is whether you're still going to help me get into Mangus, or
whether I'm going to have to do it all myself."

"I've given you my pledge once," Kruin said coldly. "You insult
me to ask again."

"Yes, well, it seems to be a day for insults," Jin said tiredly. All
the fight was draining away, leaving nothing but emotional fatigue
behind. "Daulo spoke of work parties hired from Azras. Can you
ask your friend the mayor to get me into one of them?"

Kruin glanced at his son. "It may be possible," he said. "It could
take a week to make the arrangements, though."

"We can't afford that much time," Jin sighed. "I've got to be
in and out of Mangus within the next six days."

"Why?" Kruin frowned.

Jin nodded toward Koja's letter on the low desk. "Because that
note changes everything. There won't be any six-month debate now

as to whether or not another mission should be sent here. Koja will have burned space getting back, and there'll be a rescue team on its way just as soon as it can be scrambled together."

Kruin's lips compressed slightly. "Arriving when?"

"I don't know exactly. I'd guess no more than a week."

Daulo hissed between his teeth. "A *week?*"

"Bad," Kruin agreed calmly. "But not as bad as it might be. With a new supply of metals on its way to Mangus, they should be needing to call in extra workers soon."

"How soon?" Jin asked.

"Within your six-day limit, I'd guess," Kruin said. "I'll send a message to Mayor Capparis this afternoon and ask if a member of my household can be worked into one of the parties."

"Please ask if he can make it two members," Daulo said quietly.

Kruin cocked an eyebrow at his son. "A noble offer, my son, but not well thought out. For what reason—besides curiosity—should I allow you to accompany Jasmine Moreau on this trip?"

"For the reason that she still knows so very little about Qasama," Daulo said. "She could betray herself as an offworlder in a thousand different ways. Or worse, she could fail to understand or even to notice something of vital importance once inside."

Kruin cocked an eye at Jin. "Have you a response?"

"I'll be fine," Jin said stiffly. "I thank you for your offer, Daulo, but I don't need an escort."

"Are his arguments invalid?" Kruin persisted.

"Not necessarily," she admitted. "But the risks outbalance the benefits. Your family is well known here, and probably at least slightly known in Azras. Even with the disguise kit I've got in my pack, there's a good chance he'll be recognized by someone in the work party, or even by Radig Nardin or someone in Mangus itself. At least as much chance, I'd guess, as that I'll be caught in an error." She hesitated; *no, better not say it.*

But Kruin saw through the hesitation. "And . . . ?" he prompted.

Jin clenched her teeth. "And if there is trouble . . . I stand a much better chance of getting out alone than if Daulo is with me."

An instant later she wished she'd kept her mouth shut. Daulo sat up stiffly on his cushion, face darkening. "I don't need the protection of a woman," he bit out. "And I *will* go with you into Mangus."

And there was no longer any room for argument, Jin realized with a sinking heart. Logic was fine in its place; but when set against the emotions of threatened manhood, there was only one possible outcome. "In that case," she sighed, "I would be honored to have your company and protection."

It was only much later that it occurred to her that perhaps she'd been guilty of the same kind of nonrational thinking . . . that perhaps the very fact she'd forgotten something as basic to Qasama as the expanded male ego meant that she really *did* know too little about Qasama to tackle Mangus alone.

It wasn't a particularly encouraging thought.

Chapter 27

"I looked up what records we had this afternoon," Daulo's silhouette said from beside Jin, "and it looks like my father's guess was a little pessimistic. It should be only two to three days before Mangus asks Azras to organize a work party."

Jin nodded silently as they passed through the darkened courtyard toward the steady splash of the fountain. It was odd, she thought, how easily a place could start to feel familiar and comfortable. *Too comfortable, maybe?* she wondered with a twinge of uneasiness. Layn had warned them against losing the undercurrent of mild paranoia that every warrior in enemy territory ought to maintain, and she could remember thinking it incredible that anyone in such a position could possibly relax that much. Now, it seemed, she was doing just that.

Which made it all the more urgent she move on to Azras and Mangus as soon as possible.

"You're very quiet," Daulo said.

She pursed her lips. "Just thinking how peaceful it is here," she told him. "Milika in general; your house in particular. I almost wish I could stay."

He snorted gently. "Don't worry too much about it. If you lived here for a few months you'd quickly find out it's not the Eden you seem to think." He paused. "So . . . what are your people likely to do if it turns out you were right? That Mangus is a base for striking back at you?"

Jin shrugged. "It probably depends partly on what *you* do in that case."

He frowned. "What do you mean?"

"Come on, Daulo Sammon, don't play innocent. If Mangus isn't a threat to Milika, you and your father have no reason to help me further. In fact, you have every reason to betray me."

His eyes grew hard. "The Sammon family is a family of honor, Jasmine Moreau," he bit out. "We've sworn protection to you, and we'll stand by that bargain. No matter what."

She sighed. "I know. But we were . . . warned not to get over-confident."

"I understand," Daulo said quietly. "I'm afraid you'll just have to take my word for it."

"I know. But I don't have to like it."

In the darkness, his hand tentatively sought hers. It brought back memories of Mander Sun . . . blinking back tears, she accepted the touch. "We didn't ask to be your enemies, Jin Moreau," Daulo said quietly. "We have enough to fight against right here on Qasama. And we've been fighting against them for long time. Haven't we earned the right to some rest?"

She sighed. Thoughts of Caelian flashed through her mind . . . and thoughts of her father and uncle. "Yes. So has everyone else I know."

For a few minutes they continued to wander around the court-yard in silence, listening to the nighttime sounds of Milika beyond the house. "Is there a meaning to the name *Jin?*" Daulo asked suddenly. "Jasmine, I know, is an Old Earth flower, but the only use of Jin I've ever heard is for the mythological spirit."

She felt a touch of heat in her cheeks. "It was a nickname my father gave me when I was young. He said—at least to me—that it was just a shortened version of Jasmine." She licked her lips. "Maybe that's really all he meant it to be . . . but when I was about eight I found an old Dominion of Man magcard in the city library that listed several thousand common names and their meanings. Jin was given as an Old Japanese name that meant 'superexcellent.'"

"Indeed?" Daulo murmured. "A great compliment for your father to give you such a name."

"Maybe too great," Jin admitted. "The listing noted that it was rarely given, precisely because its meaning placed so great a demand on a child."

"And you've been trying to live up to it ever since?"

It was a thought that had often occurred to her. "I don't know. It's possible, I suppose. I remember that for weeks afterward I felt like everyone was looking expectantly at me, waiting for me to do something superexcellent."

"And so here you are on Qasama. Still trying."

She swallowed through a throat that suddenly ached. "I guess so. Or at least trying to make my father proud of me."

It was a long moment before Daulo spoke again. "I understand, perhaps more than you realize. Our families are not so different, Jin Moreau."

A flicker of movement from one of the windows overhead caught Jin's eye, saving her from the need to find a good response to that. "Someone's in your father's office," she said, pointing.

Daulo stiffened, then relaxed. "One of our people—a messenger. Probably bringing Mayor Capparis's reply to my father's message this morning."

"Let's go find out," Jin said, changing direction back toward the door. Beside her, Daulo seemed to draw back. "If that would be all right with you," she added quickly.

The extra tension vanished as male pride was apparently assuaged. "Certainly. Come with me."

Alone with Jin, Daulo had lost track of time a bit, and it was with mixed embarrassment and guilt that he led her down the empty corridors toward his father's office. Most of the household had retired to their chambers by now, and the corridors echoed oddly to their footsteps as they walked. *I should have returned her to her rooms half an hour ago,* he thought, hoping the heat rising to his cheeks wasn't visible. *Father will probably be angry with me.* For a moment he searched for an excuse to give Jin for changing his mind and getting her upstairs instead, but nothing occurred to him that didn't sound limp or contrived.

The guard at Kruin Sammon's door made the sign of respect as they approached. "Master Sammon," he said. "How may I serve you?"

"The messenger who came to my father—is he still within?" Daulo asked.

"No, he left a moment ago. Do you wish to speak to him?"

Daulo shook his head. "No, I seek to speak to my father."

The guard nodded again and turned to the intercom box. "Master Sammon: Daulo Sammon and Jasmine Alventin are here to see you." An inaudible reply and the other nodded. "You may enter," he said as the door's lock clicked open.

Kruin Sammon was seated at his desk, a stylus in his hand and an oddly intense look on his face. "What is it, my son?" he asked as Daulo closed the door.

"We saw from the courtyard that a messenger had arrived, my father," Daulo said, making the sign of respect. "I thought it might be news from Azras."

Kruin's face seemed to harden a bit more. "Yes, it was. Mayor Capparis has arranged housing for two people, and promises to facilitate your entrance into the work party whenever Mangus announces its formation."

"Good," Daulo said, feeling his eyebrows come together in a frown. His father's expression . . . "Is anything wrong, my father?"

Kruin licked his lips and seemed to take a deep breath. "Come here, Daulo," he sighed.

A hollow feeling settled into Daulo's stomach. Squeezing Jin's hand briefly, he left her side and stepped to his father's desk. "Read this," the elder Sammon said, handing him a piece of paper. His eyes slid away from Daulo's gaze. "I'd intended that it be delivered to you tomorrow morning, an hour before dawn. But now . . ."

Gingerly, Daulo accepted the paper, heart thudding in his ears. To have discomfited his father so . . .

> DAULO:
> IN MY MESSAGE TO MAYOR CAPPARIS THIS AFTERNOON I ALSO INFORMED HIM THAT THE YITHTRA FAMILY HAS DISCOVERED AN ARTIFACT FROM OFFWORLD. HE HAS INFORMED ME IN TURN THAT MY MESSAGE HAS BEEN FORWARDED TO THE SHAHNI, WHO WILL BE SENDING A FORCE TO QUESTION THE YITHTRA FAMILY AS TO THEIR REASONS FOR NOT INFORMING THEM ABOUT THIS ARTIFACT THEMSELVES.
> YOU AND JASMINE MOREAU WILL NEED TO LEAVE AS SOON AS IS PRACTICAL—TOO MANY PEOPLE OUTSIDE OUR HOUSEHOLD HAVE SEEN HER FOR HER TO REMAIN HIDDEN HERE. A CAR HAS BEEN PREPARED FOR YOU, CONTAINING ALL THE SUPPLIES YOU SHOULD NEED FOR A WEEK IN AZRAS. MAYOR CAPPARIS HAS OFFERED YOU THE USE OF HIS GUEST HOME WHILE YOU WAIT FOR MANGUS TO BEGIN ITS HIRING.
> BE CAREFUL, MY SON, AND DO NOT TRUST JASMINE MOREAU MORE THAN YOU MUST.
> KRUIN SAMMON

Daulo looked from the paper to his father. "Why?" he asked, dimly aware that his heart was thudding in his ears.

"Because it was necessary," Kruin said simply. But the look in his eyes belied the confidence of the words.

"You had no right, my father." Daulo could hear a tremor in his voice; could feel his face growing hot with shame. *The Sammon family is a family of honor*—he'd said those words to Jin not half an hour ago. *We've sworn protection to you* . . . "We had a bargain with Jasmine Moreau. One which she has not broken."

"And which I've not broken, either, Daulo Sammon. You've known you'll need to go to Azras eventually. Now it'll simply be sooner than we'd expected."

"You swore not to betray her—"

"And I have not!" Kruin snapped. "I could have told Mayor Capparis everything about her; but I didn't. I could have kept from you both the knowledge that the Shahni were sending investigators; but I didn't."

"Fancy words do not hide truth," Daulo bit out. "And the truth is that you swore to her the protection of our house. Now you drive her from both our house and our protection."

"Take care, Daulo Sammon," his father warned. "Your words are dangerously lacking in respect."

"My words echo my thoughts," Daulo shot back. "I'm ashamed for my family, my father."

For a long moment the two men stared at each other in silence; and it was almost a shock for Daulo to hear Jin's voice come from close beside him. "May I see the paper?" she asked calmly.

Wordlessly, he handed it to her. *And now the world ends,* the thought came distantly to him. *The vengeance of a demon warrior betrayed.* The memory of the headless corpse of the razorarm she'd killed brought bile into his throat . . .

It seemed a long time before she lowered the note and looked Kruin in the face. "Tell me," she said quietly, "would the Yithtra family have kept the pod secret for long?"

"I doubt it," the elder Sammon said. His voice was even . . . but Daulo could see a trace of his own fears in his father's eyes. "As soon as they've gained all the secrets they can from the pod, they'll alert the Shahni themselves."

"Within the week, you think?"

"Probably sooner," Kruin said.

She looked at Daulo. "You agree?"

He worked moisture back into his mouth. "Yes. Doing that would still gain them favor in the eyes of the Shahni and yet let them have first look at anything of value."

She turned back to Kruin. "I understand," she said. "In other words, as you said, it was inevitable that I would eventually be chased out of Milika anyway."

Daulo suddenly realized he was holding his breath. "You . . . I don't understand. You're not angry?"

She turned back to him . . . and he shrank within himself from the smoldering fire in her eyes. "I said it was inevitable," she ground out, "and that I understood. I *didn't* say I wasn't angry. Your father had no right to do such a thing without consulting me first. We could have left this afternoon and been safely hidden away in Azras by now. As it is, if we wait until dawn we stand a fair chance of being trapped in Milika. By then they'll not only be swarming around Milika, but they'll also have aircraft flying around looking for the wrecked shuttle. *And* they'll have roadblocks set up." She looked at Daulo. "Which means we leave tonight. Now." She seemed to study him. "Or at least *I* have to leave. You can stay if you want to."

Daulo gritted his teeth. Under normal conditions, a supreme insult to suggest he would go back on his word. Under these conditions, it was no more than he deserved. "I said I would go with you, Jasmine Moreau, and I will." He looked at his father. "Have the supplies you mentioned been assembled yet?"

"They're already in the car." Kruin pursed his lips. "Daulo—"

"I'll try and send word when the work party is formed," Daulo interrupted him, not especially in the mood to be polite. "I hope you'll at least be able to stall any investigations into Jasmine Moreau's identity until then."

The elder Sammon sighed. "I will," he promised.

Daulo nodded, feeling a bitterness in his soul. His father's promise . . . a word that had always seemed to him as immutable as the laws of nature. To see that word deliberately broken was to lose a part of himself.

And all of it because of the woman at his side. A woman who was not only not a Sammon, but was in fact an enemy of his world. It made him want to cry . . . or to hate.

Clenching his teeth, he took a deep breath. *We've sworn protection to you,* they'd said to her, *and we'll stand by that bargain. No matter what.* "Come, Jin," he said aloud. "Let's get out of here."

Chapter 28

In the daytime, Jin knew, it took about an hour to drive from Milika to Azras. At night, with Daulo taking it a little easier, it took half again that long, with the result that it was just about midnight when they crossed the Somilarai River and drove on into the city.

"So now what?" Jin asked, peering with some nervousness down the largely deserted streets. The last thing she wanted was for them to be conspicuous.

"We go to the apartment Mayor Capparis is lending us, of course," Daulo said.

"Did he send you the key, or are we going to have to wake up someone?"

"He sent the combination," Daulo told her. "Most temporary homes in Azras use keypad locks. That way all you have to do is change the combination when the occupants leave."

Which was basically the same system the Cobra Worlds used. "Oh," Jin said, feeling a little silly.

They passed the center of town and continued into the eastern part of the city, pulling up at last in front of a large building very reminiscent of the Sammon family house in Milika. Unlike that structure, though, this one had been carved up into apartments which—judging from the size of theirs—weren't appreciably bigger than the two-room suite the Sammon family had given her. In that space were squeezed a tiny foodprep area, a living room, and a bedroom.

A single bedroom.

"Small wonder the city people resent us," Daulo commented, dropping his cases in a corner of the living room and taking a few steps to peer around the corners into each of the rooms. "The average worker in my family's service has a larger home than this."

"Must be lower-class housing," Jin murmured. A hundred ways to approach the issue occurred to her; but there was no point in cat-footing around it. "I see there's just one bed here."

For a long moment he just looked at her—not at her body, she noted, but into her face. "Yes," he said at last. "I really shouldn't have to ask."

"Qasaman women are that pliant?" Jin asked bluntly.

He pursed his lips. "Sometimes I forget how different you are.... No, Qasaman women aren't overly pliant; just realistic. They know that women don't function well without men ... and as the heir to a powerful family, I'm not exactly someone they want to refuse."

A shiver of disgust ran up Jin's back. For just a second the polite veneer around Daulo had cracked, giving her a glimpse of something far less attractive beneath it. Rich, powerful, probably pampered, as well—he'd likely had life pretty much his own way since the day he was born. On Aventine that type almost always grew up into selfish, immature adults. On Qasama, with the pervasive male contempt for women, it would be far worse.

She shook the train of thought away. *It's a different culture,* she reminded herself firmly. *Assumptions and extrapolations may not be valid.* She'd seen his discipline in regards to the family business, after all; some of that must have seeped into his personal life, as well.

But whether it had or not, she had to lay down the ground rules right here and now. "So," she said coolly. "Does that mean you've taken advantage of your family's power to prey on young women who haven't got any choice in the matter?—and, worse, with the underlying hint that you might marry them someday? At least the razorarms are honest with their victims."

Daulo's eyes flashed with anger. "You know *nothing* about us," he spat. "Nothing about us, and even less about me. I don't use women as playthings; nor do I make promises I don't intend to keep. You of all people should know *that*—else why am I here?"

"Then there should be no problem," she said quietly. "Should there."

Slowly, the fire faded from Daulo's eyes. "So now it's you who toy with me," he said at last. "I risk my honor and position for you, and in return you stir up anger in me to drive away all other feelings."

"Was that the reason you agreed to come with me?" she

countered. "And as long as you've brought it up, tell me: if I accepted your advances, wouldn't you some day wonder whether I had manipulated you that way?"

Daulo glared at her in silence for a moment. Then he sighed. "Perhaps I would have. But is it any better this way? Perhaps now you're manipulating me through the aura of mystery about you, an aura that might disappear if you showed an ordinary woman's behavior with a man."

Jin shook her head. "I'm not manipulating you, Daulo Sammon. You're helping me for the reasons of rational self-interest that we've already discussed. You're too intelligent to make decisions based on your hormones."

He smiled bitterly. "And so now you make it a point of honor for me to stay away from you. You play your games well, Jasmine Moreau."

"It's not a game—"

"It doesn't matter. The end result is the same." Turning his back on her, he stomped to the bags they'd brought in and began rummaging through them. "You'd best get some sleep; we'll need to rise early for worship." Pulling out a blanket, he strode to the living room couch and began tucking it in.

Worship? she wondered. *They never did that in Milika. Do the proper places only exist in the cities?* She opened her mouth to ask . . . but it didn't seem like a good idea to prolong the conversation. "I understand," she said instead. "Goodnight, Daulo."

He grunted in return. Pursing her lips, Jin turned and went into the bedroom, shutting the door behind her.

For a long minute she sat on the bed, wondering if perhaps she'd played the whole thing wrong. Would it really have been so bad to go ahead and accept his advances?

Yes, of course it would have . . . because she'd have been doing it for the wrong reasons. Perhaps to avoid having to argue the point with him, or to pay back his family for their hospitality, or even to cynically ensure his continued cooperation by bonding him emotionally to her.

Her Cobra gear provided her an arsenal of awesome weapons. She had no intention of adding her body to that list.

Daulo would understand someday, too. She hoped.

Daulo woke her shortly after sunrise, and after taking turns to clean up in the cramped bathroom they left the apartment and set off on foot down the street.

Azras by day was a strikingly different place than it had seemed the night before. Like the cities Jin's Uncle Joshua had seen on his visit to Qasama, the lower parts of Azras's buildings were painted with wild forest-pattern colors that seemed sometimes to throb with movement. Above the colors, the buildings were glistening white, demonstrating the kind of careful maintenance that bespoke either a healthy city budget, a strong civic pride, or both.

It was the people, though, that attracted most of her attention.

They were out in force—perhaps three hundred within sight— all walking the same direction she and Daulo were going. *All of them going to worship?* she wondered. "Where exactly are we going?" she asked Daulo quietly.

"One of the *sajadas* in the city," he told her. "Everyone—even visitors—are expected to go to worship on Friday."

Sajada. The word was familiar; and after a moment it clicked. Daulo had pointed out Milika's *sajada* to her on that first tour of the village, but at the time she'd still been posing as a Qasaman and had been afraid to ask what the place was. But then why had they never gone there . . . ? *Ah—of course.* Presumably this type of worship was a weekly event, and her only other Friday on Qasama had been spent flat on her back recovering from her crash injuries.

Which immediately brought up another problem: she hadn't the foggiest idea of what she was heading into, or how she'd be expected to behave once they got there. "Daulo, I don't know anything about how you worship here," she muttered.

He frowned at her. "What do you mean? Worship is worship."

There were several possible responses to that; she chose what she hoped was the safest one. "True, but form varies widely from place to place."

"I thought you learned everything about us from your father's trip here."

Jin felt sweat breaking out on her forehead. Walking through a crowd of Qasamans was hardly the time to be making even veiled references of this sort. "His hosts didn't show him everything," she murmured tightly. "Would you mind keeping your voice down?"

He threw her a brief glare and fell silent. *No,* she thought morosely, *he hasn't forgiven me yet for last night.* She just hoped his bruised ego would heal before he did something dangerous.

They reached the *sajada* a few minutes later, an impressive white-and-gold building that looked to be a scaled-up version of the one she'd seen in Milika—and now that she thought about it, almost identical with similar structures she'd spotted in the tapes from the previous mission. A conformity which, taken with Daulo's comment about worship being worship, implied a strong religious uniformity all across Qasama. A state-controlled religion, then? Or merely one that was independently pervasive? She made a mental note to bring up the subject if and when Daulo ever calmed down.

Joining the flow of people, they climbed the steps and headed inside.

"Well?" Daulo asked an hour later as they left the *sajada*. "What did you think?"

"It was like nothing I've ever experienced before," Jin told him honestly. "It was . . . very moving."

"Or primitive, in other words?"

His voice was heavy with challenge. "Not at all," she assured him. "Perhaps more emotional than I'm used to, but a worship service that doesn't touch the emotions is pretty much a waste of time."

A little of the stiffness seemed to go out of his back. "Agreed," he nodded.

The crowds heading home seemed to be thinner than they had been on the way into the *sajada,* Jin noticed, and she asked Daulo about it. "Most of them will have stayed at the *sajada* with their *heyats,*" he told her.

"*Heyats?*"

"Groups of friends and neighbors who meet for further worship," he explained, throwing her an odd look. "Don't you have anything like that on—at home?" he amended, glancing around at the scattering of other pedestrians within earshot.

"Well . . . they're not called *heyats,* anyway," she said, thinking hard. It was evident the Qasamans took their religious expression very seriously. If she was going to win Daulo back as a more or less willing ally again, she had better find an answer that emphasized the similarities between Qasaman and Aventinian worship and minimized the differences. "But as you said earlier, worship is worship," she continued. "Only our style is different. The intent is certainly the same."

"I understand that. It's the style I'm trying to find out about."

"But style isn't really what counts . . ." She trailed off as something ahead caught her attention. "Daulo . . . how obvious is it that we're not city people?"

They took another three steps before he answered. "Those *ghaalas* up there, are they what you're worried about?"

"I don't know that word," she murmured, "but if you mean those teens leaning against the building, yes, that's who I mean. Can they tell from our clothing that we're from a village?"

"Probably," Daulo said calmly. "But don't let it worry you. They won't bother us." He paused. "And if they do, let me handle it. Understand?"

"Sure," Jin said. Her heart, already pounding in her ears, picked up its pace a bit. The scruffy-looking youths—seven of them, she counted—definitely had their eyes on her and Daulo.

And were definitely drifting away from the wall onto the walk-way. Moving to block their path.

Chapter 29

A drop of sweat ran down between Jin's shoulderblades. *Cross the street,* she wanted to urge . . . but she knew full well what Daulo's reaction would be. She might as well suggest they turn and run back to the *sajada* for sanctuary.

At least none of the youths blocking the walkway appeared to be armed. That was something, anyway.

"But if you have to fight," she murmured suddenly, "stay as far back from them as you can. Understand?"

He glanced at her; but before he could comment one of the youths swaggered a step forward.

"Hello there, baelcra-keeper," he said conversationally as she and Daulo stopped. "Your own *sajada* burn down last night or something?"

"No," Daulo replied with a touch of ice in his voice. "Though if we're going to mention the *sajada,* you don't seem to be dressed for a visit there."

"Maybe we went earlier," another youth said with a sly grin. "Maybe you and your woman were too busy *pharpesing* to go then, huh?"

Another word the Troft translation tapes hadn't covered; but Daulo jerked as if he'd been stung. "And who'd know all about *pharpesing* better than *ghaalas* like you?" he snapped.

Insult traded for insult, clearly; but none of the toughs seemed especially disturbed. In fact, to Jin's eye they almost looked pleased by Daulo's reaction. As if they'd been deliberately trying to get him mad.

Which may have been exactly what they'd planned. At seven-to-one odds, picking a fight would be little more than a game to them. And a game with potentially rich rewards, too, if Daulo's clothing also identified his social and financial positions. It might not even take an overt robbery, in fact—depending on how Qasaman law was written, it was possible that if they could get Daulo to throw the first punch, they could claim damages from him. It could explain why the youths hadn't moved to encircle them: they might have to be able to claim afterwards that Daulo hadn't been threatened.

And in that case . . . there might just be something Jin could do to throw salt water on their little scheme.

" . . . ought to slink back to your little drip-water village now and tend your *pharpesing* little women, okay?"

Beside her, Jin could feel Daulo trembling. Whatever the incomprehensible slang was they'd been tossing back and forth, he was tottering on the brink of losing control. Gritting her teeth, Jin took a deep breath. This was it—

"All right," she snapped, suddenly stepping forward. "That's just about enough of *that*. Get out of our way."

The toughs' jaws sagged with astonishment, instant proof that she had indeed just kicked the supports out from under their game plan. Picking a seven-to-one fight with a man was one thing; picking the same fight with a woman was something else entirely. Not even a financial settlement would make up for what a fiasco like that would do to their reputations.

"Shut your mouth, woman," the first youth snarled at her, his cheek twitching with obvious uncertainty. "Unless this *fhach*-faced friend of yours prefers hiding behind—"

"I said *get out of our way!*" Jin yelled. Raising her arms, she charged.

The move caught him totally flatfooted, and she'd slammed her shoulder into his ribs before he could even get his hands up to stop her.

It didn't hurt him, of course—she was taking enough of a chance here without exhibiting Cobra strength in the bargain. But the damage to his pride was all she could have hoped for. Snarling something incomprehensible under his breath, he grabbed her arms and thrust her into the grip of two of his companions—

And stepped past her just in time to catch Daulo's fist in his face.

The blow staggered him back. Daulo followed it with a punch to his solar plexus, knocking him to the ground. "Leave him alone!" Jin wailed as the two holding her arms pulled her back out of the

way and the other four belatedly moved in to circle Daulo. The
hands on her upper arms tightened their grip; crossing her arms
across her chest, she reached up with opposite hands to press theirs
against her arms.

Pinning them solidly in place.

One down, two out of the fight, she ticked off mentally. Daulo
and his opponents were crouched in what seemed to be variants
of the same fighting stance, the toughs continuing to circle as if
unsure of whether or not they really wanted to take on the man
who'd just decked their leader.

And then, almost in unison, they moved in.

Daulo knew enough about street fighting not to let all four reach
him at the same time. He took a long stride to his left, flailing a
wild punch at the youth on that side to force him back.

He seemed as surprised as anyone when the punch actually
connected. Even more so when the youth went down and stayed
there.

A second tough got within range and snapped a kick in Daulo's
direction. Daulo leaped belatedly out of its way; but his move
turned out to be unnecessary. The kick missed by at least twenty
centimeters, and even as Daulo stepped forward to throw a count-
ering punch, the youth lost his balance totally and toppled to the
walkway.

It was enough for the other two. Backing away, they glanced at
each other and at their two companions still holding—and being
held against—Jin's arms. Then, turning, they took off down the
walkway.

Daulo swung around to face Jin and her warders. "Well?" he
demanded.

Jin recognized a cue when she heard it. She released her pressure grip on their hands, senses alert in case they tried something
last-ditch foolish.

They didn't. Letting go of her, they sidled past Daulo and ran.

Daulo watched them go. Then, turning back to Jin, he looked
her up and down. "You all right?" he asked at last.

She nodded. "You?"

There was a peculiar expression on his face. "Uh-huh. We'd better
get out of here, before there are any awkward questions asked."

Jin glanced around. No one was approaching them, but several
of the passersby were eyeing them from a healthy distance. "Right."

They'd covered another block before he finally asked the inevitable question. "What did you do to them?"

She shrugged uncomfortably. This could be extremely ticklish . . . "Well, for starters, I was hanging onto the ones who were holding my arms, keeping them out of the fight. The others . . . I gave them each a blast of focused ultrasonic in the head before you hit them."

"Which is why you wanted me to keep back, I suppose. And that knocked them out?"

"No, I didn't want to hit them that hard. I just gave them enough of a jolt to rattle their brains and throw their balance off track."

Walking closely beside him, she could feel his arm begin to tremble. *Uh-oh*, she thought tensely. *Too much for his Qasaman ego to take?* "Daulo? You okay?"

"Oh, sure," he said, a noticeable quaver in his voice. "I was just wondering what their friends are going to say when they hear about this. Seven of them, beaten right into the ground by a villager and a woman."

She frowned up at him . . . and only then realized that the trembling she heard and felt wasn't rage or shame.

It was suppressed laughter.

She fell silent after that . . . which gave Daulo the rest of the way back to their temporary home to try and figure out just why the whole thing was so funny.

On one level, it shouldn't have been—that much he was acutely aware of. For him to have been defended by a *woman* was something that should have him red-faced with shame, not shaking with laughter. Even if she *was* a demon-warrior woman, and even if the alternative *had* been to get himself beaten to blood-pulp.

No, he told himself firmly. *That's not the way to think of it. It's more like a couple of villagers putting one over on a bunch of jerkfaced city ghallas. Or a villager and a villager-by-adoption, anyway.*

The thought startled him. *Villager-by-adoption.* Was he really starting to think of Jin Moreau in such friendly terms? No— *impossible*, he assured himself. She was a temporary ally, temporarily under his protection as a point of honor. Nothing more. In a few days her rescuers would come, and she'd go, and he'd never see her again.

And he wondered—though not very hard—why that thought finally stilled the laughter within him.

"Are all the formalities over for the day?" she asked as they reached the apartment. "I'd like to change clothes."

"They're over at least until sundown," Daulo told her, keying the lock and opening the door. "And that service is optional."

"Good," she said, stepping inside. "I think it must be a basic human failing not to be able to come up with formal clothing as comfortable as day-to-daywear—what's that light?"

"Phone message," Daulo explained, frowning. Who might have known to call them here? Walking over to the instrument, he keyed for the message.

The phone beeped, and a thin strip of paper slid out from the message slot. "What?" Jin asked.

"It's from Mayor Capparis," Daulo told her, reading it quickly. "He says Mangus has called for a work party to be assembled at the city center this Sunday morning."

"How do they pick the workers?"

Daulo skimmed the paper. "Looks like it's on the basis of need. Unemployed and poor first, based on city records—"

"Wait a second," she interrupted him. "Aren't they even going to try and contact any of the workers they've had out there before? Ones they've already trained?"

"Maybe they already have."

"Oh. Right."

"Um. Mayor Capparis recommends we stick to the marketplaces' second-booths when we pick up city-style clothing."

Jin nodded. "Good idea. What about those city records, though? How are we going to fake that?"

Daulo shrugged. "Presumably Mayor Capparis will take care of that."

"Um." Jin stepped toward him. "May I see the message?"

He handed the paper over. She gazed at it for what seemed to be an unnecessarily long time. "You having trouble reading it?" he asked at last.

"No," she said slowly. "I was just wondering . . . It's addressed to you. By name."

"Of course it is. So?"

"So doesn't it strike you as odd that those toughs just happened to be hanging around directly between the *sajada* and here?"

He frowned. "I don't see the problem. You're the one who pointed out we were dressed in villagers' clothing. They were just after some fun."

"Maybe." She chewed at her lip, an annoying habit of hers. "But suppose for a moment that there was more to it than that. Suppose that whoever it is who doesn't want villagers snooping around inside Mangus found out we were going to try for one of their work parties."

"That's ridiculous," Daulo snorted. "How would they find out . . ." He trailed off, eyes dropping to the paper still in her hand. "Mayor Capparis wouldn't tell them," he said flatly.

"I'm not suggesting he did," Jin shook her head. "But this message presumably came from his office. Couldn't someone there have found out about it, either before or after it was sent?"

Daulo gritted his teeth. It *wasn't* all that farfetched, unfortunately. If one of the mayor's enemies had gotten wind of the scheme, putting them into the hospital would be a safe and simple way for him to thwart it. "It's possible, I suppose," he admitted aloud to Jin. "But if you're suggesting we pick up and run, forget it."

"We don't have to run," she said. "Just move. Find somewhere else, where no one—including Mayor Capparis—knows where to find us."

"We still have to show up at the city center," he pointed out.

"True. But there's nothing much we can do about that."

"Then what's the point of hiding now?" he countered. "All it does is buy us a couple of days."

"A couple of days can mean a lot. Among other things, it gives us more time to prepare."

She was right; and down deep he recognized that. But on the surface, his honor had surged once again to the fore. "No," he shook his head. "I'm not running. Not without better proof than that."

She took a deep breath, and he braced himself for an argument. "Then the deal's off," she said bluntly.

He blinked with surprise. "What?"

"I said the deal's off. You might as well head back to Milika right now, because I'm going into Mangus alone."

"That's ridiculous. I'm not letting you do something that— that—" He shut up, realizing with annoyance he was starting to sputter. "Besides, what do we have to worry about? With your powers—"

"My powers are designed to protect *me*," she cut him off. "Not friends or people around me; just me. And if you're not going to cooperate, I can't take the risk of something happening to you."

"Why?" he snarled. "Because my father would call the Shahni down on your head?"

"Because you're my friend," she said quietly.

For a moment he just glared at her, feeling his arguments melt and drain away. "All right," he gritted at last. "I'll offer you a compromise. If you can prove we're under direct attack, I'll agree to anything you say."

She hesitated, then nodded. "Fair enough. Well . . . let's see. I suppose the best way to start would be for you to call up Mayor Capparis's office and leave a message telling him that we're moving to a new place. We won't really be going anywhere," she hastened to add, "but if there's an informant there, he'll get the word out to his fighters. Then we can find a place on the sidelines and watch what happens. If anything."

He clenched his teeth, trying without success to find some grounds on which to object. Then, silently, he stepped to the phone.

Mayor Capparis wasn't in, of course, probably still meeting with one of the *heyats* at his own *sajada*. Leaving the message, he hung up and turned back to Jin. "Okay. Now what?"

"Now we load everything back in the car and drive off as if we're leaving," she told him. "We need to go out and buy some city-style clothes, anyway. First, though, we'll want to find some place near here that would be a plausible hiding place."

"Easy enough," Daulo grunted, stepping over to where he'd laid out his clothing the night before. "We just look for an apartment whose door has no protector."

"Protector?"

"Yes," he said. "The traditional carved medallions every household places near their doors to protect them from the evil eye. Didn't you notice the ones in Milika?"

He had the minor satisfaction of seeing her blush with chagrin. "No, I'm afraid I completely missed them," she admitted. "Well . . . good. That'll make the hunt easier, anyway."

"So what happens once we've found this empty apartment?"

She smiled lopsidedly. "With any luck, sometime tonight it'll be attacked."

And with that she disappeared into the bedroom. *No,* Daulo told himself firmly, *you don't want to know.* Swallowing, he returned to his packing.

Chapter 30

"You're actually going out in public like that?" Daulo asked.

Standing before the apartment's largest mirror, Jin took one last look at herself in her gray night-fighter garb and turned to face him. Seated on the couch, his hand rubbing restless patterns on the end table beside him, Daulo glared back with barely controlled distaste. "If it's the outfit that offends you," she said coolly, "you'd better get used to it. From what you've told me it sounds like Mangus will be hiring mainly men for their work party, and if I'm going to get in it'll have to be disguised as a man."

He growled something under his breath. "This whole thing is ridiculous. Even if someone *was* out to get us, what makes you think they fell for that little game of yours? Suppose, for starters, they haven't noticed that that's our car parked outside the other apartment?"

"I told you one of those toughs was watching when we drove off this morning," she reminded him, pulling her full-face mask from the back of a chair and fitting it on. "You have to make it a *little* hard for them, Daulo—everyone gets suspicious of prizes handed over on silver platters."

"It'll serve you right if they're too stupid to catch your subtleties," he snorted. "Then while you're out there watching an empty apartment, they'll break in here instead."

"That's why you're going to have this," she told him, pulling a small cylinder from her belt and handing it over. "Short-range signaller—flip the top cap back and push the button if you're in trouble. I'm only going to be two blocks away; I can be here before you've stopped insulting each other."

Sighing, he took the device. "I just hope all this is nothing but a fever-trick of your imagination."

"I hope so, too," she admitted, scooping up the pack she'd prepared and settling it onto her shoulders. "But if it isn't, then tonight is the obvious time for them to strike."

"I suppose so. Well, at least we'll know one way or another by morning."

Probably a lot sooner than that, Jin thought. "Right. Well, I'm off. Lock the door behind me, and don't be afraid to signal if you hear anything suspicious. Promise?"

He managed a smile. "Sure. You watch yourself, Jin Moreau."

"I will." Activating her optical enhancers, she cracked open the door and looked outside. No one was in sight. Slipping out, she closed the door behind her and headed off down the street.

She'd been ensconced in her chosen place of concealment, halfway under an outside stairwell, for barely an hour when they showed up: the same seven toughs who'd accosted her and Daulo on the street that morning.

And it was quickly clear they weren't total amateurs at this. Moving silently down the deserted street, taking advantage of shadows and cover, they approached the vacant apartment from both directions. Two stopped at the car, presumably making sure no one was watching from there, before joining the rest at the apartment door. One crouched over the lock, and after a few seconds swung it open. Moving quickly, the group filed inside the darkened apartment.

They probably hadn't even realized yet that the place was deserted when she caught up with them; and it was for certain that none of them had a chance to shout before her disruptor's ultrasound washed over them from close range, hammering them into instant unconsciousness. They dropped into seven heaps on the floor and lay still.

Jin nearly wound up joining them. For a long minute she staggered against the wall, gripping her stomach and fighting to keep her balance. Layn had warned them about the dangers of using sonics in such enclosed spaces; but there had been no other way to silently disable the toughs without killing them. And questions of ethics apart, with the Shahni now aware that there was an outworlder on Qasama, leaving laser-ridden corpses lying around would be about as clever as standing up at the *sajada* and identifying herself as a demon warrior.

Eventually, the throbbing in her head and gut faded away, and she set about tying up the would-be assailants with rope from her pack. That accomplished, she stepped to the door again and scanned the street. Still no one in sight, and she gave silent thanks that Azras's night life shut down so early in the evening. With a little luck, she might get back to the apartment in time to get at least a few hours' sleep.

Thoughts of the apartment reminded her of Daulo; Daulo, who still didn't believe they were under deliberate attack. Pulling her signaller from her belt, she flipped back the lid . . . and paused. True, she could show him evidence that the toughs had indeed tried it again, but given the Qasaman sense of personal honor, they might conceivably have launched this second attack entirely on their own. What she needed was some kind of admission from one of them as to who had put them up to this job.

And until she had such a confession, there was no point in dragging Daulo out here. Putting the signaller back, she returned to the unconscious youths. Assuming the one who'd thrown the first challenge this morning was the leader . . . locating him, she hoisted him to her shoulder and carried him across the street to the car. It would have been nice to have a supply of those sophisticated interrogation drugs they were always using in the telvide fictions, but in their absence she would just have to fall back on one of the more traditional methods. And for that, she was going to need a little more privacy.

Starting the car, she headed off through Azras's deserted streets.

The knock on the door jolted Daulo awake, and for a disoriented heartbeat he stared in confusion at the darkened ceiling. Then it clicked. "Coming," he growled, getting stiffly out of the chair where he'd fallen asleep. Jasmine Moreau, returning from her little hide-seek game—and the stupid woman had managed to forget the door's combination. *If this is the kind of people who become Cobras,* he thought sourly as he straightened his tunic and stomped to the door, *we haven't got much to worry about.* The knock came a third time; "I'm *coming,*" he snarled and threw open the door.

Three men stood there: one middle-aged, the other two much younger. Their city-style clothing was all similar; their grim faces were almost identical. "Are you Daulo Sammon of the village Milika?" the middle-aged man asked.

Daulo got his tongue working. "I am," he nodded. "And you?"

"May we come in?"

It wasn't really a question. Daulo stepped aside and the three filed into the room, the last flicking on the light as he passed the switch. "And you are . . . ?" Daulo asked again, squinting as his eyes tried to adjust to the sudden light.

The door was closed with a thud, and when Daulo could see clearly again he found the middle-aged man standing in front of him, holding out a gold-rimmed pendant from around his neck. "I am Moffren Omnathi; representing the Shahni of Qasama."

Daulo felt an icy shiver run up his back. "I am honored," he managed through stiff lips, making the sign of respect. "How may I serve you?"

Omnathi's eyes flicked around the room. "Your father, Kruin Sammon, sent the Shahni a message through Mayor Capparis of the city Azras yesterday. Do you know the content of this message?"

"Ah . . . in a general way, yes," Daulo said, wishing he knew what, if anything, his father had told this man. "He said he was going to inform the Shahni that the Yithtra family had discovered an offworld artifact."

"Essentially correct," Omnathi nodded casually. "Do members of the Yithtra family find such artifacts regularly?"

Daulo frowned. "No, of course not, sir."

"Oh? An unusual event, then?"

"Most certainly."

"An event most people would think worth staying to see?"

Daulo fought to keep his expression neutral as he finally saw the net the other was weaving. "I suppose most people would, yes."

"Yet you chose to come to Azras instead. Why?"

A drop of sweat trickled between Daulo's shoulder-blades. "I had an errand to perform here."

"One that couldn't wait a few days?"

One of Omnathi's companions emerged from the bedroom and stepped to the older man's side. "Yes?" Omnathi asked without taking his eyes off Daulo.

"Nothing but some of his own clothing," the other reported. "Certainly nothing a woman would wear or use."

Omnathi nodded, and Daulo thought he saw a brief flicker of annoyance cross his face. "Thank you," Omnathi told the other. "You see now, Daulo Sammon, that we're aware you didn't come to Azras alone. Where is the woman you brought here?"

Two blocks over, the thought flashed through Daulo's mind, and his stomach tightened with the realization that she could wander back at any time. "I really don't know where she is—"

"Why not?" the older man snapped. "According to Mayor

Capparis, your father asked him to get you and an unnamed companion into some sort of work party. Was this woman to be your companion?"

"Of course not," Daulo said, trying for a combination of amusement and insult at the very idea. "I had planned to ask my brother to go to Mangus with me, but decided against it when this other matter came up."

He watched Omnathi, holding his breath, but the mention of Mangus didn't spark any reaction he could see. "You didn't tell Mayor Capparis about your change in plans. For that matter, we were rather surprised to find you here, since you'd told him you were moving elsewhere."

Daulo shrugged. "I thought that Mangus might have a listening ear in Mayor Capparis's office," he said, adopting Jin's theory for lack of anything better to say. "I thought if they were watching for two people instead of one, I might have a better chance of getting in."

Omnathi's forehead creased slightly. "You sound like you're preparing to assault an armed camp. What do you want with Mangus, anyway?"

Daulo hesitated. "I don't believe the place is what it seems," he said.

Omnathi flicked a glance to one of his aides. "Tarri?"

"Mangus is a private manufacturing center about fifty kilometers east of here," the other said promptly. "High-quality electronics, both research and manufacture. Run by the Obolo Nardin family; I believe the last full check by the Shahni was carried out approximately two years ago. No hints then of any unusual activity."

Omnathi nodded and turned back to Daulo. "You have recent evidence to dispute that last?"

Daulo drew himself up a bit. "They refuse to allow villagers in," he said stiffly. "For me, that's adequate reason to be suspicious."

Omnathi's lip twisted. "Hard though it may be for you to understand, city-bred prejudices are often as ridiculous as those of villagers," he growled. "At any rate, you'd do better to save your pride for more important matters—the safety and protection of your world, for example. Tell us what you know about the woman."

"She told me her name was Jasmine Alventin," Daulo said, again wishing he knew what they'd learned from his father. "We found her on the road, injured, and brought her into our house."

"And . . ."

"And she told us she was from Sollas and that she'd been in an accident. That's all."

"Didn't you think it advisable to press for further details?" Omnathi persisted. "Or even to check up on her story?"

"Of course we did," Daulo said, trying to sound offended. "We sent men out to search the roads for her car and companions."

"Did you find them?"

"No." Daulo glanced at the other two men, looked back at Omnathi. "What is this all about, anyway? Is she an escaped criminal or something?"

"She's an offworld invader," Omnathi said bluntly.

Daulo had expected him to ignore or evade the question; the very unexpectedness of the reply startled him almost as much as if he were hearing it for the first time. "She's—*what?*" he breathed. "But . . . that's impossible."

"Why?" Omnathi snapped. "You said yourself the Yithtra family had found an offworld artifact. Didn't it ever occur to you that an offworld artifact might be accompanied by someone to use it?"

"Yes, but . . ." Daulo floundered, hunting desperately for something to say. Jin's words just before she'd left popped back into his mind: *you have to make it a* little *hard for them, Daulo— everyone gets suspicious of prizes handed over on silver platters.* "But it was Jasmine Alventin who told us it was an offworld artifact in the first place," he said. "Why would she do that if it were hers?"

Omnathi frowned. "What do you mean? Told you how?"

"Well, when I heard there was a truck bringing something unusual into Milika I drove off to take a look," Daulo explained, trying to keep his voice and face under control. "Jasmine Alventin was with me at the time, and at a slow section of the road she suddenly got out of the car and climbed in the back of the truck to see what it was."

Omnathi seemed taken aback. "Your father didn't mention that," he said.

Daulo took a deep breath. "Well, actually . . . I believe I told him it was *I* who looked into the truck,"

Omnathi's eyes were steady on him. "You *believe* you told him?"

Daulo licked his lips. "I . . . suppose I wanted to . . . take the credit."

For a long moment the room was silent. Omnathi and the others just looked at him, contempt showing in varying degrees in their expressions. "You told us you didn't know where the woman was," Omnathi said at last. "Why not?"

"Because she left me just after sundown," Daulo said. "She said she was anxious to get back home and asked me where she could pick up a bus heading north. I took her to the waiting area at the city center and left her there."

"Did you, now." Slowly, Omnathi ran the tip of his tongue along his upper lip, gazing hard at Daulo. Daulo stared back, listening to his heart thudding in his chest. "Tell me," Omnathi said abruptly, "did you actually see her get on any of the buses?"

"Ah . . ." Daulo considered. "No, not really. She *was* walking toward the one for Sollas when I drove away, though."

One of the other men cleared his throat. "Shall I have the bus intercepted?" he asked.

"No," Omnathi said slowly. "No, I think that would be a waste of time. She didn't take that bus. Or any of the others."

Daulo blinked. "I don't understand—"

"Tell me, Daulo Sammon," Omnathi interrupted him. "Where is your car?"

"Uh . . . just outside the building, in the parking area."

Omnathi shook his head. "No. In fact, it's nowhere for six streets around you. We looked for it."

Daulo's heart skipped a beat. He and Jin had left the vehicle parked in plain sight only two blocks away . . . "That's impossible," he managed. "I left it right outsi—"

"Do you have the keys?" Omnathi asked.

No; he'd given them to Jin in case she had some need of the vehicle while she was out. "Of course," he said. "They're on the table over there."

One of the men moved over to look. "No, they're not," he reported, sifting through the personal items Daulo had piled there.

"Find them," Omnathi ordered. "Have you been gone from this apartment since she left, Daulo Sammon?"

"No." Daulo watched as the two men began searching the room, feeling the sweat begin to gather on his forehead again. It was all very well to ease them toward the conclusion that Jin had stolen his car, but they weren't going to believe it unless he came up with a plausible mechanism for that theft. "I *was* asleep when you arrived, though—"

"What's this?" one of the searchers interrupted him, holding up a small black cylinder.

The signaller Jin had given him.

"I . . . don't know," he said through stiff lips. "It's not mine."

"Be careful with it," Omnathi said sharply, stepping over to the other's side and taking the signaller from him. He studied it for a moment, then carefully lifted the top cap. *Push the button if you're in trouble, and I'll be there,* Jin had said . . .

But Omnathi made no move to do that. "Interesting," he murmured. "Looks like a radio transceiver of some kind—here's the antenna." He looked back at Daulo. "Did you tell her how to work the lock combination on the apartment door?" he asked.

"Uh . . . not directly, no. Though she might have seen me key it."

Omnathi nodded grimly. "I'm sure she did." He hefted the signaller in the palm of his hand. "Do you snore when you sleep, Daulo Sammon?"

The question took Daulo by surprise. "Ah . . . I really don't know. Perhaps a bit."

Omnathi grunted. "Doesn't really matter, I suppose. The sound of a sleeper's breathing is fairly distinctive to someone who knows what to listen for."

"Sir . . . I—"

Omnathi impaled him with a glare. "She planted this on you," he grated. "All she had to do was pretend to get on that bus, then follow you back and wait for you to fall asleep. Then she slipped in, took your keys, and left. Any idea how long you were asleep?"

Daulo shrugged, feeling a little dazed. They were practically writing his alibi for him. "An hour, perhaps. Maybe longer."

Omnathi muttered something under his breath. "An *hour*. God in heaven."

Daulo licked his lips. "Sir . . . I don't understand any of this. What is Jasmine Alventin's interest in my family?"

"I don't think she has any interest in you whatsoever," the older man sighed. "She's simply been using you: first to help her recover from her spacecraft's crash, and after that to create a diversion."

"A diversion?"

"Yes." Omnathi waved toward the northwest. "Once she realized her discovery was inevitable, she simply took charge of the time-table, letting your father know about the supply pod in Yithtra family hands and perhaps encouraging him to notify the Shahni before they did. Then, while the focus of our attention was on her spacecraft and your village, she persuaded you to bring her here, distracted you further with a feint toward the bus, and proceeded to steal your car." He paused, eying Daulo thoughtfully . . . and when he spoke again his voice had taken on a hard edge. "But innocent victims or not, the Sammon family nevertheless has aided an enemy of Qasama. It's possible that you may yet be punished for that."

Daulo swallowed hard. "Yet we *did* inform the Shahni about the offworld artifact as soon as we knew about it," he reminded the other.

"That may weigh in your favor," Omnathi nodded. "Whether it does or not will depend on how quickly we capture this Jasmine Alventin. And what we learn from her."

He signaled his men, and they headed for the door. There, Omnathi paused and looked back. "Tell me, Daulo Sammon; your father said the woman asked many questions. Did she ask about anything specifically about our culture or technology?"

The question caught Daulo by surprise. "Uh . . . no, not that I can remember. Why?"

"It occurs to me that this penetration of Mangus might originally have been her idea."

"It wasn't," Daulo shook his head. "Getting into Mangus has been something I've wanted to do for a long time."

"Perhaps. Then again, perhaps the idea was yours and the timing hers." For a moment Omnathi gazed thoughtfully at him. "Very well, then. Satisfy your pride as you will, Daulo Sammon. But remember while you do so that your real enemies aren't in Mangus or anywhere else on Qasama."

Daulo bowed and made the sign of respect. "I will, Moffren Omnathi."

They left. Daulo stood where he was for a handful of heartbeats; then, moving carefully on weak knees, he wobbled to the window and peered out at the car's taillights pulling away down the street. An emissary of the Shahni themselves . . . and Daulo had lied through his teeth to him.

For an enemy of Qasama.

He spat an oath into the empty room. *Curse you, Jasmine Moreau,* he thought viciously. *For God's sake, be careful. Please.*

Chapter 31

The tough gasped as the ammonia fumes rose into his nostrils and he returned abruptly to consciousness. "I'd suggest you keep quiet," Jin advised him, making her voice as deep and manly as she comfortably could.

He obeyed . . . but his eyes suddenly came wide open as he got his first clear look around him. Jin couldn't really blame him; sitting on the edge of a high roof, with nothing between him and a long fall but two thin ropes belaying his trussed wrists and ankles to a stubby chimney five meters away, he had a perfect right to be scared. In fact, she rather admired his self-control in not screaming his head off. "Let's start with your name, shall we?" she said, squatting down beside him.

"Hebros Sibbio," he managed, eyes focused on his lifelines.

"Look at me when I speak to you," Jin ordered. He did so, eyes almost unwillingly shifting up to her masked face. "That's better. Now tell me who told you to break into the apartment you hit tonight."

"I . . . no one," he said, his voice cracking slightly.

Jin sighed theatrically. "Perhaps you don't fully understand the situation here, Hebros Sibbio," she said coldly. "Your hairy butt is hanging well past the edge there. All I have to do is cut these two ropes and you'll be off to explain all this to God instead of to me. You think He'll be more lenient with you?" He shuddered and shook his head. "Neither do I," she agreed. "So tell me who put you up to this job."

"I don't know!" he gasped. "As God is my witness, I don't *know.* A man—he didn't give his name—called me up this morning and told me he wanted us to beat up a village man who would be at an apartment at Three-forty-six Kutzko Street."

"And kill him?"

"No! We don't kill—not even villagers. I wouldn't have agreed if that had been the bargain."

"Keep your voice down. What *was* the bargain, then? What payment did he promise you?"

Sibbio shivered again. "There was to be no payment. He promised only not to reveal some of our other . . . activities to the rulers of Azras."

"Illegal activities?"

"Yes. And he named some of them . . ." He trailed off, staring pleadingly at her. "It's the truth—I swear by God's presence it is."

Blackmail, then . . . which unfortunately eliminated the chance of backtracking a payment drop. "Did he tell you the villager's name, or say *why* he wanted him beaten up?"

"No."

For a moment the rooftop was silent as Jin considered. If Sibbio was telling the truth, it meant his mystery caller had at least a passing familiarity with Azras's underworld and its activities. At the same time, paradoxically, that knowledge must be fairly limited for him to have picked such an obviously small-time group as Sibbio's to handle his dirty work.

Unless this was as well organized as Azras's criminal underworld got. She made a mental note to check with Daulo on that one.

Either way, Sibbio was clearly a dead end. "There's a small knife by the chimney over there," she pointed, getting to her feet. "You can roll or otherwise work your way over to it and cut yourself free. Your friends are still at the apartment you broke into; collect them and all of you get out of Azras."

Sibbio's mouth fell open. "Get out . . . but this is our home."

"Too bad," Jin said, letting her voice harden. "Because for the next few days it'll be *my* home, too . . . and if I see you again while I'm here, Hebros Sibbio, you'll be taking that premature trip to see God that we discussed earlier. Understood?"

He nodded up at her, a single nervous motion of his head. Jin didn't especially like threatening the boy, but she liked the thought of him talking to Mangus even less. "Good. Let's both hope I never see you again."

Moving quietly across the roof, she reached the stairwell that she'd brought Sibbio up by and opened the door. He would make it to the knife, eventually, unless he lost his balance first and fell off the roof. As far as she was concerned, it didn't much matter what happened.

Nevertheless, she waited silently at the open door until he was safely away from the roof's edge.

She was two blocks from their apartment, visions of a soft bed hovering siren-like in front of her eyes, when she spotted the two cars parked at the building.

Instantly, she shut off the lights and pulled over to the curb, keying in her optical enhancers' telescopic and light-amp capabilities as she did so. Both cars were empty, but—she flipped briefly to infrared—the tires and drive shafts were still warm. And though her angle was bad, it looked very much like the lights in their apartment were on.

A cold chill ran up her spine. From what she'd seen of both village and city life, midnight visitors weren't exactly commonplace on Qasama. Could they be messengers from Milika, perhaps, bringing news from Daulo's father?

Or had Mangus hired a back-up set of muscle?

Jin cursed under her breath and started the car forward again. The direct route through the front door was out, of course—even if it was something as innocuous as a message from home, there was no plausible excuse she could think of as to why she, a woman, would be out alone at night. And if Daulo was in trouble, she had no intention of walking straight into his attackers' arms, anyway.

But there were always more indirect routes to be had ...

She pulled around the next corner, parking the car a block away in a handy row of similar vehicles. Keeping to the shadows, enhanced senses alert for trouble, she made her way back to the apartment building, arriving at the side opposite to theirs within a couple of minutes. The building didn't offer much in the way of handholds, but she didn't have time for a long climb, anyway. Taking one last look around, she bent her knees and jumped.

She made it onto the roof without any sound louder than a slight scraping of shoes on roof tiles. Crossing it, she squatted down at the edge and scanned the courtyard below for signs of life. There weren't any that she could see. Not surprisingly; with no access to the courtyard from outside except through the individual apartments, there would be no reason for anyone to watch the place once they'd established she wasn't hiding there. Setting her jaw, she eased over the edge, scrabbled for handholds that weren't there, and dropped to the ground.

The downside landing wasn't nearly as quiet as the upside one had been, and for what seemed like a long time she crouched motionlessly, auditory enhancers at full power as she waited for some kind of reaction. But the inhabitants of Azras must have had the city dwellers' traditional ability to sleep through noise, and after a minute she rose and loped across the courtyard to the rear of their apartment.

Through the sliding glass door, she could see the diffuse glow of lights from either the foodprep area or living room. Unfortunately, that was *all* she could see—the arrangement of the rooms didn't allow a direct view into the front of the apartment. An ear pressed against the glass yielded nothing. *Into the valley of death, and all that,* she thought grimly; and, pointing her little finger at the door's lock, she fired a burst from her metalwork laser.

The crack and spitting of flash-vaporized metal seemed to thunder in her ears, but there was no reaction from inside. Sliding the door open a crack, Jin slipped inside, closing it behind her. From the living room ahead came the faint scraping of shoes on rug.

She held her breath and keyed her auditory enhancers to full power. The sound of breathing came to her . . . the sound *of one* person breathing.

So all the company's left? Apparently . . . but there was no point in taking chances. Curling her hands to rest her thumbs lightly against the triggers in her third-finger nails, she straightened her little fingers into laser firing position and stepped around the corner.

Daulo, standing at the window, spun around as if he'd been stung. "Jin!" he gasped, seeming to wilt. "God above, you startled me."

"Sorry," she apologized, glancing quickly around. Daulo was indeed alone. "I thought you might be in trouble," she added, dropping her hands back to her sides.

"I am," he sighed, walking unsteadily to the couch and sinking into it. "But you're in more. They know who you are."

"They who?" Jin asked, her heartbeat picking up again. "Mangus?"

"Worse. The Shahni." He hissed between his teeth. "I just had a visit from one Moffren Omnathi and two of his men. They've identified you as the outworlder they're looking for. I managed—maybe—to persuade them that you'd stolen my car and headed north toward Sollas."

Jin took a moment to digest that. She'd known it would happen eventually. But she hadn't expected it quite so soon. "Did you tell them we'd been working together?"

"Do I *look* stupid?" he snorted. "Of course not. I played the total innocent, telling them you were a stranger who'd talked me into bringing you to Azras and then disappeared. Fortunately—I guess— they found that signaller you left, and decided you'd used it to listen for me to go to sleep so you could sneak in and take my car keys."

Jin bit at her lip. "As good a theory as any, I suppose. I just hope they didn't make it up just to make you think they believed you."

"Well, they left, didn't they?"

"Maybe. Did you actually see them go?"

"I saw the car pull away, yes."

"*One* car? Because there were two here when I drove up."

Daulo muttered something under his breath and started to get to his feet. "Should I—?"

"No, don't look out," Jin stopped him. "If they spotted me coming in, it's too late. If they didn't, you don't want to seem unusually suspicious."

Daulo exhaled a ragged breath. "I thought they seemed too willing to believe me. God above. I hoped they were accepting my words because of my family's position."

"More likely they just weren't sure enough to arrest you. Or else backed off in hopes that you'd lead them to me." Jin glanced at the curtained window, wondering what devices the Qasamans might have for looking through cloth and glass. But if they were doing so, again it was already too late. "They didn't have any photos of me, did they?" she asked.

"Not that they showed me," Daulo shook his head. "Though it hardly matters. As my father pointed out, there were plenty of people in Milika who saw you."

"Well enough to provide the investigators with a good description?"

He threw her an odd look. "Using hypnotics? Of course."

Jin gritted her teeth. She should have realized they'd have something like that available—her father's mission had noted the Qasamans' penchant for mind-enhancement drugs. "Yeah, I forgot about those. Well, maybe the disguise paraphernalia in my pack will be enough."

"You're not going to stay in Azras, are you?"

"Not with the alert already out for your car," Jin shook her head. "I'll head out of town, try to find a place off the road to hide the car in. With luck I'll be able to stay with it until the work party is formed on Sunday. Let me take a set of that cheap city clothing we bought—"

"Hold it a second," Daulo interrupted her, eyes narrowing. "You're not still going to try to get in there, are you?"

"Why not? Unless you told our friend Moffren Omnathi that was what we were planning. Oh, my God," she interrupted herself as the name suddenly clicked.

"What?" Daulo asked sharply.

"Moffren." The name tasted sour on her tongue. "Moff. The man who played guide to our first survey mission, thirty years ago. And very nearly nailed it." She shook her head. "Well, that's the end of the game for you, Daulo. First thing in the morning you find yourself a ride back to Milika and get out of here."

Daulo frowned at her. "Why? Just because the Shahni sent an old enemy of yours to ask me some questions?"

"No—because whatever pits there are in the story you told him, he'll find them," she retorted. "And when he does, he'll act. Fast."

"And you think running back to Milika will keep him from getting to me?"

Jin braced herself. "Of course not. But maybe it'll slow him down enough to let me get into Mangus."

For a long moment his eyes were steady on hers. "So that's what it comes down to, isn't it?" Daulo said at last. "Your mission."

Jin forced her jaw muscles to relax. "Would you have me run somewhere and hide?" she asked.

"Would you have *me* do so?" he countered quietly. "Would you have me go back to my father and tell him I gave up a chance to perhaps uncover a threat to our family because I was afraid?"

"But if they're watching you and you try to go into Mangus—"

"And if they're watching me and I try to run back to Milika?"

Again, they locked gazes. "Daulo, look," Jin sighed at last. "I know this isn't something a woman says to a man on Qasama . . . but I feel responsible for your safety. I talked you and your father into this scheme, after all, and if I can't be right at your side I may not be able to protect you."

"You didn't promise me any protection."

"Not to you, no. I *did* promise it to myself."

To her surprise, he smiled. "And I made a promise to myself,

Jasmine Moreau: to protect you from your cultural ignorance while in Mangus. I can't do that from Milika."

"But—" Jin took a deep breath, sighed in defeat. She simply didn't have time to argue the point any further. The longer she lingered here, the more time Moff would have to weave a net around Azras, and she had to get Daulo's car out of town before that happened. "Will you at least think about it? Please?"

He rose from the couch and stepped forward. "I will," he said softly, reaching out to take her hand. "You be careful, all right?"

"I will." She hesitated, looking up at his eyes. *Cultural differences,* she reminded herself distantly. *He might take this wrong,* but for once, she didn't care; the need to hold someone tightly was almost overpowering in its intensity. Leaning toward him, she put her arms around him.

He didn't pull away, nor did he attempt to make the hug into anything else. Perhaps with potential danger all around them, a simple nonsexual contact from a friend was something he needed right now, too.

For a minute they held each other tightly. Then, almost unwillingly, Jin pulled back. "You take care of yourself, too, okay?" she said. "And if you decide to stay . . . don't look for me in the work party."

He nodded, reaching up to stroke her cheek. "I understand. You'd better go now."

Three minutes later, the city clothing Daulo had given her knotted into a bundle on her back, she was back at the car. No one lay in wait near the vehicle; no one jumped out of the shadows or shot at her as she climbed in and drove away. Either the Shahni's people hadn't gotten the Azras part of their operation fully organized yet, or else Moff was growing careless in his old age. Personally, she wouldn't bet much money on the latter.

But for the time being she appeared to have gained a little breathing space, and she was determined to use it to the fullest. A few kilometers south of Azras—an adequate gap between trees in the forest—and she would have a place to hide for the next day and a half. A little face-shaper gel from her pack, perhaps a wig and some skin darkening, and she'd be able to walk into Azras Sunday morning without being recognized. And after that . . .

But there was no point in trying to think too far ahead. With Qasama's official government actively in the game, she had to be ready to play every move by ear. And hope that her Moreau family heritage counted for something besides just a name.

Chapter 32

"Like this?" Toral Abram asked, shifting his left foot in front of his right.

"Right," Justin nodded. "Now just uncurl your legs and drop onto your back onto the floor, pulling your knees to your chest as you do so."

The young Cobra obeyed, and a second later was spinning around, belly-up, in an awkward-looking fetal position. "And this is a *military* maneuver?" he asked wryly as he came to a halt.

"Trust me," Justin assured him. "You try that with your anti-armor laser firing and you'll look *very* military."

"If there's anyone left nearby to see you," one of the other Cobras lined up against the walls muttered.

"That is the basic idea," Justin nodded as a nervous chuckle swept the room. "Okay, Toral, off the floor. Dario, your turn."

One of the other Cobras took Abram's place in the center of the room and got into ready position. "Ceiling flip," Justin ordered; and a second later the *Dewdrop* shook as the Cobra jumped upward, bounced feet-first off the ceiling, and landed a handful of meters away from his starting point.

"One of these days," a voice at Justin's elbow muttered, "one of you is going to kick a hole in the deck doing that."

"Hello, Wilosha," Justin nodded to the middle-aged man who'd slipped unnoticed into the room. "Just can't get enough of the show, can you?"

"Watching the ship's structural integrity beaten into rubble always gives me a thrill," Second Officer Kal Wilosha retorted. "Haven't you practiced these more violent maneuvers enough?"

"No, but unfortunately we don't have the time to do it right."

Justin raised his voice. "Okay, Dario, nice job. Don't forget to keep your hands up when you land so that you'll be able to fire if you need to. Now give the backspin a try."

"Yes, sir."

He did marginally better than Abram had. "Again," Justin ordered. "Remember that your nanocomputer will do a lot of the work on these basic maneuvers if you'll let it. Just get things started, relax, and let your body take it from there."

Dario nodded and set himself for another try. Beside Justin, Wilosha hissed through his teeth. "Problem?" Justin asked him.

"Just . . . wondering."

"What about?" This time Dario did better.

"Oh . . . Cobras." Wilosha waved his hand vaguely. "The nano-computers, if you insist on specifics. Has it ever occurred to you that no one on the Cobra Worlds really knows anymore just exactly how the things are programmed?"

"I don't let it worry me," Justin told him. "The Academy super-vises every step of the nanocomputer manufacture."

"Oh, right. So they supervise a bank of automated circuitry replicators—what does that prove? Does a list or printout exist anywhere showing *exactly* what the nanocomputers are or are not capable of?"

"What are you worried about, that the Dominion of Man may have planted a program bomb?" Justin asked quietly. The conver-sation, he noted, was beginning to attract his students' attention.

"No, of course not," Wilosha shook his head. "But there doesn't have to be deliberate malice involved to make something dangerous."

Justin looked at him for a long moment. It would serve the man right to expose him here and now, in front of a roomful of Cobras . . . but it would be a childish trick, and Justin was long past the age for childish tricks. "Cobras, take a break," he called. "Be back in fifteen minutes."

The others filed out without comment or question, and a minute later Justin and Wilosha were alone. "I hope it wasn't something I said," Wilosha commented, his voice almost light but his expres-sion tight and wary.

"Just wanted a little peace and quiet," Justin told him, and threw a punch at the other's face.

Wilosha could never have evaded a serious attempt to hit him, not with Justin's Cobra servos driving the punch. But his reflexes tried their best, throwing his arm up in front of his face . . . and because Justin had his audio enhancers on and knew what to listen for, he caught the faint whine of servos from the other's arm.

"What the hell was *that* all about?" Wilosha snarled, taking a hasty step back toward the wall.

Justin made no move to follow. "Just showing you how easy it is for a Cobra to identify a Ject. Even with the restraints your nanocomputer puts on your servos, they still kick in to that limit when you react as quickly as you just did."

Wilosha's lip twisted. "A great technique, for sure. I can just see you walking down the streets of Capitalia throwing punches at everyone you pass. You could have just asked me, you know."

"Asked you what? I already knew what you were. This was just to prove to you that I knew."

"Of course. You probably had me spotted ever since we lifted, right?"

Justin snorted gently. "No. Only since you started showing up at every other practice with your mouth spitting venom and your eyes looking envious. What conclusion would *you* have come to?"

"I don't envy you," Wilosha snapped. Too quickly. "I come to your workouts to keep an eye on you—nothing more."

"Keep an eye on us for what? What is it about us that you're so afraid of?"

Wilosha took a deep breath. "I don't think this is the right time for a debate, Moreau. So you might as well get your team back in here and continue—"

He broke off as Justin took a long step toward the door, blocking the other's quiet move in that direction. "Actually, Wilosha, I think this is an excellent time for a debate," he told the other coldly. "Or at least for a little chat. There are some things I'd like to know, starting with why the hell you Jects are trying to make a lifelong career out of sour grapes."

For a moment Wilosha glared at him in silence. "You're not more than a couple of years younger than I am," he growled at last. "You must be feeling the first twinges of Cobra Syndrome arthritis. That's what the Lord High decision-makers of the Academy did to us: sentenced us to a premature death, and for nothing. Don't you think that's enough reason for us to be bitter?"

"No," Justin said flatly. "I'm sorry, but it's not. Nobody beat you over the head and forced you to apply to the Academy. You knew the risks going in; and if it didn't work out, then those are the breaks. Life requires certain sacrifices—on everyone's part. And as long as we're on the subject of premature deaths, you might recall all the Cobras who've died a hell of a lot younger than you are fighting spine leopards."

A muscle twitched in Wilosha's cheek. "I'm sorry. But it's not the ones who've died for Aventine that we object to."

"All of us have risked our lives," Justin reminded him. "You can't single out those who happen to have survived to vent your contempt at."

"It's not contempt," Wilosha insisted. "It's an honest and legitimate concern over the problems we see in the whole Cobra system."

Justin felt his stomach muscles tighten. "You sound like Priesly banging his fist over the net."

"So Governor Priesly's done the best job of putting it into words; so what?" Wilosha countered. "The point is still valid: that when you're on the outside looking in you get a different perspective on things. You Cobras see the prestige and physical power and political double vote; while we see the elitism and the arrogance that goes with absolute job security."

Justin favored him with a cold smile. "Absolute job security, hm? That's very interesting . . . especially given that that's exactly what Priesly's gotten out of you and the other Jects."

Wilosha blinked. "What are you talking about? The governorship isn't a permanent position."

"I wasn't talking about the governorship. I was referring to his status as head and chief speaker for a highly vocal political group. Think it through, Wilosha. Aventine can't simply get rid of the Cobras, for reasons you know as well as I do."

"We don't want to get rid of you, just alter your power structure to—"

"Just shut up and listen, will you? So all right; if the Cobras are always going to exist, why shouldn't an organization whose sole purpose in life is to oppose the Cobras do likewise?"

For a moment Wilosha stared at him. "Are you suggesting," he said at last, "that Governor Priesly started this whole movement solely to create a political base for himself?"

Justin shrugged. "You know more about the inner workings of your group than I do. *Is* that how he's using it? You might start by deciding whether or not you were this bitter about being rejected from the Cobra Academy before Priesly told you you ought to be."

"You're twisting the facts," Wilosha growled. But he didn't sound totally convinced. "Through Priesly we threaten your elite status, so of course you try to impugn his motives and activities."

"Perhaps," Justin said quietly. "But *I* didn't send someone charging into *his* office trying to make the Jects look like dangerous homicidal maniacs. Think about it, Wilosha. Do you really want to be on the side of a man who deliberately mangles truth in the name of political power?"

Wilosha snorted. "You're skating pretty close to slander," he said. "Unless you have some proof that that incident happened the way you claim it did. Some proof besides your brother's word, of course."

Justin felt disgust rising like bile in his throat. "Oh, for—" He took a breath, released it through clenched teeth. "Just get out of here, Wilosha. I haven't got time to waste arguing with someone who's already decided to let the party do his thinking for him."

Wilosha's face darkened. "Look, Moreau—"

"I said get out. We've got work to do."

The other opened his mouth, closed it again. Eyes on Justin, he sidled past the Cobra and out the door. The dull metal panel slid closed, and for a moment Justin stared at it, listening to his heartbeat slowly settle down and wondering if the talk had done any good at all. He could almost sympathize with Wilosha; the man was, after all, a would-be Cobra, and a strong sense of loyalty was high on the list of qualities the Academy screened its applicants for.

On the other hand, so were intelligence and integrity . . . and if he'd knocked even some of the stars out of Wilosha's eyes, the other might at least start watching Priesly's moves and words more closely. And if he found sufficient truth to the idea that Priesly was being corrupted by his own power . . .

It might help blunt Priesly's power. But it wouldn't help bring Jin back.

Clenching his teeth, Justin took a ragged breath. *She's alive,* he told himself firmly. Just as he had through the long and sleepless nights of the past four days. *She's alive, and we're going to get her out of there.*

Stepping up to the door, he slid it open and stepped out into the corridor. "Cobras!" he bellowed. "Break time's over. Get back here—we've got a lot of work ahead of us."

Chapter 33

The crowd milling around the Azras city center was large and noisy, composed mainly of youths and seedy-looking older men. Some, the younger ones especially, seemed to be radiating a combination of impatience and desperation, but in general the mood of the crowd was that of slightly bored normality. At one end, seated at a table, city officials took names of each of the would-be workers, keying them into portable computer terminals where the names were—presumably—ranked according to previous work history, skills, and other pertinent information. Working his way slowly toward the table in what the city dwellers probably considered a neat line, Daulo fought against his own nervousness and tried to look inconspicuous.

"Ah—Master Sammon," a voice came from behind him; and Daulo's heart skipped a beat. As casually as he could, he turned around. "Greetings, Master Moffren Omnathi," he nodded gravely, making the sign of respect and then shifting his eyes to the young man standing at Omnathi's side. "I greet you as well, Master . . . ?"

"I am Miron Akim," the other answered. "If you'd like, I'll be glad to hold your place in line while you and Master Omnathi confer."

Daulo swallowed hard; but before he could say anything, Omnathi had taken his arm and eased him out of line.

"You'll excuse this unorthodox approach, I hope," Omnathi commented quietly as he led Daulo away toward a relatively empty part of the center.

"What's this about?" Daulo demanded. Or rather, tried to demand; to his own ears his voice sounded more guilty than threatening. "I thought we'd settled everything two days ago."

"Yes, so it seemed," Omnathi nodded calmly. "But a couple of things have come up since then that I thought you could possibly help us with."

"Such as?" Daulo asked, stomach tightening.

Omnathi waved a hand at the assembled crowd. "This Mangus place, for instance. Your determination to gatecrash struck me as being rather a waste of time and energy, even given the stiffneck pride often associated with villagers." Daulo snorted; Omnathi ignored him. "So I had my men do a complete file check and confirmed that, as we told you, Mangus is indeed nothing more than a private electronics development center."

"And you'd like me therefore to leave and go home?" Daulo growled.

"Not at all. It occurred to me that perhaps you'd been mistaken about the timing of this gatecrash being your idea . . . and that Jasmine Alventin might still think this work party was the best way to get in."

Daulo's lungs seemed to have forgotten how to breathe. For a half dozen heartbeats the only sound was the dull buzz of the crowd around them, a buzz that seemed distant behind the roar of blood in Daulo's ears. "Understand, please," Omnathi said at last, "that at the moment I'm not accusing you of anything except unknowing cooperation with an enemy of Qasama. I'm even willing to believe that her prompting may have been so artfully buried that you honestly think all this *was* your idea. But from now on, that's over. You know now that she's an offworld spy . . . and you'll be expected to behave accordingly."

"All right," Daulo said. "Threat received and understood. So what exactly do you want from me now?"

Omnathi sent a leisurely glance around the crowd. "If the electronics information in Mangus is truly her goal, than a little thing like a planetary search isn't likely to slow her down much. She'll find a way in . . . and if she does, I want someone there who can identify her."

"Someone like me, I suppose?" Daulo asked.

"Exactly," Omnathi nodded. "Of course, spotting her is only the first step. You haven't had any training in methods of fugitive capture, and it's a little too late to teach you. Fortunately, I remember that you'd originally planned to have your brother along on this trip."

Daulo glanced at the line behind him. "Which is why Miron Akim is here, isn't it? To go in with me?"

"And to command you." Omnathi's face hadn't changed . . . but his voice was suddenly covered with ice. "From this moment on, Daulo Sammon, you're under the direct authority of the Shahni."

Daulo swallowed hard. So Jin had been right—the story he'd worked so hard to spin for Moffren Omnathi two nights ago had been that much wasted effort. The Shahni knew enough—or at least suspected enough—and Miron Akim was their countermove. Placing him under Shahni authority and Shahni surveillance . . . "And under their sword, too?" he asked.

Omnathi gave him a long look. "If you aid us in capturing the Aventinian spy, all other questions concerning your involvement in this will be forgotten. Otherwise . . . as you say, the sword will be waiting." He glanced over Daulo's shoulder. "You'd better get back into line. Miron Akim will give you any further information you may need."

"You realize this is probably a waste of time," Daulo pointed out, driven by something he didn't quite understand to make one final effort. "She probably won't even show up in Mangus."

"It's our time to waste," Omnathi said calmly. "Farewell, Daulo Sammon."

And with that he turned his back and disappeared into the crowd. Daulo looked after him for a long moment, wondering what to do now. If he simply turned the opposite way and left Azras right now . . .

But of course it wasn't just him under the Shahni's sword. Taking a deep breath, he tried to quiet the thunder of his heartbeat and headed back to the line.

Akim was waiting for him. "Ah—Daulo Sammon," he nodded. "You had a pleasant talk, I take it?"

"Oh, certainly," Daulo said irritably, stepping back into line beside him. The man behind them muttered something about the end of the line; Akim sent the man an icy look and he fell silent.

They reached the table about ten minutes later, and it was only then that Daulo realized that Mayor Capparis himself was overseeing the operation. "Ah!" the mayor beamed at Daulo as he and Akim stepped up to the table. "Daulo Matrolis and his brother Perto. I'm glad you heard about this opportunity."

"I also, Mayor Capparis," Daulo said politely, making the sign of respect. He'd never heard the name *Matrolis* before, but knew a cue when he heard it. So did the man at the computer; he was busy tapping keys before Daulo even had to repeat the name. "Thank you," he nodded when he'd finished. "You can find out

over there whether or not you'll be accepted." He pointed to
another table at the edge of the city center, near a half dozen parked
buses.

"Thank you," Daulo said, making the sign of respect to both
him and the mayor. Akim followed suit, and they headed off
through the crowd.

"Daulo and Perto Matrolis, eh?" Akim murmured as they walked.
"Do I assume that the files matching those names will show us
highly suited for this work party?"

"This whole exercise would be a waste of time if it didn't,
wouldn't it?" Daulo returned tartly.

"Agreed. Interesting, too, that you got Mayor Capparis himself
to take a hand in this."

"Is it that hard to believe?"

Akim shrugged. "Perhaps not in this part of Qasama. For myself,
I find it refreshing to see cooperation between city and village
leaders. More often we see you at each other's throats."

"Um." Daulo looked around the buses, estimating their capacity. If they were to be filled completely, it looked like the work
party would be something on the order of a hundred-fifty men.
Odd that they'd elect to go through this routine every two weeks,
he thought. *Permanent workers would be a lot easier . . . though
perhaps they don't have any long-term housing facilities out there.*
His eyes drifted to the area near the table . . . "Uh-oh."

"What is it?" Akim murmured.

"Over there—those men watching the proceedings?" Daulo said,
turning his head partly away.

Akim glanced the indicated direction. "That's the group from
Mangus," he identified them. "Drivers and a couple of higher
officials."

"One of the officials is the director's son, Radig Nardin," Daulo
growled. "He knows me."

Akim frowned. "How well?"

"Well enough to identify me," Daulo gritted.

"Is he likely to keep you out if he spots you?"

Daulo thought back to the attacks on him and Jin. "I think
so, yes."

"Um." Akim considered. "I suppose I could identify myself to
him . . . but that would probably start rumors floating around
Mangus, and I'd just as soon avoid that. All right. Wait here; I'll
go find one of our people and arrange for a distraction."

"Good." Daulo looked back over—

And felt a shock run straight through his core. In the center of the group from Mangus, talking earnestly to Nardin, was a smallish man. Or rather, a smallish figure wearing a man's clothing. Clothing he recognized . . .

It was Jin Moreau.

God above. The scene seemed to waver before Daulo's eyes. Right there, in the middle of Azras, with people all around. If Akim turned to look—if he identified her—they would both be dead.

But Akim was already gone.

Licking his lips, Daulo tried to still the shaking of his hands. Whatever Jin's purpose in doing something so insane, if she would just hurry it up and get *out* of here, she might still have a chance.

And as he watched, Jin did indeed turn away. Accompanied by Nardin and one of the other men, she walked to the end of the line of buses—

And got into a car parked there.

Daulo watched the vehicle pull away onto the street; watched it disappear behind the buildings surrounding the city center; and was still gazing after it when Akim returned. "All set," he reported. "Which one is Radig Nardin?"

"He's gone," Daulo said mechanically. "Drove off a couple of minutes ago."

"Oh? Well, that solves *that* problem."

Daulo took a deep breath. "I guess so."

Chapter 34

Azras was twenty kilometers north of the section of forest where Jin had hidden Daulo's car—a healthy run even for a Cobra, and one that allowed plenty of time for worrying about what lay ahead. Just one more reason to be thankful that the predawn jog itself was totally uneventful.

Her timing, for a change, was good, and she arrived at the city just as the sky to the east was growing light. Already some of the shopkeepers in the nearest marketplaces were beginning to prepare their booths for business, and she drifted through the streets pretending to be on various errands, feeling safer than she had since landing on Qasama. Disguised in lower-class male clothing, her hair covered by a carefully trimmed wig and her features altered slightly with face-shaper gel, she ought to be totally unrecognizable, especially to people who thought they had a good picture to go by.

That was the theory, at any rate . . . and as the morning progressed, it appeared to work in practice. She bought herself some breakfast—a nice treat after a day of emergency ration bars—and spent an hour wandering around the marketplace, observing the citizens of Azras as they began their new day.

She'd forgotten to ask Daulo when the work party selection would get underway, but when she made her first pass by the city center she saw that timing wasn't going to be critical. The park-like open area was teeming with men, most of them standing in a ragged and snaky line running up to a set of tables at one end. She watched for a few minutes, timing the procedure and estimating how long it would take to process the entire line, and then wandered off. Without Daulo it would be foolish to try and get into the work party in any straightforward way, and there would be little opportunity to try anything less obvious until the workers were ready to move out.

An hour later she returned, to find perhaps thirty minutes' worth of line left. Easing through the milling crowd of those who'd had their turns at the tables and were awaiting the results, she made her way across the center toward where a line of buses were parked along the street. Transport to Mangus, presumably. Also the simplest way for her to penetrate the place, assuming she could find some private hiding place atop, beneath, or inside one of them.

And with most of her attention on the buses, she suddenly found herself walking directly toward Daulo.

Fortunately, he was nearing the front of the line and seemed to have most of his own attention on the tables ahead. *Bless the angel who watches over fools,* Jin thought to herself, shifting her path to give him a wide berth. Beyond him, near the buses, another official-looking table had been set up; beyond that, a group of men were loitering near the vehicles. Together they effectively canceled any chance for approaching the buses from this side. If she swung around to the other side, made her approach from there—

Her thoughts froze in place. One of the men in that group, eyes ranging alertly over the crowd . . .

Was Radig Nardin. Watching, presumably, for Daulo.

For a half dozen heartbeats she just stood there, oblivious to the men milling around her. With Moffren Omnathi and the Shahni occupying her worries lately, she'd almost forgotten Mangus's own attempts to discourage her and Daulo. But Mangus obviously hadn't . . . and having seen Daulo in Milika less than four days ago, there was little chance Nardin would fail to recognize him.

At least, assuming he was able to continue looking . . .

She chewed at her lip, thinking hard. Step close and stun him with her sonic, hoping the others would assume he was ill and rush him away for treatment? But she would have to be practically up against him to deliver that kind of jolt without the others feeling some fringe effects. Use her lasers to set one of the buses on fire? No good; with his rank Nardin wouldn't be one of those fighting the fire. Besides which, any large-scale trouble she caused would more than likely just hold up the loading of the workers without guaranteeing that Nardin wouldn't still be around to watch it.

Unless . . .

She gritted her teeth. It was a borderline crazy idea . . . but if it worked, it would solve both her problems at one crack.

Across the city center, near the rearmost of the line of buses, was a small shedlike building, possibly a public toilet. Jin crossed to it and, positioning herself facing the wall away from the would-be workers, she worked her fingernails under the edges of the face-shaper gel and began tearing it away. It wasn't a pleasant task—the stuff wasn't supposed to be removed except with a special solvent—and her cheeks and chin felt raw by the time she'd finished. The wig and men's clothes she would have to leave as is; but if Nardin had been paying attention during his trip to the Sammon mine it ought to be enough.

In Milika she'd noted evidence of gaps between social classes, and as she walked up to Nardin's group it became quickly apparent that city dwellers worked under a similar set of rules. A lower-class man, wearing the clothing Jin was, would never have tried to barge right up to someone of Nardin's status, a fact that registered clearly in the startled expressions of those around Nardin as she passed between them. She was within arm's reach of the other, in fact, before two of the entourage broke their astonishment enough to step into her path. "Where do you think you're going?" one of them snarled at her.

"To speak to Master Radig Nardin," she said calmly. "I have a message for him."

Nardin turned to glare at her. "Since when do—?"

The words froze on his lips as recognition flashed onto his face, followed immediately by a whole series of startled emotions. "You—what—?"

"I bring a message for your father, Master Nardin," she said into his confusion, touching fingertips to her forehead. "May I approach?"

Nardin glanced at his companions, seemed to pull himself together. "You may. Let her pass," he ordered.

She sensed the shock pass through the others as she slipped between them—apparently they hadn't yet realized that she was in fact a woman. Dimly, she wondered if transvestism was a crime on Qasama, then dismissed the thought. "I bring a message for your father from Kruin Sammon of Milika," she told him. "Will you take me to him?"

Nardin's face had become an unreadable mask. "I remember you," he said. "You were in the village Milika in the company of Kruin Sammon's eldest son. Who are you that he trusts you with messages?"

"My name is Asya Elghani, Master Nardin."

"And your relation to the Sammon family?"

"That of a business professional," Jin said, choosing her words carefully. She had no idea if the service she was about to describe even existed on Qasama; but with the widespread Qasaman use of drugs, there was no reason why it shouldn't. "I'm a messenger, sent as I said to your father, Obolo Nardin."

Nardin cocked an eyebrow, his gaze flicking pointedly over her clothing. "And what is so special about you that you should be trusted with messages of any importance? Aside from the fact that few people would think you so trustworthy?"

Jin ignored the snickers from the others. "What makes me special," she told Nardin, "is that I carry an oral message . . . the contents of which I don't know."

Nardin's eyes narrowed. "Explain."

Jin let a look of barely controlled impatience drift across her face. "The message was given me while I was in a special drug-induced trance," she said. "Only in your father's presence will I be able to return to that trance and deliver the message."

He gazed at her for a long moment, and she mentally crossed her fingers. "How important is this message?" he asked. "Is the timing of its delivery crucial?"

"I have no way of knowing either," Jin told him.

One of the other men stepped close to Nardin. "With your permission, Master Nardin," he murmured, "may I suggest that the timing of this supposed message is extremely suspicious?"

Nardin's eyes stayed on Jin. "Perhaps," he muttered back. "However, if this is a ruse, it does little but buy him some time." Slowly, he nodded. "Very well, then. I'll take you to my father."

Jin bowed. "I'm at your disposal, Master Nardin," she said.

He turned and headed to the rear of the line of buses. Jin followed, sensing a second man join them. A car was parked behind the buses; the other man slid into the driver's seat as Nardin and Jin took the back, and almost before she had her door closed the vehicle swung out into the street and headed east.

Carefully, Jin took a breath, exhaled it with equal care. Once again, it seemed, the pervasive Qasaman disdain of women had worked in her favor. Nardin might have swallowed the same "private message" routine coming from another man, but he almost certainly wouldn't have let a male stranger into his car without some extra protection along. But as a woman, Jin was automatically no threat to him.

Settling back against the seat cushions, she watched the cityscape go past her window and tried to figure out just how best to turn that blind spot to her advantage.

Chapter 35

It was a fifty-kilometer drive from Azras to Mangus, along a road that was clearly newer and in better shape than the highway Jin had jogged alongside earlier that morning. Neither Nardin nor the driver spoke to her throughout the trip, which gave her little to do but study the scenery outside and—more surreptitiously—the two of them.

Neither examination was all that impressive. Nardin rode impassively, eyes flicking to her occasionally but generally staying on the road ahead. The driver, too, seemed stiff and distant, even toward Nardin. Their few exchanges were short and perfunctory, and she could sense none of the easy camaraderie that she'd seen between Daulo and his own driver. *A strict master/servant relationship,* she decided eventually, *without a scrap of friendship or even mutual respect to it.* In retrospect, given her first impression of Nardin four days previously, it wasn't all that unexpected.

The landscape outside wasn't quite as unfriendly, but it more than made up for that in sheer dullness, consisting mainly of flat tree-dotted plains. Further to the east, she knew, the dense forest that surrounded Milika began again, extending across Qasama to the villages at the opposite end of the Fertile Crescent. But here, at least, the forest had failed to take.

Which meant that there would be far fewer deadly predators between them and Azras, should she and Daulo need to get out of Mangus in a hurry. Fewer beasts, and considerably less cover. All things considered, she would have preferred to take her chances with the predators.

Mangus was visible long before they reached it . . . and the satellite photos hadn't nearly done the place justice. From what she could see of the high black wall surrounding it, the compound appeared to be shaped roughly like a diamond, in sharp contrast to the circular shape of Milika and the villages her father had visited on Qasama. The diamond's long ends seemed to point southeast and northwest—*along the direction of the planet's magnetic field,* she decided, remembering the similarly angled streets in Azras and the other cities. Qasama's migrating bololin herds took their direction from magnetic field lines, and builders either had to deflect the huge beasts around human habitations or else give them as free a passage as possible.

Impressive as the wall was, though, it paled in comparison to the shimmering dome-shaped canopy arching over it.

The Cobra Worlds' satellites hadn't been able to make much of the canopy. It was metal or metal coated; it wasn't solid, but a tightly woven double mesh of some sort whose varying interference patterns actually blocked the probes more effectively than a solid structure would have; and it was almost entirely opaque to every electromagnetic wavelength the satellites were able to work with.

Now, seeing it at ground level, Jin found she couldn't add much more to that list. It was anchored, she could see, by tall black pylons set into the ground outside the wall, which were in turn held in place by pairs of guy cables. How the canopy was being held up in the center was still a mystery, especially since its slight but visible rippling in the wind showed it to be more akin to fabric than to rigid metal. She was peering toward it, trying to see through the slight gap between its lower edge and the upper part of the wall, when a movement past the wall to her left caught her eye. Keying her optical enhancers to telescopic, she focused on it.

It was a bus. Identical to the ones that had been waiting to bring Daulo and his fellow workers to Mangus . . . except that this one was heading northward on a different road. As was the bus that followed it. And the next. And the next.

"They're going to Purma," Radig Nardin said into her thoughts. Startled, she looked at him, to find him gazing hard at her.

"I see, Master Nardin," she said, remembering to show proper respect. "May I ask who they are?"

His forehead creased a fraction more. "Last week's workers. On their way home."

Jin hesitated. Another question might be out of Qasaman character . . . but, then, she'd already established herself as an anomaly, anyway. "Do you hire from Purma often?"

"Every other week or so," he said. "It alternates with the hiring from Azras."

"I see." Carefully, Jin settled back into her seat, returning her eyes to the wall and dome ahead. So Mangus *did* have enough work to keep what amounted to a full-time force busy. So why didn't they simply go ahead and hire permanent workers, instead of going through all this trouble every week?

They had passed the line of pylons now, and as they neared the end of the road a gateway swung open up in the wall ahead. The only gateway on this side of the compound, she noticed, and built furthermore along the lines of a minor bank vault. Bololin-proof, for certain.

There were half a dozen buildings visible as the car drove through the gateway and into Mangus proper: an office-looking one directly ahead, a residence-type building beyond it, a guard station and garage flanking the road to right and left. But Jin saw them only peripherally. Her full attention was grabbed by the totally unexpected black wall rising off to her right.

It ran, as near as she could tell, between two of the diamond-shape's corners, cutting Mangus into two roughly equilateral triangles. A single gate was set into it at its center, a gate that looked to be just as strong as the one they'd just passed through. *The only way into that section?* she wondered, remembering that there'd been just one gateway into Mangus on the western part of the outer wall.

If so, that implied that Mangus's dark secrets came in two distinct shades. Now if only Radig's father Obolo Nardin kept his office beyond that internal wall . . .

But it wasn't going to be quite that easy. "The administrative center, Master Nardin?" the driver called over his shoulder.

"Yes," Radig said, looking at Jin. "You'll be given—" his eyes flicked down "—more suitable clothing before being brought before my father."

"Thank you, Master Nardin," Jin nodded gravely. Leaning slightly toward the window, she saw that another of the black pylons rose from the top of the interior wall, reaching upward to the center of the overhead canopy. The shield's primary support, clearly, with perhaps medium-strength ribs extending from it to the outside pylons to maintain the dome shape. Simple but effective. "I trust you'll provide me with transportation back to Azras once I've delivered my message," she added to Nardin.

He cocked an eyebrow. "That may depend," he said coolly, "on just what the message is."

✧   ✧   ✧

They kept her waiting a long time, far longer than it took her to change into the clothes they'd given her. Long enough, in fact, that she was beginning to wonder if they were secretly monitoring her; and if so, when she as a supposedly busy professional ought to start looking annoyed at having her time wasted. But eventually someone came, and she was taken down a series of corridors to Obolo Nardin's throne room.

There was no other way to think of the place. Larger and far more elaborate than Kruin Sammon's study—larger even than the bigcity mayor's office she'd seen tapes of—it was clearly designed to intimidate all who came in. A light breeze continually played across her face as she was led through and around the maze of hanging curtains to the center. A quick mental picture flashed across her mind, a picture of a spider waiting in the center of his web . . .

"What is your name?" the man on the cushion throne growled at her.

With an effort, Jin forced the spider image from her mind. *I'm a Cobra*, she reminded herself. *Spiders aren't supposed to scare me.* "I am Asya Elghani, Master," she said, making the sign of respect and studying his unnaturally bright eyes. Excessive use of Qasama's mind drugs? "Are you Obolo Nardin?"

The man's face didn't change . . . but an abrupt shiver ran up her back. "I am," he said. "What have you to say to me?"

Jin took a deep breath. This was it. Now if only he bought her performance. . . . Letting her face go slightly slack as if entering a hypnotic state, she dropped her voice an octave. "This is Kruin Sammon," she intoned. "I know what you are doing here in Mangus, Obolo Nardin, and I know what you are risking. With that knowledge I can destroy you . . . but I can also aid you. You need the resources I possess, as well as the strength of the western villages whose loyalty I command. I propose therefore an alliance between us, with the rewards shared equally. I await your reply."

Carefully, Jin brought her eyes back into focus. "Did you receive the entire message, Master Nardin?" she asked in a normal voice again.

Obolo Nardin's eyes were steady on her face. "Indeed I did," he grunted.

"I've already been paid to bring Kruin Sammon a reply, should you wish to send one," she continued, struggling to keep her face and voice impassive. Deep in the back of her mind, alarm bells were beginning to go off. Something here wasn't quite right . . . "However, in that event, I would need time to prepare myself—"

And without warning the scene ahead of her was abruptly rimmed by red.

A jolt of adrenaline surged through her as, reflexively, she held her breath. Suddenly it all clicked: the long delay back at the changing room, the careful scrutiny Obolo Nardin was giving her, the breeze blowing in her face . . . a breeze undoubtedly laden with sleeping drug. They'd considered what to do with her, decided that the message cover was nonsense, and were taking the appropriate action.

At her sides, Jin's hands curled into fists, nails digging into the skin of her palms to ward off the drug's effect. She might be able to stun Obolo with her sonic and get out of here . . . but the hanging curtains could hide a hundred other men, and even now she couldn't afford to give herself away. On the other hand, she couldn't hold her breath forever, either, and she'd probably already inhaled enough of the stuff to put her under before she got too far, anyway. And Obolo was still staring at her. Still waiting . . .

Waiting for her to collapse? *All right,* she decided suddenly. "I—Master Nardin—" she began drunkenly, using the last of her reserve of air; and rolling her eyes up, she collapsed to the floor.

She'd made sure to let her head roll so as to face away from the direction of the sleep breeze, but the stars of her impact had barely cleared away before the air now playing at the back of her head was shut off anyway. Footsteps came slowly around one of the curtains . . . stopped at her side . . . "That was quick," Radig Nardin's voice said. "Even for a woman."

"She's a soft offworlder," Obolo replied contemptuously. "If this is the best our enemies can do, we have little to fear from them."

An iron spike seemed to drive itself up through Jin's stomach. *God above—they know who I am!* But how—?

"Perhaps." A hand pulled at Jin's shoulder, rolling her over on her back. Keeping her eyes closed, she activated her optical enhancers, keying for zero magnification and the lowest light-amp setting. Radig peered at her face a moment, then straightened up again to face his father. "I'll have her body searched for tiny instruments before we confine her."

"As you choose, my son, but I doubt there's any need."

"Her clothing yielded nothing—"

"You're forgetting the crash of her spacecraft," the elder Nardin cut his son off. "She carries no devices because none survived with her."

"Perhaps. Have you decided yet what to do about Daulo Sammon?"

"Why, nothing, of course—his father has offered us a deal," Obolo said, heavily sarcastic. "Didn't you hear his message?"

Radig glanced down at Jin again. "You'll forgive me, my father, if I fail to see any humor in the situation. Or do you consider it impossible that the Sammon family has in fact made an alliance with this spy?"

"Hardly impossible," Obolo grunted. "Unlikely, though."

"Then let me get rid of him," Radig urged. "As long as he's here, he presents a danger to us."

"True. Unfortunately, removing him at this point may be even more dangerous. Tell me, have you identified the man who came into Mangus with him?"

Radig's lip twitched. "Not yet. But he's probably just someone else from that bololin dropping of Milika."

"'Probably' isn't good enough," Obolo said coldly. "The Shahni know the woman is on Qasama, and they know she stayed in the Sammon household while in Milika. This man could well be a Shahni agent assigned to Daulo Sammon, either as protector or as jailer."

"But in either case, why accompany Daulo Sammon *here*?"

"*She* is here, is she not? Whatever she and our enemies know or suspect, it's not impossible she might have shared that knowledge with Kruin Sammon."

"But then allowing an agent of the Shahni—"

"Radig Nardin." Obolo's voice was like the crack of a whip. "Control your fears and *think*. As far as the Shahni are concerned, Mangus is an electronics firm—nothing more. If we behave openly, they'll have no reason to doubt that. If, on the other hand, we make an inflated presentation of plucking Daulo Sammon from among the workers and throwing him outside our wall, will this agent's curiosity not be aroused?"

Radig took a deep breath. "It's still dangerous, my father."

"Of course it is. There's no profit without danger, my son. If your nerve threatens to fail you again, concentrate on that."

"Yes, my father." Radig glowered down at Jin. "And for what potential gain do we risk keeping *this* one alive?"

Obolo snorted. "You consider keeping a *woman* alive to be a risk?"

"She's not a normal woman, my father—she's an agent of the Cobra Worlds. That makes her dangerous."

Abruptly, Jin noticed that the red border was still around her vision . . . that it was, in fact, getting thicker . . . as the view itself seemed to be fading away . . .

No! she told herself furiously, trying to fight the sleep flowing over her mind. *Come on, Jin—hang on.* But it was too hard to muster the necessary emotion. And it was so comfortable here on the floor . . .

Her last memory was that of rough hands digging under her armpits and legs, lifting her up and floating her away . . .

Chapter 36

" . . . The screen in front of each of you will display a brief summary of each of the steps I've just outlined," the instructor concluded his presentation, waving his hand over his podium toward the rows of equipment-laden tables in front of him. "If you have any questions tap the 'help' key; if that still doesn't do it, tap the 'signal' key and someone will come to your work station. Any questions? All right, then. Get to it, and remember that the future of communication on Qasama may depend on you."

Shifting his eyes to the screen attached to the work table, Daulo suppressed a grimace and picked up a circuit board and a handful of components. He hadn't really expected to be given a missile casing and told to load a warhead onto it . . . but assembling telephone circuitry was hardly what he'd hoped for, either. "Not wasting any time getting us to work, are they?" he murmured.

He glanced to the side in time to see Akim's shrug. "They're paying all of us quite well," he pointed out.

Daulo gritted his teeth and plugged the first component into the circuit board. He'd been trying to pique Akim's curiosity about Mangus itself ever since being ushered off the bus, and had yet to make any impression on the man. Akim was on the trail of a female offworlder, and he clearly had no intention in being distracted from that single-minded path. "At least it explains why they don't bother hunting down their previous workers," Daulo commented, trying another approach. "If everything they do here is this simple-minded it's just as easy to teach a new group from the beginning."

Akim glanced up and around, and for a moment Daulo hoped he might argue the point. But he merely nodded. "Inefficient, to some degree, but not overly so," he said, and returned his attention to his own circuit board. "Certainly helps spread a little extra wealth around to Azras's poor."

"Right," Daulo muttered under his breath. "Obolo Nardin is just as noble as all creation."

"If I were you," Akim said coldly, "I'd try and forget my village prejudices and concentrate on the task at hand. Do you see anyone here who could be the woman in disguise?"

With a sigh, Daulo gave the room a careful scan, the image of Jin getting into Radig Nardin's car rising up to haunt him. "I don't think so."

"Keep an eye out," Akim told him. "They may occasionally rotate workers between groups."

Daulo nodded and turned back to his work.

It was perhaps an hour later when he suddenly noticed Akim had stopped working and was gazing straight ahead into space. "Something?" he asked.

Akim turned sharply to look at him. "Something's wrong," he whispered hoarsely. "There's—" he licked his lips, eyes darting all around him. "Don't you feel it?"

Daulo leaned close, fighting against the sudden dread rising in his throat. Akim's barely controlled panic was contagious. "I don't understand. What is it you're feeling?"

Akim drew a shuddering breath. "Treachery," he said, hands visibly trembling. "There's . . . treachery here. Don't you feel it?"

Daulo threw a quick look around the room. So far no one else seemed to have noticed them, but that wouldn't last long. "Come on," he said, getting to his feet and gripping Akim's arm. "Let's get out of here."

Akim shrugged off his hand. "I can manage myself," he snarled, standing up unsteadily.

"Whatever you want," Daulo gritted. The door they'd come in by was all the way at the back of the room; much closer was another exit near the front podium. Taking Akim's arm again as the other staggered slightly, he headed that way.

The instructor intercepted them as they got to the door. "Where are you going?" he demanded. "The exit is back that—"

"My friend is sick," Daulo cut him off. "Is there a lavette out there somewhere?"

The other seemed to draw back, and Daulo took advantage of his hesitation to push past. Outside was a corridor he hadn't seen on their way into the building, with a heavy-looking door at the far end. Halfway toward it was the lavette he'd hoped for; guiding Akim through the door, he all but pushed the other down onto a cushion in the lounge section.

For a long moment neither man spoke. Akim took several slow, deep breaths, checked his fingers for signs of trembling, and after a bit rose and studied his face in the mirror. Only then did he finally look Daulo in the eye. "You didn't feel it, did you?" he demanded. "You didn't feel anything in there?"

Daulo spread his hands, palm upwards. "You'll have to be more specific," he said.

"I wish I could." Akim leaned back toward the mirror, gazed deeply into his own eyes. "I felt—well, curse it all, I felt treason. There's no other way to put it; I felt *treason*. Whether it makes any sense or not."

It didn't; but it almost didn't matter. Whatever the reason, Akim had finally been jolted out of his indifference toward Mangus, and it was up to Daulo now to fan that flame. "I don't understand," he admitted, "but I trust your instincts."

Akim threw him a baleful glance. "Instincts be cursed," he ground out. "There's something wrong in this place, and I'm going to find out what it is."

He started toward the door. "You going back in there?" Daulo asked carefully. "I mean, considering what just happened—"

"I'm fully under control now," the other said stiffly. "As far as you're concerned, I just had a bad reaction to something I ate for breakfast. Understand?"

The instructor was watching from just outside the assembly-room door when they emerged from the lavette. He accepted Akim's suitably embarrassed explanation and escorted them back to the room and their tables. Returning to his work, Daulo stretched out his senses to the limit, trying as hard as he could to pick up the feeling Akim had described.

Nothing.

What was perhaps worse, Akim could apparently no longer sense it, either. Grim-faced, he sat at his table and worked on his circuit boards, without even a mild recurrence of his earlier reaction.

Which meant either that whatever it was had passed . . . or that it had never been there in the first place.

It was, Daulo decided, probably the oddest sunset he'd ever seen. Ahead, the sun was invisible below the level of Mangus's outer wall, while overhead it still sent multicolored light patterns across the shimmering canopy. "I wonder if that thing keeps the rain out," he commented, twisting his head to gaze upward out their window at it.

"Why else would it be there?" Akim growled from his bed.

To keep Jin's people from seeing in. But he couldn't tell Akim that. "You still bothered by what happened in the assembly room this afternoon?" he asked instead, keeping his eyes on the canopy.

"Wouldn't you be?" the other snapped. "I behaved like a fool in public, and then couldn't even discover why I'd done so."

Daulo pursed his lips. "Could it have been some chemical they use in the manufacturing process?" he suggested. "Something that might still have been evaporating from the circuit boards?"

"Then why didn't anyone else react? More to the point, why wasn't it still there when we came back into the room? And it *wasn't* still there."

Daulo chewed the inside of his cheek. "Well, then . . . maybe it was something meant for me, something you got caught in by accident."

Behind him, Akim snorted. "Back to your paranoia of Mangus wanting to keep villagers out, are we?"

"It fits the facts, doesn't it?" Daulo growled, turning to face the other. "A stream of gas, maybe, designed to make me feel frightened and leave on my own?"

"It wasn't fear I felt."

"Perhaps you're braver than I am. And then when *you* reacted instead of me, they may have panicked and shut it off."

Akim shook his head. "It doesn't make any sense. You're talking something far too sophisticated to be used in what amounts to a telephone assembly plant."

"And how do you know those *were* telephone circuit boards we were putting together?" Daulo countered.

Akim's forehead creased. "What else would they be?" he asked.

Daulo took a deep breath. "Weapons. Possibly missile components."

He'd expected at least a snort of disbelief and scorn. But Akim merely continued looking at him. "And what," the other said quietly, "would give you that impression?"

A cold shiver ran up Daulo's spine. *He knows,* was his first, horrible thought. *The Shahni are in this with Mangus—the cities redly are preparing for war against the villages.* But it was too late to back out. "Rumors," he said through stiff lips. "Bits of information, pieced together over the months."

"As well as suggestions from the Aventinian spy?" Akim asked bluntly.

"I don't know what you mean," Daulo said as calmly as possible.

For a half dozen heartbeats the two men stared at each other. "You slide dangerously close to treason, Daulo Sammon," Akim said at last. "You and the entire Sammon household."

"The Sammon family is loyal to Qasama," Daulo said, fighting a trembling in his voice. "To *all* of Qasama."

"And I, as a city man, am not?" Akim's eyes flared. "Well, let me tell you something, Daulo Sammon: you may *think* you love Qasama, but any loyalty you possess pales against mine. We of the Shahni's investigators have been trained and treated to be totally fair in our dealings with Qasama's people. *Totally* fair. We cannot be corrupted or led astray from what we see as our duty. And we do *not* show prejudice, to anyone on our world. If you remember only one thing about me, remember that."

Abruptly, he got to his feet, and Daulo took an involuntary step backward. But Akim merely walked past the two beds and seated himself at the writing desk. "So you think we've been assembling parts for missiles, do you?" he said over his shoulder as he picked up the phone and turned it over. "There ought to be one quick way to settle that."

Daulo stepped over and crouched down beside him as Akim pulled a compact tool kit from his pocket and selected a small screwdriver. There were, Daulo noted, about a dozen screws holding the bottom of the phone to the molded resin top. "Why so many fastenings?" he asked as Akim got to work.

"Who knows?" Akim grunted, getting the first one loose. "Maybe they don't want anyone messing around with his phone unless it really needs fixing."

Akim was working on the last screw when Daulo first noticed the odor. "What's that?" he asked, sniffing cautiously. "Smells like something's burning."

"Hmm. It does, doesn't it." Frowning, Akim lifted the phone to his nose. "—uh-oh."

"Did we ruin it?"

"Sure smells that way. Well . . . the damage is probably already done." He got the screw free and carefully pulled the bottom plate out.

Just inside the plate was a circuit board—the same board, Daulo saw immediately, that they'd been working on all day.

All the same components, plus a tangle of connecting wires, plus—

"What are those things?" he asked, pointing to a row of slightly blackened components. "We didn't put those on our boards."

"No, we didn't," Akim agreed thoughtfully. He raised the board to his nose again. "Whatever they are, they're where the smell is coming from."

A knot began to form in the pit of Daulo's stomach. "You mean . . . we tried to take the phone apart, and they burned themselves out?"

Akim held the board closer, peering at it from different angles. "Take a look," he said, lifting a bundle of wires and pointing beneath it. "Right there. See it?"

Daulo tried to remember what that component was. "A capacitor?" he hazarded.

"Right. And *there*—" he pointed beneath it "—is what releases its stored current into that section of the circuit."

The knot in Daulo's stomach tightened an extra turn. "That's . . . right over one of the screw holes."

"Uh-huh," Akim nodded. "And now that we've got it open, it's clear that screw doesn't help hold the phone together at all." He looked up at Daulo. "It's a self-destruct mechanism," he said quietly.

Daulo had to work moisture into his mouth before he could speak. "Any way to find out what those burned-out components are supposed to do?"

"Not now. Not this set, anyway." Akim gazed at the board another moment, and then put it back into the phone and picked up one of the screws. "I'll have to find out where they finish this part of the assembly and get in there." He paused, a strange look flashing across his face. "You know . . . phones manufactured in Mangus have been the most advanced on Qasama for the last two or three years. They're very popular among top city officials."

"And the Shahni?" Daulo asked.

"And the Shahni," Akim nodded. "I've got one on my desk . . ." He took a deep breath. "I don't know what we've got here, Daulo Sammon, but whatever it is, I need to check it out, and quickly."

"Are you going to call for reinforcements?"

Akim gave him a sardonic look. "Over these phones?" he asked pointedly.

Daulo grimaced. "Oh. Right. Well . . . look, it probably wouldn't take more than an anonymous tip to the right person to get me thrown out. If you want to give me a message, I'll make sure to deliver it to Moffren Omnathi in person."

"Even if Radig Nardin decides to make sure you never try to enter Mangus again?" Akim asked.

Daulo licked his lips, remembering the toughs who'd attacked him and Jin. "And what do you suppose they'll do to us if they find out we know about their phones?" he countered.

Akim set the phone back on the table and stood up. "I'm a representative of the Shahni," he said flatly. "They wouldn't *dare* harm me."

There was no response Daulo could make to that. "Were you planning to try and find that extra assembly room tonight?" he asked instead.

Akim hesitated, looking out the window. "It's getting late . . . but I don't remember them saying anything about us being confined to quarters in the evenings." He turned back to Daulo. "I suppose you want to go, too?"

"If I may. Unless you don't trust me."

Akim looked at him steadily. "To be perfectly honest, no, I don't. I don't think you're the innocent bystander you try to appear, and until I figure out just what the game is you're playing I'm not going to like having you at my back." He snorted gently under his breath. "Unfortunately, if you're working against me I risk just as much by leaving you here where I can't watch you."

Daulo grimaced. "Is there anything I can say or do to convince you I don't oppose you?"

"Not really."

"Then I guess you'll have to make up your mind on your own. Bear in mind that I can't come with you and stay here at the same time."

Akim's lip twitched. "True." He inhaled deeply. "All right, then. Come on, let's go."

Chapter 37

It was something of a surprise to Jin to awake and find herself still alive.

She took a moment first to listen with her eyes closed. Silence, except for the hum of distant machinery or forced air venting. No sounds of breathing except her own.

Which meant that, along with leaving her alive, they'd left her alone.

Opening her eyes, she found herself in a small room, perhaps three meters by four, bare except for the thin mattress on which she was lying and a somewhat thicker sitting cushion in one corner. Set into the ceiling was an air vent, too small for anything larger than a cat to get through; on one wall was a metal door.

Carefully, she got to her feet. There was no dizziness, no pain except for a mild ache from the bruise where she'd allowed her head to hit the floor. *And no way to know how long the stuff had me under, either,* she reminded herself grimly, wishing she'd thought to start her clock circuit before going under. Stepping to the door, she pressed her ear against it and activated her audio enhancers.

The faint sound of cloth on skin came from outside, followed by a cough.

At least they thought enough of me to lock me up, she thought, feeling a little mollified. Even recognizing on an intellectual level that her supposed feminine weakness was greatly to her advantage, it still somehow rankled to be so casually treated by her opponents.

Whoever these opponents were.

She frowned as the memory of that last overheard conversation came back to her. Obolo Nardin had known about the shuttle crash—had known she was an offworlder and that she'd been staying with the Sammon family in Milika. Had the Shahni made that information public? Or was Mangus in fact a government operation? Neither option was especially attractive.

And yet . . . unless the drug they'd been blowing in her face had thoroughly scrambled her memory . . . hadn't they also been openly worried about the risk of having an agent of the Shahni in their midst?

Which implied they *were* hiding something from the Shahni. But how then did they know things only the Shahni were supposed to know?

Could Mangus be some kind of chip in an internal power struggle among the Shahni themselves? One side's jealously guarded effort, perhaps, to come up with a way to fight back against the Cobra Worlds?

Cobra Worlds. Cobras. Mangus. Mongoose . . .

God above.

For a long moment Jin just stood there, rooted by horror to the spot. *God above.* It'd been staring her right in the face the whole time, and she'd managed to completely miss it. *Mongoose* . . .

Angrily, she shook her head, the movement sending a stab of pain through her bruise. It still wasn't too late to redeem her error . . . assuming that she could get out of this room. Gritting her teeth, she crouched down and examined the door's lock.

It was instantly obvious that the room hadn't originally been designed to hold prisoners. The door had been locked by the simple expediency of removing the inner knob mechanism and welding a metal plate over the resulting opening.

Moving back from the door, she gave the room a quick but careful scan. There were no hidden cameras that she could find, though there could still be subsurface microphones buried out of sight in the walls. Those could be dealt with, though. A more pressing problem would be to find something she could use to bend back the metal covering the lock. Pulling off one shoe, she experimented with the heel. Not ideal, but it would do. Taking a deep breath, she wedged the heel beneath the edge of the plate with one hand and activated her other hand's fingertip laser.

It was easier than she'd expected it to be; clearly, the man assigned the job of securing the door hadn't wanted to make a career of the task and had used a soft metal that he could spot-weld in place in a couple of minutes. It took Jin even less time than that to free three of its edges and soften the rest enough to pry it back from the hole.

Waiting for it to cool was the hardest part, but the door itself was a fair heat sink, and within a few minutes she was able to get close enough to see into the opening.

Inside the door was the minor maze of wiring and equipment: an electronic lock. She knew a dozen quick ways of dealing with such a device, ranging from frying it with her arcthrower to slagging it with her antiarmor laser. Unfortunately, most of them tended to be extremely noisy, and the last thing she could afford right now was for the guard outside to hit whatever panic button he was equipped with.

Fortunately, there were more subtle approaches available to her. The solenoids and deadlock bolt of the actual mechanism were easy enough to locate; easing a finger into the hole, she found the bar that blocked the deadbolt in place when the lock was engaged. Pushing it out of the way with one finger, she teased the deadbolt back with two others . . .

There was no click, just a slight inward movement of the door as it was suddenly freed to swing on its hinges again. Straightening up, Jin slipped her shoe back on and licked her lips. This was it. Activating her omnidirectional sonic to interfere with any microphones that might be operating, she got her fingernails on the door edge and pulled it open.

The two guards standing with their backs to her probably weren't even aware the door behind them had opened before she dropped them where they stood with a blast from her sonic. Gripping the door jamb, her own head ringing from the sonic's backwash, Jin leaned out into the hallway and looked around. No one was in sight; and from the level of light coming in a window down the hall, it was already early evening out there. She'd slept the whole day away . . . Gritting her teeth, she bent to the task of disposing of the unconscious guards.

The next door down the hall turned out to be a small washroom, its size indicating it had been designed for use by one person at a time. Carrying the guards inside, she propped them up in such a way that they would help wedge the door once she closed it. Her trainers had warned them repeatedly that the duration of sonic-induced unconsciousness varied so wildly between people and situations that it couldn't be relied on, but with nothing around to secure them with, she would just have to hope that they wouldn't wake up too soon.

Her next stop was the window down the hall. The sun was indeed well down past Mangus's western wall, though its light was still sending a rainbow of color across the canopy overhead. More importantly, the view outside told her that she was still in the building she'd first been brought to that morning.

Which gave her a very good idea of where she ought to start her investigation ...

There were still a handful of people roaming around the building, but in the relative stillness their footsteps carried clearly to her enhanced hearing, and she found it an easy task to elude them. It took her several minutes and a few false turns, but eventually she made it to the hallway leading to the ornate door of Obolo Nardin's office-cum-throne room.

There hadn't been any guards outside the door when she'd been first brought before Obolo, and there weren't any now, either. Which implied either very good electronic security on the entrance itself, or else human guards waiting out of sight behind some of the hanging curtains inside. She was just starting around the corner to check out the door when another set of footsteps caught her ear and she ducked back.

It was Radig Nardin.

Jin gnawed at her lip. The messenger who'd taken her to Obolo earlier had announced their arrival on an intercom set beside the door and they'd been admitted by someone inside. But given Qasama's culture, it seemed unlikely that the son of Mangus's director would have to go through such a routine. On a sudden hunch, she clicked her optical enhancers to telescopic and focused on the door.

Radig stepped up to the panel, tapped six buttons on a keypad she hadn't noticed before, and opened the door.

Jin was gliding down the hallway toward the closing door before it occurred to her on a conscious level that sneaking into Obolo's office right on Radig's heels might be an unnecessarily stupid risk to take. But she kept going. Obolo presumably had a perfectly adequate communications system available in his office, and if he and Radig needed to speak in person, perhaps it would be worth listening in on.

She reached the door unseen and repeated Radig's code on the keypad. Too late, she wondered if the system might also be sensitive to fingertip pattern ... but Obolo hadn't bothered with extra refinement, and with a quiet click the door unlocked.

She opened it just enough to slip through, closing it again behind her and moving immediately to the cover of the nearest hanging curtain. The room seemed hazy, and she nearly choked on her first breath. *Chemical smoke,* she realized, remembering the unnatural glow in Obolo's eyes earlier. Presumably one of those wonderful mind-stimulating drugs. Keying in her audio enhancers, she slid off her shoes and moved out cautiously in Radig's wake.

Two guards were near the door, hidden from view behind a pair of curtains. Pinpointing them by the sounds of their breathing, Jin moved silently past on her bare feet. Radig's footsteps were easy to follow, and she was within a single curtain of Obolo Nardin's cushion throne when they came to a halt. Squatting down behind the curtain, Jin held her breath.

"My son," Obolo's voice said, his tone oddly grating in Jin's ears—the vocal equivalent, perhaps, of the drug user's shining eyes.

"My father," Radig greeted the elder Nardin in turn. "I've brought you the manifest of the latest shipment. Unloading has already begun; transfer of the special components to the assembly building will begin as soon as it's dark and all the temporary workers are properly confined in their houses."

The familiar *shisss-click* of a magdisk into a reader . . . Obolo grunted. "Good. Have they begun work on the second computer system yet?"

"They're still setting it up," Radig told him. "They estimate it'll be ready in about two days."

"Two and a quarter," Obolo said with casual certainty. "They consistently underestimate the actual time they'll need."

"Perhaps this time—" Radig stopped as a ping came from the work table.

"Obolo Nardin," Obolo said. Something inaudible even to Jin's enhanced hearing . . . "Command," he bit out angrily. "Specified recorder; last playback."

More inaudible speech . . . but even without visual cues, Jin could sense a sudden tension on the other side of the curtain.

As Radig clearly also did. "What is it?" he asked tautly when the voices had stopped.

Obolo took an audible breath. "The Shahni agent who came in with Daulo Sammon has found the key to the Mongoose Project."

"The Shahni—? You know for certain that's what he is?"

"If I hadn't already, his last conversation with Daulo Sammon confirmed it." Obolo's voice was settling down, drifting almost toward boredom. "His reaction this morning to the subliminals was actually all the proof I needed."

Radig seemed to be having trouble catching up. "You say he knows? How?"

"He was pushed into the discovery by Daulo Sammon, as it happens. There was some fantasy about missile production here, and it goaded the agent into disassembling the phone. Perhaps you were right; perhaps we should have removed the villager right at the beginning."

"But the phone's self-destruct—"

"Worked properly, of course. But you don't suppose for a minute that that really helped, do you? Destroyed evidence is as intriguing to such people as undestroyed evidence."

Radig cursed. "We'd better get some guards to their complex right away."

"Why?"

"*Why?*" Radig echoed in disbelief. "Because if he gets that information to his superiors—"

"He can't." Obolo was almost glacially calm. "Mangus is sealed for the night, and I've had all outside phone contact except that from this building shut off since he betrayed his identity this morning. Quiet, now, my son, and let me think."

For a moment the painful thudding of her own heart was all Jin could hear. It had happened, her worst fear about this whole penetration: Daulo was in deadly danger. Her legs trembled with the urge to leap out of concealment, cut both Obolo and Radig in half with her antiarmor laser, and get herself and Daulo out of here . . .

"Yes," Obolo said abruptly. "Yes. You will assemble a small force, my son—four men—and take them to the assembly building. The agent's next step will be to try and find some of our special components in undamaged form to take out of Mangus with him."

"How will he know—"

"He'd have seen the final assembly room door this morning when he and the villager left their own area in reaction to the subliminals. He'll remember it and go there first."

"I understand. Do you wish them killed there, caught in an act of burglary?"

Jin's hands twitched involuntarily into combat position: little finger pointed straight out, thumb resting on ring-finger nails . . .

"Of course not," Obolo snorted scornfully. "That would merely bring others from the Shahni to investigate why one of their preconditioned agents would stoop to simple thievery. No, my son, bring them back here, alive and unharmed."

"We *will* eventually kill them, though, won't we?" Radig asked, almost pleading. "A Shahni agent's training won't allow—"

"Of course we won't kill them," Obolo said evenly. "*We* will do nothing. It'll be the offworlder spy who'll handle that task for us."

Chapter 38

The door to the assembly building was locked, but an unusual-looking tool from Akim's kit took care of it in short order. "Now where?" Daulo whispered as they slipped inside.

"That room we saw when I—" Akim pursed his lips. "You remember—at the end of the hallway the instructor tried to keep us out of?"

"Right," Daulo nodded, glancing out the window beside the door. At Akim's insistence they'd taken a leisurely, roundabout route here from their housing complex, and the earlier twilight had faded now into deep dusk. "What do you want me to do?"

Akim stepped past him to relock the door. "You might as well stay here," he said, not sounding entirely happy with the decision. "This is the door any visitors would be most likely to use. If you see anyone coming, give a whistle."

"A whistle?" Daulo frowned.

"Whistles carry as well in a building as shouts do with less chance of being heard from outside," Akim explained briefly. "Watch carefully."

And he was gone. Daulo listened as his footsteps faded down the hallway, trying to ignore the gnawing sensation in the pit of his stomach. So Jin had been wrong all along. It wasn't missiles . . . or was it? There was still that walled-off section of Mangus that none of their instructors had even referred to.

But then what was all this business with the phones?

The tap on the window barely ten centimeters from his face nearly threw him across the hall in reaction. *God above!* He staggered, trying to regain his balance—tried to shape unsteady lips for a whistle—

"Daulo!" The whisper was barely audible through the glass. His whole body trembling, Daulo moved back to the window.

It was Jin.

Taking a shuddering breath, Daulo stepped to the door and unlocked it. "Jin—God above, but you startled me—"

"Shut up and listen," she growled, brushing past him to peer out the window. "Obolo Nardin's on to you and your Shahni friend. Radig Nardin's gone to assemble a guard force to come here and pick both of you up."

Daulo felt his mouth drop open. "Over *here*? But how did they know we were coming here?"

"Obolo deduced it. He seems to be running on one of those mind-expanders you Qasamans are fond of." Jin turned back from the window. "No sign of them yet—Radig must figure there's no hurry. Where's your Shahni friend?"

"Miron Akim's down the hall." He pointed. "And he's not exactly a friend."

"Go get him anyway—he's dead too if Radig catches him here. If we can hide you somewhere until you can get out of Mangus—"

"Wait a second, we've got to talk first. I think you were wrong about the missiles. They're playing some sort of game with the phone instead."

She hissed between her teeth. "It's no game, Daulo. My guess is that they're systematically planting bugged phones all over Qasama."

"Bugged?" Daulo frowned.

"Equipped with microphones. Listening devices."

"God above," Daulo murmured. *Phones manufactured in Mangus are very popular among top city officials,* Akim had said. And among the Shahni, as well. "But even with microphones in the phones . . . God above. The long-range phone system."

Jin nodded grimly. "That's it, all right. Your marvelous detection-proof underground waveguide has been turned against you. It's tailor-made for this sort of thing."

Daulo clenched his teeth hard enough to hurt. She was right. With virtually every phone in the Great Arc linked through the natural waveguide beneath the planet, it would be childishly simple for any phone conversation to be picked up, duplicated, and the copy routed via that same waveguide back here to Mangus.

With the villages west of Azras one of the few areas immune

to that surveillance. One reason why they'd tried so hard to keep him out of Mangus? "Milika's in danger," he murmured.

"All of Qasama's in danger," Jin retorted. "Don't you get it, Daulo? Once this system's completed—if it isn't already—Mangus will have access to practically every communication and data transfer on the planet. And that kind of information translates directly into power."

Daulo shook his head, forehead tight with thought. "But only if they can sift out the specific information they're looking for. And the more microphones they've got planted, the more they'll have to sort through to get it."

Even in the dim light he saw something flicker across her face. "I've got an idea how they might be handling that," she said, her voice heavy with reluctance. "For the moment, though, there's a rather more immediate threat to us: I think they're trying to build themselves an army among their temporary workers. Did Miron Akim have some kind of reaction this morning? I heard Obolo Nardin mention it."

"Yes—said he felt treason in the assembly room. We left for a few minutes, and he was fine afterwards."

"Presumably because they turned the thing off. You ever heard of subliminals?"

Daulo gritted his teeth. *Treason . . .* "Yeah," he breathed. "If you mix a mild hypnotic gas with subaudible vocal messages, you're supposed to be able to create minor attitude changes in a person."

"We don't use anything like that on Aventine, but the theory's known well enough," Jin nodded. "Is it something common here?"

"I've only heard of it being used as a last-try method with chronic criminal types. It's not supposed to be all *that* effective." Abruptly, another piece of the puzzle fell into place. "Of course— the temporary workers. That's why they keep hiring new men; they're trying to run as many of Azras's people through their conditioning as they can."

"Azras and Purma both," Jin grunted. "On the way in this morning I saw some loaded busses heading back to Purma. They're rotating their work force between the two cities, maybe hoping neither city will notice what they're doing."

"Yeah. You think they've found a way to make subliminals powerful enough to force people into treason?"

"I don't know," Jin shook her head. "I hope all they're trying to do is sow discontent among the cities' poor. Given your current political climate, even that might be enough."

Daulo nodded, feeling cold all over. "God above. We've got to get this to the Shahni."

"No kidding—and may I suggest as a first step that you go collect your friend and we all get out of here? Radig Nardin could arrive any minute now, and if he finds us we probably won't have any choice but to kill them." She stooped again to look out the window.

Daulo shivered. The way she just automatically assumed who would win such a faceoff . . . "Yeah. Okay, I'll go get—"

"Too late." Peering out the window, Jin hissed a curse between her teeth. "They're coming."

Stupid, Jin bit out silently at herself. Yes, it'd all been information the Shahni were going to need; and *yes,* Daulo was the best person to give it to them. But she still should have gotten him and Miron Akim out first.

Clenching her teeth, she looked around the entrance hallway. There was nothing here she could use to fight with; nothing that might realistically allow Daulo to defeat five alert men without killing them. And it *had* to be Daulo who did all the fighting; if Akim found out Daulo had been talking to her he would probably have the entire Sammon family up on treason charges.

Her eyes fell on an electric socket. *Unless,* she amended, *no one actually sees who it is fighting them . . .*

Radig's men were almost to the door now. "All right," she muttered to Daulo. "Get back there—across the hallway—and cover your eyes. Cover them *good.*"

"Then what?" Daulo asked, moving obediently to the spot she'd indicated and raising his forearm across his eyes.

"With luck, you'll grab their full attention when they come in and they won't have a chance to see me. So I wasn't here—you understand? If anyone asks, you took them all out by yourself." Her enhanced hearing was picking up footsteps outside now. "Get ready; here they come."

She flattened herself into the corner behind the door, keying her targeting lock to the electrical outlet and raising her right fingertip to the ready position . . .

And abruptly, the door was flung open.

"Well, well," Radig Nardin said sardonically, sauntering into the entrance hallway. "What have we here?—one of our trustworthy employees overanxious for tomorrow's work to begin? Put your stupid arm down, Daulo Sammon—"

And as the last of the guards stepped across the threshold, Jin squeezed her eyes shut and fired her arcthrower.

Even through closed eyelids the flash was dazzlingly bright. Someone gasped, someone else bit out an oath—and then Jin was in their midst.

It was no contest. Temporarily but totally blinded, facing a sighted opponent with Cobra servos behind her punches, the five men went down like randomly flailing target dummies.

The last *thud* of a falling body was still echoing in Jin's ears when she heard the gasp from Daulo's direction. "God above," he breathed. "Jin—you—"

"No; *you* did all this," she snapped at him. The door was still open; throwing a quick look outside, she caught its edge with the tip of her foot and swung it closed. "Don't forget that—it could cost you your life."

Daulo took a deep breath. "Right." He swallowed and tried another breath. "You'd better get going—Miron Akim's sure to have heard all of this."

"I know." Jin hesitated. There was so much more she needed to tell him, but for now they'd run out of time. "You and Miron Akim had better do the same. If you can get out of Mangus before they realize you haven't been captured, you ought to have a good chance."

"What about you? Aren't you leaving with us?"

"Don't worry, I'll be right on your tail," she assured him. "There's something else I have to check out first, but then I'll be heading for Azras with you. Or behind you, anyway—we don't want Miron Akim seeing me."

Daulo clenched his teeth. "Right. Good luck."

"You too. Remember not to use any of the phones in Azras." The faint sound of running footsteps could be heard from down the hallway now. "And be careful," she hissed. Opening the door, she took a quick look around and slipped outside.

Again, the nearby area was deserted. Moving around the corner, where she'd be out of sight when Daulo and Akim left, she crouched down against the building and made a more leisurely scan of the area. There was occasional movement near the center of the black wall dividing Mangus in half, as well as some quiet activity around the housing complex backed up to the wall. Otherwise, nothing. Keying her optical enhancers for telescopic, she focused on the wall.

It was too tall for her to jump—that much was quickly obvious.

Half again as tall as the three-story housing complex near it, it was at least a meter beyond her leg servos' capabilities. She'd been taught a lot of climbing techniques, but all of them assumed some kind of hand and foot grips in the surface to be scaled, and a quick study of the wall didn't look especially promising.

Which left ladders, grappling hooks, or the armored gateway. The first two would require equipment she didn't have. The third, on the other hand . . .

It was the obvious way for her to get in, and for a long moment she seriously considered it. Radig Nardin had mentioned a transfer of material, and if they were going to open the gate anyway, all she had to do was properly disguise herself and walk on in.

Except that her disguise kit was twenty kilometers south of Azras in Daulo's abandoned car. And anyway, if her suspicions were right, Obolo Nardin would hardly have trusted the secret to more than a handful of his closest family members. A stranger—any stranger—would be caught instantly.

A movement from her right caught her eye: Daulo and his companion, walking with forced casualness in the general direction of the gateway she and Radig had entered Mangus by that morning. For a second she wondered if she should perhaps sneak on ahead and help clear the way.

But if and when their escape was discovered, the evidence Jin needed to get could literally go up in smoke. And besides, Daulo had a new protector now. She could only hope that the Shahni picked competent people for their agents.

Taking a deep breath, she headed at a crouching run across the compound toward the wall.

Chapter 39

The courtyard of the housing complex was bustling with quiet activity, the intermix of voices including those of women and children as well as men. *Must be the permanent workers,* Jin decided as she crept carefully along the roof. Members of Obolo Nardin's family, if the Milika pattern held here; the trustworthy ones, who could be relied on to ignore odd sounds that might come from beyond the wall towering over them.

Though presumably they wouldn't ignore odd sounds coming from directly over their heads. No one seemed to have noticed any noise from her jump up to the roof, but now that she was silhouetted against the overhead canopy all anyone in the courtyard below had to do was look up . . . Gritting her teeth, Jin crouched down a little more and concentrated on keeping her footing.

But she reached the far side of the complex without incident, to find that she hadn't gained as much of an advantage as she'd hoped to. Her rangefinder put the top of the wall at eight meters away and six meters up, and from a standing start—on uncertain footing—it was going to be close. Stepping back a pace, she checked her balance and jumped.

She made it with scant centimeters to spare, her nanocomputer jackknifing her horizontally to let her absorb the impact with her legs as she slammed into the smooth ceramic. Her fingers lunged forward, locked hard over the edge, and for a few moments she hung there motionlessly, listening for any sign that she'd been seen. But the compound remained quiet. Pulling herself up into a prone position atop the wall, she looked down over the edge.

And found she'd been right.

A cold chill shivered its way up her back, *Mangus,* she thought to herself, bitterness at her stupidity bringing a knot to her stomach. *Mangus. Mongoose,* An utterly obvious and natural name for a group seeing itself as the Qasaman answer to the Cobra threat. She and Kruin Sammon had both caught the name's significance, even to the point of having an argument about it ... and in all of that fuss both of them had still managed to miss one small fact.

The fact that no one on Qasama had any business naming such a group *mongoose* in the first place ... because no one on Qasama had ever heard the hated demon warriors referred to as Cobras.

Until now.

The Troft ship below was only about half visible, its long neck disappearing into a Troft-style maintenance building while a squat siege-tower unloader partially blocked her view of the main drive nozzles at the aft end. But enough was showing for her to see that the usual inkblot/sunburst indicators of ownership and demesne identification were missing.

There were figures moving down there—mostly Trofts, but a handful of humans as well. If the Trofts hadn't bothered to remove the equivalent identity marks from their clothing ... but a quick telescopic examination showed they had. Something on the oddly shaped residential building across the compound from the ship, then? She shifted her attention to it—

And without warning there was a hooting of alarms from behind her.

Reflexively, she flattened herself to the top of the wall, biting back a curse as the human half of Mangus seemed to explode with light. Her light-amps automatically shut off in the glare; clenching her jaw, she kicked in her audio enhancers to compensate. Her opponents had the edge in sheer numbers, but if she could spot their positions before they started shooting, she might be able to eliminate them before they could do her too much damage.

Trained responses took over from the momentary panic ... and it was only then that she realized that the floodlights weren't being directed at her. In fact, the placement of many of them—fastened to the wall a meter below her—had actually wound up leaving her in relative shadow. Lifting her head a few centimeters, she keyed her optical enhancers to telescopic and scanned the compound for the focus of the commotion.

It wasn't hard to find. Daulo and Akim, the latter limping slightly, were being half dragged away from the outer gate by an escort of six armed men.

Jin ground her teeth savagely. *I should have gone with them,* she told herself bitterly. For a long minute she watched the group walk toward the administrative center, a hundred wild schemes for saving them rushing tornado-like through her mind. Then, with a shuddering breath, she forced her emotions aside. *All right, girl, knock it off. Calm down and think it out.*

Daulo and Akim had been captured. All right. Obolo Nardin would know soon that they were on to his secret; but then he'd already suspected that much, anyway. Furthermore, since neither man had escaped or otherwise breached Mangus's security, there was no reason for Obolo to panic. Which meant that the inevitable interrogation would presumably be handled in a relatively leisurely fashion, and also that the Troft ship down there wouldn't be sent scurrying prematurely off to space with its cargo only half unloaded.

Until, that was, Obolo discovered his offworlder spy had escaped. Damn.

Jin chewed at her lip, trying hard to come up with an alternative . . . but there wasn't one. Not if she wanted Daulo to live past the next hour or so. And the whole idea wasn't as crazy as it looked at first glance, anyway. Obolo was smart enough, but for all his chemically-stimulated mental abilities, he still lacked one crucial fact . . . and as long as he thought Jin was just an ordinary Aventinian, she and Daulo would have a chance.

The floodlights bathing the compound were still on, but the activity at the gate was dissipating now as the prisoners and their escort marched down the road toward the administrative center. Sliding along on her belly, Jin eased forward until she was between two of the wall-mounted lights. The ground directly below wasn't exactly dark, but it was as good as she was going to get. Taking a last look around, she slid off the wall to hang for a second by her hands, and dropped.

And gasped in shock as the impact of landing sent a stab of pain up through her left knee.

"Damn!" she hissed under her breath, rolling awkwardly over to a sitting position and clenching her leg tightly. For a long and terrifying minute she was afraid the vaunted Cobra equipment had failed her, that she'd actually succeeded in spraining or even breaking the joint. But finally the pain began to ease, and in another minute she was able to scramble carefully to her feet and start limping toward the administrative center.

She hadn't yet figured out how she was going to cover that much floodlit ground without being seen, but fortunately that problem solved itself. She'd taken only a few steps before the lights abruptly cut off, plunging the compound again into darkness. *Excitement's over, folks; go to bed,* she thought, increasing her speed to a sort of syncopated trot. Now if the freshly relaxed security extended to the doors of the administrative center . . .

Surprisingly, it did. Even more surprisingly, it also extended to the lower levels of the building where her cell was located; though once she thought about it it was obvious that any preliminary interrogation of their new prisoners would be taking place upstairs in Obolo's throne room. She hoped Daulo would remember to leave her out of whatever story he and Akim told them.

The guards she'd stunned were still lying unconscious in the washroom where she'd left them. Retrieving them, she treated each to another blast from her sonic as a precaution and then carried them back to their posts. A quick study of the cell door; then, raising her fingertip lasers, she burned a spectacular but shallow arc part of the way around the lock area. *Not too much, she* warned herself. *Your theoretical rescuer didn't get very far, remember.* When Obolo sent someone to check on her—as he eventually would— there had to be a plausible explanation as to why the guards had been knocked unconscious but Jin still a prisoner. Whatever con- clusion Obolo came to, it ought to be possible to bend it to her own ends. She hoped.

A minute later she was back in her cell, relocking it behind her via the exposed mechanism. Replacing the metal plate over the opening was somewhat trickier, but by softening it first with her lasers she was able to smooth it back without leaving any major stress wrinkles to show it had once been off.

And after that there was nothing to do but wait. *We'll let the offworlder spy kill them for us,* Obolo had told his son. Jin had no idea how he planned to do it; but if he wanted to do it properly he would need to at least have Jin in the same room with Daulo and Akim before they were killed.

She hoped to God that Obolo would want to do it properly.

"In the name of the Shahni," Akim intoned formally, "I hereby charge you with treason against Qasama. All here are released of vows of loyalty to others and ordered to surrender to my authority."

A fine speech, Daulo thought; delivered with just the right combination of command and righteous anger.

It would undoubtedly have sounded even better if he and Akim hadn't been on their knees with their hands manacled behind them.

Seated on his cushions, Obolo Nardin raised a bored eyebrow.

"You maintain your dignity well, Miron Akim," he said in a raspy voice. "So. You have said the required words. Now tell me the reason for which you charge my household with treason."

Akim's lip twisted. "Or in other words, what do the Shahni know about your treachery? Don't be foolish."

Obolo chuckled humorlessly. "Better and better. Now you seek to plant doubt within me as to whether any of my plans are known outside the walls of Mangus. Unfortunately, your attempts are useless. You forget that I know exactly what the Shahni know of me . . . which is nothing at all."

There was a flurry of movement behind them. Daulo risked turning his head away from Obolo Nardin, received a slap from one of his guards for his trouble. But not before he saw that it was an unsteady Radig Nardin who was being helped into the room. He focused on Obolo again, but if the other man was concerned over his son's health, it wasn't visible. "Well, Radig Nardin?" he asked. "You were sent to detain them. Why did you fail?"

Radig passed the two prisoners, throwing acid looks at them as he did so. "They ambushed me, my father. One of the guards who was with me may not survive the night."

"Indeed?" Obolo's voice was cold. "Were five then not enough against two?"

Radig refused to shrivel under his father's gaze. "No, my father. Not when they were armed with devices of offworld origin."

Daulo felt his stomach knot up. "Explain," Obolo ordered.

Radig nodded to one of his men, who stepped forward and made the sign of respect. "We found severe burns on and around an electrical socket in the hallway where Master Nardin was attacked," he told Obolo. "Clearly the source of the bright flash that was used against him."

"Indeed." Obolo shifted his eyes to another man standing by. "Bring the offworlder woman." The other nodded and hurried out.

Beside him, Daulo felt Akim stiffen. "What is this about an offworlder woman?" he asked cautiously.

"We have the Aventinian spy you've been seeking," Obolo told him calmly. "She's been our prisoner since morning."

Akim seemed to digest that. "Then perhaps your activities this evening can yet be overlooked," he suggested slowly. "The Shahni are very anxious to find and interrogate this spy. If you release her to me, I'm sure any other problems between you and the Shahni can be . . . worked out."

Daulo held his breath . . . but Obolo merely smiled. "You

disappoint me, Miron Akim. The lie saturates both your face and your voice. However—" He raised a finger "—I'll grant you this much: you'll have your chance to interrogate the spy before we kill her."

Akim didn't reply.

"And you, Daulo Sammon," Obolo said, turning his eyes on Daulo. His *shining* eyes, Daulo noted, feeling a tightness in his throat. Jin had been right; the man was high on mind stimulants. "What is your interest in Mangus?"

Daulo considered fabricating a lie, decided it wasn't worth the effort. "The same interest any rational Qasaman would have in a nest of treason," he bit out. "I came to find out what you were doing here, and to stop you."

For a long moment Obolo continued to gaze at him. "You aren't yet defeated, are you, Daulo Sammon?" he said at last. Thoughtfully. "Your friend there is, though he hopes against hope for rescue. But you are not. Why? Is it simply that you don't realize what's at stake here?"

Daulo shook his head silently. "Answer!" Radig snarled, taking a threatening step toward him.

"Peace, my son," Obolo told him calmly. "Whatever secret Daulo Sammon thinks he possesses, it'll be ours soon enough." Abruptly, he leaned over toward his table and touched a button. "Yes?"

The voice was unintelligible from where Daulo knelt, but even so he could hear the nervous excitement in it. A tight smile tugged at Obolo's lips . . . "Interesting, though not entirely unexpected. Alert all guard posts and have a full sweep made of the grounds."

He leaned back into his cushions and glanced up at Radig. "As I said, my son, Daulo Sammon's secret is now ours. It seems the woman wasn't the sole survivor of her spacecraft's destruction."

Radig's hand strayed to the grip of the pistol belted at his side. "She's gone?"

"Her associate was fortunately not that competent," Obolo told him, eyes drifting to Daulo again. "Or perhaps he was sent on an errand. Did she tell him through the door that you needed aid?"

"If you're suggesting I would associate myself with an offworlder spy—" Daulo began.

"It hardly matters anymore," Obolo cut him off coldly. "Except possibly to you. You may be able to buy yourself a painless death if you can tell us where the other offworlder is."

A shiver ran up Daulo's spine. "I don't know what you're talking about," he growled.

Obolo shrugged. "As I said, it hardly matters."

For a minute the room was silent. Daulo concentrated on steady breathing, trying to stay calm. Could Jin have lied to him about being the only survivor? No, she wouldn't have done something like that. Whatever was going on—whatever evidence Obolo's men had found or thought they'd found—Jin was in control of the situation. His life, and Akim's, and possibly the entire future of Qasama—all of them were in her hands now.

It was a strangely comforting thought. More strange yet was the complete lack of resentment accompanying it.

There was the sound of an opening door back behind the curtains. This time he resisted the urge to look around at the approaching footsteps; and a minute later Jin and her escort came into his view.

Her appearance was a shock. Hunch-shouldered, almost visibly trembling as she was half led, half dragged toward Obolo, she looked like nothing more than a simple farming girl being hauled toward terrifying matters totally beyond her understanding. It was as if the Jin Moreau he'd come to know had never existed, and for a horrible moment he wondered if they'd gotten to her with one of their drugs.

And then he caught a glimpse of her eyes as she flinched back from Obolo . . .

Unfortunately, Obolo saw it, too. "Your act is amusing but useless, woman," he said, voice dripping with contempt. "I'm perfectly aware you're not a helpless Qasaman female. You many start by telling me who you are."

Slowly, Jin straightened up, the aura of fear dropping away from her like a dark robe. "Not that it's any of your business," she said evenly, "but my name's Jasmine Moreau."

Beside him, Daulo felt Akim react. "You know her?" he murmured.

"We know her family," Akim muttered back. "They are . . . rather deadly."

Daulo glanced up at the guards towering over them. "Good," he murmured.

Akim snorted gently.

Obolo's eyes flicked to Akim, back to Jin. "I recognize the family name from our histories," he told her.

"The family name is important on Aventine, too," Jin returned. "Which means they'll eventually be coming to look for me."

" 'Eventually' is a long time." Obolo's eyes suddenly narrowed. "Where's your accomplice?" he barked at her.

Jin remained unshaken. "Well beyond your reach," she said calmly. "Somewhere on his way to Azras by now, I'd imagine."

"Leaving you—a woman—to die?" Obolo snorted.

"Women die approximately as often as men do," Jin said icily. "Once per customer. I'm ready to take my turn at it if need be. How about you?"

Obolo seemed taken aback, and Daulo fought to hide a grim smile. Obolo's experience, his secret information network, his expanded mental abilities—none of it could have quite prepared him to face someone like Jin Moreau. Possibly for the first time in years, the man was actually flustered.

But he recovered quickly. "My turn at the cup of death will not be for some time," he snarled. "Yours, on the other hand, will be very soon now. If your companion is lurking about Mangus, we'll root him out quickly enough. If instead he's truly run away . . . he'll return far too late to help you."

Abruptly, he turned to look at Daulo and Akim. "Take them to the north chamber," he ordered their guards. "Her as well," he said, gesturing back at Jin. "Chain all three together, where they may share a last half-hour together." His lips curled back in a sardonic smile. "You see, Miron Akim, I keep my word. You will have your chance to interrogate your prisoner. Before she kills you."

Chapter 40

The north chamber turned out to be a cozy corner of the curtain-walled maze that was Obolo's throne room. "Quite a mouse track you have here," Jin commented to Radig as he supervised the chaining of her ankles to Daulo's and Akim's. "I'll bet someone who knew what he was doing could hide out for hours without being spotted."

Radig threw her a glower. "A feeble attempt, woman. Your companion isn't here."

"You sure?" she asked blandly. The more she could get them chasing each other in circles, the better.

But he just ignored her, and a moment later left with the other guards. *Well, it was worth a try,* Jin told herself, and turned her attention to Daulo.

To find him glaring bitterly at her. "So," he growled. "It seems Moffren Omnathi was right—you *did* come here to spy on us. We took you in and healed your wounds . . . and in return for our hospitality you lie to us."

The tirade was totally unexpected, and for an instant she stared at him in confusion. But only for an instant. In her peripheral vision, she could see Akim watching them closely . . . "I'm sorry, Daulo Sammon," she said with cool formality. "I regret having had to deceive your family. If it helps any, I never planned to involve you or anyone else on Qasama with my mission."

"That mission being . . . ?" Akim put in.

"I suppose it doesn't matter anymore if I tell you," she sighed, looking around the curtain walls surrounding them. No sounds of breathing; no body-sized hot spots showing on infrared. Which meant Obolo was relying on more sophisticated electronic methods

780

of listening in on the private moments he'd so graciously granted his prisoners. Smiling grimly to herself, Jin activated her omni-directional sonic. "My mission," she said quietly, turning back to Akim, "is essentially the same as yours: to stop Obolo Nardin and Mangus."

"Indeed," Akim said coldly. "So once again you reach down from the sky to interfere in matters that are ours alone."

"Can we forget politics for a minute and concentrate on the problem at hand?" Jin growled. "Or don't you understand just what Obolo Nardin's got going here?"

"He's tapping into Qasama's communications network," Akim shrugged.

Jin stared at him in disbelief. "And that doesn't *worry* you?"

"Of course it does," he said, eyes steady on her face. "But the scheme is self-limiting. Yes, he can listen into the Shahni's conversations, and that certainly must be dealt with. But you have to realize that the more communications he copies, the longer it's going to take him to find the ones he wants. At the rate he's making and distributing these phones, his entire system will eventually collapse under its own weight. If it hasn't already done so."

Jin shook her head. "I wish it were that simple, but its not. You see, he doesn't need to sift all these conversations and data transfers by hand. He can do it with computers."

"With computers?" Daulo frowned. "How?"

"It's very simple. All he has to do is have the computers scan each conversation for preprogrammed words or names—"

"And he then has to listen personally only to the ones containing those words," Akim interrupted her. "Credit us with a little sophistication, offworlder—the method is well known. But for the scope you accuse Mangus of indulging in—" He shook his head. "Perhaps you don't realize just how much information is transferred around Qasama in a single day. It would take computers far more advanced than any available on Qasama to handle it all."

"I know," Jin said quietly. "But Obolo Nardin's computers didn't come from Qasama. They came from the Troft Assemblage."

For a half dozen heartbeats the others just looked at her, Daulo with his mouth hanging open, Akim only marginally less thunderstruck. Daulo found his voice first. "That's insane," he hissed.

"I wish it were," Jin said. "But it's not. There's a Troft ship parked right now in the other half of Mangus."

"Which you can't show us at the moment, of course," Daulo growled. "How convenient."

Jin flushed. Daulo was carrying this hostility act entirely too far. "I'll see what I can do later to remedy that—"

"And what," Akim interrupted her, "would the Trofts stand to gain from such a deal?"

Jin turned back to him. "I don't know how much you know about the Trofts, but they're not the monolithic structure you might think. The Assemblage is basically nothing more than a loose confederation of independent two- to three-system demesnes in constant economic and political rivalry with each other."

"Like the villages and cities of Qasama," Daulo muttered under his breath.

Jin glanced at him. "Something like that, yes. My guess is one of those demesnes has decided humans are more of a threat than we're worth, and is trying to do something about it."

"By helping Obolo Nardin gain political power?" Akim frowned.

"By uniting Qasama," Jin corrected quietly. "And then using your world as a war machine against us."

Akim's eyes flashed. "We don't need alien help to hate you, offworlder," he bit out. "But we don't make war under alien orders, either."

"If Obolo Nardin succeeds, you may not have much say in it." A sound caught Jin's ear. "Someone's coming," she hissed, shutting off her sonic.

A second later the curtain was pulled aside to reveal Radig and a handful of men. Radig looked rather annoyed, Jin noted; at a guess, his eavesdropping on their discussion had been something less than successful. "You—offworlder—put these on," he snarled, throwing her a tangle of male clothing.

The same clothing, she saw, that she'd worn as a disguise that morning in Azras. "And then what?" she asked as one of the guards stepped forward to unshackle her.

He ignored the question. "That one—" he pointed at Akim "—will be coming with us to the assembly building. You, on the other hand—" he smiled chillingly at Daulo "—we'll keep alive a little longer. Though you probably won't like it."

"What's that supposed to mean?" Jin demanded.

"Get undressed!" Radig snapped.

"Tell me what you're going to do to Daulo Sammon."

One of the guards stepped forward, raised his hand to slap her—

"No!" Radig stopped him. "She's to remain unmarked." He glared at Jin as the guard reluctantly stepped back. "And you ought to be thankful my father doesn't want your body to show evidence of any *other* activities, either. Otherwise we would be postponing your execution by a few hours."

Jin glared right back at him. "You would have found it surprisingly unrewarding," she said evenly. "What are you going to do to Daulo Sammon?"

"Interrogate him, probably," Akim spoke up grimly from beside her. "They're still looking for your companion, remember?"

Jin glanced at Daulo's expression. "I've already said he's beyond your grasp," she told Radig.

"Get undressed," the other repeated coldly. "Before I allow my men to forget my father's orders. *All* of his orders."

For a long moment Jin seriously considered letting them try it. But this wasn't the time or the place for that kind of a confrontation. Swallowing her anger, she changed into the other set of clothes, doing her best to ignore the watching eyes.

It seemed darker, somehow, out in the compound, and it took Jin most of the short walk to the assembly building to realize that it was because the housing complexes were now completely dark. The timing was no doubt deliberate; whatever Obolo and his son had planned, they wouldn't want any witnesses around to see it.

The suspense didn't last long. "Let me explain what's going to happen," Radig said in a conversational tone as the two men holding Jin's arms positioned her in front of the building's entrance. "You, a spy and enemy of Qasama, were trying to steal our technology. Fortunately for Qasama, this alert Shahni agent—" he waved at Akim, held by two burly guards a few meters in front of her "—was here to stop you. Unfortunately for him, you were also armed." He nodded to one of Jin's guards and the man reached a gloved hand into his holster to produce a standard Qasaman projectile pistol. "He shot you, but you managed to kill him before you died. A pity."

"And you then put the gun in my hand to get my fingerprints on it?" Jin asked coldly, watching the pistol being held at her side. The second he raised it to shoot she would have to to act . . .

"Ah—something else you don't know about Qasama," Radig said sardonically. He nodded again, and to her surprise the man with the gun pressed the weapon into her hand, keeping his own gloved hand around hers in a firm controlling grip. "Our science is quite advanced in such matters—more so, obviously, than yours. Here it's possible to prove from a careful residue analysis that a specific shot was fired by a specific gun held in a specific hand.

Therefore, each of you will have to fire the fatal shots yourselves. With our help, of course."

"Of course," Jin said sarcastically. A reddish haze seemed to be stealing across her vision, and for a second she wondered if they'd decided to risk drugging her after all. But it wasn't that kind of haze ... and after a moment she realized what it was.

It was fury. Simple, cold-blooded fury.

A good Cobra is always self-controlled, the dictum ran through her mind ... but at the moment none of those platitudes seemed worth a damn. Daulo had looked quietly horrified as he'd been led off for his interrogation; Radig's own self-satisfied expression here and now was in sharp contrast as he choreographed his double murder ... and it occurred to Jin that up till now Mangus had been gaining all the benefits of treason without having to pay any of the costs.

It was time for the balance to be evened up a bit.

A third guard was moving up to Akim's side now, pressing his pistol into the other's clearly unwilling hand. Consciously unclenching her teeth, Jin activated her multiple targeting lock, keying for the centers of the three guards' foreheads. "I presume it's almost time," she said coldly, glancing at Radig before focusing on Akim. "Tell me, Miron Akim: what's the penalty for attempted murder on Qasama?"

Radig snorted. "Don't try to scare us, woman—" he snarled, taking a step toward her.

"Miron Akim?"

"This is more than simple murder, Jasmine Moreau," Akim replied, his eyes on Radig. "It's murder combined with treason. For that the penalty is death."

"I see," she nodded. "I trust, then, you won't be too upset if I have to kill some of them?"

One of the guards snorted something contemptuous sounding. But Radig didn't even smile. Stepping to her side, he grabbed the barrel of the pistol in her hand and brought it up to point directly at Akim. "If you're waiting for your companion to save you, wait for him in hell," he snarled, eyes glittering with hatred. "In fact, I almost hope he's watching. Let him watch you die."

Jin glared straight back, twisted her right arm free of the hands holding it, and slammed the gun across the side of Radig's face.

He flopped over backwards onto the ground without a sound. The guard holding Jin's left arm spat a curse, but he'd gotten no farther than tightening his grip on her arm before she turned partly around in his direction to slam the pistol against his head. The grip abruptly loosened; and even as the guard to her right threw his arms around her shoulders, she twisted back that direction to swing the weapon into his face. Simultaneously, her left hand whipped up, swept across the group around Akim—

Her peripheral vision caught the triple sputter of light as her nanocomputer fired her fingertip laser, and she turned back just in time to see the three guards drop like empty sacks to the ground.

Leaving Akim standing among the carnage. The pistol they'd meant him to kill her with still gripped in his hand. Not quite pointed at her . . .

For a long moment they stared at each other. "It's all over, Miron Akim," she called softly, the haze of fury evaporating from her mind. The hand holding the pistol was noticeably trembling now. "May I suggest we get out of here before these men are missed?"

Slowly, the pistol sagged downward; and after a moment, Akim stooped and laid it on the ground, his eyes on her the whole time. He flinched slightly as she stepped toward him, but didn't back up. "It's all right," she assured him quietly. "As I said earlier, we're on the same side here."

He licked his lips and seemed to finally find his voice. "A demon warrior," he said. A shiver abruptly ran through him. "A demon warrior. Now it finally makes sense. God in heaven." He took a shuddering breath. "On the same side, you say, Jasmine Moreau?" he said with a hint of returning spirit.

"Yes—whether you believe it or not." She risked a glance around the compound. He hadn't tried to jump her by the time she looked back at him. "If for no other reason than because Obolo Nardin wants both of us dead. So which will it be?—you want to join forces, or would you rather we tackle Obolo Nardin's private army separately?"

Akim licked his lips again, glancing down at the three dead men around his feet. "I don't really have much of a choice," he said, looking her firmly in the eye. "Very well, then, Jasmine Moreau: in the name of the Shahni of Qasama, I accept your assistance in return for my own. Do you have a plan for getting us out of Mangus?"

Jin breathed a quiet sigh of relief. "A plan of sorts, yes. But first we're going to have to go back into the administrative center. Or I have to, anyway."

He nodded with far too much understanding for her taste. "To rescue Daulo Sammon?"

She gritted her teeth. "His family saved my life, long before they knew who I was. No matter what Daulo Sammon thinks of me now, I owe them his life in return."

Akim looked back at the administrative center. "How did you plan to get him out? More of the same firepower you just demonstrated?"

"Hopefully less of it." Jin grimaced, locating Radig's unmoving form. "I'd hoped to persuade Radig Nardin to tell me where they'd taken him. Unfortunately, it doesn't look like he'll be up to talking for a while."

"He'll be on the lowest level," Akim said thoughtfully. "Probably in a corner room. An airtight one, if possible."

Jin frowned at him. "How do you know?"

He shrugged. "Historical precedent, coupled with the nature of the drugs used in the kind of interrogation they're probably doing. Drugs that are reported to be extremely unpleasant, incidentally. The sooner we get him out, the better for him."

Jin bit her lip. "I know. Unfortunately, there's something else we have to do first."

"Such as?"

"Such as getting our escape route set up. Come on."

Chapter 41

The hard part wasn't taking the high road for the second time that night, jumping from ground to housing complex roof to the top of the wall. The hard part wasn't even inching along the wall on her stomach, leaning precariously down to cut the power cables linking the spotlights and splice them together into a makeshift rope.

The hard part was wondering the whole time whether Akim would still be waiting down below when she finally finished the chore.

But he was. Evidently, she decided as she carefully pulled him up, Shahni agents were not as fanatic as she'd feared they might be. A true fanatic would probably have preferred death to dealing with a perceived enemy of Qasama.

She got him up and spreadeagled in a safe if not entirely comfortable position atop the wall, and for a long minute he gazed in silence at the Troft ship below. "May God curse Obolo Nardin and his household," he spat at last. "So you were telling the truth after all."

"Keep your voice down, please. You know anything about Troft ships besides what they look like?"

He shook his head. "No."

"Me, neither. Which could be a problem . . . because that's where we're going to hide out for the next day or two."

He didn't fall off the wall, or even gasp in stunned astonishment. He just turned a rock-carved face to her. "We're *what*?"

She sighed. "I don't much like it either, but at the moment we're slightly low on options." She waved back toward the administrative center. "As soon as they find out we're gone, they'll turn their half of Mangus upside down looking for us. And since they're already scouring the countryside between here and civilization for my theoretical accomplice, going outside the wall isn't going to be any safer. What's left?"

"If we're discovered here, it will be Trofts we'll have to fight," Akim said pointedly, "Will you be as effective a warrior against them as you would be against Obolo Nardin's men?"

Jin snorted, the image of her father battling the target robots in the MacDonald Center's Danger Room flashing through her mind. "We were *designed* to fight the Trofts, Miron Akim," she told him grimly.

"I see." Akim exhaled a thoughtful hiss. "I suppose it really is our best chance, then. All right, I'm ready."

"Yes, well, I'm not. First I've got to go back and get Daulo Sammon, remember?"

"I thought perhaps you'd changed your mind." Visibly, Akim braced himself. "All right, then. Tell me what you want me to do."

He didn't think much of the idea—that much was evident from the play of emotions across his face as she explained it. But he didn't waste any time arguing the point. Unlike Daulo, Akim didn't seem particularly disturbed by the thought of taking orders from a woman. Perhaps he'd had experience with female agents of the Shahni; perhaps it was simply that he knew better than to let pride get in the way of survival.

A moment later she was moving silently through the darkness toward the administrative center as, behind her, Akim pulled the cable back up. At least this time, Jin knew, she wouldn't have to worry about him leaving before she returned.

She hit the wall a little harder this time, rekindling the ache in her left knee. For a moment she hung by her fingertips, gritting her teeth tightly as she waited for the pain to subside.

"You all right?" Akim asked softly from half a meter in front of her.

"Yeah." Pulling herself up, she rolled onto her stomach facing Akim and took the end of the cable/rope from him. "Knee got hurt in the crash and hasn't totally recovered yet. How about you?"

"Fine. Any trouble?"

"Not really," Jin replied, trying not to pant. Even before that last leap over from the housing complex, the jog from Daulo's interrogation cell with the boy in fire-carry across her shoulder had worn her out far more than it should have. A bad sign; it implied she was getting too tired to give her servos as much of the load as they were capable of. "You were right about him being on the lowest level," she said as she began pulling Daulo up. "Obolo Nardin thoughtfully left a pair of guards outside his door to mark the spot for me."

"Did you kill them?"

Jin's cheek twitched. "I had to. One of them recognized me before I could get close enough."

Akim grunted. "They're all parties to treason. Don't forget that."

Jin swallowed. "Right. Anyway, I found Daulo Sammon strapped to a chair with a set of tubes in his arms and smoke curling around him from a censer under his chin."

"Was he alone?"

"No, but I was able to stun the interrogator without killing him. Okay, here he comes. I'll take his weight; you protect his head."

Between them, they got Daulo up on the wall, draping his limp body over it like a hunting trophy across an aircar rack. "Any idea what they might have used on him?" she asked, trying to keep the anxiety out of her voice as Akim peered closely at Daulo's slack face. The boy was so quiet . . .

Akim shook his head slowly. "There are too many possibilities." He took Daulo's wrist. "His heartbeat's slow, but it's steady enough. He should be able to simply sleep the drugs off."

"I hope you're right." Notching her light-amps to higher power, Jin gave the Troft side of the compound a quick scan. "Did you see any activity over there while I was gone?"

"No. Nor on the other side, either."

Jin nodded. "Hard to believe our escape still hasn't been noticed, but I suppose we should be grateful for small favors."

Akim snorted gently. "Perhaps Obolo Nardin expected his son to disobey the order about leaving you untouched."

"You're a cheery one," Jin growled, shivering. "Well, there's no point in postponing this. Watch his head again, will you, while I flip him over the side?"

A minute later Daulo was down, half lying and half slouching at the base of the wall. "Your turn," Jin told Akim. "Don't step on him."

"I won't. How will you get down?"

She felt her stomach tighten. "I'll have to jump," she said, trying not to think about what had happened the last time she'd tried that stunt. "Don't worry, I can manage it."

Akim's eyes were steady on her. "That last jump from the housing roof—you didn't make it by very much."

"I'm just getting a little tired. Look, we're wasting time."

He gazed at her another moment, then pursed his lips and nodded. Pulling a handkerchief from his pocket, he wrapped it around the cable and held on there with both hands. Rolling off the wall top, he slid down to the ground in a military-style controlled fall. Waving once to her, he knelt and began to untie Daulo from the cable.

This is it. Dropping her end of the cable to fall beside Akim, Jin lowered herself over the edge to hang by her fingertips. Knees slightly bent, she set her teeth and let go. The ground jumped up to meet her—

And she clamped down hard on her tongue as a hot spike jabbed up through her left knee.

"Jasmine Moreau!" Akim hissed, dropping to the ground beside her.

"I'm all right," she managed, blinking back tears of pain as she lay on her back clutching her knee. "Just give me a minute."

It was closer to three minutes, in fact, before she was finally able to get to her feet again. "Okay," she breathed. If she consciously turned over to her servos the job of keeping her upright . . . "I'm fine now."

"I'll carry Daulo Sammon," Akim said in a voice that allowed for no argument.

"Okay by me," Jin said, wincing as she eased back down to a sitting position. "I'll let you carry the cable, too, if you don't mind. But first we have to figure out how we're going to get into that ship."

Akim looked over at it. "Security systems?"

"Undoubtedly." Jin adjusted her enhancers to a combination telescopic/light-amp and made a slow sweep of the unloading tower nestled up to the ship's stern. "Looks like the twin horns of a sonic motion-detector over the doorway there," she told Akim. "As well as a—let me see—yes; there's also an infrared laser sweep covering the loading ramp and a fifteen-meter wedge of ground in front of it."

"What about that one?" Akim asked, pointing at the maintenance building. "The one the craft's nose is buried in."

"Probably something similar." Jin glanced back along the wall behind them. "More motion detectors and monitor cameras over the gateway to the other half of Mangus. A reasonably layered intruder defense."

"Can you defeat it?"

"If you mean can I destroy it, sure. But not without setting off a dozen alarms in the process."

"Well, then, what *can* you do?"

Jin gnawed at her lip. "It looks like our only chance will be to approach the ship from the side. If I can get on top of it, there'll probably be a way to get through the coupling between the unloading tower and the ship proper."

Akim considered that. "That almost sounds too easy. Except for a demon warrior, of course."

"No, their security wasn't planned with demon warriors in mind," Jin said dryly. "On the other hand, they haven't been totally stupid, either. You can't see it, but for about thirty meters out from the side of the ship there's a crisscross infrared laser pattern running a few centimeters off the ground."

"Can *you* see it well enough?"

"Seeing it isn't what I'm worried about. The problem is that the pattern of crisscrosses changes every few seconds."

Surprisingly, Akim chuckled. "What's so funny?" Jin growled.

"Your Trofts," he said, the chuckle becoming a snort of derision. "It's nice to know they're neither omniscient nor even very clever. That laser system is a Qasaman one."

"What?" Jin frowned.

"Yes indeed. Perhaps Obolo Nardin deliberately gave it to them to keep a little extra control over the bargain."

"Meaning there's a weakness in the system?" Jin asked, heart starting to beat a little faster.

"There is indeed." He pointed toward the ship. "The pattern changes randomly, as you noted; but there are between three and six one-meter-square places in every system of this sort where the lasers never touch."

"Really?" Jin looked back at the ship. "Doesn't that sort of negate the whole purpose?"

"There's a reason behind it," Akim said, a bit tartly. "It gives those using the system places to mount monitor cameras or remote weapons. The gaps are normally set far enough back from the edge to be useless to the average invader . . . but of course, you're hardly an average invader."

"Point." Bracing herself, Jin eased to her feet. A flicker of pain lanced through her knee as she did so; she tried hard to ignore it. "Okay. Wait here until you see me wave to you from the top of the tower ramp over there. *Don't* move until then, understand?— I don't want you wandering into range of the detectors by mistake before I figure out how to shut them down."

"Understood." Akim hesitated. "Good luck, Jasmine Moreau."

❖   ❖   ❖

Akim had been right: the gaps were indeed there, though she had to spend a few tense minutes out in the open watching the lasers go through their paces before she had all four of the spots identified. The pattern led like meandering steppingstones back toward the ship itself, with distances between them that under normal conditions would have been child's play for her. But with her knee the way it was, it wasn't going to be nearly that easy.

But then, it wasn't as if she had any real choice in the matter. Clenching her teeth, she jumped.

Akim had said the gaps would be a meter square each; to Jin they'd looked a lot smaller. But they were big enough. Pausing just long enough at each point to regain her balance and set up the next leap, she bounded like a drunken kangaroo through the detection field. The second-to-last jump took her to within three meters of the ship's hull; the last took her to the top of the stubby swept-forward wing.

For a long minute she crouched there, watching and listening and waiting for her knee to stop throbbing. Then, standing up again, she made her way aft along the wing, passing over the blackened rim of the starboard drive nozzle to the forward edge of the unloading tower.

The tower, like the ship, was of Troft manufacture, and the two had clearly been designed to mate closely together. But "closely" was a relative term, and as she approached it Jin could see that the metal of the tower proper gave way to a flexible rubberine tunnel half a meter from the entryway cover. Rubberine was inexpensive, flexible, and weatherproof, but it had never been designed to withstand laser fire. A minute later, Jin had sliced a person-sized flap in the soft material; a minute after that, she was inside the tower.

Inside the tower . . . and standing on the threshold of a Troft ship.

The emotional shock of it hit her all at once, and her mouth was dry as she stepped through the vestibule-like airlock into the ship. *Inside a Troft ship,* she thought, a shiver running up her back as she paused in the center of the long alien corridor. A *Troft ship . . . with Trofts aboard?*

Her stomach tightened, and she held her breath, keying her auditory enhancers to full power. But the ship might have been a giant tomb for all the activity she could detect. *All of them ashore?* she wondered. It seemed foolish . . . but on the other hand, if Troft shipboard life was anything like what she'd experienced on the way to Qasama, the crew was unlikely to spend their nights here by choice. And if there were only two or three duty officers aboard, they'd probably be all the way forward in the command module.

It was a good theory, anyway, and for now it would have to do. Returning to the airlock, she went back out into the loading tower.

She'd half feared the controls to the approach-detection system would have been routed to the command module, but it turned out the Trofts had elected convenience over extra security. All those long hours of catertalk classes were paying off now; scanning the labeled switches, she figured out the procedure and shut off the system.

Akim was on his feet against the wall, Daulo already hoisted onto his back, when she stepped out into the cool night air and waved. He headed toward her at a brisk jog, and a minute later had reached the ramp. "Is it clear?" he hissed as he started up.

"Far as I can tell," she whispered back. "Come on—I don't want the security system to be off any longer than it has to be."

A handful of heartbeats and he was beside her. "Where to now?" he puffed, pulling back from her attempt to take Daulo's weight from him.

"Forward, I think, at least a little ways," she told him. "We need to find an empty storeroom or something where we won't be getting any company."

"All right," he nodded. His eyes bored into hers. "And when we're settled and have time to talk, you can tell me exactly why you came to Qasama."

Chapter 42

The confrontation was fortunately postponed a few minutes by the necessity of covering their trail. Switching the motion detectors back on was the work of five seconds; trying to seal the hole Jin had made in the rubberine took considerably longer and with far less success. She was able to use her lasers to fuse the edges back together, but the procedure left shiny streaks that stood out all too well against the duller background material. Roughing up the shiny parts with her fingernails helped some, but not enough, and eventually she gave up the effort. As Akim pointed out, anyone coming in through the tunnel would probably be more concerned with his footing than with watching the walls, anyway.

The ship was still quiet as they started down the long central corridor. Jin had hoped to hide them in an empty storeroom where they could be assured of privacy, but it was quickly apparent that that plan would have to be altered. Most of the rooms they found along their way were locked down, and the few that were open still had a fair assortment of scancoded boxes guardwebbed to walls and floor. Akim pointed out at one stop that even with the boxes there was enough room for the three of them; Jin countered with the reminder that the Trofts would probably be coming in to continue their unloading in the morning.

So they kept going. Finally, in the forward part of the main cargo/engineering section, just aft of the ship's long neck, they found an unlocked pumping room with enough floor space for at least two of them to lie down comfortably at the same time. "This ought to do, at least for now," Jin decided, glancing around the vacant corridors one last time before shutting the door behind them. "Let me give you a hand with Daulo."

"I've got him," Akim said, lowering the youth to a limp sitting position against one wall. "Is there a light we can turn on?"

The glow filtering in from the corridor was enough for Jin's light-amps to work with. Locating the switch, she turned on the room's wall-mounted lights. "We shouldn't leave them on long," she warned Akim.

"I understand," Akim nodded, giving the room a quick once-over.

"Do you see anything we can use as a pillow?" Jin asked, lowering herself carefully to the deck beside Daulo.

Akim shook his head. "His shoes will do well enough, though." Stooping down, he removed Daulo's shoes and leaned awkwardly over the unconscious youth.

"I can do that," Jin offered, reaching over.

"I'm all right," Akim said tartly, avoiding her hands. The motion threw him off balance, and he had to drop one hand to the deck to catch himself.

"Miron Akim—"

"I said I was all right," he snapped.

"Fine," Jin snapped back, suddenly fed up with it all.

Akim glared up at her as he slipped the shoes beneath Daulo's head. "You'd be advised to show more respect, offworlder," he growled, moving back and sitting down across the room from her.

"I save my respect for those who've earned it," Jin shot back.

For a long moment he and Jin eyed each other in brittle silence. Then Jin took a deep breath and sighed. "Look . . . I'm sorry, Miron Akim. I realize my personality grates against your sensibilities, but right now I'm just too tired to try and fit into the normal Qasaman mold."

Slowly the anger faded from Akim's face. "Our worlds would have been enemies even without the razorarms, wouldn't they?" he said quietly. "Our cultures are just too different for us to ever understand each other."

Jin closed her eyes briefly. "I'd like to think neither of our societies is *that* rigid. Just because we're not the best of friends doesn't mean we have to be enemies, you know."

"But we *are* enemies," Akim said grimly. "Our rulers have shown it in their words; your rulers have shown it in their actions." He hesitated. "Which makes it very hard for me to understand why you saved my life."

Jin eyed him. "Because you're not the Shahni and their thirty-year-old words, and I'm not the Aventinian Council and their thirty-year-old actions. You and I are right here—right now—facing a threat to Qasama that both of us want to stop. *We* are not enemies. Why shouldn't I save your life?"

Akim snorted. "That's a false argument. We're extensions of our rulers—no more, no less. If our rulers are at war, we are, too."

Jin chewed at her lip. "All right, then. If I'm such a threat to Qasama, why didn't you call Obolo Nardin's men while I was off rescuing Daulo Sammon?"

The question seemed to take Akim by surprise. "Because they would have killed me along with you, of course."

"So? Aren't you supposed to be willing to die for the good of your world? I am."

"But then—" Akim stopped.

"But then what?" Jin prompted him. "But then the threat Mangus represents would remain hidden?"

Akim's lip twisted. "You're subtler than I'd thought," he said. "You fight me with my own words."

"I'm not trying to fight you," Jin shook her head wearily. "Not verbally or any other way. I'm simply trying to point out that you're doing exactly what you're supposed to: you've evaluated the potential threats to Qasama, you've figured out which of those threats is the most immediate, and you're throwing every weapon you possess at it." She smiled wryly. "At the moment, I'm one of those weapons."

He smiled, too, almost unwillingly. "And I one of yours?" he countered.

She shrugged. "I could hardly stop Obolo Nardin on my own, even if I wanted to. Besides, he's one of your people. Dealing with him should be *your* business."

"True." Akim glanced around at the metal walls surrounding them. "Though dealing with him from here may prove difficult."

"Don't worry, we'll get out all right," Jin assured him. "Remember, Obolo Nardin seems to be very big on mind-expander drugs, which means he'll be thinking about this very logically. If we aren't in his half of Mangus—and he'll be able to confirm that pretty quickly—then he'll have to assume we got out somehow. It's a solid fifty kilometers back to Azras and we're on foot, so he knows we can't possibly be there before midday tomorrow—today, I mean. Then we either have to contact the Shahni by phone—"

"Which he would know about instantly."

"Right. And since he knows *we* know about his rigged phone system, he knows we'll have to try something else instead." And now came the crucial question. Jin braced herself, trying to keep her voice casual. "So. Are there any radio systems in use on Qasama? Big ones, I mean, not like the little short-range things the Sammon family uses inside their mine."

She held her breath; but if he noticed anything odd in her voice or face he didn't show it. "The SkyJo combat helicopters have radios," he said thoughtfully. "But the nearest ones we could get to are in Sollas."

Her heart skipped a beat. "There aren't any at Milika?" she asked carefully. "I'd assumed your people would come in by helicopter when you heard about the supply pod."

"We did, but those SkyJos have since been sent into the forest to guard your spacecraft's wreckage."

Jin began to breathe again. "I see. And of course, Obolo Nardin will know all that," she said, getting back on the logic of her argument. "So he'll know that we'll have to go all the way to Sollas to find any kind of assault force to hit him with. How far is that by car?"

"Several hours. And more time after that to assemble a force and get it back here, especially since we can't use the phone system. Yes, I see now where you're heading. You think Obolo Nardin will feel secure enough not to panic and begin destroying evidence of his treason?"

"Not for at least the next half day, no. Face it; he's got too much to lose if he cuts and runs when he doesn't have to. Not to mention the fact that if he pulls up stakes here he also loses his best chance of finding us before we can talk. I doubt he'd do that without a specific and imminent threat swooping down toward him." She shrugged. "Now, if another day goes by without him catching up with us, then he probably *will* start worrying. But by then his search parties ought to either be back home or spread out too thin to bother us. And Daulo Sammon will hopefully be back on his feet, too."

Akim looked down at Daulo. "I hate the thought of hiding here while Obolo Nardin has full freedom to operate," he admitted candidly. "The damage he could do to Qasama . . . but I also see nothing better for us to do."

"Well, if something occurs to you, please don't hesitate to speak up," Jin told him. "I might have more of this tactical military training than you do, but you know the planet far better than I ever will."

He grimaced. "Most of it, perhaps. But apparently not enough. Tell me, how did your people discover Obolo Nardin's treason?"

Jin snorted gently. "They didn't. They knew there was something wrong with Mangus, but they got their conclusions almost completely backwards."

She described the satellite blackouts and the missile-test theory the Qasama Monitor Center had come up with. "Interesting," Akim said when she'd finished. "I hope you aren't suggesting the Trofts have given Obolo Nardin advanced weapons, too."

"No, I don't think they'd do anything like that," Jin shook her head. "Trofts never give anything away for free, and certainly not to a human society that's still considered a threat. They'll be keeping a very tight control over what Obolo Nardin gets, and any technology that could conceivably be used against them won't be on the list."

"Hence the security around this ship," Akim nodded. There was an odd note of disappointment in his voice. "Yes, I suppose they would be careful about such things. I take it that it wasn't Obolo Nardin who was knocking out your satellites, then?"

"No, it was the Trofts playing games with them. Trivial to do, too, from close range. They probably sneaked up behind the one they needed to knock out and left a remote chase satellite slaved in orbit to it. That way they could remotely arrange blackouts to cover both landing and liftoff and still leave no hard evidence of tampering when our ships came by to pick up the recordings."

Akim snorted gently. "Yes, your ships. Odd. We've watched them come by for many years, Jasmine Moreau. In the early days we prepared for attack each time we spotted one, wondering if *this* would be the one that would bring warriors down to the surface. Then we discovered the satellites, and began correlating your ships' movements against them, and realized what you were actually doing. But still we watched . . . and two weeks ago, when the long-expected invasion actually came, we missed it entirely." He eyed her. "I trust you appreciate the irony of it."

Jin shivered. "I gave up on irony when my companions were killed."

His expression was almost sympathetic. "We didn't shoot your spacecraft down, Jasmine Moreau," he said quietly.

"I know."

"The Trofts?"

She nodded. "You appreciate irony, Miron Akim? Try this one: given that they never came out to investigate, I don't think they even knew who and what they'd hit."

He frowned. "They attacked without knowing what they were attacking?"

"It was probably some kind of automated hunter/seeker missile patrolling the airspace, programmed to hit anything flying too close to Mangus. We must have just happened to arrive at the same time one of their ships was landing or lifting; they surely wouldn't have missiles flying around the area all the time."

"Uncontrolled weapons." Akim spat. "And they consider themselves civilized, no doubt."

Jin nodded. "There are things Trofts won't do . . . but some of the things they *will* do are pretty disgusting. We'll have to try and scramble the controls for launching the missiles before we leave the ship or any helicopters you send will be shot out of the sky before they get past Purma."

"Shall we go do that now?"

Jin glanced down at Daulo's slack face. "No. There'll probably be Trofts on duty on the bridge, and we don't want to risk starting anything right now. Tomorrow night, when Daulo Sammon's recovered and you and I have caught up on our sleep, we'll give it a try."

Akim stifled a yawn. "All right. Should one of us stand watch?"

Jin shook her head. "Just lie down against the door, if you don't mind. As long as we're alerted the second anyone tries to get in, I'll be able to deal with them."

"What about you?" Akim asked, sliding across the floor to parallel the door. "There's not really enough room for all of us to lie down."

"Don't worry about me," Jin yawned. "I used to sleep sitting up all the time when I was a girl. I should be able to recover the technique."

"Well . . . all right." Reaching to his feet, Akim pulled off his shoes and slid them beneath his head as he stretched out on his back against the door. "But if you have trouble sleeping, let me know and we can trade off partway through the night."

"I'll do that," Jin promised. "Thank you, Miron Akim. Goodnight."

For a moment his dark eyes bored into hers. "Goodnight, Jasmine Moreau."

Reaching up, Jin flicked off the light. The room fell silent, and for a long while she just sat there in the darkness, feeling utterly drained in body, mind, and spirit. *Two weeks,* Akim had said, since Jin's "invasion" had begun. Two weeks, now, she'd been marooned on this world.

And with an almost shocking suddenness, the end of it was upon her.

With an effort of will, Jin activated her optical enhancers and looked over at Akim. His eyes were closed, his body limp, his breathing slow and steady. Sleeping the sleep of the righteous. *And why not?* she thought, almost resentfully. After all, she'd done her best to convince him that there was nothing for them to do *but* sleep for the next half day or more. This was the eye of the storm, the lull before embarking on what he surely knew would be a long and perilous journey to Azras to sound the alarm.

Except that, with any luck at all, it wouldn't be.

Two weeks. Eight days for the *Southern Cross*, six days for the *Dewdrop.* Fourteen Aventinian days were . . . Briefly, she tried to make the conversion to Qasama days, but her brain wasn't up to it and she gave up the effort. It was close, though; the two planets' rotation periods didn't differ by more than an hour or so.

Which meant that the rescue team could be here almost any time.

We'll listen for your call at local sunrise, noon, sunset, and midnight, Captain Koja's supply pod message had said. *If you can't signal, we'll come down and find you.*

How long would they wait before landing and beginning a full-scale search? Not more than a day, surely. Especially once they confirmed that the shuttle's crash site was being guarded by military helicopters. Twelve hours in orbit, no more, and they'd be coming down.

And when they did . . .

Jin shivered. *We aren't enemies,* she'd told Akim. And she'd meant it. Whether he liked it or not, they really *were* allies in this battle to tear Obolo Nardin's sticky fingers off Qasama. The landing team, though, was unlikely to see things that way.

Which meant she had to get in touch with them before they landed. Probably within the next day. Almost certainly before it was safe for Akim and Daulo to leave.

Her stomach knotted at the thought. What would they think, she wondered uneasily, when she abandoned them here tomorrow evening and made her solitary escape from Mangus? Would they understand that all this really *hadn't* been a cold-blooded scheme to trap them here out of her way? Would they believe her when she repeated that this was still the safest place for them to wait for their own reinforcements to arrive?

And would either understand if she had to kill someone in order to get access to one of those helicopter radios out at the shuttle crash site?

Probably not. But ultimately, it didn't much matter. Whether they understood or not, it was something she had to do. As much for Qasama's safety as for her own.

With a sigh, she turned off her optical enhancers and tried to sink into the darkness surrounding her. Eventually, she succeeded.

Chapter 43

She woke abruptly, and for a moment just sat there in the darkness, heart thudding in her ears as her fogged brain tried to figure out what it was that had startled her so thoroughly out of a deep sleep. Then it clicked, and she surged to her feet, stifling a groan as pain lanced through sleep-stiffened joints and muscles.

"What is it?" Akim hissed.

"Trouble," Jin told him grimly, keying in her optical enhancers. Akim was sitting up now, a hand dabbing at his eyes as he grabbed his shoes; Daulo was still stretched out in sleep. "That deep drone you can hear sounds very much like a pre-flight engine test."

Akim's eyes widened. "A *what?*" he demanded, jamming his shoes on and scrambling to his feet.

"A pre-flight engine test," she repeated, squatting down beside Daulo and shaking his shoulder. "Daulo Sammon?—come on, wake up."

"What time is it, anyway?" Akim asked. His groping hand found her arm, squeezed with painful force.

"Take it easy," she growled, shrugging off his hand and checking her nanocomputer's clock circuit. The readout stunned her: they'd been aboard the ship barely seven hours. "Only about mid-morning," she said.

"*Mid-morning?* But you said—"

He was interrupted by a sudden gasp from Daulo. "Who is it?" he croaked.

"Shh!" Jin cautioned him. "Relax—it's Jasmine Moreau and Miron Akim. How do you feel?"

He paused, visibly working moisture into his mouth. "Strange. God above, but those were bad dreams."

"Some of them may not have been dreams," Jin told him. "Do you feel up to traveling?"

Clenching his teeth, Daulo pushed himself into a sitting position, a brief spasm flicking across his face. "I'm a little dizzy, but that's all. I think I'll be all right if we don't have to go too far or too fast. Where are we, anyway?"

"Inside the Troft ship." Jin turned to Akim, noting with relief that he seemed to have recovered his balance. "I'm going to make a fast reconnoiter outside," she told him. "See if I can figure out just what's happening."

"I'll come with you," the other said.

"It might be better if you stayed here with—"

"I said I'll come with you."

Grimacing, Jin nodded. "All right. Daulo, you stay here and get all the kinks out of your muscles. We'll be back in a couple of minutes."

The corridor directly outside the door was deserted, though the sounds of activity coming from all directions indicated that that was probably a very temporary condition. "Where to?" Akim hissed in her ear as she stepped out.

"This way," she whispered back, leading the way back to the ship's central corridor. Glancing both ways along it, she started forward at a fast jog. "We need to find a room with a full-sweep monitor," she added as he caught up and matched her pace, "and most of these'll be in the neck and command module."

"You're certain?" he snarled. "As you were certain that Obolo Nardin wouldn't be reacting until tomorrow?"

She glanced back over her shoulder at his tightly hostile face. "So maybe I overestimated Obolo Nardin's nerve," she growled. "Or maybe the Trofts decided the odds of us getting recaptured weren't all that good and decided to offload and run before your people caught them here."

"Or maybe—"

And barely three meters ahead, a door slid open and a Troft stepped into the corridor.

The alien was fast, all right. His hand went instantly to the gun belted against his abdomen, closed on the grip—

And Jin leaped across the gap, one hand grabbing the gun to lock it in place as the other jabbed hard against the Troft's throat.

The alien dropped with no sound but a muffled clang. "Come on," Jin breathed to Akim, looking over at the door the alien had emerged from. *Port drive monitor station,* the catertalk symbols read. "Here we go," she muttered to Akim, and jabbed at the touchplate. The door slid open onto a roomful of flashing lights and glowing displays and a second Troft seated in a swivel chair in front of them.

The alien was just starting to turn around toward the door as she took a long step forward. It was doubtful he ever knew just what had hit him.

"Bring that other one in," Jin whispered to Akim, glancing around to make sure there was no one else in the room. Akim already had the unconscious Troft halfway through the door, leaning over to throw one last look each way before he let the panel slide closed.

"Are they dead?" he asked, letting the limp form drop to the deck with a shudder.

"No," she assured him. "They'll be out of action for at least an hour, though. Better leave that alone," she added as Akim gingerly picked up the Troft's laser. "Those are extremely nasty weapons, and I don't have time to teach you how to use it properly. Right now you'd be as likely to damage yourself with it as shoot anyone else."

Reluctantly, he let the laser drop onto the Troft's torso, and Jin turned her attention to the control boards. Somewhere here had to be . . . there it was: *Monitor camera selection.* Now if she could find a camera that covered the rear loading hatchway, or even outside . . . there. "Here goes," she said, tentatively touching the switch.

The central display shifted to a fisheye view that seemed to be coming from somewhere near the starboard drive nozzle. At one edge was a corner of the loading tower's ramp; at the other was the gateway to the human half of the Mangus compound. In the center about a dozen people were running motorized load carriers both ways between the gateway and the ship.

Akim spotted it first. "They're not unloading," he said abruptly. "The carriers leaving the ship are empty—see?"

"Yeah," Jin agreed, stomach tightening into a hard knot. "Damn. Perhaps you were right after all, Miron Akim. Obolo Nardin's apparently packing his alien gadgetry onto the ship and deserting Mangus."

Akim swore under his breath. "We can't let him escape," he said.

"With those alien computers he'll be able to set up somewhere else in the Great Arc and continue his treason."

"I know." For a half dozen heartbeats Jin watched the display, trying to think. "All right," she said at last. "Wait here; I'm going back to get Daulo Sammon."

"And then what? Everyone out there is armed; and even if we could get past them all, there's still no way we could call for reinforcements in time."

"I know." Stepping to the door, she slid it open and glanced out. Again, no one was in sight. "We'll have to do something else. Like take over the ship."

Daulo was waiting when she reached the pumping room, pacing restlessly around the cramped space. "What's going on?" he demanded as she slipped back into the room.

"It looks like Obolo Nardin's preparing to leave," she told him, giving him a quick once-over. "How are you feeling?"

"I can make it. What do you mean, leaving?"

"Just what I said. He's got his people loading stuff onto this ship right now."

"And the aliens aren't stopping him?"

"Hardly. They're helping him. Shh!"

A double set of hurrying footsteps passed by out in the corridor. "But how are we going to get off before they leave?" Daulo hissed.

"We're not." The corridor was quiet again. Sliding it open a crack, Jin looked out. "Okay, looks clear. If we meet any Trofts, let me handle them."

They slipped out and headed forward. "Where are they all?" Daulo hissed, glancing around as they jogged.

"A lot of them are probably in the stern, helping with the loading," Jin murmured back. "Most of the rest will be busy back in the engineering rooms or up front in the command module."

The latter being where they were headed. It didn't seem a good idea to worry him with that.

They reached the port drive monitor station without incident, collected Akim, and continued on. "Stay at my sides," Jin warned the two men as they neared the end of the neck. "If I have to shoot it'll probably be straight ahead or behind, and I don't want you getting in the way."

They left the neck and entered the flat-steeple command module beyond it. Jin had been braced for an immediate battle; to her mild surprise, again there was no one in sight. "How many aliens are we going to be up against?" Akim muttered.

"Probably thirty to fifty in a ship this size," Jin told him, trying to remember what little she knew about Troft ship layouts. The bridge ought to be near the top of the command module, just below the sensor blister. A collision door slid open at their approach—

And they found themselves in a spacious monitor intersection.

It was a design, Jin remembered, peculiar to Troft ships. A circular area seemingly carved out of the intersection of two major corridors, its walls were covered by monitor screens and displays. In its center, a wide spiral stair led to the level above. "I think we're here," Jin murmured to the others. "Now stay behind me and—"

"Stop, humans!" a flat, mechanical voice shouted in Qasaman from behind them.

Jin spun around, dropping into a crouch at the base of the stairway and shoving Akim and Daulo to either side. A flash of light and heat sliced the air above her, and an instant later her nanocomputer had thrown her in a flat dive to the side. She rolled up onto her right hip, left leg sweeping toward the Troft as he swung his own weapon toward her. She won the race, barely, and the corridor lit up with the blaze of her antiarmor laser.

She was on her feet in an instant, sprinting back to the stairway. "Follow me up," she snapped at Akim and Daulo, leaping onto the stairs and starting up them five at a time. Whoever was up there couldn't possibly have missed hearing the ruckus, and she had to get to them before they sealed off the bridge.

And for one heart-stopping second it looked like she was going to be too late. Even as she came around the last turn of the staircase she looked up to see a heavy blast hatch starting to swing down over the opening.

Her knees straightened convulsively, hurling her in a desperate leap straight up. Her hands caught the rim of the opening, barely in time—

And she gasped with pain as the rubberine rim of the hatch slammed down on her fingers.

For a long second she hung there, vision wavering with the agony in her hands, mind frozen with the realization that she was completely and utterly helpless. The triggers to her fingertip lasers were out of reach, her sonics useless with a metal hatch blocking them, her antiarmor laser impossible for her to aim.

Servo strength . . . Pressing upward with the back of one hand did nothing but send a fresh wave of pain through her fingers like an electric shock—

Electric shock!

Her mind seemed to catch gears again; and, gritting her teeth, she fired her arcthrower.

There was no way to tell if the random lightning bolt actually hit anything; but the thunder was still echoing in her ears when the pressure on her hands abruptly eased a little. Again she shoved upward, and this time it worked. Arm servos whining against the strain, the hatch swung open; simultaneously, she pulled down hard on her other hand, launching herself up and through the opening.

They were waiting for her—or, rather, those who hadn't been leaning on the hatch in the path of the arcthrower blast were waiting for her—but it was clear they didn't really understand what it was they were facing. Even as she shot out of the hatch-way like a cork from a bottle, the room flashed with light as a crisscross of laser fire sliced through the air beneath her.

There were five of them in all, and they never got a chance to correct their aim. Jin reached the top of her arc, head coming perilously close to banging against the ceiling, and her left leg swung around in a tight crescent curve across the crouching Trofts, antiarmor laser spitting with deadly accuracy.

By the time she landed, stumbling, on the deck, it was all over.

For a moment she just sagged there, teeth clenched against the throbbing pain in her fingers. The ceramic-laminated bones were effectively unbreakable, but the skin covering them had no such protection, and it was already turning black and blue with massive bruising.

"Is it all right?" a muffled voice called tentatively from behind her.

She turned to see Akim poke his head cautiously over the level of the deck. "Yeah," she grunted. "Come on, hurry up. We've got to close this place off."

Akim came all the way in, followed closely by Daulo. "What happened to your hands?" Daulo asked sharply, stepping forward to take one of them.

"They tried to slam the door on us. Never mind that; you two get that hatch closed and sealed, all right?"

They moved to obey, and she moved past the line of smoldering Troft bodies to give the control boards a quick scan. A dull *thud* from behind her signalled the closing of the hatch, and a moment later Akim stepped to her side. "I don't hear anything that sounds like an alarm," he commented quietly. "Is it possible they didn't have time to call for help before they died?"

Jin frowned at one of the displays, which was showing the same outside scene she and Akim had watched earlier from the port drive monitor station. She wouldn't have thought it possible . . . but on the other hand, this craft was clearly built more along the lines of a small freighter than a warship. If there hadn't been laser alarms built into the corridors, perhaps there weren't any on the bridge, either. "It looks like they didn't," she agreed, gesturing to the display. "They're certainly not showing any signs of panic out there."

"Which means we have some time," Akim nodded. "That's something, at least."

"Only if we move fast," Jin said grimly. "I doubt that hatch will hold them for very long once they realize what's happened." A vague, half-formed plan was beginning to take shape in her mind . . . and unfortunately, she wasn't going to have enough time to work out all the details in advance. "You two stay here; I'll be back as soon as I can."

"Where are you going?" Akim frowned, his voice dark with suspicion.

"To try and put a wrench into Obolo Nardin's plans. Seal the hatch after me, and don't open it again until I signal—three knocks, two knocks, four knocks; got it?"

She turned back toward the hatch . . . paused at the odd expression on Daulo's face. "You all right?" she asked.

He tried twice before he got the words out. "You shot them down in cold blood."

She glanced down at the dead Trofts. "It was self defense, Daulo Sammon," she bit out. "Our lives or theirs, pure and simple."

But the words sounded strangely hollow in her ears; and even through the agony in her hands she could feel a twinge of guilt. Her grandfather, in very similar circumstances, had only destroyed his enemies' weapons . . . "And anyway," she snarled abruptly, turning her back on him, "whoever's running this operation needs a good object lesson. They're going to learn that fiddling around with human beings' lives is a damn costly proposition."

She stepped to the hatch and unsealed it. Or, rather, tried to. But her fingers seemed dead on her hands, and Daulo had to come over and do it for her. "Can you tell us what you're planning?" he asked quietly.

"I'm going to try and short-circuit Obolo Nardin's escape route." She paused for a moment, listening. If anyone was in the monitor intersection, he was keeping quiet about it. "I'll be back as soon as I can."

Chapter 44

The monitor intersection was still deserted, but Jin knew it wouldn't be that way for long. Slipping through the collision door, she left the command module and headed aft down the neck, taking long loping strides that gave adequate speed while still allowing her time between steps to listen.

She was about halfway down the neck when she heard approaching footsteps, and she risked taking another two strides before ducking into one of the rooms lining the corridor. Standing just inside, her ear pressed against the door, she listened as four Trofts hurried past. *Have they realized they've got intruders on their bridge?* she wondered uneasily. But it wasn't a question she could afford to dwell on. Daulo and Akim wouldn't have been any safer anywhere else . . . and anyway, the Trofts would surely try to get their bridge back intact before resorting to anything violent.

She waited until the footsteps had faded completely before opening the door and slipping out. Luck continued to be with her, and she reached the end of the neck without encountering any more Trofts. She stepped from the neck into the large cargo/ engineering section with a sigh of relief—here, at least, she would have room to maneuver if it came to a fight. And with many of the Trofts presumably working back here . . .

She paused as a sudden idea struck her. Interfering with the loading back there was all well and good . . . but if she could cut down the opposition at the same time . . .

She retraced her steps to the base of the ship's neck. Sure enough, the edge of a blast door was visible right where the cargo/engineering section began. The manual control for it had to be nearby . . . there. Hauling on the lever, she watched as the heavy metal disk slid silently across the corridor, cutting her off from the front of the ship. If the door was connected to an automatic alarm . . .

But no sirens or horns went off. *Must be tied into the decompression sensors instead,* she decided, looking for a way to seal the door. There was of course no lock; but she still seemed to be unobserved, and a two-second burst from her antiarmor laser did an adequate job of spot-welding it. The welds wouldn't hold longer than a half-hour or so, even if they were trying not to completely destroy the door in the process. But if she was lucky, a half-hour would be all they'd need.

She continued on into the cargo/engineering section, switching from the main corridor to a smaller—and hopefully less traveled—parallel one. Staying alert, she headed back toward the aft entryway and the loading tower there.

With voices and drones and clangings coming from all around her, her audio enhancers were all but useless; but even so, she heard the Trofts well before she saw them. They were talking, and with all the noise around them they were talking loudly, and for a moment Jin hung back behind a corner and listened.

[—not allow them to board yet,] one voice was saying. [The Commander, he does not want them aboard until all equipment has been loaded.]

[The isolation area, it is ready,] a second voice objected. [The humans, they would be out of our way if they were there.]

[More equipment, it must yet be brought to the ship,] the first said.

[The loading, we could handle it more efficiently alone.]

[The equipment to come, much of it is beyond the wall. Would you have the humans there see us?]

The second Troft gave a piercing, almost ultrasonic bray of laughter. [Why not? Their mythos, does it not allow for the existence of demons?]

The first alien didn't echo the laughter. [A risk, it is not worth taking,] he said sternly. [Return to your post. The humans, inform them that anything still beyond the wall in fifteen minutes will not be loaded.]

Jin licked her lips, setting her mind into full combat mode. Clearly, the Trofts weren't wildly enthusiastic about having their Qasaman clients aboard their ship, and while that was good for long-term plans, it did nothing for the upcoming near-term confrontation. The Troft outside the port drive monitor station had drawn on her without challenge or question; she had no intention of letting the ones back here do likewise. Setting her teeth, she stepped out from around the corner.

Just in time to see the two Trofts turn a corner of their own back toward the noise and commotion at the airlock.

She breathed a quiet sigh of relief and hurried after them . . . and was just two steps from the main corridor when the thin wail of an alarm abruptly split the air all around her.

The bridge? Or the welded blast door? She had no way of knowing which the Trofts had discovered . . . but it didn't much matter. Either way, her short grace period was over. Increasing her stride, she swung around the corner—

And skidded to a halt a bare three meters from a scene of chaos.

The rubberine tunnel she'd burned a flap in barely eight hours ago had become a bottleneck of activity, with a half dozen humans, an equal number of Trofts, and several equipment-laden load carriers all traffic-jammed together. The reason for at least part of the congestion was obvious: like a bucket brigade with a single node, the humans were bringing the equipment to the airlock and then passing it on to Trofts to haul into the ship proper.

And as she stopped every eye in the cramped space swung around to lock solidly onto her.

[You!—halt and identify yourself,] one of the nearer Trofts called toward her, his hand swinging toward his belted pistol. "You!" the Qasaman translation boomed from his translator pin an instant later. "Stop where—"

And the rest was swallowed up in the thunderclap as her arcthrower hurled a lightning bolt into one of the boxes of equipment lying against the airlock wall.

Someone gave a choking scream; someone else cursed violently. Then all was silent, save for the wail of the alarm in the background.

The six Trofts were all armed, as were one or two of the Qasamans. But no one made any move toward a weapon. No one made any move at all, in fact . . . and as Jin gazed back into their frozen faces she realized why. They all finally understood what it was they were facing.

It would be easy to kill them all. A single swift crescent kick with her left leg, and her antiarmor laser would cut through them like a blazing knife. And it was surely the tactically intelligent thing to do. It would lower the number of opponents facing her, increase the odds of her and Akim and Daulo getting out alive.

You shot them down in cold blood.

She ground her teeth . . . but the memory of Daulo's quiet horror at her handiwork was too vivid to ignore.

And the Trofts on the bridge had fired first. These people hadn't even drawn their guns.

Damn them all. "You Qasamans will leave the ship," she grated. "Now."

No one tried to be a hero; no one tried to argue the point. Those farthest back on the ramp turned and fled, and the others followed immediately, abandoning their load carriers where they were.

Jin's eyes flicked across the Trofts, their arm membranes stretched wide with shock, fear, or anger. Or possibly all three. [Your hands, you will place them on your heads,] she ordered in catertalk.

One of the aliens looked around at the others, his arm membranes rippling for a second before going rigid again. [But you are a female,] he said, clearly bewildered. [A cobra-warrior, you cannot be that as well.]

[One of many things you don't know about cobra-warriors, consider this one of them,] Jin told him. [You and your companions, you will obey my order.]

Slowly, reluctantly, the Troft raised his hands away from his weapon and placed them on his head. After a long second, the others did likewise.

Jin stepped sideways to the edge of the airlock. [You will go into the ship now,] she instructed them. [The loading of equipment, it is now at an end.]

The first alien looked at his companions, gave the Troft equivalent of a nod. Carefully, they filed past Jin into the main corridor. [What about the humans?] the first Troft asked as he joined them.

[Your dealings with them are ended.] Carefully, Jin backed through the airlock toward the loading tower, trying to watch the Trofts and still keep an eye on the ramp behind her.

[A promise, our demesne made them.]

[The promise, it is broken.] At her side now was the control plate for the airlock, and her eyes flicked over to it. The large emergency button was, as she'd expected, easy to identify. Bracing herself, she set her feet, jabbed the button with her elbow, and simultaneously leaped back out of the lock onto the entryway platform.

The outer lock slid shut at high speed, just barely in front of her face. The *boom* of it echoed in the rubberine tunnel—

And a flash of laser fire sliced through the rubberine and metal behind her.

Instantly, she dropped to her belly, twisting over to face down the ramp. A handful of Trofts were visible below, loping cautiously toward the tunnel with lasers drawn. She targeted them, her hands automatically starting to curve into firing position—

She hissed a curse as a stab of pain shot through the injured fingers, belatedly reminding her that the triggers of her fingertip lasers were out of normal reach. Another laser blast sizzled the air above her head; swiveling on her hip and shoulder, she pivoted her feet around to point down the ramp and fired her antiarmor laser.

Her left leg seemed to jump of its own accord, the nanocomputer guiding the blasts with deadly accuracy, and the laser fire from below abruptly ceased.

Though presumably only for the moment. There would be other Trofts down there, as well as armed humans; but with luck, all such opposition would be concentrated on the ship's starboard side, between the Troft housing complex and the gateway to the human half of Mangus. Swinging her leg back toward the airlock, she repeated the welding procedure she'd used a few minutes earlier on the interior blast door. Then, shifting her aim, she lasered a chunk out of the rubberine tunnel. Rolling to her feet, she threw a last quick look down the ramp and leaped through the hole onto the ship's portside wing.

The heat rising from the drive nozzle hit her like something solid as she ran across and past it. Keeping low, she kept going, sprinting forward along the wing. Directly ahead loomed the maintenance building, a familiar-looking rubberine collar molding itself around the last few meters of the ship's neck. To her right, the upper deck of the engineering/cargo section hid her from most of Mangus. To her left—

To her left, a large section of the outer wall had vanished.

It was obvious, of course, once she thought about it. The overhead canopy that hid the Trofts' presence here so well also blocked all normal landing approaches. Building a sliding door into the wall was the most straightforward response.

And from her point of view, a highly useful one. It meant that if she and the others were able to get out of the ship, they wouldn't have any walls to climb.

She reached the rubberine collar without any shots or shouts being directed at her. Once there, however, she realized she had a new problem. There was no gap between collar and ship she could get through, and while her antiarmor laser would make short work of the rubberine it would do so spectacularly enough to alert any Trofts inside the building to her presence out here. But with her fingertip lasers out of commission . . .

Pursing her lips, she knelt down, bringing one knee up and resting the third finger of her right hand on top of it. Straightening the little finger, she mentally crossed her fingers and pressed down on the third-finger nail with her left thumb.

Somehow, she'd always thought that the triggering mechanism depended on having the finger of the appropriate hand curled. Apparently, that wasn't true. This way was awkward, but it worked; and within a few seconds she had a ragged flap burned through the rubberine. Taking one last look behind her, she ducked through into the building.

She'd seen a starship maintenance facility on Aventine once, and this one seemed built along similar lines. The ship's command module—a standard Troft flat-steeple design, as near as she could tell from her perch—stuck out into the center of a huge bay, with movable stairways and ramps leading to the entryways and equipment access areas. Scaffolds and boom cranes lined the bay's walls, all of them retracted away from the ship now in preparation for the imminent lift.

A dozen Trofts were also visible, standing on the ramps or milling about the bay floor. All had weapons drawn, and all were clearly agitated.

And none of them had yet noticed her.

Jin permitted herself a grim smile. They were rattled, all right; rattled and almost totally unsure of what they were doing. *But they're all armed*, she warned herself. *They're all armed, and there are a hell-and-crackling lot of them.*

The reminder sobered the wave of adrenaline-spurred cockiness. Crouching lower, she licked dry lips and considered her next move.

Below and to her left, leading to the rear/port side of the command module, she could see the lower end of one of the movable stairways. It seemed unlikely that it would still be against the ship unless there were an open entryway at its upper end. It was also unlikely that it would have been left unguarded.

But it was the best chance she had; and she had to take it quickly, before the Trofts outside figured out where she'd gone and alerted the rest. If she could get just another few meters along the neck

and reach the rear edge of the command module before one of
the aliens below happened to look up—

She'd made barely two meters of that distance when the bay
suddenly echoed to the sound of excited catertalk.

Jin cursed under her breath, straightening and shifting from a
crouch to a flat-out run. A laser split the air in front of her, sending
a wash of heat and light over her. Automatically, she closed her
eyes against the purple blob now floating in front of them and
shifted to optical enhancers. She reached her target spot; skidding
to a halt, she twisted forty-five degrees to the side and jumped.

And soared over the rear port corner of the command module
to land squarely on the entryway stairs.

For a second she fought for balance, throwing her hands out
to the sides and hooking her thumbs onto the railings in a desperate attempt to keep from falling backwards down the steps. For
that second she was a sitting duck . . . but once again, the Trofts
arrayed against her had been taken by surprise. The alien standing at the head of the stairs in front of the entryway simply stood
there, frozen in shock; he was still standing like that when Jin's
antiarmor laser all but cut him in half.

Another second was all she got before the weapons around the
room opened up again; but it was all she needed. Regaining her
balance, she took the remaining steps in a single leap, and an
instant later was loping down what she hoped was the right corridor to get her to the bridge.

The corridor was deserted; and ten meters later, she reached the
monitor intersection beneath the bridge to discover why. Nearly
twenty Trofts filled the intersection, grouped around the circular
stairway as they watched two more at the top working on the hatch
with a laser torch. They turned en masse as she skidded to a halt,
twenty lasers tracking toward her—

And with a *boom* that rattled her own skull, Jin fired her sonic
disrupter.

A multiple flash of laser fire lit up the room as a wedge-shaped
group of the Trofts collapsed into folded heaps, twitching hands
firing almost at random as they went down. Again Jin fired,
twisting her torso to a new firing angle; and again, and again,
clenching her teeth tightly against the backwash from the sonic
and the scorching near misses from lasers only marginally under
their owners' control. By the time the first victims had ceased their
spasmodic firing, the last group was collapsing to the deck; by the
time the last group lay still Jin was on the stairs, pounding on

the hatch with the heel of her hand in the three/two/four code she'd left with Akim.

She finished, and waited. And waited . . . and as some of the Trofts beneath her began stirring again there was the sound of released catches above her and the hatch suddenly swung open.

"Jin!" Daulo gasped, eyes wide as he stared down at her. "Are you—?"

"I'm fine," she grunted. "Get out of my way, will you?—they'll be able to fire again any second now."

He stepped back hastily, and she leaped up the last steps into the bridge. Akim was waiting to the side, and she'd barely cleared the rim before he slammed the hatch back down again. "You came back," he said, squatting down to seal the catches.

"Didn't you think I would?" Jin countered. Suddenly her knees were going all wobbly; staggering over to one of the chairs, she collapsed into it.

Akim stepped over to her, eyes flicking down her body. "We'd thought you might go for help."

"Help from where?" Jin countered. "Didn't we agree that we couldn't even reach any of your people for several hours?" Her foot touched something metallic; leaning back, she spotted a row of five laser pistols beneath the panel. "You making a collection?" she asked.

"We thought it would be good to have all the weapons together," Daulo told her. "For when . . . we weren't sure you were coming back, you know."

"Why *did* you return?" Akim demanded. "Let me be honest: I don't want to share my death with an enemy of Qasama."

Jin took a deep breath, exhaled it raggedly. "With any luck, you won't have to. Has the Troft commander tried to communicate with you?"

"He wants us to surrender," Daulo put in from behind her, clearly fighting against a tremor in his voice. "He says we can't possibly win and that they don't want to kill us if they don't have to."

"I don't blame them," Jin nodded. "Especially since he'd probably wreck his bridge in the process." She leaned forward, studying the control panels before her.

Akim followed her gaze. "What exactly are you planning, Jasmine Moreau?" he asked. "Are you going to fly this spacecraft out of Mangus?"

Jin snorted. "Not a chance. I've never flown anything bigger than an aircar in my life, and this isn't the time to start." She paused, looking over her shoulder as a faint crackling sound wafted into the bridge. The sound was coming from the hatch. . . . "They're back again," she said, stomach tightening as she turned back to the controls. Somewhere here there had to be—

There it was. Taking a deep breath, Jin hunched forward and tentatively touched the switch. "What are you doing?" Akim demanded suspiciously.

"You remember, Miron Akim, how surprised we were that Obolo Nardin would panic this early?" she asked. The volume control . . . there. Microphone? . . . clipped to the wall over there. "We wondered why both he and the Trofts would throw away their listening ear when there couldn't possibly be any enemies on their way here yet?" she added, working the mike free of its clip and gripping it awkwardly between palm and thumb.

"I remember," Akim growled. "Are you leading up to giving us the answer?"

"I hope so." She took a deep breath. If she was wrong . . . Raising the mike to her lips, she touched the operating switch. "This is Jasmine Moreau," she said in Anglic. "Repeating, this is Jasmine Moreau. Please respond. This is Jasmine Moreau; please respond. This is Jasmine—"

And abruptly the board speaker boomed in reply. "This is Captain Koja; commanding the *Dewdrop*. We read you, Cobra Moreau, and we're ready to come down and pick you up."

Chapter 45

It took Jin three tries to relax her throat enough to speak again. "Understood, *Dewdrop*," she managed at last. "I—" she glanced up to see Akim gazing darkly at her. "Please tie in your Qasaman language translator."

There was a slight pause from the other end. "Why?"

"I have some Qasamans here with me," Jin explained, switching back to their language herself. "I think they ought to be in on the discussion."

"Who are you talking to?" Akim demanded.

"An Aventinian ship," Jin told him. "Here to rescue me. Captain, are you still in orbit?"

"Yes." The word was Qasaman, the voice the artificial one of a translator program. "Where are you?—wait a minute, the head of the rescue team wants to get in on the conversation."

"Jin?" a familiar voice said in accented Qasaman . . . a voice fairly dripping with relief. "Jin, it's Dad. Are you all right?"

Jin felt her mouth drop open. "Dad! Yes, yes, I'm fine. You— but—"

"What, you didn't think I'd drop everything to come get my daughter back? Oh, God, Jin—look, where are you?"

"In that covered compound west of Azras—Mangus, they call it. Wait a minute, though, you can't come down just yet."

"Why not?"

"You might run into a hunter/seeker missile. Courtesy of the Trofts whose ship I'm talking to you from."

There was a long pause. "We were wondering how you'd gotten on this frequency," the *Dewdrop* translator said at last. "What in blazes are Trofts doing there?"

"At the moment, trying to get us out of their bridge so that they can airlift some Qasaman allies to safety."

"*Allies?* You mean the Trofts and Qasamans have made an alliance?"

"No, no, it's not that bad. There's nothing official about this; it was a private deal with some Qasaman thugs making a power play."

"A power play which may yet succeed," Akim muttered.

Jin glanced up at him. "Yeah, right. The problem, Dad, is that we've got to find a safe passage out of here for the three of us and at the same time make sure Mangus's owners don't get away before the Qasaman rulers can deal with them."

"Now, wait a minute, Jin," Justin said cautiously. "We'll get you and your friends out, certainly, but the rest of it sounds like internal politics. Nothing we ought to get involved with."

Jin took a deep breath. "We're already involved, Dad, just by my presence here. Please just trust me on this one."

"Cobra Moreau, this is Koja," the translator interrupted him. "Let's table this discussion until you're safe, all right? Now, you said you were on the bridge?"

"Yes, and we're sort of trapped—"

"Can you describe the ship? Is it a warship, or what?"

"From the way the crew fights, I doubt it. Let's see: the ship's got a large cargo/engineering section with sagging swept-forward wings over twin drive nacelles. The front section looked like a pretty standard flat-steeple command module, and there's a long neck connecting the two sections. No identification marks anywhere I could see."

"Okay. I'll see if we've got anything on this design on file."

"Jin?" Justin's voice came back on. "This is Dad. Now, you say you're trapped on the bridge?"

"Yeah, and they're trying to burn up to us through the emergency blast hatch. I can fight them if necessary, but I'd prefer it if we could find a way to convince the commander to just let us go."

"It's worth a try. Can you tie him in to us?"

Jin peered at the board again. "Hang on . . ."

[That will not be necessary,] a burst of catertalk cut in. [I have been listening.]

"I thought you might be," Jin said, only lying a little. "In Qasaman, please, Commander—as I told the *Dewdrop*, my companions need to hear all this, too."

There was a momentary pause. "Very well," the Troft's translator voice said. "I will listen, but you must realize that I cannot allow you to escape."

"Why not?" Justin asked.

"Our demesne-lord's agreement with the Qasaman Obolo Nardin will come to nothing if his plan is ruined."

"The plan's already ruined," Jin told him. "How are you going to get your allies into your ship for transport, now that I've sealed off the cargo section? And where are they going to stay during the ride?"

"Foolish human! How many other ways into our ship do you think there are?"

"Several," Jin agreed. "But you really don't want to let them see the areas you'd have to take them through. True?"

"The Qasamans can learn nothing from a casual glimpse of our equipment."

"Maybe. But if you're wrong, the Qasamans might advance a little too quickly . . . possibly quickly enough to break your grip on them before you have a strong enough puppet government in place. Is your demesne-lord willing to take that chance?"

"It is a negligible risk," the Troft insisted.

"Perhaps," the *Dewdrop*'s translator put in. "Let's put it another way, then. Would your demesne-lord be willing to let an entire Crane-class starcarrier fall into Qasaman hands?"

For a long moment there was silence; and in that hiatus, a keen awareness of her body's condition seemed to flood into Jin's consciousness. Awareness of the throbbing ache in the stiff fingers of both hands—of the burning sensation in her left ankle from excessive use of her antiarmor laser—of an even more painful burning along her ribcage where one of the laser shots fired earlier must have come closer than she'd realized. Her eyes drifted around the bridge, and she realized for the first time just how much equipment was really here. Would she have the ability and stamina to systematically destroy all of it if she had to? Because that was the only realistic threat they had to bargain with.

And the Troft commander clearly knew it. "Our ship can be flown without the use of the bridge," he said at last.

"Oh, certainly," the *Dewdrop* agreed. "Most ships can. But not very easily. Besides which, the bridge isn't the only thing in danger here. There's a sensor bubble directly over her head, for one thing— it wouldn't take all that much for her to punch through to that. Oh, now *there's* an interesting idea," Koja interrupted his own thought. "If your ship follows standard design, there should be parallel connections between all your sensors for making synchronicity checks. A good jolt of high voltage along that connector cable might just take out every navigation sensor you have on the ship."

"Ridiculous," the Troft snorted.

"Maybe. There's one sure way to find out."

Again the Troft was silent. "You may have the Cobra," he said at last. "If she will leave the ship now, she will be allowed safe passage away from here. The Qasamans with her may not leave, though."

"Jin?" Justin asked.

"No," she said firmly. "My companions leave with me, or I wreck the ship. But I'm ready to make you a counter offer."

"I am listening."

"Okay. You let the *Dewdrop* land—safely—and allow the three of us to leave here, and there'll be no further damage to your ship."

"And . . . ?"

"No ands. We'll leave Qasama, you'll leave Qasama, and it'll all be over."

Akim snorted and turned away from her. Jin frowned over at his stiff shoulders, then turned back to the panel. "Face reality, Commander; your demesne-lord's scheme has failed, and all you can do is cut his losses."

"The scheme has not failed until the Qasaman authorities have been made aware of Mangus's true purpose," the Troft countered.

"Then your ship is dead," the *Dewdrop* said flatly. "Not just the bridge and sensors, Commander, but the entire ship. If Jin wrecks the bridge, it'll be hours before you can fly—you know it and we know it. Long before then we'll be there, even if we have to drop down outside your hunter/seekers' patrol range and come in on foot. And we have thirteen Cobras aboard."

A movement caught Jin's eye, and she looked up as Daulo stepped over to the spot at her side that Akim had just vacated. "Do you think he'll accept?" he asked in a whisper.

"He'd be a fool not to," Jin murmured back. "He has to have some idea of what a ship full of Cobras could do to him. Even just by myself, I could have killed half his crew if I'd wanted to."

"You should have done so," Akim growled from behind her.

"I'd like to end this mess with as little bloodshed as possible," she shot back over her shoulder. "It's enough that we chase the Trofts off Qasama; we don't have to kill them all just to underline the point. Unless the commander insists on that kind of lesson, of course."

"I do not so insist," the Troft commander said with something that sounded almost like a sigh. "Very well, Cobra: I agree to your terms. To your left is a keypad. Enter the following words."

Jin swiveled to the keypad as the Troft shifted into catertalk and gave a series of commands. "What's he telling you?" Daulo asked.

"Looks like the procedure for recalling the roving hunter/seeker missiles to the ship," she told him. A display above the keypad came alive. "Yes," she confirmed, studying it. "The missiles have been deactivated . . . they're on their way back to the ship."

"We're ready to break orbit, then, Jin," the *Dewdrop* said. "Shall we land near Mangus?"

"Better not—the Qasaman military may track your path in." She paused, thinking. Presumably the Qasamans weren't listening in . . . but Akim was, and she didn't want Qasaman helicopters getting to the *Dewdrop* before she did. On the other hand, if she shifted back to Anglic now, both Akim and Daulo might worry that she was giving the ship secret instructions.

And that bothered her. For reasons that weren't clear even to her, it had become very important to her to show that Qasama and the Cobra Worlds could trust each other at least this once. "Okay, here's how we'll do it," she said at last. "Picture Qasama as Aventine, with Mangus where Capitalia would be. Get down low where they can't track you and then take a circumspect route to Watermix. You get that?"

"Got it," the *Dewdrop* came back immediately. "You ready to head out to meet us?"

Jin looked at the hunter/seeker readout. If she was interpreting it correctly, the missiles were within fifteen minutes of reaching Mangus. "Yes, we're ready," she said into the mike.

"No, we're not," Akim said.

Beside her, Daulo turned and inhaled sharply. Slowly, carefully, Jin swiveled around in her seat, to find Akim standing against the opposite side of the bridge, a small device in his hand pointed at her. "What do you mean by this, Miron Akim?" she asked quietly.

"Exactly as I said," he replied, equally quietly. "We're not leaving yet. I'm claiming this ship for the Shahni of Qasama . . . and I intend to make certain it won't escape us."

Chapter 46

For several heartbeats Jin and Akim just gazed at each other. "I wondered why you went along with me on all this," Jin asked at last. "Now I know. You want the stardrive in this ship, don't you?"

"The stardrive?" Akim snorted. "You think too small, Jasmine Moreau—or perhaps too big." He waved his free hand around him, keeping the other pointed at her. "There's literally nothing aboard this ship we won't be able to use. The stardrive, the computer systems, the powerplants—even the crew's personal effects will give us information about these new enemies we face." He nodded his head slightly toward the lasers behind her under the panel. "Daulo Sammon and I had time in your absence to learn how to use those hand weapons. You were right; they are indeed powerful. All by themselves they will be worth a ransom."

Jin's eyes flicked to his hand. "Weapons mean a lot to you, don't they? That's, what, a breakapart palm-mate dart pistol?"

Akim nodded. "Designed from the one Decker York used on our people thirty years ago. We learned a great deal from your last invasion; we'll learn even more from this one. Get up, now, and go over to the hatch."

"Why?" she asked, not moving from her seat.

"I want one of those lasers behind you. This ship is staying here, and your people were kind enough to tell me how to keep it from leaving."

I can stop him, she thought. My sonic—

Would be slow enough to leave Akim time for a reflexive shot. And if the poison they'd coated the darts with was anything like the ones the original model used . . . *Okay, okay, don't panic girl,* Jin told herself firmly. *You're still in control here.* With a flick of

824

her eyes her nanocomputer's autotarget capability was locked onto the palm-mate in Akim's hand; and with a casual curving of her hands—

She inhaled sharply as a fresh wave of agony lanced through her injured fingers. Once again, she'd forgotten about her hands.

And it left her only the antiarmor laser and arcthrower to use against the palm-mate. The first of which would vaporize Akim's hand in the process . . . the second of which would kill him outright.

A hard knot began to form in Jin's stomach. *I won't kill him,* she told herself firmly. *I won't.* "Miron Akim, listen to me—"

"I said *get up!*"

"No!" Jin snapped back. "Not until you hear me out."

Akim took a deep breath, and Jin could see the knuckles on his gun hand tighten momentarily. "I don't intend to break our truce, Jasmine Moreau," he grated. "You've been of great help to us, and I won't kill you unless I have to. But I mean to have this ship."

Jin was suddenly aware of the mike still in her hand, and of the total silence from the speaker behind her. Both the *Dewdrop* and the Troft commander were waiting. Listening. "Miron Akim, listen to me," she said, fighting hard against the trembling in her voice as she reached behind her to set the mike down on the panel. "You don't want this ship. Qasama isn't ready for it yet."

He spat. "And you of Aventine are omniscient enough to know that, are you?"

"How are you going to control it?" Jin persisted. "You've seen how Obolo Nardin used the computers he was given—how are you going to keep someone else from doing something similar?"

"The Shahni will control the technology. They'll make sure it's used properly."

"Used by whom? Are the Shahni going to become a technocratic oligarchy, then?—doling out new technology to those they deem fit?" She shook her head. "Don't you see, Miron Akim, how something like that would change the whole texture of Qasaman society? I've seen how you do things here, the way your cities and villages each have their own unique political balance, independent from that of the next town over. Your people take great pride in this, and well they should; it's one of your society's greatest strengths. For that matter, search your records and legends—it was to escape from an overly centralized government that your ancestors left the Dominion of Man in the first place."

"Then perhaps it's time we grew up," Akim said stubbornly. "Would you have us hold onto petty quarrels and pride at the cost of civil war?"

"Civil *war*?" Jin snarled. "God above—you worry about civil war, and you want to add new *weapons* to the mixture?"

"The weapons will be controlled by the Shahni—"

"For how long? Months? Days? And what do you think will happen once a single village or city gets hold of one of them?"

Akim clenched his teeth. "I'm an agent of the Shahni," he grated out. "I'm charged to obey their orders, and to do that which benefits Qasama as a whole. It's not my place to make these larger policy decisions."

"Why not?" she countered. "For that matter, you've already made a policy decision. If standing orders are all that count, why haven't you killed me?"

"If keeping Qasama defenseless is all that counts to *you*," he countered, "why haven't *you* killed *me*?"

She sighed. "Because ultimately it doesn't matter. No matter what you do, Qasama won't get this ship. If the Trofts can't get it off the planet, they'll destroy it."

"Even damaged, it'll be worth—"

"Not *damaged—destroyed*," Jin snapped. "They'll turn the engines into a minor fusion bomb and blow the ship, themselves, and Mangus into dust and scatter it into the upper atmosphere. You heard me talking to the Troft commander—they're scared to even let Obolo Nardin's people get a glimpse at their readout displays. You think he'll let you take his crew alive and his ship intact?"

For a long moment the only sound in the room was the muffled hiss of the laser torch coming from the direction of the hatch. Jin kept her eyes on Akim, acutely aware of the targeting lock on the other's weapon . . . acutely aware, too, of Daulo's stiff presence a meter to her left. She wished she could see his face, try and get some feeling as to which side of this confrontation he was on. But she didn't dare look away.

"No," Akim said suddenly. His face was rigid, eyes almost unfocused, and Jin felt a sympathetic ache for him. But the other's voice was firm, with no hesitation left for her to work against. "No, my duty is clear. Even if it doesn't seem that I can win, I still have to try." He took a deep breath. "Stand up, Jasmine Moreau, and move over to the hatch."

Slowly, Jin stood up. "I beg you to reconsider, Miron Akim."

"Move over to the hatch," he repeated stiffly.

Licking her lips, her eyes still on Akim, Jin took a sidling step to her left toward the lock—

And gasped as her left knee collapsed beneath her.

Perhaps Akim had been expecting a trick; perhaps he merely reacted reflexively to her sudden movement. Even as Jin's hands snapped out toward Daulo's chest, she heard the faint *snap* of the palm-mate, and the hoarse whisper of the poisoned dart piercing the air bare centimeters from her right arm. She could almost sense her nanocomputer assessing the situation; could feel it preparing to take control of her servos and launch her into a defensive counterattack that would leave Akim burned to ashes—

And at the last instant before her outstretched hands reached Daulo's chest, she flipped her left hand over, curving the palm inward, and jammed the heel of her right hand against the left's fingertips. The fingernails slammed into Daulo's breastbone with the full force of her right hand behind it—

And with a flash of heat against her right wrist her left-hand fingertip laser fired.

Akim jumped violently to the side, swearing viciously as the blackened remains of his palm-mate went spinning to the deck. With a curse, he leaped toward Jin, hands curving into talons.

Jin waited, feet braced against the deck; and as his arms curved toward her shoulders she jabbed her arms out, the heels of her hands slamming hard into his upper chest. The impact stopped him dead in his tracks; sliding one hand around each of his shoulders, Jin twisted him around and shoved him hard into the chair she'd just been sitting in.

For a moment he just sat there, looking up at her in dazed astonishment as he caught his breath. "All right," she told him, taking deep breaths herself as the pain in her fingers slowly retreated again to a dull ache. "Let's get out of here before the Trofts get nervous and blow the ship regardless."

"Jin!" The *Dewdrop*'s translator called faintly from the speaker. "What's happening? Are you all right?"

"I'm fine," she called back. "All of us are. Commander, call your men off and we'll open up the bridge."

"Understood," the Troft translator said. "You will not be harmed."

Slowly, Akim got to his feet and faced Jin. "Someday," he said bitterly, eyes boring into hers, "we will repay you in full for all you have done to us."

She met his gaze without flinching. "Perhaps. At least now you'll have a chance of surviving to do so."

Silently, he moved toward the hatch. She followed, keeping her attention on him . . . and because of that they were halfway there before she suddenly realized Daulo wasn't following. "Come on, Daulo Sammon," she called over her shoulder. "Time to leave."

"Not quite yet," he said quietly.

Frowning, she threw him a quick glance . . . and then looked again.

Daulo was standing well back from her, pressed against the communications board. In his hand was one of the captured lasers. "Daulo Sammon?" she asked carefully.

"Thanks to you, your world is now safe from us," Daulo said tautly. His face was pale, but the gun was steady. "At least for now. But *you*, Jasmine Moreau, aren't nearly so safe . . . and the repayment Miron Akim spoke of can begin with you."

"Hold it!" Justin shouted. "You—whoever you are—if you harm her, you'll never get off that ship alive."

"You'll have to catch us first," Daulo called to the mike. "And by that time, we'll have figured out just what to do with her."

"Damn you! If you so much as—"

Stepping to one side, Daulo shifted his aim and fired a long burst into the communications board.

The *Dewdrop*'s voice was suddenly cut off . . . and the clatter of Daulo's laser as he tossed it casually to the deck again was almost shattering in the taut silence.

"Daulo . . . ?" Jin asked, feeling her eyebrows come together in bewilderment.

Daulo looked at her, took a deep breath. "*Now* we can leave," he said quietly. "And we'd better go quickly. Before, as you said, the Trofts get nervous."

Beside Jin, Akim took a step toward Daulo. "Would you mind explaining," he grated, "just what in God's name *that* was supposed to prove?"

Daulo gestured upward. "Her father is up there," he said simply.

For a long second the two men eyed each other . . . and then a smile tugged at Akim's lips and he snorted gently. "Clever. Very clever. Or it will be if it works."

"I think it will," Daulo nodded. "Like a good Qasaman family, they are very close." He looked at Jin. "Well, come on, Jasmine Moreau," he said briskly. "Let's get out of here."

The walk down the corridor was a nerve-wracking one. Jin had rather expected a large escort to tag along to make sure they actually left Mangus, but to her uneasy surprise they rated only a single Troft to lead them out of the ship, and he abandoned them just beyond the portside entryway where Jin had earlier shot her way back into the ship. "I don't like this," Akim muttered as they hurried down the steps into the now deserted maintenance bay. "Obolo Nardin's men may be waiting to gun us down out there."

"If Obolo Nardin's got any brains, he'll have his people behind their own wall by now," Jin said as they ran across the bay toward an exit door that would let them out of the maintenance building near the gap in the outer wall. "The Trofts seem to be in a flat-out hurry—that drive rumble is getting louder, and I wouldn't want to be on this side of Mangus when they fire up the engines for real."

The words were barely out of her mouth when, abruptly, the rumble swelled to a roar and a piercing ultrasonic whine rose to accompany it. "It's moving!" Daulo shouted over the noise, waving back at the ship.

Jin glanced over her shoulder. *My God, he's* right, she thought, stunned, as she watched the command module sliding smoothly back through the now retracted rubberine collar along the reddish haze of the ship's gravity lifts. "Run!" she shouted to the others. "Outside, to whatever cover you can find."

They needed no urging. Flinging open the building door, they sprinted out across a short patch of bare ground to the wall. Even here the air was becoming noticeably warmer; if they were anywhere near the nozzles when the Trofts kicked the drive to full power, Jin knew, they would stand a good chance of being charred on their feet.

They passed the edge of the wall at a dead run, and it took only a glance to see that there was nothing anywhere that could possibly serve as cover. "That way!" Akim shouted into the din, waving his arm to the right as he turned to run that direction. "Around the corner of the wall!"

It was the best they were going to get. Akim in the lead, they tore along the wall toward the south-east point of the Mangus diamond-shape a hundred meters away. Jin's left knee flashed stabs of pain with each step; gritting her teeth against the agony, she forced herself to keep going. Behind and to her side, she heard Daulo panting with the effort—sensed him stumble—

"Daulo!" She skidded to a halt and grabbed for his arm, gasping with pain as she reflexively tried to close her hand.

"No!" he panted, waving her forward. "Just go—never mind me—"

The rest of his protest was swallowed up in a sudden blast of sound from beyond the wall. Jin didn't hesitate; throwing one arm across Daulo's back and the other behind his knees, she lifted him bodily and ran.

She nearly made it. Akim was around the corner, and she and Daulo were within five paces, when the landscape in front of them abruptly flared with light and an incredible wave of heat washed over them from behind. In her arms Daulo cried out; blinking back tears, Jin fought to keep her balance against the hurricane wind-storm behind them. She reached the corner—tried to turn—

And from seemingly out of nowhere Akim's arm darted out, grabbing Jin's just above the elbow and spinning both her and Daulo around the corner to sprawl to the ground.

For a few seconds Jin couldn't speak . . . but then, for that same time neither of the others would have been able to hear her, anyway. The roar from the Troft ship was deafening—far louder than she would have expected it to be—and seemed to go on forever. Finally—finally—it began to ease, and within a few seconds had faded to a whine in the distance.

Leaving behind it the crackling of fire.

"God in heaven—they've set Mangus on fire!" Akim snarled suddenly, leaping up and disappearing around the corner in the direction of the wall opening.

Jin scrambled to her feet and took a few steps back from the wall. Sure enough, the overhead canopy was flickering with reflected light from the flames beneath it. On the ground in front of her, Daulo said something under his breath. "What?" she asked, stepping closer.

"I said they were fools." Gingerly, Daulo propped himself up on an elbow, took a deep breath. "If they'd wanted to destroy their half of Mangus properly, they should have had a self-destruct set up ahead of time. Now they're always going to wonder what they left behind we might be able to use."

"Good," Jin said grimly. "Maybe that fear will keep them from coming back and trying this again. Odd that they'd panic like that, though; once they were rid of us, they really had all the time they needed to do their cleanup properly."

Daulo chuckled. "No, they didn't." He squinted toward the sky. "Take a look."

Frowning, Jin peered skyward . . . and felt her throat tighten.

Above them, a dark shape ringed with red haze was dropping swiftly toward the ground. "The *Dewdrop*? But . . . I told them not to land here."

"Of course you did. And I expect your father had a very sharp argument with the others about that after I threatened you and then destroyed your link with them."

Jin looked back down at him, suddenly understanding. "Is *that* why you did it? To get the *Dewdrop* down here faster?"

"Not faster, really. Just more directly."

"More—?" Jin clamped her mouth shut. "Oh. Sure. Wherever they track the *Dewdrop*, that's where they'll send the helicopters. Perfectly obvious."

His eyes were steady on her. "I had no choice, Jin. Even if you'd been willing to take us directly to Azras, we still might not have gotten the military here before Obolo Nardin covered his trail and cleared out."

"Agreed," Jin nodded. "Very clever, as Miron Akim said. I wish I'd thought of it myself." The *Dewdrop* was showing a recognizable shape now. Lying down on her back, Jin raised her left leg and sent three antiarmor laser bursts in the ship's direction. "That should let them know I'm all right," she explained.

Daulo slid over to sit next to her. "I'd rather . . . hoped we'd have a little more time together once this was over," he said, almost shyly. "Before you had to leave."

Jin reached over to touch his hand with her fingertips. "I did, too," she said, and was mildly surprised to find how much she really meant it. "But I don't think we can afford to stay. Miron Akim told me there were two of those SkyJo helicopters based near my shuttle; if they get the tracking data fast enough, they won't be more than a few minutes behind us."

Daulo nodded, and for a moment they watched the *Dewdrop* dropping through the sky toward them. Then, with a grunt that was half sigh and half groan, Daulo climbed to his feet. "Speaking of Miron Akim, I'd better go and track him down. Make sure he hasn't found some weapon and is lying in wait for your ship with it."

Jin got up too, conscience nagging uncomfortably. "Daulo . . . look, I . . . well, I want you to know that I really *did* plan to fulfill my half of our bargain."

He frowned at her. "What are you talking about? You don't think that my finding the way to capture Obolo Nardin and Mangus isn't going to raise my family's status?"

"But that was all *your* doing, not—"

"Could I have done it without you?"

"Well . . . no, not really. But—"

"Jin." He stepped close to her, put his hands on her shoulders. "The bargain is satisfied. Really."

Over the plain behind him, the *Dewdrop* was sweeping down toward Mangus. "Okay," Jin sighed. "Well, then . . . I guess there's nothing to say but goodbye. Thank you for everything, Daulo."

Leaning forward, Daulo kissed her gently. "Goodbye, Jin," he said, smiling at her. "I hope this will let your uncle keep his power among your people."

Jin had almost forgotten about that. "He will," she nodded. "There's no way even his enemies can twist what's happened into failure."

"Good." He smiled again, this time with a touch of mischievousness. "Then perhaps he can talk them into letting you visit Qasama again."

She smiled back. "If I can, I will—that's a promise. If I can't . . . you'll be getting back into space again someday. You can come visit me."

The background whine that had been growing steadily louder over the past few minutes suddenly shifted pitch. Looking over Daulo's shoulder, Jin saw the *Dewdrop* had landed. "I've got to go," she said, disengaging herself and stepping away from him. "Goodbye, and thank your father for me."

There were five men crouching in a loose arc around the *Dewdrop*'s entryway before she was halfway there—Cobras, all of them, by their stances—but she didn't pay any real attention to them. Silhouetted against the hazy glow from the gravity lifts, another man was running toward her. Moving with the slightly arthritic gait she knew so well. "Dad!" she shouted to him. "It's all right—no one shoot!"

A moment later she was in his arms. A minute after that, they were aboard the *Dewdrop*, heading for space.

Chapter 47

" . . . it is therefore the opinion of the undersigned members of the Directorate that the Mangus mission in general, and the actions of Cobra Jasmine Moreau in particular, be considered a success."

Corwin sat down, letting the end of the joint opinion—and its four signatures—linger on the syndics' displays for another moment before blanking it and pulling the magcard from his reader. At the center of the speakers' table, Governor-General Chandler stood up. "Thank you, Governor Moreau," he said, eyes flicking once to Corwin before turning away. "One might expect that, with virtually none of the facts or testimony from the Mangus mission in dispute, it would be a straightforward matter for this body to come to a conclusion as to its success or failure. However, as will soon become apparent, it's often possible to interpret things in more than one way. You've heard Governor Moreau's interpretation, and that of his co-signers; I yield the floor now to Governor Priesly and a different point of view."

Priesly stood up, his eyes fairly flashing with righteous fervor as he inserted a magcard in his reader . . . and Corwin braced himself.

It was even worse than he expected.

" . . . and so let me now summarize the main points:

"Cobra Moreau failed to keep her identity as an Aventinian spy hidden from the Qasamans, in clear violation of her orders.

"Cobra Moreau furthermore failed to keep her identity as a Cobra hidden from those same Qasamans, spoiling any future chance we might have of taking them by surprise with a similar ruse.

"Cobra Moreau voluntarily spent a great deal of time in close proximity to a member of the official Qasaman government. She spoke at length with him, cooperated with him, and—even more damaging—repeatedly demonstrated her Cobra weaponry in his presence.

"Cobra Moreau deliberately allowed the Troft meddlers to escape, thereby ruining any chance we might have of identifying them and making sure any threat of this alliance between them and Qasama is at an end.

"And finally, as a direct result of her actions, Cobra Moreau permitted the other mission members' bodies to fall into Qasaman hands, allowing the Qasamans to examine them and denying us the opportunity to give them decent and proper burials.

"It is therefore the opinion of the undersigned members of the Directorate that the Mangus mission in general, and the actions of Cobra Jasmine Moreau in particular, be considered a failure."

Jin was sitting by the window of her room, curled up into her old loveseat and staring outside at the waning light of sunset, when the tap came on the door, "Jin, it's Dad and Uncle Corwin," her father's voice said quietly. "May we come in?"

"Sure," she said, not turning around. "I've already heard, if that's what you want. It hit the net a couple of hours ago."

"I'm sorry," Corwin said, pulling up a chair to just inside her peripheral vision and sinking tiredly into it.

"May I?" her father asked, stepping to her side and waving at the loveseat. Jin nodded, shifting her legs off the seat to make room for him and wincing as her knee protested the action. The injury was probably going to lead to early arthritis in the joint, the doctors had told her; earlier even than the usual Cobra average. Just one more little sacrifice for the Mangus mission.

One more sacrifice for nothing.

Justin sat carefully down beside her. "How do you feel?" he asked.

"How *should* I feel?" she countered.

He sighed. "Probably about the same way we do."

She nodded. "Probably."

For a few moments the room was silent. "Look, Jin," Corwin said at last, "you really shouldn't be taking any of this personally. *I* was Priesly's target, not you. You just happened to be the most convenient conduit for the attack he had in mind."

"Oh, I was convenient, all right," she said bitterly. "Everything I did—everything I said—he just twisted all of it into knots like a snake pretzel. And everyone just rolled over and believed him."

Corwin and Justin exchanged looks. "Well, now, that may be

open to debate," Corwin said. "I take it you stopped reading after the opinion reports and final vote came on?"

"I'd already seen how Priesly mangled what really happened," she said, blinking back tears of frustration. "I didn't need to see what the public would do with it."

"Oh, then, you missed a real treat," Justin said. Jin frowned over at him, to find a smile quirking at his lips. "It seems that about fifteen minutes after the vote came out an anonymous transcription hit the net: purportedly, that of discussions in the upper ranks of the Ject camp over the past couple of days. It shows several men, including Priesly himself, deciding how best to distort what happened on Qasama to their own political benefit."

Jin stared at him. "But who would . . . you two?"

"Who, us?" Corwin asked, radiating wide-eyed innocence. "As a matter of fact, no, we had nothing to do with it. Apparently it was some unidentified Ject of Justin's acquaintance who decided that perhaps Priesly was going a bit too far on this one."

Jin took a deep breath. For one brief moment it had felt better . . . "But it really doesn't help any. Does it?"

Corwin shrugged. "Depends on whether you're talking short-term or long-term results. Yes, I've resigned my governorship, so as far as that goes Priesly's won; and yes, your supposed failure will probably make it difficult, if not impossible, for other women to be accepted into the Cobras."

Jin snorted. "So what are all the big long-term gains? The fact that Qasama is temporarily safe from Troft meddling?"

"Don't sell that one short," Justin chided her gently. "Mangus was indeed as great a threat as we'd thought all along, just not quite as immediate a one. *That* part of your mission was a complete and resounding success—and everyone on the Council knows it, whether they admit it publicly or not."

"And we've made at least two other long-term gains, as well," Corwin told her. "First of all, Priesly may not yet realize it, but in kicking me out of the Directorate he's shot himself in the foot."

"How?" Jin asked. "Because it makes him look like a bully?"

"More or less. Never underestimate the power of a sympathy backlash, Jin, especially when it involves a name as historically revered as ours." Corwin smiled wryly. "In fact, I've been preparing a campaign for the past few days to try and guide the expected public reaction straight down Priesly's throat. Now, with all this other stuff coming out, I don't think I'll have to bother."

Jin closed her eyes. "So the Jects lose power, and all it costs is your career," she sighed. "Standard definition of a Pyrrhic victory."

"Oh, I don't know," Corwin shrugged. "Depends on whether I was tired of politics anyway, doesn't it?" Gently, he reached over to take one of her bandaged hands. "Times change, Jin, and we have to change with them. Our family's had more than its fair share of political power over the past few decades; perhaps it's time for us to move on."

"Move on to what?" she asked.

"Move on from politics to statesmanship," Corwin said. "Because we've now got the one thing neither Priesly nor anyone else in the Cobra Worlds can take away from us." He lifted a ringer and leveled it at her. "We've got *you*."

Jin blinked. "Me?"

"Uh-huh. You, and the first ever genuinely positive contact with the people of Qasama."

"Oh, sure." Jin snorted. "Some contact. The twenty-year-old niece of an ousted political leader and the nineteen-year-old heir to a minor village mining industry."

Her father made an odd sort of sound, and Jin turned her head to look at him. "What's so funny?" she demanded.

"Oh, nothing," Justin said, making a clearly halfhearted effort to erase his amused smile. "It's just that . . . well, you never can tell where something like that will lead."

He took a deep breath; and suddenly the amusement in his smile vanished, to be replaced by a smile of pride and love. "No, you never know, Jasmine Moreau, my most excellent daughter. Tell me, have you ever heard the story—the *full* story, that is—of your grandfather's path from Cobra guardian of a minor frontier village to governor and statesman of Aventine?"

She had; but it was worth hearing again. Together, the three of them talked long into the night.